TRACI HARDING

DREAMING OF ZHOU GONG

THE TIMEKEEPERS [1]

時間守衛

夢見周公

HARPER
Voyager

Harper*Voyager*
An imprint of HarperCollins*Publishers*

First published in Australia in 2013
This edition published in 2014
by HarperCollins*Publishers* Australia Pty Limited
ABN 36 009 913 517
harpercollins.com.au

HarperCollins*Publishers*
Level 13, 201 Elizabeth Street, Sydney NSW 2000, Australia
Unit D1, 63 Apollo Drive, Albany, Auckland 0632, New Zealand
A 53, Sector 57, Noida, UP, India
77–85 Fulham Palace Road, London, W6 8JB, United Kingdom
2 Bloor Street East, 20th floor, Toronto, Ontario M4W 1A8, Canada
10 East 53rd Street, New York NY 10022, USA

National Library of Australia Cataloguing-in-Publication data:

Harding, Traci.
  Dreaming of Zhou Gong / Traci Harding.
  ISBN: 978 0 7322 9267 6 (pbk.)
A823.3

Cover design by Darren Holt, HarperCollins Design Studio
Cover images: Woman by Chris Nicholls; all other images by shutterstock.com
Typeset in Goudy 11/16pt by Kirby Jones

Traci Harding, best selling author of 'the Ancient Future Series', has published in excess of twenty books through through HarperCollins/Voyager Australia, Brio Books and Bolinda Audio. Her work blends fantasy, fact, esoteric theory, time travel and quantum physics, into adventurous romps through history, alternative dimensions, universes and states of consciousness. Her books have been published in several languages throughout the world.

To find out more about Traci and her books
visit her website at: traciharding.com

For autographed copies of Traci's books visit her store at:
allthingstraci.com.au

Get Exclusive Content at Patreon:
patreon.com/user?u=20034469&fan_landing=true

Find Traci on Facebook at:
"Mastering Your Reality with Traci Harding" Group -
All Things Traci Store - Traci Harding Fans - Trazling

Traci is also on:
Twitter: @tracharding
Instagram: traciharding_author
YouTube: youtube.com/c/TraciHardingChannel
& Redbubble: redbubble.com/people/traciharding/shop?asc=u

Books by Traci Harding

The Ancient Future Trilogy
The Ancient Future: the Dark Age (1)
An Echo in Time: Atlantis (2)
Masters of Reality: the Gathering (3)

The Alchemist's Key

The Celestial Triad
Chronicle of Ages (1)
Tablet of Destinies (2)
The Cosmic Logos (3)

Ghostwriting

The Book of Dreams

The Mystique Trilogy
Gene of Isis (1)
The Dragon Queens (2)
The Black Madonna (3)

Triad of Being Trilogy
Being of the Field (1)
The Universe Parallel (2)
The Light-field (3)

For
Harold Hopkins,
who died 11 December 2011.
You were a dear friend,
a great actor,
and a wonderful human being.
You are sorely missed.

ACKNOWLEDGEMENTS

First and foremost, a huge credit goes to Lee Pou Lon, who meticulously checked all my research for this book, aided with the Chinese translations and proofread this manuscript for errors. His painstaking attention to detail saved me from making some very embarrassing errors (like a 30-foot long qin, for example) and awarded myself, my editors and now my readers, with a greater understanding of Chinese history and culture. Lon's input was invaluable, and thanks to his guidance and polish, I feel far more confident in presenting this story to the world.

Thanks also to my editors, Sue Moran and Stephanie Smith, and to my new commissioning editor, Deonie Fiford, all of whom are a pleasure to work with and, along with all the wonderful people at HarperCollins/Voyager Australia, continue to support my creative aspirations.

I also wish to thank my agent, Selwa Anthony, for her ongoing guidance and belief in me. Also my daughter, Sarah Harding, who listened to me read this story as it was written, and aided me to create the floor plan of the House of Yi Wu Li Shan and a map of ancient Zhou. To my son, John, a big hug for letting Mum get on with writing, and to Mum and Dad, all my family and friends — who don't really get to see me much, but are always there when I need them most.

I am very grateful to Cheryl Hesketh for maintaining my Trazling Messageboard and Facebook Page, to Trish Borg for taking care of my Traci Harding Fans Facebook page, and to David Harding for maintaining traciharding.com. Thanks to the moderators on all my sites and to my readers, near and far, who keep me gainfully employed as a writer and who email and post messages of encouragement — your excitement and enthusiasm are always inspiring!

Thanks to my pre-readers on this book, Rob and Christine; your feedback was very helpful.

The beautiful Chinese clock featured in the front pages of the book, I use with the kind permission of theabysmal.wordpress.com

The Holy City of Chengzhou map and illustration of the magic square, on page 415, were created by Lamassu Design.

All the speeches written by Ji Dan (Zhou Gong) in this tale were adapted from the translation of 'The Great Document' featured in *Sacred Books and Early Literature of the East: Ancient China* (see bibliography for details).

CONTENTS

PRONUNCIATION GUIDE

Tian — Tien (one syllable)
Li — Lee
Yi — Yee
Ji — Jee
Wu — Woo
Jiang — Jee-ahng
Huxin — Hoo-sin
He — Huh
Hu — Hoo
Hudan — Hoo-d'ah'n
Nuan — Nwhan
Haojing — Hou-jing
Zhou — Joe
Wen — Wun
Bo — Bow
Fen — Fuhn
Diji — Dee-Jee
Fa — F'ah'
Dan — D'ah'n
Shi — Shur
Chi — Chur
Zhu — Joo
Xian — Shee-en
Du — Doo
Chu — Choo
Hui — Hwee
Ru — Roo

LIST OF CHARACTERS

Li Shan

The Great Mother — Yi Wu

Wu Master — Shanyu Jiang Hudan

Shape-shifter — Shanyu Jiang Huxin

Healer — Wu Fen Gong

Wu Initiate — He Nuan

Cook — Ling

Haojing

Xibo Chang — Ji Chang (Zhou Wen Wang — deceased)

1st son of Xibo Chang — Bo Yi Kao (deceased)

2nd son of Xibo Chang — Ji Fa (Zhou Wu Wang)

4th son of Xibo Chang — Ji Dan (Zhou Gong)

9th son of Xibo Chang — Ji Shi (Shao Gong Shi)

Prime Minister of Zhou — Jiang Taigong

Wife of Ji Fa — Yi Jiang

Son of Ji Fa — Ji Song (Zhou Cheng Wang)

6th son of Xibo Chang — Ji Zhenduo (Cao Shu Zhenduo)

7th son of Xibo Chang — Ji Wu (Cheng Shu Wu)

Storeman of Ji family treasure house — Heng

Were-tiger twins — Zhen and Kao

Spirit Tiger — Ling Hu

Fenging

3rd son of Xibo Chang — Ji Xian (Guan Shu Xian)
5th son of Xibo Chang — Ji Du (Cai Shu Du)
8th son of Xibo Chang — Ji Chu (Hui Shu Chu)
10th son of Xibo Chang — Ji Zai

The Shang

Emperor — Zi Shou (Di Xin)
Emperor's wife, Wu and General — Su Daji
Emperor's son — Wu Geng
Emperor's uncles and Ministers — Bi Gan and Jizi
Minister Jizi's granddaughter — Hui Ru
Emperor's brother and Minister — Weizi
Affiliate with the Jade Book — Dragonface

Sons of the Sky

Ex-Governor of Kila — Rhun (Hreen)
Lord of the Otherworld/Elementals — Avery (Ang-wei)
The Akashic Memory — Telmo (Taliesin)

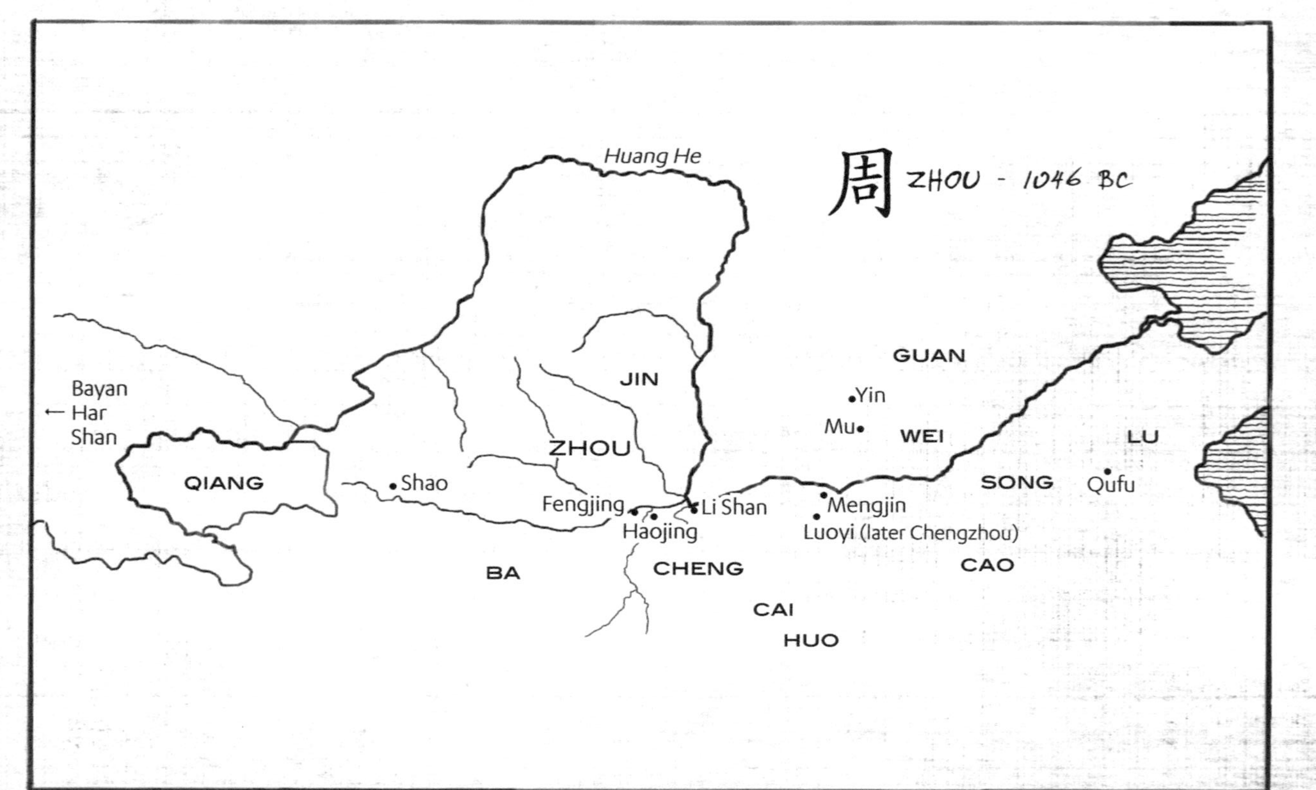

周 ZHOU - 1046 BC
Huang He
Bayan Har Shan →
QIANG
JIN
ZHOU
Shao
Fengjing
Haojing
Li Shan
BA
CHENG
Mengjin
Luoyi (later Chengzhou)
CAI
HUO
CAO
GUAN
Yin
Mu
WEI
SONG
Qufu
LU

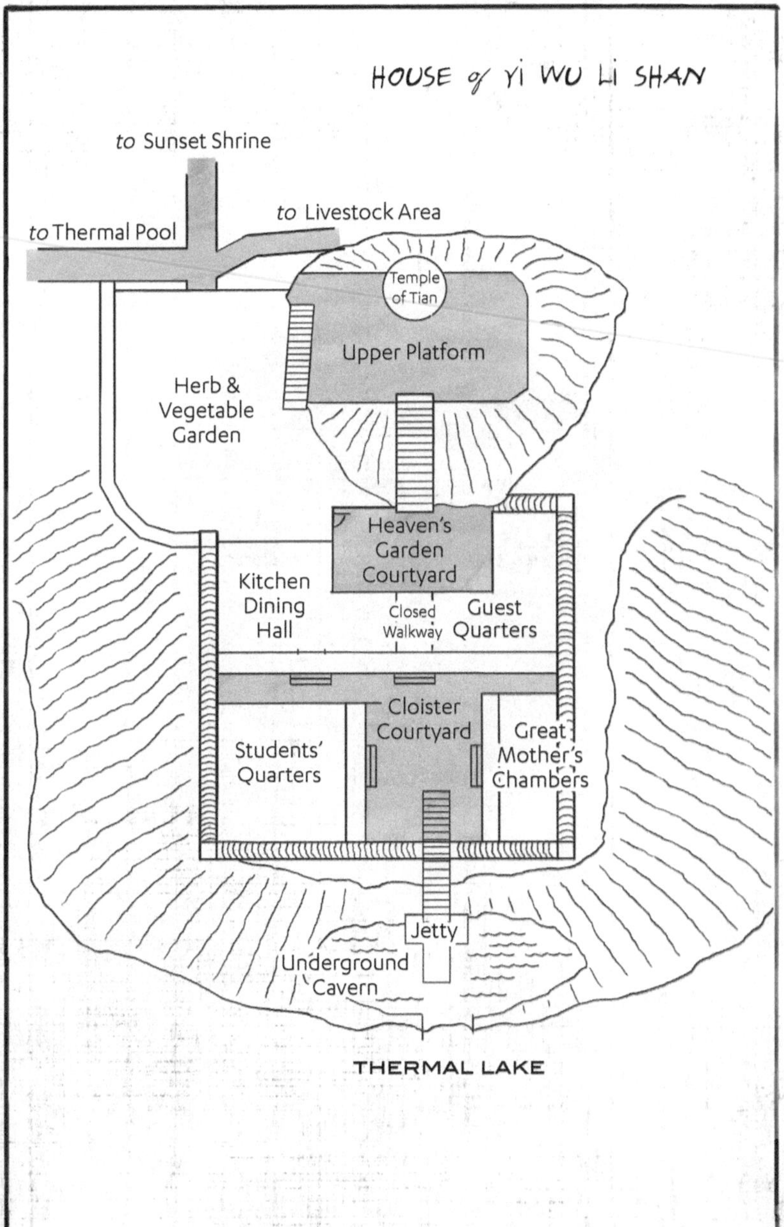

HOUSE of YI WU LI SHAN
to Sunset Shrine
to Livestock Area
to Thermal Pool
Temple of Tian
Upper Platform
Herb & Vegetable Garden
Heaven's Garden Courtyard
Kitchen Dining Hall
Closed Walkway
Guest Quarters
Cloister Courtyard
Students' Quarters
Great Mother's Chambers
Jetty
Underground Cavern
THERMAL LAKE

CHINESE CLOCK

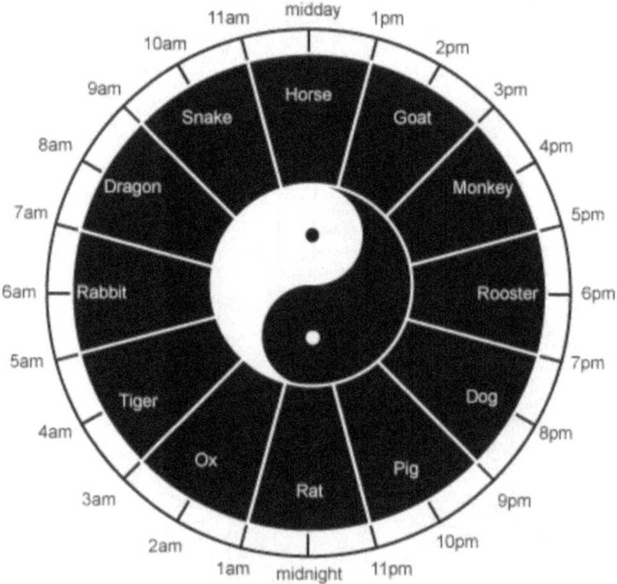

'I must be slipping.
It has been so long since I dreamt of the Duke of Zhou.'
— Confucius

HEAVEN'S MANDATE

In the past, the Shang king Zhongzong solemnly attended to heaven's mandate with the utmost care, fashioning ordinances to rule the people, always fearfully alert lest he should dare to become self-indulgent. For this reason, Zhongzong enjoyed his throne for seventy-five years.

When the throne passed to Gaozong, who had toiled long away from the capital, joining together with the common people, he observed the three-year mourning period in perfect silence, living in a hut by his father's grave. And when he did, at last, speak, his words were joyful, yet he did not dare become self-indulgent. He brought peace to the state of Shang, and none, whether great or small, had any complaint. For this reason, Gaozong enjoyed his throne for fifty-five years.

When it came to Zujia, he was at first unrighteous as king and was forced to dwell for long away from his throne, and so came to know the lot of the common people. He learned to succour the common people and never to disgrace those who were alone, without husbands or wives. For this reason, Zujia enjoyed his throne for thirty-three years.

Otherwise, from the reign of the Shang founder Tang to that of Diyi, none performed the proper sacrifices to make their virtue bright; none were a suitable match for heaven.

Now Diyi's son, Zi Shou, is greatly dissolute and lax; he attends neither to heaven, nor to the needs of the people. His people are all under a sentence of death.

In the meantime, King Wen of Zhou did not take the time even to eat a meal while the sun was in the sky, and so he enjoyed the throne of the Zhou people for fifty years.

— Zhou Gong Dan (Duke of Zhou)
The Book of Documents

There was a time, not so long past, that the Shang government had tenfold the population and wealth of the Zhou territories. It was my great father, Xibo Chang, renowned for his wisdom, fairness and tireless dedication to his people, who inspired so many citizens and provinces, once allied to the Shang, to quietly defect to the Western Lands under his rulership. By the advent of my father's untimely death, the land was divided into three parts, two of which were Zhou.

At the end of the three-year mourning period for Xibo Chang, my eldest brother, Ji Fa, rallied Zhou's troops with the intention of finishing what our great father started — the total defeat of the Shang. But the signs were not good for success. There were landslides at the mountain of Yao, and Ji Fa, Zhou's new Xibo, was urged by his advisors to be patient and await more favourable conditions to strike.

Three years have passed and Ji Fa is still uncertain whether the time to strike the Shang Empire is nigh.

Our prime minister, Jiang Taigong, is in agreement with him and whilst in private conference in the Xibo's council chambers at our ancestral home at Haojing, he advocated this path to Ji Fa and myself: 'While I was fishing, on the fateful day when I first met your great father, I realised one truth — if you want to succeed, you need to be patient. We must wait for the appropriate opportunity to eliminate the emperor, Zi Shou, and his Wu concubine and general, Su Daji.'

'I agree,' Ji Fa stated, although his tone implied he was only half in accord. 'However, those who flocked to support me, and mourned in patience for three years and refrained from action for another three, will not be content to delay further without good reason.'

I had to sympathise with my eldest living brother's reluctance to delay, as there was much bad blood between the Ji family and the

Shang ruler, Zi Shou. Yet, in this instance, I felt we could not allow our personal feelings to influence such an important political decision. We had to trust that, by the grace of Tian, Ruler of Heaven, a chance to avenge the deaths of our great father and beloved eldest brother would come in time. 'I believe I may have a solution.' I spoke up, for there was an observation I had made some time ago that weighed heavily on my mind.

Ji Fa looked my way. 'Your counsel is always welcome, Dan. Heaven knows you are the smartest of us all.' In saying 'us all', the Xibo referred to our nine brothers — eight since the death of our eldest brother, Bo Yi Kao.

I found my brother's flattering view abstruse, as it was Kao's goodness and intellect that I had always aspired to emulate, for in reality he was the most sagacious and beloved son of Xibo Chang. 'I believe, dear brother, that your hesitation to attack stems from the fact that the heavenly order to conquer the Shang has not been given.'

The troubled expression on the Xibo's face transformed into one of complete clarity. 'The mandate of Tian.'

Tian was the name the Zhou people used to refer to the Ruler of Heaven, who was neither male nor female.

'Exactly! The order to attack can only be given by heaven,' I concurred. 'The people will understand and respect this.'

'Are you suggesting that we consult the Wu?' The prime minister was concerned, as the Wu were an ancient holy order of female shamans who were in the service of heaven, and they were known to have extraordinary powers. 'The emperor's wife, Daji, is Wu. The people fear her supernatural power and despise her inhumanity.'

I served our dear advisor a look that implied that he was preaching to the converted. 'Daji murdered our eldest brother because she was sick with lust for him. No one hates that shapeshifting witch more than I. But the fact remains, mere warriors are never going to be enough to destroy her.'

'We need a Wu to kill a Wu.' Ji Fa nodded as he began to see the wisdom behind my reasoning.

'No man can give you permission to destroy the Shang.' I pointed out another benefit. 'Only the Wu in the service of the supreme god, Tian, can communicate the will of heaven to the people. And only the Great Mother of the Wu can bestow upon a family Tian's heavenly mandate.'

'Yi Wu Li Shan.' Ji Fa uttered the Great Mother's name with reverence. 'My great-grandfather told me tales when I was a young boy about the oracle woman and her House of Wu on Li Shan. Could she possibly still be living?'

'She is said to be immortal, highness.' Jiang Taigong stated his understanding of the matter. 'There has never been a report of her death, only of her miracles.'

'A prophecy of the downfall of Shang is said to have sprung from the Wu of Li Shan,' I added further weight to my argument. 'And the prophecy states that Zi Shou will go up in flames, and along with him the Shang Dynasty will end. So who, in heaven's eyes, should take his place, I wonder?'

My brother was inspired. 'You think the Great Mother may have foreseen that also?'

'It is entirely possible,' I answered. 'And, of course, the legendary Shanyu Jiang Hudan is said to reside at Li Shan, along with her tigress sister, Shanyu Jiang Huxin.'

The mere mention of their names put the look of horror back on my brother's face, for all Wu had supernatural power, but none, bar the evil Su Daji, were so famed as these women. 'Why would they help us? Our family has neglected to pay homage to the Great Mother ever since the emperor was bewitched by his wife, Su Daji, and turned into a compassionless tyrant.'

I agreed that the notion of seeking the aid of the Wu was daunting — there were many unknowns and variables to my strategy — yet my gut instinct told me this was the way forward. In reality, we had no other feasible option, as far as I could surmise.

'We nobles fear being bewitched in such a manner by the Wu,' I stated. 'But love for the women of the heavenly orders has not been lost among the common people, who still readily seek their advice, healing and spiritual counsel. I have been looking into the history of the Wu, as they have always advised and anointed the emperors in the past. However, never — before Su Daji — has a Wu left the service of heaven to pursue an earthly life of such debauchery and self-pleasure.'

'So, you're saying that Daji would be considered a disgrace to her heavenly sisters?' Jiang Taigong was most interested to learn this fact.

'Actually the Wu refer to each other as brothers, to reinforce that they are equal in status to men. Their Great Mother they call Shifu for the same reason, for no man on earth has dominion over her, or any of the students of her house, not even the emperor. The Wu answer only to Tian.'

'That could be dangerous.' The prime minister voiced the concern that was clear in his expression.

'The Wu are not interested in earthly affairs or pleasures, only in heavenly service. But the fact that one of the Wu is preventing us from achieving peace could certainly help us to gain their favour,' I concluded happily, for I was deeply curious about the Wu. They were said to have abundant knowledge about the inner and outer workings of heaven and earth and, as a scholar, I could not help but wonder what they could teach me. 'The Zhou must return to honouring Tian and his mistresses if the Ji family is to win heaven's mandate.'

Ji Fa smiled. 'This path sits well with me.' He looked to his prime minister for his approval.

'There is certainly no harm in making initial contact with the Wu and testing the waters for an alliance between heaven and earth,' Jiang Taigong granted. 'That would certainly appease the people, who miss the great festivals once presided over by the Wu, before Su Daji forbade all Wu within Shang states to practise.'

Fortunately, the temple of the Great Mother on Li Shan was deep in Zhou territory, almost inaccessible, and so the House of the Great Mother had been left in virtual peace to thrive.

The Xibo nodded, most pleased. 'We shall keep this quiet for the moment.' He looked at me. 'Dan, I charge you to go to Li Shan and seek the blessing of the Great Mother on my behalf.'

Of course, the notion pleased me greatly; it was a rare opportunity to satisfy some of my curiosity regarding the Wu. Yet I shook my head — not to disobey, but in warning. 'I am fairly certain that gaining heaven's mandate will be no simple matter, brother. There will be tribute to pay for our neglect of the holy House of Tian, trials to accomplish and sacred rites to observe in order to appease heaven and —'

'Then find out exactly what is required,' the Xibo interjected. 'For even if I was to depose Zi Shou, he has a son to whom heaven's mandate may be passed. Do I kill the son, Wu Geng, for fear of the same madness erupting if he lives to rule? Some divine insight is exactly what I require. If I am granted heaven's mandate, only then can I be sure that the demise of the Shang state is the will of Tian and in best interests of the people.'

This conclusion was personally satisfying, for I too needed some divine reassurance that the blood feud we were about to embark upon was indeed divinely meant. Hence I rose and bowed to my eldest brother and the prime minister to take my leave of them. 'I shall depart for Li Shan at once.'

Never had I been assigned a quest that so inspired me, and with this sense of purpose I hastened my exit from the Xibo's council chambers. My interest in the mysterious ways of the Wu had been ever growing since the untimely deaths of my father and my eldest brother at the hands of Su Daji. There had to be a way to combat her supernatural advantage — the laws of divine polarity dictated that it be so. As I proceeded down the stairs and into the grandly cobbled central courtyard at Haojing, I was determined to discover that counterforce, and prevent Su Daji from unleashing her evil power ever again on any member of my family, or the good people of Zhou.

PART 1

THE WU

1

YI WU LI SHAN

The sky above was dark and flashed electric with the promise of a storm that might break the long drought. Thunder growled in the distance. Through the steam clouds rising off the thermal waters, the torches of summons burned brightly in the night on the jetty ahead — this was the only means to request an audience with the Wu of Li Shan and she had been sent in response to the summons.

A team of hooded ferrywomen at her back were moving the ferryboat across the surface of the shallow thermal lake, using the power of their chi; no oars or ropes were required. This vessel was the only official means for supplicants to gain access to the temple of the Great Mother, for everyone knew that any man who attempted to reach the house of the Holy Orders uninvited never returned. The occupants of the ferry had their faces shrouded by the hoods of their long dark robes, but, as the representative of the Great Mother, she herself was dressed in white and stood on the bow of the ferry to address the seeker of their counsel. As their vessel neared the jetty, the noise in the rumbling sky was 3 13matched by the din before them. The rattle of battle armour, warrior chatter and horses served to tell her that a small army lay in wait. She motioned for the ferry to halt on the water at a good distance from the pier.

'Speak,' she requested and the commotion quickly hushed to silence. 'The Wu of Li Shan are listening.'

'I am Ji Dan, come to seek the guidance of the Great Mother on behalf of my brother, Ji Fa, Leader of the West.'

Both names were legendary. The sons of Xibo Chang were increasingly idolised by the common people of Zhou — the mightiest warlords in the land had come to the temple, just as the Great Mother had predicted.

'We were deeply saddened to hear of the death of Ji Chang, your great father,' she said in condolence. 'He brought a lasting peace and calm to the West.'

During the course of his life, Ji Chang had been recognised as a well-educated, conscientious and benevolent leader, dedicated to educating the population, promoting good ethics, assisting agricultural development and the migration of superior people into the state. Well-qualified advisors and functionaries, fleeing the chaos of Shang imperial rule, had flocked to the leadership opportunities in the West. As the Zhou state's popularity increased, the Shang emperor's rule became more ruthless and abusive in equal measure. When Ji Chang was invited to the capital to advise the emperor, he was instead arrested on a charge of conspiring to foment revolution. Ji Chang was locked up at Youli, where he remained imprisoned for seven years. The Zhou ruler spent this time studying the trigrams of old, and reinterpreted their meaning by sorting them into a system of sixty-four hexagrams for strategic divination called the *Yi Jing: The Book of Changes*. The *Yi Jing* had then revealed to Ji Chang the rise of the Zhou Dynasty.

During his imprisonment, those with wealth who secretly supported Ji Chang presented the emperor with beautiful girls, fine horses and other riches on Ji Chang's behalf to prove his loyalty to the emperor. His suspicions dispelled, Zi Shou released Ji Chang and named him Xibo — leader of all the Zhuhou of the lands in the West. Upon his release, Xibo Chang immediately began scouring the country for talented men who could help him destroy the Shang empire.

'His sons hope to continue his legacy,' Ji Dan told her in a strong voice that carried across to the ferry, 'and are here to seek heaven's mandate to depose the emperor, who no longer serves heaven, our great ancestors or the people. We understand a prophecy of the downfall of Zi Shou hailed from the House of Yi Wu Li Shan and I am here to discover if my great and noble brother Ji Fa is the one whom the Great Mother foresees will put an end to the madness of Shang oppression.'

'You want the permission of the Great Mother to go to war,' she clarified.

'We are already at war,' the lord replied, 'but, yes, if that is the will of heaven.'

'The will of heaven is that we live in peace.'

'That is our greatest wish also.' Ji Dan was amused; she could hear it in his voice. 'My brother respectfully asks the Great Mother to consider, given it is one of the Wu who inspired much of Zi Shou's madness, whether you would aid us to defeat her?'

'Daji is not of the House of Yi Wu Li Shan,' she replied coolly. Ji Dan's attempt to use of guilt tactics did not impress her. 'We cannot be held responsible for her corrupt ideology and destructive practices. She has permanently damaged the reputation of *all* the Wu in the eyes of the people.'

Where once there had been numerous temples of practising Wu throughout the land, many had been destroyed upon the Shang emperor's word. Other cloisters had been destroyed by the local people, who feared Wu were all evil like Su Daji, or the emperor's wraith, for allowing the local Wu to remain practising in their vicinity.

'That is because none of the Wu has done anything to depose her,' Ji Dan offered. 'If our armies are to have any chance of overthrowing Zi Shou, we must first deal with Su Daji. The Wu have powers beyond that of mortal man, and the Wu of the House of Yi Wu Li Shan are the most famed and respected in the West. Where else could we possibly find Daji's equal?'

The notion of combatting Daji, who had shamed the Wu so greatly, appealed to her very much. 'The Great Mother will only speak with the candidate for her heavenly mandate about such matters.'

'I can only bring forth the candidate once I know his safety in your house is assured,' Ji Dan bartered. 'At the very least, I would have to accompany Ji Fa as far as your cloister.'

'You have my word that you and your brother will have a safe passage to Yi Wu Li Shan and back,' she avowed.

'And who are you, lady?' the lord asked. 'May I have a name to report to my brother as our contact among the Wu?'

'I am Jiang Hudan,' she announced, and her name incited gasps and muttering among the soldiers. The reverence and fear she detected were very pleasing to her.

'I have heard of you, Tiger Courage,' the lord stated, for 'tiger courage' was what her name meant. 'They say you have a sister who is a white tiger, but how can that be?'

'Mortal men are not expected to understand all the wonders of heaven,' she replied.

'This mortal man would very much like to try,' Ji Dan announced humbly.

Beneath her hood, Jiang Hudan was smiling. 'Your thirst for knowledge precedes you, Ji Dan, and I hear that you are quite the diviner yourself.'

'To divine strategy for wars and hunts is one thing, but to divine the will of Tian, without human bias, is quite something else,' he granted.

His words were pleasing and unexpectedly insightful for a man. Hudan was about to respond when her birth sister leaned over her shoulder to hiss in her ear: 'Stop indulging in this pointless banter and dismiss him.'

'As you command, Xi Wangmu,' Hudan quipped quietly to her, and her sister gave a low, barely audible growl of resentment.

Xi Wangmu was not her sister's name, for it was a title that meant 'Great Mother of the West', and was currently held by their Shifu, Yi Wu. But Hudan had foreseen, long ago that her sister, Huxin, would someday be given this title, so the nickname was a private joke between the sisters; Hudan referred to Huxin thus whenever she thought her twin was being a little high and mighty. Huxin meant 'tiger heart', and she was not renowned for her diplomacy or her patience.

'Return with your candidate in five days' time, Ji Dan. The Great Mother will see him then,' Hudan advised. Huxin backed off to focus, along with her brothers, on powering the ferry for them to return to the cloister.

'As you request, lady,' Ji Dan called. 'Ji Fa greatly looks forward to this audience.'

As there was nothing more to be said, the ferry began to move and Hudan took a seat, nursing a rather overwhelming feeling that she had been in this circumstance before — although, in reality, she knew she had not.

'What is it?' Huxin sensed her sister's discomposure, just as she had sensed her delight with Ji Dan's comments only moments before. 'Do you suspect something untoward?'

'Quite the reverse,' Hudan whispered back. 'I feel like I've had this meeting before … perhaps I foresaw it while in trance and am only now remembering? But, for whatever reason I feel this way, it must be significant.'

Huxin was amused. 'You are about to help bring about your own prophecy. This meeting is the proof you saw correctly … I would say that is sufficient.'

Hudan wished she was as pleased about her prophecy as everyone else was; she'd never foreseen such a major event before. Everyone wanted the cruel Shang regime to come to an end, herself included, but only war on a massive scale was going to bring that about and she feared that her prophecy had only added fuel to the fire of that horrendous prospect. Many people were going to die attempting to fulfil her vision, and she could only pray to heaven that their ultimate sacrifice would bear sweet fruit for following generations — for this too, she had foreseen, and it gave her the strength to stand by her prophecy.

The ferry docked at the House of Yi Wu Li Shan, so named after their Great Mother, Yi of the Wu, who resided on Mount Li. The name Yi meant to heal, whilst Wu marked their Great Mother, or Shifu, as an oracle, seer, shaman and mistress of Tian; Shan simply meant mountain. Shanyu, which was a nickname that was at times used to refer to Jiang Hudan and Jiang Huxin, simply implied that they were 'mountain born'.

Hudan made her way from the jetty and walked under the raised iron gate and up the long flight of stone stairs that cut through the mountain and into the central courtyard of the cloister. The iron gate dropped closed behind her. Although it was late, and long past the dog-hour that marked curfew, she knew her Shifu would be awaiting her report. Hudan headed straight for the Great Mother's private council chamber.

'Enter,' Shifu said when Hudan announced herself and the doors opened wide.

The Great Mother was seated comfortably in her chair of council, radiant and serene, as Hudan entered. She had not aged a day in Hudan's lifetime. All the Wu had great longevity, but none so much as Shifu Yi, who always appeared old enough to be wise, but young enough to preserve her beauty — she had not one grey strand in her long thick hair. The Wu were not vain, but Shifu maintained that, against a man, beauty was a weapon more effective than any sword.

Head bowed, her right fist pressed into her left palm and held out before her, Hudan came forth, knelt and lowered her head. 'Shifu Yi.'

'Be at ease, Jiang Hudan,' the Great Mother granted, and Hudan sat back on her haunches.

'I have come to report that Ji Dan seeks your heavenly mandate for his brother Ji Fa, leader of the West, just as you predicted.'

'Yes,' she concurred, 'and he will return with the candidate in five days' time.'

'Shifu, why request my report, if you already know the outcome of my meeting?'

'You cannot fathom the answer?' she inquired.

Hudan's heart sank, as she had a fair idea what was on her Shifu's mind. 'You wish to speak with me about another matter entirely. Is this about brother Fen?'

'Must we go through this every year?' her Shifu appealed and thus confirmed Hudan's fears. 'I will not have a rooster in my henhouse, no matter how well you try to disguise him as a chicken. Every year I threaten to sacrifice him at the Spring Festival and every year he mysteriously goes missing!' she scolded. 'Every year I tell you if he is not gone from here by next spring he will be sacrificed, and is he gone?'

'No, Shifu,' Hudan replied, her head bowed, 'but among our brotherhood there is no one who is a better gardener, healer or herbalist —'

'I am well aware of his talents, Hudan. Why do you think he is still breathing? But the fact remains he is not a cute little child any longer. In a year he will be a full-grown man!'

The idea of her adopted baby brother being a man sounded like a joke, but she caught her urge to laugh before it escaped her lips.

'All men have desires, Hudan,' Yi said in all seriousness, 'and I know for a fact that sweet little Fen Gong is already bestowing his earthly favours on one of our order.'

Hudan gasped — shocked, bewildered, betrayed! She'd been valiantly defending Fen's right to remain here as a faithful servant of this house, but if what her Shifu said was true, no amount of arguing would save him from the spring fires, banishment or some other severe punishment.

'It is only because the woman in question is not a vestal virgin of this house, that I have not already had him seized and quartered.' Her Shifu was clearly most displeased.

Hudan suspected that, secretly, the Great Mother did not want the celebration preparations disrupted by sacrificing the head of her garden. 'It was He Nuan, wasn't it? She's been making eyes at Fen for years —'

'It makes no difference *who* it was,' her Shifu insisted. 'The point is, Fen must go.'

'Not before the festival, surely?' Hudan pleaded. As angry as she was, she wasn't ready to bid him farewell. Next to Huxin, Fen meant more to Hudan than anyone else in her world … including her Shifu.

'Of course not.' The Great Mother seemed frustrated by that fact. 'I need him in the garden until then. And once the festival comes, we shall need a human sacrifice,' she concluded, smiling.

Hudan knew Shifu Yi didn't mean what she said. She was as fond of Fen as everyone else under her roof. 'We have other prisoners,' she appealed, as she always did.

'Ah, but none are as young, talented and pretty as your brother, Fen — *sacrifice* is not just a figure of speech!'

Hudan breathed deeply to calm herself. She felt frustrated and angry for being put in this uncomfortable position with her Shifu.

'So,' Yi Wu concluded, 'I want your personal assurance that our beautiful sacrifice will not go mysteriously missing this year.'

Hudan nodded her head in agreement. 'Right now, Shifu, I believe I would push him into the flames myself.'

Fen Gong had been Hudan's ward since he'd been left on their jetty as a child of three years. She'd been barely eight years on this earth herself at the time, and had taken an immediate shine to him.

A man-child left for the Wu was only ever intended to be a sacrifice to Tian, Ruler of Heaven. It was common knowledge that only women occupied the House of Yi Wu Li Shan. Whoever had delivered the boy and lit the torches of summons, would have believed they were sealing his fate.

But fate has its own agenda. Fen was living proof.

Caged in the kitchen at first, Fen was only to be kept alive until the Spring Festival. But so pretty and well behaved was the boy-child that none of their order could spurn him. They may have called themselves brothers, and were hardened fighters all, but the hearts of women still burned in their chests and fed their instinct to protect and nurture the child as a mother might.

Hudan, an orphan herself, empathised with the lone youngster, who did not have a twin to cling to, as she had. She took to creeping down to the kitchen to keep him company and stop him fretting at night — and Huxin did too. They started dressing the lad in their old clothes, so that he could sit at the table with them and the other female initiates without looking out of place. As all her brothers were as charmed by the boy as Hudan was, no one complained, and as Shifu Yi rarely ate at their table — for she rarely ate at all — it was some time before she discovered that her spring sacrifice had become the new and beloved pet of her household.

When their Shifu realised she'd have a rebellion on her hands if she burnt the boy, she gave Hudan charge of him as a punishment, but Fen had brought them all nothing but happiness, wonder and joy. Once given liberty to roam the house, garden and mountain top beyond, it became apparent that Fen might have been left to the Wu for reasons other than appeasing heaven as a sacrifice. For the boy showed an unnatural talent for growing and healing just about any living thing, hence his name Fen Gong, which meant 'fragrant magic'; he could make flowers bloom with a touch, even in the coldest winter. This was the by-product of another supernatural ability Fen possessed. Through skin contact, Fen could influence the emotions of others with his own. Had the person who abandoned the boy-child on Li Shan known this? Such influence over others at such a young age would have been a terrifying prospect to one of the common folk and nobility alike! Maybe they wisely surmised that, if such a child was ever to belong anywhere on this earth, that place would be among the Wu?

Only Hudan and Huxin were close enough to Fen to have discovered the emotional influence he could command over others — if Shifu Yi had discovered it, she had said nothing. In the event of Fen ever needing this talent to save his life, his adopted sisters kept it secret. As Fen was so extraordinarily pretty, he'd blended in for years. Even now, although obviously lacking in the breast department, Fen could pass for one of the prettiest females in the house.

So Shifu Yi had turned a blind eye to Fen's existence: he'd made himself indispensable in the garden and infirmary, and he'd exhibited exemplary behaviour and aptitude in his lessons. But these past few years, some of those in her order had begun regarding Fen differently. The younger girls, especially, were all soft smiles and fluttering eyes ... which Hudan had instructed Fen to ignore.

'Their silly vanity is going to get you banished,' she had warned him.

But had he listened? Clearly not.

As two of the most prized students of the House of Yi Wu Li Shan, Hudan and Huxin had their own room; sharing with them had kept Fen out of the dormitory of the younger initiates and away from the private rooms of the highly adept students and the older matrons — many of whom had chosen a cloistered life after being widowed. Most of these matrons were not trained Wu but were welcome to serve in the cloister in exchange for the protection and security the Wu could provide them.

When Hudan reached their sleeping quarters, her anger at boiling point, she stopped outside the door, to calm and centre herself.

Anger is one step away from disempowerment, her Shifu always said.

She could not just storm in and give Fen a serve of her mind without waking the entire household and making them aware of his shame. But there was no way she was going to sleep on this; her fury would ebb by morning, and Hudan wanted Fen to feel the full brunt of her disappointment and betrayal.

Hence she entered quietly, and finding Huxin and Fen sleeping, Hudan moved to the end of Fen's bed and clasped her hands into a single fist in front of her chest in order to summon her chi to serve her intention.

Everyone in residence at Yi Wu Li Shan trained in Dao Yin every day. Dao Yin was a system of gymnastic exercises that combined flighting techniques with ritual dance. Breath combined with motion cultivated internal energy — chi. With practice, chi could be harnessed, directed and unleashed by the practitioner on their mental command, enabling them to perform feats that the uninitiated considered superhuman.

Once Hudan felt confident, she raised her clasped hands and extended only her first two fingers upward to form a peak. She aligned her sights with the peak of her fingers and directed her will at her unsuspecting victim. Fen's body began to rise off his bed and he continued sleeping like a baby as Hudan directed his form to follow her through the abandoned walkways of the house, down through the huge kitchen area and into the herb and vegetable garden.

The storm had cleared without a drop of rain — a sign of Tian's continuing disfavour of the rulership of their land — and the waxing moon lit the way through the dark. At the end of the garden path was a gate that led into the sacred gardens; here Hudan turned right and eventually came to the livestock area. A large stone trough was, in more prosperous times, constantly fed icy cold water from a mountain stream, but lately, due to drought, they'd been forced to fill the trough for the livestock from the well.

Once Fen's sleeping form was positioned above the trough, Hudan released her hold over him and let him drop into the water. Shocked into awareness, Fen screamed and floundered until he managed to fathom where he was and jump out of the trough. For a moment he stood shivering, bemused by how he'd got there. Then he solved the conundrum. 'Hudan!'

'Yes, Fen.' Her close proximity in the darkness startled him to an about-face.

'What kind of cruel joke is this?' He controlled his shivers.

'Oh, it's not a joke,' she informed him, 'it's a punishment.'

'A punishment?' he queried, warily. 'What have I done to displease you?'

'You know what you have done ...' Hudan said harshly, and Fen's head sank into his shoulders and he began shivering again. '... and Shifu Yi knows also.'

Fen's head shot back up, and even in the moonlight Hudan could see his horrified expression.

'You told her!' He was deeply hurt by that notion, and so was Hudan.

'She told me!' Hudan's voice conveyed her humiliation. 'So know that your days here on Li Shan are numbered.'

'Then I hope the Great Mother means to kill me this time.' He took a seat on the side of the trough, clearly devastated. 'I cannot live without this place,' he said, and his voice dropped to a whisper, 'I cannot live without her.'

'You idiot!' Hudan slapped him across the back of the head. 'It was He Nuan, wasn't it?'

Fen turned his large brown eyes to Hudan, and they were filled with tears of sorrow. 'It has always been He Nuan,' he confessed. 'I have waited a long time for her to see me, as I have always seen her.'

'Ooh ...' Hudan was frustrated, but refrained from hitting him again. 'Idiot! Was it worth your vocation? Worth giving up your family, home, *your life* for?'

He nodded confidently.

Hudan was completely baffled by his lack of regret. 'I have fought so hard for your right to remain here on Li Shan, and then you commit the one truly forbidden act of our Order!'

'We are permitted to pleasure ourselves.' He stood to defend himself. 'And I did nothing that Nuan could not have done to herself … except for the tongue thing —'

'Fen!' Hudan, shocked to her core, covered his mouth. 'I don't want to know. For goddess' sake, the woman is old enough to be your mother!' She shoved him backward in disgust.

'Holy Tian, you don't think she could be, do you?' He was horrified by the notion.

Hudan was inclined to let him suffer, but could not. 'No, she was already with us when you were dropped off.'

'Phew.' He began breathing again, and Hudan was annoyed.

'Well, if you had picked a girl anywhere near your own age, you wouldn't have to wonder!' Hudan vexed. 'Still, good thing you didn't or you'd be in several pieces by now.'

'I should warn her.' Fen made a move, but Hudan stopped him.

'It's over, and the matter is in Shifu Yi's hands,' she said pointedly. 'You'll not be allowed to see her again —'

'Is she in trouble?' Fen was clearly more concerned about his lover, than himself.

'Forcing Shifu into a position where she must sacrifice her head gardener at festival time? I can't imagine that is going to be a picnic,' Hudan acknowledged. 'But if Shifu doesn't punish her for this, I surely will.'

'No, Hudan, *please*, brother.' He got down on his knees and begged.

'I don't understand you, Fen.' She felt she was conversing with a complete stranger.

'How could you understand, when you have never been in love?' he appealed.

'Nor will I be,' Hudan insisted, '*ever*. It is not *permitted*!' Hudan grabbed his arm and dragged him to his feet. 'We are the servants of Tian, and have sexual union through the divine instruction of heaven only.'

'Maybe this was the will of heaven,' Fen reasoned, 'or why would I feel so compelled?'

'It is far more likely that this was a test,' Hudan replied, 'and you failed *miserably*.'

'If that is the case, I am completely to blame.' Fen appealed to her: 'Please don't punish Nuan for my shortcomings.'

Hudan could only roll her eyes. 'If you think she cares for you just as much, you are naive. She has preyed on you due to lack of choice!'

'Take that back!'

Hudan had never seen a look of such intensity on Fen's face before.

'You are implying she is a whore and she is —'

'So! That was her profession before she came here.'

This news came as some surprise to Fen. 'That's a lie.'

'It is the truth,' Hudan insisted, crushing him emotionally with her certainty. 'And if her lust gets you killed, I will not be happy. You need to be more worried about what is going to happen to you!'

'I am for Shifu's fire at last.' He sounded completely resigned to his fate.

'Not if I have anything to do with it.' Hudan was passionate, even if Fen wasn't.

He shook his head. 'I told you, brother; I cannot live without her.'

Hudan felt for him, and then realised he'd gently taken hold of her arm, which she immediately pulled from his grasp. 'I guess you should have kept your tongue to yourself then.' She flashed a smile and left him for her bed.

The next morning after meditation, when Hudan and Fen were not speaking to each other, it was clear to everyone that something tense had transpired between them.

'Enough.' Huxin could not stand the silence over breakfast any longer. 'What has happened?' She looked at Hudan across the small table that the three of them occupied at every meal that was not an official occasion. Her brother completely ignored her and continued eating. So Huxin looked to Fen, whose head was hung in shame as he shrugged. 'And where is He Nuan this morning?' she queried more loudly, addressing the entire room to discover if the absence was relevant.

An answer came from the far end of the dining hall where the kitchen was open to the rest of the room. 'She left last night,' Ling, the head cook, informed the room, and her statement sent whispers flying around the many full tables.

'What!' Fen had leapt to his feet and his protest startled everyone to silence, as he was normally so quiet and reserved.

'Aha.' Huxin was granted some clarity about the situation between Fen and Hudan.

'How could she leave voluntarily?' Fen asked, somewhat less as though his life depended upon the answer.

'How would I know? I'm only the cook,' old Ling barked. 'Ask Shifu Yi!'

Fen had gone pale and Hudan yanked him back into his seat.

'Although He Nuan never really belonged here, nobody just *leaves*,' Huxin said in a low voice, so that only the two brothers at her table could hear. She raised her eyebrows as if expecting some enlightenment from them.

Both her brothers declined to respond, however.

'So, I guess He Nuan has either been banished or butchered,' Huxin added and this time her comment fetched a reaction.

Fen was back on his feet and out the door. Hudan went straight after him, and Huxin playfully followed their lead.

'Fen, I would not vex Shifu Yi about this right now,' Hudan warned, as she trailed him through the covered walkways of the central courtyard. Thankfully, everyone was still at breakfast.

'I must know what has really happened,' he called back, staying one step ahead of her grasp.

'You don't need to know,' Hudan stressed, and, sick of the pursuit, she employed her will over matter, whereupon Fen's feet stuck to the stone beneath them and he was rendered immobile. 'He Nuan is none of your concern,' she said for Huxin's benefit, as she was still with them, seeking answers.

'If she is dead, then I wish to join her,' he said honestly, much to Hudan's distress and Huxin's insight.

'Come on,' Huxin said. 'You think I don't know our little

brother has been getting a bit of slap and tickle.' She extended her tongue and wriggled it about.

'You told Shifu Yi,' Fen exclaimed in horror.

'Hell no,' Huxin laughed. 'The day I, or anyone, has to tell Shifu Yi what goes on under her own roof will be the day the walls of this house crumble. You think I do not sneak out for a little romp every now and again.'

Both Hudan and Fen were shocked, but Huxin smiled. 'Not with humans, of course.' Huxin shrugged when the other two looked even more horrified. 'But then it is my heavenly duty to do so, lest I be one of the last were-tiger in the land.'

'Are you condoning what brother Fen has done?' Hudan hissed quietly, almost panicking to learn that she alone among her siblings was virtuous in mind, body and spirit.

Huxin rolled her eyes at Hudan and approached Fen, running her fingers through the black hair that fell, perfectly straight, to his shoulders.

He and Hudan could easily pass as blood sisters. They had the same chiselled features, pitch-black hair, ebony eyes and slim form that made them appear as beautiful and regal as princesses. Yet Huxin, although Hudan's birth twin, could not have been more different. They were equal in height and slim of form, but Huxin had the rounded face of a cheeky waif and a mane of long, golden brown waves that hung to her waist and matched her eyes which were the colour of dark, amber jewels.

'It was bound to happen,' Huxin stated, 'but look on the bright side, Fen.'

'There is a bright side?' he queried, on the verge of losing his mind.

Huxin nodded. 'If Shifu has truly banished He Nuan, then perhaps she will show mercy and banish you, too, then you may get your wish to be together.'

'Oh, my heavens!' Fen's mood lifted considerably having been thrown a thread of hope. 'You're right, brother Huxin.' He threw his arms around her and hugged her with delight.

'Don't encourage his wanton desires!' Hudan was disgusted with them both.

'Why not?' Huxin replied. 'Fen deserves a happy life, just like anyone. More than most!' she concluded, proud of him, and received another squeeze from their little brother in appreciation of her support.

'Do you really think Shifu might have a happier plan for us?' he beseeched Huxin, who began to nod.

'All Shifu has in mind for you at present is a prize place upon the ceremonial fire,' Hudan said sombrely, bringing them back into the realm of reality. 'She made me vow you would not go missing this year and would present when you were called for.'

When all the joy and positivity had fled from their brother once more, Huxin was very annoyed. 'Way to go, *brother*.'

'Fen is my charge!' Hudan was surprised that no one seemed to be considering this fact. 'He has shamed me in the eyes of our Shifu.'

Again Huxin rolled her eyes. 'I doubt very much Fen's actions have left the shadow of a stain upon your perfect life of sacrifice to Tian.'

'Why do you mock my aspiring to greatness?' Hudan asked, offended, as Huxin did this often.

'I'm just saying,' Huxin retorted, 'that it is unreasonable to expect everyone to be as perfect as you.'

Hudan knew Huxin was right. It was more her pride than her concern for Fen, that was driving her anger. 'The point I am trying to make is … if Fen storms off and starts demanding information from Shifu, she will be less inclined to be lenient on him. Do not tempt fate … just wait until she summons you.'

'So you forgive me, brother Hudan?' Fen ventured to ask.

'No,' she replied, 'I'm just less mad at you.'

'Less mad enough to allow me my feet back?' he requested, and then added by way of an inducement: 'Or we will all be late for Dao Yin.'

Satisfied that he was not going to do anything rash, Hudan let go of her hold over her little brother and Fen was grateful to be back in control of his body.

'To your lessons then,' she prompted as he grinned thankfully at her.

'Thank you, my brothers,' he bowed as he withdrew. 'Your support means everything.' He quickly turned to make his way to class, leaving Hudan gaping and Huxin giggling in his wake.

'If he thinks I am going to support him setting up house with a whore twice his age —'

Huxin thumped Hudan's arm quite hard. 'Oh, lighten up, brother. He's in love.'

'The ultimate excuse to forget one's duty and honour, I'm sure.' Hudan was dark about the whole affair. 'And if you think He Nuan wasn't using our brother as a means to escape the cloistered life, you're as deluded as he is!' Hudan stormed off, leaving her sister musing on the truth of Hudan's statement.

2

THE JI FAMILY

In the hour of the dog, five days after his first dialogue with the Wu, Ji Dan had his soldiers light the torches on the jetty extending out over the steamy waters of the thermal lake, in the foothills of Li Shan. He then ordered all the men to withdraw a good distance, make camp and await further instructions.

For Ji Dan the evening was alive with great expectation, but his brother, the Xibo, he'd never seen so nervous.

'We are not going into battle.' Dan felt it needed saying. 'For once we are in search of wisdom, not destruction.'

'You know me, Dan,' Ji Fa replied. 'Anything of this world I can deal with. But events and creatures otherworldly?' He twitched his head, not so confident. 'What if they bewitch us all? Who will run Zhou? They will, probably!'

Dan was amused by his brother's fears. 'An imperial appointment requires an emperor's courage. If the Wu wanted to kill you, they would kill you in your bed with no witnesses, not on their holy mountain. They have as much to gain by joining forces with us, as we do with them … we have a common enemy.'

Fa nodded, liking his brother's reasoning, but he was only partially set at ease by it.

'I am not afraid of the Wu,' Ji Song, the Xibo's young heir, announced. When Song had discovered his father's intention to visit the mysterious Wu of Li Shan, he had insisted on accompanying him.

'Are you not?' Fa was impressed with his boy's steely countenance.

'I have had dreams about them,' Song said, 'the maidens of

Tian who are vestals belonging to the emperor *alone*.' He grinned and his father laughed — his uncle did not.

'Well, no one could accuse you of not having a vivid imagination,' Dan responded.

'Or a one-track mind,' the Xibo added jovially.

'It was a vision, not a dream, Uncle,' Song assured him in all seriousness, the cocky grin never leaving his face.

'And I suppose in this vision the Wu were young and of unsurpassed beauty?' Dan challenged the reality of the lad's premonition.

'They were,' Song stated surely, 'for they are immortal and forever virtuous, despite any sexual relations they might be called upon by Tian to have with their emperor.'

Dan found Song's ideas rather more vivid than expected. 'Where on earth have you been getting your information?'

'From my visions, of course,' Song replied.

'Well, I'd be very careful of assuming anything about the Wu that you might take for granted with the women of your court. They will not answer to you or any man, only to heaven,' Dan said seriously. He did not want to cause any offence when they met the Wu.

'Well, who do you think sent me the vision?' Song challenged, and the sound of rippling water drove their conversation to a whisper.

'Do and say nothing that might bring their wrath upon us,' Dan cautioned Song more sternly. 'You do not need to fear them, but you *need* to show respect. If you are not sincere, they will know it.'

'Your uncle is the wisest man I know next to Jiang Taigong,' Fa instructed his son. 'Heed his words, now and always.'

'Even when I am emperor?' Song asked, not entirely happy to get such advice.

'Especially then.'

The Xibo and Dan turned to face the incoming ferry and, much to their amazement, the vessel, carrying nine hooded figures — eight in black and one in white — glided to the dock of its own accord and stopped alongside the steps without any of its occupants flinching from their standing pose.

The hooded figure in white came forth onto the dock to greet them. 'The House of Yi Wu Li Shan bids welcome to the noble warriors of Zhou.' The white hood slid off the wearer's head onto her shoulders without any physical movement on her part, and Dan was not the only one stunned by the beauty of the Great Mother's messenger; his brother and nephew were equally enchanted. 'I am Jiang Hudan —'

When Song gasped, her eyes turned his way. 'You are a legend,' he said by way of explanation, his eyes scanning the vessel they were about to board.

'You are wondering where my famous tiger sister is at present?' the lady asked, as if able to read the lad's mind. He nodded, and Jiang Hudan grinned. 'She is very close,' she teased, 'and although you cannot see her, she definitely has her eye on you, Ji Song.'

Song gulped, and both Dan and the Xibo had to suppress their amusement. 'How did you know who I was?' he asked.

'I have seen you all whilst in trance,' she explained. When her eyes looked Dan's way before she looked across to the Xibo, he wondered if this meant she had foreseen something of his future also, or whether she was confused as to which one of them was Ji Fa?

'You were the one who made the prophecy about the downfall of the Shang?' Dan voiced what he suddenly suspected.

'I was,' she confessed, and clearly the weight of that responsibility hung heavy on her young shoulders, yet she bore the fact with pride nonetheless.

Jiang Hudan was easily ten years Ji Dan's junior, and she was as fragile as a lotus flower to look at, yet her demeanour was as forceful as the fiercest warrior. She was exactly as her legend described — beautiful, dauntless and mysterious. There was a power that emanated from her that left Dan feeling like he was on the threshold of a greater awareness. Even Song could feel it, as he was sincerely humbled and awed by her presence.

'The Great Mother expects your visit will last a few days, for she has much to discuss with the candidate,' and she tipped her head respectfully to the Xibo, although she was not required to do so.

Jiang Hudan was a highly adept Wu and even if he were emperor, she would still be Ji Fa's equal. This was how balance had been maintained in the days of the great Yellow Emperor: men ruled the earth, but women ruled the heavens. It was also clear that Jiang Hudan knew exactly who was who.

'Yi Wu of Li Shan hopes this will be pleasing to her guests,' Hudan continued.

'My time is at the Great Mother's disposal.' Ji Fa found his tongue, and bowed his head to their hostess, before turning to his son. 'Run and tell the men I shall return in a few days, or send you back with a message if I am to be delayed longer.'

Song hesitated, frowning. 'Do not leave without me.' Clearly the lad thought this might be a ploy to be rid of him.

'I cannot send you back with a message, if you are not with us,' the Xibo said patiently. 'Now, please run, and let us not keep legends waiting!'

Their hostess was amused by their banter, watching Song run off as fast as his legs would carry him.

'Thirteen years on this earth and they think they know everything,' Fa looked back at the lady in white.

'We were no different,' Dan commented. Despite the young heir challenging him at times, Dan thought a questioning nature was healthy, and not insulting.

'Only in your case, Dan, you *did* know everything,' the Xibo said, embarrassing him with the extravagant compliment.

'I am far from all-knowing —' Dan began to say, feeling more like a blind idiot than an esteemed scholar in the present company.

'The wisest man in the land, so we hear,' Jiang Hudan said in an aside to the Xibo, only compounding Dan's embarrassment — he could feel his cheeks burning bright red.

'Truly, I still have so much more to learn.' He bowed his head a little to hide the heat in his face, quietly thanking Tian for the cover of night.

'As do we all,' Jiang said graciously. 'My Shifu has prepared a feast to welcome you to our house and a demonstration to give you a greater insight into our order. Yi Wu vows that tonight you will dine in heaven.'

'Heaven is somewhere I should very much like to dine.' Fa looked at Dan, not too sure how he felt about Jiang's claim.

'That sounds splendid,' Dan replied. 'Shall we climb aboard whilst we await my nephew?'

'Follow me.' Hudan turned and led them onto the ferry where her eight hooded brothers stood at attention. When they were aboard, Ji Song appeared, racing along the dock. He jumped into the ferry to join Dan and his father.

'Please be seated,' Hudan instructed, as the barge began to move off into the darkness beyond the torchlight of its own accord. The Xibo and his son found the gentle, steady glide of the boat off-putting and quickly sat down before they fell down. Ji Dan, however, waited for Jiang Hudan to take a seat at the bow, and took a seat close by her.

'Jiang Hudan, I have made an observation I would like to ask about?' he politely requested.

'I am here to answer any question you may have, Ji Dan. Tell me of your observation.'

'I sense there is a very strong energy around you,' he began somewhat awkwardly, as he'd never broached supernatural topics with anyone before now, despite a very keen desire to do so. However, in his world Ji Dan was already the greatest authority on the subject. 'I was wondering if it is this energy that you somehow harness and use to propel our vessel forward?'

'Always the thinker, Ji Dan … you are supposed to be in awe of the ways of heaven! How are we to impress you if you figure out all our tricks?'

'Such a feat is far more than a trick,' he insisted.

'That is very true,' she concurred. 'The control of chi energy, a discipline known as Dao Yin, has taken many years of study to master, and I still have much to learn.'

'But it is something you mastered, not something you were born with?' he queried, most curious, and as he could not see his hostess' face clearly, he hoped he was not causing offence by asking.

'A little of both, I expect,' she replied.

'I see.' Dan was deflated, as he'd hoped he might be able to be taught this art. 'Well, I very much envy you this gift.'

'But we are all born with such gifts,' Jiang Hudan replied kindly. 'Is that not right, my brothers?'

'*Shi!*' they replied in the affirmative, and either began to float upward into the misty night sky, or bound across the water, barely disturbing the surface with their contact. Some vanished completely! And from among those of the Wu who had scampered off across the water, the sound of a tiger's growl echoed back and startled them.

'Tian preserve us!' Fa was on his feet, and Song was gasping in wonder.

'I don't believe it!' The young heir was astonished. 'Jiang Huxin was on the boat with us?'

'I did tell you she was close.' Only Jiang Hudan was left on the barge with their royal party. She turned her attention back to Dan, who could not wipe the astonished grin off his face. 'You see, Ji Dan, all of us have talent, but only some can pursue a lifestyle that allows the development of our full potential. Human beings are capable of so much more than just multiplying and making war.'

'I have always had faith that it was so,' Dan granted, 'but before today I have seen very little evidence to support that hope. But I wonder, and I wish to cause no offence in asking, whether —'

'Are men born with such gifts, or is it only women?' Jiang Hudan guessed.

'Yes,' he agreed, 'that was my very question.'

'The simple answer is yes. However,' she was quick to add, 'it is rare that male psychic talent is discovered, and even if it is, it is even more rarely nurtured.'

'Why is that?' Song wanted to know.

Dan knew the reason. 'In the hands of a man such power would be dangerous.'

'Where women are creators, men tend to be destructive. They think with their heads and love with their hearts.'

'Well, how else should we do it?' Song was perplexed.

'We should love with our head, our mind, and think with our heart,' Dan surmised, and Jiang Hudan nodded.

'That is a rare man, indeed,' she conceded, 'and even if, when a boy starts his training, he is committed to Tian, by the time he grows to manhood he is *easily* distracted and led astray.' There was a real annoyance in her tone, that made Dan think she was speaking from experience, but he dared not pry.

'Daji is a woman who does not seem to comply with your perfect scheme of things,' Song was quick to point out.

'The emperor's witch is the perfect example of what happens when a daughter of heaven attempts to live among men, on earth.' Jiang Hudan was civil and patient with the Xibo's heir. 'That is why Wu lead a cloistered life.'

'Well, father told me what lies in store for us this night and I, for one, can hardly wait to see your demonstration.' Song's claim that he did not fear the Wu was obviously holding firm. Like Dan, Song was an adventurer. Dan sought knowledge, while Song sought the thrill of the unknown.

'It promises to be quite something,' Ji Fa said. He was still reserved, but more curious now.

The steam from the water thinned suddenly and the full moon lit a rock face in front of their barge. This caused a brief panic as they were headed straight for it.

'Please duck your heads,' Hudan told them as she bent her torso flat into her lap. When the vessel was set to pass under a small opening at the base of the cliff, all her company was quick to do likewise. The barge passed through a low rocky tunnel and entered a high cave that harboured another dock, at the end of which were lit torches. Torches also burned each side of the entrance to a stairway that led up through the rock at the other end of the jetty.

Their hostess disembarked the vessel in one slow, graceful bound and stood on the jetty. 'My brothers await you in the temple of Tian,' she said as the three guests climbed onto the dock in the clumsy, regular fashion. 'Please follow me.'

Jiang Hudan turned and proceeded down the jetty and up the steep incline of the stairway.

The peace of the warm cavern, heated by the steamy water within it, enveloped Dan and he felt like he could relax for the first time in an age. His instincts for danger were sharp, but he felt nothing other than harmony within these walls. He couldn't help but note the raised iron gate at the base of the stairs as he passed beneath it. Once he had ascended the long flight of stairs that cut through the mountain he also spied the large metal grate that was presently open at the top. If under attack, the base gate could be raised and, once the enemy battalions scaled the stairs, they would find themselves confined between the grated trapdoor and the lowered iron gate at the bottom of the stairs. The large cauldrons that sat either side of the grating would be filled with oil, heated and then tipped, pouring the scorching hot contents through the bars of the trapdoor and down the steep stairs. The oil would be set alight, effectively burning the caged enemy alive.

'Nice defences,' Ji Fa noted as they walked through the open courtyard of the cloister. 'No wonder they have been left in peace.'

Dan smiled at this, pleased to see his brother had found his sense of humour.

'I hear music, and singing!' Song pursued Jiang Hudan, who was still moving straight ahead.

Dan and the Xibo pricked their ears and, upon hearing a beautiful melody being woven between voices, bells and bamboo flute, they picked up their pace as they were already moving toward the music.

'If heaven has a sound, I believe we are hearing it,' Dan commented to his brother.

They left the central courtyard and, up a few more stairs, entered a long hall that had large double doors flung open at each end, like a tunnel through the main house. The walls were washed red, and two green dragons, one on each side of the walkway, were depicted fleeing in the opposite direction from them.

'The Green Dragon of the East,' Dan commented to his brother. It was the symbol of the Shang and the emperor whose capital lay in the direction toward which the dragons were fleeing. 'What are the dragons running from, I wonder?'

The dragons' tails extended down the long hallway and ended at a garden courtyard, where many torches and candles burned, highlighting the magnificent statues of warrior women and white tigers, the beautiful colours of the exquisite blooms and plants, the pools and water features.

'This is beyond belief,' the Xibo said in an aside to Dan.

'Heaven,' Dan agreed, his senses swimming from the sweet smell of burning oils. He thought it interesting that the Green Dragons were depicted fleeing from the garden of paradise; a perfect portrayal of the prophecy they were here to ask about.

The euphonious choir of women's voices was much closer now and the tone of their song sent a deep vibration rippling through Dan's being — his heart felt to be tearing open, as if he'd just fallen in love, and the intensity of the emotion moistened his eyes. He looked aside to his brother to see the Xibo flick a tear from his cheek.

'The music is very moving.' When Fa spoke, his voice was choked with emotion, and he held a hand over his heart. 'It is a long, long time since my being has been stirred by joy and beauty, instead of pain and suffering.'

'It seems to me now, that it is exactly what heaven is,' Dan said. 'We have yet to even reach the celebration and already I know this will be the most memorable night of my life.'

The Xibo and Dan reached Song, who had come to a stop in front of a fountain featuring a beautiful statue of a half-naked woman with tiger's ears and a tail, holding a babe in one arm and a tiger cub in the other. 'I think I want to live here,' the lad uttered, awed by the intense beauty he was experiencing.

'Well, for the next two days, you get that wish,' his father granted.

'Provided none of your flights of fancy get us expelled from here prematurely,' Dan interposed.

'You've seen what they can do ... do you think me mad, Uncle?' Song had found his respect for these women suddenly, and Dan was most relieved to note it.

'I have a feeling that we haven't seen the half of it,' Dan speculated.

At the far end of the courtyard, Jiang Hudan had scaled a set of candlelit stairs cut into the mountain which rose to a height twice that of the courtyard walls. She was awaiting them patiently at the top, but what lay beyond her they could not see.

They watched Song sprint double-time up to the top and Dan felt old as he began ascending the steps.

'Very glad we decided against wearing armour,' the Xibo commented halfway up — they were both fit men, but the steep stairs were murder on the legs.

'It is becoming painfully clear why they learn to float,' Dan grinned.

As they neared the top of the stairway, a beautiful white temple, round in shape and pillared around the exterior, came into view. The structure itself was not very large and appeared nowhere near big enough to house the choir they were hearing. Yet the holy dwelling was an impressive sight in the light of the full moon, for it glowed with splendour.

'How on earth did all this get built?' Fa said quietly to his brother, as they trailed Jiang Hudan and Song across a plateau to the stairs of the temple.

'No one seems to know how long the House of Yi Wu has been on Li Shan,' Dan advised. 'I scoured the land for information, but the local peasants proved to be the best source … they say that it has always been here. Since the time of the Yellow Emperor.'

'But that's well over a thousand years!' Fa emphasised in a whisper.

'They also say that the House of Yi Wu Li Shan,' Dan continued, 'cannot always be found here on earth, as it drifts between the earth realm and heaven. The Great Mother is said to manifest her house on earth only when the land is in great peril.'

The Xibo stopped to look at his brother and gauge if he was serious.

Dan nodded and raised his eyebrows. 'It seems to be a commonly held belief in these parts. And one of many myths about the Wu that will work to our favour if tonight goes well.'

Fa bit his lip and nodded, conceding Dan's point.

As they joined Jiang Hudan at the temple's large double doors — painted gold and inset with a white tiger motif — the music fell silent, creating a dramatic effect.

'Before we enter the temple of Tian …' Hudan waylaid them outside the closed doors, '… Shifu Yi has asked me to stress that the Ji family have our greatest respect and you have nothing to fear within these walls. The mistress of this house hopes you will feel at ease to enjoy the experience and hospitality of the House of Yi Wu Li Shan.'

'We are greatly honoured by such heavenly favour,' the Xibo replied, his tone somewhere between apprehensive and humbly intrigued.

As Jiang Hudan turned back to face the double tiger doors, a cacophony of tiny bells sounded. The doors parted and the voices again rose to weave harmonious awe-inspiring notes.

Shock began vibrating through Dan's entire being as he realised the inside of the temple was much larger than the outside had suggested, and he had to resist the urge to run outside and double-check that his eyes had not deceived him. His brother was wide-eyed as was his young son, and all were completely lost for words.

Echoing the external design, inside the temple of Tian were pillars, this time set around a large central circular pool where the ceiling was open to the clear night sky. Where they entered was candlelit, but the far side of the temple had only natural light at present. The moonlight streamed through the open centre of the temple and hit the water so that it sparkled around the throne on the far side of the pool. Upon the throne sat a veiled woman dressed in sparkling silver and white. This was Yi Wu, the Great Mother, and it was she who led the choir of young women in song. Her initiates stood to either side of her on the stairs that descended into the pool. None of the Wu initiates were veiled and all were beautiful — just as Song had claimed they would be. Although not all the women were young, they appeared youthful and alive! Their song had no words, simply long harmonious notes, akin to the flute, weaving beautifully through their melody.

On this side of the pool, a candlelit table was laden with covered platters and surrounded by cushions, and Jiang Hudan directed their party to be seated behind it, facing the pool and the Great Mother. The youngest initiates of the order stood at attention at each end of the table, waiting to serve their guests.

Dan was actually quite thankful to take a seat, as his head was swimming from the mellifluous sounds echoing around the high chamber.

Once they were comfortable, Jiang Hudan joined her brothers and took the position to the right side of the Great Mother's throne. The young Wu rushed to remove the covers from the platters of food on the table, and to pour the warm wine, before quickly dispersing. The song came to an end and the Great Mother spoke through her veil to them.

'It is my great pleasure to finally welcome you, Ji Fa, Ji Dan and Ji Song, to the temple of Heaven,' she began. 'I have been anticipating your visit for some time, for it is seen that we have a long and historic future association. I expect that you have many questions and, over the next few days, myself and my initiates will endeavour to answer them. But this evening is for celebration and demonstration. You know what earthly warriors are capable of, so now please relax, eat, drink and allow us to show you what the warriors of Tian can do.'

With a clap of her hands, drummers positioned behind the Great Mother and her choir began pounding out a beat.

More of the Wu entered the temple from the side and converged on the pool. They were dressed in white trousers and long-sleeved jackets that crossed and were belted at the waist. Their shin-high boots were of black leather and were bound with criss-crossing laces to the lower leg. Astonishingly, their feet did not break the surface of the water; it was as if a transparent barrier lay between them and the pool. Clearly, this was not the case as the front row of the choir behind stood knee-deep in the water.

Once the Wu were aligned in four perfect rows, the drums were silenced, and the bamboo flutes and bells played, creating a sublime ambience. Very slowly, and in perfect unison, the Wu began to perform a dancing exercise. It became apparent to Dan that this was a demonstration of the Wu discipline of Dao Yin that Jiang Hudan had spoken of earlier. As he observed the movements, he could see the practitioners were focused on an invisible something that they consciously moved around their bodies — their dance was mesmerising to watch.

The beautiful flautist, who was seated to the left side of the pool playing the bamboo dizi, did manage to capture Dan's attention; however, there was something about her that didn't seem right.

Song noted his uncle's interest and leaned behind his father to convey a thought. 'I think that particular brother is truly *a brother*,' Song whispered, raising a conspiratorial eyebrow.

This was a little hard for Dan to digest because she was a stunning beauty, despite the fact that she was clearly not as well-endowed as the other Wu her age, and that her hands, although soft and supple in their movements, did seem a little large.

'How can you be sure?' Dan asked, excited by the possibility that a male might have been accepted and trained by the Wu already!

'The flutist is the only woman in the room I'm not attracted to,' Song told him in a whisper, grinning broadly.

Dan studied the musician in question again and saw the brother with new eyes. He was definitely male, and that was inspiring … Dan had to speak with him.

In the hours that followed, their party feasted, and were treated to death-defying feats of gymnastics and fighting displays with staff, sword, dagger and fan. The women then turned their weapons on themselves! They slashed themselves with knives, drew blood and then instantly healed. They swallowed swords, then juggled fire, swallowed it and spat it out their mouths. Once the performance was over, Dan and his party applauded heartily, as they had many times while watching the many amazing feats.

A solo voice began a soulful chant, and from behind the rows of warriors, Jiang Hudan rose into the air. Her hair and flowing garments swirled around her as if she were submerged in water — it was like watching a spirit dance. Her voice was incredibly moving and expressive.

'Goddess …' uttered Song, enchanted.

'My thoughts exactly.' The Xibo glanced aside to see Dan's jaw dropping, and so closed it for him.

'Is this not the most splendid spectacle you have ever witnessed?' Dan was too enthralled to be embarrassed.

'It certainly is,' Fa agreed in delight, his eyes again glued to Jiang Hudan's flying form. 'We can enchant the enemy into laying down their arms.'

Dan was stunned to hear this, as he felt that the last thing he could stomach in the presence of such a supernatural event would be fighting.

As Jiang Hudan's chant drew to a close, she maintained her lofty position above the proceedings. The drums sounded, slow and ominous, like a predator stalking its prey, and the Wu warriors scattered evenly to each side of the pool and bowed down. This created a clear corridor across the pool between the throne of the Great Mother and the table at which the Ji warriors sat. The drums found a slow, primal rhythm, while the flautist's melody and Jiang Hudan's chant changed and became more seductive.

'What could possibly top what we have already seen?' the Xibo asked his brother.

Dan could only shake his head. 'I cannot imagine.'

'I can,' Song grinned, as a beautiful woman, with long wavy hair the colour of honey, glided from behind the throne of the Great Mother.

She wore only a sheer, white silk robe, loosely tied at the waist, and they could see a clear impression of her naked form beneath.

'Here we go.' The young man rubbed his hands together as the seductive beauty reached down and undid the tie at her waist, her eyes fixed ahead as she walked toward them. 'Yes,' he uttered under his breath in hopeful anticipation.

The silk belt dropped away, and as she clasped her robe to pull it open, she ducked down and the silk garment gently folded over her form. All the music stopped, and beneath the silken fabric the woman's form seemed to be expanding.

With bated breath the warriors watched a full-grown white tigress emerge from beneath the silk and she continued to walk across the water toward them.

'Jiang Huxin.' Song's fantasy had shattered into fear.

'Shh!' Dan advised as the beast drew closer. Jiang Hudan's vow that 'they had nothing to fear' was resounding in his brain and doing battle with his urge to reach for his weapon.

Before the animal got uncomfortably close, it stopped and took a seat on their side of the pool and the men could only stare, breathless at its close proximity and the transformation they'd just witnessed.

Jiang Hudan's chant had stopped and she spoke. 'The Ji family rule the West and, according to the sacred geomancy of Wu Xing, the heavenly guardian of the West is Baihu, the White Tiger. Baihu's colour is white, her element is wind, her stone is white jade, and her virtue is righteousness.' Jiang Hudan returned to the ground and came to stand beside the tiger, which she stroked without fear. 'Her associated material is metal, as opposed to the associated material of Qinglong, the Green Dragon of the East, which is wood.'

'Metal chops wood,' Ji Dan deduced, for he had studied the mnemonic charts of Wu Xing, otherwise known as the Five Movements, Phases or Elements.

'Yes,' Jiang Hudan confirmed. 'In such a conflict, the White Tiger will prevail.'

'That is what you saw?' Ji Fa queried. After what he'd witnessed this night, he would not doubt her word.

'Whoever has the favour of the White Tiger and flies her colours on their banner will be emperor.'

'And how do I secure the favour of Baihu?' Fa asked.

'Tigers are an amazing judge of character, Ji Fa, and if you are truly a man worthy of heaven's mandate, Baihu will know it and Jiang Huxin will know it too.' Jiang Hudan crouched down beside the animal, and hugged it around the neck tightly with great affection. 'So if you seek Tian's mandate, come forward now and be judged worthy.'

Dan's heart stopped upon the request, and Ji Fa turned to him for an opinion. Dan looked to Jiang Hudan for reassurance.

'If you know your leader is a good-hearted man, he has nothing to fear,' Jiang Hudan insisted, whereupon Dan looked back to his older brother and gave him a nod.

'I believe you are the best of us, dear brother,' Dan advised, 'but only you truly know if your intentions are pure.'

Fa rose, decidedly undaunted. He removed his weapons and put them aside ahead of walking around to the front of the feasting table, where he crouched down on one knee. The candidate held forth both hands, palms up, and bowed his head in reverence to the powerful animal before him. 'I humbly await Baihu's judgement.'

Song shot Dan a worried glance as the tiger rose and moved toward Ji Fa. When she reached the Xibo, she sniffed his outstretched hands and then his bowed head. She hesitated a moment and then pulled back to release an almighty roar, which drove Dan and Song to their feet in horror, but Ji Fa did not flinch. After a moment, the Xibo dared to raise his eyes, only to find the tigress in very close quarters and, although he held her gaze, he maintained a bowed submissive stance. When the tigress leaned in close and opened her jaws, Dan's heart stopped, then the animal began licking his brother's face, and nudging him playfully with her head.

'Not so terrible.' Ji Fa gave a nervous laugh as the tiger placed her head under his hand to encourage him to stroke her, which he did happily. As the Xibo's fear fled altogether, he was utterly delighted to unexpectedly find himself a playmate of the beast.

'Baihu has spoken,' Yi Wu stated. Her initiates bowed their heads as the Great Mother vanished from the temple, leaving her veil fluttering down to settle upon her vacated throne.

'I think we have established Baihu's will now, brother Huxin.' Jiang Hudan looked to the tigress, who had the Xibo pinned to the ground as she licked his face.

Before their eyes, and in an instant, Jiang Huxin transformed back into a woman, her naked form pinning Ji Fa to the ground. 'I shall protect you, Ji Fa,' she told him. 'You shall please the goddess.' The next moment, the tigress returned and with a friendly growl, she romped back across the pool, and out a side door.

'Dismissed,' Jiang Hudan gave the Wu warriors permission to leave and the choir and musicians followed them out. 'Ji Fa.' She reached down and offered the Xibo a hand to help him to his feet, as he was a little intoxicated.

'Your sister is quite something, Jiang Hudan,' the Xibo granted as he found his feet. 'If only my people could have seen that spectacle.'

'Oh, they will know of Baihu's decision,' Hudan assured Fa.

'Unbelievable … what a demonstration!' Song was deliriously satisfied. 'That was the most fun I ever had when I wasn't —'

Before Song could offend their hostess, Dan redirected her attention. 'Ah, the flautist?' he asked, indicating the departing musician.

'Brother Fen,' she advised.

'I would very much like to speak with her … ah, him?' The smile on his hostess' face told Dan she already knew what his interest in Brother Fen was.

'He is the only male ever to be trained here on Li Shan.' She was clearly not comfortable with the subject, but Dan persisted anyway. If she got mad at him, he could blame his persistence on the wine.

'But may I speak with brother Fen?' Dan repeated.

'I'm afraid that is impossible.' She was embarrassed to have to explain. 'He is currently in disgrace.'

'What did he do?' Song had been following the conversation, and Dan was glad, because he would have felt rude asking. The boy could get away with it.

'To live among the Wu you must vow to live by our creed,' Jiang Hudan began.

'What is your creed?' the Xibo wanted to know as did Dan.

'We agree to abstain from causing harm and taking life, both human and non-human, without ritual or purpose. We do not take what is not given; we abstain from hurtful speech and lies; we do not take intoxicating drinks or drugs outside of ritual purpose. We abstain from eating at the wrongful time, and from singing, dancing, playing music or decorating ourselves for any other reason than to celebrate the glory of Tian. And we abstain from overindulging in sleep or engaging in improper sexual conduct,' she said.

'For reasons other than ritual purpose,' Song added for good measure and to confirm whether what he'd foreseen in his visions regarding the Wu's ritual relations with the emperor was true.

Jiang Hudan seemed perturbed by the correction, but replied, 'That is correct.'

Song didn't say anything, but Dan could hear the lad cheering on the inside.

'So which vow in your creed did brother Fen break?' Dan got back to his original query.

'I bet you it was the last vow,' Song posed with half a grin.

Jiang Hudan was pained to say it. 'Yes, he allowed himself to be seduced by one of the less devoted women here,' Hudan informed Song, who could not wipe the smile from his face, until she added, 'So now Fen is bound for the Great Mother's spring fire as a sacrifice.'

'What?' Dan was mortified that the only male Wu in existence was going to be burnt in less than a month.

'But he ought to be given a medal for making it this far!' Song said.

'Clearly brother Fen is most talented —' Dan argued.

'Far more than you know,' Jiang Hudan was forcibly restraining her emotion now. 'But as the Great Mother pointed out to me, if what you are giving up to Tian is not truly precious then where is the sacrifice? Now if you gentlemen will excuse me, our underlings will see you to your rooms.' She bowed her head slightly in leaving, and then vanished from their midst.

All three men were left flabbergasted, until an array of delightful little warriors huddled around to aid their tipsy guests to their accommodation for the night.

Sleep was impossible for Dan at the best of times; he had trouble shutting his mind off and tonight it was doubly difficult. Thanks to his intoxication and the sensory overload from this evening's performance, he was buzzing. Usually he would wander the house or the campsite until he was ready to drop. However, being caught wandering around this sacred house at night, would hardly make the right impression, so Dan lay there listening to his brother snore in the next room.

The most disturbing thought for Dan was that he might have caused their hostess offence with his questions about brother Fen. She was obviously emotionally attached to the lad — surely she had not been the one who had seduced him? *No*, he decided,

Jiang Hudan seemed far too honourable for that. Maybe he could ask his brother to barter for the life of the flautist when he spoke to Yi Wu on the morrow? Perhaps then brother Fen could train him in the art of Dao Yin?

A memory of Jiang Hudan's performance made Dan's heart swell to bursting for a moment, and then the memory of her sister transforming into a tiger sent shivers of wonder shooting through his being. *How can they be sisters? How can they be human at all?* These Wu seemed more spirit than mortal, and the vow that he and his male counterparts would feel as if they had been delivered into heaven had certainly been kept. But without all the pomp and pageantry, what were the Wu really like?

Curiosity finally drove Dan from his bed.

He'd watched the comings and goings of the young Wu serving their table at the celebration, so Dan was very sure he knew where the kitchen might be located. Beyond that would be a garden and he felt he could not get into trouble for being there.

It was a great relief to make it out to the herb and vegetable garden without encountering any weapon-wielding women, a phantom or a wild beast. In retrospect it was rather brave to have ventured out weapon-less and alone, but the ambience of the house was so tranquil, it seemed sacrilege to be armed.

Brushing his hand over the plants in the herb garden produced an array of amazing aromas — it was difficult to tell one plant from another with only the moonlight to see by.

At the end of the path Dan was pleased to find a gate that led into open gardens with paths running in several directions. As he stood there in the moonlight contemplating which path to follow, he heard his name called.

'*Ji Dan.*'

When it was repeated in the same mocking tone, his attention was drawn to the path that led downhill to the left.

'*Ji Dan!*'

'Be quiet!'

He heard splashing, then laughter, and could not resist investigating.

Nestled within the garden was a thermal pool and stone stairs leading down to it. There were three people swimming naked; the full moon illuminated their heads and shoulders above the waterline but he could not see who they were. One woman was trying to drown another whilst the third just chuckled at their antics.

When the submerged woman broke away and surfaced, she was not perturbed. 'The only mystery Jiang Hudan has yet to fathom … *men*.' Huxin laughed at her sister's discomfort. 'Did you see the way Ji Dan was admiring our brother, Fen?' She swam over to the onlooker.

'Don't tease her, Huxin, you know how she hates it,' a male voice replied, and Dan's heart suddenly jumped into his throat when he realised it was brothers Fen, Hudan and Huxin in the pool.

'Ji Dan is interested in our little brother Fen, *not* in me,' Hudan insisted.

'Why me?' Fen was stunned. 'Does he like boys, do you think?'

'Heavens, no!'

Dan was relieved to hear Hudan say so.

'I believe it is because you are the only male Wu in existence.'

'Not for long,' Fen said solemnly.

'Shifu Yi is not going to kill you, Fen,' Huxin said in an attempt to lift his spirits. 'What you did was only human.'

'We are not "only human"!' Hudan protested. 'Stop defending his offence against Tian, this house and me! I didn't raise him for near on fifteen years, just so he can throw it all away on a —'

'I raised him too!' Huxin declared. 'And I think you have the same desires.'

'I do not!' Hudan defended adamantly.

'Tell me honestly that you don't think Ji Dan is the handsomest man you've ever seen.'

Hudan opened her mouth to flatly deny it and then thought longer on it. 'I think he would be handsomer without that little beard.'

Dan absently began stroking the short growth on his chin, which he was rather attached to, wondering what was wrong with it.

'It makes him appear much older than he is,' Hudan explained, 'but otherwise I concede you are probably right; he is a handsome specimen. Still, I find the fact that he is a thinking man far more attractive than his appearance.'

'You should tell him about the beard.'

'Huxin, why on earth would I do that?' Hudan said, smiling. 'It is none of my business how he grooms himself.'

'You are so clueless!' Huxin laughed, and Fen with her.

'What is so funny?' Hudan appealed to Fen.

'You would tell Ji Dan because it is a way to find out if he admires you in return,' Fen explained. 'If he does favour you, he will shave the beard off to please you.'

'I am not so vain as to care if he likes me or not,' Hudan stated emphatically. 'Love is the addiction of unfulfilled people seeking to suck the vital energy out of someone else, because they fail in their ability to generate that vital energy for themselves.'

'I rather thought that love was two people in a perfect exchange of energy,' Fen said humbly.

'How right you are, brother! I am so glad I have entirely different instincts and reasoning faculties to you, Hudan,' Huxin stated deadpan to her sister, 'because yours are completed whacked!'

'I made an oath —'

'Yes, but that doesn't mean you can't have, or be, any fun! Our Shifu has said beauty is a weapon as great as any sword, and I'm telling you, brother, your sword is dull, dull, dull.'

'Righteousness is my weapon.' Jiang Hudan glided over to the side of the pool, launched herself up and twisted about to take a seat on the edge.

Moonlight glistened on the droplets running down the front of her naked body as she squeezed the water from her long dark hair. This vision filled an empty cavity in Dan's chest with a warm glow, and he had to disagree with Huxin — Jiang Hudan's weapon was as flawless as her character.

'She'd be the choice for an emperor's bounty,' a voice whispered from beside Dan.

A split second later Dan was clutching Song by the throat. 'What are you doing here?' he hissed quietly, releasing the lad, but covering Song's eyes to prevent him gawking at Jiang Hudan. 'We should go.' He turned Song around and gagged him with one hand as he led him away.

'What was that?' Huxin was heard to ask, and the tiger's growl urged them to move faster.

Back in the guest rooms, Dan finally let Song go.

'You cannot drag me around like that!' the lad protested. After all, he was Ji Fa's heir.

'I can, and I will,' Dan stated firmly, looming over the lad to intimidate him a little, as Dan was still quite a bit taller and broader than Song. 'We said you could come provided you didn't cause an *incident*.'

'Do not act all high and mighty with me, Uncle. You could have landed this negotiation in strife just as easily,' Song accused, and Dan decided he was not going to waste his breath arguing.

'Stay in your room until someone sends for you,' Dan instructed and turned to leave.

'I stand a far better chance of having her than you ever will,' Song boasted to spite his uncle, but Dan was not so easily baited into exposing his feelings on any matter.

'We can all dream,' Dan granted, coolly, and departed for his own quarters. He was suddenly feeling very tired.

3

TIAN'S TRIBUTE

A restless sleep drove Jiang Hudan out into the garden before meditation. She'd had strange dreams of working with a heavenly race, only fragments of which she could remember. She assumed they were Tian's people, as they were not like the humans of her world in appearance. Their skin was whitish pink, their eyes were round and wide and, like their hair, the colour varied greatly from person to person. This was not the first time she'd dreamt about these people, and although the dreams were truly wondrous, she always awoke feeling panicked, as if there was something very important she'd forgotten. It seemed that the harder she tried to focus on the details, the more elusive the dream became.

'Jiang Hudan.'

It was Ji Dan, and she felt quietly flustered to be alone in the garden with him. Huxin was right: Hudan saw most men as the enemy, but what she was really afraid of was liking one of them. 'Good morning, Ji Dan. I trust you slept well.'

'Not really,' he said honestly, 'but it was not from a lack of comfort and hospitality. I assure you.'

'Too many questions,' she supposed, as she went to rise from where she was seated by the pond.

'Indeed.' He was quick to approach, motioning for her to be seated once more. 'Please.'

'I will be late for mediation.' Hudan wanted to quickly excuse herself.

'But Yi Wu said you would be happy to answer my questions today. So surely the Great Mother would excuse you this once.'

'What we do here, we do by choice, not because we will be punished,' she parried.

'But brother Fen will be punished,' Ji Dan noted.

'Wu Fen Gong has been destined for the spring fire since he was three years old,' Hudan said by way of explaining his harsh punishment. 'He was spared because he was innocent … but he is innocent no longer.'

'So love is a crime?' Dan asked her bluntly and without any dramatic overtones.

'No,' she said, 'love is never a crime. If Fen and Nuan had truly loved each other, they would have stayed away from one another and not caused the other so much pain and grief. Lust is the crime. Any sexual relations with another person without Tian's consent is forbidden to the Wu — Fen knew that.'

Ji Dan gave half a laugh and broke the tension with his beaming smile. 'Here I was, coming to apologise for any offence I might have caused you with questions about brother Fen, and it seems I have done it again.'

'You wish for Fen to train you.' Hudan was forthright about his interest and shook her head. 'The disruptions of court life and battlefields are not conducive to Dao Yin.'

'Just because no one has ever managed it before, does not mean it cannot be done,' Ji Dan argued politely. 'I rarely sleep, so I always have extra time on my hands, no matter where I am.'

'What troubles your sleep?' Jiang Hudan wondered.

Dan both smiled and frowned. 'There is so much to be done for this land, so much to learn, that I fear rest is a precious waste of time.'

Hudan was quietly impressed by his answer. 'Perhaps there is Wu in you?' she mused. She made to move back toward the house, not wanting to stay and chat.

'I see things …' he announced to keep her there, '… that are not of this world, not of this time.'

Hudan was surprised by his claim and, doubtful, she swung around to look him in the eye. 'What kind of things?'

'Come, sit, and I shall tell you.' He smiled winningly, confident of getting his way.

Hudan found his subtle power play infuriating. 'I'm sure the ladies of your court find you very charming, Ji Dan, but I have better things to do than indulge your ego.' Hudan turned and strode toward the house not to be diverted again, but he came after her.

'I meant no offence —'

'Really?' Hudan swung around to confront him. 'Would you ask a man to come sit with you in the same fashion?'

Ji Dan realised his error. 'No,' he conceded, 'you're quite right. Please forgive me. I sought only to get you to stay in one place long enough to have a conversation.'

'When you truly consider me your equal, maybe then I shall consider bestowing on you the wealth of my knowledge.' She nodded curtly, turned and continued on through the garden gate.

'Brother Hudan …' Fen came rushing out to meet her. 'Shifu Yi is requesting your presence in her private council chamber.' Fen noted one of their visitors trailing her, as Hudan swung him around to walk with her.

'You must be late for mediation, dear brother.' She noticed the men exchange glances, but she was not prepared to allow their guest an audience with Fen without the Great Mother's permission. 'You'd best hurry back and save yourself any more grief.'

'Yes, brother.' He dutifully sped off ahead of her and disappeared into the house.

Dan trailed Jiang Hudan as far as the main courtyard, which she crossed to enter the private house of the Great Mother. Then he headed right, toward the stairs to the guest rooms on the upper level.

As he ascended and rounded the corner to the next flight, he was surprised to find brother Fen awaiting him. 'Brother —'

'Shh!' Fen urged.

Dan saw the desperation in the boy's eyes and so suggested, 'Follow me.'

Fen looked a little wary as he trailed the dignitary to the beautiful guest room and entered behind him.

'Have no fear, I am not interested in young boys.' Dan knew of his worry, and Fen gasped, startled.

His eyes widened, understanding. 'It was you watching us in the pool last night?'

'Well, I heard my name being called, so …' Dan shrugged off the incident and then smiled. 'Now you know one of my secrets, care to return the favour?' He invited Fen to offload whatever was on his mind.

'I don't know what has become of the woman I am to burn for,' Fen began. 'I know I have nothing to offer you in payment, but —'

'You hoped I might help you discover her fate,' Dan concluded for him, and Fen nodded.

'I need to know that she will be taken care of …' his eyes glistened with tears '… and live a happy life.'

As naive and misguided as Fen's love for his first sweetheart probably was, Dan was touched, for he'd never felt so intensely about a woman, not even his wife. 'I will see to it,' he resolved. 'You are wrong in the belief that you have nothing to offer me in exchange for this service, for it would be my great honour to call you my mentor.'

'Mentor!' Fen nearly had a fit. 'I'm just the gardener.'

Dan had to laugh out loud — the boy was clearly as talented and well trained as any of the Wu here and yet felt humbled to be the mentor of a mere man. 'I think we both know that you are far more than *just* a gardener. You are trained in Dao Yin?'

'Half-trained,' Fen thought it fair to say. 'Dao Yin takes a lifetime to master.'

'Then we could do that together, Wu Fen Gong. What do you say?' Dan appealed.

The boy just appeared bemused. 'But I am to burn —'

'I say you won't.' Dan rebuffed his objection confidently. 'So if I get my way, and you are only banished, what say you?'

Brother Fen was still completely bewildered. 'What you suggest is a very great honour …'

'But?' Dan urged him to be out with the remaining impediment to such a partnership.

'I just always expected to burn in the end, or live out my days here …' Fen attempted to explain his odd reaction to the offer of a lifetime. 'I never ever considered that I would *leave*.'

Clearly, the prospect was as heartbreaking to Fen as losing his love, or being under sentence of death. The lad had probably never ventured beyond Li Shan in over fourteen years, so the thought was bound to be daunting.

'Look at it this way,' Dan said upfront. 'Come with me, and when we find your lady love, I'll let you keep her.'

Fen's spirits radically improved. 'I do not even dare to dream of such freedom.'

'Just agree,' Dan assured him. 'I will take care of the rest.'

'It would be my honour to serve the House of Ji.' Fen bowed as he would to his Shifu.

'The honour will be all mine.' Dan returned the gesture. 'I shall speak to my brother at once, before he visits with Yi Wu.'

'Shifu Yi is the only one who knows what happened to Nuan,' Fen clarified.

'You have not asked your Shifu?' Dan queried.

'I cannot,' Fen explained, frowning. 'Shifu Yi has never seen me.'

'But you live under her roof.' Dan was confused. 'You have trained here.'

'You misunderstand,' Fen rethought his explanation. 'She *sees* me, but she pretends not to. It is her way of allowing for me to be here. If she were to recognise me, she might see I was a male, and males are not permitted to live on Li Shan.'

Dan nodded in understanding. 'I will make my brother aware of your problem and see what we can find out.'

Fen finally smiled as he backed up to the door. 'I am forever in your debt, my lord.'

Dan shook his head to deny any debt. 'Let us just hope that forever outlasts the month.'

In the course of their meeting, Hudan told her Shifu about her strange dreams and of the unsettling feeling left behind in their wake.

'These visions need not concern you at this time,' the Great Mother gave her standard response. 'They portend a future quest that is part of your birthright, but you have other trials to see to first.'

Every time Hudan had one of these heavenly dreams she hoped that her Shifu would say it was now time to learn the meaning — alas, today was not that day. This morning, Shifu Yi was far more concerned about her meeting with Ji Fa.

'If it goes well this day, then tonight you will act as oracle for the Xibo,' Shifu Yi advised.

Hudan nodded dutifully. 'I shall prepare.'

'In your absence, I shall have brother Huxin show our other guests around,' she said, and Hudan gave a quiet sigh of relief at hearing that.

'Very good, Shifu. Is there anything else?' Hudan sought dismissal.

'You may tell the Xibo that I am ready to see him now.'

Hudan exited the Great Mother's abode, sent for the Xibo, and then her sister, Huxin.

When Ji Fa arrived with his brother and son in tow, Huxin stood alongside Hudan at the doorway to Yi Wu's abode. 'Good morning, lords,' Hudan began, noting that Ji Fa's companions seemed much more wary of Huxin than did the Xibo himself; he appeared to be delighted to see her again.

'Made better by your esteemed presence, brothers.' The Xibo bowed to them both.

Huxin glanced at Hudan with a satisfied grin on her face; clearly, Ji Fa was completely enchanted by her.

'Yi Wu will see you now, Ji Fa,' Hudan passed on her instructions, 'and has directed Huxin to show your escort our house and grounds and answer any questions they may have.'

Dan and Song appeared quite alarmed to hear this, but Ji Fa looked at Huxin, disappointed. 'I very much envy my companions,' he told her and she smiled, pleased by his obvious adoration.

'If you will kindly follow me, Ji Fa.' Hudan opened the door to lead the Xibo to her Shifu.

'What will you be doing this day?' Dan couldn't help asking Hudan, before she disappeared inside after his brother.

'I must prepare myself for this evening,' she explained coolly, and then held up a hand to prevent their guest wasting his breath on more questions. 'All shall be revealed in good time, Ji Dan … enjoy your day.'

Hudan closed the door to escape his interrogation, and then turned to Ji Fa, who raised both brows. 'My little brother has a voracious thirst for knowledge.'

'He certainly does,' Hudan replied.

'He means no offence in his persistence.' Plainly, the Xibo saw how his brother annoyed her.

'I am sure he seeks only to protect his lord,' Hudan granted politely, and Fa grinned, as if not entirely convinced that was the reason.

'I believe his interest lies more with you,' said Fa.

'Why me?' Her stern tone and glare seemed to disconcert the Xibo, as he absorbed the fact that she was not of the same amicable, flirty nature as her sister.

'I meant the Wu as a whole,' Fa clarified to dispel any ill will or misunderstanding. 'Dan and I have always been mentored by men and have never before met women more knowledgeable than ourselves.'

Hudan softened a little; the comment was half-flattering, but did not say much for the intelligence level of the noblewomen of their land.

'Or perhaps I should say we never met a *good* woman more knowledgeable,' Fa added.

'You speak of Su Daji,' Hudan guessed. She was at once sympathetic. 'It is said that she ordered the death of your eldest brother.'

'She had him ground into mincemeat and fed to our father in jail,' the Xibo told her, obviously trying to suppress his fury, and Hudan wished she'd not mentioned the incident.

'She will be brought to account for her crimes against humanity,' Hudan vowed, and she meant it.

'I never believed that until I met you, Jiang Hudan.' The Xibo raised a smile. 'I have seen what the emperor's witch is capable of first-hand. She can enchant entire armies to carry out her insanity. She can topple entire battalions with a wave of her hand.'

'You have encountered her in battle?'

The Xibo nodded, and shrugged. 'I was knocked unconscious. It was Dan who fought her off and got me out, I still don't know how. But Dan does look a great deal like our first brother.'

'You think Daji may have a soft spot for Ji Dan?' Hudan was suddenly finding Dan more interesting than expected. If he had confronted her nemesis and lived to tell the tale, then perhaps she had something to learn from him after all?

'Daji may have a desire to possess Dan, but there is nothing soft about her,' Fa concluded, leaving Hudan with food for thought.

'I should announce you,' she said, recalling the business of the day. 'The Great Mother is most eager to converse with you.'

'The feeling is mutual,' the Xibo assured her, whereupon Hudan entered the council chamber to complete this task for her Shifu and then move on to the more serious preparations of the day.

'You may now enter, Ji Fa,' Jiang Hudan invited, fully opening the doors to the Great Mother's private council chamber.

The Xibo was a little nervous about making the right impression on the Great Mother of Li Shan, recalling how his great-grandfather had venerated her in his yarns. Ji Fa had not been submissive to a woman since his mother had passed, and even then it was an entirely different kind of veneration. Dan had instructed Fa, prior to this meeting, that he must see Yi Wu as his most esteemed *male* associate; Dan had stressed this point several times.

When the Xibo entered, Hudan withdrew and closed the doors behind him. The chamber was flooded by the morning sun, so despite the chill of the late winter air, having the shutters open on the huge windows opposite him did not detract from the warmth of the room. They did, however, offer stunning views of the mountainside and steaming thermal lake below.

Fa turned to the right to face into the long room, and more stunning than the view was the woman seated in a large, gold, cushioned throne at the far end of the chamber that Fa could only assume was the Great Mother; unlike the night previous, she was unveiled. She was robed simply yet elegantly in white, and her hair was drawn back into a bun at the back of her head. Two floor statues of a tiger, carved from white jade, sat each side of her throne and before it, between Ji Fa and his hostess, was a table set for tea, with a large golden cushion placed on the floor each side.

'Good morning, Ji Fa.'

Ji Fa bowed. 'A very good morning, Yi Wu. I am deeply honoured for this audience.' What he meant to say was that he was honoured to be permitted to see her face, as from all reports, no man had ever seen the face of the Great Mother.

'Arise, Ji Fa. No need to venerate me, for I am not your sovereign, nor are you mine. We are equal, and may speak as brothers.'

Ji Fa stood upright, amazed by the youthful aspect of the Great Mother — he'd been expecting an old, *old* woman — but as he also did not want to seem to be staring and admiring Yi Wu's beauty, he didn't know where to look.

'You are surprised to see me unveiled?' she queried, as if she had picked up on his thought, and the Xibo nodded. 'We are to work together,' Yi Wu said as she rose to standing, 'and if I cannot trust heaven's mandate, then who can I trust? Tea, brother Fa?' she offered, descending the stairs to kneel on the cushion on her side of the table.

'How kind of you, brother Yi. Yes, I would like that,' replied the Xibo, advancing to kneel at the table — feeling comfortable with regarding the great Wu master as a brother.

He watched in silence as Yi Wu poured the tea, wondering all the while about her assertion just now. When she had placed his tea in front of him and he'd thanked her, he could not refrain from asking: 'Am I the one, brother Yi? Do I have heaven's mandate?'

The Great Mother smiled, amused by the question. 'That is my prediction, Ji, but it is for you to prove to yourself and Tian.'

The Xibo was concerned by her response, but before he could voice his worry, Yi Wu continued. 'Yet, if the journey to be emperor is one you wish to take,' and she raised her eyebrows in expectation, 'then I can supply you with the map.'

Fa was most relieved to hear this, but he also knew nothing in life came without a cost. 'And what does the House of Yi Wu Li Shan stand to gain from its partnership with the House of Ji? Of course, our treasury and resources are at your disposal. No tribute is too high for such an honoured ally.' Ji Fa proffered politely, and again Yi smiled at his lack of understanding.

'The Wu are not interested in earthly treasure, and we have all the resources we need right here,' she advised, raising her tea to him in salutation. Ji Fa returned the gesture and drank with her.

Deeply savouring the wonderful brew, he waited patiently to pursue the conversation until after he had complimented his hostess and requested another cup.

'Surely, brother Yi, you would require some remuneration for your aid to our house?' Ji Fa proffered.

'No, brother Fa. This house serves Tian,' she clarified as she poured, 'and it is to Tian that you must give tribute for our service to the House of Ji.'

'Ah,' he replied, sounding enlightened, but wary.

'As you can imagine, the aspirations of heaven are very different to the desires of earth, so the tribute expected by Tian will be very dissimilar to the simple material homage you would normally pay an ally,' his hostess stated seriously and Fa was even more concerned.

'Dear brother,' Fa softened his tone and expression to make his plea, 'I am very ignorant to the ways of the Wu. If you could give me some idea of what Tian expects of me, I would be very grateful.'

'It is not wise to speculate,' she advised. 'Tian's expectations will be revealed to you this night via the oracle.'

His eyes parted wide in wonder and apprehension.

The Ji family had court diviners who were very good at interpreting the *Yi Jing* hexagrams his late father had refined. Since the death of Xibo Chang, Dan had been working on a companion text to the *Yi Jing: the Book of Changes*. This was the *Yao Ci: Explanation of Horizontal Lines*, in which Dan elucidated the significance of the horizontal lines in each of the sixty-four hexagrams. The philosophy of *Yi Jing* was based primarily on the literature and administration of government; an oracle reading, on the other hand, was divination at its most sacred. Since he'd been enchanted by Su Daji, the emperor had decreed only he held a right to consult an oracle.

Fa recalled Jiang Hudan saying she had to prepare for this evening, and as she was the one who claimed to have predicted the downfall of the Shang, the pieces fell into place.

'Jiang Hudan is the oracle?' the Xibo asked, needing his guess to be confirmed.

'Only the very best for you, brother Fa.' Yi Wu raised her cup to him and Fa again joined her, feeling calmer in the knowledge that tonight many of his questions would be answered directly by heaven.

'Shall I be allowed to query the oracle when she is in trance?' Fa wondered.

'A good oracle will leave you with no questions to ask,' Yi Wu assured him.

'Of course,' Fa smiled. 'As with last night, I expect this evening to be a memory I shall treasure for the rest of my days. I hope, at some point, to be able to return the favour you have shown me.'

Yi Wu placed her cup aside. 'Actually, brother Fa, there is one favour you could do for me personally,' she entreated him.

Fa felt he knew what this request might be. 'If it is within my power, brother Yi, know that I shall be happy to oblige.'

'That is well.' Her smile was tinged by sadness now. 'For this matter is very dear to my heart ...'

Surprisingly, Huxin was more hospitable than her sister, and nowhere near as intimidating, in Dan's opinion — at least when occupying her human form.

Dan and Song had been taken to view the balance of the morning meditation session, then had tea served to them privately in the heaven's garden courtyard. Afterward, brother Huxin invited them to join the daily session of Dao Yin with the junior initiates, which was held on a large plateau in front of the temple. Dan was fascinated by the accomplished movements of even the five-year-olds and their ability to concentrate. They were also very attuned to one another. Ji Song, who was barely a teenager, was having trouble keeping up with their gymnastic movements and challenging postures — designed to target energy trapped within the body. Dan realised very quickly that he had energy trapped everywhere and that releasing it was painful; he might be a fit warrior, but he was far from supple. He quietly bowed out of the class and returned to where his tour guide had been standing back, discreetly observing them.

'I feel like an old tree stump amidst a field of flowing reeds,' he commented, and Huxin smiled, amused by his imagery. Dan took her silence to be polite agreement. 'Please don't tell me that is how it looked?'

She drew her brows together, apparently concerned about answering that question. 'Would you like a tour of our gardens? Our sunset shrine has beautiful views of the thermal lake and the river beyond.'

A *change of subject, very tactful*, Dan thought. 'That sounds marvellous.'

When Song noted his uncle moving off with their guide, he left the class to come after them.

'No, you stay and finish the session,' Dan instructed. 'You're young, it will do you good.'

'But I'm dying,' Song said in an overly dramatic fashion to Dan, who obviously had no intention of relenting. The lad looked to Huxin. 'How much longer does the session go for?'

'Until the hour of the monkey,' she replied.

Song was horrified. 'But that's three hours away!'

'That is our regular regime,' Huxin informed him.

'Will you be shown up by a group of little children?' Ji Dan challenged and with a lady legend watching on, Ji Song could not maintain his tactic to avoid Dao Yin.

'Hardly.' Song glared at his uncle and was quietly fuming, no doubt dreaming of the day when he would give the orders.

'We will come back for you later, then.' Huxin led Dan toward another set of stairs at the far end of the platform, which gave access to the kitchen courtyard and to the gardens beyond.

On the way past the temple of Tian, Dan halted, curious about its illusion of having a larger interior than exterior. Huxin turned back upon noting his distraction.

'May I?' he queried, pointing to the temple door.

'You will find it is as it was last night,' she advised, but gave a nod giving him leave to investigate.

When he opened the door, the empty interior was patently larger than the exterior, yet as he backed up trying to view them in comparison to each other, there was still no logic to be drawn from it. Brother Huxin watched his investigations with some amusement.

Dan threw his hands up, as what he was seeing was impossible. 'How can you explain that?'

'Simple,' Huxin shrugged, 'there is no temple.' She turned and headed back down the temple stairs, and Dan came after her.

'I don't understand. Clearly, there *is* a temple?'

'Is there?' Huxin emphasised, as though he was talking nonsense. 'What if I told you none of this is really here? *We ...*' she motioned to him and then herself '... are not really here, and all perception is just the dreaming of Tian? Time, space, reality, *individuality*, are an illusion created by heaven to understand earth.'

It took a moment for Dan to digest the notion, yet with the suggestion he felt his consciousness expand.

'If you can comprehend that, then the so-called miracles we perform by our manipulation of matter, the elements and our very forms are really just our greater ability to see matter as energy in motion — that is all.'

'That is very profound,' Dan conceded, still trying to fully wrap his mind around the concept while he followed his guide down the stairs into the kitchen garden.

At the garden gate, brother Huxin took the central path leading up a gentle incline in the direction of the mountain peak.

'Brother Huxin, am I allowed to ask you what is planned for us this evening?' Dan trailed her out of the formal gardens and onto a forest trail.

Huxin turned to address him, but continued to walk backward up the slope. 'For you, we have nothing planned,' she said.

'Tonight's festivities are for heaven's mandate alone.' She turned about and continued walking forward.

'I don't like the sound of that.' Dan felt he had to protest.

'You don't trust us?' She turned abruptly to confront him, and her pretty face was right in his. 'It doesn't matter what you like, court scholar. The fate of the land is now in your brother's hands, and the deal he strikes tonight with heaven is strictly between Tian and the candidate.'

Dan swallowed, rather taken back to be so put in his place. 'I have no part in heaven's plan?'

Huxin moved away a step or two. 'That remains to be seen,' she said in a friendlier tone, 'although my sister predicts you will play a far greater part in bringing peace and order to this land than anyone else of your generation.'

Dan gasped, partly honoured, partly fearful.

'But not yet,' stressed his guide. 'Now is your brother's time, and you must trust his judgement.' Huxin traipsed on up the track.

But she had struck the fear of heaven into Dan now. 'How could I play a bigger role than my brother, who would be king and bring down the Shang?'

Huxin shrugged. 'You'd have to ask brother Hudan.'

The thought of asking Jiang Hudan anything after he'd insulted her this morning made him cringe. 'I don't think brother Hudan likes me very much.'

'Really? I think just the opposite is true,' Huxin mused. 'And that in liking you, a man, she finds it easier to be hostile than to analyse the dynamics of a relationship that she does not know how to handle.'

'So what could I do to make the situation more comfortable?'

'Ignore her,' she suggested.

'Ignore her?' Dan thought her advice was a little extreme.

Huxin nodded. 'Wait for her to come to you.'

'I think I'll be waiting a long time.' Dan didn't hold out much hope for the success of this tactic.

'Trust me —' She walked on a few steps then came to an abrupt halt, her eyes fixed ahead. 'Sorry.' His guide did an about-face and headed down toward him. 'We cannot go up to the shrine at present. It is in use.'

Dan's curiosity immediately spiked. 'May I see?' He pointed in the direction they'd been moving, as he walked past her.

'Quietly,' she hissed, 'we must not create any distraction.'

'I understand,' he whispered, silently creeping up the steep track with Huxin alongside him.

Dan crouched low and his eyes followed the trail to where it flattened out and led around the mountainside to a set of stone stairs. These led up to a stone platform, in the middle of which was an altar block. Behind the altar was Jiang Hudan, dressed in a robe — azure blue, just as the sky was this clear winter day. Her long dark hair was flowing in the breeze as she burned oils to honour and call upon Tian.

'What is her offering in aid of?' Dan was wondering if this had something to do with this evening's events.

'She is preparing her body to act as an oracle for your brother this night.'

Hudan was brewing something on the altar and poured herself a cup of the steaming liquid, which she held toward heaven and then drank down.

'What is that?' Dan asked softly.

'A mixture of hemp seed oil, ginseng and other sacred herbs,' Huxin advised. 'It assists us to see within …' she placed her palms together and reversed her hands so that her fingers pointed toward her heart '… and then without.' She now opened her hands and held them palm up to the heavens.

'It enhances your powers?' Dan queried.

'It enhances perception,' she explained. 'The source of individual power is internal, never external, and anyone or anything telling you otherwise is seeking to enslave you.'

Dan looked back to the altar to see Hudan relinquish her robe and bare her naked form to the world. 'Goodness sake!' Dan closed his eyes and turned away, but the beauteous vision burned into his mind. How liberated she looked with her arms flung wide to the heavens, hair blowing in the breeze as the morning sun beat down upon her bare skin.

Huxin was having a little chuckle at his discomfort.

'The Wu do not seem to value modesty as much as other women.' Dan quietly made his way back down the track.

'We do not consider nakedness shameful.' Huxin caught up with him. 'On the contrary it is empowering!'

Dan halted, finding the statement curious for two reasons: firstly, because empowered was exactly how Hudan appeared, and secondly, because deep down he envied them such freedom and social abandon. 'I imagine standing naked on a mountainside would feel quite empowering,' he said cautiously.

'You should try it, brother Dan,' she suggested. 'I would not object.'

Dan was briefly lost for words and embarrassed by the suggestion, but he could not wipe the grin off his face. 'Thank you, no, not today.'

'Aw,' Huxin pouted, and Dan was shocked.

'Isn't flirting against your code?' Dan ventured to inquire.

'Not my code,' the tigress grinned. 'I am the exception to the Wu rule, as I have to mate eventually. And besides, seeing you naked wouldn't be flirting. It would just be *enjoying the scenery*. You're very beautiful for a man.' She openly observed him, very matter of fact, regarding him as a man might a pretty young woman.

This was very off-putting for Dan and he now understood why Hudan had taken offence this morning.

'Not quite so *masculine* as your brother, though …' Her smile broadened and she gave a little growl and shimmy of delight.

Dan was relieved to note the tigress' amorous mood shift toward his brother. 'The Xibo was very taken by you also, brother Huxin.'

'I know,' Huxin boasted, gleefully. 'He pleases me.' Dan's guide lost interest in seeing him strip and led off down the track toward the house.

'You won't mention our presence here today to brother Hudan?' Dan felt Jiang Hudan would surely think him disrespectful again.

'Brother Hudan will not care what you saw,' Huxin scoffed at his fear. 'She would tell you that she is not saving her modesty for a man or marriage. She will gladly strip bare to do battle and distract her enemies unto their death … as would we all.'

Dan was absolutely astounded to hear this. He considered being confronted by a beautiful naked female in battle and decided he would surely be stunned long enough to lose his life — even a naked man would be distracting enough. 'You are all very dauntless and clever.'

'I am a beast, brother Dan. It is in my nature to have such traits.' She brushed off his flattery. 'My natural state of being is naked in the wild.'

'And your sister?'

Huxin smiled at the question, and shook her head 'I got the animal nature and desires. Hudan is my polar opposite, a goddess, pure in body and thought, more spirit than human. She spends most of her time out of her earthly body, so whether that body is clothed or not is of no consequence. Her body is just a vessel that enables her to serve Tian on an earthly level.'

Her answer got Dan to wondering about the legend of these two sisters. 'Brother Huxin, may I ask —'

'How could Hudan and I possibly come from the same mother?' She guessed his query.

'I mean no offence,' Dan explained. 'It is the scholar in me who must ask … for who shall record your legend correctly if no one outside these walls knows about where it all began?'

'You've been researching us, brother Dan.' His guide seemed flattered, and then not so amused. 'There is a good reason you cannot find that information, and that is because some mysteries are better left secret.'

'I am sorry if I —'

Huxin held a hand up to prevent an apology. 'You have caused no offence. In fact, I'm surprised it took you this long to ask. Perhaps, one day in the future, we will reveal to you the mystery behind our birth, but at this moment in time, it is vitally important that those details remain hidden from the uninitiated in the human world.'

'Vitally important to you and brother Hudan?' He couldn't help probing further.

Huxin shook her head. 'To everything in existence,' she replied. 'One secret mystery tends to lead to another and before you know it, you are confronted by all manner of enigmas and phenomena that you are not equipped to fathom.'

Dan had always been one of the smartest people he knew, and that was not vanity; his intelligence was what he was most famed for throughout the land. As he trailed Huxin to the gardens, he felt like a complete novice for the first time in twenty years! *I must secure Wu Fen Gong for my instruction.* The brief glimpse he'd had of Wu disciplines this day had only emphasised to Dan how much work he had to do on himself and he could barely wait to get started.

'No! She said no?' Dan queried his brother in his chamber, where Ji Fa had withdrawn following his meeting with Yi Wu. There was barely enough time left for him to eat, change and leave for the evening ceremony.

'I am sorry, Dan, but brother Yi was most insistent that Wu Fen Gong is not going to escape her verdict,' Fa conveyed as he ate. 'But she did invite us to witness the rite in question.'

'Did you tell her we would pay handsomely for him?' Dan stressed.

'I did.' Fa looked bored with the conversation. 'The Wu are not interested in earthly treasure. They have more resources than we do, and they don't want their doctrine passed on to the uninitiated beyond these walls.'

This news seriously deflated Dan's ambitions. 'What of Fen's woman, Nuan? Did you ask about her?'

'I did.' The Xibo looked at his brother. 'It is as the Great Mother said … Nuan was banished and what became of her after the ferry dropped her at the jetty, Yi Wu does not know.'

'I see.' Dan did not consider the information very helpful. 'At least we know she is probably still alive.'

'What good will it do you to find her, if you cannot have the boy?' Fa asked. 'You're not thinking of doing anything that might offend our hosts, I hope. With the Wu, every situation is a test of character.'

'I assure you, my brother,' Dan replied, trying not to take offence, 'I seek only to fulfil a promise I made to Wu Fen Gong. And speaking of concern, I am not happy about you attending this ritual alone tonight —'

'No need to be unhappy, Dan.' Fa brushed off his protest. 'As the candidate, there will be several rites I will be required to attend alone, so I'm afraid you will have to get used to it.'

Dan was a little affronted. 'My opinion is usually more valued by you.'

'In earthly affairs, I have no greater advisor, Dan, but in regard to the will of heaven, brother Yi is the expert and I trust her more than I would our own mother.'

'One day with a veiled woman can convince you —'

'She was not veiled,' the Xibo advised with a sly elitist grin, and Dan was shocked by the claim.

'You saw her face?' He was fascinated.

His older brother nodded, his smile growing wider. 'She looks my age, and very beautiful … serene,' he added, 'just as great-grandfather claimed.'

'How can that be?' Dan was sceptical. 'How can you be sure it was Yi Wu that you spoke with?'

'She is not like any other woman I have ever met, or any man for that matter. She is almost like a spirit: wise, composed, selfless —'

'But not forgiving,' Dan interrupted his Xibo's litany of praise.

'She does not view earthly affairs as we do, Dan. Just because the Great Mother will not give you what you want, that does not mean her judgement is unwise.'

'But she is going to burn him?' Dan was beginning to wonder if his brother had been bewitched.

'We kill men every day!' Fa roared, standing to defend his new ally.

'This boy is not your average man,' Dan argued, although clearly his brother was at his wits' end. 'He may be the only one of his kind —'

'End of subject!' Fa decided, most annoyed. 'I will not have this issue interfering with our true purpose for being here.' The

Xibo drew a deep breath to compose himself. 'Can't you be a bit philosophical about this, Dan?'

That query, coming from his brother, was decidedly odd.

'Trust that everything will unfold according to the will of heaven,' Fa advised. 'Nothing we simple folk on earth can do will prevent that. In which case, we must trust that Tian knows best and that everything is as it should be.'

Ji Fa was never philosophical, so this suggestion made Dan's jaw drop. 'Who are you? And what have you done with my brother?'

The Xibo was amused by Dan's reaction. 'I feel like I have been touched by a greatness this day that I cannot explain ... I only know that I have never felt as calm, focused and as sure about the future in my life.'

Dan finally realised what was driving his suspicion of the Great Mother. It was envy — envy of Ji Fa's privileged relationship with the Wu. 'That is well,' he said, resolving to be supportive. After all, he'd been the one who had convinced the Xibo to seek out the Wu — he should be pleased that the bonds of a strong partnership were forming. 'I shall not detain you from your engagement any longer.'

'I wish it was you, Dan.' Fa delayed his departure. 'I know you'd understand so much more —'

'If it was meant to be me, I would have been born second, not fourth. You are right, brother, everything is as it should be. I accept it,' he said, to put his brother at ease on the previous matter. 'Thank you for your help, and may the oracle show you favour this night.'

The Xibo smiled, sincerely grateful for Dan's support. 'You'd think I would be afraid of meeting the ruler of heaven ...' Fa quietly consulted his feelings a moment to be sure. '... but I'm not.'

'Nor should you be,' Dan insisted. 'Tian needs good service and we shall provide it.'

The brothers each braced their hand around the other's wrist and shook firmly, nodding in full agreement that this was destiny.

When Ji Fa entered the temple of Tian, the large interior had been transformed.

The water in the pool had been drained and replaced by a number of huge drums — some also strapped to the central pillars — and there was no space between the instruments for the drummers to stand. Drums were pounding as Ji Fa entered, but these drummers were positioned around the outer wall.

Yi Wu sat upon her throne on the far side of the performance area and, unveiled, she smiled in greeting. Ji Fa returned the gesture.

Where the feasting table had been, a large cushioned chair was placed, facing into the temple. Beside the small throne stood Jiang Huxin, wearing only her thin transformation robe of white.

'Welcome, my candidate.' In her hands was a cup of steaming liquid, which she brought forward and held out in offering to him. 'This is an elixir of waking sleep. It will expand your consciousness and aid you to comprehend the oracle.'

Without questioning the contents, Fa accepted her offering and drank it down. The taste was very floral with a touch of spice. 'Delicious.' He smiled, and returned the vessel to her, whereupon it vanished from her hand.

'I shall be beside you all the way.' Huxin removed her robe and dropped to all fours.

As she transformed into the tigress, the Xibo could barely breathe until the animal arose and, circling around behind him, came to stand at his side. The tigress then accompanied him to his seat and settled alongside him.

The drums fell silent, and the haunting sound of Jiang Hudan's voice filled the heavenly space. Singing canon, Yi Wu followed, echoing her note, and the rest of the women present followed their Shifu.

The sound sent the Xibo's senses reeling in a most pleasurable, emotion-fuelled way. His body began to tremble and his eyes floated with tears of pure joy.

Jiang Hudan emerged from behind the throne of the Great Mother in a swathe of colourful silken fabric and with one high, graceful leap, she came to land solidly atop the grouping of drums in the empty pool. The pounding sound of her landing was echoed by the drummers around the walls. In her hand, Hudan held a hooked staff of carved wood and inset atop the staff, where the head began to curve, was a glowing gemstone, a ball of fiery red.

This staff was as much of a legend as its wielder and was called Taiji, which meant the supreme, or ultimate, pole. Not only in the sense that Taiji was a staff, but also in the sense of opposing poles: yin–yang, light–dark, above–below, right–left, front–back. Hence, Taiji granted the wielder a supreme polarity which was non-polar — a perfect state of non-judgement, through which to channel the will of heaven.

Hudan chanted another note, echoed by Yi Wu, and then her brothers, before somersaulting over to hit the drums which were strapped to pillars, with her feet; bouncing off a drum below with her staff, she then swung her feet over to hit drums on the opposite side of her stage. Drummers with instruments of a corresponding tone echoed her notes and timing from the periphery. Each note sung was higher, and with each new octave the glowing ball in Jiang Hudan's staff changed, moving through the colour spectrum. The ball progressed from red to orange, to yellow, to green, and a beautiful scent arose from nowhere, and grew more and more intoxicating.

When the highest note was sung, the light in the staff turned bright blue. Hudan whirled into the air, until her body suddenly stilled and floated in mid-air.

The temple fell silent and a strange darkness descended, sending a chill of awareness through Fa's being, for he recalled a poem about the Wu his great-grandfather had told him.

> *See the Wu, how skilled and lovely,*
> *whirling, dipping like birds in flight.*
> *Unfolding the words in time to dancing,*
> *pitch and beat all in perfect accord!*
> *The spirits descending,*
> *bring darkness to the world.*

Had Tian descended?

A small blue light pierced the darkness, and as its intensity grew, Fa realised it was the glowing ball of Taiji. But it was not

Jiang Hudan holding the staff of polarity now, but a tiny little person, half Hudan's height.

The tigress left the Xibo's side to welcome the visitor, circling and rubbing gently against it, whereby Huxin received a pat on the head for the warm welcome.

'Dear little puss, you've brought me a candidate for a new mandate, so I hear … shall we take a look at him?'

Fa was rather shocked to hear the voice of a woman, when he'd been expecting that a man ruled heaven. Not only was the voice female, but high-pitched like a child's; surely the Ruler of Heaven was not a little girl?

'You flatter me, Ji Fa, for in truth, I am much older than you.'

The figure got close enough to perceive clearly by the light of her staff, and what Fa saw was a fully grown woman in a body barely big enough for a five-year-old girl. Her skin was as white as the finest Shang porcelain, and although she was clearly a mature woman, there was not a single wrinkle on her tiny face. Her eyes were large, round and the most mesmerising shade of brilliant blue. He could not see the shading of her hair, for her head and body were completely covered by her deep blue robe and hood.

'You are Tian?' Fa inquired with a squeak of surprise in his voice.

'And you are Tian, in some higher consciousness,' she replied, 'and a very old soul indeed.' She looked aside to Huxin and stroked her. 'He is the one we foresaw.'

'You foresaw?' Fa was confused. 'But I thought Hudan —'

'We are but messengers who bring you a missive from your future, Ji Fa.' She reached out and placed the palm of her tiny hand against Fa's forehead, and a string of visions began streaming into his mind, answering his questions faster than he could conceive of them. With his entire being trembling, Fa's mind reached information overload and he passed into a fitful sleep.

4

THE YEAR OF GENGYIN

When the Xibo awoke, the morning after his oracle reading with the Wu, Dan had been present to check on his brother's wellbeing and ask him about the events of the previous night. Ji Fa assured Dan he was in excellent health and spirits. When asked if he had discovered what tribute Tian expected of them for the service of the Wu, the Xibo said only that he had been advised and wished to return to Haojing immediately to get to work. He added that they'd been invited back to the House of Yi Wu Li Shan to celebrate the New Year, which, coincidentally, was to be the year of Gengyin — metal tiger. Despite Dan voicing his desire to avoid Wu Fen Gong's execution, which was to be part of the festivities, Fa insisted his brother must come, as the Great Mother intended to grant Dan a private audience on the first day of the New Year. For some reason, the honour felt more like entrapment, but Dan did not voice this feeling to his brother.

'When are we going to war?' Dan had hoped to get a straight answer to that question at least.

'As soon as Tian sends me the sign,' was Fa's reply.

When asked what this sign would be, Dan had been assured that Fa would know it when he saw it, before requesting that Dan trust and have a little patience.

Huxin had repeatedly advised Dan to trust his elder brother's judgement, and he did. Dan just hoped that Fa's aims were not being distorted by the grandeur and mystery of the Wu and their heavenly agenda.

As a rationalist, Dan decided to avoid forming an opinion until he'd spoken with the Great Mother directly. If Yi Wu had somehow enchanted his brother, could she enchant him also? He could only pray to his ancestors that his decision to guide his brother to the House of Yi Wu Li Shan had been the right one, and that his fears of manipulation were completely groundless and only a sad projection of the old fears the evil Su Daji had ignited in him.

In the month that followed, Dan had to concede that, at least initially, he was surprised and rather pleased by the form their tribute to Tian had taken. Yi Wu had not asked for riches, veneration, labour, protection or property, but for massive political and social reform to be implemented across the land once it was united under the Zhou banner. The basis of these reforms was the creed of the Wu.

Yi Wu had told Ji Fa that she was concerned that only nobles were bound to marry, have children and be responsible for those children. Meanwhile, no one was bound to take care of the children of the lower classes, who were, more often than not, bastards, or orphans. Young unwanted local girls were always welcome at Li Shan, but unwanted boy children were left to make, or lose, their way alone. What she had suggested by way of a solution was that those of the lower classes who got married should be granted a plot of land, so they could build a house for themselves and their offspring and could feed themselves, and then be given another plot to farm for the state. This practice, which would solve many problems in the long run, would take a massive effort to implement. In preparation, the prime minister, the Xibo and Dan worked on creating an entirely new feudal system and writing down a detailed code of social conduct that would be enforced under law once the land was united. It was Ji Fa's goal to have a draft of their proposal ready to present to the Great Mother for Tian's consideration on the eve of the New Year.

The day the Xibo and Dan were due to depart for the House of Yi Wu, there was a miraculous occurrence at their residence in Haojing.

A heavy mist had settled over the city during the night. Only a day away from new moon, the night was near to pitch dark and shadowless. In the dawn hour of the rabbit, Ji Fa and Dan were summoned from their beds to see that hundreds of large sealed bronze urns had appeared overnight beneath a cloud in the central courtyard. As they stood gaping from the top of the stairs, looking over the mist-filled yard of urns, the Xibo was handed a note written on silk.

'I have questioned my entire guard and no one saw anyone arrive, my lord,' informed the very embarrassed captain of the night watch. 'I found that message tied to one of the urns.'

'Is this the sign?' Dan brushed his unbound hair from his face. He was sure it must be, this being the miracle it was.

'No.' The Xibo remained absorbed in the missive he was reading. 'Some of these urns contain wine, but most contain *water*,' Ji Fa said with immense relief. Fresh, clean water was scarce, as the drought had continued unabated. 'This is a New Year's gift to the people from the Great Mother of Li Shan.'

'The Wu!' The night watchman looked at the anomaly in a whole new light.

Dan smiled at the thoughtful and timely gift. Approval of the Wu by the people would be strengthened, right before Ji Fa was about to announce his allegiance with their house. 'Very clever.' The fact that the urns had just appeared in the courtyard overnight only added to the validity of the gift being heaven sent.

'Rain would be more clever,' Fa commented, for if the Wu could accomplish this feat, surely just making it rain would be easier and more widely beneficial?

'The Wu will not make it rain, as that would look good for the emperor,' Dan pointed out. 'They will wait until they can be seen by the people to make it rain in your honour and not that of Zi Shou. This way there can be no doubt as to who the gift has come from.'

'Only one tenth of this gift is for the House of Ji and its troops; the rest must be distributed to the people in the name of the Great Mother of Li Shan,' the Xibo instructed the head of his watch. 'See that it is done.'

The guard confirmed the order and departed to see it carried out.

'News of this will spread during the course of the festival like wildfire. It will be the talk of the entire land before long.' Dan was happy to see the Great Mother's plan finally taking form.

'And I'm not sorry that I won't be in town to hear the gossip.' The Xibo grinned, already basking in the glory of his association with the Wu. 'You were right, Dan. We are witnessing the birth of a legend.'

'Indeed.' Dan was not feeling quite so confident. 'We can only hope it ends triumphantly.'

'No doubt of it.' Fa headed indoors to be met by a flock of squires — yet to dress their Xibo properly — and officials waiting for an explanation. 'Let us depart as soon as possible,' he called back to Dan, who nodded in agreeement.

Although he'd had mixed feelings about the Wu, Dan couldn't wait to return to their home. Maybe he could yet save Wu Fen Gong from the fire. If not, he expected to have the death of the only male in the Wu's temple explained the following day, when he met with the Great Mother herself.

Their departure from Haojing had not been as effortless as they had hoped, so it was well after noon by the time the Xibo, Dan and a small guard departed the city. The ride to Li Shan was swift however; because of the drought, fording the rivers proved to be no major problem.

Ji Song, as Fa's heir, had been left to be Master of Ceremonies on New Year's Eve in Haojing. The festival would run from the new moon until the full moon, so the Xibo would only be absent from his family for the first day of the two-week festival.

The sun had only just set in the hour of the rooster when they arrived and lit the jetty torches to summon the Wu. The Xibo's guard were ordered to leave and return the following day.

'Alone at last!' Ji Fa threw his arms wide and took a deep breath of mountain air, which was tinged by the warm humidity rising off the thermal lake. 'If not for the Great Mother's heavenly gift this morning, I would never have heard the end of this from my wife.'

'I gather she does not approve of you leaving the family at festival time?' Dan offered a sympathetic ear.

'She is fearful and opposed to my association with the Wu.' Fa was obviously annoyed by this, but then his mood took an upswing. 'Yet the gift from the Great Mother now has the woman thinking twice about rejecting divine assistance. *And* it gave me justification to leave the city and family on the eve of the New Year, because I must thank Yi Wu personally. But then, I am sure Yi Wu foresaw that.'

'I think it is Huxin you wish to thank personally,' Dan bantered.

Fa had a chuckle at this, something Dan had not heard him do since they were lads. 'But seriously ...' the Xibo chose not to comment further on that subject '... this visit is much more than just a social call. I have important acquisitions to collect, and our proposal to deliver.'

'Acquisitions?' queried Dan.

'Yes, indeed,' Fa replied, spirits soaring, until he spied Dan's excess luggage, in the form of a long wooden case. 'You brought your qin,' he uttered, stunned.

Dan had only played the instrument on a couple of occasions since their brother's death, when their father had commissioned that a sixth string be added to the instrument to mourn the loss of Bo Yi Kao, who had been the greatest master of the qin. The sixth string was sorrowful, and Dan found it emotionally disturbing to play.

'As the Wu are not interested in material tribute, I thought a performance might please the Great Mother.' Dan forced a smile. 'Still, I have not played in so long that I hope I do not cause more offence than favour.'

'I hardly think so.' Fa was delighted. 'You are as great as Bo —'

'No,' Dan insisted, 'there will never be a greater qin master then Bo Yi Kao.' Even now, the loss of their eldest brother still hit a raw nerve. 'But I thank you for the compliment and the faith you place in my ability.'

'I fear that too often you sell yourself short, Dan, so that those around you — even *the dead* — appear to shine more brightly,' Fa said gravely.

Dan was touched by his brother's appraisal, and would have said so had the sound of lapping water not drawn their attention to the lake, where the ferry, bearing its hooded occupants, could be seen approaching through the mist.

It was not Jiang Hudan wearing the white robe who greeted them this day, but Huxin and Ji Fa was beside himself with delight.

'Brother Huxin, what a wonderful surprise,' he exclaimed when she disembarked at the jetty.

'The pleasure is all mine, brother Fa.' She inclined her head slightly in greeting.

'But where is Jiang Hudan?' Dan asked — with a tinge too much disappointment for his own comfort.

'She has fled our order, never to return,' Jiang Huxin told him coolly. His horror must have reflected on his face, for she smiled suddenly. 'Forgive me, brother Dan, I am just teasing you. Brother Hudan is in vigil with our brother Fen ...' the humour slipped from her face '... who shall be leaving us this night.'

'Of course.' Dan quietly damned his own impetuosity, and was forced to admit to himself that it was Jiang Hudan whom he was really here for. What was disturbing to him was that there was no purpose behind wanting to see her in particular, but he craved her company more than anyone he'd ever met, despite how she confused and humbled him on many levels.

'Fear not, brother Dan,' his hostess said, forcing a smile to disperse the heavy mood, 'you shall surely see brother Hudan, for she is eager to speak with you.'

'Really?' The news shocked him out of his melancholy. 'Why is that, brother Huxin? Have I done something else to offend her?'

Brother Huxin's smile became altogether more sincere. 'Quite the contrary, I would think. I told you she'd come to you *eventually*.' Dan found Huxin's words mind-boggling, and wondered what he might have done to earn Jiang Hudan's favour.

Jiang Huxin turned her attention back to his brother to escort him onto the ferry.

Whatever Jiang Hudan's interest, Dan was grateful she was now willing to converse with him, and this time he would show the proper humility and not undermine his purpose. He'd never considered himself as particularly conceited before he'd met Jiang

Hudan, but since meeting her he'd become acutely aware that true wisdom lay in knowing that he knew next to nothing, compared to everything there was to know and learn under heaven. In that new belief, Dan was truly humbled and hoped to fare better among the Wu.

Upon their arrival at the House of Yi Wu, the Ji brothers were shown to their rooms to refresh themselves. As the Xibo was the guest of highest honour, he was shown to his room first — although that was probably not the order Fa would have preferred. Dan was grateful, however, as once she had opened up his quarters he had a moment alone with Jiang Huxin.

'Is there any way I might be able to see Wu Fen Gong before …' Dan tipped his head, not wanting to mention this evening's event out loud. 'I have a gift for him.' From his qin case he pulled a beautifully crafted jade dizi. 'I know he will have little time to play it —'

'A very generous gift!' Jade was more valued than gold and Huxin seemed a little torn over the situation. She had a peek out the door to see if the way to the kitchen was clear — most of the brothers were decorating the temple, and collecting wood for the sacrificial fire. 'You know Hudan is with Fen. She will surely disapprove of your meeting, when Fen is in shame and the Great Mother has not given permission.' She gave Dan fair warning.

Dan was not thrilled that his short-term wish was contrary to his long-term ambition. He'd seen thousands of young men die, but for some inexplicable reason, he felt a connection to this one; even though Fen would not be Dan's Shifu as hoped.

'In that case, would you give brother Fen this for me?' He handed over the dizi to Huxin. 'When Fen stands before Tian he will have a fine instrument to play for heaven's favour.' His hostess was almost moved to tears, but she did not shed them. 'Tell him that I will keep my promise to him, even though he cannot return the favour in this life.' Fen's love, the banished Wu, had proven elusive so far, but Dan had men out searching for her. If Fen could not be his Shifu, perhaps Nuan could? 'Tell brother Fen that the wheels are in motion.'

Brother Huxin appeared a little surprised that Fen and Dan had obviously already met for long enough to have a private understanding. 'I will tell him,' she vowed without asking questions and immediately left to deliver the missive.

When Huxin returned to the kitchen where she had left her siblings, Fen and Hudan were still there. Fen was finishing off the arrangement of a beautiful wreath of azalea, peony, water lily, narcissus and pussy willow. He was running his hands over the barely budding stems of these flowers, whereby they burst into full bloom and he added them to the wreath.

'That is beautiful work, Fen.' Huxin admired the arrangement. Fen went about his task solemnly, with great care and eye for detail.

'This is my death wreath,' he told Huxin without looking up. 'I want it to be a thing of perfection, so that when I stand before Tian he will know that I was good for something.'

Huxin looked to Hudan, who was leaning against the wall, seemingly distant and unmoved as she rolled her eyes.

'He still won't consider repenting and begging the forgiveness and mercy of Shifu Yi,' Hudan explained, annoyed.

'I cannot ask for forgiveness for something I am not sorry for,' Fen barked, and then nearly collapsed into tears. 'Please, I don't want spend my last hours in this world arguing with my only family.'

'I don't want you to depart this world at all,' Hudan stressed, 'but you seem resigned to the notion.' She gave his wreath a nudge to emphasise her point. 'Where is your fight?'

'It left with Nuan,' he said sadly, and Huxin had to intervene to prevent Hudan from hitting him. Fen didn't flinch.

'Spit on heaven's gifts to you then,' Hudan jeered, at her wits' end. 'Die for the egotistical illusion that is the love of other! Your sacrifice will make no difference to Nuan's plight —'

'I never want her to learn that I regretted us,' Fen insisted. 'I would rather die.' He went back to work, and Hudan, fuming, left the kitchen.

'I have a gift for you from Ji Dan,' Huxin uttered quietly to Fen once Hudan had left, and the jade dizi certainly served to get Fen's attention.

'Dear heavens!' Fen smiled for the first time in a month as he took possession of the treasure.

'And I have a message,' she advised, peering about to ensure no one could overhear before she conveyed it. The news came as a great relief to Fen.

'Then Tian has already blessed me.' He went back to work on his wreath. 'I have nothing to fear from death now.'

Huxin had mixed feelings about making her little brother feel more relaxed as a prelude to his impending doom. Like Hudan, she would have preferred to see Fen trying to escape the fire, as he had done every year since he'd been there. But today was not about Huxin or Hudan. It was about Fen, and she could only support his wishes.

The sound of drums summoned everyone at the house to the large platform outside the temple of Tian, where the sacrificial bonfire had been erected and now lit the entire area with the light from its blaze. The throne of the Great Mother was positioned at the top of the exterior steps to the temple and there her veiled person sat, surrounded by her Wu brothers, awaiting the arrival of her sacrificial offering.

Dan and his brother stood apart from the proceedings, as they were outsiders and only present to observe. As they waited for Wu Fen Gong and his sisters to arrive, Dan got curious. 'What is that you have tucked under your arm?'

'Clothes,' Fa replied.

'Where you expecting to be cold?' Dan queried.

Fa shrugged, nodding toward the stairs that ascended from the courtyard to alert Dan that Jiang Hudan had arrived.

As opposed to her usual lightness of being, today Jiang Hudan appeared as hard as the stone platform beneath them. She fronted up to kneel before the Great Mother and slammed her clenched right fist into the open palm of her left hand — as a soldier might yield before his commanding officer or king. 'Shifu Yi, I deliver to you my ward, Wu Fen Gong, as promised and beg that you will show mercy and spare him from the fire of Tian.'

Fen followed Hudan onto the platform and came to a standstill while Hudan pleaded his case to the Great Mother. Jiang Huxin came to stand alongside Fen, and placed an arm around him in support.

'Has your ward repented his sins against this house?' Yi Wu asked, and Hudan was clearly vexed by the question.

'No, Great Mother, he has not,' Hudan was pained to say, 'but —'

'Sh!' Yi Wu held up a single finger and Hudan bowed her head in obedience. 'You may step back.'

She rose and backed up, slightly sideways, to grant Yi Wu line of sight to the accused. Hudan finally came to a stop beside Dan. This was just a happy accident Dan realised when Hudan looked aside to see him and maintained the same stony glare she'd worn into the gathering. She may have been as cold as ice on the outside, but inside she was fit to explode. Without comment or even a nod of recognition she looked back to the proceedings as Fen was called forth and knelt before their Shifu.

'What say you, Wu Fen Gong? Are you not sorry that you have broken our creed and in so doing offended and hurt those who have kept you alive all these years?' The Great Mother acknowledged Fen directly for the first time since he'd been led before her at the age of three.

'My sorrow has as many levels and branching paths as a river in the wet season, Great Mother.' He took the flower wreath from around his neck and, placing it on the ground before his Shifu, he remained kneeling, head bowed in shame. 'I am sorry for the harm and offence I have caused you Shifu Yi, my sisters and everyone in this house. But I am not sorry that I love He Nuan, and I shall never be sorry for receiving her love,' he stated bravely, sealing his own fate.

'So ... you *are* a man, after all,' she said with some humour, having ignored the fact for years, but at the same time she was emphasising that their creed, and men, didn't mix. 'But, if that is how you feel, then you leave me no choice. Remove your clothes, Fen Gong, for you are Wu no longer.'

As the lad stripped, Dan glanced aside to Hudan, who was visibly shaking from restraint, her eyes moist with panic.

Fen stood, clothes in one hand, jade dizi in the other.

'Yours was a crime of passion, Fen Gong, but it is not how much we loved that Tian will measure us by, but by how much we were loved.' The Great Mother looked up from Fen to address the gathering. 'Is there anyone present who does not love this man and would see him fed to the fire?'

There was a great gasp from everyone; then all that could be heard on the plateau was the sound of wind and flames.

'Hear that, brother Fen? See how you are loved and treasured by those who have known you. It would seem that others cherish your existence far more than you do.' The Great Mother stood and came down the stairs to confront Fen Gong. When she removed her veil to speak with him, Dan nearly died from shock. He was honoured — maybe Yi Wu had forgotten he was present? The Great Mother was very beautiful, and her face was rather ageless, neither young nor old. Her appearance certainly did not betray the number of years she had reportedly been on earth.

Fen Gong was also astounded to be looking at the woman who had kept him for most of his life. 'Great Mother ...' he began and his eyes bulged momentarily as they drank in her image, and then he dropped to his knees before her, 'I am not worthy.'

Yi Wu dropped to her knees before him and forced him to look her in the eyes. 'You are most worthy, my dearest only son,' she told him, and Fen was moved to tears. 'There is no one sorrier than I to be losing you this day. Your talent is rare and will be sorely missed, but a soul as beautiful as yours is even more hard to come by. I shall miss you, Fen Gong.' Yi Wu kissed his forehead and stood once more, leaving Fen completely shellshocked with delight, pride, and confusion.

Yi Wu addressed the gathering. 'Who claims this man?'

'I do!' Fa and Dan were quick to say at once, but when Dan noticed Fa holding up the clothes he'd been carrying, Dan realised he was speaking out of turn. 'Actually, he does,' and Dan motioned to Fa with some embarrassment while his brother went forth to claim Fen Gong.

'I claim your son for the House of Ji.' Fa came to stand by Fen Gong. 'He shall be treated well and will be prized by my house as the honoured son of Yi Wu Li Shan that he is.'

'Throw your old clothes into the flames and with them your old life, Fen Gong,' Yi Wu instructed the lad. 'They are the only things that shall burn this day.'

'But Great Mother,' Fen said, wondering if this outcome was too good to be true. 'I have sinned, I —'

'— have done nothing that any boy your age would not have done,' Yi Wu explained. 'I knew the time would come when you would have to leave, and now an opportunity in the wider world has opened up to you. Tian has spoken, Fen Gong; this is what heaven wants for you.'

As Dan watched Fen Gong toss his old clothes into the flames and don his new attire, he was simply bursting with happiness and relief. The atmosphere was electric with goodwill.

When Fen was dressed and ready to embark on his new life, his sisters were called forth to kneel beside him before their Shifu.

'Are you both still angry at your Shifu?' she queried them light-heartedly.

'No, Shifu,' they said as one.

'Yet you will both miss your little brother. Am I right?' she proffered.

'Yes, Shifu,' they chanted, looking at Fen fondly.

'Wrong,' Yi Wu contradicted. 'You will both accompany Ji Fa back to Haojing, and may return to Li Shan once the Shang emperor and Su Daji have been deposed. You have Tian's permission to use your abilities to their fullest extent to bring about heaven's will.'

'Yes, Shifu,' Jiang Huxin replied, much keener to confirm her obedience than Jiang Hudan.

'If it pleases Tian,' Hudan said, accepting the assignment with some reluctance.

'Ji Fa, you have my best oracle, my best warrior and my best healer to aid your mission,' Yi Wu advised. 'May they serve you well and bring you ultimate victory.'

Dan assumed Hudan was the oracle and Huxin was the warrior, but he was rather surprised to hear Fen's greatest attribute was healing.

'It is my greatest wish to rid this land of tyranny and restore order and peace,' Ji Fa said, humbled. 'With the support of your house and these three masters, I feel far more confident of achieving that vision.'

'Our business here is done.' Yi Wu motioned to the temple doors behind her, which opened wide with no visible assistance. 'A celebration awaits!'

The Wu responded with loud chattering wails of approval, and they migrated into the temple of Tian to celebrate the passing of the old year.

Hudan and Huxin lingered beside the fire as their freshly acquitted brother picked up his death wreath and, throwing it on the fire, he played upon his new jade dizi as he watched his offering burn.

'I guess Tian shall have to wait just a bit longer to have you tend heaven's gardens,' Hudan commented to Fen once his tune was done. 'I am so very happy about that.' She smiled and embraced her little brother.

'So you are not mad at me any more?' Fen ventured.

'I was never mad at you in the first place.' Hudan nearly wept as she stressed the point. 'Just worried.' She hugged him close.

'I knew Shifu wouldn't kill him.' Brother Huxin waved off the close call.

'She has sacrificed others who have broken the law,' Hudan argued. 'How could you know she would spare Fen?'

'Because he is so *pretty*.' Huxin pinched Fen's cheeks affectionately. 'How could you kill anything so *adorable*!'

Hudan glanced about and spotted Dan loitering outside the temple observing them. Upon being caught out, he immediately made a move toward the interior, when Fen called out to stop him. 'Ji Dan, I owe you everything!' He ran over to convey his gratitude. 'Now I have a chance to fulfil my end of our bargain.'

'What bargain?' Hudan marched over, hands on hips. 'When did you two have time alone to strike a bargain?'

Both Dan and Fen were stumped by the question, so Huxin intervened to spare them the confession.

'Can't you just be grateful to Ji Dan for saving our brother's life!'

'But —' Hudan protested.

'Hudan! Everyone got what they wanted.' Huxin emphasised how unreasonable she was being. 'All due to Ji Dan's efforts.'

'Fine,' Hudan relented, 'I don't want to know.' Her dark mood retained its hold on her, and she left them to enter the temple.

Dan gave a heavy sigh, although he was grateful to Jiang Huxin. 'I told you, she hates me.'

Huxin began to giggle, and Fen repressed amusement.

'That is not helpful.' Dan felt they were mocking his attempt to befriend their mysterious sister.

However, Huxin shook her head to assure him. 'You don't need any help.' She took his arm to escort him inside. 'You are doing just fine.'

Dan looked to Fen, who nodded to agree. 'She just needs time to wind down, then she'll be in a much better mood. You'll see.'

During the festivities, Hudan kept her distance from their guests and her siblings — well aware that her mood was not at all hospitable.

It might have been her brother's impending sacrifice that had sparked her objectionable mood, but it was the notion of leaving Li Shan to accompany the Zhou army into battle that was continuing to fuel her angst. No matter how many premonitions Hudan had about the future, it was disconcerting to watch them manifest in the present.

She had foreseen the Great Mother charging her to assist Ji Fa's campaign before the Xibo had ever set foot on Li Shan. Some of Hudan's future observations had been buried so deep within her psyche, she did not even acknowledge them to herself; she felt that if she didn't acknowledge them, or speak of them, she gave her undesirable visions less power. Yet the river of blood and bodies that would result from this war had left such a vivid imprint on her psyche that she could not deny her knowing. As the war grew nearer, she was not eager to see the terrible consequences manifest.

At the height of a Dao Yin demonstration by some of the most advanced adepts of their house, Hudan slipped quietly out of the temple and stole away into the gardens for some quiet and space.

In the darkness of the moonless night, she practised Dao Yin until she felt her undesirable emotions abate and her clarity returning.

'There is no instance in the future that is set in stone,' is what her Shifu would say. *'The gift of precognition is the ability to see into the future and either accept or deny the possibilities presented to you. One wilful thought in the present could change everything that was predestined just a moment before … for willpower is stronger even than psychic knowledge. The only thing more powerful than willpower is imagination.'*

There had to be a way to avoid all the bloodshed, but if Hudan allowed her emotions to get the better of her, she would not find it. If this quest was Tian's will, it was not for her to question or judge; she had only to execute her role to the best of her ability. That decision gave her some peace.

No longer angst-ridden, Hudan felt grateful to Ji Dan for what he'd done on Fen's behalf, and resolved to thank him properly at the first opportunity.

Her exercise session must have taken longer than she imagined, for as Hudan passed through the kitchen garden she found the novices clearing the temple in the wake of the gathering — the day's celebration was over and the household had all but headed for bed.

In the kitchen the sound of music was wafting faintly through the hall from the inner courtyard of the cloister, but it was not the sultry tones of Fen on his new dizi, nor the pounding of drums, nor the clang of bells that she heard, it was the gentle strum and pluck of a string instrument.

The qin was most popular among nobility and scholars, for to master the qin's strings required great dedication, skill and refinement. Such an instrument had not been heard on Li Shan in Hudan's lifetime and she was compelled to follow the beautiful composition to its source.

On approaching the stairs leading to the guest rooms, Hudan was amazed to find half the students of the house nestled low, quietly listening.

'*Brother Hudan*,' one girl called in warning, and the stairs cleared as students scattered silently for their dorms.

Calm and centred as she was at present, Hudan regretted that she was so feared by her students — still, her path had been cleared without her having to raise more than an eyebrow. She ascended the stairs until the stirring notes from the strings brought her to a standstill and she was compelled to close her eyes and just listen.

It was such a unique and heady sound and it resonated so well with her. The music reached into the core of her being and stirred her higher emotions — chi energy welled in her chest, generated by the sheer admiration and appreciation she felt for such genius.

One of their two guests was the source of this profound enchantment, and Hudan's skin began to tingle as she realised it had to be Ji Dan playing. A feeling of shame swept through her, as no shallow being could ever produce such a heavenly sound. She had clearly been far too quick to judge the lord.

The door to the guest chamber was open, and Hudan watched Ji Dan complete his performance. Fen Gong, who was seated inside listening to the lord play, noted her presence in the doorway, but did not acknowledge her, as the last note resounded into silence.

'What do you think?' Dan queried his new ward. 'Shall I offend the Great Mother?'

'Oh no, lord.' Fen had tears in his eyes, he was so moved. 'Shifu Yi will feel exalted.'

'Please do not compliment me just because you are in my charge. I want your honest opinion.' Dan pressed for a critique.

'That was the most extraordinary musical performance I have ever heard,' Hudan interrupted, drawing the lord's attention her way. 'You have a talent that is surely second to none, brother Dan.'

'Brother Hudan,' Dan said, both startled and quietly delighted by her presence. 'I am greatly honoured that you would say so.'

'I should get some sleep.' Fen rose abruptly, ready to be dismissed. 'Leaving home tomorrow,' he explained., 'I need rest for such an adventure.'

'Of course.' Dan rose, placing his instrument on a cushion in front of him. 'Until tomorrow.'

Fen placed his fist against his open palm and gave a respectful bow. As soon as Dan returned the gesture, Fen was gone.

'Please, come in,' Dan invited Hudan, who was still loitering outside his door. 'Would you like to take a closer look?' He referred her to where Fen had been sitting.

'Yes, I would.' Hudan settled on the seat facing the instrument, and Ji Dan sat on the far side, facing her.

'Do you know of the symbology behind the qin?' Dan asked as he seated himself.

'Nothing at all,' she admitted, but was quite fascinated by the appearance of the beautiful piece.

'The qin measures,' Dan held one hand at each end of the item in question, 'three chi, six cun and five fen in length —'

'— to represent the days of the year?' Hudan guessed.

Dan grinned broadly. 'Correct. The upper surface is rounded to represent the sky, and the bottom is flat to …' he invited her guess this time.

'… to represent the earth,' she concluded, and he nodded to acknowledge she was correct again.

'The thirteen mother-of-pearl inlays along the outer edge symbolise —'

'— the thirteen months of the lunar year?' Hudan posited, and was pleased when Dan ticked his head in agreement.

'These five strings are the five elements.' He plucked them in turn as he announced their corresponding element: 'Metal, wood, water, fire and earth.'

'And the sixth string?' Hudan wondered. Looking up from the instrument at Dan, she noted the joy had gone from his face, and a great shroud of sadness weighed down his shoulders.

When Dan explained that the string was added to mourn the death of his eldest brother, Bo Yi Kao, Hudan felt for Dan, having come so close to losing a member of her own family this night. 'My brother was the greatest qin master who ever lived, and it was he who taught me the craft.' He plucked the string, and the sound was deeply reflective of Dan's current expression.

'It is sorrowful,' Hudan agreed. 'It must be difficult for you to play.' Obviously, Dan had adored Bo Yi Kao, and Hudan realised that his intention to play for her Shifu came at some personal and emotional cost to Dan, which made his gift all the more honourable.

Dan forced a grin. 'I have only played twice since my brother's death. At my father's funeral, and ...' The pain that crossed his face, mixed with repulsion, rendered him speechless a moment. He looked away from Hudan, seeming ashamed to voice the rest '... I performed for Su Daji.' He continued to stare out the window at the dark night, tears rimming his eyes.

'That's how you saved Ji Fa from her sorcery?' Hudan guessed, and Dan looked at her, shocked that she knew about that event, but he nodded.

Even though they had stumbled onto the very subject that Hudan had wished to quiz Dan about, she could clearly see how disturbed he was by the event in question and she felt questioning him would only cause him further distress.

'I did not thank you for saving my brother this day.' She found a more uplifting topic. 'I am most grateful for the kindness you and brother Fa have bestowed on Fen.'

'But you know my reasons are entirely selfish.' Dan found his smile.

Hudan also smiled, as she rarely did, amused that she and brother Dan seemed forever destined to disagree. 'I misjudged you, brother Dan,' she admitted, and Dan feared his comment had been mistaken as a taunt.

'I did not mean —'

Hudan held up a hand and silenced the lord, but her smile reassured him that he'd not been misunderstood. 'You cannot hide your wisdom and compassion from me. I have seen your future,

Zhou Gong, and you are the brightest star in Tian's sky.' The words left her mouth like prophecy, said before she could think or object.

Dan's face was devoid of all expression — he was completely lost for words. Her reference to him as Zhou Gong implied that he would one day be a duke of their own family dynasty.

Hudan's shock at her own declaration ebbed as she found Dan's stunned reaction most gratifying. 'I had no intention of ever telling you that,' she added, at a loss as to why she had. 'Please, do not let that prediction go to your head.'

Dan gave a laugh. 'What do I do that is so pleasing to Tian?'

'You are who you are.' Hudan got up to leave, as the amicable mood made her uncomfortable.

'Well,' Dan stood also, 'that shouldn't prove too difficult for me.'

'Happy new year, brother Dan,' she said, inclining her head to him in leaving.

'And to you, brother Hudan.'

'I know Shifu Yi will be most enchanted by your musical gift,' Hudan assured him, as she inched closer to the door. 'Perhaps your desire to learn the way of the Wu will be granted.'

Dan was most inspired by her words. 'Is that a prediction, brother Hudan?'

Hudan raised half a grin and left before she disclosed any more of what she'd foreseen.

The remains of that night passed slowly. Dan was more expectant about his private audience with the Great Mother than he wanted to admit. He'd envied his older brother's sacred connection with the Wu, never expecting that Tian would have cause to summon him, a mere lord, to a private meeting with the Great Mother of Li Shan. One meeting with Yi Wu had transformed Ji Fa from a diffident conqueror into a confident, spiritual warrior of heaven. Dan wondered what the Great Mother would make of him, both figuratively and literally. Would she cast her spell over him, like she had Ji Fa, and make him feel more confident and calm about his future than ever before? Each time Dan recalled Jiang Hudan referring to him as

Zhou Gong, butterflies fluttered in his gut. It was difficult to determine if it was excitement or fear driving the frenzy of sensation, but regardless of the cause, the feeling had not been conducive to sleep.

'Perhaps your desire to learn the way of Wu will be granted?' This was the memory playing on the lord's mind as he was led into the private audience chamber of Yi Wu, and whether or not it was a prophecy didn't matter. It was uplifting to know that Jiang Hudan was on side.

The Great Mother sat unveiled, dressed simply in white, on her throne of cushioned gold. There was a table set for tea, and Dan's instrument had been set up and was ready to play. 'Welcome, brother Dan. I understand that you come bearing a gift for me?'

Dan went down on one knee before her, as her adepts did. 'I do, Great Mother. I would like to play my qin for you, if that would be pleasing?'

'That would please me greatly, brother Dan. Be at liberty.' She rose from her seat and motioned to his qin. 'Would you mind if I take tea as you play. I assure you my ears are entirely yours.'

'Please, Great Mother,' Dan granted with an easy smile. 'Whatever is your pleasure.'

As Yi Wu seated herself at the table, Dan moved to where his instrument sat by the windows in the sunlight, and taking a seat, he made himself comfortable and checked the tuning of the qin. Once he was satisfied with the sound, he sat motionless and stilled his mind.

To the sound of liquid pouring into a cup, Dan closed his eyes and breathed in the tranquil atmosphere of the crisp clear morning on Li Shan. The sun through the open shutters at his back permeated his being to warm his soul. The morning song of the birds beyond their dwelling filled him with the joy of this moment, so pregnant with possibility and free of care.

On that note, the lord began a composition that expressed the wonder he'd felt upon meeting the Wu and being granted glimpses of their sacred world. For quite a good part of the piece Dan managed to avoid the sorrowful sixth string of Bo Yi Kao. Yet, when he considered his own longing to learn their ways, he could only feel sadness, and the sixth string expressed this. With the little hope given to him the previous evening by Jiang Hudan's comments and smile, he struck a happier chord, his composition concluded.

When Dan looked at the Great Mother, her eyes were still closed. Her cup was balanced in both her hands and she could have been a statue, she appeared so serene.

'Magical …' she said, her eyes parting. 'Beautiful, masterful, powerful and a little sad.'

'But there is always hope,' Dan assured her.

Yi Wu smiled a knowing smile. 'Come, take tea with me.' She rang a bell for a fresh pot, and her request was met, with graceful poise, by one of her initiates even before Dan was fully seated. 'You have a very great talent, brother Dan. Your gift is one I shall treasure always. It is a shame that more souls have not had the opportunity to be inspired by your art.'

Dan felt the pressure of sorrow welling in his chest and battled his desire to please the Great Mother. 'I shall try harder to set aside my grief,' he allowed, with some difficulty.

'Tian will aid you in this,' Yi Wu stated with confidence. The Great Mother waited for her initiate to depart before she spoke again. 'What I deduced from your composition is that you deeply desire to learn the way of the Wu.' She was straightforward in her speech, and Dan opened his mouth to confirm. 'But have you really considered how a nobleman could possibly manage to abide by our creed?'

'I have, Great Mother,' Dan assured her, 'and I am certain that I can.'

'But what of your wife?' she reasoned calmly — all noblemen had at least one, to ensure an heir.

'My wife died giving birth to my son, Bo Qin, twenty years ago,' he informed her without sentiment. 'We were very young and I did not choose to remarry.'

Yi Wu found this interesting. 'And what of your concubines?' Every nobleman had several of those.

Dan grinned, stating for the record: 'I am quite able to appreciate beauty without feeling a need to possess it. I find companionship in study, and as I am married to the government, that is truly all I have time for. So you see, Great Mother, I already live by your creed, in that regard.'

Yi Wu smiled, as if she knew something that he did not. 'I think the reason you find beauty so easy to pass by is because you know you can have any beauty you desire … but what happens when beauty is forbidden you. Will it be so easy to resist then?'

'Great Mother,' Dan began, 'I —'

'If I were to send one of my Wu to seduce you, could you resist?'

'Su Daji herself tried and failed,' he contested, matching the Great Mother's challenging gaze with his own.

'But Daji disgusts you,' Yi Wu pointed out. 'What if beauty came in the form of someone who makes your heart soar and fills your dreams with the possibilities of an amazing future?'

Dan's eyes had not wavered from those of the Great Mother, but there was a sinking feeling in his gut — her words were more accurate than anyone could have known. Was she aware of the dreams he'd been having? Was his inexplicable attraction to Jiang Hudan so obvious?

'If I sent Jiang Hudan to seduce you, what then, brother Dan?'

The feeling in his gut went from sinking to plummeting, and his sights wavered as he gave the query due consideration. He was actually surprised by how panicked the premise made him feel inside, but he looked at Yi Wu to answer her honestly. 'If Jiang Hudan were ever to offer herself to me, I believe that I would remember this meeting, Great Mother, and the challenge you pose to me. Then I would see the seduction for the test that it is.'

Yi Wu smiled warmly. 'You see through my mind games so easily, brother Dan, and it pleases Tian that you are so clever. I too am clever. If I were to initiate you as Wu, then you would be bound to protect your brothers, rather than seduce one of them for information.'

Dan was feeling decidedly uncomfortable as his cheeks began burning with more heat than he'd ever known. 'I greatly respect and admire brother Hudan, Great Mother —'

'Admire or *desire?*' she probed, and Dan felt affronted.

'I would never wish to dishonour a legend in such a manner,' he defended. 'I have never entertained such thoughts.'

'That is well,' Yi Wu proffered, 'because if you were to allow personal feelings to overwhelm you, you would disempower your best weapon against Su Daji.'

Dan was breathless in the wake of this statement, realising that the inquisition was far more than just a lecture in ethics; it was a warning about a potential misstep that might cost them victory.

'In order to channel chi energy to its greatest advantage one needs to feel clear, centred and powerful,' the Great Mother said. 'The whole reason you have not taken another wife or lover is because you know what a distraction they can be.'

Dan was shocked by how right she was and was able to understand the point with blinding clarity.

'You could easily become the distraction, brother Dan.' Yi Wu eyed him over with an admiring gaze. 'Or you could be the arrow that Tian launches straight into the heart of the enemy.'

'Why me, Great Mother?' Dan was bewildered. 'Why do you not say these things to my brother?'

'I had other matters to discuss with Ji Fa, brother Dan. But you are who you are and must accept that your destiny may also be great,' she advised him light-heartedly, dispersing the heavy mood. 'As for your aspiration to be a pupil of this house ...'

Dan regained his focus very quickly and looked at the Great Mother to hear her decision.

'I am prepared to allow Fen Gong to instruct you on a trial basis,' she granted. 'Come and see me again when your quest in the East is complete.'

'Thank you, Great Mother,' Dan bowed his head low to hide his elation. He felt like such a child. 'I shall make you proud, Shifu Yi.'

'I know,' she said, with such sureness that Dan was forced to look at her. 'The brightest star in Tian's sky.'

'Brother Hudan told you of our conversation about Zhou Gong,' Dan assumed.

The Great Mother was surprised. 'I was not aware Jiang Hudan knew about Zhou Gong?'

The response sent shivers down Dan's spine when he realised that what had seemed a playful compliment the previous night, was really some deep, dark destiny that Tian was only telling to those in psychic circles.

'Why do you fear greatness, brother Dan?' Yi Wu asked.

Dan cocked an eye; he was about to be cynical. 'Could it be because great men end up dead men, or married men, and either way a man cannot study?'

Yi Wu had a chuckle, finding his view very amusing. 'So then, brother Dan, what is the secret to my success?'

'You were born a woman.' The lord never thought he'd say that with envy.

'Bah!' Yi Wu discarded his knee-jerk response, and challenged him to try again. 'That gives me a far greater disadvantage than you, my lord.'

'You are Wu.' Dan's reply was tinged with realisation.

'As are you, brother Dan,' she concluded, 'the first beyond these walls to be so honoured. Does such an honour not hint at a certain potential for greatness in the future?'

Dan was suddenly a little embarrassed by his premature doubts. 'Yes, Great Mother, one would hope it does.'

'One would.' She raised her tea in a toast. 'To the dreams of Zhou Gong.'

Dan had to smile at her sentiment, thinking the prophecy somewhat ironic, although he hesitated to return the gesture, saying: 'To the dreams of a man who cannot get to sleep.'

'I have never known a Wu to have trouble sleeping ...' The Great Mother dismissed the last of Dan's worries with a reassuring smile. 'And neither will you.'

Exultant was the emotion Dan was coming to associate with the Wu. Every encounter with them induced an inner lightness and harmony that nothing in the mundane world seemed able to replicate. He exited into the cloister from the Great Mother's chambers, feeling as if he were floating. The cares that had weighed him down before today had simply melted away.

His father had been hesitant to oppose the Shang out of respect for heaven's mandate and fear of the repercussions of Su Daji's sorcery upon the Zhou people. But today, Ji Fa and he had all but secured heaven's mandate for the Zhou, and had three Wu to aid them in combat with Su Daji. No matter the outcome of this war, Dan would never again be answerable to the emperor or his witch. The laws of imperial rule no longer applied to him, for the Wu were only answerable to heaven.

In those very comforting thoughts, Dan felt that his feet might just lift off the ground and he would soar into the heavens — just as he had seen the Wu do, in fact. Dan couldn't help but wonder what psychic talents might be lying dormant within him, waiting to be activated by the right spiritual training.

'Dan, my brother!' Ji Fa's call snapped Dan from his whimsy, and he looked to find his older brother crossing the cloister to meet him.

'At last I can treat you as a true brother again, instead of a subservient.' Fa embraced Dan, who was taken aback that his Xibo had even considered this — Dan certainly hadn't.

'That is not the reason I desired to be Wu,' Dan ventured, 'and I'm only being taken on as a student on a trial basis.'

Fa was not surprised by Dan's modesty, and held him at arm's length to state, 'If there was a perfect student ever born into this world, it was you, Dan.'

Dan smiled to accept the flattery.

'I see your meeting with Yi Wu has done wonders for your self-esteem, little brother. That is well.' Fa admired him fondly. 'You should take pride in your achievements. I have just visited the sunset shrine to leave offerings to our ancestors who, I feel, support our quest and are gratified at the role you played in bringing our alliance with the Wu into being.'

'Since when do you pay homage and chat with our ancestors?'

No one openly honoured the ancestors any more, as homage was due to the emperor, and he alone, with Daji, was allowed to pay homage to Shangdi — the Shang name for the ruler of heaven.

'I have always done so inwardly,' Fa confessed, 'but now I shall do so outwardly and free our people to do the same.' He waved off that matter, still beaming with pride. 'And you are to be Wu … what an honour upon the House of Ji.'

'Our great-grandfather would be especially proud.' Dan reflected on the old Xibo's stories and reverence of the Wu. Ji Danfu had desired to break with Shang law and consult with the Wu of Li Shan about deposing the emperor and his witch, but fearing the reprisals of the emperor, or worse Tian, on his newly established colony in the valley at the foot of Li Shan, Ji Danfu had refrained from seeking out heaven's warriors. Still, their great-grandfather had many a tale to tell about the Wu mysteriously coming to the aid of the people in the valley during his rule.

Fa chuckled and nodded in agreement. 'The Great Mother confirmed our great-grandfather's claim that our family are descended from the Yellow Emperor, and I plan to raise shrines to his honour and to the honour of our many great forefathers!'

Dan could not wipe the silly smile from his face, nor could his brother. 'With such allies, how can we possibly lose?'

'We cannot.' Fa clapped Dan on the shoulder and then released him. 'Wish me luck.' Fa entered the chambers of the Great Mother, where he would deliver their proposals for the new Zhou state for Tian's final approval.

If Yi Wu approved of the tribute they intended to pay Tian for supporting their quest, then all that was left to do was to inform the rest of their brothers, and allied states, of their new affiliation with the House of Yi Wu Li Shan. In light of the bad reputation Su Daji had cast upon the Wu, Dan did not expect this would be the most popular political alliance the House of Ji had ever made, but it was by far the boldest. Zi Shou would not anticipate the move and the Zhou would need to attack before the emperor learned of the Wu's involvement.

However, Ji Fa was still waiting for a divine sign to declare war on the Shang. 'Trust in Tian,' his Xibo kept telling him. Till now, Fa's refrain had proven wise — they had waited this long for the Wu to ally with them, which was essential to their victory.

If Tian's timing was indeed divine, the omen would be delivered soon, before the Zhou lost the element of surprise and with it, their advantage.

PART 2

THE ZHOU

5

HAOJING

At the jetty Ji Fa's personal guard witnessed their leaders disembark from the Li Shan ferry with a quiet young man, a white hooded figure and to their great alarm, a large white tigress, who kept pace with their Xibo and growled at anyone who got too close to her charge.

'This is Jiang Huxin,' Ji Fa said, patting the head of the tigress as he introduced her to his guard, and every man took a step backward upon hearing the legendary name. 'She is the representative of Baihu, heavenly guardian of the West.' The commander of the Xibo's guard was overwhelmed by the news, and when he kneeled before his lord and the tigress, his men followed suit. 'She has been sent by the Great Mother of Li Shan to protect me, and is the living proof that Tian supports my right to claim heaven's mandate!'

The men gave a mighty cheer, then the Xibo silenced them with a simple hand motion. 'These Wu,' Fa motioned back to Fen and Hudan, 'are my honoured guests and are here to aid our cause. Your task is to ensure that no one discovers who they are or what their purpose is. If anyone asks, the lad is the son of a fallen ally who is now my ward, the hooded lady is a concubine given as a gift to my brother —' Hudan gave a grunt of disapproval, resenting this cover, but bit her tongue for the sake of the mission '— and the white tiger is my new pet and constant companion. Understood?'

His soldiers unanimously confirmed their Xibo's instruction, but Fa raised a finger to give them fair warning.

'Jiang Huxin will walk among you now and as long as you are true to your Xibo and Zhou, and are confident you can keep to the vow you have just made, then you have nothing to fear. However, if there is treachery in your heart, Jiang Huxin will sense it.' He watched as the tigress moved among his men, her sniffing nose causing even the most hardened of his warriors to wince in fear of her harsh judgement.

When at last she returned to Ji Fa's side, the tigress rubbed against him, satisfied that all was well.

'Very good,' the Xibo commented, pleased that he did not have to see any of his personal guard slaughtered, and gave them leave to rise. 'Let us proceed to Haojing.'

To prevent Jiang Huxin driving too much fear into the hearts of the locals, Fa had her ride in an open cart — as long as the tigress lay at leisure therein, he hoped to avoid any undue panic. It might have been easier for Huxin to travel in human form, but they hoped to keep her human persona a secret for the present. In her tiger form she would generate rumours and talk among the people of Ji Fa's divine favour, for only someone who carried Tian's favour could befriend a wild beast!

It had been some time since Jiang Hudan had left Li Shan. The Wu had been outlawed for over a decade and had kept to themselves — only coming to the aid of those who were daring or desperate enough to light the torches of summons. The height of Li Shan and the thermal lake at its base meant that despite the drought and shallower waters of the lake, there was always moisture in the air and the mount remained green. It was not unusual to see the valley parched just before the wet season — which was still months away — but every year in the last ten, the wet season had been shorter and shorter. Last year, barely a dusting of rain graced their fields and the Wu could do nothing but watch the green valley wither. Until the people of the earth entreated heaven's aid, heaven could not act. Powerful as heaven's forces were, Tian's might needed righteous human channels through which to manifest, and any action the Wu undertook had to be in the best interests of the land and people as a whole. When Ji Dan lit their torches of summons and requested aid to overthrow the Shang, he gave the Wu permission to act. Had Zi Shou lit their torches and requested their aid to put down the

Zhou, the Wu would have refused, for his intention was not pure like Ji Fa's.

The further their party descended into the valley, the more obvious became the dispiriting effect of the drought. The land, like the people, appeared to have been bled dry of life and hope; anything still living on the landscape was silently screaming for sustenance and moisture.

'The quicker we find a battlefield, the sooner I can put an end to this suffering,' Hudan commented from beneath her hood to Ji Dan, who was riding alongside her, for she had a notion — she'd foreseen how the bloodshed might be avoided.

'You think deposing the emperor will break the drought?' Dan queried.

'No,' Hudan replied coolly, 'I believe quite the reverse.'

Dan found her response most curious. 'You can summon rain?'

'Any Wu worth her salt can summon rain,' Hudan replied confidently, although in truth she had never attempted the feat herself. She had seen it done by Shifu Yi, and Hudan realised a deep spiritual commitment was required to accomplish the feat. 'I shall seek yin by means of yin.'

'Surely you don't mean to offer yourself on a pyre in the hope that Tian will send rain and prevent your incineration?' He sounded fearful and appalled, for seeking yin by means of yin required a female shaman to expose herself to open flames, to scorch the water element within herself in order to bring rain. 'I thought we were progressing beyond pointless human sacrifice —'

'The practice is not pointless!' she interjected, and put aside her intolerance to explain. 'It is strategic. I will not perish. I will bring rain. Can you think of a better way to intimidate Daji, before battle, than to achieve what she herself could not.'

'Actually, no,' Dan admitted, warily. 'But here are many other feats you could preform —'

'In the eyes of the people, the breaking of a drought is undeniable proof of divine favour, and in this particular battle there could be no better harbinger of heaven's will.' Hudan closed her eyes, remembering what she had foreseen of the battle ahead.

'But surely, brother Hudan —' She realised he had no faith in her ability for she could hear the concern in his tone.

'You forget, brother Dan, that I have foreseen this battle.' Hudan spoke up over his argument.. 'There *is* rain. So you had better hope that that miracle is my doing and not Daji's.'

'Maybe it will be a natural phenomenon?' Dan suggested, and Hudan rolled her eyes beneath her head cover.

'That would be good news for the masses, but not so good for us while Zi Shou is still emperor.' Hudan lowered her voice, since the royal party was now attracting attention from local people as they moved through one of the small villages on route to Haojing.

'Point taken,' Dan admitted, sounding none too happy about it. 'It is just that I vowed to Shifu Yi to protect my brothers, and allowing you to cast yourself onto a pyre doesn't really seem to fulfil that promise.'

Hudan could have been annoyed by his assumption that he knew better than she did, that she needed his consent to do anything, or that he could possibly protect her from something that she could not defend against herself, but instead she laughed.

'What is so amusing?' Dan asked, unsure whether to laugh, or be offended.

His hooded companion chose to be distracted by the villagers who were cheering as they passed by — the locals were wishing the Xibo and his family a Happy New Year and thanking him for the water they had received from the House of Ji.

'Thank the Great Mother of Li Shan,' was the Xibo's reply.

'Praise Yi Wu!' the cry went up and was echoed loudly by everyone.

Dan smiled, and he felt Hudan was also smiling beneath her hood. 'It must be inspiring to hear our Shifu's name being venerated after so many years of silence.'

'The common people have always venerated her,' Hudan replied, with a smile in her voice, 'but now they are free to do so openly, and that is pleasing to —'

'Brothers! Brothers!' A voice was heard amid the din, and when Hudan and Fen turned about on their horses to see where the call had come from, a second cry was heard. 'Fen!'

Dan's sights were drawn to the second storey of a house, where he saw someone being torn away from an open, barred window.

'He Nuan!' Fen dismounted his moving horse and began to run toward the dwelling.

'Fen!' The desperate call turned into a scream of agony that was suddenly silenced.

Dan rode after his ward and, noting that Jiang Huxin had raised herself, he gestured for the tigress to stay put and not alarm the crowd. 'Fen!' The lord dismounted, managing to head the lad off at the door to the establishment. 'Let me assist you. You have no idea how rough the common folk can be, especially when disrupted from their leisure.'

'It is He Nuan. She is here!' Fen was anxious to find her as Jiang Hudan rode up and dismounted.

'At a house of jun ji,' she commented. 'What a surprise.'

Jun ji were military prostitutes, and the most common of all in the profession. These woman had no talent with song, instrument or dance, or were too old to fetch a high price. Thus jun ji were considered good for nothing more than satisfying the sexual thirsts of common men who could not afford to buy a woman of quality.

Fen served his eldest brother a hate-face for her lack of compassion. 'He Nuan does not belong in such a place,' he insisted, and the deadly look in his eye warned Hudan to keep her derogatory opinion to herself. 'If this is a house of ill-repute, then why are there bars on the windows?'

'To keep the whores in and prevent customers slipping away without paying,' Hudan snapped. 'You are delaying the Xibo's journey and jeopardising his safety for a —'

'*Do not* call her that again.' The once-passive gardener-cum-musician was more agitated and tense than Dan had ever seen him. 'I'm not asking any of you to stop. I'll handle this on my own.'

Fen pushed forward, but Hudan waylaid him. 'You have no idea how the world works —' she began.

'Please, brothers,' Dan intervened. 'This does not have to delay us long. Allow me.' The lord headed into the dilapidated double-storey dwelling, and was met in the service foyer by a chubby woman, who bowed low upon recognising him.

'My lord, welcome. We are so honoured by your presence in our house.'

'The woman we saw calling out from upstairs, just a moment ago. Where is she?' Dan got straight to the point.

'I apologise for the insult, lord,' she said. 'We've quietened her down. She won't be any more bother.'

'What do you mean by that?' Fen was concerned, but Dan urged him to be patient.

'I wish to purchase that woman from you.' Dan tossed a jade piece on the table in front of the aging proprietor which was worth enough to buy every woman in the house. Despite the exceptional price, the woman's reaction seemed to indicate the offer posed a dilemma for her. 'Respectfully, I advise my lord that we have many more girls who are younger and more beautiful than this woman,' she offered.

'In that case, to sell this woman to us shall be no great loss to your business,' Dan insisted.

'So true,' she agreed. 'However, please allow us some time to clean her up before presenting her to you.'

'No!' Fen took charge of the negotiation, sensing the woman was stalling. 'You will take us to her *now*.'

Brows drawn with worry, the old proprietor finally nodded. 'If that is your wish, but I warn you, she has not been well. Follow me —' She turned to lead the way, but Fen pushed past her and headed for the stairs.

'He Nuan!' he called, scaling the stairs quickly, with Dan and Hudan in hot pursuit. There were a couple of young women at the top of the stairway who wished to waylay Fen, but he bypassed their advances by jumping the rails straight onto the open landing above, where the upstairs rooms were located.

When the scantily clad ladies spotted Dan in pursuit, they were even more excited, but as Hudan let loose an unearthly snarl of disapproval from beneath her hood, both the girls fled in fear. Dan was grateful to avoid the scene and to have their path cleared to pursue Fen.

'He Nuan!' Fen called again, and when he received no answer, he stopped dead still, closed his eyes and took three deep breaths, before looking to one door in particular.

'Fen, wait —' Dan called in warning, but the lad was already charging the room.

'What do you want, little girl?' Dan heard another man grumble as he approached the open doorway and perceived the horrendous scene within.

A woman sat on the floor, her arms extended over her head and tied to the bars of the window above. Her clothes had been torn open down the front, and hung off her in rags, covering nothing of her modesty. Her long body was skeletal thin, and she was badly bruised all over. The man leaning over her, who had beaten her nearly unconscious, was double Fen's size. Still, as he rose to confront the lad, Fen charged at the burly fellow and gripped hold of his throat.

Dan was horrified, expecting the larger man would throw Fen off like a rag doll, but instead the thug buckled to his knees. He became short of breath and his face began to turn bright red — he appeared fit to explode!

'No, Fen!' Hudan pushed past Dan, flinging her hood back to speak with her brother. 'If you waste your energy killing him, you'll never be able to save her.'

Fen began seething with conflict: his hate for this man versus his love for Nuan.

'Stop now or they will both die!' Hudan reasoned. 'Love or hate, you cannot accommodate both successfully.'

Fen threw the man backward, out of the way, and the fellow gasped for breath.

'Yield,' Dan commanded the stranger, 'or I shall have you arrested. This woman has just been purchased by the House of Ji.'

'You are welcome to her!' The man hauled himself to his feet. 'She may look like a weak bag of bones, but she has a will of bloody iron.'

'Cut her loose.' Dan noted the man carried a large knife. He must be an employee of the house and not a customer, as customers would have to leave weapons at the door. With a grumble of resentment the man cut his prisoner's bonds, and she fell unconscious into Fen's arms.

'Leave us!' Fen demanded through gritted teeth.

Dan closed the door behind the fellow as Fen laid He Nuan on the floor. As her own clothes were in such a state of disrepair, Dan removed his cloak, covered the patient with it and knelt down beside her. He was no doctor, but the woman was obviously having trouble breathing and was in a very bad way. In fact, she didn't look like she'd survive the journey to Haojing, but he wanted to offer the services of the court physicians. 'We could —'

'Shhh,' both Hudan and Fen requested at once, as they completed lying the patient flat on her back.

Their reaction was puzzling to Dan, but as he knew little about the Wu, he was silent and observed. Instead of crying over his lover's injuries and near-death state, Fen had calmed himself. He knelt close to He Nuan, breathing deeply, his eyes closed; then he smiled and brought his hands together at his chest.

Hudan grabbed Dan by the wrist and quietly guided him back to standing. He wanted to ask what was happening, but in response to his quizzical frown, Hudan only referred him back to Fen.

In between the lad's palms an illumination now flared — as if he held a tiny sun inside his hands. Fen bent forward and laid his palms between He Nuan's breasts, at which point the light disappeared inside her and the woman's injuries began to heal and vanish. Dan had seen the Wu heal themselves, but had no idea they could heal others in the same fashion. Or was it only Fen who could do this? Yi Wu had referred to the lad as a healer and now it was clear why.

'No wonder your house was loathe to let Fen go,' Dan uttered aside to Hudan.

'A great boon for the House of Ji,' Hudan confirmed.

'Indeed.' Dan was so overcome with excitement it momentarily left him breathless — he had secured himself a far more gifted teacher than he'd imagined.

When Fen's patient showed signs of coming around, he scooped her up into a supported, seated position to welcome her back to consciousness. 'Nuan?'

It took her a moment to focus on his face. 'Fen?' she rasped, and he nodded eagerly, tears filling his eyes as she smiled. 'You're alive!' She shed tears of relief, although still weak from lack of food and water. 'I was devastated when that old witch said she was going to burn you.'

'Old witch?' Hudan protested, but one glare from Fen and Hudan lapsed into silence.

'I offered myself in your place,' Nuan wept, caressing his cheek with her trembling hand, 'but she said I was not worthy.'

'Yi Wu freed me,' Fen told Nuan to encourage her to stop worrying. 'I am an honoured son of the House of Ji now, and free to take a wife of my choosing.' His announcement brought tears of joy to Nuan's eyes, but Hudan could only roll hers. 'And I choose you, He Nuan,' Fen whispered.

'Oh, brother,' Hudan muttered to herself, shaking her head in disapproval.

'I have died, Fen,' Nuan gasped through her sobs, as Fen scooped her up to carry her out of her prison, 'and this is heaven.' She leant her head upon his shoulder and closed her eyes.

The gushing love talk and heightened emotions made Hudan very uncomfortable. 'Can we leave, please?' She placed the hood over her head, opened the door and led the way outside.

As they emerged from the house of jun ji, the tigress gave a roar which sent the villagers running for their lives.

'Shut up!' Hudan growled back at her sister, in a mood.

Dan repressed a smile of amusement and only shrugged at the tiger, who returned to her reclining position. When he was again seated on his horse beside Jiang Hudan, Dan felt satisfied to have been able to fulfil his end of the bargain with Fen.

'What are you looking so happy about?' Hudan queried. 'Now your new teacher has the distraction of a lover.' She dug her heels into her horse and galloped off down the road after their party.

Perhaps he hadn't entirely thought that bargain through. Because of He Nuan's association with Fen, Dan's happiness was again running contrary to Jiang Hudan's. 'Damn.'

A little way down the road a soldier riding at the head of the party came back to advise Dan that the Xibo would like a word with him.

'We found the banished Wu, I gather?' Ji Fa commented as Dan joined him.

'It would seem so,' Dan glanced back at his new ward, whose arms were filled with a bundle of woman — he'd never seen a lad so happy. 'But I do not think Jiang Hudan is very pleased about the event.'

'Brother Hudan has no say in Fen Gong's life any longer,' Ji Fa said, seeking to cheer up his brother. 'He is your ward now.'

'An enviable position,' Dan replied sarcastically, and Ji Fa saw his point.

'Ah well, we are all on the same side and want the best for brother Fen, so I'm sure the situation will work itself out. The hint of a wedding turns any woman to mush.'

Dan was a realist. 'Not Jiang Hudan.'

'I fear you might be right,' Ji Fa quietly chuckled.

'Is our new acquaintance the reason you wanted to speak with me?' Dan queried.

'No,' Fa admitted. 'The Great Mother was very impressed by your performance this morning,' he began, a little awkwardly. 'She wanted me to pass on her desire that you play for our troops to rouse them before battle.'

It felt as if someone suddenly reached down Dan's throat and yanked his heart into his windpipe — he couldn't breathe.

'I know that you have found playing the qin difficult since our brother's death, which is why I am going commission a new instrument for you, with a seventh string, and its tone shall be joyous!'

Dan had promised the Great Mother that he would try to set aside his grief in order that he might share his gift with others, and Yi Wu had vowed that heaven would aid him to do this. Was this new instrument the answer?

'Thank you. I eagerly await your gift.' Dan resolved to remain open to the possibilities inherent in a new instrument. He had truly adored playing the qin once, and he wished to find the joy in it again.

'Then you will do it?' Ji Fa concluded, seemingly surprised by the lack of argument.

'I shall do my best,' Dan conceded, his gut churning with inner resistance. If the Great Mother was intent on him overcoming his musical block, then Dan knew that the challenge was important and he must endure; he did not wish not give Yi Wu a reason to think him unworthy of her tutelage.

Their party was greeted with a mixed reaction in the open courtyard at the Ji family residence in Haojing. Most notably, Jiang Huxin caused a commotion as she paced beside the Xibo through the courtyard toward the steps to the interior where the household were assembled.

Ji Song was obviously delighted to see the Wu again, but as he opened his mouth, his father held a finger to his own lips to urge Song to keep silent for the moment.

Fa had decided that how much his subjects were told about their guests would be based on a need-to-know basis. So their family members, including Fa's wife and three of their most trusted brothers, Zhenduo, Wu and Shi, were told that the tiger was Fa's personal protector, given to him by Yi Wu; that Fen was Dan's new ward; and Hudan was a gift to Dan from Yi Wu, in appreciation for his performance.

'Such a gift is surely wasted on Dan,' commented Zhenduo, brother number six. 'What does she look like under there?'

As Zhenduo neared to draw back her hood, Hudan let loose her unearthly snarl, and the warrior decided he was no longer curious, much to the amusement of the rest of the menfolk.

'What a beauteous specimen!' Shi, brother number nine, who looked to be a younger twin of Ji Fa — even though they did not share the same birth mother — was fascinated by the tiger. Shi kept a couple of tigers that he'd raised from cubs, and he was by far the biggest animal lover among Xibo Chang's sons. 'The tigress is tame?' he asked, excited to see that she was not on a leash.

'That really depends on whether she likes you,' Fa replied.

'May I?' Shi decided to try his luck, as he was not as fearful as most.

Fa gave a laugh and shrugged. 'They're your limbs.' The Xibo patted Huxin's head. 'My little brother has a bit of an obsession with tigers. He's raised orphaned cubs, who are still thriving in our garden.'

'I have never seen a *white* tigress before!' Shi's wide eyes were fixed on Huxin as he stepped forward and then slowly sank onto his haunches. Shi bowed his head submissively, and holding his hands out before him, palms up, he inched closer.

'This is madness,' uttered the Xibo's wife, but Fa hushed her to silence, intrigued.

As Shi got closer, a sound began to reverberate from deep in the tigress' throat, and there was a gasp from the court, as most thought the sound was a warning that the animal was about to strike. As Shi's hands were now right under Huxin's nose, the sound she was making increased and she began to purr loudly. Shi ventured to touch her fur, and gave a sigh of delight. 'You are amazing, girl.'

Huxin nudged her head against his, and the next thing Shi knew he was being bowled over and having his face licked.

'Well,' exclaimed Fa, rather surprised by the outcome, 'it seems Baihu will protect me from everyone but you, Shi.' Fa could not refer to the tigress by her real name, as it was known far and wide.

The tigress suddenly returned to Fa's side — as if she realised she'd got carried away.

'May I try?' Ji Fa's wife asked, thinking she'd test where she stood with her husband's new pet. She'd barely taken one step toward Huxin before the tiger let loose a roar that sent every woman and child fleeing for the house interior, including Ji Fa's wife.

Huxin sat back on her haunches, obviously pleased with the chaos she'd created, and most of the men found the scene highly amusing.

'She really looks like she's about to attack,' Shi exclaimed, still seated on the ground before the tiger, laughing at the scene.

Fa agreed with a nod. 'However, Baihu, if you don't want my wife to have you locked up, best keep your opinion of her to yourself,' he remonstrated, a chuckle still in his voice.

'You are always welcome in my part of the house, Baihu,' Shi declared and crawled over to give her another pat.

'Odd!' Fa watched their fond interaction with some bemusement. 'She has not let anyone else get near her besides me.' Obviously Huxin felt Shi was very trustworthy. 'You always did have a way with wild creatures, Shi.'

'They have a way with me,' Shi corrected. 'They make so much more sense than people do.' He got a lick up the side of the face for that comment. 'See, she understands me.'

'More than you could possibly know.' Fa was perturbed that Huxin was so taken with their much younger brother, but Huxin again withdrew from her cuddle with Shi to return to Fa's side.

'That growl was fierce!' Ji Song came forward to express his opinion, but he was not game enough to actually pat the tigress.

'You and I need to talk, son,' said Fa, indicating that Song should follow him to somewhere quiet. Fa wanted to explain their strategy, and ensure his heir remained tightlipped about the Wu.

Huxin rose to accompany Fa inside the house, but could not resist looking back to Shi, who sat gazing at her with total love and adoration.

'Just what we need,' Hudan muttered, under her breath. 'Another distraction.'

'City life is full of them, I'm afraid,' Dan said to acknowledge her concerns.

'Then, with Tian's grace, we shall not be forced to linger here long.' Hudan was already craving solitude and a chance to practise Dao Yin.

'Indeed.' Dan could not have been more in agreement. 'Still, I think you will find my rooms quiet and conducive to st—'

'Your rooms!' Hudan protested.

'Your cover denotes,' Dan whispered to her, 'that you are my respons—'

'I shall not be shut up with the rest of your women!' Hudan had lowered her voice to a stressed whisper.

'I do not *have* any other women,' he hissed in reply, and as Hudan remained silent beneath her hood, he continued. 'There is only me, the interior house staff and now Fen, Nuan and you.' Hudan was still quiet, and Dan could feel her resistance to being put in his charge — if only covertly. 'Allow me to show you around, and you can make up your own mind,' he proffered.

Finally, she nodded, resigned. 'Lead the way,' Hudan said, so that she could trail him through the house as a 'gift' might.

En route, Dan instructed one of the house staff to fetch the physicians to his quarters to see to He Nuan.

'I realise this is awkward for you,' Dan said, waiting for her to catch up and, insisting on walking beside her despite her cover. 'I am not accustomed to sharing my space either, so ... we'll just have to make the best of it.'

He pushed open the double doors at the end of the hallway and they entered a huge Hall of Records, complete with a few writing desks near the windows in the sunlight and a vast amount of floor space.

'What do you think?' he asked, with a hopeful frown.

Hudan's hood fell back to expose a large smile on her face. 'It is so quiet in here.' She could hardly believe they were in the middle of the city.

'The garden is private and fairly quiet also,' Dan replied, relieved to see her in good spirits. That was a first since they'd left Li Shan.

Dan directed his master of the interior to show Fen and his patient to sleeping quarters. Fen was surely finding his load heavy, but the lad was not about to allow anyone to relieve him of his burden.

'It is clear to me that you do not approve of Fen's choice of wife.' Dan waited until Fen had gone to broach the subject, and Hudan's brow collapsed into a frown once again. 'I can have them separated, if you wish.'

Hudan seemed confused by Dan's consideration. 'You have an agreement with Fen, not me. Your allegiance should lie with him.'

'As far as my personal education is concerned, that is true,' Dan conceded. 'In the larger scheme of things it is far more important that I keep you on side, Jiang Hudan.'

Hudan nodded, conceding his point. 'Fen is a free man now. I do not have a say in his life any more, and I do not resent you for honouring your arrangement with him. Still, I would like to know your honest opinion about Fen's choice … do you think He Nuan will make Fen a good wife?'

Dan was overwhelmed by the question, as he didn't really know the woman in question. 'I think that Fen believes that He Nuan will make him happy, and that is what counts really.'

Again Hudan nodded, yet her expression was melancholy. 'Fen had the potential to be one of the greatest of us. Now his chance for true mastery will be severely diminished.'

'Why so?' Dan wondered.

Hudan was shocked that he should need to ask. 'The Wu refrain from sexual relations because vital chi energy can be wasted by both parties if the act is not handled properly, to their mutual benefit.'

'Really?' Dan was discomfitted, and yet aroused, by the information.

'But more so for men,' Hudan clarified.

Dan's curiosity was making him grin and he had to ask. 'Why is that?'

An uncomfortable grin graced Hudan's face also. 'Because women have an inexhaustible supply of yin essence, until such time as they pass childbearing age. But men have only a limited supply of yang for the extent of their lives. So if a man were to expend his yang before sufficiently raising his partner's yin, then the entire act is nothing but a waste of chi.'

This was most interesting to Dan. 'My first and only wife, long deceased,' he explained, 'might have been a lot happier had I been taught that at school.' He made light of the awkward, rather tantalising, moment. 'Has Fen been made aware of this?'

'Only so far as to know that he would waste his yang if he amused himself too much,' Hudan said, coyly, and shrugged. 'As to how much he knows about raising a woman's yin essence … He Nuan would be more insightful than I.' She then held up a finger to add: 'Still, I am told Fen is very handy with his tongue.'

Dan burst out laughing, he couldn't help himself. It was a pleasant surprise to find that Jiang Hudan was not the frightful prude he'd thought, for she was laughing right along with him.

'Well, that certainly sounds promising.' He drew deep breaths to contain his amusement. 'I'll talk to him,' Dan squeaked, short on breath.

'Whatever you think is best.' Hudan took a breath and gazed around the room. 'Maybe our jaunt in the city won't be completely terrible, after all.'

'Would you like to see the rest?' Dan offered, gratified that Hudan seemed to now be relaxed in his house.

'I would, although I don't need to.' Hudan smiled, drinking in the atmosphere of the Hall of Records. 'I can work here.'

'I have always found it congenial here,' Dan said proudly.

Before he had left Haojing, the Xibo had arranged to have half the Great Mother's miraculous gift of water- and wine-filled urns delivered to Fengjing, Haojing's sister city on the opposite side of the Feng River, late on New Year's Eve. Subsequently, the brothers Fa had assigned to rule there — Xian, Du, Chu and Zai — whom he did not trust so well as the brothers he kept by him at Haojing, did not become curious about Fa's sudden divine favour until after Fa's unusual overnight trip away on the eve of the New Year was complete. The holiday meant the Xibo had plenty of time to return to Haojing with his prized companions before his rebellious siblings arrived to seek answers.

The day following the New Year celebrations, the Xibo and his trusted brothers — Dan, Zhenduo, Wu and Shi — along with the prime minister, Jiang Taigong, awaited the party from Fengjing in the war council's chamber.

Huxin was the only outsider, and certainly the only female permitted to be present, and she sat proudly beside Ji Fa, observing all.

The gong sounded to announce the arrival of the brothers from Fengjing, who entered the hall in a diamond formation: Xian was in the lead; his two full-blood brothers, Du and Chu, flanked him; their youngest brother, Zai, brought up the rear. The first three brothers were very similar in appearance and their round faces held no trace of joy — they were warriors and from all accounts had no appreciation of culture or refinement, unlike the brothers who stood alongside Ji Fa. The youngest brother, Zai, seemed the odd one out; he was not a warrior like the brothers he ran with, yet there seemed to be something dubious about him nonetheless — Huxin considered Fa wise to keep him at a distance.

'My brothers,' Fa stood to greet them, 'you've come to see if the rumours are true, I expect.'

Xian and party came to a halt some distance from their brother's throne and bowed their heads briefly, their eyes never leaving the tigress at the Xibo's side. 'So, it is true; you have had dealings with the Wu,' Xian said in dismay.

'Only the Great Mother can award heaven's mandate.' Ji Fa sat down and stroked Huxin's head. 'What of it? Did you not enjoy the New Year's gift from the Great Mother?'

'Hexed water, not fit for human consumption,' Xian spat back.

'You did not distribute it to the people?' Dan could scarcely believe what he was hearing.

'Is everyone to be enchanted out of their wits like Su Daji has done to Zi Shou?' Xian appealed.

'We need a Wu to defeat a Wu,' Ji Fa said. 'Unless you wish to confront her ill-prepared again? We all know how we fared last time.'

'*Some* know more than *others*.' Xian flashed a glare in Dan's direction, and the look he received in return was just as resentful. Xian looked back to Fa. 'So we are to go to war, after all,' he stated, gratified about that, at least.

'Once Tian sends me the omen expressing his will,' Fa awarded, 'I shall obey.'

'We must wait for an omen now?' Xian made a joke of it, and the brothers in his company found it amusing. 'Those witches from Li Shan have hexed you all —'

The tigress gave a roar and silenced Xian. She didn't think much of his opinion.

'What is it with the tiger?' Xian motioned toward it, undaunted by her gaze.

'Tigress, you idiot!' Shi corrected, and Fa interrupted before Xian could provoke further argument.

'This is Baihu, guardian of the West,' the Xibo advised his brothers with a grin. 'She was given to me by the Great Mother of Li Shan to be my treachery detector.'

Xian was clearly discomfitted by the news, but strangely, young Zai seemed even more so.

'So far, she has not found cause to attack any of my subjects,' Fa advised, looking to his Fengjing brothers in challenge; as he did Huxin detected panic amongst them and sprang forth to tackle the cause.

To the shock of everyone in the room, Huxin bypassed Xian, Du and Chu, to pursue young Zai who had begun to flee before she had left Fa's side. Zai looked back, knowing the animal was close and she bowled him over onto his back and held him to the ground. Her face was close to his as she gave a low growl, warning him not to flinch.

'Zai?' The Xibo queried the meaning of his guardian's hostility toward him, as he strode forth to claim his youngest brother from her.

'Get her off,' Zai whimpered, tears in his eyes as she growled at him again. 'I'll confess,' he assured her, 'I'll confess ...'

With a touch from the Xibo's hand, Huxin withdrew, and Ji Fa dragged his brother to his feet. 'And what are you confessing to?'

'I haven't done anything lately,' Zai said in his own defence.

'What did you do?' The Xibo rephrased in hopes of getting a straight answer. The brothers gathered round, curious as to Zai's shortcomings.

'It was years ago,' he justified. 'I was a kid!'

The Xibo came to the end of his patience. 'I can have Baihu chew off your leg if you wish?'

'No!' Zai was still shaken from her first attack. 'I'll tell you,' he said beseechingly, and drew a deep breath for strength. 'I might have told some of my friends about Dan finding the Jade Book.'

'What!' Dan was immediately infuriated.

'So, that is how she found out that we had it,' Zhenduo, the warrior amongst the Xibo's favoured brothers, said thoughtfully.

'That book cost our father his life!' Zhenduo and Wu had to stop Dan from hitting Zai.

'Said you ... *alone*,' Xian redirected some of the heat Zai was copping back at Dan. 'You were the only one the witch left awake that night, *Dan*,' he shot back in accusation.

'And we are all still alive,' Fa pointed out, 'and have Dan to thank for it.'

Xian scoffed at this. 'Pity Dan didn't factor our father into his little deal with Zi Shou's magical whore!'

Again Zhenduo and Wu had to restrain Dan, as Du and Chu held down Xian. Huxin trotted away from the riot, shocked by the extent of the family secret she'd unearthed.

'Enough!' The Xibo threw himself in the middle of the huddle. 'This meeting is over!'

'Over?' Xian objected. 'You haven't told us anything!'

'Nor will I until there is something to tell.' The Xibo returned to his seat, having prevented Dan and Xian from strangling each other. This was nothing new. As brothers number three and four, they always came to loggerheads, having nothing whatsoever in common.

'But —'

'It is not for any of us to question the will of Tian,' Ji Fa insisted, as Huxin settled alongside him. 'When the omen has come, you will be the first to know.'

'Wu, beasts, *omens* — this is no way to run a nation!' Xian threw up his hands in disgust.

'The Shang have not honoured Tian, or the ancestors, and look at the state of our land,' Wu spoke up in support of the Xibo.

'Politically speaking, timing is everything,' Jiang Taigong said, also backing the Xibo.

'Seven years we've been waiting!' Xian argued. 'If you ask me, you have lost the stomach for war.'

'No one is asking you,' the Xibo pointed out. 'You shall all return to Fengjing, distribute the Great Mother's gift to the people as previously instructed and await further orders.'

Xian opened his mouth to argue, but Huxin's roar made him reconsider. He bowed and left, with his lackeys in tow.

6

YOU LING

During the months that followed, as they awaited Tian's omen, the weather grew warmer and the drought grew worse. Ji Fa had his armies and allies prepared and ready to move East as soon as the sign from heaven arrived, but after months of waiting without knowing his motive, his followers were beginning think Ji Fa was stalling, or had lost the will to go to war. Jiang Huxin's constant presence at Ji Fa's side prevented anyone openly challenging the Xibo's delay, for people feared that the tigress would take their head off, but the Xibo's heavenly appointed guardian would not be able to hold off Ji Fa's doubters forever; Xian would see to that.

It took some time for He Nuan to recover her full health and strength, and while Fen was attending to his patient, Hudan had taken it upon herself to begin Dan's tuition in Dao Yin meditation and the ancient doctrine of the Wu. It was no surprise that Dan proved a highly intelligent and focused student who was able to comprehend the spiritual principles he was being taught and then devise means to apply those principles on earth. What did come as a delightful surprise to Hudan was her enjoyment in teaching him. She'd never spent so much time in one person's company and not felt drained by the end of the day — not even with her siblings. To the contrary, Dan's energy and nature blended so well with her own that Hudan went to sleep feeling as fresh and energised as she felt when she first awoke.

Jiang Huxin was not adjusting to city life as well as her brothers, and was sure she was going to die from boredom and apathy. As she watched Ji Fa freshen himself before dinner, Huxin

120

transformed into her human form and wrapped her naked body in the large fox fur on the Xibo's bed to complain about her plight.

'How do you stand it? All the meetings, the endless chatter and complaints, the lack of air, the confined spaces, the *monotony*, the —'

'I agree.' Ji Fa knew being his bodyguard was not the most exciting of assignments for Huxin. 'You should take some time off, get out, see your brothers, or whatever it is you want to do. I am in no danger so long as Ji Xian and our brothers remain in Fengjing.'

The atmosphere had been very tense at Haojing during their visit. Huxin didn't trust Ji Xian or any of the brothers that ran with him; they were a pack of wolves waiting to tear Ji Fa to shreds at the first opportunity. Exactly the opposite could be said about the brothers Ji Fa kept close to him at Haojing, and there was one brother that Huxin had taken a particular shine to.

'Perhaps I should go visit with your brother, Shi,' Huxin purred, lying back on the bed in a seductive fashion. Although taking pleasure in the sight of her naked form in his bed, the Xibo was the perfect gentlemen. 'I think that if you go wandering, it might be best to do so in human form. Wear a hood, like brother Hudan does. Everyone will just assume you are she, and no one dares to approach her apart from Dan and Fen.'

It was a good plan, but Huxin resented the implication. 'So, you are saying I cannot go and visit with Shi.'

There was an apologetic look on Fa's face as he shook his head. 'Nothing could come of it. You would only be toying with his affections and distracting him from what he should be doing.'

'Which is?' Huxin queried. What could be more important than her own fun?

'Choosing a wife,' Fa advised her seriously, and Huxin frowned in protest. 'I need my brothers married, and soon, so that when I rule the land, my governing lords will be setting the right example. If they don't marry, they don't rule. It's that simple.'

'Even brother Dan?' Huxin spotted a bug in his ointment.

Fa was somewhat perplexed by the question. 'No, Dan is Wu now. But every other brother,' he insisted, 'Shi included … his marriage is *long* overdue.' Shi, nineteen, was the last of the brothers bar Dan and Zai — the youngest — to court a wife.

Huxin released a huge, bored exhalation.

'I feel sure your brothers will be happy to see you,' Fa encouraged, 'and in all honesty, my wife will be beside herself with joy if I arrive to celebrate our anniversary without you.'

'Subtle.' Huxin tried not to sound offended. 'I shall vanish for the night.'

'Much appreciated,' Fa smiled. 'If my wife saw you as you are at present, this anniversary would be our last.'

'Not really the example that a marital enforcer wants to set,' Huxin affirmed, and Fa nodded to agree. 'Well, if your piousness would kindly fetch me some clothes, I shall be happy to *recede* from view.'

'Of course.' Fa was hard pressed to pry his eyes away from her, but he left to see to her request personally and avoid any servant's gossip.

Under her hood, Huxin wandered the halls of the house and the occupants avoided her like the plague. Hudan had been dubbed You Ling — spiritual entity — as most in the household were convinced that the Great Mother had given Dan some manner of supernatural creature as a gift, and Huxin considered that it was not so far from the truth.

Hudan rarely left Ji Dan's rooms, as she was required to keep a low profile until their call to arms. That was where Huxin was headed at present, but she really had no desire to see Hudan, who would be studying, or Fen who was busy planning his marriage to He Nuan. What Jiang Huxin really wanted was to run, and so she reset her trajectory toward the Ji family gardens.

The gate that led from the main courtyard garden to vast outlying gardens was usually wide open in the mornings when Fa took her for a brisk walk before the day grew too hot. The gate must be shut at sundown, as it was now closed, but a simple latch released the barrier and Huxin slipped past into the more open grounds.

It was easy to see her way through the mazed garden, as all the structures that would normally support a vast array of plants and shrubs were bare, or sported withering vines at best. However, the statues, tiny shrines and waterless water features could still be admired by the light of the waxing moon, which was near full in the cloudless night sky. Huxin really had to resist her urge to shift into animal form, but remembering the Xibo's wishes she did not. Her human form was nowhere near as exhilarating to run in, but once she'd hitched up her skirt and excess cloak, she was happy that she could squeal with delight as she bounded along.

At the end of a long tree-lined path, she found a more open walkway and immediately came to a halt, having picked up on a scent downwind, and then she spied two southern red tigers eyeballing her. 'Hello,' she said winningly, as one of the tigers was a very handsome male.

Clearly, the pair did not know what to make of the fearless newcomer and growled in warning.

When Huxin growled back just as fiercely, the pair romped over to welcome her. 'Hello, dear friends,' she stroked and admired them. 'How beautiful you are —'

'Stop!' a voice called through the darkness. 'Are you mad?'

In the moonlight Huxin's tiger's eyes had no trouble perceiving Ji Shi running toward her whilst trying to finish dressing himself at the same time.

'They will eat you!' he called, when his first warning provoked no reaction.

I'll eat you, thought Huxin, with a grin, as Shi was having some trouble getting his shirt on, and Huxin noted with delight that Shi had a more strapping physique than either Fa or Dan.

'Jia, Jin!' Shi called the tigers to him, and both hesitated until he let loose a growl that Huxin considered rather impressive.

'You speak tiger?' Huxin jested, as the pair relented and ran to him.

'Well, they had to learn human, so I thought it only fair,' Shi replied with good humour. 'Didn't Dan tell you we let the tigers loose at night. They're our night security patrol.'

'Why would Dan tell me?' Huxin wondered. She'd barely seen him since she'd arrived.

'Aren't you the one they call You Ling?' Shi motioned to the hooded cloak that hung about her shoulders when it should have been over her head, masking her identity. 'Are you not assigned to my brother Dan's charge?'

'Ah, yes! Well ...' Huxin finally got the gist of the conversation. 'Extreme spirits do not fear going where the wild things are. Why are you half dressed?'

'I was about bathe, when I heard the tiger alarm.' Shi finally finished fiddling with his shirt.

'No alarm,' Huxin emphasised 'we were just saying hello.'

'You are Wu, aren't you?' He sounded very sure of that.

'That is an odd assumption?' Huxin played naive.

'There is not a woman of this earth Dan would choose to keep in his quarters. Only the women of Tian have ever interested him.'

'I am whatever Ji Fa needs me to be.' Huxin neatly sidestepped the query.

'I knew it,' Shi said, reassured. 'My brother does have a plan.'

'You are right to believe in your eldest brother. Xian would be a pale shadow of a king compared with the Xibo. You've backed the right sibling, believe me.'

'I do not doubt that,' Shi stated for the record, 'but as one of the youngest brothers, I rarely get told anything before we march into battle!'

Huxin could sympathise, but as she was not at liberty to enlighten him, she turned their exchange toward the animals they were stroking. 'They are brother and sister,' Huxin commented, seeing the family resemblance.

'They are, how did you guess?' Shi was very impressed, but Huxin only shrugged.

'Where did you find them?'

'*Some* of my brothers like to hunt,' Shi was ashamed to say. 'These two were left orphaned in the aftermath of one of those slaughters.'

Huxin could barely breathe in the wake of the short tale. 'Yet another reason to dislike Ji Xian and his minions.'

'Master Shi!' A manservant was yelling from the garden gate.

It was obvious that no one bar Shi would venture any further at night. 'Master Shi, your dinner guests are waiting!'

Shi gave a heavy sigh. 'I have to go, my brother is forcing me to seek a wife … but I prefer Jia's company, don't I, girl?' He cuddled the female of the pair.

'So you wish to rule a city like Fa and Xian?' Huxin asked, as he seemed compelled to comply with the Xibo's rule.

'Not really,' Shi admitted, 'but I shall be whatever Ji Fa needs me to be, so …'

'*Master Shi!*'

'Coming!' Shi called as he backed up. 'If you would come back to the house with me, I'd feel much more at ease.'

Huxin shook her head and backed away in the opposite direction. 'Sorry … but this extreme spirit is running wild tonight.' With a swirl of her cloak and a laugh of delight, she took off into the shadows of the night garden, Shi's tigers in pursuit.

When Dan arrived in the Hall of Records to meet Jiang Hudan for morning meditation, she was not awaiting him as usual. He sent one of the house staff to see if she had overslept, and the servant returned to report that the bed did not appear to have been slept in. Dan was about to instruct the servant to ask after her whereabouts around the house, when Fen Gong arrived.

'Brother Fen, have you seen brother Hudan this morning?' Dan queried.

'No, lord.' Fen replied. 'Last night Hudan told me that she was going for a walk and if she was not back in time, I should conduct your lessons today.'

'Where would she have gone?' Dan was deeply concerned that she would wander around the city on her own at night.

'I have no idea where she went,' Fen replied. 'There is no need to worry —'

'I know she is Wu,' Dan conceded, 'but so was He Nuan.' When he considered how *she* had ended up, the lord started to panic.

'Nuan is a novice compared to Hudan,' Fen stressed. 'But if you really wish to know where Hudan is now, she is in conference with the Xibo. He Nuan was summoned also.'

'You could have said so in the first place!' Dan breathed a sign of relief. 'What has happened, I wonder?' He decided to go and investigate.

'Begging my pardon, lord, but if the matter does concern you, the Xibo will have you summoned.'

Dan was rather shocked to be put in his place by his young ward-cum-Shifu. 'Are you pulling rank on me, Fen?'

Fen grinned at the challenge. 'If that is what it takes to get you to focus and not be *distracted* from your lessons. Hudan is unharmed, that is all you need to know.'

Dan hated that his motives were so obvious to the lad. 'I do have an obligation to attend to matters of state, you realise?'

'Hudan is not interested in matters of state, only matters of heaven,' Fen said patiently. 'Any more excuses, or shall we begin?'

With a smile of defeat, Dan relented. His curiosity would have to wait to be satisfied.

That afternoon, Dan was excited to have the Xibo visit him in his Hall of Records. He and Fen were nearing the end of their Dao Yin practice for the day, and Dan was hot and completely exhausted. As disciplined as he was, the lord had been unable to prevent questions about Hudan's absence from entering his mind, so Fa's visit felt like a gift from Tian. Finally, he could ask what was going on.

'I don't wish to disturb your study, Dan ...' The Xibo left his guard outside the Hall of Records whilst another fellow followed Fa into the hall, carrying a large polished wooden case. '... but your new qin is finished, and I wanted to present it to you personally.'

Fa smiled broadly, and the craftsman laid it on a table. 'I hope your lordship is satisfied with the workmanship.' The fellow withdrew, and was about to leave when Fa stopped him.

'Surely, after you have spent so many months crafting our new qin, you would like to hear it played?'

'I would, very much, my lord,' replied the craftsman, whereby Fa looked back to Dan.

'Play for us,' Fa implored Dan, and took a seat, motioning for the qin's maker to do the same.

The last thing Dan had the patience for right now was playing the qin, but the craftsman did deserve to hear the results of his work. 'Do you have your dizi?' Dan queried Fen, who whipped the item from inside the leg of his boot.

'Set a mood for us,' Dan requested, approaching the case and opening it to behold the one-of-a-kind instrument. He'd been the first to play the six string qin and his performance for Daji with that instrument had sealed his father's fate. Dan could only hope that this performance did not hex his brother in the same fashion.

Placing it on a low writing table, Dan checked the qin's tuning. When he plucked the new string, the sound was so uplifting it brought tears to his eyes, inspiring him to play and enrich Fen's enchanting melody. The moment was soul stirring for Dan; he almost regretted having abstained from playing for so long. Bad memories were surfacing, but when he played the new seventh string, they melted away.

Ji Fa and the craftsman applauded loudly. 'That was just beautiful!' the Xibo exclaimed. 'However, for battle, perhaps something a bit more compelling might be in order.'

Fa rose to say his farewells but his companion preceded him. The craftsman bowed to his Xibo and to Dan. 'It has been an honour. My ears will never want for another note, for today I heard perfection.'

Dan smiled. 'Any artist is only as good as his tools,' he said humbly, and the fellow was speechless at being so honoured. He bowed again and left the room.

'I wanted to ask —' Dan began.

Fa held up a hand to prevent Dan's query, before he'd even verbalised it. 'I am not at liberty to say.'

Dan was immediately deflated.

'But I will say,' Fa added in consolation, 'that you will know before day's end. Brother Fen, would you come with me, please. Your assistance is required.'

'Of course.' Fen put his dizi back in its hiding place. 'I can send for He Nuan to finish your lesson,' Fen offered to Dan, but the lord shook his head to decline.

'I'm having trouble focussing today,' Dan retorted, somewhat reproachfully, for Fa's benefit.

'Not like you to waste time being distracted,' Fa commented, 'and by a woman!'

'The most knowledgeable woman … correction, person, on *earth*,' Dan replied, stressing the exceptional circumstances.

'Well, that being the case,' Fa posited, 'I should be confident, if I were you, that she knows what she is doing.'

'*What* is she doing?' Dan had to know. He remembered Hudan had mentioned she was considering performing an ancient rite to 'seek yin by means of yin'.

He knew this rite was a form of sympathetic magic. Women, especially Wu, represented metaphysical water in human form and by exposing themselves to the sun, or to an open flame, they drew water down from the sky, by scorching the water element in themselves and provoking a storm.

'By sundown, Dan,' Fa said, and he would say no more on the matter.

'I shall report to you as soon as I have word.' Fen reassured Dan.

'Come along, Fen,' Fa called, waiting by the door for the lad, who then closed it in their wake.

Usually Dan was the one keeping others in the dark, and he did not like having the tables turned on him. He realised his distraction was misplaced energy, and as he did not wish to waste the remains of the day in this manner, he imagined what advice Hudan would give him in this moment. 'Redirect your energy into something constructive,' he concluded, and his sights came to rest upon his new qin.

Last night Hudan had walked the valley, viewing the disheartening effects of the drought by the cover of darkness. She entreated Tian to allow her to bring an end to the hardship of the Zhou people and everyone in their lands. She wept in empathy for their suffering, and for the dead and dying animals, as she trekked on, increasingly convinced that something had to be done.

It was the early hours of the morning when Hudan broke from her near-trance state to discover she had wondered into a star-field. This was one of many similar configurations of huge flat-topped, earth prisms — sloping or stepped — that littered the Zhou plains. These ancient structures, some the size of small mountains, were called by the people, jinzita. Legend said that the jinzita had been constructed by the sons of the sky, long ago, to map out the heavens on earth. What Hudan found most interesting about this legend was that the sons of sky were said to have golden hair, white skin and blue eyes ... like many of the people of Tian that she had seen in her dreams.

The silhouette of the tallest and largest jinzita in this field's nine-tower array was very distinctive against the night sky and it sparked in her mind's eye the recognition of a vision she'd had during Ji Fa's oracle reading. She'd seen herself scaling a similar structure toward a flaming pyre, and the impression sent a wave of awareness surging through her being. *This is the place...* The thought brought tears of relief to her eyes. *This is where it all begins.*

Hudan struggled to remember the chill on the air that she'd felt sitting in this very spot the night before. Now, twelve hours staked to the ground on the top of the jinzita, had melted any memory of coolness from her mind. During this day she had focused on a fragment of a vision of a son of the sky that she had seen in Ji Fa's oracle. The son of the sky was the Lord of Elements and he was the key to manifesting a cloud to give her naked skin and the land around her some moist relief. Hudan had only to remember the lord's name. Tian was testing Hudan's tenacity and faith in her own abilities, but Jiang Hudan would not relent. She would come and lay on this pyramid every day until the lord's name was forthcoming, and when it was Ji Fa would light a pyre atop the stepped jinzita next to this one, and she would enter the flame and bring down the rain.

The sun was now only shining down one side of her body; the end of the long day neared and not a cloud could be seen.

When she felt her foot being unbound from its stake, it felt like a beautiful dream, and Hudan did not have the strength to raise her head to see if it was reality.

'Fen is on his way up.' Nuan lay a light, damp cover over Hudan and then removed the rest of Hudan's bonds. 'Will you take a little water?'

'No, nothing,' she said, seeking to hold all the fire energy she had absorbed. 'But thank you … for standing vigil for me this day.'

'It will always be my honour to serve you, Jiang Hudan,' Nuan advised in all seriousness. 'Only now we shall be sisters, not brothers.'

The comment made Hudan want to cringe, but in a way it was comforting to know that, when this war was over and they returned to Li Shan, Fen would have someone to take care of him. 'You have won my greatest treasure, Nuan,' Hudan told her, but internally choking on a strange mix of resentment and goodwill. 'I hope you know how blessed you are.'

'I promise you, Shanyu,' Nuan's words were more heartfelt than any that had passed between them before today, 'I do know, and I praise Tian for him every day.'

'Hudan!' Fen said as he arrived, alarmed by her weakened appearance.

'Little brother,' she smiled, and the expression made her entire face sting. She had requested that Ji Fa send Fen to carry her down from the jinzita, and she had been looking forward to seeing his sweet face all day. 'I made it.'

Fen nodded, as if he was not entirely convinced about that. 'You should have told me.' He was annoyed at her and Nuan. 'I could have been here to stand vigil for you.' He eased his hands under her shoulders and legs, and as he lifted her, she growled in pain.

'No one knew we were here,' Hudan wheezed.

Nuan came over to pull the cool cotton wrap over Hudan's beaming red face, and Hudan saw a soft smile pass between Fen and his wife-to-be. The moment warmed Hudan inside more efficiently than the entire day in the summer sun. Hudan knew that much of her warm, fuzzy feeling was being fed by Fen's love-struck emotions, but she didn't care. After the day she'd had, this small comfort was bliss.

'You must not heal me, Fen,' Hudan said as she dozed against his shoulder.

'I know,' he answered, 'but there is nothing in the rules that says I am not allowed to make you feel content.'

'Like you,' Hudan replied.

'Yes, like me.' Fen kissed Hudan's head, as she'd done in the past to comfort him, before he began the long trek down the side of the jinzita.

He Nuan drove the horse-drawn cart through the city streets whilst Fen kept Hudan company in the back. Inside the main courtyard of the Ji residence, Fen lifted Hudan from the cart and carried her up the steps to the interior, where the Xibo and his tigress awaited.

Ji Shi came running from another direction. 'Is that You Ling?'

'Shi!' The Xibo held up a palm and stopped his brother in his tracks.

'But what has happened?' the young lord appealed.

'This is none of your affair.' With a frown and a wave of his hand the Xibo dismissed Shi, who reluctantly withdrew.

When Fen reached Fa, the Xibo drew aside Hudan's face cover to speak with her.

'I am sorry, brother Fa,' she said, apologising for the cloudless sky. 'Tomorrow I *will* go deeper.'

The Xibo was frowning and seemed quite upset as he nodded. 'We both know you are on the right track, brother Hudan,' he conceded. 'I hope, for your sake, that our vision is fulfilled swiftly.'

'Tomorrow,' Hudan insisted, barely able to keep her eyes open. 'I will go deeper … I will find him, and know his name …' Her words trailed off as she drifted out of consciousness.

The timeless realm of the creative that Dan had been lost in for the past few hours vanished as Fen walked into the hall with the body of Jiang Hudan draped in his arms. Nuan followed them, along with the tigress who was obviously concerned for her sister.

'What did she do?' Dan rose quickly to investigate.

'She has begun her preparation for seeking yin,' Fen replied, to Dan's horror.

Dan pulled back the cover to see Hudan's red and swollen face. 'Can you heal her?'

'I am not permitted,' Fen replied, his voice sorrowful. 'If Tian is with us, Hudan will absorb the heat hovering on the surface of her physical body into her spirit and heal herself by morning.'

Dan's heart and mind were thrown into complete conflict. If he was to learn the way of the Wu, he must trust them, although his human logic told him Hudan needed urgent medical attention.

Jiang Huxin gave an annoyed growl. 'Is something the matter?' Dan looked to the tigress.

'She wants a robe,' informed Fen, as he moved off toward the door at the far end of the hall which led to the sleeping quarters.

'Here.' Nuan removed and offered hers to the lord.

'Thank you,' Dan said, holding onto it, whereby Nuan gave a bow and hurried to catch up with Fen.

The lord turned away from the tigress, held the robe over his shoulder, and she retrieved it promptly.

'You must vow that you will not let any of your physicians near my sister.' Huxin walked around in front of him, still tying her robe.

'She must be in terrible pain,' he stalled, not wanting to show his lack of belief in their method.

'That is the point,' Huxin advised. 'Beyond the pain barrier is the euphoria of a whole other world, and it is there that the Lord of Elements resides. Only he can break the drought and spare Hudan from the flames.'

Dan felt his jaw hanging open, so he closed it. 'How —'

The lord's master of the interior entered, and Huxin quickly ducked behind Dan to hide herself. 'What is it?' The lord was annoyed by the interruption.

'Your brother, Shi, is here to see you,' he announced, and Huxin gave a quiet gasp of delight.

'Give me a moment,' Dan requested, and the sly grin on his servant's face made Dan a little embarrassed. 'This is not how it looks, I assure you.'

'All of my lord's secrets are safe with me,' the servant assured his master as he left the room.

'Why would Shi want to see me?' Dan was perplexed by the visit. Shi was the outdoors type and thus their paths and interests seldom crossed.

'Yes, I wonder?' Huxin played dumb.

'Well, he can't see you here,' Dan insisted, looking around for a hiding spot in the sparsely furnished hall, but when he looked back, Huxin was gone.

'Brother Huxin?' Dan called quietly and, startled to hear a roar, he looked down to see the tiger crawl out from beneath the robe.

'Good thinking.' Dan grabbed up the robe, tossing it onto a pile of cushions.

'Brother Dan!' Shi exclaimed, sounding pleased to see him.

'Brother Shi ...' Dan made his surprise clear in his voice. 'What brings you indoors?'

'Baihu!' Shi was even more excited to see the tigress, who responded to his call by romping over to him, He awarded her his full attention. 'What are you doing in Dan's rooms?'

'I am, ah ... tiger sitting,' Dan explained.

'Fa could have asked me to do it,' Shi said, surprised. 'I would be honoured any time!' Dan realised 'tiger sitting' was a rather flimsy excuse, but Shi didn't comment further.

Huxin licked Shi's face, who delighted in the show of affection, but Dan felt he was watching his brother be seduced in plain sight. 'Was there a reason for your visit?'

'Um ... well ...' Shi lost some of his enthusiasm, realising his presence must be unexpected. 'I was wanting to inquire after the condition of You Ling?'

Dan was frowning now, deeply puzzled. 'Why should you be interested in You Ling?'

'We met in the garden one evening, not too long back,' Shi advised, with a smile that indicated it was a fond memory.

'Really?' Dan thought it odd that Hudan had not mentioned the encounter.

'She is amazing, Dan,' Shi said, complimenting his brother. 'You are a very lucky man indeed.' The lovelorn look on Shi's face made Dan very uncomfortable, and Huxin released a loud purr of pleasure that sounded rather like a cow mooing. 'Over all the women the Xibo has forced me to meet ...' Shi acknowledged the tigress with a caress on the head '... I would choose her as a wife in a heartbeat.'

The tigress' loud purring was cut short by Dan's protest, and she scampered out of the way as he came close to his brother. 'You cannot hope to marry this woman!' Dan was angry that Shi even knew about her.

'I know she belongs to you.' Shi raised both hands, palm outward, hoping to calm Dan.

'She does *not* belong to me, or *anyone!*' Dan said firmly. 'Nor will she *ever*.'

'Forgive me, Dan, if I have caused offence.' Shi was overwhelmed by Dan's adverse reaction.

Dan look a deep breath and reeled in his emotions. He'd always been very fond of Shi — he may be the feral of the family, but he was a good and gentle soul. 'Apologies Shi, you have no idea what I am talking about, so I can —'

'You Ling is Wu,' Shi guessed. 'And that is why she is so amazing and free.'

Dan nodded, conceding the truth of it. 'She is here to serve the will of Tian.' When Hudan performed the rite she was preparing for, the Xibo's full intention would be known. If she managed to break the drought, then the numbers joining their army — and their allies — would grow, as defectors flocked to join the side of the righteous.

'If there is anything I can do to help?' Shi offered.

'You can keep silent about what you know,' Dan replied, directing his brother to the door. 'Now, you'll have to excuse me. I have a lot going on at present.'

'Of course,' Shi bowed out. 'Please give You Ling my best regards.'

'I will do that,' Dan granted, glad to see his brother depart.

'Did you hear what he said?' Huxin whispered in excitement, as she pulled on her robe again and tied it off.

'I did,' and Dan sounded not quite so amused. Huxin began giggling, which rubbed Dan the wrong way, as brother Huxin seemed to love teasing him about his admiration for her sister.

'Dear brother Dan,' she said, pressing her hands together to imply she thought him sweet, 'how I would love to tease you further, but it saddens me to see you in such torment.'

'I am sure I have no idea what you mean.'

'It was me that Shi met in the garden,' Huxin said, enlightening him, and watched an expression of relief sweep across his face with some amusement.

'Oh.'

'Shi just assumed I was You Ling, because of the robe.' Huxin's huge grin made the lord feel rather over-exposed.

'Well, you should not be seducing my brother at every given opportunity,' Dan scolded, to cover his own embarrassment. 'That is not why you are here.'

'We only talked,' Huxin explained in a sultry tone. 'If I had intended to seduce Shi, I would have had him already.'

There was a delicious, awkward pause in the conversation. Dan suddenly found her confidence and her amber eyes mesmerising.

'The truth is, Ji Fa has leashed me in that regard.' Huxin released him from her engaging stare and gave a confident grin. 'But good luck to the Xibo's attempts to get Shi to pick a bride now.' She turned on her heel and headed off to attend to her sister.

As Dan watched her sway down the hall, barefoot and silent as a mouse, he was thinking that if Jiang Huxin had not been Wu, she would make the prefect bride for Shi. The tigress' secret would probably only add to Shi's admiration as a were-tiger, in theory, would be Shi's ideal woman — a woman to love and a tiger to run wild with.

7

SEEKING YIN BY MEANS OF YIN

It was a long night for Dan. It had been an age since he had conversed with his ancestors or Tian, but he played his new qin in their honour, hoping that, in return, they would bestow their good graces on Jiang Hudan during her spiritual trials.

The lord awoke the next morning hunched over his instrument, and immediately sat upright and began to play once more, before his mind had the chance to fill with worry and conflict.

At the end of the composition, Dan observed a moment of silence and then raised his hands to play again.

'Brother Dan.'

Dan turned about and then stood when he saw Hudan waiting to speak with him; to his enormous relief she appeared entirely well.

'Do you still believe I cannot survive the fire and bring rain?' she asked in a non-judgemental fashion, raising the sleeves of her robe to show him the radiant, pale complexion of her arms.

It appeared a miracle had occurred, for even a hardy soldier would have died from such exposure. 'I have infinite faith in you, brother Hudan,' Dan assured her, 'it is heaven I have cause to doubt.'

'You evoke heaven with your art,' Hudan advised with smile. 'At least, you did for me last night. So I wanted to thank you … your music made the healing process easier. Would you play for me again tonight?' she requested.

'I shall play every night until your vigil is over,' he vowed solemnly, grateful to be able to aid her.

'I shall look forward to it.'

The young Wu left to endure another day exposed to the elements, and from a glance out the window Dan thought the heat would be as relentless this day as it had been the day before. It felt as if his chest might burst from the conflict raging within it. Dan had never known anyone to be so selfless or courageous; he wanted to take Hudan's place, or find a justifiable reason to stop her self-inflicted suffering! Had Dan not taken the vow of the Wu, he could have put a stop to the ritual, but as things stood, he had to respect Hudan's authority in this matter and it was a most harrowing test of his faith.

On top of the highest jinzita, Nuan bound Hudan's hands and feet to stakes, to anchor her will in moments of weakness. There was not a cloud to be seen in the sky above. Hudan was well practised in the art of projecting her perception beyond her physical body in order to roam the material world, but today she planned to launch her conscious perception into the spirit world and that was something else again.

When Hudan had informed the Xibo of her intention, he had wanted to send a battalion of troops to guard her during the rite, but Hudan felt this would only attract attention to their activities and they did not want the Shang catching wind of their tactics before they were prepared to execute their plans. In the end, Hudan agreed to take two plainly clothed guards to walk the base periphery and keep watch, whilst Nuan guarded the apex.

'Are you ready?' Nuan prompted.

Hudan nodded, giving Nuan the go-ahead to feed her the elixir of waking sleep.

The brew had been heated, as Hudan was permitted to consume warm liquids only, and it tasted like a sunny spring garden smelled.

'Ah,' Hudan relaxed in the wake of her refreshment. 'Make sure I am not disturbed.'

Nuan nodded to affirm the order and Hudan closed her eyes and turned her attention inward.

She knew who she was looking for; she'd seen the blond, blue-eyed lad when she had been oracle to Ji Fa.

'*I am the lord of the elemental realms,*' he'd said. '*Just call my name and I shall answer.*'

A channel rarely remembered everything that was foreseen in trance. The conscious recognition of events were fragmented, and seldom in chronological order. Much like memory, the channel remembered more when there was a conscious trigger, such as when Hudan had wandered into the star-field. Certain objects or instances aided recollection, but no matter now hard she tried, Hudan could not remember the name of the son of the sky that she needed to call, or even if he had told her his name? She had spoken with Ji Fa, who had shared her vision of his future and although he remembered seeing the blond master, he could not recall a name either. But Fa did remember the lord saying that '*their storm would start a war that would end conflict in their land for a hundred years!*'

At the time Ji Fa thought the lord had been referring to the amassing of their forces, not the weather, but Hudan had understood the lord's meaning. She had expected to be performing this rite *after* Ji Fa had received Tian's omen to attack, but as time and the drought had dragged on, Hudan had had an increasingly uneasy feeling that there was some vital clue in her memory of Ji Fa's oracle that she had missed. However, her request for guidance and clarity had been answered that first night on top of the jinzita. She did, of course, know as well as Ji Fa what the omen to attack would be, and upon revisiting the oracle's vision that night atop the jinzita, she finally realised a vital clue she'd missed about the sequence of the events to unfold — that the omen arrived *wet*! As the Lord of the Elements had told Ji Fa, their storm would *start* a war. There was just one vital piece of information missing — the name of the Lord of the Elements.

Yesterday, deep in trance, Hudan had failed to recollect any more of her original prophecy and her attempts to summon the Lord of the Elements by his title had proven futile. But, with the elixir of waking sleep, she hoped to travel deep within and enter that timeless realm of spirit and elemental that was the abode of the sons of the sky and the great immortal ancestors; those who, like her Shifu, had achieved Xian — the heightened state of awareness that promoted material immortality.

It took a considerable amount of time, as it had the previous day, to move beyond the constant burning sensation down the front of her body, and the light beating down on the outside of her eyelids. She had only managed to punch through that pain barrier in short bursts the day before. Today, however, the elixir she'd taken aided her mind to slip straight into the dark passage that led to sleep, with her senses and consciousness still very much alert.

It was cool in the passage; Hudan couldn't feel the suffering of her physical form and the ease of movement via intentional thought was far more blissful than dragging a heavy body around. She conjured up the image in her mind of the Lord of the Elements and willed herself down the long tunnel to him.

The pinpoint of light at the end of the tunnel welled in size as it rushed up to meet her.

Hudan was inside a crystal cave, and the walls shimmered like jewels in the light that was emanating from her own being.

'Here you are, finally!' Her attention was drawn to the blond lord she'd been seeking, who was dressed only in trousers and an open vest. He was slouched in a throne-like rock formation and his being was light-filled, as if composed more of spirit than matter. Beside him on a flat rock sat another young man, who was dressed in a tight-fitting black bodysuit from his neck to his calf muscles, from where the suit disappeared into black metal boots. This lord had dark hair and dark eyes, but his skin and facial features matched those of the Lord of the Elements — they could have been brothers. Yet his form appeared far more dense than the body of the elemental lord, and had the dark-haired lord not emitted a subtle glow from his form also, Hudan would have thought him mortal.

'Didn't you get my message?' the fair lord asked curiously. *'I cannot come to your aid unless I am summoned by name.'*

'What is your name, lord?' Hudan politely responded.

The dark son of the sky shook his head, disappointed. 'She really doesn't remember anything, does she?'

'I try, my lord,' Hudan appealed in her own defence, 'but prophecy is difficult to recall afterward —'

The fair-haired lord held up a hand to prevent her apology. 'We are not questioning your dedication, believe me. We were warned this would happen. My brother is just being overly dramatic.'

'So you are brothers?' Hudan's statement caused the dark lord to roll his eyes.

'Yes, we are,' the fair lord said, happy to answer her.

'Is your brother a lord too?' Hudan felt there wasn't any harm in taking a little knowledge back with her.

'Yes,' snapped the dark lord. 'I'm the Lord of Time, and all this waiting around is pissing me off! Let me say the word and get, at least her, with the program!'

'I told you, oh Lord of Time, that what they have to do here first is too important to history at large,' the fair lord emphasised by waving his arms wide. 'You should know that well enough from the disaster you created the last time you tried to push your agenda in this scenario. Just wait until their contribution to this age is over, then you can have your team back.'

'Damn it, Avery, if you weren't the Lord of the Otherworld, I swear —'

'That's your name!' Hudan interrupted. 'Ang-wei.'

'No, it's A-ver-ree.' The lord rose from his seat to approach her and pronounce the name for clarity.

'A—bi—wei,' she tried again.

The lord waved off the problem as a minor hitch. 'You know what? Ang-wei is fine. I'll know who you mean.'

'And you will bring the rain?' Hudan appealed.

'I am the Lord of the Elements. Our storm will start a war that will end the conflict of your people for a hundred years!'

'You're worried about one little drought?' the dark lord protested. 'I'm talking about the utter obliteration of the most advanced race in the universe!'

'Once you were just as passionate about the fate of Zhou!' Avery defended. 'Go do a little past-life regression, Ji Fa, and then tell me you don't care?'

'Ji Fa?' Hudan queried. 'That is your name?'

Both lords appeared a little discomfitted in the wake of the disclosure.

'It might have been better not to bring that up,' said the dark lord to his fair brother, who nodded his head to agree. But the dark lord looked back to Hudan to clarify. 'Ji Fa was my name when I lived in the age you are from.'

'I know you,' Hudan gasped, perplexed.

'You have always known me,' the dark lord smiled, seeming more kindly disposed toward her.

'But you are a son of the sky now — the Lord of Time!' Her heart began beating with excitement so intense that it felt more like panic.

'A Lord of Time,' said Avery. 'Technically speaking,' he added with a shrug, when his brother served him an unappreciative glare.

'We call ourselves the Time —'

'Ah!' Avery cut off his brother. 'Nice try, but no using the T-word.'

With a roll of his eyes the dark lord looked back to Hudan and, getting up from his rock, he held up one finger and beckoned her closer.

'Yes, lord?' she said as she neared him.

He waved a hand over the smooth surface of the rock he'd been sitting on, whereupon it turned silver and reflective. 'Look,' he invited her to lean over and peer into the mirrored surface.

She was surprised to see the face of a daughter of Tian staring back at her: blonde hair, fair of skin and wide eyes that were a soft grey-mauve.

'What you are viewing is what your soul-mind looks like,' he announced.

Hudan was stunned speechless, as she'd felt sure she was seeing a heavenly vision.

'You are one of us,' he concluded.

The panic in her heart exploded as Hudan heard her name being yelled from far away. 'No!' she protested at the interruption, and felt herself losing focus.

'Just call my name and I shall answer.' Avery reaffirmed his vow, as she was engulfed by a vacuum of darkness leading back toward the heat and discomfort of her physical form.

The intense burning of re-entering her body was not as great as Hudan had expected, and upon opening her eyes she saw a dark cloud unfolding above her.

'Hudan!' Nuan called, and Hudan looked over to see Nuan at a standoff with several men, whom she was keeping at bay with her staff.

What happened to the guards? she wondered. *Why is Nuan not calling for them?*

'Ah, our gift from the sons of the sky is awake,' commented one of the men, as another attempted to circle around Nuan.

'She is Wu of Li Shan! And those are the Xibo's men you just attacked.' Nuan attacked the man trying to move around her and sent him toppling down the side of the jinzita, then quickly swung back to prevent the other three getting by her. 'So I would start running if you know what is good for you.'

'And I'm the emperor!' bantered one of the men, and they laughed.

Even when emerging from a deep trance naturally, Hudan would be exhausted, as it took a while for the spirit to realign with the physical body. The danger of being brought out of trance too quickly, as in this instance, was that the bodies were completely out of alignment and she could not get her physical body to respond to her mental commands. Hudan was filled with chi, but without her spirit and body being as one, she could not utilise any of it — she was powerless! If any of these men were to steal her virtue, she would be ruined and unable to perform the yin rite.

The three men remaining ran in different directions, laughing loudly as they toyed with Nuan. She pursued the pair that ran to her right, who split in two directions to make her defence even more difficult, but the fellow she chose to pursue was quite nimble and hard to strike.

'She's ready for me!' The first man to reach Hudan dropped to his knees to straddle her and unhitch his trousers.

Hudan had never felt this kind of intense panic before. Her body was burning with frustration and anger, but she could not even speak to curse him.

Like a warrior sent from heaven, a white tiger leapt out of nowhere and clamped its jaws around the man's head to drag him off Hudan, taking his head clean off in the process. The tiger turned to confront the other man who had escaped Nuan, blood dripping from its fangs as it roared loudly. Hudan was shocked to the core, for she knew better than anyone the sound of her sister's roar and this tiger was not Huxin.

Nuan finally overpowered her nimble opponent and sent him flying down the steep earthen structure as she had the first man, but she did not dare go after the one man remaining, as he was in the tiger's sights.

'Come on!' The man drew a large blade from his belt. 'You'll make a handsome rug.'

The tiger leapt and overpowered the man, who managed to cut the tiger's front leg to make it back off as he escaped, casting himself down the side of the jinzita.

The animal turned its sights toward Nuan, who lowered her weapon and dropped to one knee to bow her head in thanks for the tiger's aid. By the time she raised her head the animal had fled.

'Hudan!' Nuan ran to her side, and gently took Hudan's head in both of hers to look her over. 'Look!' She motioned to the cloud above. 'You did it … a storm is forming.'

Hudan blinked her eyes. It was all she could do; that last burst of excitement had completely drained her. She had to sleep.

'Hudan!' Nuan slapped her cheeks in an attempt to keep her conscious, but as Hudan's physical body was not connecting with her senses, she slipped back down the corridor toward sleep and into unconsciousness.

Once Hudan had been delivered to a recovery bed, He Nuan reported to Ji Fa and his tigress on what had transpired and why they had returned the city before sunset.

'A cloud has formed?' Ji Fa moved to the window to see a cloud expanding out from the star-field in all directions. 'We must have the pyre built immediately.' He was excited that something from his oracle reading was finally coming to pass.

As the tigress gave a roar, Nuan untied her outer robe and held it out for Huxin, who transformed into her human form to question Nuan.

'A white tiger, you said?' Huxin draped the cloak about herself.

'That's right.'

'Male or female?'

'I don't know,' Nuan said apologetically. 'It happened so fast.'

'Your gut feeling,' Huxin said, pressing for details. 'Was the animal large or small?'

'Larger than you,' He Nuan stated hesitantly, but Huxin seemed gratified by the answer.

'Probably male then,' she mused, with a smile.

'I really could not say.' Nuan obviously wanted to avoid any disappointment the tigress might experience down the track. 'Perhaps it was Baihu herself? For it seems to me that the animal was heaven-sent. The tiger's arrival could not have been better timed, nor more precise. It left not so much as a scratch on Jiang Hudan when it took the man from on top of her … there was no doubt as to whose side the tiger was on.'

'Heaven is truly with us,' Fa conceded, happily. 'I will have the men responsible for the attack on my men, brother Hudan and you hunted down,' Fa assured Nuan. 'There cannot be too many men running around with tiger scratches on them.'

'There ought to be a law against harming tigers,' Huxin said, as according to what they had just heard, the tiger was the only victim in the attack.

'There is such a law,' Fa quickly assured her. 'Shi hounded my father to pass a bill protecting tigers to force some of our brothers to abstain from the pastime.'

Huxin smiled, gratified.

A gong sounded from outside the Xibo's council chamber. Huxin transformed back into her animal form and Fa dismissed He Nuan, who took up her cloak and left the Xibo to attend to his other affairs of state.

*

For the remainder of that day and night, Dan played his fingers raw, hoping Hudan would heal herself and awaken, but Fen could only report that she continued to rest peacefully. The lord would have continued his musical vigil but for a summons to a meeting with the Xibo and prime minister, Jiang Taigong.

The aging prime minister had a huge smile on his face as Dan entered the war room. 'Here is the man of the moment,' he announced.

'My Xibo,' Dan acknowledged, inclining his head before his brother. Although he was no longer required to venerate Fa as a superior, it was against his nature not to do so. 'Prime Minister,' he said to their chief advisor. 'What have I done to make you both so happy?'

'The alliance with the Wu that you encouraged us to form,' Jiang Taigong replied. 'It must be wonderful to see your efforts about to bear fruit.'

The statement surprised Dan. 'Are we going to war?'

'I am rallying our armies as we speak,' Fa confirmed with a smile.

'Tian's sign has arrived?' Dan assumed, secretly hoping that this meant Jiang Hudan would not be casting herself onto a pyre.

'It will, and very soon,' the Xibo told him.

'How can you be so certain?' he questioned, baffled by his brother's pre-emptive strategy. 'If we rally our armies and allies and fail to go to war *again*, we'll be the ones needing to defend ourselves.'

Fa gave a hearty laugh, and Jiang Taigong did not look worried either. 'The Great Mother told me that you would have difficulty in accepting the validity and importance of the actions Jiang Hudan and myself will undertake in the next few days, but I can assure you it is integral to our success.'

'You still intend to burn her,' Dan concluded sadly.

'She will not burn,' the Xibo stated categorically, and Dan, as much as he admired the Wu, could not refrain from stating the obvious.

'She is human, Fa, she *will* burn,' Dan insisted, panic gripping his chest. 'Then where will we be, trying to confront Su Daji without her?'

'You know as well as I do, Jiang Hudan is more than human,' Fa corrected calmly, which only emphasised how contrary Dan was being. 'You knew the nature of the Wu when you met her, and you were warned not to become attached to any one of these women.'

'I —'

'They are not here to satisfy our lust for knowledge or power,' Fa lectured. 'They are here to serve Tian and the heavenly agenda, and despite what we might think of their methods, it is not for us to question *the will of heaven*.'

'I am not questioning the will of heaven,' Dan said in defence. 'I am questioning whether casting Jiang Hudan into a pyre is indeed truly the will of heaven. How can you be sure … the Great Mother?'

'It is the will of Tian as revealed to both Jiang Hudan and myself, during my oracle rite,' Fa explained patiently. 'Bringing down the rain was part of the deal we struck with Tian for his mandate.'

Dan's mouth was gaping as he considered the unlikely event of two people having the same vision at once. 'You both foresaw this?'

'In part,' Fa said, honestly. 'We both remember fragments, but the rite itself we definitely both saw. I am sorry, Dan, but there is no avoiding it. You have no choice but to place your faith in Tian. Is that not what being Wu is all about?'

Dan inhaled to steady his emotions; for the first time he was starting to doubt whether he could truly commit to the way of the Wu. Clearly, the Great Mother had foreseen he would have difficulty with the faith side of their vocation, and that is what this trial period of training was designed to establish. From a scholarly perspective, Dan had never failed in any endeavour he'd put his mind to. His logical mind told him this rite was utter insanity and that he was about to lose a dear friend, and the notion caused a panicky feeling in his gut. Yet, when he thought about the wonders that the Wu had shown him to date, the butterflies in his gut calmed. The Wu had control of forces he couldn't even begin to understand, and Dan felt that if he would just let go and accept the will of Tian freely, as the Wu did, he might discover numerous amazing aspects of existence that were beyond logic. 'It was my suggestion to pursue heaven's mandate ...' Dan wondered what other deals Fa had struck with heaven. Surely none worse than this? 'And I will not obstruct any event you have foreseen,' Dan agreed resolutely, with a look of challenge in his eye.

Fa picked up on the warning. 'I can assure you, Dan, that two weeks after we perform the yin rite, the reason why it is so important will be perfectly clear.'

Dan thought he understood the strategy. 'When Zi Shou and Daji learn we have conscripted the Wu to bring down the rain, the emperor will declare war on us.'

'They cannot afford a war, in fact that is why they have kept a safe distance since the death of our father,' replied Fa, confusing the issue. 'But as a precautionary measure, Xian, Du, Chu and Zai are quietly amassing our armies at Mengjin,' Fa explained, 'on the Zhou side of the Huang He.'

'So we are going to attack without provocation,' Dan exclaimed with a frown, as this was the very situation they'd wanted to avoid.

'Did I say that?' the Xibo questioned, and Dan felt exhausted and perplexed.

'I want my pre-Wu brother back,' Dan complained, 'he was so much easier to understand.'

'Easier to win an argument against, you mean,' and Fa served him a cocky grin.

'I have no desire to argue with you, Jiang Hudan, or the Great Mother,' Dan relented, 'and if all of you agree this event must happen, then ... so it must.'

'Good man!' Fa slapped a hand down on Dan's shoulder. 'For your faith in Tian, a reward will await you in heaven.'

The lord was not very interested in rewards at present. 'For Jiang Hudan to live through this will be reward enough.' Dan fished for more information from Fa, but a gong sounded from outside the war room and Dan cursed the timing of the interruption.

'Ji Fen Gong,' the crier announced, and the lad entered purposefully to inform them: 'Brother Hudan is awake.'

'Splendid,' Fa said. 'Then we shall spread the word that the mighty Shanyu Jiang Hudan of Yi Wu Li Shan is seeking yin by means of yin this night to the glory of the Ji family and the peoples of Zhou.'

'I shall see that the word is spread,' Jiang Taigong confirmed.

'I want a barrier of soldiers surrounding the stepped jinzita, at a distance of one hundred paces from the base,' Fa instructed. 'And I shall need our finest chariot polished. It will carry Jiang Hudan to the ritual site.'

'Would you like to be the charioteer, Dan? That would be fitting considering it was you who brought this alliance about,' Fa suggested, and Jiang Taigong nodded in agreement.

It all sounded like utter madness to Dan, and he really didn't wish to discuss any of the arrangements. 'Whatever you think is best,' Dan replied. 'May I be excused. I wish to inquire after brother Hudan's wellbeing, personally.'

'Of course,' the Xibo granted. As Dan turned to head for the door, Fa added, 'She will validate everything I've told you.'

The lord did not turn back to argue the assumption. Dan was feeling somewhat nauseated by his brother's cockiness and good cheer regarding the rite — he needed some air.

Recollections from the events she'd experienced on top of the jinzita, in both spiritual and physical realms, reoccurred as consciousness dawned. Beyond her memory of blacking out after the ordeal, there was music. She recollected floating around in the Hall of Records watching Ji Dan play his qin, and the experience had filled her with peace and contentment until she saw his tears.

'Hudan?'

It was her sister's voice beckoning her back to consciousness, and Hudan responded with a groan.

'Storm clouds are covering Zhou,' she advised, 'you need to wake and finish what you have begun.'

Hudan opened her eyes to find Huxin and Fen leaning over her.

'I shall run and tell the Xibo that she is awake,' Fen advised Huxin and left quickly to do so.

'So,' Huxin looked at her sister, her eyes wide with wonder, 'how did you do it? Tell me everything! Did you find the Lord of the Elements?'

'I am feeling fine, thank you, brother Huxin,' although Hudan was not surprised by her sibling's lack of concern.

'Do not tease me, Hudan,' Huxin warned. 'Did you find him or not?'

'I did.' Hudan motioned to the storm clouds beyond the window. 'I also met his brother, the Lord of Time ... he was really amazing!' Hudan shivered when she recalled herself in his mirror of souls, and then a second shiver ran through her as she remembered that the Lord of Time was Ji Fa at some distance point in the future ... or the past?

'And you learned the name you require to bring down the rain?' Huxin asked to speed the tale along.

Hudan nodded, still preoccupied with her own thoughts.

'And then after you awoke on the jinzita?' her sister prompted.

Hudan gasped, as she suddenly recalled those terrible moments. 'The white tiger!' Hudan exclaimed. 'It wasn't you!'

'Yes, I know that,' Huxin said, annoyed. 'Male or female?'

'Male,' Hudan said surely, and Huxin wanted to explode with happiness.

'You would not tease me about something like this, would you?' Huxin felt it was too good to be true and needed certainty.

Hudan shook her head. 'He was amazing, Huxin.' Hudan fuelled her sister's excitement with the tale of the tiger's defence of her.

'Brother Dan has requested to speak with you,' Fen interrupted, having quietly entered and waited for Hudan to finish telling her tale. 'May I show him in?'

Hudan nodded and Huxin rose to leave. 'I shall investigate this mysterious appearance,' Huxin decided. 'I'll let you know what I discover. Brother Dan,' Huxin acknowledged him as he passed. She raised her hood to cloak her identity and left them alone.

'You kept your promise, brother Dan,' Hudan said, and Dan frowned as he wondered at her meaning. 'Your fingertips must be sore from playing.'

'Ah,' Dan replied, enlightened. 'You have been awake a while then,' he assumed, as he'd stopped playing several hours ago.

'No,' Hudan advised, 'I spirit walk in my sleep often.'

'Really?' Dan seemed both fascinated and discomfitted by her claim. He toyed with the little beard on his chin, as he did whenever he was discomfitted or uncertain.

'Perhaps you should be the one resting?'

The suggestion made Dan smile and also choke with emotion. 'There is too much anticipation in the air to sleep this afternoon, I fear.'

It was clear to Hudan that Dan was distressed. During her spirit walk she'd seen him crying, and she hoped her mission was not the cause. 'Why are you so gloomy, my brother? Tell me what it is you really fear.'

Dan seemed a little affronted and frustrated. 'What I fear ...' he came and sat on the floor by Hudan's bed '... is ... whether this rite you are to perform is really necessary, when I know, no matter what we do, Fa will rule.'

Hudan found this curious. 'Have you had a vision, brother?'

Dan shook his head, very uncomfortable suddenly. 'I have never told anyone, beside Jiang Taigong, what I am about to tell you now, and I have killed good men to keep this secret.'

'I swear by the creed of the Wu I will not repeat anything you tell me in confidence,' Hudan asserted, sitting upright.

'Have you heard of the Jade Book?' he asked, and Hudan's heart skipped a beat.

'The book that awarded the mandate of heaven to Shun of Yu, when he found it in a cave at Li Shan?' Hudan knew her history as well as any educated person.

'The book could grant heaven's mandate, as it is an ancient calendar that lists the critical dynastic eras and changes of the past and future, in chronological order.'

'The legend never mentioned what the Jade Book contained,'

Hudan said, her head cocked to the side, intrigued by his knowledge.

'I have seen it,' Dan whispered, 'and I can assure you that Fa will rule regardless of whether it rains or not.'

'How did you come by such a treasure?' Hudan was more interested in the tale than Dan's reason for telling it. 'Where is it now?'

'It is a very *long* story.' Dan really didn't want to dig up that history. The Jade Book had caused him nothing but pain and anguish since the day he'd found it, locked up and hidden amongst the important family documents in the royal storehouse. 'The point I am trying to make is —'

'I know your point, brother Dan, but without rain, our troops will suffer and there will be but a desert for Ji Fa to rule over.' Hudan appreciated his concern, although she knew it was unnecessary. 'I need to prepare for tonight, but will you tell me your long story tomorrow, when the rite is done?'

Dan was deflated by her insistence, but managed to conjure a smile. 'I shall even let you see it.'

Hudan froze in place and only dared whisper her query. 'You still have possession of it? I heard rumours that Su Daji claimed to have it?'

'The book Daji has is a forgery,' Dan assured Hudan. 'I know because I gave it to her. If she read the authentic item, she would have pre-empted our attack.'

'Of course,' Hudan said in amazement, as He Nuan entered to advise that the hour of the monkey had arrived and it was time for Hudan to bathe and ready herself for her audience with heaven.

'You will come?' Hudan queried Dan as he rose. She knew he was still sceptical about her surviving the yin rite. 'I cannot wait to defy your logical analysis.'

Dan was amused and cheered by her attitude. 'Apparently I am to be your charioteer.'

'I shall not disappoint,' she assured the lord.

'From all accounts, you never do.' Dan seemed to have resigned himself to the event, as he left her with He Nuan to prepare.

'He is really is quite extraordinary for a man,' Hudan commented to her sister-to-be in the wake of Dan's visit.

'Like attracts like,' He Nuan shrugged, as if it went without saying that any man Hudan attracted would be exceptional.

'How right you are,' Hudan said thoughtfully, finding the comment comforting. For weeks now she had felt almost ashamed because she enjoyed Dan's company, but this simple law explained their connection as perfectly natural and not to be feared. Hudan told herself that she was not just rationalising a deeply buried fear; for she suspected she'd solved the puzzle that had prevented her forming an honest opinion of Dan.

Years ago, in trance, Hudan had seen herself kiss a man of this earth, but she told no one, not even her Shifu, and wiped the vision from her mind. Apart from the fact that such an action was against the Wu creed, Hudan also often dreamed of another lover who was not of this earth. He was a son of the sky, who looked rather similar to the Lord of Time, with dark hair and wide dark eyes. As a Wu in the service of Tian, Hudan had always fancied that she was meant for this heavenly suitor, and thus no man of the earth would ever interest her.

But the vision of her earthly kiss had reoccurred the night after she had first met Ji Dan, and it was why she had gone to such great lengths to avoid him. Now that Hudan knew Dan better, she'd come to realise that he was not the kind of man who would try and force himself upon her, nor would she ever break her vows, so how then could this prophecy ever come to pass? Hudan believed she knew the answer — this earthly kiss must have a divine purpose and she now believed she knew what that purpose was.

From the top of the highest jinzita in the star-field, Huxin watched the Xibo's soldiers carefully constructing the pyre on the stepped jinzita one over from her. Other officials were marking out the boundary where the Xibo's guard would form a barrier around the site to prevent anyone interfering with the ceremony.

Tonight the nobility and common people would crowd onto the jinzita that Huxin stood upon to get the best view of the sacred rite, as no one would be permitted near the site itself, other than the Xibo, his guards and the Wu.

'You Ling.'

Huxin turned around to see Ji Shi and was, at first, delighted to see him.

'But you are not You Ling, are you?' Shi said surely, which caught Huxin off-guard.

'How ...'

'I saw the face of You Ling when she was carried into the house unconscious earlier today,' he explained. 'So, who are you?'

'Ah, well.' Huxin shrugged off his discovery. He would never guess the truth. 'I am whoever Ji Fa needs me to be.'

'Just how many Wu is my brother hiding in our house?' Shi was curious.

Huxin raised her eyebrows in an anticipatory manner. 'Everything will be revealed in its time,' she said, and looked to the pyre being constructed in the distance.

Shi looked from the pyre to the cloud cover above and took a deep breath, releasing it slowly. 'It doesn't smell like rain,' he commented casually.

'The rite has not yet begun,' Huxin defended, as she had to agree with him. There was not a hint of moisture on the hot air. 'How did you find me?'

'A happy coincidence,' he said. 'I came up here to investigate a white tiger sighting that, according to reports, was not my brother's beauteous pet, but another tiger altogether.'

'I am here to investigate that also.' Huxin was glad of the excuse to get on with her task. She moved to the bloodstained ground next to where her sister had been lying, and crouching down, she sniffed and looked around.

'Do you have a name?' Shi came to squat beside her, and he smelled delicious as always.

'You Ling is fine.' Huxin leaned in closer to the blood and took another deep whiff, before she sat back on her haunches to be frank with Shi. 'All I can smell is you,' she explained in a direct manner.

'Oh.' Shi was apologetic. 'I just bathed. Shall I move away?'

'Sadly,' she said, flirting just a little, 'that would be helpful.' She continued her investigation with little success. The ground was too hard and dusty for prints and, besides the scent of the man who had died in the attack, Huxin couldn't detect the scent of a tiger, although her sense of smell was not as acute as her vision or her hearing.

'Nothing?' Shi assumed when Huxin stood and shrugged.

'Perhaps he was heaven-sent?' She gazed up at the heavens a moment and back to Shi, who was smiling.

'Why are you so interested in tigers?' Shi sounded suspicious.

'I have an affinity with them,' she said, skirting around the question. 'Like you, Ji Shi.'

An unconscious micro-shake of his head indicated that he did not believe her. 'A Wu from Li Shan who has an interest in tigers?' Shi advanced that notion that was on his mind. 'It seems to point to one legend in particular, Jiang Hudan.'

Huxin burst out laughing that Shi was about to confuse her with her sister once again, and the thought of Ji Dan getting the wrong impression of Shi's infatuation a second time was just too funny.

'Heavens, no, I am not Jiang Hudan!' Huxin waved off his guess. 'Jiang Hudan is spiritual, intellectual, and pure as the freshly fallen snow.' Huxin laughed again at his mistake.

'But you seem so,' Shi retorted, unable to see what was so funny. 'Please don't toy with me.'

'I'm not toying with you,' Huxin defended. 'I am being honest.'

'Then tell me if you are Wu, at least?' Shi appealed. 'And if it is you who will burn this night?'

'No one will burn this night,' she assured him. 'As to whether I am Wu, why do you need to know?' Huxin knew why, but she wanted the guilty pleasure of hearing the reason from his lips.

'Because if you are not Wu and are not spoken for by any man, I should like to ask whomever I must for your hand in marriage.'

'You have only met me twice,' Huxin pointed out with an apologetic look upon her face. Shi was sweet and handsome, but unfortunately not the species she was looking for in a mate.

'Enough to know that I have more in common with you than any other woman I have met to date,' he assured her.

Huxin didn't want to see the disappointment in his face when she told him the truth and that she could belong to no man. She should have listened to Ji Fa and left Shi to his wife-hunting. 'Close your eyes, and then I'll tell you what you wish to know,' she requested.

He smiled as he complied. 'All right.'

'The truth is, Ji Shi …' Huxin planted a kiss upon his lips and then summoned her chi to render herself invisible.

When Shi opened his eyes to find himself alone on the top of the jinzita, the answer was plain enough: 'She is Wu.' He closed his eyes to endure the disappointment, and Huxin fled down the earthen prism, unable to watch the pain she'd caused him. The Xibo was right: she could never make Shi or any earthly man happy, so from this day forth she vowed to never again flirt with a human. She had her eyes on another prize … she only had to hunt him down. Tonight, when her sister's rite was complete, Huxin would scour the outskirts of the star-field — if this tiger was of the earth, she would find him.

Nuan wound strings of seashells through Hudan's hair to prevent it being singed by the flames, while the rest of the initiate's body had been shaved smooth with a sharpened shell. Lightheaded from her two days of fasting, Hudan felt light in spirit as well — another cup of the elixir of waking sleep had heightened her emotions, including her empathy. 'The timing of our mobilisation will delay your wedding plans, He Nuan. I am sorry for that.'

Nuan was taken aback. 'I am surprised that you would even consider such a trivial matter amidst current events.'

'My brother's happiness is always foremost in my mind … and yours,' Hudan added, so that Nuan might know she no longer disapproved of her engagement to Fen Gong. 'The fact that you found each other again, despite the odds, would seem to indicate that your association is divinely meant. There are no accidents,' Hudan said and knew it was true. 'Fen would not renounce his love for you, even in the face of death.' She had to admire Fen's persistence in that regard, for his unfailing will had secured him that which he wanted most.

'Nor I for him, mistress.' Nuan had tears in her eyes, and Hudan could see how sincere her feelings were.

'See,' Hudan touched her cheek and wiped the tear from it, 'divine. It is people like you and Fen who give me the faith to keep aspiring for a more prosperous future on earth.'

'You give me faith that we shall have one.' Nuan's tears flowed freely.

It was unusual for Hudan to be touched by sentiment, but Nuan's words moved her. Nuan had never really shown Hudan admiration in the past, and had gone out of her way to avoid her. 'I thought you despised me?'

'I envied you, Jiang Hudan,' the older woman confessed, 'so admired, feared and accomplished. Whereas I —'

'Did not have the same fortunate beginning in life that I had,' Hudan finished for her. She took hold of Nuan's hands to reassure her. 'I misjudged you, sister. You have proven invaluable to me throughout this trial and are truly worthy of the title Wu.'

Nuan smiled through her tears. 'I no longer care about that title. That you call me sister means one thousand times more.'

The goodwill that was forming drove them to embrace for the first time in their long association.

A sound drew their attention to Fen, who could clearly not believe what he was seeing. 'Am I dreaming?' the lad asked, astonished and overjoyed.

'All our conscious hours upon this earth are but a dream,' Hudan replied with a smile, as Nuan brushed away her tears and hurried to finish Hudan's hair.

Fen assumed a more official tone. 'Ji Fa and the royal procession await your presence in the courtyard.'

'One moment,' Nuan appealed. She wound the last few strands of shells through Hudan's hair and sat back to admire her work. 'There! Fit for a king.'

Or even a son of the sky, thought Hudan, suppressing a smile of delight. She stood up, dressed only in her white silk robe, and Nuan raised the hood over her head and handed Hudan her staff, Taiji. The crystal in the staff was in its dormant state at present — a dull, clear sphere.

Perhaps it was the elixir working its magic, but Hudan felt she hadn't a care left in the world as she rose to follow Fen. She was to meet with the Lord of the Elements this night, and the excitement this inspired in her was almost debilitating. Hudan wished that everyone suffering on this earth could know, as she did, that beyond the pain and death of this life there awaited a realm where humanity's dreams were being formulated into plans by the sons of the sky, to once again bring their earth more closely into alignment with the splendour and harmony of Tian. The sons of the sky clearly had their own agenda, and although Hudan knew very little about their scheme, she was proud to do whatever she must to be of service.

In the courtyard, the Wu arrived to catch the end of a confrontation the Xibo was having with one of his brothers. 'You are not Wu and you do not have heaven's mandate, so you can view the rite from the tallest jinzita with the rest of the household,' Fa was saying. 'Not even Jiang Taigong is allowed at the site of the ritual.'

'Dan is permitted,' the younger man, who looked like Fa, said pointedly.

'And Dan is Wu,' the Xibo announced to the shock of the one he was speaking with.

'But … he is male?' The lad argued, although he also sounded inspired by the news.

'So he is,' Fa replied light-heartedly.

'But —'

'We'll explain later,' Fa insisted as he spied Hudan descending the stairs into the courtyard with the other Wu. 'Right now, Shi, you need to leave.'

'But I —'

'Must I have soldiers escort you?' the Xibo demanded, his patience at an end.

Shi finally backed away, glancing curiously toward the Wu before he turned and departed. The tigress made a move to pursue Shi.

'Baihu!' The Xibo's call halted her in her tracks, and with a growl of reluctance she returned to Fa's side.

Two four-wheeled chariots, pulled by four horses each, were standing ready. One of the chariots would carry the Xibo and his tigress, and the other was for Dan to use to convey Hudan to the star-field. Fen and Nuan would follow on horseback, with a large guard at the front and rear of the convoy.

Hudan hardly recognised Dan without his lordly finery. Dressed simply in black, Dan had shaved his face clean of hair and, as predicted, looked ten years younger. His long dark hair was unbound and left to fall free — as the Wu wore theirs — and Hudan had to suppress a gasp of recognition. This was just how Dan had appeared in her vision of their kiss, though if her reckoning of future events was correct, it would not happen for some time yet. Still, seeing Dan appearing thus had set her heart to pounding in her chest. Why now? Why pick this moment to test her commitment to her creed? She had fought to deny the truth that was now blindingly obvious to her; that Dan was as desirable as any son of the sky, including the elusive lord who seduced her in her dreams.

But to be enticed by earthly desires was not an option for Hudan at this time. She shut off her heart and looked away.

'Brother Hudan, are you well?' Dan queried, as she'd hesitated so long before greeting him, and he could see nothing of her face beneath the hood. Hudan collapsing from hunger and exhaustion would be an answer to his prayers — then they could cancel the event.

'Wu becomes you, Dan,' Hudan commented as she stepped up into the wooden four-wheeled chariot that was to take her to her audience with heaven.

The comment took him aback momentarily. He had forgotten he'd shaved and was stunned that Hudan noticed, let alone commented. She regarded him as an object rather than a person most of the time.

'My thinking was that if I appear Wu, perhaps my mentality will follow,' he lied. The truth was, he remembered Hudan saying, long ago at the thermal pool, that he'd be more attractive without his facial hair. Why he sought her personal favour was beyond reasoning, when he knew she could not give it. Perhaps he had a vain hope that she might secretly love him. If he could only bypass the pomp and ceremony and make Hudan realise that her life was precious to someone, then perhaps she would not be so eager to throw herself to the flames! It was no longer about what she could teach him, because he could learn Wu doctrine from another Wu. It was Jiang Hudan herself who he craved — every time she left his presence he longed to see her, until next he did — but after tonight, there might be no next time.

'And has your faith been strengthened?' Hudan asked as he climbed into the chariot with her and took up the reins.

'Sadly, no,' he replied, feeling like he'd swallowed a stone that was now stuck in his gullet.

'That will change presently, I expect,' Hudan assured him as she sat down on the seat, somewhat lower than the driver's, at the rear of the carriage. 'I have the protection of the sons of the sky. You have nothing to worry about.'

As the procession began moving forward, Dan had to focus on getting his team of horses to move at a steady pace before he raised a subject that he'd been wanting to discuss with Hudan for a very long time. 'Do you remember that first morning at Li Shan, when I told you I saw things that were not of this time and world.'

'Yes, I remember.' Intrigued by the subject, she came to stand near him, so she could hear him more clearly over the sounds of the procession and the crowds lining the way to the star-field. She used her sacred staff to anchor herself.

'I have had dreams about a race of people who fit the description of the sons of the sky,' he admitted to her, but what he had to say next felt even more outrageous. However, he felt compelled to tell someone who might be an authority on such matters, and with Hudan he was now pushed for time. 'I even think I may have been one of them.'

Dan heard a distinct huff of breath from Hudan, and wished he could remove the hood from her head. 'Do you recall hearing any of the names of Tian's children?'

Dan certainly did, although the knowledge made him blush. He remembered intimate moments spent with a beautiful fair-skinned woman with mauve-grey eyes and hair the colour of undyed silk. As they'd made love she had uttered his name over and over, as if she were afraid she might forget it. 'Lu Chen.'

Hudan gripped her stomach. 'You met *this* lord?'

She sounded so stunned, and Dan had to wonder why — did she know something of this son of the sky? 'Lu Chen was the name they called me.'

Hudan returned to her seat, and Dan was alarmed by her reaction — without even seeing her face he could tell she was harrowed by his confession.

'Do you know something of Lu Chen?' he ventured.

Hudan shook her head to the negative.

'You are unwell then?' Dan was beginning to feel anxious.

'I am perfectly fine.' She held up a hand to hold him at bay, but her tone did nothing to reassure Dan.

'I have offended —'

'No. Just … drive.' She bowed her head, and drew deep breaths, still clutching her stomach.

'I should not have mentioned it,' he concluded, annoyed at his continual quest for answers.

'It explains a lot,' she commented, so faintly that he barely heard her. Despite wanting to pursue the conversation, for once he reined in his curiosity and bit his tongue.

There was a reason for everything, and just because that reason was not yet clear was no cause for alarm, Hudan lectured herself.

The son of the sky who filled her dreams went by the name Lu Chen, she knew that, as she remembered calling him by this name. If Ji Fa was to be one of the sons of the sky, wasn't it likely that Ji Dan, even more cultured and wise, would be a son of the sky also? Was her divine suitor the same soul now leading her through the Xibo's guard toward the jinzita with its peak ablaze? The possibility made her feel ill, for how could she then continue to regard Dan as a mere mortal, unworthy of her favour and interest? Hudan so wanted to take the last hour back and do it differently — she envied the Lord of Time his ability.

With a few deep breaths Hudan ceased feeling sorry for herself and found her equilibrium. *There are no accidents. You have discovered this now for a reason ... knowledge is power.*

The wall of guards lining the perimeter of the site were facing inward when the Xibo's party arrived. As Ji Fa and the Wu entered the inner sanctum formed around the jinzita by the human wall, the soldiers turned so that they faced outward and were required to remain thus until the rite was complete — to disobey this order was punishable by death. Only the Xibo and the Wu were permitted to watch the rite from close quarters; the jinzita, from where the rest of the house and local people observed, was too far afield to see the event in any detail. The guardsmen and spectators felt they had already received a good show, as the men who had attacked Jiang Hudan earlier in the day had been caught and thrown onto the pyre prior to the Xibo's arrival, which served to prove that the fire would incinerate an ordinary moral. Ji Fa's head guard reported that the men died screaming. If Hudan had known that the men who had attacked her were going to be sacrificed, she would have appealed to Ji Fa for mercy.

'Very good,' the Xibo commented, in fine spirits, while Dan looked like he was going to be sick.

The sky above rumbled black as the Xibo and his tigress led the way toward the base of the stepped jinzita. Dan and Hudan followed at several horse lengths distance, while Fen and Nuan followed at the rear. Were it not for the torches held by the guard wall and the huge pyre raging on the artificial mount, the night would have been pitch black. Other torches had been staked into the ground either side of the walkway to the site.

'Jiang Hudan,' Dan requested permission to speak as they proceeded slowly down the path toward their fiery destination.

'Yes, Ji Dan?' she replied just as formally.

'Do you value your life?' he asked.

'I value all life,' she replied, knowing that the answer was not going to satisfy Dan. 'But I am perhaps more indifferent to dying than most, because I know that beyond this life my soul has other lives, like the one you have experienced among the sons of the sky.'

'That was just a dream,' Dan said, sounding sorry he'd mentioned it.

'No, brother Dan, *this* is the dream,' Hudan assured him.

'It scares me when you talk that way,' he replied quietly, and Hudan could hear the fear of loss in his voice.

'There is nothing to fear,' Hudan replied calmly,.'Even if I were to perish, you know as well as I do that your Xibo will prevail over the emperor and our quest will be a success.'

'The quest is not my concern,' he uttered aside to her. 'I care that one of the most amazing people I have ever known is about to dance with death, unaware of how devastating her loss would be to those she would leave behind.'

Waves of shock began radiating through her, but Hudan drew a deep breath and stayed her course. 'If you would be a true brother to me, you will not distract me with such matters.'

Hudan could not see his face and was spared the awkward moment as a disruption occurred among the guard wall to the west of them.

Ji Fa's head guard immediately ran to investigate and reported back. 'It is a tiger, my Xibo. A *white* tiger,' he advised without turning to face the jinzita, whilst his soldiers struggled to do the same and fend off the encroaching animal.

Huxin gave a roar, and Hudan spoke up on behalf of her brother. 'I owe that tiger my virtue,' Hudan called ahead to Ji Fa, and Dan gave a gasp of shock.

'How?' Dan queried. He must not have been informed about the attack, which Hudan considered very fortunate, as he was emotionally unstable enough already.

'Let the tiger through,' the Xibo decreed, whereupon his guard gladly parted, and the large white tiger trotted into the inner sanctum to join the ritual party.

Huxin went bounding up to greet and challenge the newcomer — just to establish who was in charge — and upon confirming the tiger was male, Huxin became far more accommodating. Once the formality was over, the pair of tigers returned to where Ji Fa stood.

'Welcome, friend,' the Xibo said, holding out a hand toward

the new arrival, who circled and nudged Fa as gently as Huxin did. 'Two white tigers,' he murmured in amazement, 'must be a promising sign.'

'I grant that it is, my lord,' Fen agreed, as he and Nuan joined the huddle at the base of the structure. Nuan bowed graciously to the Xibo on her way past, and to the male tiger in recognition of his aid, before she proceeded up the jinzita to await Hudan by the pyre at the top. Fen moved to take his place behind a large drum positioned at the base and took the drumming sticks in hand.

As Hudan made a move toward the stairs Dan turned and faced away from the jinzita.

'You are Wu, you are required to watch,' Hudan said, removing her hood to speak with him.

Dan shook his head. 'Remember how you felt when you thought Fen was to burn.' He finally looked her in the face, his fear melting into sorrow and moistening his eyes. 'And you have never even been kissed.'

Hudan had to smile at his priorities, but she wanted to reassure him if she could. 'True as that may be, I believe Tian is saving that honour for you, brother Dan.'

A spark of hope shot through the lord's expression.

'But not today.'

Dan forced a smile and nodded in understanding. 'You toy with me.'

Obviously, Dan still thought she was going to die and that she was making a prediction that would never be honoured. 'That would be against our creed,' she stated confidently, 'which you know I shall never break.'

'Then —' Dan frowned, obviously as confused about how the event could happen, as she had been.

'Have more faith in my abilities, for I have foreseen many earthly events that lie beyond this night for me,' Hudan told him, finally feeling better about her little revelation regarding Dan, and she was about to meet with an entity who might be able to explain the reasons behind the dreams they'd both been having.

Patently, Dan was still struggling to accept that this rite was fated.

'Use what I have taught you, to calm yourself and focus on the desired outcome,' she said, giving him her best advice.

'I will,' he said, but remained facing away from the proceedings, as Hudan went to see Ji Fa.

'Brother Fa.' She came to a stop before the Xibo.

'Brother Hudan,' Fa greeted her with a warm smile, before they got down to business.

The white tiger had been invited to join them for the ceremony and now sat at the side of the path to the jinzita, while Huxin sat on the opposing side, admiring her new friend. Hudan could not continue up the jinzita without thanking her saviour, and moved to crouch before him.

'If not for you I would have been ruined and unable to perform the rite, so I and the land are in your debt.' She held a hand out to touch the creature and he gently pushed his head into her hand to encourage her. 'Thank you, you have the lasting gratitude of Hudan.' She massaged around his ear and then leaned in close to whisper: 'You take good care of my sister.' When Hudan leaned back, the tiger's jaw had dropped open — it seemed he comprehended her words!

A beat from Fen's drum urged Hudan to rise and return to Ji Fa and they both regarded each other with more formality now.

'Ji Fa ...' Hudan increased the volume of her voice — the cloud above may have been agitated, but there was not a breath of wind in the hot valley — so the Wu's voice carried a long way. 'You have called upon the services of the Wu of Li Shan to break the drought that has plagued your lands.'

'I have,' he responded, equally loudly.

'Such a request is against the law of the Shang emperor, Zi Shou, and his Wu, Su Daji —'

There followed a wave of ill will from among the distant audience. 'Glory to Yi Wu!' someone shouted, and the crowd repeated his sentiment until the Xibo raised a hand to quieten his people.

'I am well aware of this law, but I cannot watch my people suffer any longer. I accept full responsibility for the imperial ramifications of our actions this night.'

A cheer from the surrounding guard inspired a corresponding cheer from the crowds beyond.

'Then I, Jiang Hudan of the House of Yi Wu Li Shan and student of the Great Mother, shall seek yin by means of yin. If Tian favours Zhou, heaven will ease the drought that heaven's displeasure with the Shang caused your lands, and will bring down rain to the glory of Zhou,' she pronounced boldly, and the crowd hushed. 'Touch the staff, Taiji, and declare this as your will to heaven!'

Hudan held out her staff toward Fa, who gripped the sacred treasure just below her hand. Together they raised the staff and then hammered its base into the earth. The crystal in the head of the staff began to glow red, and there was a gasp from the spectators on the jinzita beyond, for the sphere of light emanating from Taiji was so bright it served to blind its holder from the view of everyone.

Ji Fa released his hand from Taiji and took several steps backward to come to a stop beside Dan, who was still facing in the opposite direction.

'What is happening?' Dan looked aside to see Fa shielding his sight against the blinding red light.

Fa looked at Dan, his eyebrows raised sympathetically. 'Brother Hudan has divested herself of her robe and is moving up the stairs toward the pyre with the staff, Taiji.'

The mental image in Dan's head and the sound of Hudan's beautiful voice rising into the stillness of the hot night, fuelled the slow fire that had been simmering in his chest since the night he'd seen Hudan in the thermal pool with her siblings, and his desire felt like it would burn a hole right through his soul.

At the end of each beautiful note, Fen pounded his drum twice, and the light in the crystal of Taiji changed colour, moving through the spectrum. She sang five long perfect notes in all.

'She is almost there,' Fa advised Dan, as the light reflecting on his face changed from green to blue.

Fen beat his drum twice to conclude the sequence, then continued to pound out a beat to heighten the suspense.

'What now?' Dan begged to know, as Fen gave a mighty drum roll and when the drums fell silent the distant crowd gasped in terror and awe.

'She is entering the fire ...' Fa uttered, so enthralled by the event that he could not drag his sights from it.

The suspense was too much: Dan was compelled to turn around.

By the time Hudan reached Nuan, Taiji glowed brilliant blue, the colour frequency allied to communication, healing, water and yin. The expression on Nuan's face was very grave for the heat from the furnace above was scorching, even at this distance.

'May Tian protect you,' she said, kneeling in homage as Hudan passed her, 'and reward your courage.'

Hudan appreciated the sentiment, but her mind was in another dimension. *Ang-wei, I summon you, lord, to aid me to transmute fire into rain.* Hudan held her staff ahead of her and its light deflected the heat to the sides, so she was able to proceed closer to the pyre, which had been constructed carefully to leave an opening into the central furnace. 'Ang-wei!' she cried out loud, as she prepared to step into the flames lapping around the entrance. 'Ang-wei?'

'*Jiang Hudan.*' An image of the lord formed inside the central furnace and then turned as blue as the light in her staff as he held his hand out toward her. '*Come on inside. It's really quite lovely.*' He grinned in encouragement.

As Hudan made contact with him, a coolness rushed over her and formed a barrier against the heat, whereupon she was able to step into the huge flaming cone of timber as if it were just an illusion of fire that surrounded her. It was surprising to sit on fresh green lawn beside the lord, who was admiring the inferno raging around them and overhead — a living tent of blazing hues.

Hudan perceived now that the lord was not himself blue in colour, but had a blueish barrier around him — a blob-like emanation that acted as if it were full-body armour against the heat. A glance at her own arm confirmed that she was wearing one too, and there were several other of these huge entities crowded around them.

'Undines,' explained the lord. '*They're water spirits.*'

She observed the cool spirit-forms interpenetrating her own and could not wipe the smile of wonder from her face. '*What next?'* she asked, feeling like they were a couple of mischievous children hiding from their parents, as the lord had a boyish playfulness about him.

'Well ... I thought we could do a little sightseeing around my realm,' he suggested winningly, *'or we could —'*

'— make it rain?' Hudan suggested.

'Ah, yes ...' Avery grabbed the staff she was holding. *'That's what the reserves are for.'* He referred to the oversupply of water spirits around them. Guiding her to raise Taiji, they hammered its end back down into the ground, whereupon the excess undines shot up through the top of the pyre.

There were no screams as Jiang Hudan walked bravely into the sacrificial fire at the top of the jinzita.

Dan held his breath as the light of Taiji was gobbled up by fire and as the bright blue illumination ebbed, the site plunged back into the shadows of torchlight and flame. 'Now what?' he asked his brother, when the fire merely continued to burn.

'Patience ...' Fa encouraged, his eyes fixed on the flaming peak.

As Dan glanced back to the pyre he got the shock of his life, as did everyone, when a burst of blue light shot forth from the centre of the pyre and into the storm clouds directly above. An almighty clap of thunder sent lightning shooting out across the skies and large droplets began to fall around them; within minutes there was a steady shower of rain.

The barrage of water felt so amazing after the long dry spell, that all anyone could do was stand there and drink it in. Dan's euphoric moment ended as he noted the torches being extinguished, and his sights returned to the pyre that Hudan was still beneath. Dan grabbed a dead torch from the ground, determined to knock the remains of the pyre out of the way with it. He sprinted toward the jinzita, ascending the stairs as fast as his legs would allow. Fen and Fa were right behind him.

'No!' Nuan moved into Dan's path to stop him. 'The pyre is enchanted. You must not disturb it before morning!'

Dan attempted to run round the Wu, but she grabbed hold of his arm.

'You will kill her if you break the spell!' she implored, waylaying him long enough for Fa and Fen to catch up.

'She speaks the truth,' Fen said, and in case Dan had other ideas, both tigers had scaled the jinzita and now stood between Dan and the pyre, growling at him.

'We must come back in the morning,' Fa advised, and Dan struggled to accept the delay.

'I will not leave.' He took a seat in the pouring rain to await the dawn.

'The guard will be in place all night,' Ji Fa said, trying to reason with Dan. 'Come celebrate our deliverance from the drought with the rest of the family. There is nothing more we can do here.'

'I'm not moving,' Dan insisted, to Fa's annoyance.

'Dan,' Fa was frank, 'I feel, in this instance, I cannot trust you to adhere to my orders.'

'I shall wait with him,' Fen volunteered, and took a seat beside Dan.

'Very well, then,' Fa said, reluctantly, 'but if one piece of coal has been moved before I arrive tomorrow, I'll have both your heads.'

Hearing this, Nuan appealed to Dan. 'Please, lord, why risk temptation? Come back to the house —'

'I do not need supervision!' Dan said firmly, standing up. 'Go, celebrate with your wife-to-be.' Dan gave Fen a nudge.

'I cannot.' Fen wouldn't budge either. 'Hudan is my brother, sister, parents! I will sit in vigil this night.'

'Suit yourselves,' Fa decided. 'I'll see you both at dawn.' Fa descended the structure and after she bowed to Dan, He Nuan followed him down the jinzita, and the tigers followed.

At the base of the jinzita the male tiger split away from Huxin and headed west a few paces, then looked back at her in invitation. Huxin was torn in two: it was her duty to follow Ji Fa, but the male tiger was so very enticing. She gave a roar of frustration, and the Xibo looked back to note her quandary.

'Go!' He gave her leave and waved her toward her heart's desire. 'See you at sunrise.'

Huxin did not hesitate to bound off after her suitor, and Fa's head guard ordered his western wall of guards to move and let them depart.

'At least brother Huxin shall be in fine spirits tomorrow,' Fen commented as they watched the tigers leave the field and darkness fall, broken only by flashes of lightning.

Dan shook his head, appalled. 'Does she not care that she may have just lost her sister?'

'Huxin trusts in Hudan's mastery in matters of the spirit,' Fen replied, 'and believes our sister is in an enchanted place this night. Huxin probably figures they both may as well have a good time.'

For some reason Fen's little anecdote made Dan feel better. 'Is that what you believe?'

Fen shrugged. 'I was too young to really remember the time the Great Mother performed this rite ... but I do know Yi Wu is still with us, and that gives me hope that my brothers are right.'

'That gives me hope too.' Dan raised his face to the heavens and allowed Hudan's gift to the earth to flow over him. Against all odds Hudan had broken the drought, and if that much of her prophecy could be true, then perhaps her prediction of survival could be true as well. With a glance at the smoking woodpile behind him, tears of doubt filled his eyes, and Dan turned back around to try and find a little faith again.

'We must expect the best outcome,' Fen advised. 'Envision seeing Hudan and speaking with her beyond today, then you'll find it easy to think constructively and clearly.'

'I fail to see how what I believe will make any difference to the outcome,' Dan replied, thinking that the exercise sounded rather childish.

Fen was totally shocked. 'You call yourself a learned man, and you do not even grasp how thoughts mould future events?' Fen thought this was ironic to the point of almost being funny. 'How do you think you brought all this about?'

'Thank you for the reminder ... this was my doing.' Dan felt like throwing himself on his own sword.

'You do not deserve to call Jiang Hudan "brother".' Fen was appalled at Dan's self-absorption. 'Your lack of faith in her ability is an insult.'

Dan hadn't had such a dressing-down in twenty years, and it wasn't the first time this lad had rattled his sensibilities. 'I mean no offence, Fen, but my logic —'

'Logic!' Fen barked. 'How dare you assume to know more than a Wu master about the nature of life and death!'

'She cannot be dead!' As they'd been busy arguing, neither man had noted Ji Song had scaled the jinzita to join them.

'She is not,' Fen assured Ji Fa's heir, and looked to Dan for support.

'We hope,' Dan temporised. 'You should not be here, Song. Your family will be looking for you.'

'She cannot be dead,' Song repeated, caught up in his own concerns. 'She was to be my goddess!'

'Song!' Dan grew tired of Ji Song's wet dreams about the Wu master, dating from when he had first met her at the Wu temple with his father.

'You just keep thinking that,' Fen encouraged Song. 'At least your wish does not run contrary to our desired outcome.' He looked back to Dan with a challenging glare.

'What would favour our outcome would be to dig Hudan out of there and heal her,' Dan reasoned, and he stood to take action. 'You can do that, Fen, I know you can.'

'Really?' Song was amazed to hear this. 'Then do it, Fen. I command you.'

'Ji Fa will have our heads if we disturb anything!' Fen was not going to be bullied. 'What you both fail to understand is that Hudan is not injured, so she does not need healing! She is under the protection of the lord of the elemental realms this night, and that enchantment will last until dawn, when the fire will have cooled and her body can be removed in safety. Touch that pyre now and the enchantment will break and the coals still simmering underneath will burn her alive!'

'I'll wait,' Ji Song decided and took a seat on the stairs, but Dan was still staring at the pyre, not knowing what to believe.

'If logic is your game, then it will tell you Hudan died the moment she entered the fire.' Fen softened his speech as he came to stand between Dan and the pyre to break his gaze and gain his full attention. 'But, if I am right, you will have done the right thing in waiting. The only reason you would take action now would be to serve your own desire to be relieved of worry.'

The truth hurt Dan, but it was the truth. 'You make a good argument,' he awarded Fen, backing down.

'You are my lord, and Hudan is dearer to me than *anyone*. You must know, then, that I have advised you to the best of my knowledge and whether you choose to heed my warning or not I cannot let you pass this point before dawn.'

Dan nodded in resignation. He had to concede he had no choice but to have faith that events had unfolded, and would continue to unfold, as Fen claimed.

'Who is this elemental lord Jiang Hudan is with?' Song wanted to know.

'Ji Song!' The captain of the guard called as he scaled the jinzita, and Dan breathed a sign of relief that he was not to endure his nephew's lovesick drivel any longer. 'Your presence is required at the house.'

'If my uncle can stay, then I can stay!' Song objected.

'The Xibo grants that you may return here with him at dawn to conclude the rite,' the guard advised as he reached them.

'Stay alert, Fen Gong,' Song instructed, accepting this condition of retreat. 'Keep my goddess safe until morning.'

'She is safe in our hands,' Fen replied, diplomatically including Dan in the equation as Ji Song bid them farewell.

'He assumes too much,' Dan said crossly as he watched the Xibo's son depart.

'The Great Mother would say that what we despise in others is a reflection of what we dislike about ourselves.' Fen abandoned his defensive stance and came to stand by Dan.

'I would never assume to have intimate rights to your sister,' Dan insisted, finding the comment offensive.

Fen grinned, amused. 'Really? You've never once thought of it?'

Dan felt ridiculous, a grown man having his morals questioned by a youngster? And he was unsure whether it was because Fen was Hudan's brother and close confidant, or because Fen was his Shifu, that he did feel compelled to answer honestly.

'Enough said.' Fen ended the awkward moment for the lord, and took a seat on the step.

'I am not permitted to love her. No man is.'

'Sure you are,' Fen said.

Dan conceded his point, but was frustrated by it. 'Yes, but that love can never be fulfilled. I would never be content.'

'That is what I thought,' Fen argued, 'and look what happened to me!'

'Yes, but the Great Mother warned me against Hudan in particular,' Dan emphasised.

Fen nodded to acknowledge the problem, and then shrugged. 'I spent years defying the Great Mother's will, and I believe she only ever admired me for it. I think sometimes her warnings are just challenges in disguise … and challenges are our chance to collaborate with fate.'

'I don't think I would earn Yi Wu's admiration for deflowering her treasured vestal.' Dan laughed at that, and Fen joined in with him.

'Unless it was the will of Tian?' Fen posited. 'Nothing is impossible. You are always permitted to dream about your heart's desire, and wait for circumstance to supply the means to achieve it fairly.'

The supposition sent pangs of shock and realisation shooting through Dan's being as he recollected Hudan's promise of a kiss for him. *'Tian is saving that honour for you, brother Dan.'*

He couldn't say he'd never had intimate thoughts about Jiang Hudan, because the truth was he constantly imagined kissing her and loving her. The one thing he had always despised as a distraction from his study had lately become a guilty pleasure he had no desire to forego.

'What happens when beauty is forbidden you? Will it be so easy to resist then?'

Dan could now see the wisdom in those words of the Great Mother, but it was exceedingly hard to heed. 'You are supposed to be instructing me in the way of the Wu, Fen Gong, not leading me into temptation with your sister.'

'I *am* teaching you,' Fen grinned triumphantly. 'You speak of Hudan in the present tense. You *do* believe that she is still alive.'

The fact made Dan smile. It was true, his previous certainty had shifted. Given no choice, he would believe her alive until he learned otherwise.

'Amazing what a little motivation will do for one's focus,' Fen said.

'It is,' Dan agreed, finally taking a seat, emotionally exhausted and soaked to the skin. 'So … who is this lord that Jiang is under the protection of?' It was very difficult to ask the question without sounding like a jealous hypocrite.

'As the lord in question is of the spirit world, I feel we have no need to be concerned about our brother's welfare,' Fen replied, trying not to sound amused. 'Hudan lives for nights such as this.'

'I am sure she does.' Dan felt rather deflated; no wonder she wasn't interested in mortal men. Still, he had to wonder, if Hudan survived the rite, was she unconscious now, or was she dreamwalking with this lord? It seemed insane that that suggestion made him infuriatingly jealous. 'I just hope he delivers her back to us safely, as pledged.'

'He will,' Fen stated. 'I am sure of it.'

'Your little brother always did have faith in me,' Avery advised Hudan as he returned from his observation of the unfolding scene near the enchanted pyre; her consciousness was hovering high over the scene of the rite, at a distance. *'I believe he will see the rite is respected. Your body is safe until dawn.'*

'Fen?' Hudan picked up on his first statement. *'You know Fen?*

'Know, have known, will know. Yeah,' Avery concluded.

'He is a son of the sky?' she inquired.

'Of course,' he shrugged, *'he is elite.'*

'So, Ji Dan …?' She was almost too afraid to ask the question.

'*Elite*,' he confirmed, and the knowledge left Hudan almost breathless.

'*You called him "Lu Chen"?*' The subject was on the table so she might as well pursue it.

The lord looked pleased. '*You are starting to remember.*'

Hudan nodded. '*I remember a lord by this name. And Ji Dan claims he was once known by this name amongst you.*'

'He certainly *was*,' Avery confirmed, sounding like a proud parent. '*Rhun said he'd linked into the Akashic memory before he left us to join the rest of you in this time. That would explain why he remembers more than you do.*'

'*He remembers more … about what?*' Hudan was perplexed on so many levels. '*Who is Hree-un? And what do you mean by "the rest of us"?*'

After a moment considering her questions, the lord clapped his hands decisively. '*We are getting way off track here. I have more important revelations to share with you.*' He held his hand out to her and she took it without question. '*What I show you now will not be easy to witness, so I hope you do not horrify easily, Jiang Hudan.*'

'*I have lived an idyllic cloistered life, but I suppose we shall find out.*'

The lord conjured a white cloak to wrap around her glowing naked form.

'*Nakedness does not bother me,*' Hudan said, but allowed him to wrap her in the cloak; her inner light shone straight through the ethereal garment.

'*I know,*' he smiled, '*but keep it on anyway.*'

'*If it makes you more comfortable,*' she conceded, wanting to please him.

'*It does.*' The gaze of the lord's beautiful mauve eyes held her spellbound. '*You are safe with me; no one can see or hear us,*' he said, as the space around them appeared to blur and shift.

8

DRAGONFACE AND THE JADE BOOK

Glancing away from her guide, Hudan found herself in a palace, but the debauchery and torture taking place in the grand courtyard was completely horrific. A festive orgy was in full swing around her, whilst other people were being roasted alive for entertainment.

'Which level of diyu is this …?' Hudan could not understand why the lord would bring her to such a vile place.

'This is not the underworld, Jiang Hudan. This is the Shang capital at Yin,' he explained.

Hudan's disgust turned to anger, realising that the depravity, gluttony and cruelty of the emperor and his witch had gone far beyond anything she could have imagined. This was truly hell on earth; the pleasured sighs and laughter of the guests only thinly disguised the underlying terror and disgust in the hearts of everyone around her.

There was a huge pool of wine in the middle of the courtyard, deep enough for naked guests to float in gondolas and dip their goblets into the pool to refill them. There was a large centrepiece in the pool, resembling a tree, from which hung meat to be plucked and eaten at leisure. A coal fire had been constructed to one side of the pool, and on top of the coals were several bronze cylinders covered with oil. On top of these cylinders men convicted of crimes against the emperor were screaming in agony as they danced upon the slowly heating metal, shifting their feet to avoid the pain, the oily surface making it even more difficult to keep their balance.

175

Inevitably, the men would slip, one by one falling into the charcoal bed below, where they were burnt alive.

'*Stop this!*' Hudan yelled at the guests, who were laughing at the gruesome entertainment, and when she recalled no one could see or hear her, she turned back to Avery.

'*It is up to you and Ji Fa to stop this. It is way out of my jurisdiction,*' the lord told her, and Hudan now wished she had acted sooner.

Into the madness of the festivities came two old, well-dressed gentlemen. Hudan watched them move through the chaos and make their way toward the pool of wine.

'Your imperial majesties,' the more regal of the two gentlemen called out.

'What is the matter now, Bi Gan?' A woman in one of the gondolas arose to a seated position to address the minister. She was the only woman present who was fully dressed, and wore a shimmering, sheer silk gown of gold and jewels. 'Can you not see that your emperor is busy?'

This had to be Su Daji, for only she would dare speak on the emperor's behalf, and Hudan felt compelled to approach and observe her more closely.

The men addressing her must have been Bi Gan and Jizi, brothers of the previous emperor, Diyi. These men were known to be two of the most honourable men remaining in the Shang emperor's court.

'We have had grave news from Zhou,' Bi Gan said. 'Ji Fa has engaged the services of the Wu of Li Shan to break the drought.'

'Insolence!' Daji was furious, but the emperor was obviously too drunk to be concerned about anything. He could barely sit upright.

'Let them do what they will.' Zi Shou waved off everyone's worry. 'In fact, command them to send me a large consignment of water. The Jade Book states I shall rule for *seventy years* and nothing on earth is going to change the will of heaven.'

Clever. Dan's fake Jade Book had made the emperor complacent and Hudan was very proud of her brother for his brilliant strategy and fast thinking.

'And shall it be Yi Wu who performs this ceremony?' Daji asked, her voice full of contempt as she floated up and out of the gondola to stand before the ministers. 'I want to know who dares to challenge our imperial ban.'

I do, Hudan fronted right up to her to eyeball her closely, *and I am coming for you.*

The empress appeared a little unnerved as the hairs on her body suddenly stood on end. 'I want a name!' she shouted.

'Shanyu Jiang Hudan,' Bi Gan said, plainly delighted to grant her request.

A smug smile crept across Su Daji's face. 'Finally, the legend surfaces. I suppose Jiang Huxin is with her?'

'I have heard that a white tiger escorts Ji Fa everywhere,' he answered. 'He calls the animal Baihu.'

'Guardian of the West!' Daji scoffed. 'Send out a command to kill any white tiger on sight.'

Hudan wanted to grab the enchantress and squeeze every ounce of life from her body.

'If we do that, then we may as well declare war on Ji Fa and those two-thirds of the land who are allied to him,' Bi Gan said, questioning her order … which was a mistake, given Daji's current mood.

'Then as general of our armies, I say it is high time we remind the Zhou who holds heaven's mandate!' she challenged him.

'Due to many grand affairs such as this,' the minister motioned around them, 'we do not have the budget to go to war.'

'Then raise taxes!' she demanded angrily.

'The drought, which your greatness has chosen to ignore, has caused widespread crop failure, and the people have been taxed to the brink —' Bi Gan gasped, whereupon Daji's temper frayed and she directed her chi energy toward Bi Gan's chest.

From Hudan's perspective in the spirit world, it looked like a large dark hand reached out from the shadow that shrouded Daji's spirit body and gripped hold of the minister's heart.

No! Hudan wished she had her body present so that she could combat the attack. '*Do something,*' she said, turning to appeal to Avery. '*Protect him.*'

'*He has not sought my protection,*' Avery answered, with an apologetic look on his face, '*so I cannot give it.*'

This was cosmic law and Hudan could not argue with it. She turned back to the confrontation, helpless to intervene.

'Such a *good* man, always pleading the cause of the people. Yet you fail to fathom that the people are here to serve *the emperor*,' the empress lectured, mocking him, as Bi Gan stood breathless and unable to speak. 'I've read that a good man's heart has seven apertures,' she proposed, glancing around to find the emperor looking alarmed, though he quickly smiled to appease her. 'Shall we verify that?'

Zi Shou hesitated for a second over the life of his greatest and longest serving minister and uncle, before he gave his lover the nod.

'No, empress, I beg you —' Jizi folded to his knees to implore her to spare his brother, only to have his face splattered with blood as Bi Gan's heart was torn through his chest.

When Daji caught the organ, it was still beating. The minister's body fell twitching to the ground beside his brother, who bowed down to the ground to wail out his grief.

The brutal and heartless act shocked Hudan to her core, yet she deliberately kept looking at this offence against Tian so that heaven might see all through her eyes and appreciate her ambition to depose Zi Shou and his evil enchantress.

Daji observed the minister's heart momentarily. 'It looks fairly ordinary to me.' She cast the organ aside. 'Jizi,' she called for him to rise, 'will you carry out my orders without argument, or shall I find another minister who will? Jizi!' She kicked him when he only trembled at her feet. 'Lost your mind, old man?'

When a whimper was all she received in response, Daji called for the guards to throw Jizi in prison, and Bi Gan's body in the pit, 'Throw it in while it is still fresh,' she added, bidding them to hurry it along. 'Come to think of it ...' She eyeballed the surrounding guests and picked a man and woman at random. 'Toss them in also, so there will be no complaints.'

'No! Bi Gan deserves a decent burial! Not the pit!' Jizi emerged from his shock to yell, as he was dragged away.

The young couple chosen to accompany Bi Gan to his grave had also begun to scream in horror and beg mercy, but their pleas fell on deaf ears. Daji returned to the gondola to join the emperor.

The horror in the minister's voice urged Hudan to turn back to where Avery was observing events. *'The pit?'*

'Dragonface ... the other peril I need to make you aware of while we are here.' The lord fell in behind the soldiers taking away the dead body of Bi Gan and the two screaming sacrifices.

As Hudan followed, her foreboding caused her to shudder.

It was the greatest of compliments to say an emperor had a Dragonface. This custom stemmed from the legend of the Jade Book.

'Shun of Yu, who obtained the Jade Book from a cave and won heaven's mandate, was said to have a Dragonface,' Hudan mentioned, wondering if there was a connection.

'Funny about that,' Avery commented, as the soldiers came to a stop at a walled-off section of the garden. A thick wooden plank secured the entrance, and to pull it aside required two guards — these men waited where they were and the rest of the party entered the enclosure.

Both the guards and their hostages fell silent in trepidation once the heavy gate slammed closed and was bolted shut from the outside. On full alert, the men used their torches to check that the barren area was deserted, before they approached the large pit.

The lord's response to her observation just now had Hudan perplexed. *'Are you implying that Shun of Yu is still alive? That was over a thousand years ago.'*

'A cleverly written legend conceals the true burden of being emperor in this land,' he said, arms folded as he observed the proceedings with calm disappointment. *'Some rulers have been shrewd and learned how to control the curse that came with being named in the Jade Book.'*

Hudan looked up and noted the large crisscrossing poles that caged in the top of the fortress containing the pit — whatever was in that dark abyss, the emperor clearly did not want it to escape the enclosure.

'But, eventually, their descendants are always seduced by the power the curse vows to award them, not realising the cost will be their soul and hundreds of thousands of innocent lives.'

'Then I will break this curse.' Hudan approached the large pit alongside Avery, some distance from where the guards had placed their torches to carry out their orders.

After tossing Bi Gan's body into the darkness of the pit, the couple who had been chosen to follow him, attempted to bribe the guards for their lives. 'Anything you want,' the man begged, 'no one will know you let us go.'

From down in the pit came a slithering, scuttling sound, echoing along a tunnel and getting louder; something was approaching the opening in the ground before them.

'Dragonface will know.' The guard cued his men to toss in the victims, who fell, screaming. Then silence. 'Let's get out of here.' The men turned and scampered for the gate.

From the pit, a huge lizard wearing armour leapt forth. Fast as lightning the creature grabbed a lagging guard by the leg and hauled him back into the pit.

Petrified, Hudan turned to her guide. 'That is Dragonface?'

'No,' Avery replied, 'that's one of his minions. You cannot break this curse, Hudan, you must contain or destroy it.'

'But what nature of creature was that?' Even in her spirit form she didn't want to pursue it.

'Let's find out, shall we?' Avery took her hand, and although she wanted to withdraw, she was under the lord's protection this night and was bound to him for the duration.

They descended into the darkness, and their light-bodies — undetectable to the living — illuminated a huge open grave on the floor of the cavity beneath. The immense pile of bones was a harrowing sight, for it denoted a loss of human life in numbers impossible for Hudan to fathom.

The fall into the pit was not deep enough to kill, but deep enough to maim. The couple who had been cast in alive lay writhing in pain from injuries sustained when rebounding off the jagged rocks on the way down. Five armour-clad lizards scampered over the large, unstable pile of bones and rotting corpses in order to reach their prey and lick the fresh blood from their wounds or slash a new cut to drink from. Another two of the lizard warriors were fighting over the captured guard, each wanting to stick a long metal implement into him. One warrior won out and carried out the deed while the victim was still alive: the creature bent its victim's head forward and drove the metal spike into his brain. When the attacker began to suck furiously from the spike, Hudan was too repulsed to watch any more. The corpse of the late and great minister was left on the pile while the young couple were snatched up by the strongest of the creatures, who made off with them back down the passage which ran beneath the royal palace. The other predators retrieved their metal straw from the dead guard and loped off down the tunnel — the creatures moved with as much ease along the walls and roof of the passage as they did along the floor.

'*Are they human?*' Hudan was petrified, anchored to the spot. She had felt apprehensive about descending into the pit, but that foreboding had increased tenfold now.

'*No. They are earth native, but their ancestors were not.*' Avery began moving down the tunnel, and she was drawn along with him.

'*If their ancestors didn't come from earth, then where did they come from?*'

'*The sons of the sky brought them here.*' Hudan didn't want to believe that Tian's warriors would release such a horror on the people of the earth.

'*A good deduction, but no,*' Avery corrected. '*It was our creators who brought them here, but unfortunately it has fallen to us to rid the earth of this particular Dragonface.*'

'*How many of them are there?*' Hudan was further alarmed.

'*That is not the concern today,*' Avery replied, attempting to keep her focused. '*This is the one that has been secretly controlling the dynasties of this land for centuries. These creatures have a hive mind and he is their leader.*'

The tunnel ended at another deep pit, only there was firelight at the bottom of this one, and Hudan braced herself for more horror. Though she did not act upon the compulsion, every survival instinct she had was rebelling against their descent. Yet as harrowing as the truth promised to be, she knew there was a great advantage in knowing one's enemy, and thus stayed her course.

The narrow pit ended in the centre of a huge throne room adorned with gold, treasures and all manner of luxury fit for an emperor. There was a large fire burning in the centre of the room and Hudan imagined it probably kept this chamber rather toasty. However, she could not feel the warmth of the blaze, only the bitter cold; for this chamber, in a spiritual sense, was damned; hence it felt as if the atmosphere of the place was sucking the life right out of her.

'*This would explain where the royal treasury has gone.*' Hudan boggled at the spoils. '*What could these creatures possibly gain from hoarding such wealth?*'

'*The satisfaction of watching their prey suffer,*' Avery responded.

The lizard warriors, carrying the moaning remains of Daji's human offerings, were sprinting down the gentle curve of the dome-shaped chamber toward a stepped platform at one end of the room, where a large throne, fashioned from polished human bones and crowned by several skulls, was located. Upon this throne Hudan saw the epicentre of all the horror, and he was the largest creature she'd ever seen standing on two legs.

'*Shun of Yu had a Dragonface,*' Hudan whispered, realising this discovery shed new light on the old legend. Dragonface was described as having a huge mouth, protruding brow ridges and eyes with double pupils — the perfect description of the creature she was now looking at. The legend was hinting that Shun of Yu did not have dragon features but had a dragon-like creature in his possession — thus the legend's wording was cunning and misleading.

'*He is the reason you and the other Time — ah,*' the lord cut himself short, '*um, and the other sons of the sky are incarnated on earth at this time … to bring this son-of-a-curse to justice.*'

'*How?*' Hudan looked back to the cause of their woes, who had taken a particular interest in the naked female offering and she had just about passed out.

'Don't you dare!' The huge warrior slapped her face hard, and coming around to see the creature leering over her, she screamed in terror. 'That's the spirit.' He threw her body forward over the arm of his throne, and she coughed blood, which his minions rushed to lick up.

'*Time to leave.*' Avery began pulling Hudan's light-body out of there.

'*What is he going to do to her?*' Hudan became hysterical as she was hauled back up the tunnels. She knew the answer, and the realisation was so revolting that she felt ashamed. How could any human being condemn another to such horror?

When Hudan finally stopped reeling from repulsion and shock, she found herself sitting quietly in a huge hall of records.

'*I am sorry you had to see that,*' the lord said, addressing her directly, '*but someone needed to.*'

'*Yes, they did.*' The last thing on Hudan's mind was her own wellbeing. Ji Fa and his brothers knew something of the emperor's cruelty, but could not imagine the horrors awaiting them at Yin. '*You said earlier that some emperors throughout history had managed to control the curse of the Jade Book — how did they do it?*'

'*That's what you need to find out,*' Avery stated.

'*You don't know?*' Hudan was under the impression that the lord knew everything.

'*I never inhabited the earth plane during the time in question, so I cannot help you.*' He was apologetic.

'*There must be some action we can take!*' Hudan could not allow this challenge to delay the attack on the Shang — people were suffering, it had to stop!

'*Sending Tian's omen to Ji Fa might be a good start,*' suggested Avery.

The lord's words sent a frightening jolt of awareness shooting through her body, because the omen in Ji Fa's oracle had taken the form of the Shang's sole remaining minister of note. '*Weizi.*'

Avery motioned her over to a desk in the corner, where the minister had fallen asleep at his work. Hudan rushed over to the sleeping man. '*He has no idea what has happened, or that they will be coming for him too. Weizi was the last remaining minister of note, and Su Daji was looking for someone to carry out her orders to slaughter all white tigers and declare war on Zhou.*' She looked at Avery for help. '*What should I do?*'

'*What can a disembodied spirit do?*' he asked, in challenge.

Hudan was encouraged to be creative. She understood his implication, although she had never attempted to possess another body before. She warily moved her light-body into alignment with the minister's physical form, and feeling the weight of the sleeping body bearing down on her being, she was excited to be able to make him sit up and take a soft-tipped brush in hand. The scholar had been writing on a stretched piece of silk prior to falling asleep, and on it Hudan wrote her missive: 'Su Daji has killed Bi Gan and imprisoned Jizi. Take your family and flee to Zhou!'

As Hudan withdrew from the minister's body, Weizi's head dropping back onto the desk served to wake him.

When he read the missive, written in large red characters before him, he was startled. 'No!' Fearful that Su Daji would see it, he poured ink all over the silk, obscuring the message. The minister backed away, petrified to the point of tears, looking warily about him — no doubt wondering about his muse. 'I cannot believe that my brother would do this to close family.'

The sound of armoured guards were heard approaching the room, and the scholar froze in fear.

'*He's going to be seized.*' Hudan, frustrated, flew back into Weizi's form, and aligning herself with it, she used her chi energy to expand his lightness of being and as he began to float off the floor, Weizi whimpered in horror. '*Hush!*' She thought, and to her delight the minister fell silent, as his body came to rest flat against the ceiling facing downwards. '*Don't make a sound,*' she thought as the guards entered the room — there were only a couple of bronze lamps burning low in the huge area, so it was quite dark.

'*Who are you?*'

Hudan heard her captive wonder, but she did not dare answer before the guards had completed their search and left. '*I am Shanyu Jiang Hudan —*'

He gasped in recognition, which was the very reason Hudan had waited to answer his query. '*You are allied to Ji Fa,*' he added as his body floated toward the open window.

'I am here to ensure you and your family are delivered safely to him.'

'Are you now?' objected Avery from the sidelines.

'Why am I so honoured?' The minister refrained from squirming as he was floated down to pass through the open window.

'With your word, Ji Fa can put a stop to this madness, before every good soul in the land has had his spirit damned or broken.'

Hudan did not set him down until the minister was on his doorstep. 'Be quick and be quiet,' she cautioned ahead of giving him back control of his form.

Weizi staggered briefly, and regaining his equilibrium, he rushed inside.

Hudan was feeling satisfied to have gotten their omen this far, but the journey to Zhou would take weeks with a family in tow, and was bound to be perilous.

'Hudan?' Avery cautioned her against her intent.

'I need to accompany him,' Hudan concluded.

'Then return to your physical form and teleport yourself to his side,' he suggested. 'You are now aware of his appearance, so it should not prove too difficult.'

'My physical form will be weak once I return to it. The minister could be unprotected for days,' she argued. 'But my spirit form is strong and more versatile.'

The lord was shaking his head. 'You cannot expect to vacate your physical form for weeks. It will wither and die, and now is not your time.'

'My brother Fen will ensure my body remains healthy enough for me to reinhabit,' she appealed desperately.

'But then your recovery could take weeks, you may never fully recover!' Avery implored her to see reason.

'If Weizi does not make it to Haojing, there will be no reason for me to recover!'

The lord was still shaking his head to deny her request, but Hudan was not going to take no for an answer.

At the first hint of light in the sky, his eyelids wavered open; even with so little sleep his senses were sharp as a razor. The rain was still falling but had eased to a sprinkle, and it was pure joy to awaken completely drenched. His wound was itching and leaning over to give it a lick, Shi was startled to feel skin against his tongue and cheek, instead of fur. *Huh? I must have transformed in my sleep.* He glanced aside expecting to find the white tiger, Baihu — who he'd learned the night before was really the legendary tigress, Jiang Huxin — but in the tiger's place was the naked form of the mysterious Wu who'd captured his human heart.

'Seriously?' he exhaled in a whisper, as he silently sprang to his feet. *She is like me!* The shock discovery sent pangs of joy and horror shooting through his being. Here was his perfect mate, yet she was a Wu of the House of Li Shan and a vestal of Tian, whose favours were intended for an emperor only!

Shi raised his eyes to heaven, hoping Tian would not judge him too harshly. *Dear Lord, how was I to know?* It certainly explained how Jiang Hudan could have a sister who was a tiger. *I swear I never suspected, and if I had, I would never have …* His mind got lost in the memories of their playful romp the previous evening and he could not honestly regret what they had done. Shi hoped his deception did not cause the legend any strife, but she had certainly not seemed particularly concerned about her virtue last night. *Still, she was under the impression I was a tiger.* As a human being, this woman had not been as interested in him.

His beautiful distraction gave a pleasured groan and she began to stir — the sound of her human voice was as arousing as her roar.

What if she wakes and sees that I am a man and not the beast she took me for? No one knew Shi's secret bar their deceased father, and he'd advised Shi repeatedly to never tell anyone, lest his brothers banished him from his family or hunted him down for sport.

Yesterday she suspected that the white tiger had been sent from heaven … he silently considered it was better that she continue to believe that he was one of Tian's own. Accordingly, Shi returned to his animal form to flee the scene of his transgression, vowing to never again interfere in the affairs of heaven.

Dawn was harder to detect than usual, as heavy cloud and drizzle obscured the presence of the sun's light. But once Dan could clearly see Fen playing on his dizi, his patience ran out and he stood.

Fen's tune ended abruptly as he quickly moved to stand between Dan and the wet, blackened pile of wood at the top of the jinzita.

'It *is* dawn,' Dan emphasised, soaked through and too weary to fight or delay any longer.

'We must await Ji Fa's word.' Fen motioned into the distance, where Dan could see that the guards at the periphery had parted and Ji Fa, Ji Song and He Nuan were proceeding toward them. The approaching party were joined by the tigress, who entered via the guard wall to the west. When Ji Fa spotted Dan, he waved him on. 'Go ahead!'

Dan and Fen wasted no time in removing the largest logs from the dead pyre, yet upon finding nothing but a huge pile of soot and coals beneath, Dan's eyes flooded with tears and he lost his enthusiasm. Fen continued digging into the charred remains of the pyre, which seemed pointless to Dan — even if Hudan hadn't burned to death, she'd been buried all night. Fen's furious digging uncovered a large hunk of wood that had not burned, and he raised Taiji from the ashes, perfectly intact but in need of dusting off. To Dan's great surprise, a soot-covered hand was still clasped around the staff, attached to an arm that disappeared beneath dead coals. Fen grabed and pulled on the limb gently, thereby exposing the rest of the ash-covered body of a woman. Shock reverberated through Dan's being and then exploded into relief as Fen announced that she was still breathing.

'Tian is great and merciful.' Dan ripped the cloak from his back to wrap her in.

Once swaddled, Fen lifted his sister up and, to Dan's surprise, handed her over to him. 'You've been waiting patiently to carry her out of here all night,' he explained.

Holding her in his arms and feeling her breathe was something that only moments ago Dan had thought could never happen. The Wu had defied all his logic and he was so very grateful.

'I shall take her!' Song insisted, as he beat his father up the jinzita stairs, and approached to relieve his uncle of his bundle.

'Watch it, boy.' Dan was in no mood to be challenged and his baleful gaze was enough to stop Song in his tracks and await his father's ruling on the matter.

'Dan is Wu,' Ji Fa decreed as he arrived at the top. 'He shall carry his brother back.'

Thankful for the Xibo's ruling, Dan carried Hudan past Song.

'I won't be a boy forever,' Song said defiantly, setting Dan's blood to boiling.

'That is entirely open to debate.' Dan kept moving.

As Fen moved to follow Dan down the stairs, Song waylaid him to ask, 'She is going to live?'

'She is alive,' Fen told the young master as much as he knew, 'and that is an excellent sign … more than that, I cannot promise.'

'Stay with her, Fen,' Ji Fa instructed. 'I need her.'

'I shall do all within my power,' Fen vowed, joining Nuan to sprint down the structure after their charge and lord.

'This will be hailed as clear sign of heaven's favour.' Song was very excited by the events of the past few days, as he and his father fell in behind.

Fa, like Dan, knew they were far from out of the woods yet. In breaking the drought they had challenged imperial rule, and without Hudan to aid them to challenge the Shang and Daji for heaven's mandate, this situation could turn on them very quickly. Ji Fa could end up rotting in prison for years, just as his father had.

After the initial drenching, rain continued to fall in Zhou in a light, steady misting. The local people were rejoicing and singing the praises of Ji Fa and the House of Li Shan, but since Jiang Hudan had yet to wake from the rite that had brought about their salvation, the House of Ji had fallen into melancholy.

The Wu residing at Haojing held a round-the-clock vigil at their ailing brother's bedside. Fen barely left Hudan's side, and slept with his hand in hers to ensure her vitality was constantly being fed by his own. With every day that passed, Dan's hope for her survival ebbed as he watched Hudan waste away. Nobody could live on love alone … Fen's emotional healing could only sustain her for so long. Without proper physical nourishment she faced the strong possibility of organ failure, brain damage and death. They could only hope that Su Daji did not get wind of Hudan's ailment and attempt to finish her and the House of Ji before the battle even started.

'I think it might be best if the Great Mother was made aware of our brother's sad plight,' Dan ventured, testing the suggestion on Fen on the sixth night of their vigil.

'Yi Wu will be aware,' Fen replied.

'Then why has she not come to aid her most beloved student?'

'Obviously Yi Wu feels that Hudan does not need aid beyond that which we are supplying.'

'But look at her,' and Dan motioned to Hudan's pale, diminished form.

Instead, Fen observed Dan with a compassionate expression. 'I wish you could know, as I do, that everything Hudan does has a purpose. She would not tarry in the spirit world without good reason.'

'But what if the reason is that she cannot get back into her form?' Dan countered.

Fen was stunned and even slightly amused. 'Forgive me, lord, but I believe that if Hudan was here at present, she would laugh at that reasoning.'

He gave up! It was beyond Dan's comprehension how everyone could stand idly by while Zhou's best hope of victory slowly perished. 'Am I the only person in this house who is concerned for her welfare?'

'To show concern would be to doubt my brother,' Fen replied honestly.

'Doubt her, or let her die. Which is preferable?' Dan asked, and the answer seemed perfectly clear to him.

'What is preferable,' Fen advised, 'is to observe all situations from a place of non-judgement. Hudan's fate is of her own design and is only for Tian to question.'

Wise words were no consolation, although in any other circumstances Dan would have been content to follow the advice.

The lord left Fen to his vigil and headed toward the Hall of Records, where he always found it easier to think.

One lamp was burning low on his desk, but as he had no inclination to work or study, he did not call for more light. Dan sat at his desk and collapsed over it, his head on his arms, feeling that his ancestors and heaven had abandoned him.

Never had Dan's faith in Tian and the ancestors been so tested. What was heaven's plan? Why would Tian miraculously spare Hudan from the fire, only to have her waste away in an unconscious state? The lord was further frustrated that Hudan's welfare was all he could think about; his ambition for knowledge, the war against the Shang, nothing seemed to matter. But then, without Jiang Hudan neither of these or other objectives would come to pass. Confronting Su Daji without Jiang Hudan would be suicide, but what Dan longed to hear more than anything was Hudan's account of her experiences since they last spoke. What was she experiencing now? He knew he was allowing emotion to cloud his perspective, and if his lustful thoughts about Hudan had offended heaven, then it should be his life under threat and not hers.

It might have served him better to have retired to his sleeping quarters, which he'd not seen for days as, overwhelmed by exhaustion, Dan fell asleep.

'Brother Dan. Brother Dan, I need you to wake.'

Dan woke at his desk in the large hall, now devoid of light, and sat immediately upright to see Hudan standing before him, her form as colourful and visible as day. 'Brother Hudan ...' Dan wanted to rise and greet her and found that he could not.

'I need you to send for soup from the kitchen, and tea, at once.'

'Of course, you must be famished,' he sympathised.

'I am!' she assured him, with a broad smile. *'And I know, and you soon shall, that you are developing Wu skill. For my sake, do not doubt yourself.'*

The statement was puzzling. 'I'm not sure I know what you mean.'

Hudan leaned over the desk toward him to suggest once more that he *'Wake up!'*

*

The sound of his own gasp woke Dan and he sat up to find he was indeed at his desk. The hall was in complete darkness and it was silent. He was very much alone, panting and sweating in the wake of the sudden change in his perception. It was most disheartening to realise his meeting with Hudan had been naught but a dream, brought on by his desire to see her well again.

'Another cruel deception on the part of heaven,' Dan concluded, bitterly. But as he rose to stretch the kinks from his body, Fen's piece of advice played on his mind: '*Observe all situations from a place of non-judgement.*'

It struck Dan that if he was truly to follow this advice, then he should be heading straight to the kitchen to fetch soup and tea for Hudan as he'd been instructed. Any Wu would consider such a dream prophetic and would act upon it. His logical reasoning told him that the only way to swing the Wu around to his way of thinking was to prove that their way was not foolproof, and here was the perfect chance to build his argument.

When Dan's servant of the interior brought the tray to him in the Hall of Records, the lord apologised for the unearthly hour and insisted that the servant return to bed.

Dan delivered the tray to Hudan's chamber himself and set it down on the table beside her bed — Fen was fast asleep on the far side, and the lord was feeling a little foolish acting on his dream. Hudan was as absent as she had been all week, and even if he did prove his point to Fen, it would be at the expense of a precious few hours the lad had taken to rest. To simply leave the tray and exit quietly seemed the most mature course of action to take.

After a restless few hours of no sleep, Dan returned to Hudan's chamber to find everything as it was before, except that the tray had been emptied and the bedpan had been used. When he woke Fen to query him about this, the lad maintained he'd been asleep and did not even realise the tray of food had been brought in, so he'd certainly not devoured it, nor had he relieved himself.

'Brother Hudan has realised the risk to her physical form,' Fen concluded. 'She is attempting to sustain it while she is away.'

Dan felt it was more likely one of the servants had snuck in and devoured the meal, although it did not seem likely that they would also stop in an esteemed guest's quarters and use the bedpan, especially considering Hudan's Wu status — everyone in the household feared her.

'What compelled you to have a tray delivered at such an hour?' Fen was curious, and Dan was hesitant to enlighten him.

'While I was sleeping, Hudan asked me to send food to her chamber,' he finally confessed, and Fen gasped in excitment. Dan found his ward's reaction predictable.

'You spoke to her spirit,' Fen pointed out. 'Mediumship is a Wu talent.'

Opening his mouth to argue, Dan refrained and instead admitted: 'Hudan claimed that I was developing a Wu talent, and warned me not to doubt myself, for her sake.' He looked back to her tiny, still form. It wasn't quite so pale as yesterday. 'So, despite my suspicions, I believe we should have food delivered to this chamber at the same time tonight, and every night, until Hudan returns to her body permanently. I shall have guards posted at the door and around the exterior to ensure no one is playing us for sport.'

Fen was pleasantly surprised by his lord's resolution. 'I shall be more vigilant tonight, my lord.'

'It would be impossible for you to be any more attentive than you already are, Fen. Tonight, I shall sit vigil with you.' Dan was determined to get to the bottom of this little mystery, which he inwardly prayed was no deception at all.

That night, in the hour of the ox, a meal tray was brought in and left on the bedside table in Hudan's quarters where Fen and Dan sat in quiet attendance. By the hour of the tiger, Dan watched Fen drift into slumber — his hand still clasping Hudan's — at which point Dan moved closer to the lantern to read and keep his mind alert.

It was most unusual for Dan to sleep against his will, so when the lord awoke with his bamboo text still in hand, he was genuinely stunned. His attention diverted immediately to the meal tray, which had again been emptied.

The guards insisted no one had passed in or out of the room, or were even sighted in the vicinity.

As vexing as these events were, after a few more evenings had unfolded in exactly the same manner, Dan was forced to concede the possibility that his dream had steered him right. Hudan no longer appeared emaciated, and was regaining her colour.

'I imagine this is Hudan's way of avoiding having to explain herself,' Fen said when he woke Dan on the fourth morning of their dual vigil and motioned to the empty meal tray.

'Then there seems little point in us persisting.' Dan rose and stretched — he was really beginning to miss his bed.

'But Hudan's health looks so much better,' Fen said, alarmed.

'I meant there is no point in trying to converse with her. We will continue to have the meal tray prepared and left beside the bed,' Dan explained to put his ward at ease. 'As the crisis seems to have passed, I believe I have neglected my stately duties long enough, and must leave Hudan's wellbeing in your very capable hands.' Dan took up his reading matter ready to leave, then looked at Fen, who was grinning broadly.

'You have found your faith,' Fen informed him.

Upon reflection, Dan realised he was feeling decidedly more at peace with himself, and this situation, than he had been at this time last week, and the fact that he'd been part of the solution was very satisfying. If and when Hudan did finally awake, she would be proud that he'd followed his intuition and that was also pleasing.

It was nigh on a fortnight since Hudan had performed the yin rite, and Dan was in council with Ji Fa and the prime minister, Jiang Taigong, discussing what should be done if Jiang Hudan did not awake soon. Their meeting was interrupted by an announcement that the Shang minister, Weizi, was at the door, requesting an audience with Ji Fa and protection for himself and his family in Zhou.

'The emperor's own brother!' Jiang Taigong was troubled by the declaration, but Ji Fa wore a satisfied grin.

'This is it, Dan,' and the Xibo gripped his brother's shoulders. 'This is the sign we've been waiting for.'

This assertion only compounded Dan's confusion regarding heaven's agenda. What was the use of sending them the sign to go to war now, when their major weapon was out of commission?

When minister Weizi and his family entered Ji Fa's council chamber, soaked to the skin, the sight made Ji Fa smile as the royal family actually seemed quite happy with their lot. 'Minister Weizi, you are most welcome in Haojing … I see you have already received our complimentary shower.'

'Indeed I have, Xibo,' the minister smiled in gracious thanks. 'I have greatly enjoyed the last week of our journey here, despite the grave circumstances that have driven us to seek your protection.' He fell on his knees and bowed to the ground before Ji Fa, and his entire family followed suit.

Dan was stunned at the implications of the brother of the emperor surrendering to the Zhou, and yet Ji Fa was not at all surprised.

'Arise.' Ji Fa approached the minister and urged him to stand. 'There is no need for you to kowtow yourself before me. Let us talk as brothers.'

The Xibo arranged for his servant of the interior to take the minister's family to lodgings in the guest quarters until a more permanent housing arrangement could be found.

Once the family had departed, the minister sat in council with them and conveyed the tale of the conditions in the imperial court that had driven him from his home. The news of Bi Gan's murder at the hand of Su Daji was deeply disturbing and it stirred the mood for war anew.

'How did you manage to escape?' Dan was suspicious, despite his brother's assurance that this was Tian's omen. It could also be a trick.

'A benevolent lady spirit led us here,' Weizi said. 'She claimed to be allied to Ji Fa —'

'Did she offer a name?' Dan's heart began beating so hard he could feel the pounding in his throat.

'Shanyu Jiang —'

Dan fled the room before Weizi could finish his announcement.

Suddenly the cosmic agenda was perfectly clear, and as the lord rounded a corner toward his rooms, he collided with He Nuan.

'She is awake,' she conveyed excitedly as Dan steadied her in the wake of their collision.

'Is she lucid?' he asked as they both made haste in the direction He Nuan had come from.

'Surprisingly so,' Nuan was happy to announce.

When Dan arrived in her bedchamber, Hudan had recovered from her initial light-headedness and was now propped upright in bed. Apart from a little weakness and fatigue, she felt perfectly well.

'Minister Weizi?' she asked, before Dan could get a word out. The question appeared to come as some relief to the lord.

'The minister is in council with Ji Fa.'

With official confirmation that the Shang minister had been well received, Hudan breathed easier.

As spirit guide to Weizi en route to Zhou, Hudan had witnessed the sad plight of the people in the East, and it was in vast contrast to the celebration, hope and goodwill that had spread across Zhou with the coming of the rains. Weizi had noted the huge disparity too, and despite the emperor's claim to know what was written in the Jade Book, clearly heaven's blessing had shifted to the West.

At this moment, the last great minister of the Shang government was begging Ji Fa to declare war on his brother Zi Shou and rescue the people of the East from the madness and cruelty of Su Daji. The reason this appeal for justice was so significant was that, to the best of the minister's knowledge, he was heir to the Shang throne, for it was reported that, at Daji's suggestion, Zi Shou had locked up his own son and then killed him.

Weizi knew he did not have the support or means to overthrow his brother, further that there was no one in the imperial court who did, and none dared even contemplate conspiracy. For the first time in the twenty long, dark years since his brother had attacked the state of Yousu and taken Daji as his prize, Weizi saw hope for the future. After his miraculous rescue from Yin, the minister was finally convinced that there was someone in this land who could oppose Su Daji. If heaven saw fit to give Ji Fa and Zhou victory, then Zi Shou would be the last Shang emperor to rule and Weizi would be content to honour the will of heaven.

Hudan knew the minister's intention was true, but she had wondered if his eagerness to hand over imperial rule to the Zhou had something to do with wanting to avoid the curse that came with being named in the Jade Book. So Hudan had mentally quizzed the minister closely and discovered he didn't know anything about the pit, beyond that it was to be feared and that to be sent there meant you were never seen again. Hudan wondered if the Jade Book contained any information about Dragonface and his curse. Ji Dan was the only person living who had read the authentic item.

'I need to speak with brother Dan, alone,' Hudan requested politely of Fen and He Nuan. 'Brother Fen, would you be so kind as to ask one of the gardeners to collect some lizards for me?'

'Lizards?' Fen wondered if he'd heard her correctly.

'That's right,' she confirmed. 'I need to study them.'

'As you wish,' said Fen, sounding a little nonplussed, but he left to follow through on her request without further question.

'It is a joy to see you well, sister.' He Nuan bowed out and followed Fen from the room, leaving Hudan and their lord to converse.

Dan took a seat on the floor by Hudan's bed. 'Something vexes you, brother?'

Considering the question, Hudan thought it was an understatement. 'Several matters are of concern to me at present, but regarding the greatest of these I believe you may be of some assistance.'

'Of course I shall assist if I can,' he assured her.

Hudan had broached this subject several times with Dan and seen fit not to probe too deeply, but now there was no avoiding the issue. 'I do not wish to be insensitive by prying into matters that are clearly painful to you —'

'You wish to know about the Jade Book,' he pre-empted, sounding none too keen on the choice of topic.

'No, Dan, I do not wish to know, I *need* to know,' she said, stressing the difference, 'everything you can possibly tell me.'

'Does this have some bearing on our mandate?' he queried. 'As I said, it is written that Ji Fa will rule.'

'Did the book mention Dragonface, or a curse?' Hudan probed, but the perplexed look on the lord's face was enough of an answer.

'It is a chronological calendar of succession, that is all,' Dan insisted, puzzled by her line of inquiry. 'Won't you please tell me what you have learned in your absence?'

'If you tell me about the Jade Book first,' Hudan bargained. 'I would not insist if I did not think it vitally important.'

Before Dan could reply, a servant entered to announce the Xibo's arrival.

Ji Fa had come to express his joy and relief to have Hudan back with them, and to announce that they would depart Haojing to meet the armies at Mengjin on the morrow. The Xibo hoped to join with their brothers and allied forces and cross the Huang He to begin the advance toward Yin within the week.

In the wake of the Xibo's departure, and news, Dan's expression was eager when he turned his attention back to Hudan. 'I did promise I would let you see the aforementioned item if you survived the yin rite. In view of our tight schedule, we really only have right now … if you feel up to it?'

Hudan smiled in relief and gratitude. 'I think I can manage, if you would be so kind.' She held both hands toward him, and Dan graciously aided her to stand. Her knees immediately gave out, so he grabbed her close to prevent her collapsing back onto the floor.

'Not the result I was hoping for,' Hudan joked. Having Hudan pressed close against him was awkward and titillating at the same time. 'Shall we abandon our adventure then?' he proffered, as Hudan was forced to grip him around the back of the neck in order to help support herself.

'I really must see that book.' When Hudan raised her big brown eyes to look Dan in the face, she knew she was flirting, but to achieve Wu ends this was allowed.

'In that case, pardon my means,' Dan said gruffly, and scooped her into his arms to carry her to the royal storehouse.

Hudan gave an uneasy laugh. 'I am much obliged to you, brother.' She looked ahead, feeling uncomfortable observing him from this snug vantage point.

'You do not find it humiliating to have a man carry you about?' he asked, conveying her shamelessly down the busy halls of the house, while everyone pretended not to see them.

'You are not just any man,' she replied, and was surprised that the admission made her feel a little choked up. 'I feel I must thank and commend you for following your spiritual insight and attending me in my infirmity, despite your logical mind telling you otherwise.'

Dan forced a smile. 'I am fast learning that there is no logic so far as you are concerned.'

Inside the walls of the small fortress that housed the treasury at Haojing was another dwelling, with high walls, no windows and only one iron door, which was bolted shut from the inside.

As Dan had his hands full with Hudan, she reached out and banged on the door. 'The storeman is here at present?'

'Heng is always here,' Dan explained simply. 'He is the most trusted and highly paid servant of this house.'

The iron peep hatch slid aside to reveal another iron plate with tiny holes that revealed nothing of what was within.

'Heng, it is I, Ji Dan.'

'The voice is convincing,' said Heng, 'but how might a blind man know for certain?'

Blindness explained how someone could live in the windowless dwelling and not suffer for it.

'My apologies, Heng.' Dan realised his oversight, ahead of rattling off a string of names in close succession, which Hudan could not fully catch.

'Very good, lord,' Heng conceded. 'And who is with you?'

Hudan looked to Dan curiously. She hadn't breathed a word.

'It is clear to me by your tone that you are under some duress, lord,' Heng explained, and Hudan had to chuckle as Dan rolled his eyes.

'Am I heavy, Ji Dan?' she teased.

'Not at all,' he told her. 'It is Jiang Hudan who is accompanying me and as she is still infirm from her recent trials —'

'Say no more!' Heng obviously got the picture. 'What an honour this is! Wait one moment, lord. I shall light some lamps for your convenience.' The iron speaking hole was closed off and silence reigned in the yard.

'Let me try my feet again,' Hudan suggested, to break the awkwardness of the moment.

'As you wish.' He placed the Wu's feet on the ground, facing her away from himself so he could steady her from behind. Although she managed to balance herself against Dan, as soon as she attempted to bear all her weight with her knees, Hudan folded, and Dan was forced to grab her around the waist with both arms to support her.

'Damn,' she muttered. Feeling him hugging her close from the back was more pleasurable than being cradled against him. 'This isn't working at all.' Her heightened emotion was making her feel decidedly ill.

'I don't mind the imposition, truly.' His voice had softened and lost its jovial tone and for the first time in her life Hudan had no idea what to do next. Her yearning to stay exactly as they were was eating at her conscience, and Hudan feared if she looked at him he'd see her desire.

'You are trembling?' Dan noted. 'Are you cold?'

They were sopping wet, having walked through the rainy courtyard to get here, but the humidity made the damp enjoyable. No, it was fear giving Hudan the shakes, an emotion altogether unfamiliar to her. She shook her head in response. 'A little weak, perhaps.'

'I should take you back —'

'No!' Hudan finally found the courage to look Dan in the eye. 'Please, I …' The longing in his expression intensified the welling emotion in her chest, and for a moment it was as if they had passed into the spirit world, where time had no measure. She completely forgot what she was saying.

The sound of the door unbolting startled them both from the enchantment and they laughed in the wake of the scare — or, rather, to hide the reason why they were so distracted in the first place. On the inside Hudan was thanking Tian for bringing them to their senses before they shamed both their houses.

'May I?' Dan sought permission to sweep her off her feet once more. 'There are stairs,' he warned.

'That does seem the wisest course,' she agreed, avoiding eye contact as he gathered her into his arms, and proceeded to enter the Ji family storehouse.

This building stood apart from the treasury, as this was where the House of Ji stored their personal valuables and historic records.

'What treasure brings my lord and such an honourable Wu legend to the storehouse this evening?' Heng inquired as he led them down the stairs, carrying a lantern for their benefit.

'The very one you gave up your life and eyes for, I'm afraid,' Dan informed.

Heng halted, perturbed. 'Pardon, my lord, but you expressly said no one was ever to know of that treasure, much less see it … I gave my eyes to ensure that promise was kept.'

'I realise I said that —' Dan began, whereby Hudan held a hand up to explain herself.

'The reason for this unusual request,' she said, 'is that I have learned that there is a curse connected to being named in the Jade Book.'

'What?' Both men gasped at once.

'What kind of a curse?' Dan probed further, horrified for his brother.

'I do not understand it fully myself,' Hudan replied, avoiding the gruesome particulars, unsure if anyone would believe the truth if she told it. 'Which is why I need to see the Jade Book.'

Clearly Heng understood what her assertion might mean to the Ji family. 'I am the humble servant of this house. You pay me to protect its secrets and this is greatest of them, but I shall always abide by your will, lord, for in this matter you are the highest authority.'

Dan's soft affectionate gaze had changed to one filled with alarm, which Hudan felt cruel in thinking was a blessing — as clearly, he was no longer feeling so amorous toward her. 'Lead the way, Heng.'

The storeman bowed and gravely resumed his descent down the stairs.

'Your reluctance to be forthcoming with information is a worry,' Dan told her, voicing his frustration.

'I would have thought that as an advocate for logic, you wouldn't pay much heed to something so intangible as a curse,' Hudan said, trying to make light of her secrecy, knowing full well that the curse was very tangible.

'That depends on what form the curse might take?' he reasoned. 'You mentioned Dragonface in the same breath as this curse earlier. What does having a Dragonface have to do with anything?'

'It would seem that having a Dragonface *is* the curse.'

'I do not think you could really describe Ji Fa as having a Dragonface,' Dan said, thinking that his brother would be fine.

'At present he does not,' Hudan concurred, 'but once we reach the Shang capital at Yin, that could change.'

The deep frown on the lord's brow conveyed how confused he was.

'Here it is.' Heng placed the oil lamp on a low table, next to a tall wooden chest that was bolted closed in several places. 'I shall leave you to your business.' Heng returned upstairs.

'He gave his eyes to ensure he never read this,' Hudan remarked, as Dan put her feet to the floor and lowered her down to seated position beside the low table.

'And lives his life in this storehouse to guard it always,' Dan added. 'In return his family thrives and prospers from his sacrifice.'

'All the names in the long password that Heng uses to identify you,' Hudan deduced, as Dan pulled the bolts from their fasteners and each side of the the wooden chest fell open to expose a book of thin jade tablets, bound with silken rope and engraved in gold. On top of the volume, a serpentine creature was depicted, and the image made Hudan draw a sharp breath. 'Dragonface.'

'I took it to represent the Green Dragon of the East.'

'The physique is rather humanlike though, do you see?' she asked Dan, and he frowned as he'd obviously failed to notice that the depiction of the dragon was not perfect.

'Were the rest of the book not so exquisite, I would have said it might be a lack of skill on the artist's behalf,' Dan said.

'Quite right,' Hudan agreed, 'but in this case I suspect the misrepresentation was quite purposeful.'

'Are you saying Dragonface is an entity rather than an imperial term of flattery?' There was no scepticism in his voice, only interest, so Hudan figured she may as well come clean with him.

'That is correct,' Hudan confided in a hushed tone, 'and he is not a solo entity either. He has minions under his command who feast on good people and live under the palace at Yin, at the emperor and Su Daji's pleasure.' The memory of the pit of bones made Hudan sick to her core, and that horror must have reflected in her tone and expression, for Dan's cynical streak did not come bursting forth. To her surprise and relief, he took her claim quite seriously.

'Dear heaven,' Dan exclaimed, repulsed by the allegation. 'Hence your sudden interest in lizards?'

'I need to figure out how to deal with these creatures before we get to Yin.' Hudan laid out her problems and raised her eyebrows at the challenge ahead.

'I was fairly fond of lizards when I was a lad, and I can tell you that there is very little they dislike or fear.' Dan thought hard. 'They dislike the cold, anything with a sour taste, or any creature bigger than they are … how big are they?'

Hudan cringed, as the answer was daunting. 'Dragonface, the tallest of them, stands at nearly twice your height —'

Dan whistled to emphasise he was impressed. 'There are not many creatures bigger than that!'

'I saw roughly eight more, exactly like him.' Hudan was somewhat agitated by that fact. 'You say they dislike cold, but as we are heading into summer, cold is not going to be easy to come by.'

'I heard you were acquainted with the Lord of the Elements,' Dan said. 'Might he not be of aid in that regard?'

Hudan considered the suggestion. 'Maybe,' she nodded in response. 'My hope was that the Jade Book might give me some insight, as the lord made it quite clear that these creatures are our problem. He did mention that emperors had learned how to control the curse in the past, but not how they had avoided paying Dragonface's tribute to have a long and prosperous reign.' She took hold of the jade tablets and carefully laid them out on the table from left to right to read.

'Well, as I said, to the best of my knowledge this volume is a list of kingship past and future, which is in itself extraordinary.'

'Yes, it is,' Hudan agreed. 'One has to wonder about the author ... who would have had to be a very skilled clairvoyant, or ... a time traveller.' Hudan was encouraged by her own suggestion. 'The Lord of Time.' She gazed at the Jade Book in wonder and awe. 'Could he have something to do with this?'

'You have met the Lord of Time?' Dan was starting to sound sceptical again.

'I met *a* Lord of Time, who claimed there were many sons and daughters of the sky who could time-shift as he did ... so this could have been penned by any one of them.' Hudan cast her eyes over the text, lost in speculation. 'But what is the connection between this book and Dragonface? Could he be a time lord, or even the author?' She looked at Dan, who had taken a seat alongside her, and his expression was one of utter bewilderment.

'Maybe Dragonface merely stole the book so he could check which individual he needed to exploit next in order to maintain ultimate power over his food supply?' Dan suggested.

'Either way, we know that when Shun of Yu found the Jade Book at Li Shan, Dragonface came with it, so the creature has surely read the original and would know that the jade volume that you gave Daji was a fake. Yet she and the emperor still believe they have the original and that Zi Shou will rule for seventy years!' She smiled proudly at Dan. 'The fake treasure you gave Su Daji has made the emperor complacent.'

'Some good news is better than none,' he warranted, obviously more preoccupied by the point she was trying to make. 'So why has Dragonface not told Su Daji the truth?'

Hudan nodded at him, as that was also her worry. 'If he knows the end for the Shang is nigh, then perhaps he's just waiting for Ji Fa to arrive at Yin? But if that was the case why send Su Daji to fetch the book?' Hudan looked at the book, lost in her own line of inquiry. 'Perhaps he'd forgotten the exact year of the uprising? Did Su Daji say how she knew about the book? Why she wanted it?' Hudan looked at Dan who had gone ghostly white.

He meekly shook his head. 'She just claimed it was the property of the emperor and that she wanted it returned. I only recently discovered that my youngest brother, only a boy at the time, had gotten wind of my discovery and shared the news with some of his friends. I can only assume that this was how word of the treasure got back to the emperor.'

'So, if you gave Su Daji the book and she believed it to be the genuine article, then what cause did she have to hex your father and cause his death?' This was the only piece of the puzzle that didn't fit for Hudan, and Dan appeared distressed again.

'She wanted me to ...' Dan was clearly discomfitted by the reminiscence '... to pleasure her.'

'But instead you consented to play the qin,' Hudan said, sparing him from relating any more of the details.

Dan nodded. 'But, afterward, she decided that as I had refused her prior request, she would allow everyone under her sleeping spell at Haojing to awaken, bar my father.'

Hudan covered her mouth, as the notion of being placed in such a predicament turned her stomach. No wonder Ji Dan had never played the qin again! 'I'm so sorry.'

'It was not your doing,' he replied, breathing deeply in the wake of the confession.

'I should not have pried,' she insisted, her eyes tearing up in empathy. She was truly sorry to have upset him.

'Actually,' he confessed, 'it is liberating to finally tell the truth about that night.'

Hudan realised that Ji Dan had carried his guilt a long time, and she was disarmed that the lord would choose her as his confessor, but as such, she felt she must reassure him. 'In order to discourage opposition, evil will always seek to offload responsibility for its ill deeds onto the good people who are its greatest adversaries. You must not believe whatever lies Su Daji fed you that night. You were in no way responsible for your father's death.'

Dan closed his eyes, although a few tears escaped to trickle down his face and he bowed his head to compose himself. 'I wish I could believe that.'

Hudan gripped Dan's shoulder with her hand for strength. 'She is playing you, brother, do not allow it.'

'But I could have saved him.' Clearly, it still pained Dan, even in light of what Hudan had just said; Su Daji had stuck her dark esoteric knife deep into this one.

'His time was nigh, Dan,' Hudan pointed to the Jade Book, 'or your father would be listed as the first King of Zhou. Subtract a three-year mourning period from the date of Ji Fa's victory, and even if your father had survived *that* night, he would have been struck down within a few years.'

When Dan raised his head to look at her he'd calmed slightly.

'I believe it likely that it was your father's time,' Hudan outlined another possibility, 'and Su Daji simply used the fact to her advantage … if she has any skill with the oracle at all, it is likely she could have foreseen Xibo Chang's death. Even if you had obliged her whim, the chances are your father would still have passed away, and Daji would have undermined your self-respect in the bargain.'

Dan was suddenly seeing the situation in an entirely different light and his guilt turned to rage and hardened his resolution. 'I concede that I may have been seriously deceived.' He was annoyed at himself, 'How gullible!'

'You knew next to nothing about the Way of the Wu at that time.' Hudan felt he was too hard on himself. 'How could you have guessed her game?'

After a moment of silent torment, Dan decided to smile. 'I am most obliged to you. I might have gone on carrying that guilt unto my grave.'

'She'll not be able to taunt you or use that against you in the future,' Hudan could see he'd been lightened of a great load. 'Let us never speak of it again.'

'That will be my pleasure,' Dan agreed.

With a reassuring smile, Hudan looked back to the golden text. 'So there was no mention of Dragonface in here at all?'

Dan shrugged. 'I must admit I did not read all of it, only as far as the year Ji Fa comes to rule — the year of Gengyan.'

Hudan was surprised to hear this. 'You weren't tempted to see how long Ji Fa and your family will rule or who should rule after him?'

'No!' Dan was clearly opposed to the notion. 'Such information is the domain of heaven and I am not Tian. But you are free to read beyond the present, if you so wish.' He rose to leave her to her reading, and began to slowly pace around the storehouse.

Hudan quickly scoured through the text to find the present and then read on in silence. *In the fifty-second year of the reign of Zi Shou, the year of Gengyan, Zhou start fighting Shang. The Shang are defeated as Zi Shou burns.* Hudan was surprised to see one of her own prophecies quoted back at her. 'That is why you persuaded Ji Fa to seek me out. You'd read my prophecy in the Jade Book and so it rang true for you.'

'It did seem a clear sign from heaven,' he conceded. 'The treasure is not without its blessings as well.'

Ji Fa of the Zhou will unite and rule over the land. Here the tablet ended and needed to be turned over, and as she proceeded she noted Dan watching her closely. 'My reaction may be as telling as reading the text yourself,' she advised. He then turned his attention elsewhere and she continued reading. '*— but will die two years thereafter.*' Hudan tried to keep her breathing natural, but still Dan was alerted by it.

'What?'

'You are right, brother.' Hudan began stacking the treasure to replace in its box. 'I do not wish to know any part of the future that Tian has not seen fit to show me personally.' Her heart was pounding in her chest — a few years was not much time to establish a dynasty. As Hudan placed the treasure in its casing she was already regretting not reading who was meant to rule after Ji Fa, as Ji Song would still be immature and not respected enough to maintain rule in the wake of the rebellion they were about to start. *One catastrophe at a time.*

'What changed your mind?' Dan was overtly curious.

'I just realised that if this text ever did contain information pertaining to Dragonface and his curse, the creature would have removed it to protect itself, so there seems little point in reading on,' Hudan fibbed, and although Dan was not entirely convinced this was her reason, he approached to help pack the treasure back in its chest and noticed she was trembling.

'I think we both need to get some rest before our early departure tomorrow.' He locked in the last of the bolts.

Hudan had to agree; her head was beginning to ache. Her quest for solutions seemed to only have presented more challenges. 'I fear rest is a waste of precious time.'

'On route to Mengjin there will be plenty of time to think,' Dan pointed out as he gathered her up to carry her back to the house. 'I cannot say the same about sleep however.'

'I envy the sons of the sky their immortality.' Hudan rested her head upon his shoulder, weary. 'It must be wonderful to never hunger, thirst or tire …' Her words trailed off, for despite the cacophony of problems flighting for precedence in her head, her awareness rushed away down the corridor of sleep.

PART 3

THE SHANG

9

LU CHEN

The sound of tea being poured into a cup stirred Hudan from her slumber, and her eyes parted to see her twin doing the honours.

'At last …' Huxin held out her steaming offering as Hudan dragged herself up to a seated position. 'I thought I would never get a chance to see you in a conscious state, but I've been checking in on you, every chance I found.'

Hudan accepted the tea and returned the smile. She'd never thought to say so, but she'd missed Huxin these past months. 'I have had the best of care,' she assured her, 'and you have responsibilities to Ji Fa.'

Huxin's eyes widened with excitement. 'Speaking of responsibility,' Huxin sat tall in her kneeling position, and flicked her hair back over her shoulders. 'Do you notice anything different about me?'

Hudan cast a discerning eye over her sister and could note only one thing that was different, and she voiced the observation just to tease her. 'You've put on weight?'

'I'm pregnant!' Huxin blurted out, too eager to contain her excitement any more.

Hudan's jaw dropped, yet as this fulfilled her sister's long-held desire, her expression melted into a grin. 'The white tiger … you did have fun the night of the rite.'

'Oh, Hudan … *so* much fun!' she emphasised. 'Look.' She pulled her long honey waves aside to expose her neck and its scabbed sores. 'I still have his teeth marks.' She seemed genuinely thrilled about that.

211

'And that's a good thing?' Hudan marvelled, eyebrows raised in concern.

'Yes!' Huxin emphasised in a dreamy fashion. 'He was very affectionate.'

'Have you seen him again since the rite?' Hudan drank down her tea.

'No. And I did not expect to,' Huxin stated without emotion. 'I think he has done what he came to do, and has returned from whence he came.' Huxin shrugged. 'I am content.'

That truly appeared to be the case. 'Well, dear sister, I know how much you wanted this, and I am very happy for you.' Hudan shuddered at the thought of bearing children herself.

'I'm carrying cubs for certain.' She stroked the tiny pot on her belly. 'Eight more weeks and you'll be an auntie.'

That notion was cause for joy, and Hudan couldn't wipe the smile from her face. 'We had best get this revolution out of the way swiftly then and get you home to Li Shan. Does Ji Fa know?' Hudan was suddenly concerned that he might be less than delighted.

'He does, and has had battle armour constructed for me,' she advised.

'That is well,' Hudan said, losing her joviality, 'as Su Daji has put out a shoot to kill order on white tigers within the Shang territories.'

Huxin's jaw immediately clenched. 'She'll never give another order once I lay eyes on her.'

'I will take care of Su Daji,' Hudan said, demanding her sister's attention. 'It is your job to protect Ji Fa and your cubs. I want you to be extra careful once we cross the Huang He.'

Huxin looked very reluctant to let go the idea of her own personal revenge.

'Daji's crimes against the animal kingdom pale by comparison to her crimes against humanity,' Hudan advised in a malevolent tone, but then softened her attitude. 'I too thought I hated her, but now I believe I pity her.'

'You pity that hag!' Huxin queried, incredulous.

'No one is born evil, Huxin.' Hudan repeated what their Shifu had always claimed. 'Events and experiences drive an individual to such extremes to protect themselves … the more evil the individual, the greater their trauma has been.'

Huxin was unmoved. 'Then let us put an end to her misery.' She smiled sweetly, raised her cup to Hudan and drank to that.

Hudan could only wish the solution would be so simple. *The end of Su Daji's troubles will mark the beginning of our own.*

Had their Shifu known what they'd be up against when she had entrusted them to complete this conquest? Or was Yi Wu's belief in them blind and ill-founded? Hudan had once considered that facing Su Daji would be the most daunting confrontation of her life! Now that battle felt like a tiny stepping stone on the path to a concealed mountain they had to conquer. Only Ji Dan and she were aware that the seemingly unscaleable pinnacle even existed and although it went against her usual solo nature Hudan was extremely grateful to have an ally and confidant. But after the previous night's misadventure outside the royal storehouse, she intended to keep more distance between herself and Ji Dan. Now that Fen was back to tutoring his lord, and she was no longer living under Ji Dan's roof, or under the premise of being 'gifted' to him, she was no longer required to constantly keep the lord's company.

Ironically, it was Ji Dan who arrived in Hudan's chamber to collect her. He was followed by two servants clutching the poles of a sedan chair, which they lowered to the ground.

'I am not riding in that.' Hudan leaned heavily on her staff to rise out of her seat.

'Only as far as your carriage,' Dan advised in good spirits. 'Unless, of course, you'd like me to carry you?'

'My carriage?' Hudan was annoyed. 'I am no princess bride! Wu ride on horseback or walk, as a man. A carriage will slow our passage '

'I advise you take up this issue with the Xibo,' Dan said, moving to assist her to the chair, and Hudan was agitated that she still needed his aid.

'Where is Fen … and Nuan?' she asked as a subtle protest to Dan taking hold of her free arm, yet it was a struggle for her to move her staff forward and maintain her balance. If she collapsed and the lord had to carry her to the seat, she'd have someone's head for it.

'Your family are in the courtyard preparing to depart, along with the rest of our party ... although they seem to be having a small disagreement over whether or not Nuan should be coming with us.'

'Best take me to the commotion.' Hudan was actually rather grateful to be seated, as Dan withdrew to a more comfortable distance.

There was an electric energy that danced between them every time the lord was close to her and the feeling it aroused in Hudan was far too delicious for her own peace of mind. The look of desire she'd seen in his face the previous evening made her heart leap into her throat each time it came to mind. All things considered, being transported around on a chair like a princess was preferable and more dignified than being carried about by his lordship — any thing that kept Ji Dan at a distance, was a blessing from Tian.

In the courtyard, Hudan took her objection to being carriage driven to Ji Fa, but the Xibo was adamant. 'You need rest, and my tigress cannot be expected to walk the entire distance in her condition.' Something Hudan had not considered. 'If you are strong enough to ride on horseback by week's end, we shall leave the carriage at Mengjin,' Ji Fa said to head off any more argument. 'Brother Dan, please see brother Hudan to her transport.' The Xibo bowed his head to her and swiftly departed.

'He'll be a formidable emperor, don't you think?' Dan directed Hudan's chair-men to convey her to a waiting carriage a little way off.

It did seem that the Xibo's command had a far more self-assured ring to it, she thought. 'Sister Hudan!' He Nuan's call drew Hudan's attention. She knew it was Nuan as she was the only person who ever openly called her sister.

'Please, I beg you to speak to Fen.' Nuan came to walk beside Hudan's chair. 'He is insisting that I stay at Haojing.'

'Brother Hudan,' Fen was hot on the heels of his betrothed. 'He Nuan is no longer Wu. And as my wife, I —'

'I am not your wife yet!' Nuan protested.

'War is no place for a woman!' Fen's comment gave Hudan pause; her young ward was starting to think like a man now.

'Other women are going!' Nuan pointed to a group of washerwomen and military whores.

'You are not jun ji,' Fen spluttered, angered by the suggestion. 'You are a lady of this house —'

'I would rather be a whore and be with you, than your legal wife forced to be apart,' Nuan retorted stubbornly.

'Enough!' Hudan decreed, as they reached her new carriage. Her seat was lowered to the ground. She looked at Nuan, who had returned her full attention to Hudan and waited breathlessly for her decision. 'Like it or not, dear sister, you placed yourself in Fen's charge when you agreed to marry him.'

The woman's eyes closed and her head bowed in pained defeat. 'But fear not …' Hudan felt sorry for any woman bound to do what a man told her. 'I have kept Fen Gong alive this long, and I give you my personal assurance he shall be well looked after.'

'I see.' He Nuan turned back to Fen, who appeared pleased he'd won the argument. 'Then I am left with no choice but to break our engagement.' Nuan backed away from Fen, who was completely mortified. 'I'll take my chances with the whores.' She strode off to join the cluster of females being herded onto a cart.

'No!' Fen looked to Hudan to appeal for help. 'She cannot do that.'

'He Nuan is free to do as she pleases,' Hudan informed him. She quietly admired the woman's guts and determination.

Fen looked at Dan. 'Any advice, lord?'

Dan was amused by the query. 'When it comes to women, brother Fen, I fear I am the last person to ask for advice.'

'Damn it!' Fen was at his wits' end and spinning in little circles he was so perturbed. 'I cannot allow her to ride with the jun ji. Other men might get the wrong impression.'

Hudan was finding it difficult to keep the grin from her face; she'd never seen her little brother so vexed. He Nuan could play him like a qin. 'You are the healer on this expedition. Take her as your assistant.

I dare say that in a war zone you will be grateful for all the help you can get.'

The relief that swept Fen's face was delightful, yet it was still tinged by concern. 'I would prefer she remain at Haojing, and out of harm's way.'

'I could have her put under house arrest until we have gone?' Dan suggested, as Fen moved off to retrieve his wife-to-be.

'That would only delay her pursuit,' Fen said, succumbing to defeat. 'Why fight the inevitable?'

As he charged off, Hudan noted the amusement on Dan's face. 'They go to such lengths to protect each other,' he explained, delighted. 'It must be love.'

The very mention of love from Dan made Hudan uncomfortable, and she swallowed hard to stay her nerves as he bent down to lift her from her chair and into the carriage.

'Dan!' Ji Shi came striding toward them. 'Ji Fa requests your presence a moment. I shall assist our honoured guest in your stead.'

'Someone is seeking an introduction,' Dan whispered, before he withdrew from her side. 'Shanyu Jiang Hudan, I do not believe you have been formally introduced to my brother, Ji Shi.'

'It is truly an honour.' The friendly young fellow bowed before her, eager to be of service, and Hudan breathed a quiet sigh of relief as Dan left them to attend to the Xibo.

'I recall seeing you the first day I arrived at Haojing,' Hudan said, making conversation as the young lord lifted her from her seat. 'You are the wild child of the family.'

Shi smiled at her impression of him. 'We must have something in common then, Tiger Courage?'

'I confess I do prefer the wilds,' she concurred, as he placed her inside the carriage.

The floor of her transport was flat, and it was padded so that Hudan could lie down in comfort. The carriage was completely screened on all sides, with doors that could be slid aside to permit some airflow, and a slanted roof to deflect rain and sun.

'I am most thankful to you, Ji Shi —' Hudan was saying, but as Shi withdrew she noted the large scar down his arm and she grabbed hold of his wrist to stay him — the memory of the white tiger being cut by her attacker on the jinzita passed fleetingly through her mind.

'That is a nasty knife wound you have there.' She looked at him and she saw a spark of recognition in his eyes. 'It was you?' she ventured in a whisper, immediately beholden to him and awestruck by the notion that he might be one of her sister's rare breed.

'I — I cut myself fishing.' The young lord pulled his hand from her grasp and covered the wound with his sleeve once more, unable to look her in the eyes. 'It is nothing to make a fuss about.' When Shi finally found the courage to look her in the face, his large brown eyes were appealing for mercy.

'We both know that is not true. I owe you a great debt and I would not betray you,' Hudan smiled, suspecting Shi hid a huge secret. 'Did you know my sister Jiang Huxin is pregnant?' If he was not the white tiger the statement would mean nothing to him; the shock, elation and horror that fought for precedence in his expression betrayed him.

'Shi!'

Hudan heard Dan call and he did not sound amused.

'May we speak again?' Shi asked, in a panic to leave.

'We must,' Hudan insisted, whereby the terrified lord ducked away through the commotion and was gone.

'Ji Fa was *not* looking for me.' Dan cast an annoyed gaze after his brother, but did not pursue him. 'I fear young Shi is up to mischief.'

'No doubt about it,' Hudan chuckled, but noting Dan's apprehensive expression she added, 'I think he is curious about my sister.'

Dan was mollified. 'It would not be the first time he'd shown an interest.'

This was news to Hudan 'How is that possible, when no one should even know she is here?'

'He does not know, not exactly,' Dan corrected her. 'Shi thought Huxin was you, or rather, You Ling. It was a comedy of errors that I can tell you en route to Mengjin, but I really should —' He motioned back to his horse.

'Yes, of course.' Hudan was thankful to be reminded she was trying to avoid his company, engaging as it was.

'I hope you manage to get some rest.' He waved as he moved off to join his brothers from Haojing and the other royal officials accompanying them to Mengjin.

Hardly. Hudan thought rest was going to be impossible, her mind had far too much information to process. Clearly Huxin had no idea that her lover walked amongst them, and it was not Hudan's place to enlighten her. Yet, what a miracle that two creatures so rare had managed to find each other. Hudan was sure the pair could not be immediately related, as Hudan and Huxin's mother had died giving birth to them, and Shi was younger than they were by several years. So what was his story? How had a shapeshifter been born into the royal family? Did anyone in the Ji family know Shi's secret? If the look of horror on his face just now was anything to go by, Hudan suspected not.

'Damn,' she murmured, annoyed to admit that she was already wishing to query Ji Dan about his family. *Stop finding excuses to associate with him,* she silently scolded herself, deciding to wait until Ji Shi found the opportunity to explain himself.

When Hudan caught herself admiring Dan on his horse, attired in battle fashion and armed, she began to close the door on her carriage. It was then that she noted the underlying war between her heart and her head, over whether she need deny herself the perfectly innocent pleasure of merely viewing him? *No more menial distractions.* Her head won the moment and she locked the door closed.

Hudan laid herself flat on her back to focus on more important matters, like working the atrophy from her body. The carriage was not quite tall enough to stand in, but Hudan didn't need to be erect to practise Dao Yin, and practise she would, every moment of every day until her confrontation with Su Daji — and the menace that lay beyond.

Hudan instructed her driver that she would take her meals in her carriage, and to advise anyone who might inquire, that she would be in retreat for several days and was not to be disturbed by anyone but her immediate family.

*

That night, once the camp had grown quiet, Hudan locked her carriage and focused the chi energy she'd managed to generate during the day on her intent to teleport herself to her Shifu. She hoped to discover how much Yi Wu knew about the Jade Book and its curse … having been around longer than she would disclose to anyone, surely the Great Mother must know something of the legend.

Despite her efforts, Hudan's will was not met, and she was forced to concede that her Wu powers were far more diminished than anticipated. This event begged the question — should she be attempting any psychic feats before the battle with the Shang, lest she further drain her energy reserves before the battle?

What if I cannot regain my powers in time? She felt the pressure of knowing that the defeat of the Shang depended entirely on her ability to combat Su Daji. *I should have listened to the Lord of the Elements.* He'd warned Hudan that she might never fully recover from such lengthy infirmity when her spirit form guided Weizi.

A few extra days would be more telling: she needed to give herself a better chance to recoup her strength. Yet, in the next thought, she considered trying to dream-walk to her Shifu, even though the chances were that the Great Mother would not see or hear her spirit form — for no one else had to date, except Ji Dan.

It was on the recommendation of the Lord of the Elements that Hudan had tested Dan's unrealised psychic talent. The lord had told her that Ji Dan, during his stint as a son of the sky, had been a seer of spirits and a glimpser of time eternal. Unlike Hudan who, in the main, perceived prophetic visions of events unfolding in her present lifetime, Ji Dan was said to have the underdeveloped ability to tap into the memories of his lives past and future. Where Hudan could free herself from her physical body and roam in her sleep, Ji Dan had the ability to perceive any such disembodied spirit, either living or deceased.

The Great Mother had always been very secretive about her abilities. Hudan could only hope that Yi Wu was as all-seeing and all-knowing as Hudan had always believed her to be.

219

It was a battle to keep her consciousness alert as it entered the corridor to sleep. *Shifu Yi, I need your wise counsel*, she repeated over and over in her mind, willing herself to find the Great Mother's private chambers at Yi Wu Li Shan waiting within the light at the end of the long dark passage.

Heart pounding with gentle excitement, she stared into the face of the son of the sky who graced her dreams from time to time. His large, wide eyes were as dark and deep as Ji Dan's, and his hair was just as dark and straight. The rest of his physical appearance was altogether different, as hers was — for her long hair was the colour of sunshine and fell about a more fair-skinned form.

This vision was always the same. He is standing in the doorway of the round windowless room of her sleeping quarters, requesting entry.

'What if this was our last night together? Tomorrow we may be leading completely different lives.' His words and expression are most compelling. *'If I can't make the time jump with the rest of you, I'll be left be—'*

She silences him with a kiss that sends her senses reeling. *'If you can make the jump or you can't, your soul-mind is there, Rhun said so.'* she reassures him, although she also holds concerns for their future. *'But what if we are enemies?'* The notion fills her with panic.

'That's never been the way of it before,' he reasons, *'and right now, we have no such impediment, so …'*

His smile is disarming, and she allows him to back her up into the chamber, and with a mere touch to the plate by the door, it closes to shut them inside, alone.

'The last time you left me, I knew you would not forget about us,' he says, as his lips caress her neck and his hands strip the clothes from her body. *'This time there are no guarantees.'*

'We have an eternal attraction,' she replies, feverishly, as his hands find her bare skin and she delights in his touch. *'Despite race, time, place … I shall always know you.'*

Since Hudan had chosen to go into isolation yesterday, Dan bunked down close to her carriage, in the hope that she might change her mind and wish to talk about their recent discoveries and a battle strategy.

In addition, he'd been wanting to thank Hudan for his new perspective on the past; her counsel had lifted a great burden from his shoulders and he was no longer carrying the guilt of his father's death. Dan felt a lightness in his heart that he'd not experienced in a very long time. He dreamed of his time among the sons of the sky and awoke in a fevered sweat. He could still hear her blissful groans as she repeated his name over and over: '*Lu Chen … Lu Chen … ahh … mmm … yes …*'

Dan was startled to realise that he *could* still hear her pleasure, and it was coming from inside Jiang Hudan's carriage! The sound of her ecstasy was deeply stirring to his blood and had given rise to an intense erection, which was thankfully concealed beneath layers of clothes and armour. Still, to hear his private guilty pleasure unfolding in the carriage without him was very disconcerting, and to further his dismay, Hudan's transport suddenly began to move out of the camp.

The lord was on his feet and scampering through the camp after the wagon before he was fully awake. He was thankful to note that he seemed to be the only person in camp to have been aroused by the disturbance, until he spotted Fen leading the horses of the carriage away from the camp, and a cloaked Jiang Huxin, in human form, beside him.

'What is going on?' Dan beseeched his brothers, suppressing his dismay.

'Nothing to worry about.' Huxin was alarmed by his presence, and immediately came to confront him and direct him back to bed. 'It is nothing but a prophetic dream. My sister has them now and then.'

Were they having the same prophetic dream? Dan didn't know whether to be horrified or delighted. 'There is no one in there with her?'

'No, I assure you,' Huxin insisted, while the sound of her sister's groans of rapture nearly drowned her out. 'And before you ask, I have no idea who Lu Chen is.'

I do, Dan thought to himself, and he wondered if the name Tar-rin would mean anything to Hudan?

'My sister claims he is a son of the sky.' Huxin forced the lord to stay put as the carriage moved away. 'However, I do not pretend to understand Hudan's spirit world affairs.'

'They certainly sound very pleasurable.' Dan suppressed a grin. Although the night was dark, the fires burned low and visibility was minimal. Huxin had better than average eyesight in the dark.

'We'll take her carriage away from the camp so as to cause no further disturbance.' Jiang Huxin turned to leave and Dan waylaid her. 'Someone will have to stand g—'

'I shall stand guard,' she insisted.

'You must protect the Xibo.'

'Fen will —'

'Fen has no authority,' he interjected again, 'and is not known among the men.'

Huxin was frustrated. 'You are the last person my brother will want bearing witness to this episode —'

'Why the last?' Dan found her opinion most curious.

Huxin was offended. 'Because Hudan respects you, and would not wish to be so indisposed in your presence. It will be embarrassing to her.'

'No more embarrassing that it is for me,' he confessed quietly. 'I have had the same dream, and I believe I know who Lu Chen is.'

Huxin was very agitated to hear this, but considered the circumstances carefully. 'If that is true, such an event must be of Tian's design.'

'I agree.' Dan could not imagine why their shared vision should be so sensual in nature though. Until tonight, he'd assumed it was just his own repressed sexual desire that had been at the root of this reoccurring dream, but if Hudan was having the same dream, patently there was more meaning to the vision than was evident. Unless, of course, Hudan had somehow tapped into his most private thoughts? Whatever the truth of the matter was, he needed to know it. 'At present, I fail to see the purpose in heaven tormenting us in this manner.'

'It does seem rather cruel,' Huxin warranted, appearing sympathetic. 'Come relieve my watch in an hour, the commotion should have died down by then.'

'Thank you,' Dan said, grateful for the assignment, certain that he would not sleep again tonight. 'I promise I shall be as diplomatic with our brother as I can be.'

'I do not doubt it.' She backed away, regarding him fondly, before she turned and swiftly left the campsite.

The next morning, Hudan felt completely revitalised as she stretched the kinks from her body and there followed the momentary disappointment of having failed to keep conscious control of her spirit form during sleep. A talk with her Shifu would have been most reassuring at this point in time. Her thoughts returned to where her subconscious had taken her during the night and Hudan smiled with delight — until her rational mind reminded her that Lu Chen and Ji Dan were one in spirit.

'Merciful heaven!' she gasped, and sat up. 'Why test me so?' she complained, then noted the silence beyond her carriage.

Unbolting the door, she slid it aside. Hudan was surprised to find her transport was not where she had left it before retiring the previous evening. Morning was well under way, under cloud and drizzle, and there was not a soul to be seen in the vicinity. 'Have I been left behind?'

The sound of movement in the driver's seat of the carriage assured her that she had not been entirely abandoned, yet it was a huge shock when Ji Dan jumped down to the ground and into her view.

'Good morning.' He greeted her with a strange tinge of irony in his voice, but then he was sopping wet.

'Where is the rest of our party?' She was mortified by the thought of being left alone in Dan's company — avoiding him was seemingly impossible! 'Why did you allow me to oversleep?'

The lord was not upset by her anger, but seemed rather amused as he raised a brow to advise: 'You were having a prophetic dream that brother Huxin advised was not to be interrupted ... a dream about *Lu Chen*,' he concluded, in a questioning fashion.

The news was quietly horrifying. Hudan had been informed previously, by her brothers, of how physically impassioned she would become during such dreams and how she would repeat her dream lover's name over and over. Still, that was not the only reason she felt ashamed on this occasion; she had told Dan an outright lie, of which he was clearly aware. Hudan could not bring herself to look at him.

'You claimed to know nothing of Lu Chen?' There was more hurt than accusation in his voice.

'All I know is that he is a son of the sky, who comes to me in my dreams sometimes. I have told our Shifu about the reoccurring episode, but she tells me I must put it from my mind for now as it pertains to a quest that I shall not embark on for some time yet.'

'I have had the same dream.'

Dan's claim drew Hudan's full attention and, although his expression was deadly serious, she could not believe it.

'Tar-rin,' he said.

His proof shocked Hudan into backing away from him, and now that she had made way, Dan stole the opportunity to sit inside the carriage out of the rain. 'I take it you know this name?'

There seemed no point in denying it. 'I believe it was once my name,' she admitted. 'Lu Chen was her lover.'

'And I was Lu Chen,' he concluded.

'Hence why I denied knowing the lord,' Hudan defended, 'for the conundrum is a trivial matter compared with the concerns of Ji Fa's revolution.'

'But there are no accidents; you said so yourself.' The look on his face was ardent. 'Why would heaven throw such a torment in our path, if we were not meant to, in some way, profit by it?'

Hudan was unsure if he was being reasonable or flirtatious. 'I have wondered the same thing myself, and am at a loss to explain it. I set out last night to spirit walk to the Great Mother, but I am weak and simply fell asleep. I fear my powers are so diminished that I may not recover them in time to face Su Daji.'

Dan was very alarmed to hear this. 'You must practise Dao Yin.'

'That is why I shut myself away,' Hudan clarified. 'I was hoping to build enough chi to relocate my physical form to a meeting with Yi Wu, but I failed to even convey my spirit form to her.' Hudan shrugged, trying to maintain her composure and not panic. 'Right now, I do not possess enough chi energy to exert my will over anything!'

She focused on a hair comb lying on her bed and willed it to her. It was a rude shock when the item flew into her grasp.

'I could not do that yesterday! One night's rest is not normally so beneficial,' Hudan murmured, perplexed. She looked at Dan, who was grinning.

'Did you not explain to me once how a person's chi energy can be greatly enhanced by proper sexual congress?'

'Of course!' Hudan was elated to comprehend. 'I was not being tested, but actually being aided.' Waves of relief swept over her, and she looked at Dan, most grateful for his understanding. 'That is a relief, thank you.'

'You lifted a great burden from my soul yesterday, so let's call it even.' He sounded deflated by this outcome, and looked to the rainy day beyond the open door of the carriage. 'Perhaps I am being aided by the torment also?'

The sound of the rain on the roof seemed amplified by their silence, and the good will that had been welling in her heart suddenly sank into the pit of Hudan's stomach as she realised she had hurt him. 'I am sorry that I told you about our kiss, Dan.'

He looked at her, his eyes wide and expectant. 'I am not.'

Hudan knew the lord had been waiting for her to raise the subject. Outside the Ji family storehouse in Haojing, when they'd found themselves entranced with each other, she'd seen the question 'is this it?' in his eyes. 'I fear I might have given you the wrong impression —'

'No —' he insisted.

'Or false hope that I might ever be able to offer you anything more than that one prophesied kiss.' Hudan wanted to get this out in the open and over with; they were both losing sight of their goal. 'I only told you because I didn't want you to think I was going to perish in the fire. But it was never my intention to torment you.'

Treating Dan like an inanimate object had worked fine in the beginning, but he was an intelligent man, who Hudan had come to respect above all others on this quest. He had never been anything but courteous and forthright with her, and she felt that he deserved the same from her.

'It was not my intention to imply that you have caused me torment,' he told her. 'Any torment I have experienced, I chose. You have never acted in a manner that would lead me to believe that there is anything more than a professional relationship between us … and therein lies *my* torment.' He swallowed hard on the confession and bowed his head. 'Not your fault.'

The subject matter was awkward and Hudan diverted her gaze also, not wishing to see his reaction. 'My vow to Tian forbids me to tell you what you want to hear … or to even admit it to myself.' The truth of her words brought tears to her eyes, and she caught her breath. 'My plan was to avoid you as much as possible …' Hudan looked up to find Dan appearing just as she'd imagined: stunned, vindicated, apologetic. 'But as my co-conspirator in all this, that would not be very beneficial to our cause.'

Dan shook his head to agree.

'Whatever the meaning behind the dream we share, it could not be as pressing as this war and its repercussions. So can we not put the mysteries of the sons of the sky aside, until Ji Fa's rule has been secured and our larger challenges are behind us?' she appealed. 'Issues of the heart baffle me, and undermine my confidence —'

'I understand.' Dan held up both palms, content in a weird kind of way.

'No, I don't think you do,' Hudan averred, moving closer to him. 'I feel more akin to you than to my own family.' She could barely speak the words for the emotion choking her. 'You are my *best* friend. I know that is not what you wish for, but it is the very highest honour I have to give.'

Teary-eyed, Dan gently took hold of one of Hudan's hands with both his own. Unaccustomed to being touched and as uncomfortable as it made her, Hudan did not pull away. 'I will never have any greater aspiration than that,' he said quietly.

She found his pledge endearing, even though she knew it was a fib — even she could not make the same claim and be telling the whole truth. 'Only you have the power to disarm me, my friend.'

The lord closed his eyes to process her admission in his mind, seeming gratified and pained by it. 'Like outside the storehouse?' He opened his eyes as she squeezed his hand to confirm.

'I have never truly been afraid of any challenge placed in my path, but I was more fearful of you in that moment than I am of Dragonface, Su Daji and the entire Shang army.' It felt wonderful to be speaking the truth to him, rather than trying to hide behind a façade of indifference.

'*No, please.*' He was shocked. 'If I have done anything to make you doubt my vow to your house —'

'You have not,' Hudan insisted. 'Perhaps I should have said, I was afraid of myself more than of you.'

A flash of astonished relief crossed his face, but was quickly swallowed by concern once more. 'The Great Mother warned me before we left Li Shan that I could become a distraction to you, or be your greatest ally.'

'Yi Wu told you that?' The fact was confronting. 'She *knew.*' Hudan was rather devastated that the Great Mother had given her no such caution.

'It was the main reason she agreed to my admission to your order, as she felt my vow to her would prevent any issue between us, and it has.' The statement was as flat as his mood, but then he perked up. 'I am resolved to be your ally, I promise you. The last thing I wish is to cause you any more distress. But I have been wanting to solve the conundrum of that dream for many years, so I naturally —'

'Many years?' Hudan queried. 'How many?'

Dan had a think about that. 'For as long as I can remember, really,' he replied with a shrug.

'Me too.' Hudan slipped her hand from his and took a seat beside him, rather overwhelmed by everything that had come to light.

'Who is Hreen, do you think?' Dan asked, which reminded Hudan that Tar-rin always mentioned him in the dream.

'I asked the Lord of the Elements the same question, and he avoided it,' Hudan advised. 'But I suspect that he might be the dark-haired time lord I told you about.'

'It would make sense that a lord of time would be aware of my spirit's comings and goings throughout history.'

'The Lord of the Elements claimed that you yourself possess the ability to tap into your previous and forthcoming lifetimes.'

Dan was a little rattled by that assertion. 'I've never heard of such an ability.'

'Akashic memory, he called it.'

'I have seen many other fragments of Lu Chen's life,' Dan mentioned.

'I have seen very little,' Hudan announced, 'but then I was advised that you would remember more than me, because of your talent.'

'Did your elemental lord mention *why* we remember our lifetime among them?'

'No,' Hudan was sorry to disappoint him, 'although he did seem extremely proud that you were remembering your life as Lu Chen.'

'But why should a memory of a past life have a bearing on a future quest?'

'I have never understood it, either, and Shifu Yi will not explain,' Hudan replied, frustrated by the mystery. 'Yet, I cannot help but feel Dragonface has something to do with it.'

'Do you think the Great Mother knows about him, um, it … them?'

'I would stake my life on it,' Hudan warranted. 'What I don't understand is why she did not forewarn us of the curse?'

Dan bit his lip, as he eyed off the weather. 'We are no so far afield from Li Shan, you know …'

The notion of sidetracking was appealing. 'That would put us a day behind the rest of our party. I could attempt to psychically relocate us to the House of Yi Wu.'

'You should not risk draining your chi again —' Dan suppressed a grin and bit his tongue a moment, before suggesting. 'Better to be late at the armies' rallying point and better to take the carriage … Ji Fa will not cross the Huang He without us.'

They stared at each other as they weighed up their options, and Hudan gave the deciding nod. 'Even if we learn nothing, we shall be no worse off.'

With a nod to concur and a gratified smile, Dan exited into the rain, with the aim of getting them to Li Shan before noon.

Shifu Yi was sincerely surprised to be greeting them that afternoon. 'Should you not be marching to Mengjin with Ji Fa?' Yi Wu asked from her cushioned chair. 'Or have the people of the East run to our rain, and the war is over?'

'If only our victory was to be so easy,' Hudan replied, as she knelt beside Ji Dan in their Shifu's presence.

'You sound troubled, Jiang Hudan. Yet, you have done this house proud since your departure. What has happened that is so very grave?' Yi Wu asked, and gave Dan a thoughtful look.

Hudan knew what the Great Mother was thinking and was quick to divert her. 'What do you know about Dragonface and the Jade Book?'

Yi Wu's face paled, and she motioned for them both to rise. 'You have seen the reptilian and his minions?'

'During the yin rite, the lord of the elemental realms spirited me to Zi Shou's capital at Yin, so that I should witness the lewdness and torture taking place.' Hudan felt sickened by the memory. 'And I swear to you, I thought I had been brought forth to one of the lowest levels in diyu.'

Both Dan and the Great Mother were grieved to hear her recount the experience, as Hudan physically shuddered to recall it.

'There is a great walled pit in the gardens at Yin that contains uncountable skeletal remains of our country's men, women and children. These are the remains of the lucky ones who perish in the fall into the pit. But, should you survive ...' Hudan stared at her Shifu, filled with trepidation. 'Dragonface has a device that sucks the life out of you ... and if you are female, he'll defile you first.'

'Brother Hudan, I'm sorry ...' Dan was horrified that she'd borne witness to such terrible sights.

'This creature, Dragonface, is double brother Dan's height. He stimulates the victim's fear and pain, and then feeds on it by sucking the vital fluids straight out of his victim's brain.'

'Come …' Yi Wu rose to escort her student to a seat, as it was plain that Hudan had been traumatised by what she had witnessed and was going into delayed shock.

'Please,' Hudan resisted the move. 'I do not wish to rest, I need answers!'

'And you shall have them,' Yi Wu advised sternly. 'Once you have both eaten.'

'There is no time,' Hudan objected as she was plonked onto a cushion by her Shifu and Dan.

'Oh, but there is.' Yi Wu seated herself, while Dan poured Hudan a glass of water from the pitcher on the table close by him. He passed the refreshment to the Great Mother, who in turn offered it to Hudan. 'It is clear to me that your energy has been severely diminished by your recent trials. A week's recuperation under my care should have you good as new and able to psychically relocate your physical form to the mustering point at Mengjin before Ji Fa even arrives.'

Hudan drew a deeply relieved breath. 'You are very wise, Great Mother.' Spending a week in isolation on Li Shan was a dream come true — nothing would heal her faster.

'And me?' Dan queried the sudden change in plans.

'You shall leave first thing tomorrow to catch up with Ji Fa and advise him that brother Hudan will be awaiting him at Mengjin,' she instructed.

'As you wish, Shifu.' Dan poured himself a glass of water to hide his disappointment, but if Hudan failed to notice his changed mood, the Great Mother certainly sensed it. A break from each other for a week might be exactly what they both needed to regain their perspective.

The Great Mother left Dan and Hudan to eat their meal in her private audience chamber.

To sit and admire the tranquillity of the misty mountainside beyond the open windows was a vast contrast to their recent trials and travels. Here on Li Shan it was hard to believe that the entire land was not at peace. But from what Hudan had reported of the Shang capital at Yin, it seemed nothing could be further from the truth and she had been through infinitely more of an ordeal during her spiritual retreat after the yin rite than he could have possibly imagined. As Hudan had, however, only just calmed down from discussing that subject, Dan did not think it wise to raise the topic again.

'Does our Shifu ever eat?' Dan asked cordially, as Hudan had gone very quiet.

'No.' She forced a smile, seeming thankful for the light conversation. 'Yi Wu has reached a state of Xian, and needs only water and the divine light of her own chi to sustain her … although she is very found of her tea, as you know.'

'How old is she?' Dan asked, curious about Yi Wu. As Hudan appeared somewhat taken aback by the question, he decided he should outline what he knew already. 'My grandfather was said to be the only man to have seen the Great Mother and lived to tell of it and on more than one occasion. He spoke of her as a beautiful contemporary who never aged a day!'

'I have heard Yi Wu speak of her time in the service of the Yellow Emperor,' Hudan offered, and Dan felt she must be joking.

'That would make her over fifteen hundred years old,' he said, thinking it was an extravagant claim.

'I am actually much older.' The Great Mother drew their attention to her presence in the room. 'We are all eternal, but I am in complete alignment with my spirit and you are not, as yet.' She came and sat at the table with them as Dan consumed his last dumpling and pushed his plate aside.

'That sustenance was most needed, Shifu Yi, I thank you.' He was embarrassed to have been caught out inquiring after her age, as for most women it was a taboo subject.

'You are most welcome.' She smiled graciously.

Hudan had pushed aside her half-eaten meal and looked to the Great Mother expectantly. 'Please tell us what you know about the Jade Book. Does it belong to Dragonface?'

'No,' Yi Wu replied calmly. 'It originally belonged to the Yellow Emperor —'

'Huang Di, the first name listed in the Jade Book,' Dan noted, having read the book more thoroughly than Hudan.

'Yes,' Yi Wu replied, confirming his observation. 'The Jade Book was stolen from his summer palace by the creature who later became known as Dragonface. The reptilian then used the text to locate and control every ruler who came after.'

'As you theorised,' Hudan commented, awarding Dan his due, but he was still puzzled.

'Then how did the treasure end up in the Ji family storehouse?' he wondered.

'The Jade Book was stolen during the rule of Huang Di's great-grandson, Di Ku, and it was from his grandfather, Shaohao that the Ji family are descended. The book was then recovered by Shun of Yu, who banished me from royal service.'

'But how did Shun of Yu deal with the curse of Dragonface and become such a beloved ruler? His reign lasted one hundred years.'

'An unnaturally long amount of time for any mortal ruler, don't you think?' their Shifu pointed out. 'Dragonface and his ilk have the ability to shapeshift and assume the form of those they have killed. But I suspect it is not comfortable for them to maintain the disguise and thus it is more convenient to control our emperors rather than assume their role.'

'How do you know this?' Hudan was dismayed. It would be very easy for the creature to slip through their fingers.

'We have been forced to deal with his like during our lifetimes on this earth, both past and future.'

'What?' Hudan had clearly never heard her Shifu speak this way.

Yi Wu nodded to confirm they'd heard her correctly. 'Dragonface is older than I am, and is extremely intelligent. He originated during the time of the *forefathers* of the sons of the sky, and he has seen the rise and fall of many a great civilisation. In the case of our lands, since the time of Shun of Yu it has been the case that the more obliging a ruler was to Dragonface the more information he would garner from the creature and the greater the advancements that would be seen during that emperor's reign. I was later to surmise that the emperors who died quickly, before ascending to the throne or just after, were those who attempted to oppose the curse of being named in the Jade Book.'

Hudan was appearing decidedly ill suddenly.

'Are you feeling poorly?' Dan asked, having expected the meal would perk her up a little.

'I am fine,' she muttered, her troubled gaze resting upon the Great Mother, who shook her head slightly.

'Do you both know something I do not?'

'No,' Hudan looked back at Dan to reassure him. 'I was just thinking it a shame that our good-hearted rulers never stand a chance.'

'We shall change that, starting with Ji Fa.' He was confident, and Hudan forced a smile to agree.

'So what happened to the Jade Book after Shun of Yu passed?' Dan endeavoured to steer the conversation back to the matter at hand.

'During the last, dark days of the Xia dynasty,' Yi Wu recounted, 'when the people rebelled — under circumstances very similar to those unfolding as we speak — I supported the rebellion of Cheng Tang, and my price was the return of the Jade Book to my safekeeping.'

'Return?' Dan quoted her. 'You had been its keeper before?'

'Huang Di entrusted it to me, as I was the author.'

Hudan and Dan both gasped at once. '*You* were?'

The Great Mother nodded. 'It wasn't until I went to claim the treasure back that I confronted the creature who had stolen the Jade Book from me and used it to curse our land.' Shifu Yi appeared embittered by the fact. 'I meant only to establish a clear line of rulership and avoid much of the bloodshed I had seen during my travels through time ...'

Were his eyes playing tricks on him? For Dan could see the ghostly imprint of an old man interpenetrating the Great Mother's much younger form, then he watched in amazement as the spirit of the old man regressed into a youth, younger, and very fair — akin to the sons of the sky.

'What is it?' Yi Wu queried his distraction.

'I'm sure it is nothing.' Dan gave his eyes a rub, but the impression of the young man was still as clear as Yi Wu herself. 'I mean no offence, Great Mother, but I see both the spirit of an old man and one much younger in you.' He felt rather silly stating the observation. 'And they appear to my eyes like sons of the sky.'

'Really?' Hudan was diverted, excited for Dan.

Yi Wu was smiling broadly, as was the young male spirit within her. 'Hello, Lucian.'

The mention of the name made both Hudan and Dan gasp.

'You are one of them?' Dan concluded, and Hudan was surprised again when her Shifu nodded.

'I was wondering how long it would take for your talent to develop to the point where you might perceive me,' Yi Wu and her young male inner-spirit stated calmly.

It was then Dan recognised the young man from one of his dreams 'They call you Tel Mo.'

'And Taliesin in the life before that. We have had many lives, and faced many a peril, together.'

Dan looked at Hudan, who was completely astounded, and then back to the young male spirit speaking through Yi Wu. 'Why are you here?'

'To guide you, as I have been,' their Shifu advised, 'until we could locate the whereabouts of the reptilian we came here to deal with. Not even I realised that Dragonface was back influencing the emperors ... I should have known better.'

'But you have confronted the creature before and obviously triumphed,' Hudan pointed out; otherwise her Shifu would not be here.

'Dragonface has no supernatural power of his own, but he has dabbled in the dark arts and has come to know many demons by name, having personally created more than a few hateful entities during his time on this earth. I suspect this knowledge, and his ability to shapeshift, aided him to escape my wrath, but I had not heard of, or seen him, in the seven hundred years since.'

'Pardon me, Shifu, but that still does not explain how the Jade Book ended up in our family storehouse?'

'There was a time when your grandfather was being encouraged to lead an uprising against the Shang. I was very fond of Ji Danfu and, having written the Jade Book, I knew the quest would be fruitless, so I gave the Jade Book to him and the Ji family to convince Danfu to desist and to help guide the long rule of your family so that the Zhou dynasty would eventually rule.'

Stunned, and minds on information overload, Hudan and Dan paused from their interrogation to think. But there was also something Hudan had to know.

'Great Mother,' Hudan said hesitatingly, formulating her query carefully. 'Brother Dan and I have had the same dream about our time among the sons of the sky, and we wonder why it is so sensual and personal in nature?'

Dan looked at Hudan, grateful for her tenacity and asking the question he could not ask without seeming untoward.

'You think Tian is trying to test you?' their Shifu posed, whereby they both nodded. 'It is simply the last memory you both share of that lifetime.'

'That explains why she kept repeating my name —' Dan muttered to himself, entranced by the recollection.

'— so she would not forget it.' Hudan looked at Dan across the table, with conflict and panic in her eyes.

'It is unfortunate that that has been the way of it, but it cannot be helped now,' Shifu Yi spoke up to calm them both, a slight reproof in her tone. 'I told you both to sleep that evening; it is not my fault you did not listen. Yes, Lucian and Taren were lovers … husband and wife, *in fact*. But that was another life and time, which you will revisit in due course; provided you do not allow the past to intrude into the present. You must accomplish what your incarnations were put on the earth *at this time* to do.'

Hudan's frown was as deep as Dan's at this point. 'I'm afraid you have lost me, Great Mother.'

'You cannot not allow this dream to influence your lives now.' Yi Wu stated more clearly. 'Our souls are embroiled in a rescue mission of intergalactic proportions and personal feelings cannot enter into it. If you do not want to ruin the prospects of the greatest dynasty this land will ever see, then you will focus on your lives as Shanyu Jiang Hudan and Zhou Gong Dan, until your days in this life are done.'

'Zhou Gong Dan.' He repeated the Great Mother's slip of the tongue — the title sounded so strange and daunting. 'How long do I live?' He knew the Great Mother would know, and he also knew that with such responsibility to the state, his days among the Wu were numbered.

'Quite some time yet,' Yi Wu advised. 'Such greatness as you shall achieve is never built in a short season.'

He felt ill, as the crushing reality that Hudan would be taken from him one way or another hit home.

'I know this must seem a hard and cruel cross to bear,' she advised, 'but this life is short compared to what lies beyond. I too have foregone love to pursue this quest for the greater good. Tian asks no more of you than he has asked of any son of the sky who has returned to this place and time to pursue the reptilian.'

'How many of us are there?' Dan asked, obviously more surprised by this news than Hudan.

'More than a handful, less than an army, but all talented and pure of heart,' Yi Wu concluded. 'And I shall say no more on that matter until the Ji family rule our land.'

A heavy silence fell as the questions ran out, leaving many conflicting thoughts and mixed emotions in their wake.

'You both appear in need of rest,' their hostess suggested, and Dan was more than content to end the discussion.

'A turn in your garden would be most welcome.' Dan stood, as he suddenly felt like he was going to suffocate on the emotion he was suppressing. 'If you'll excuse me, I know the way.' He left to be with his own thoughts.

1 0

THE ROAD TO MENGJIN

In the company of his brothers, Wu and Zhenduo, Shi had been maintaining a low profile during the ride to Mengjin. All the while, his conscience gnawed on the fact that the great tigress, Jiang Huxin, was carrying his offspring.

He should never have sought to meet Jiang Hudan, but he'd always been fascinated by the Wu, especially the tales of Shanyu Jiang Huxin as, from all reports, she was a shapeshifter, as he was. But his desire to know more about Jiang Hudan's sister had led to the knowledge that he was in so much more trouble with Tian than he could have possibly imagined, and worse than this, Jiang Hudan knew of his transgression ... or, at the very least, strongly suspected.

Yet Shi could not suppress the pride that kept filling his heart to bursting point every time he considered that the most beautiful creature he'd ever seen would be secretly bonded to him henceforth. His were-tiger legacy, unknown to all, would live on through their progeny. Their brood would not be forced into hiding as he had been, but rise to greatness through the guidance of the Wu, just as their mother had — he could not have hoped for a better life for his children. For in truth, he'd never expected to have a family, and would not contemplate inflicting such a birth on an earthly woman. But Jiang Huxin was designed to carry his seed, and if he died for that honour, he would die a happy man.

'You're very quiet, Shi,' Wu noted, as they made camp for the night.

'And still!' Zhenduo emphasised. 'We've been here a full hour and you haven't disappeared into the forest yet. Are you ill?'

'No.' Shi forced a smile to reassure them.

'The only other time you're this tame is when you're in trouble,' Wu jeered at him, and the suggestion rattled Shi a little, and Wu — perceptive like Dan — noted it at once. 'Are you in trouble?'

'No,' he swore, wishing he'd stated that with more conviction.

'Ji Shi!'

The brothers all looked to Dan's new ward, Fen, who announced: 'The Xibo is requesting to speak with you at once.'

'Are you quite sure you're not keeping something from us, brother?' Wu gave him one last chance to speak, as being brother number nine it was seldom that Shi was summoned without his older brothers. 'Fa's tigress eats liars, you know?'

'I am completely loyal to our brother and have nothing to fear,' he told Wu and Zhenduo, but inwardly Shi was unnerved. Of course Jiang Huxin would detect any falsehood, and with far more ease than he could most likely.

On approach to the entrance of the Xibo's tent, Shi pushed any speculation from his mind to focus solely on his Xibo's concerns, but as he entered behind Fen he saw Jiang Huxin wearing her lovely human persona. His heart leapt into his throat and he stopped breathing.

'We meet again, Ji Shi,' she said, smiling at his dazed expression.

There she stood, no trace of her condition evident in her slender figure. Only a radiant glow on her skin and hair, and a soft contentedness in her demeanour, betrayed the truth of what Jiang Hudan had told him.

'Jiang Huxin.' He drew breath to bow to her and his Xibo.

'You two have met?' Ji Fa was surprised to hear this.

'Ji Shi mistook me for You Ling one evening.' Huxin explained and the Xibo calmed. The tigress cast her sights back to Shi. 'But now you know who I truly am,' she noted.

'The revelation dawned on me recently,' he thought it fair to say. 'I apologise for any offence I may have caused you in my ignorance.'

'Offence?' the Xibo asked, worried, but the tigress pacified him with a gentle touch on the shoulder.

'Ji Shi tried to save me from his tigers one evening,' she told him with some amusement.

'Oh, I see.' Ji Fa found the idea laughable and Shi saw the humour also, happy for the jovial mood. He didn't sense that he was in trouble, just yet. 'I have an errand for you, Shi,' his brother stated. 'As you may have noted Dan and the caravan containing Jiang Hudan have still not joined us. Backtrack to where we left them and if you fail to find them, go to Li Shan.'

Shi tried not to look anxious at the thought of carrying out this instruction.

'I feel my sister may have wished to see the Great Mother, and sidetracked to Li Shan in order to do so,' Jiang Huxin explained.

'But why ask me to go?' Shi wondered why he'd been singled out.

'I cannot send any of the Wu I have with me ... brothers Huxin and Fen are indispensable at present, and He Nuan will not be allowed entry,' the Xibo clarified. 'Chances are you shall find our brothers between here and the House of Yi Wu Li Shan, but if you must light the torches and request a meeting with the Wu, Jiang Huxin feels that, amongst our present company, it is you that the Great Mother will find most pleasing.'

Shi didn't know what to say. He was terrified at the thought of meeting personally with the Great Mother and attempting to hide his guilt from her. 'It is a great honour that a legend would think of me so highly.'

'Yes, it *is*,' agreed the Xibo, with a good serving of suspicion. 'So be sure and live up to our expectations of you. Find our missing brothers and bring them back to us. If I do not see you before Mengjin, I shall await you there.'

'I will not fail you in this,' Shi vowed, and was dismissed.

As he headed for the tent flap, Shi felt his nerves fluttering in his gut and he thought he might be sick.

'Ji Shi!' the tigress called, and his stomach churned a little more as he heard her approaching to speak with him. 'You should not fear the Great Mother so,' she advised with a reassuring smile as she reached him. 'Shifu Yi is wise and just.'

That is what I fear. Clearly, the tigress had picked up on his dread of meeting her Shifu, but thankfully the tigress was not telepathic, or she would already know the reason why he wished to avoid such a meeting. 'I trust your word in all things,' Shi managed to say and kept going, eager to ride solo for a while and escape the prying gaze of everyone — his heart's desire included.

All the way to the Li Shan ferry Shi prayed to Tian and his ancestors to release him from the obligation to meet with Yi Wu. He felt that if his plea was answered and the meeting was avoided, then that was a sign that heaven had forgiven him.

But as the torches burned and the ferry approached across the dark misty surface of the lake, Shi held little hope that he was going to escape the wrath of the Wu this night.

A woman hooded in white led him on board the ferry, and eight dark hooded others stood at attention around him. The ferry moved back across the lake at a steady even pace, in utter silence, and without any physical effort on behalf of the occupants. The others ducked low, suddenly, and he was urged down with them, then their vessel floated into the mountain.

Inside the cavern was a dock, and when Shi spotted his brother Dan awaiting him, he couldn't cease silently praising his ancestors — he'd never been so relieved to see anyone in all his born days. 'Thank Tian I found you!'

'I was not lost,' Dan assured him, sounding slightly annoyed. 'Just delayed.'

'I should return at once and inform our Xibo,' Shi suggested, looking ready to jump back into the ferry, but his travelling companions flew onto the dock and departed via a stairway in the rock wall.

'I believe the ferry service is closed for the evening. Looks like you'll have to stay the night.' Dan grinned at Shi's apparent discomfort.

'I could swim back,' Shi said desperately, eyeing the distance, as he was a fairly good swimmer, but Dan laughed off the suggestion.

'The Wu won't eat you, you realise. You'll be perfectly safe.' Dan grabbed his shoulders and directed him toward the stairs.

'Now that I have found you, there is really no need for me to meet with the Great Mother,' Shi reasoned, taking small steps.

'Of course not,' Dan agreed. 'The Great Mother does not meet with any man without good reason.'

'And there is no reason for her to be interested in me?' Shi proffered.

'And why is there a question in your voice?'

'I don't claim to know the will of heaven,' Shi grinned, relieved, and Dan decided he could not be bothered pursuing the matter.

'I am returning to our Xibo's party first thing on the morrow. You can leave with me,' Dan advised, as he began to scale the stairs.

'And Jiang Hudan?' Shi asked after his other charge.

'She will be waiting for us at Mengjin.' Shi thought Dan sounded slightly agitated.

'Waiting for us …' Shi noted the wording. 'Has she left already?' he asked, wondering if he'd missed her en route, but didn't imagine that Dan would have allowed the Wu to ride off alone.

'No more questions, Shi.' Dan stopped abruptly as they reached the fresh air of the open cloister. 'Actually, I have a question for you. Why did you need to speak with Jiang Hudan alone, just before we left Haojing?'

'Like you, I am curious about the Wu,' Shi shrugged, hoping that would be the end of it.

'Well, I would have introduced you, if you'd asked,' Dan lectured. 'You didn't have to send me on a false errand so that you could speak with her *alone*.'

'You've made that point several times.' Shi hadn't realised just how possessive Dan had become. 'You sound like a jealous husband.'

Shi saw fury flare in Dan's eyes, but it ebbed just as quickly. 'I am a concerned *brother*,' he emphasised, 'that is all.'

'My mistake.' Shi was as happy to drop the topic as Dan was.

'Follow me to our rooms, and *stay there* until I come for you.'

'We leave at first light?' Shi asked, seeking confirmation so that he might sleep at ease in that knowledge.

'Those are the Great Mother's orders,' he said drily, and Shi could not have been more thankful to hear it.

When Hudan saw Dan leading his younger brother to their guest quarters, she could not believe her luck. Even though she'd vowed not to be distracted from her quest by earthly affairs of the heart, she felt she would be hard pressed to find another opportunity in the near future to speak with Shi in private without arousing suspicion.

She waited for an hour after the house fell completely silent before she staggered as quietly as she was able into Ji Shi's room.

When Shi awoke to find a hand over his mouth, he began to struggle. 'It is I, Jiang Hudan,' she whispered to calm him, and he immediately ceased retaliation. 'I wish to talk with you. Follow me,' she instructed, but he grabbed her arm to prevent her moving off and urged her near once more.

'Dan told me to stay here, until he came for me,' he whispered.

'Well, we could discuss what we must here,' she replied softly, 'but Dan might overhear details you'd rather keep secret.'

Weighing up his options, Shi nodded to confirm that he would accompany her and then noting how she struggled to raise herself, he hoisted Hudan to her feet and half carried her with him as she pointed the way to the gardens.

It felt a little awkward being dragged about by a man who was practically a stranger, yet when Hudan remembered him in his tiger form, he felt like kindred and she did not mind so much.

At the garden gate, Hudan broke away from him. 'Thank you for your assistance, lord, but I can take it from here.'

'My apologies for being so abrupt, but I feared Dan would catch us, and he's stressed enough about our last meeting.' He followed her out the gate and down the path.

'Well, I suppose he would wonder what we have to talk about,' Hudan granted.

'I don't think we should have anything to talk about either,' Shi argued.

'I am not here to judge you, Shi, and I will never tell anyone what I know, so long as you live,' she vowed. 'But what if, one day, one of my nieces or nephews asks where their father hailed from? I would like to be able to tell them something more than I have been told. I am not an animal-shifter like my sister, but I am still of your kind, and just as curious to unlock the mystery of our origins.'

Obviously, for Shi, the subject matter was awkward to discuss because he was used to being so guarded about it. 'I was very young when my father came and took me to live with him, but like you he claimed I was Shanyu. My father encountered my mother whilst exploring a mountainous region in Qiang, further east of Yong, known as Bayan Har Shan.' Shi smiled as he recalled his father's account of her. 'Father had wandered out of camp to take a ...' Shi stopped to rephrase. '... to relieve himself, when he was bowled over by a white tigress, and just when he thought she would devour him, she transformed into a beautiful woman who made love to him instead.'

Hudan smiled at his tale. 'I wonder about our father often.' The delight fell from her face. 'I wonder if he was chosen in the same random fashion?'

Shi nodded, supposing he probably had been. 'Father boasted that if he hadn't been so handsome, he would have died that night. Instead, the tigress asked him to return after two years. That's when she presented my father with me.'

'You were the only one of your litter?'

'I was the only male,' Shi said. 'If I had been female, mother would have kept me with her.'

'So you may have a sister, or sisters?' Hudan suggested, and Shi went very pale.

'You think we might be related?' He stopped breathing.

'We are *not* your sisters, Shi,' Hudan realised his worry and quashed it. 'Our mother died giving birth to us, a few years before you were born.'

Shi drew breath again, thankful for the reassurance. 'I already feel guilty enough for my offence against heaven,' he confessed. 'I swear to you that, even though I had heard the stories of Jiang Huxin being a shifter, I did not believe it until the morning after we'd mated. Only then did I realise I had seduced one of the Wu.'

'But I told you before the rite who she was, Shi,' Hudan pointed out, but not in a scolding manner.

'It is difficult to explain to anyone who is not a shifter but, when in my tiger form, animal instinct overrules intellect,' Shi shrugged. 'It was only once I returned to my human form the next morning, that I had any cause for regret.'

Rather surprisingly, Hudan nodded, empathising with him. 'When I travel in spirit form, it is the same; the desires of the spiritual and physical body are very different. Sometimes I wish I had inherited just a little of Huxin's wild abandon,' Hudan sighed. 'But alas, someone has to keep a level head.'

'You sound like Dan,' Shi noted with amusement, but Hudan did not smile.

'I would rather not speak about brother Dan,' she said coolly. It seemed she could not escape the subject of him with anyone.

'Has my brother offended you in some way?' Shi was concerned.

'No!' Hudan was quick to contest. 'Quite the contrary. Sometimes I find him a little too pleasing for my own peace of mind. But I thank you for your concern.'

Shi relaxed. 'Know I am always at your service, Jiang Hudan.'

He was so like Dan in his sincerity, but without the intellect to keep his emotions in check. Shi wore his feelings on his sleeve as Fen did, and Hudan could see what her sister found so attractive about him.

'Yes, you are.' Hudan reached out and touched his cheek, unafraid to make contact with him, for Shi felt like kindred already. He had seen her at her most vulnerable, and she would never forget the horror that he had spared her. 'I owe you my life, brother, and for that I am eternally grateful.' She leant over and kissed his cheek. Shi was completely stunned.

'I expected you would want to kill me this night.' Shi was clearly much happier with this outcome, and held a hand over the cheek she'd kissed as if to protect the gesture and treasure it.

Hudan shook her head, and smiled. 'My sister could not have found a more worthy mate to father her children. I could hardly deny my own nieces and nephews the opportunity of knowing you.'

Shi was touched by her words, but still he feared there would be repercussions. 'I doubt very much the Great Mother and Tian share your good opinion of me.'

'Well, I cannot say what the Great Mother and Tian think of Ji Shi the young lord of Zhou … but, I can tell you that the Great Mother has a *very* soft spot for the white tiger who spared me from defilement, and fulfilled Huxin's desire to bear offspring of her own rare breed. *That* tiger has effectively made the Great Mother an expectant grandmother and she could not be more excited.'

'Really.' Shi was greatly relieved. 'You mean Huxin had heaven's blessing to mate?'

Hudan nodded to confirm this. 'She is the only one amongst us who has Tian's blessing to choose her own mate.'

'Oh, brother!' He threw his arms around her, squeezed and twirled her, then let her go just as abruptly. 'That is the best news, ever.'

'As to who that tiger really was …' Hudan grinned to conclude their chat. 'I shall never tell.'

'Shi, get up, we're leaving.'

By the time Shi opened his eyes, Dan was already out the door.

'Now!' Dan yelled back to him as he descended the stairs into the cloister.

Shi caught up to his brother at the jetty in the cavern, where Jiang Hudan was waiting to escort them back to the real world.

'Good morning, lords,' Hudan bid them sincerely.

'For some, perhaps,' Dan replied, bypassing her to board the ferry.

'I think it a very grand morning,' Shi said, greeting her with a beaming smile, thinking his brother extraordinarily rude.

'I *had* thought so.' Her puzzled gaze shifted to Dan as they boarded the ferry.

On the way across the lake, Shi could not fail to notice the contrast between his happy mood and his brother's dark sulk, and clearly Hudan was perplexed by it too.

At the mainland jetty, Dan disembarked without a second glance at either of them. 'Come, Shi, we are pressed for time,' he commanded, without looking back.

Hudan and Shi disembarked after him, watching Dan storm off down the jetty. 'Do you think he saw us —' They both suggested at once and then smiled at the synchronous moment.

'That would explain it,' Shi said, frowning, dreading how the rest of the day would unfold, if that was the case.

'Brother Dan was not in a good mood when he left the Great Mother's audience yesterday,' Hudan advised. 'It may be that his mood has not improved since then.'

Shi could only hope. 'But what should I tell Dan if he did see us?'

Hudan was irritated. 'It is none of his business who I converse with. He has been told by the Great Mother to focus on other matters. Tell him nothing.'

'What?' Shi knew that was easier said than done. 'Dan is very protective of you, and if he saw you kiss me, he'll have my head for it!'

'I cannot believe he could think me so fickle.' Hudan wasn't listening; she was fuming. 'Well, better that he hates me … and as we cannot tell him the truth lest your secret be known, it serves our purpose to let him think what he will.'

'Shi!' Dan yelled from the distance, without bothering to check if he was coming or not.

'Tell him I have foresworn you to secrecy,' Hudan suggested.

'As you wish,' Shi agreed staunchly, and ran off after his brother.

At the clearing at the end of the forest track, Shi was forced to freeze to avoid cutting his throat on Dan's extended blade.

'I told you to stay in your room.' It seemed obvious now that Dan had seen him in the night garden with Jiang Hudan.

'When one of the Wu bids me follow, I follow,' Shi replied.

'What business have you with Jiang Hudan?' His brother was livid, and Shi knew that any more light banter and he'd have a good scar to show for it.

'I do not have her leave to inform you —' Shi rose up onto his toes as Dan pressed his blade deeper.

'You took liberties with her that were inappropriate no matter what secret you share,' Dan moved closer to impress on him. 'I forbid you to see her again.'

Shi took advantage of the slackening of the blade against his neck to duck away from his brother and, taking a running jump to land on his horse, he took off in the direction of Mengjin.

'This is not over!' Dan yelled in his wake.

As long as I can stay ahead of you it is, Shi thought, leaning in close to his steed to ride faster. The carriage Dan was driving would take much longer to catch up to the Xibo's party. Dan would not attempt to drag the truth out of him in the presence of anyone else, to save blemishing Jiang Hudan's reputation, so all Shi had to do was keep the company of others until Hudan returned to handle Dan.

Six days of isolation, following the strict regime of the Wu, and Hudan felt as good as new. In fact, she felt far more equipped to handle the impending battle, as she and the Great Mother had been brainstorming ways in which Hudan might contend with Dragonface and his lackeys.

Killing was not the way of the Wu, but they were dealing with an enemy who would never repent or surrender, so mere entrapment could serve no purpose.

'These creatures are not immortal,' her Shifu had emphasised, 'but they can make themselves more resistant to death by consuming the life force of others. They do this by drinking directly from the pineal gland in the brain of their living victims. As you have already surmised, the more pain and fear they incite in their victim, the more resilient to death the creature becomes. A brave soul is poison to them — if they cannot intimidate you, they will run.'

'They ran from you, Shifu?'

There was a glint of satisfaction evident in her smile as she'd replied. 'They cannot stand the presence of cosmic light ... it literally makes them sick. Divine light cuts through darkness, which must then retreat into shadow.'

'But shadows lurk everywhere.'

'That is why Dragonface must not be allowed to escape this time. You know how to take wilful control over the body of another, to have them do your bidding. You can burst their vital organs, or banish them to the ends of the earth. You also hold the favour of the Lord of the Elements, so do not hesitate to summon him to your aid. This cause is his cause, but he cannot become involved in earthly affairs without being invited.'

Armed with this knowledge, Hudan felt well prepared to greet the Xibo at Mengjin and commence the final leg of this quest for freedom that they had begun together. The affairs of the heart in which she'd been entangled only a week ago had been stored away, and it was Hudan's intention to keep them in storage.

Without a clear vision of a place or person to project to, Hudan could not psychically transfer her physical body. She had never been to Mengjin, neither was she familiar with any of the Xibo's brothers, who were waiting for him there with their armies. Unsure if the Xibo's party was still on the move, Hudan chose to focus on the inside of the carriage in which she had been travelling and, with the desire to be there, her will set the feat in motion.

'Hudan!' Huxin sounded relieved to see her as she materialised in the carriage.

'The Xibo is still en route?' Hudan concluded from the jerking movement of their transport.

'We hope to reach the camp within the hour,' Huxin was happy to say.

'The rain has eased,' Hudan said as she took a peek outside.

'We are close to the Shang border. They were not blessed with your gift.'

'Did Ji Shi and Ji Dan return and report to the Xibo on my behalf?' Hudan queried.

'Shi arrived some time before Dan to report your delay, and then volunteered to ride ahead to Mengjin to advise their brothers of the Xibo's arrival.'

Smart move, thought Hudan. 'And brother Dan?'

Huxin served Hudan a rather curious look of concern. 'He reported several days later, and has barely spoken to anyone, apart from the Xibo, since.'

'That is well,' Hudan decided. At least he was focused on the goal now.

'I hardly think so,' Huxin replied, annoyed with her sister. 'I do not know what has caused the ill will between you, but it is hardly *well* that we are going into battle with our side divided.'

'There is no ill will between us,' Hudan said, telling half a lie. 'Not from my quarter, in any case.'

'You've done *something* to upset him.'

'Everything I do upsets him!' Hudan lost her patience — not five minutes back in the real world and she was already arguing about Dan. 'He is a curse.'

'He is a blessing!' Huxin strongly disagreed. 'I have a sixth sense about people, Hudan, you know that, and I can smell fear on you!'

Hudan held her breath as she decided between rage and surrender. Perhaps Huxin could be of more aid in this matter than the Great Mother had been. 'I need help,' she admitted. 'It is like having a jealous husband without any of the marital benefits!'

Huxin was completely ambushed by Hudan's frankness, but Hudan pretended not to notice.

'Who has Ji Dan to be jealous of, so far as you are concerned?' The tigress was puzzled, and skirting dangerously close to the truth of the matter.

'He is jealous of any man I speak with!' Hudan complained, presenting half the truth, but there was still enough validity to her statement to escape her sister's built-in lie detector.

Huxin bit her lip, as she deliberated on the problem. 'If a man is jealous he usually needs reassuring.'

'I did reassure him,' Hudan informed, frustrated, 'and it seems to have gone in one ear and out the other.'

'You did?' Huxin was stunned again, and grinning. 'Well, it seems your life is no longer dull.'

'I miss dull,' Hudan stressed. 'I *crave* dull.'

'Sorry, Hudan, but I don't think your life is going to get dull any time soon. You've joined the emotional minefield that is human relationships, so you have to learn to deal with the sensibilities of others,' Huxin lectured. 'Dan is a good friend to you —'

'I agree! I told him that!'

'Then tell him again,' Huxin shrugged in response. 'Whatever happens, you must not take to the battlefield if you are at odds with one another.'

That little piece of advice was a bit of a wake-up call for Hudan. Huxin was more right than she could possibly know.

'I shall see to it.' Hudan drew a deep breath for strength. 'I'll see you at Mengjin,' she said, alerting Huxin to her imminent departure.

In the knowledge that Ji Shi would already be at Mengjin, Hudan focused her chi on joining him there.

When Hudan materialised, she found her target outside the main camp at Mengjin, facing a tree that he was urinating on. Hudan was quick to turn away and then clear her throat.

'Jiang Hudan!' Shi sounded embarrassed and very surprised to note her presence.

'My apologies for catching you indisposed. Physical relocation is not a flawless science.'

'We must not be seen together.' Shi, now dressed, moved around to face her, in a panic. 'Dan has forbidden me to see you.'

'You have managed to avoid his questions?' she assumed, but Shi's attention was elsewhere.

'Until now,' he replied, and Hudan followed his line of sight to see Dan striding toward them.

'He's here early.' Hudan figured he must have ridden ahead to catch up with Shi.

'I'm in *so* much trouble.' Shi observed his brother warily as he neared.

'No, you're not,' Hudan assured him. 'Trust me.'

'I do,' Shi stated as if he were balancing on a cliff edge.

'Thank you, Shi,' she said, once Dan had arrived. 'You may go.'

Dan did not object, although he regarded his brother with utter disdain as he quickly exited, and then looked back at Hudan with a wounded expression. 'Chosen a new favourite to seduce? Come inside, I have four other brothers you might prefer?'

The comment was so spiteful, it took a moment for Hudan to process it and forgive. 'Ji Shi enlightened me to some information that I had been seeking for some time regarding my birthright, and I was very grateful to receive it. That is all.'

Dan's expression contorted in pain. 'I have shared my deepest, darkest secrets with you and not once have you held me as you held him!'

It was clear, in that moment, where her error lay. The fear of being close to Dan was the very thing driving a stake between them, so there seemed only one thing for it. Hudan dropped her defensive stance and walked over to Dan and hugged him tight. 'There is nobody else I shall ever prefer to you,' she said firmly, tears of relief rimming her eyes as she felt him surrender his anger and collapse into her embrace. 'Not in this world or the next, apparently.'

His body shuddered as he gave a laugh. 'That was a cruel accusation I made just now,' he said, as they remained as they were. 'I am ashamed to have been so hurtful. Please forgive me.'

'It should be you forgiving me for my aloofness, secrets and cruelty,' Hudan advised, feeling that she was to blame. 'I am a poor specimen of humanity when it comes to the feelings of others.'

'Hardly ... time and again you risk your life for the greater good of everyone. I've never known anyone so selfless.'

She had no compulsion to debate their shortcomings; cocooned in his embrace, listening to his heartbeat, she wanted nothing more than to just hold onto the blissful moment. Every time her fear compelled her to let go of him, Hudan just snuggled in tighter and enjoyed the small comfort for the gift it was.

'This is so much better than fighting.' Dan broke the long silence, but did not pull away. 'You have no need to fear me, you know? I will never give you cause to regret our association.'

'That is a welcome revelation,' Hudan said, finally pulling back to look her dear friend in the face. A week apart had altered her perception of Dan, although not quite in the way she'd expected. 'I have come to realise there is nothing that disturbs me more than being at odds with you.'

'We are of the same mind on that count. Even Lu Chen claimed we were forever fated to be on the same team,' Dan recounted.

'I remember,' she confirmed, her shy smile concealing how vulnerable that memory made her feel.

Thankfully, Dan's sights had drifted back to the campsite. 'Our war party has arrived.' He noted the influx of people in the camp, ahead of looking back to Hudan. 'Are you ready to face our first test?'

'Time to meet the bad brothers?' Hudan figured the Ji brothers from Fengjing would be awaiting Ji Fa in the large temporary structure that had been erected on-site to be the centre of operations.

'Oh, they'll be very welcoming today, I'll warrant.' Dan reluctantly allowed Hudan to extricate herself from their embrace. 'You and Ji Fa have finally brought them the war they've been hankering for.'

'Shall we?' Hudan held her hand out to Dan. Surprised as he was by this gesture of friendship coming from Hudan, he took hold gladly.

'People will talk about us, Jiang Hudan,' Dan pointed out, although he was clearly not worried.

'I certainly hope so.' Hudan surprised herself with her choice of words, but at this point in time, she suspected any gossip about their close friendship would work in Zhou's favour.

'My brothers! I commend and thank you for your patience,' said Ji Fa.

When Hudan and Dan entered the council chamber, the Ji brothers and the leaders of territories who supported the Zhou, were focused on the Xibo, who stood upon a large platform at one end of the room with his tigress by his side.

'I know you have derided my delay in sending out a call to arms,' Fa continued, as Hudan and Dan loitered by the door, so as not to disturb the gathering, 'but seeking heaven's mandate is no trivial affair. It is time you, my brothers and allies, were made aware of the truth of our situation.'

'The truth of our situation, my brother, is that the emperor has hundreds of thousands of troops being led by a demon witch,' one man stepped forward to advise, 'and we have, at best, rallied forty-five thousand!'

'That is Xian,' Dan uttered aside to Hudan.

'It is not the head count that matters. It is who commands and holds more hearts on the day,' Fa advised his brother, and then addressed the entire gathering. 'And I say Shou holds the hearts of none since he allowed Su Daji to rip out the heart of that *great* man, Bi Gan; those followers Shou has left have no hearts!' he added before Xian could scoff at his optimism, and many in the room seconded the Xibo's sentiments with a war cry. 'And Su Daji is not the most powerful or revered Wu in our land either.' Silence fell in the chamber as the Xibo removed his cape and draped it over the tigress alongside him. 'Minister Weizi advises me that there are Wu that even Su Daji fears ... and I have conscripted them to *our* cause.'

When Huxin rose to stand beside Ji Fa, his cloak wrapped around her, there was a great intake of breath from the men present. 'I am Shanyu Jiang Huxin of the House of Yi Wu Li Shan, and I have been commanded by Tian to protect our Xibo, Ji Fa from treachery.' Huxin looked across at Hudan, and the gathering of men all turned around to note the second woman amongst them. Those close to Hudan backed away warily, while Dan followed in her steps to the platform on which the Xibo stood.

Hudan chose to address the gathering from the floor, however. 'I am Shanyu Jiang Hudan,' she announced and all the men gasped in awe, although they had surely expected her identity before she revealed it. 'I have been sent by the Great Mother of Li Shan to protect our Xibo and his legions from the sorcery of Su Daji.'

'Rainmaker,' said one of the western lords, and when he bowed down before Hudan, every man in the room followed suit, even Xian. 'Your sacrifice has already saved my entire kingdom from the curse of the empress. The people of Qiang are forever in your debt.'

Hudan noted this was the region that Ji Shi had claimed to hail from and quietly observed that he was not present. 'It was Tian who brought the rain to the lands of the righteous,' Hudan stated for the record. 'I only made the request to heaven on our Xibo's behalf. I performed the sacred oracle for Ji Fa and did foresee his victory under the banner of the white tiger long before he ever set foot on Li Shan. But Tian does not require you to take our word that Ji Fa holds heaven's mandate.' Hudan's eyes diverted to Xian, who met her gaze with a look of curiosity. 'Heaven will send clear omens,' she advised mysteriously, and Ji Fa smiled in understanding and nodded his head to concur.

'My dreams of late coincide with my divinations, and the auspicious omen is double!' Ji Fa continued, seconding her words

'Of what omens do you speak?' Xian was the first to stand and query this, wary of more delays.

'On the morning of the battle Tian will present Ji Fa with a flaming sword, with five sparkling jewels at the hilt,' Hudan advised her stunned audience. 'On that day the sun and moon will combine like jade and the land will be cast into darkness. Know then that the tyrannous rule of Zi Shou has ended, and a glorious new era of peace and co-operation has begun.'

Everyone, bar Ji Fa and Huxin, was completely overwhelmed by the proclamation and the task assigned to them by heaven.

'Rouse yourselves, my heroes!' Ji Fa encouraged his men to rise. 'Do not think that Zi Shou is not to be feared … better to think that he cannot be endured. Unite your energies, unite your hearts, and you will surely accomplish this work that will last for all the ages! Heaven and earth are the parents of all creatures; and of all creatures man is the most highly endowed. The sincerely intelligent among men become the great sovereign. But now Zi Shou, king of the Shang, does not give reverence to heaven above, and inflicts calamities on the people below. Abandoned to drunkenness and reckless in lust, he has exercised cruelty and oppression. He has extended the punishment of offenders to all their relatives. He has put men into office on the hereditary principle. He has made it his purpose to have palaces, towers, pavilions, ponds, and countless other extravagances erected causing injury to you, the people.'

As Fa's speech roused their passion, a cheer of agreement swept around the chamber.

'Zi Shou has murdered and burned the loyal and good. He has sliced open pregnant women!' Fa ended the list of the emperor's offences. 'Great heaven was moved with indignation, and charged my father to display the terrors of Zi Shou's rulership, but he died before the work was completed.'

Hudan noted Xian's sights shift to Dan. It was apparent that the lord suspected Dan of having something to do with their father's death.

'On this account I, Fa, the little child, have by means of you, the hereditary rulers of my friendly states, contemplated the government of the Shang and found that Shou has no repentant heart.'

It was quietly amusing to hear Fa refer to himself as 'the little child' for it was quite true that the Xibo was the shortest in stature of the brothers, the youngest included. This was not his meaning in this instance, however; Ji Fa was, in fact, inferring that he was humbled to be following in the footsteps of his great predecessor.

'Shou sits squatting on his heels, not serving Tian, or the spirits of heaven and earth; neglecting also the temple of his ancestors; and not sacrificing to those who came before. The good people of the Shang fall prey to wicked robbers, and still he says, "The people are mine, the heavenly appointment is mine," and never trying to correct his contemptuous mind.'

The warlords gave a cry of support that was even more convincing than the last.

'Heaven, giving help to the people, made for them rulers, to secure the tranquillity of the four quarters of the kingdom,' Ji Fa proclaimed loudly and with grave self-assurance. 'Yes, Shou has hundreds and thousands and myriad officers, and they have hundreds and thousands and myriad minds. I have *three thousand* officers, but they have *one mind*. The iniquity of the Shang is endless and heaven gives command to destroy it. If I did not obey heaven, my sin would be just as great as theirs! I, the little child, early and late am filled with apprehensions, but I have received the command of my deceased father and I have offered special sacrifice to Tian. I have performed the services due to the great earth and I lead the multitude to execute the punishment as adjudged by heaven. Now is the time! It should not be lost. Do you aid me, the one man, to cleanse forever all within the four seas?'

'Shi!'

The cry of support was not fierce enough for Fa's liking. 'Do you with untiring zeal support me, the one man, to execute the punishment as adjudged by heaven?' Fa challenged them again.

'Shi!' the crowd replied with more enthusiasm.

'The ancients have said that he who soothes is our sovereign, he who oppresses is our enemy. This solitary fellow, Shou, having exercised great tyranny, is your *perpetual* enemy and must be destroyed! Do you, my brothers, march forward with determined boldness to sustain me?'

'Shi!' This time the shouts and cheers nearly raised the roof, and Ji Fa grinned with delight as the leaders of his alliance chanted his name.

'Where there is much merit, there shall be much reward,' Fa vowed to his countrymen. 'Tomorrow we cross the Huang He. Heaven and Tian's warriors accompany us ... victory will be ours!'

As Ji Fa moved to leave the platform, Jiang Huxin withdrew under his cloak and emerged from beneath in her tiger form, to the consternation of the onlookers. She then gave a friendly roar to compliment the general din.

'That went better than expected,' Dan commented to Hudan as they followed their Xibo and his tigress from the war room.

'Brother Fa is quite an orator,' Hudan said, having felt her blood being roused by his words several times during the address. 'A very fine speech, brother Dan,' she told him, knowing that, as Fa's chief aide, Dan wrote the Xibo's speeches.

'It is all in the delivery,' he said, waving away the praise, then said quietly: 'Do you think we should mention what we have uncovered about the Jade Book?'

Hudan shook her head to the negative. 'We should focus our energy on accomplishing one thing at a time.'

Once outside, Hudan sped up to speak with Ji Fa. 'Ji Shi missed your rousing call to arms, brother Fa.'

'I sent him ahead to Mu,' Fa replied.

'He has crossed the Huang He, then,' Hudan said, worried to hear it. Fa was understandably confused by her reaction.

'If we are to march to Yin, that is the path we must take,' Fa explained and attempted to move off, but again she waylaid him.

'Does Shi know of Su Daji's shoot to kill order on white tigers?' Hudan queried.

'Why would I tell Shi about that?' Fa reasoned. 'It would only inspire him to go charging off on some personal vendetta.'

'Quite right.' Hudan dropped the matter to avoid suspicion, and let Ji Fa get on with the business of readying his troops. Hudan could see the wisdom in Ji Fa's reasoning, and as Shi was on government business he would surely not risk shifting into tiger form, so she felt he was safe enough for the time being.

THE BATTLE OF MU

Five days later, under cloudy, rainless skies, the armies from the west and south reached the rallying point in the open country of Mu, just within the Shang border. The location had been specifically chosen for its remoteness, far away from any towns.

Hudan kept her carriage for the last leg of the journey, rather than switching to horseback, as it saved having to erect a tent each evening and it was hardly slowing the pace of the huge force. If she had been travelling alone, or with her Wu brothers only, she would have been glad to sleep out under the stars. As it was, Hudan had never seen so many men, or even imagined there could be so many in all of existence! And these were only Zhou's troops — according to the reports of their scouts, the Shang force massing against them was ten times larger. She was now quietly grateful for Dan's constant companionship. He was well known, well respected and — as rumours of their friendship spread — on seeing a woman in Ji Dan's company everyone immediately knew she was a Wu legend who was not to be trifled with. Hudan was not afraid of taking on an army, but she would rather they were her enemies and not her allies, so keeping Dan's company meant that there were no misunderstandings.

The huge camp was utter chaos, so despite Hudan's attempts to locate Ji Shi, he remained elusive.

'He'll be out scouting,' Dan told her, insisting she was unduly worried. 'That's what Shi's good at, that's what he does ... *disappears* most of the time.'

Hudan forced a smile, more aware of Shi's real reasons for escaping. 'Perhaps I should attempt to project myself to him psychically?'

'You should not risk draining your chi the evening before battle,' Dan advised, before a shy smile graced his lips. 'However, if you did do so, I would be more than happy to aid in repairing any damage.'

The look Hudan served him was a rebuke, although she cracked a smile. 'I commend you for not saying so last time we had this conversation.'

'At that time, I do not think you would have taken the suggestion in the light-hearted, but sincere, manner that it was meant.'

She considered he was probably right about that, but Hudan had learned to relax in Dan's company now. 'Should I ever require such assistance, you will be the first to know,' she granted, with good humour.

'Honestly?' Dan asked rather more seriously than their banter warranted and Hudan suddenly realised why they were having this conversation.

'My interest in your little brother is simply maternal,' she said rather more coolly, having already reassured Dan on that front before now. 'He's just a baby, for heaven's sake, like Fen. He reminds me of Fen. He has no parents to watch out for him, just brothers, who boss him about, tell him *nothing* and —'

'*Hudan!*' Dan gripped her shoulders to stop her rant. 'I shall make inquiries. You should return to your carriage and prepare for tomorrow. I shall see you there, later.' He reconsidered. 'Much later ... as this war council may adjourn quite late.'

'I think not,' Hudan assured Dan. 'Fa knows exactly what must be done, so a good night's sleep should be had by everyone.' Dan looked doubtful. 'And the preparation I needed to do was done before I left Li Shan,' she further advised him. 'I am ready for Su Daji.'

'I envy your surety,' Dan replied, 'but I do not doubt it.' He forced a smile, and left her to join the other officers and warlords assembling in the Xibo's large tent.

*

Just after nightfall, Dan joined Hudan at her carriage, which was situated on the outskirts of the officers' section of the campsite. There he found her aiding Fen and Nuan to brew up remedies and medicines.

'Here is our night owl,' Hudan commented when she saw him approaching, and lifting a small pot from one of the fires, she set it aside a moment. 'We've made you a little something to help you sleep.'

Dan was apprehensive. 'I don't know if that is wise? I wouldn't wish to miss the battle, or wake up groggy.'

'You need some decent rest. This brew is not strong enough to give you more than a few hours respite,' she assured him. 'And I shall wake you before dawn, I promise.' She poured the steaming brew into a cup and offered it to him. 'Trust me.'

Hudan knew better than anyone how little he'd slept on this journey. The first week he'd been too agitated by Hudan's mysterious favouring of his brother, and since his Wu training had been neglected of late, his mind was back to being overactive and he could not shut it off.

Dan sat down in front of the log they were all using as a seat, and, accepting the elixir, he obediently drank it down in one gulp. 'I thank you.' He handed the empty cup back.

'Did you manage to locate Shi?' Hudan asked, and Dan was bewildered. Here they were on the eve of war, and Hudan's only concern was for Shi?

'Shi is out scouting, as I said.'

'But when did he leave?' she queried.

'Before we arrived this morning.'

'And he has still not returned to report?' Hudan's determination to seek his young brother began to stir up the resentment he'd been suppressing since he'd seen them together in the garden at Li Shan.

'It is not unusual for a scout to be gone for days, *weeks* sometimes,' he stressed, hoping that she would drop the subject.

'Shi is one of our best scouts. I am sure he is perfectly safe and will return by morning.'

'I shall pray to Tian that it is so.' Her eyes were gazing into the fire, entranced, as she said this, and Dan had to wonder if she ever expended this much worry on him.

'I think it is Fa you should be praying for,' he commented aloofly, and Hudan looked at him.

'I pray for the deliverance of all the Ji family,' she clarified, and the comment pacified him a little. Or perhaps it was the sleeping potion taking effect. 'Have you prepared the composition the Great Mother requested that you perform before the battle?' Hudan asked, changing the subject at last, although Dan did not really find the new topic any more preferable and slouched further into the log at his back.

'In my head.' He suppressed a yawn. 'How that will translate through my fingers remains to be seen.'

'Nuan and I shall be there to assist you, lord,' Fen assured Dan, with a beaming smile.

'And I am grateful,' Dan assured his ward, 'but you should keep your focus on your own preparation, as you shall have enough to deal with, treating the wounded.'

Fen shook his head at this, 'I think the medics among the Shang will have far more to deal with than I,' he said confidently. 'Hudan will protect us.' Fen's admiring gaze shifted to his sister and she didn't dismiss his claim, but gave him a smile.

These Wu had never seen a real battle and Dan had to wonder if it was they who were deluded, or himself, as logic told him they were going to be massacred. Yet whether they won, or died trying, Zi Shou would never rule over them again and that thought was liberating.

As Dan's eyes slowly closed, he worried about Hudan's claim that heaven would gift Fa a sword before the battle tomorrow. This was obviously part of the oracle Ji Fa and Jiang Hudan had shared, and a condition of the deal they had struck with Tian. But even after witnessing many a Wu miracle, Dan thought the gifting of a sword was an outrageous notion. He also hoped the sleeping brew he'd taken wouldn't prevent him from witnessing the event, so he obviously anticipated that heaven would not disappoint.

'Dan.'

A warm hand was stroking his cheek.

'Awake friend, the day of our destiny is nigh.'

The sound of Hudan's lovely voice drew him from the twilight of his dream state. When Dan opened his eyes to behold her, bathed in moonlight and smiling broadly at him, it was the most pleasant awakening he'd ever had. 'Good morning,' he said, without a hint of sarcasm, as he felt truly rested for the first time since the yin rite.

'It certainly is.' Hudan pulled back and directed his attention to the sky above them.

The clouds had departed and the starry sky appeared to have been cut open — a long gash through the belly of the heavens bled bright red light into the night sky. The streak of red was thickest in the west, and tailed off to a point toward the east. In the constellation of Fang through which the bright blade of light extended, five planets aligned like a string of jewels, glistening across the hilt of heaven's fiery weapon.

'The omen!' he gasped, sitting immediately upright.

Realising that everyone in the camp was still sleeping, he was dismayed, for the omen would not be so easily seen after sunrise.

'Alert Fa,' Dan instructed Hudan, before rushing over to rouse Fen and Nuan. 'Quickly, we must fetch our instruments.' Dan directed his ward's attention to the sky, and the lad jumped immediately into action. Heart pounding in his chest, Dan made to honour the vow he'd made to Yi Wu and his Xibo; he had been dreading this performance.

Yet heaven's spectacular gift was inspiring and warranted a magnificent salute by way of thanks. The Great Mother had fortunately foreseen this and prepared Dan for the duty, which now felt like the highest of honours.

It was no surprise to Hudan to find the Xibo awake and outside his tent, staring at the sky like a gleeful child. 'I saw it in my dreams, and still I stand in awe of its manifestation.'

'The hilt to the west places the sword of the divine clearly in your quarter, brother Fa,' Hudan said. 'Is the little child ready to become king?'

Fa smiled at her reference, and looked her way to nod. 'May that come at a small price to my countrymen.'

The sound of Dan's qin and Fen's dizi attracted their attention to the centre of the campsite, and watching the troops stir gently to the dulcet, inspiring tones and then heed the prophesied omen in the sky above was an utter delight — an enchanting scene fit for the birth of a new legend.

'Behold,' the troops and officers cried, 'Tian's gift to the one true Tianzi! Victory to Zhou! Vic-tor-y ... vic-tor-y.' The call to arms built to a rousing chant.

Tianzi meant 'son of the heaven', and this omen validated, for all to see, Ji Fa's claim to have heaven's mandate to overthrow the Shang and not be branded an usurper — for in the eyes of heaven and the people, he was now a king.

'That certainly seems to have raised morale somewhat,' commented Fa.

'Of course,' she concurred, 'for the side of the righteous in the eyes of heaven is now clear in the eyes of the people.'

As the tigress slunk out of the tent to see what the fuss was about, she released a loud roar that was not directed toward the sky, but sounded more like an alert.

Hudan followed her sister's line of sight to see Xian approaching.

'Your omen, Fa!' Xian pointed to the sky, excited. 'I didn't believe —' He choked on the tears threatening to form in his eyes, and dropped to one knee before the Xibo. 'But I understand why you refrained from war until now, and I see that your Wu have guided you wisely. Clearly, heaven's mandate lies with the West, my lord, and I am honoured to ride into battle with the one true Tianzi this day.'

If the prediction had cemented Ji Fa's claim in Xian's mind, there was not another officer or warlord in Zhou who would now doubt him, as Xian had been profoundly sceptical.

'That means a great deal to me, Xian,' Fa said, and urged him to rise. 'Today we shall avenge our father and Bo Yi Kao as brothers, and we shall see them both proud.'

Xian nodded to agree, but jaw clenched, was too emotional to speak.

'Time to address the troops.' Fa embraced Xian, and after a mutual slap on the shoulder, they headed through the din toward the music.

Huxin and Hudan followed to hear Fa's address.

Dawn of the day, jiazi, the new king came to address his army. In his left hand he carried a battleaxe, yellow with gold in laid designs, and in his right he held a white standard featuring a black imprint of his tigress, which he brandished, saying: 'Far have you come, men of the western regions! Hereditary rulers, ministers of my friendly states; ministers of instruction, of war, and of public works; the first and second officers and secretaries; and you, men of Yong, Shu, Qiang, Mao, Wei, Lu, Peng and Bo; lift up your lances, join your shields, raise your spears, and make an oath with me.'

Under the red streak of dawn, the men clattered their weapons in response to Ji Fa's call to arms.

'The ancients have said,' the king raised his voice and the crowd hushed, '"The hen does not announce the morning. The crowing of a hen in the morning indicates the subversion of the family." Now Shou, the King of Shang, follows only the words of his wife. He has blindly thrown away the sacrifices, and makes no response for the favours that he has received; he has maliciously cast aside his paternal and maternal relatives, not treating them properly. It is only the vagabonds of the empire, loaded with crimes, whom Shou honours and exalts, whom he employs and trusts, making them great officers and nobles so that they can tyrannise the people, exercising their villainies in the cities of Shang. Now I, Fa, am simply executing respectfully the punishment appointed by heaven. The virtue of my deceased father was like the shining of the sun and moon. His brightness extended over the four quarters of the land, and shone signally in the western region. Hence it is that Zhou has received the allegiance of many states. If I subdue Zi Shou, it will not be from my prowess, but from the faultless virtue of my deceased father. If Shou subdues me, it will not be from any fault of my father, but because I, the little child, am not good.'

'Victory to Tianzi!' yelled an officer, and the sentiment was echo by many. But Fa raised his hands to hush them.

'In today's business, do not rush or kill those who fly to us in submission, but receive them to serve our Western Land. My brave men, be energetic. Do not advance more than six or seven steps, and then stop and adjust your ranks; my brave men, be energetic! Do not exceed six or seven blows before you stop and adjust your ranks; my brave men, be energetic. Display a martial bearing. Be like the tigers here in the border of Shang. For if you be not energetic in all these matters, you will bring destruction on yourselves.'

As Fa's words raised a riot in the stillness of the early hour, the war drums of the Shang could be heard in the distance.

An hour past dawn the Shang army could now be seen. Their forces were spread across the horizon like an endless forest of shadow on the sunlit plain. Spearheading the seven hundred thousand-strong army was a sole rider, clad entirely in red.

'Su Daji.' Hudan, dressed entirely in white, had Taiji in hand, and could hardly wait to meet her opponent face to face.

Apart from the red and black ensign of the dragon, the Shang army was also brandishing several black and white banners, which, it became apparent as the army got closer, were the stretched pelts of several white tigers.

When Hudan saw these pelts, taunting her and Huxin, she felt sick to her stomach. 'Has Shi returned?' Hudan asked Fa who was standing in front of their forces on her right, while Dan stood to her left. Everyone else, bar Huxin, was to their backs.

'Hudan?' Dan was surprised at her, motioning to the approaching multitude. 'We have greater concerns at present.'

Fa turned and noted Shi was not with the rest of their brothers. 'Shi hasn't the killer instinct for war … he's better off wherever he is.'

Hudan looked at the tiger carcasses, struggling to contain her tears of panic, praying silently to Tian that Shi was not one of them.

The tigress was in a fury, seeing red, body armour rattling as she paced in front of them, growling with resentment.

'Huxin!' Hudan called for her sister to halt her frenzied movement, and when she did not, Hudan moved to hug her sister around the neck and whisper in her ear. 'Calm yourself, dear sister, for I promise you that I have something for Su Daji that will cut her much more deeply.'

A call from their general halted the Shang force beyond firing range and Su Daji continued to advance alone.

Fa turned to Hudan and took hold of both her hands to pray: 'And now ye spirits, grant me your aid, so that I may relieve the millions, and nothing turn out to your shame.'

'Have no doubt that Tian is with you this day, dear brother,' she said with confidence, ahead of turning to Dan and serving him a cheeky grin. 'I should like that kiss now, brother Dan, if it pleases you.'

Clearly Dan was overwhelmed, and wondering if she was joking. 'Now? In front of everyone?' Such intimacies were usually kept behind closed doors, as they were most sacred.

She nodded to confirm.

Dan eyed their approaching enemy, realising the truth of her prophecy now. 'So our kiss is simply to make Su Daji jealous.' He obviously felt cheated and put on the spot.

'To make Daji *insanely* jealous,' she emphasised, as she sidled seductively up to him. 'For the glory of Tian and Zhou, do you think you're up for the challenge?'

Dan hesitated, indignant, but resolved to shed his inhibitions, and taking Hudan in hand, he gently planted his lips upon hers to the cheers of the entire Zhou army.

The moment was electric and, infused by Dan's passion, Su Daji's rage and the expectations of her countrymen, Hudan felt an exuberance she'd never experienced before. At last and all too soon, their lips parted.

'Good enough?' queried Dan, eyebrows raised in question.

Hudan looked to see Su Daji leap off her horse and start flying at them, still screeching in protest. 'It would appear so.' Hudan took a running leap to launch herself into the air, and flew into the confrontation.

As they raced toward one another, the heads of their staffs aimed at the other, Hudan sang the note that activated the sphere in her staff and Taiji lit up bright red — the colour of Su Daji's magic — which was the base vibration of the spectrum and aligned to the lowest part of human consciousness. As the seat of fear, grounding, willpower and action, at its best red chi energy was assertive, courageous, strong and pioneering; at its worst it bred insecurity, self-pity, aggression and terror.

'You dare defy your empress!' Su Daji wielded her staff as she flew, shooting forth a sphere of force toward Hudan, which Hudan blocked with her own staff and dispersed to the four winds. After blocking the strike, Hudan awaited Su Daji's presence, and when she was just about upon her, Hudan vanished, leaving Su Daji spinning in circles to seek her. 'Show yourself, coward!' she shrieked, enraged. 'Or I shall rip out the hearts of every Ji traitor on this field, starting with Dan!'

Hudan was not far afield, focussing her chi to cloak her in invisibility. *'Ang-wei, Lord of the Elements, I summon you to my aid. Join with me, know my intention and assist me to fulfil my will.'*

'Holy mackerel, that's a big army! I hope they're ours.'

Hudan looked up to see the young, fair lord eyeing the Shang army. 'No, *they are the enemy, and thus I have no time for idle banter. Please, we must hurry.'*

'My minions are yours to command.' Avery came and collapsed to a seated position and offered her both his hands, which Hudan gripped to manifest her vision.

A mass of coloured cloud erupted above the Shang army, and as it took the form of a beautiful woman — Hudan — most of the men were at first enchanted. But when the massive billowing apparition spoke in a loud booming voice, the men cowered. 'Good men of Shang, I am Shanyu Jiang Hudan and I bring you a message from the King of Zhou.'

'No!' Su Daji directed blasts of energy from her staff toward the apparition in the sky, to no effect.

'By heaven's appointment, Ji Fa prepares to administer a great correction to Shang. The true Tianzi, Ji Fa, along with his great father, Ji Chang, has brought peace and prosperity to the north, south and west, who now equally follow and consent with him in this undertaking. Shou, King of Shang is without principle. He is cruel and destructive to the creatures of heaven, and injurious to the people of the earth. In accordance with the will of heaven, Ji Fa pursues his punitive work to the East to give tranquillity to its men and women. The virtuous men opposing you presume reverently to comply with heaven's will and make an end of Shou's disorderly ways.'

When it became apparent that the cloud was an apparition and her attack ineffective, Daji calmed herself, turned about and, setting her sights on Ji Dan, she flew in his direction to carry out her previous threat.

She came to a stop a good distance from where he stood, to admire and gloat over him. 'So much like Bo Yi Kao. Such a shame he would not play, as you would not ... not even to save your father.'

'You have no power over us, Daji, nor did you ever,' Dan replied with a good serve of resentment. 'My father died of natural causes and well you know it!'

His certainty surprised her and betrayed the truth of the matter, and that made her angry. 'But you will not!' She reached out the hand of her shadow body to grip his heart, as she had with Bi Gan, but her spirit-fist hit an invisible barrier, and the force of the unexpected impact rebounded back on her and pained her hand as if she had punched into steel.

The Lord of the Elements had a quiet chuckle at this, for he did not need to be in the vicinity to see what was unfolding, and his perception fed Hudan's. She breathed a sigh of relief that the ethereal barrier they had raised in front of the Zhou force had held firm.

Huxin took advantage of Su Daji's pain and leapt higher than any regular tiger could to grip Daji's staff in her mighty jaws and rip it from her possession. When the tigress landed, she transformed into human form to grasp the staff and turn it back upon Su Daji. Huxin's scaled body armour hung to her thighs like a sleeveless ill-fitting dress. 'Now you die, tiger slayer!' Huxin directed the force of her chi through the weapon, but Su Daji vanished and the force hit the hard dry ground, resulting in an enormous puff of dust. 'Damn it!' Huxin vanished after her.

Seeing the path to the Shang free of unearthly impediments, Fa took this as his cue. He mounted his chariot, as did Dan, and then turned and raised his voice to address his forces. 'Let all of us, with one heart and one purpose, be determined to conquer our enemy, so that the people of the world shall live in peace hereafter!'

To a roar of confirmation, and the thundering of tens of thousands of swords banging against shields, Ji Fa led three hundred chariots of war, three thousand tiger-helmeted warriors on horseback and forty thousand troops onto the battlefield in the wilderness of Mu.

Hudan continued to address the Shang army as the Zhou horde bore down on them. 'If you would see justice done this day, fight for Ji Fa and win your freedom, for you shall be rewarded and embraced as a kinsman. If you are weary of fighting, then face your sword tip to the ground and heaven's justice will bypass you, and shall not persecute you hereafter. Your destiny and the fate of the entire land are in your hands. Do you choose to fight for heaven or for Su Daji? The time to decide is *now*!' Her voice boomed and the apparition promptly dissipated in a large cloud that began spreading out in all directions, crashing thunder and flashing with electrical fury, leaving the Shang forces stunned.

The Zhou force was near upon them, and in a wave of mass consciousness, the two hundred thousand foot soldiers of Shang — prisoners and slaves granted their freedom to defend the emperor — turned on the official Shang army, and the shock of the huge turnaround caused many others in the army to join the turncoats, or drop their spears to save their skins. The small percentage of remaining loyalists turned and fled for their lives and rain finally fell in Shang and there was much rejoicing.

*

So it was that the great battle of Mu was no battle at all, only a liberation of the East. Hudan could breathe easier knowing that the river of blood she had foreseen had been avoided by clever tactics and righteous action. *'I thank you, lord, but must leave you now.'* Hudan let go of his hands and bowed her head in thanks.

'Any time,' Avery told her, waving off the favour.

'May I call on you again, when it comes time to deal with Dragonface?'

'To aid you in disposing of that monster would be an honour,' and the lord had never appeared so deadly serious.

Su Daji ... Hudan visualised her foe as she had seen her on the battlefield just now, and willed her body to wherever the enchantress was hiding. Hudan was dismayed to remain exactly where she was. *'Have I drained my chi?'* Hudan queried the lord, confused, as she felt rather empowered and not drained in the least.

'She's a bit of a fox that one,' Avery commented.

Was he referring to Su Daji? *'Sorry, lord ...'*

'Try your sister in human form,' Avery suggested, *'as she is carrying a staff.'*

Without further query, she followed the lord's instruction. Hudan visualised being with Huxin, and felt every fibre of her being infused by the intense light of transcendental teleportation as she was reduced to chi essence and swept away by her will.

'Thank heaven!' Hudan heard Huxin says emphatically, as she appeared next to Huxin in a dry glen. Their location appeared to be nowhere near Mu as this was hilly, craggy country, parched and barren.

'Here, hold this will you.' Huxin gave her sister Su Daji's staff. 'The witch is a damn were-fox, quick as lightning.' Huxin wriggled out of her armour.

'Ah, that's what he meant.' Hudan understood Avery's quip.

'But I'm faster!' Huxin cast her heavy armour to the ground, shifted into tiger form and took off through the wilting woods in the direction the fox had gone. Hudan flew after her.

In the neighbouring grotto, Huxin was set upon by several foxes that had no hope of defeating her but, like Hudan, she was confused as to which fox she was supposed to be chasing. Then Hudan spied one single fox fleeing the craggy vale via a cleft in the ridge at the far end. 'Huxin!' Hudan directed her sister to the escaping animal and the tigress bowled over her opposition and made after her prey. Hudan bade the decoy foxes to disperse, and it was so.

Beyond the cleft was a cliff edge where the tigress soon had the fox cornered, and Su Daji assumed her human form. 'You think this is a victory, but you will never be so wrong,' she said as she tottered, naked, on the verge of the deep abyss.

'I know about Dragonface,' said Hudan sympathetically, 'and I believe you have been wrongly accused of many an ill deed because your hand was forced.'

For a moment, there was a glimmer of hope in Su Daji's eyes, which her resentment quickly squashed. 'You know *nothing*,' she hissed. 'I was stolen from my father by a man I did not love! What was I to do when offered the power to bring him down! And now I have succeeded. Shou will be remembered for all time as the tyrant he was. Your brave king and his pretty brothers will be as lambs to the slaughter.' She gave a malicious laugh before her indifference turned her face to stone. 'So take the throne … you have my condolences … for you are all *damned*.' And Daji allowed herself to drop from the cliff ledge. Racing to the edge, Hudan reached out with her chi to save her, but Su Daji deflected the supernatural aid and fell to her death on the rocks below.

The tigress alongside Hudan resumed her human form. 'What a sore loser! But … Su Daji is dead!' she cheered in excitement, then noted Hudan's lacklustre mood. 'Too easy.'

'Yes, it was.' Hudan backed away from the edge, and found herself considering that the door to the throne had just been left wide open for them. 'Against the two of us, she didn't stand a chance.'

'Who is Dragonface?' Huxin summoned her armour back to herself to cover her nakedness.

'The real enemy,' Hudan commented, her thoughts turning to Ji Fa. 'We should join our forces.'

'You have some explaining to do,' Huxin said, and wriggled into her heavy armour.

'I know,' Hudan agreed, before envisioning Ji Fa and teleporting herself to his vicinity.

When Hudan and Huxin joined the Zhou army the force had slowed to a stop to regroup, just beyond the walls of Yin city. The downpour had ceased and the storm cloud had broken up and scattered across the sky. Those still loyal to Shang had been rounded up and barricaded in a stockade which the emperor had been using to keep prisoners of war. These captives had been freed to make room for the Shang — Ji Shi among them.

When Hudan recognised him, she was most relieved to see him alive and neared to converse with him. 'I thought …' Tears rimmed her eyes, and she was prevented from hugging him by the two staffs she held, one in each hand.

'I saw the skins,' Shi said, jaw clenched, then forced a smile. 'But I am well.'

'Ji Shi!' Huxin wandered over. 'I was not aware you two had formally met.'

Shi was so overwhelmed at Huxin's presence that his mind went blank and he stood silent.

'We met at Li Shan, when Shi was sent to seek out Dan and me,' Hudan explained, and Shi was grateful. 'We share a love of tigers,' she said, grinning to placate her sister, and left them both, while she sought out Ji Fa, who was not far afield.

'Post guards around the stockade … we'll see how many are still prepared to die for their emperor once Shou is pronounced dead. They may only be holding out for fear of reprisals if we fail to take the city,' Ji Fa was instructing Xian and Zhenduo. 'Hopefully, no one else has to die this day.'

'Not much chance of that now,' Zhenduo said, but as his brother's eyes shifted to focus just behind Fa, the king turned to find Hudan waiting to present him with the staff of her enemy.

'Su Daji is dead.' She handed the trophy over to Ji Fa. 'She will wreak her cruel vengeance on our people no more.'

'Now there is no one to stand in our way.' Xian was delighted by the news.

'I fear you are wrong about that,' Hudan said directly, and the brothers looked disbelievingly at each other.

Fa held up a finger to stop her from saying any more. 'Please see to the prisoners.' Fa bade his brothers to leave him with Hudan.

'Yes, my king,' Xian replied, bowing out without further question. Zhenduo followed, serving Hudan a firm nod of respect for her day's work.

'Are you aware of an impediment that I am not?' Fa turned to her, as Ji Dan spotted them and moved to join the huddle.

'Is it true? Su Daji is dead!' He was so excited he didn't realise he was interrupting something, and Hudan simply nodded to confirm. 'I thought my time had come when she flew at me, but some mysterious barrier repelled her attack.'

'Perhaps you are more powerful than you realise, brother Dan,' Hudan suggested, denying that she had anything to to with it.

'I don't think so,' he reckoned, with a soft smile of appreciation that was captivating.

'Ah-hum,' Fa cleared his throat. 'We have a war unfolding,' he reminded Hudan, hoping to get her back to their previous conversation.

'Ah, yes,' Hudan found her senses. 'Ji Dan and I have become aware of an … impediment …' It came to her attention that the daylight was fading, and looking up she saw the moon beginning to merge with the sun.

'The second omen!' a voice cried and everyone looked up in wonderment as the prophecy unfolded.

'Not now,' Fa said, annoyed. 'How am I to kill Shou by the end of the doubling, if I am not yet in the city?'

'Smoke,' exclaimed Hudan, as she spied the plume rising from a tower in the centre of Yin. 'Zi Shou will burn,' she repeated her prophecy, having never conceived that the cowardly emperor would take his own life. 'Fate has beaten us to it,' she stated. *Fate or Dragonface?* she pondered on the quiet.

The dark haze from the inferno rose and added to the eeriness of the celestial event unfolding above, and as the land was cast into shadow, the frenzied screams of many men cut through the darkness like an assassin's blade, striking fear into the hearts of all around her — for the screams were emanating from their side of the city wall.

'Your brave king, and his pretty brothers, will be as lambs to slaughter.'

As she recalled Daji's prediction, Hudan felt arms about her and she was pulled in close to another — she knew instantly it was Dan, as no one else would dare. Her first reaction was to pull away and go to investigate, but it was dark and complete chaos reigned. As the hysteria intensified, Hudan stopped resisting Dan's restraint — she'd never heard such blood-curdling shrieks of dread, and was stunned to inaction. As people scampered about them, attempting to flee from the cause of the horror, whatever it was, Hudan was glad for the solid support to cling to. As soon as the moon shifted to allow the sun's rays to again illuminate the earth, the screaming and ruckus ceased, and an unearthly silence fell as everyone got their bearings.

'Are you all right?' Dan asked as he held Hudan at arm's length and she looked for Ji Fa. When she spotted the king, still living and breathing, Hudan also began to breathe once more, and nodded to respond to the query. But Dan had been distracted and was smiling broadly as he watched Jiang Huxin peel herself away from his brother Shi, who clearly regarded her with considerable affection.

'I told you so,' Hudan ribbed him, and Dan raised both brows to admit he'd been unduly jealous.

'The prisoners!' someone yelled in horror, whereby Hudan and Dan pursued Ji Fa to the centre of the commotion. Men were running away and covering their mouths to refrain from vomiting.

Inside the stockade lay a blanket of human porridge and body parts — every single man had been torn asunder. Entrails dripped down the tall bamboo bars of the enclosure and heads were spiked on the upright poles, which stood over two times the height of any man. A river of blood oozed out one side of the enclosure, and it chilled Hudan to the bone to see it.

The look on Ji Fa's face was bleak and then wrathful. 'Who did this?' he demanded, furious to have had his orders ignored, and every man backed away to deny any part in the crime.

'A hundred men could not have accomplished such a massacre in the time this took,' Zhenduo, bloodspattered from being so close to the action, gave his opinion. 'It sounded like a hundred beasts were loose in there.'

Many eyes turned to Jiang Huxin, but Shi was quick to defend her. 'I had contact with the tigress for the entirety of the doubling. She did not move from my side.'

'Nor did Jiang Hudan,' Dan vouched, before the possibility of her involvement was suggested.

'It appears that only the prisoners were attacked.' Xian returned from surveying the area. 'So perhaps this was heaven's justice for the unfaithful?'

Fa looked to Hudan, who nodded to confirm Xian's assessment, as it was far better than stating the truth before she discussed Dragonface with Ji Fa. 'I must speak with you about that other matter,' she said urgently.

The king obviously knew there was a connection between the impediment Hudan had spoken of and this horrific act. After eyeing the carnage, he looked at Zhenduo and Xian. 'Have it burned, before the cesspit causes a sickness. And do it quickly.' Fa glanced at the sky, noting that rain clouds were again forming.

His brothers left at once to see it done.

'You four,' he singled out Dan, Hudan, Huxin and Shi, 'follow me.' Fa appeared most perturbed as he looked for a quiet place for them to speak.

At this moment the gates of the city were hauled open, and a herald exited to announce. 'The Emperor Zi Shou is dead!'

'Long live the king!' cried the high lord of Qiang.

'Long live the king!' Every man present turned and knelt down before Ji Fa, and even Hudan and Huxin bowed their heads to him in a symbolic gesture.

'This victory belongs to heaven!' Ji Fa told them. He was not entirely comfortable with being the only man standing. 'There is still much work to be done this day, so let us not waste time in idle veneration. Arise my fellow countrymen, arise and assist me to set our land to rights once and for all.'

A deafening roar of victory and a clashing of weapons evolved into a steady beat that accompanied the chant: 'Tianzi! Tianzi! Tianzi!'

'Now let us find somewhere quiet to talk,' Fa said to the other four to let them know that their discussion was a top priority, and Hudan nodded to agree it was.

'This conquest will be legendary!' the lord of Qiang said, congratulating the new king as the small group headed toward the city gate. 'We took the East in a single morning, majesty, with an army ten times smaller than that of the enemy! That is unprecedented!'

Indeed it was, but how long they could maintain control of the East and the city of Yin was quite another matter.

As Zhou and Shang troops alike rushed to help the local people to put out the fire in the central palace, more troops searched for assassins and booby-traps. Ji Fa found Shou's huge council chamber abandoned, and declared it would be his room of operations. He led his group inside.

THE DRAGON PIT

The account Hudan gave of Dragonface and the Jade Book was met with incredulity, for the story was beyond belief. However, Dan's nodding head added validity to the surreal revelation. There had been many such moments of truth this day already, and it was now clear that there would be more before the day was done.

'I believe these creatures are why this battle was such a non-event,' said Hudan. 'They know it is your time, Ji Fa, and Dragonface is welcoming you with open arms. These creatures feed to build strength and a greater resistance to death.'

'But considering the feast they've just had …' Fa was too overwhelmed to continue.

'… then our adversaries are fuelled up and waiting for us,' Dan finished.

'But note the carnage was confined to your enemies, Ji Fa,' Hudan pointed out. 'Dragonface is not burning any bridges just yet.'

'I didn't depose Zi Shou so I could be controlled by some prehistoric lizard!' Fa stood to pace out his frustration.

'Many of those who have opposed him in the past have died suddenly or been taken over by him for the extent of their rule,' Hudan informed him, passing on what she'd learned from the Great Mother. 'A truly fearless few have managed to banish the creatures, but none have managed to kill the beast, not in hundreds of thousands of years.'

'A lizard is no match for a tiger,' Huxin said, keen to get hunting.

'You are staying out of this,' Hudan replied, saying what Fa and Shi both wanted to … she had noticed both men flinch at Huxin's suggestion. 'You are responsible for other lives now.'

'Absolutely correct,' Fa said, and then unexpectedly looked at Shi, making his little brother jump. 'And how are you involved in all this?'

'I don't know,' Shi pleaded, faking innocence. 'I mean, I'm not.'

'Then why have you and Dan been at odds these past weeks?'

Both Dan and Shi were surprised that Fa had noticed.

When they both stared blankly back at him and then at each other, Fa grew impatient. 'Someone answer me.'

There was a knock on the door and Fa, still perturbed, said 'Enter'.

'We have recovered the body of Shou, my king,' Xian announced as he eyed the gathering curiously. 'He attempted to burn his riches with him in his tower, but I believe we have salvaged most of it.'

Fa gave a determined nod of approval. 'Good. See that the hoard is distributed to the people of Yin.'

'There is more hidden in the city,' Hudan said surely and Fa looked to her. 'Shou liked to pay tribute to our *friends*.'

Fa caught her drift, and shifted his attention back to Xian. 'Have the body of Shou taken to his throne room, and gather our brothers.'

Fa looked back to his company as Xian withdrew. 'I know something odd is going on here, and I will get to the bottom of it,' he vowed in a paternal tone. 'Come Dan, Shi … let us *pay our respects* to the dead.'

Huxin and Hudan moved to follow the brothers from the room, but Ji Fa claimed their attention.

'Please,' he said carefully, not wishing to offend, 'I respectfully request you remain here. This is a family affair, and I fear we shall not be at our best.'

The ire in his tone matched the look on the brothers' faces; Hudan had never seen them appear so forbidding. 'As you wish,' she granted, and Dan, for one, was relieved.

'We shall speak again after,' Fa insisted, 'and devise a means to deal with this curse before it deals with us.' As the new royal family exited the chamber, Fen entered with haste.

'Thank the heavens I found you,' Fen said, very distressed. 'He Nuan has vanished!'

'Calm down,' Huxin entreated him. 'What do you mean, she vanished?'

'During the doubling I had hold of her hand, when she was torn from my grasp in the darkness. I know not by whom.'

Huxin and Hudan looked to one another, and it horrified them both to think Dragonface had hold of her.

'I hoped that you might use your talent to join her wherever she is and bring her back,' Fen appealed and Hudan was torn.

She had become quite fond of her brother's betrothed and she hated the thought of any woman being hauled into the dragon's lair, but Ji Fa would be furious if she attempted to confront his curse alone, and without his order or permission.

'You cannot …' Huxin could not believe she was even considering it.

'Why not?' Fen realised they both knew something he did not.

'You cannot run such a risk without Ji Fa's consent,' Huxin pressed.

'Why are you both so fearful?' Fen's panic intensified.

Hudan clicked her fingers having had a thought. 'The elixir of waking sleep,' she resolved. 'To project my physical body is too great a risk, but if I spirit walk my way to her I cannot be detected.'

'Please,' Fen begged, at his wit's end, 'won't you tell me —'

'Just fetch the elixir, Fen,' Huxin instructed. 'No questions.'

With a deep frown, he turned and sped off to retrieve the said item.

'It certainly won't do any harm to see what our adversaries are up to,' Huxin added, once Fen had left them.

'My thought, precisely,' Hudan concurred.

'Still, this deed will drain your chi.' Huxin found this very concerning. 'If you are to confront Dragonface this day, that is not to our favour.'

Huxin's point made Hudan's heart flutter and she couldn't keep the smile from her face.

'Why are you smiling?' Huxin was curious to know.

'I believe I know of a means to recover my chi quite quickly.' Hudan shook her head, wondering if this predicament was heaven-sent or of her wanton design — there was only one way to know for certain. 'I shall explain everything to heaven's chosen and allow him to decide which scenario is more favourable?'

'Now to explain that to Fen,' Huxin said, glancing to the doors that she expected to see him come speeding back through at any moment.

'We tell him nothing before Ji Fa gives the nod,' Hudan insisted. 'I feel our new sovereign will want this situation handled as quietly as possible.'

The sons of Ji Chang exited the blood rite appearing both satisfied and disturbed at once. Dan's expression was utterly rueful.

The body of Shou of Shang was carried away for burial in pieces. Three arrows, shot through his heart, still protruded from the torso; his head was hung on a pole — flying the white banner of the tiger — for public viewing.

Hudan was later to learn that Fa had fired the arrows; one for his father's wrongful imprisonment, one for the murder of Bo Yi Kao, and the last to avenge the great man, Bi Gan; but it had been Dan who had swung the axe that severed Shou's head.

As Shou's crimes against heaven were read out to the gathering crowd in the palace courtyard, the clouds burst and heaven began to weep. For the people of the East the rain brought welcome relief and it was a clear sign that justice had been done. It was proclaimed that: 'The Zhou have exterminated the Shang, as per the mandate given to Ji Fa by heaven: to unite the four quarters of the land, over which the Zhou dynasty are now sovereign.'

Ji Fa did away with the Shang title of emperor and replaced it with the word 'Zhou'. He then commanded that the imperial rice store be opened immediately, to feed the starving people of this city. There was great rejoicing in Yin and the people chanted the name of their new sovereign, proclaiming him to be 'the father of the people'.

Afterward, the king summoned Dan, Hudan and Fen to his council chamber where he awaited them with Jiang Huxin.

Dan hadn't said a word to anyone since the blood rite, which had left him in the darkest of moods. He'd not realised the extent of the animosity he and his brothers had stored up toward Shou over the years and, unleashed, his own primal aggression left him rather disgusted. They had been anticipating the day when they took their revenge on Zi Shou, but desecrating a dead coward's body had given him no satisfaction. His brothers had certainly seen another side to the humanitarian son of Ji Chang this day that they would not soon forget. Dan vowed he'd never swing an axe again.

'Brother Huxin has explained to me that you suspect He Nuan has been abducted by our adversaries, and that you have the means to spy on them,' Fa said, getting straight to the point and aiming his query at Hudan. Dan was shocked to hear the news. Fen appeared to be showing great restraint, for clearly he had questions.

'I can,' Hudan began warily, 'but the feat will drain my chi.'

The news was concerning to Fa, but Jiang gained Dan's attention with the comment and his dark mood took a sudden upswing.

'Brother Hudan knows a means to quickly replenish her chi afterward,' Huxin was quick to advise Fa, and Hudan's shy smile caused Dan to smile also. Surely she was not contemplating what he thought she was contemplating.

'But there is a risk I might not fully recover.' Hudan made that very clear. 'The first rule in establishing a fact is to repeat the experiment, and the theory on which I am basing my hypothesis has been not replicated or verified to complete satisfaction.' She glanced at Dan, who was fit to burst with amusement. He dared not believe she would allow him to be involved in her restoration, but just the suggestion put a grin on his face.

After a moment's consideration, Fa made his decision. 'I believe that is a risk worth taking.' He looked to his chief advisor and was surprised to find Dan suddenly cheerful.

'I ... I,' Dan contained his delight by clearing his throat. 'I couldn't agree more.'

'What do you need from me?' Fa looked back to Hudan, and so did Dan, a playful look of question on his face.

'A few hours solace in a quiet, private place.' Hudan seemed a little nervous now Fa had approved of her course of action. 'And someone to assure I am not disturbed.' Hudan avoided making eye contact with anyone as their sovereign considered her request.

'Fen,' Ji Fa said, and looked to the lad to suggest he accompany Hudan.

'Fen has no authority.' Dan was quick to object. 'I shall assist — or rather guard brother Hudan for the duration.'

'But you are my chief advisor, Dan,' Fa objected.

'And as such I advise that you have this dragon pit in the garden grounds found and barricaded shut. Then choose on merit, not by boast, every truly fearless warrior we have, and brief them on the situation. By which time Hudan shall have completed her reconnaisance.'

Fa glanced at Hudan to see if she agreed, and Dan quietly held his breath, as if she did not welcome his involvement she would say so.

For a moment Hudan appeared unsure. 'Brother Dan does have a unique understanding of the risks involved,' she granted.

'Please my king, my lord,' Fen bowed down on one knee to beg. 'I must know what has happened to He Nuan.'

Hudan held up a finger to make a suggestion and Fa gave her leave. 'Fen could accompany us to witness my dream-walk, and report my findings back to you whilst I recuperate.'

Dan's heart leapt into his throat at her suggestion. It would leave him alone guarding Hudan whilst she attempted to regain her chi, and only the two of them knew how she planned to achieve the feat. She had vowed in jest that if she ever needed aid in this regard that he would be the first to know, and the possibility was so unexpected and uplifting after the gloom of the blood rite, that he could barely breathe. How many more times could this day swing between being the worst and the best of his life.

'Waste no time,' Fa granted, 'as daylight hours are running out and I would rather not be facing off with these creatures after dark.'

'Creatures?' Fen queried, as Hudan and Dan snapped into action and bowed to their king on departure.

'We shall explain en route,' Hudan assured her brother, who bowed to the king.

They passed Ji Chu and Ji Du, two of the king's brothers from Fengjing, who were on their way into the chamber with an old, frail man, whose soiled clothes had obviously been very fine once. The smell of him was horrendous!

'My king, look who we found in the dungeon,' Ji Chu advised happily.

'Minister Jizi?' Ji Fa barely recognised the man, and the name turned both Hudan's and Dan's head briefly.

'Xibo — I mean, your highness.' Jizi threw himself on the floor as the doors were closed behind their party.

'Dear heavens, Bi Gan's brother still lives!' Hudan commented as they set out to find a quiet place in the palace of chaos.

'You knew him?' Dan wondered how.

'I witnessed his arrest,' Hudan stated regretfully. 'I hope the remainder of his days are more blissful.'

'I feel sure brother Fa will see to that. Like his brother Bi Gan, Jizi is highly respected by Shang and Zhou alike.'

Dan knew the layout of the palace at Yin, having accompanied his father there several times in his younger days. The sleeping quarters were abandoned now Shou and Daji were gone. They'd killed off nearly all of Shou's relatives; the rest had fled or been imprisoned. The idea of performing a sacred rite in either of the grand rooms the deceased rulers had occupied gave Hudan the shudders. However, the rooms once frequented by the murdered prince, Wu Geng, would suit their purpose nicely, as there was only one door — which could be bolted from either side — that led into the rooms. The private balcony could not be accessed without rope or ladder.

'Rather more like a prison than sleeping quarters,' Hudan commented as they surveyed the room.

'To keep the prince in or something else out?' Dan wondered whether the security measures had been installed by Shou or Wu Geng himself.

'Why did you not tell me of these monsters before we left Haojing? I would never have let Nuan come.' Fen was furious, in his own quiet way.

'Brother Hudan was not to know this would happen, Fen,' Dan pointed out. 'And preventing Nuan coming was not really an option, as I recall.'

Fen, still scowling, opened his mouth to debate the matter but Dan would not hear it.

'This is a very big risk Hudan is taking on Nuan's account, so be grateful and silent.' Dan ended the argument and, releasing his anger, Fen melted into tears.

'I cannot lose her again.' He turned his big, dark teary eyes to his sibling. 'You must save her, Hudan.'

Hudan wanted to comfort him, but she would not give him false hope. 'These creatures seldom take hostages, Fen. If they have taken her, chances are she is dead already.'

'No!' Tears burst from his eyes in protest.

'Listen!' Hudan demanded. 'There is also a chance they did not take her, but if her captors are of the human variety ...' She shook her head, believing the outcome may be just as horrendous.

'No.' Fen shook his head to deny the possibility. 'Has Tian not been cruel enough to her already?'

'Brother Hudan, speculation will not help matters,' Dan said, finding her frankness rather cruel. 'Be strong for her, Fen,' he advised his ward. 'Focus on the desired outcome, isn't that what you are always telling me?'

Fen calmed himself and handed his sister the elixir she'd requested. Hudan took the item in hand, regarding it with trepidation for a moment.

'Are you sure you want to do this?' Dan asked — he was the only one who truly understood her hesitation.

Hudan was wishing that she'd never suggested the course of action. On the one hand they needed to know the movements of their enemy, and find Nuan. But, on the other, what if she was wrong about being able to restore her chi? If she enlisted Dan's aid, would she offend Tian and lose his favour? Or was this a sign from heaven that her immortal relationship to Dan was meant to be renewed? Her Shifu had certainly not thought so, but now she had the royal decree to do what she must.

'Hudan?' Dan disturbed her inner struggle.

'No, I'm not sure,' Hudan admitted, 'but now the king has commanded me, what choice do I have?'

A loud whistle drew their attention to the Lord of the Elements, who was waving at them from a slouched stance against a pillar. *'Might I be of assistance?'*

'My lord!' Hudan was very relieved to see him; Dan could only see a glimmer of a spectre. 'I had completely forgotten I'd not dismissed you.'

'Is it a ghost?' Dan asked unable to make out any detail at all.

'You can see him?' Hudan was astonished.

'See who?' Fen was baffled by the turn in the conversation.

'Not really,' Dan replied to Hudan's query, 'but I can hear him quite well.'

Lord Avery was impressed, and commented to Hudan. *'His talent is coming along.'*

'I am right here,' Dan offered. 'You can speak to me directly.'

The lord grinned and approached Dan. *'But I have no business with you … yet. My business at present is with your lovely companion here, so if you wouldn't mind I should like to converse with her.'*

'Go right ahead.' Dan had trouble getting the words out, his jealousy coming to the surface, and the lord was quietly amused.

Hudan could see Avery was only teasing Dan, and thought he was being rather childish for a son of the sky. 'The lord of mischief was not in your deity description,' Hudan subtly protested. 'You're supposed to be helpful.'

'Is aiding you to do what that potion in your hands would do, without any of the draining side effects, not helpful? he proffered, to her bitter-sweet relief, and then wandered back in Dan's direction to add: *'Then you won't have to waste time or energy trying to regain your chi.'*

Dan smothered all reaction to the announcement and his expression turned to stone.

Again the Lord of the Elementals was highly amused, but Hudan thought he was being cruel now.

'Then let us not tarry,' she urged, to escape the awkward moment.

'*Well, you might want to lie down first,*' he suggested.

'Who is Hudan talking to?' Fen pestered his lord, who was back to being in the darkest of moods.

'I don't know,' he retorted. 'One of her spooky friends.'

'Can they help find Nuan?' Fen found his hope returning.

'That seems to be the plan,' Dan said, finding a chair. He was seated as Hudan climbed onto the bed.

'Be still, Fen,' Hudan advised. 'You know I shall always do my best for you.'

'*Lovely,*' said the lord, with a good serve of satisfaction, as Hudan lay down. He then chuckled when Dan served a dark look in their direction.

'Stop it,' Hudan said, tired of his games, when the impending confrontation would define the next thousand years of history. 'There are millions of lives at stake. This land needs a sovereign who is *humane*.'

'*Sorry.*' Avery contained his amusement. '*He always was so easily baited where you are concerned.*'

That comment took some of the sting out of Dan's glare, and his expression was one of questioning. 'What —'

'*Sh!*' the lord hissed insistently as Hudan closed her eyes. '*We require complete silence until she wakes. Do not disturb her for any reason, understood?*'

As requested, Dan remained silent and merely gave a nod. Fen didn't know what was going on, but he followed Dan's example, took a seat and stilled himself to await an outcome.

'*Right then.*' Avery floated up to stand over her on the bed, and crouched low to place both hands over her face. Her eyelids, feeling as weighty as lead, fell closed, and her body felt cemented to the bed. '*Out you come.*' As his hands lifted from her face, he drew her spirit right out of her slumbering form.

'Huh!' she gasped, reeling from the speed of it, and her attention diverted to Dan, who was staring at them in wonder.

'*Can you hear me?*' she asked.

Dan grinned. 'I can.'

'*We shall return presently.*'

He nodded to confirm, whereby she looked at Lord Avery, who took hold of her hands. '*Remember, even if they sense us, they can neither see nor hear us,*' her guide advised, as their present location began to morph into their desired destination.

The firepit burned brightly in the Dragonface's lair, where the creatures were prowling around the throne of bones on which He Nuan was perched like a brave little bird being stalked by a throng of feral cats.

'*She's still alive!*' Hudan broke away from Avery to fly to her aid, but Avery stopped her. '*Your powers will not work here, this place is devoid of cosmic light.*'

'*What!*' Hudan was mortified to learn this. '*Then how am I to combat them?*'

'*Battle strategy number one,*' Avery proffered, '*is to draw the creatures out.*'

Dragonface was the only lizard standing upright and he was leering over He Nuan, who was staring straight ahead, doing her best to ignore them all. 'A beautiful woman on a battlefield … you must be the whore of someone important?'

'I am,' Nuan said confidently and with pride, 'and heaven help you when he comes for me.'

The creature laughed, amused by her threat. 'Heaven! There's no such place or animal. But we do want your keeper to come fetch you,' he informed and licked the side of her face, and her expression turned even more stony. 'Do you think he will bring Ji Fa with him? Hmmm?'

When Nuan did not answer, the creature released a loud growl and gnashed his teeth in her ear, but Nuan did not flinch.

'Just a little fear is all I require!' The creature gave up attempting to intimidate her. 'There is something wrong with this one.'

'Screw her, boss,' snarled one of his companions, licking his lips in anticipation. 'Give us all a go; we'll break her.'

'It would not be wise to offend our new hosts just yet,' Dragonface decreed, and then looked back at Nuan. 'Besides, even having her in my presence is making me ill.'

Nuan smiled at this, and the creature was back in her face. 'That might prevent me eating you, but it won't stop us tearing you apart!'

'My confidence in my love remains unaltered.' She closed her eyes to meditate.

'*Clever girl,*' Avery commented. '*Battle strategy number two: courage and love are your best weapons. They will not consume the vital essence, or even feast on a fearless, loving soul. If they cannot feed on you, they cannot assume your identity.*'

Hudan felt emboldened by this information and it hardened her resolve to remain confident. '*Interesting.*' She drifted over toward Dragonface to observe him at close range, and via her etheric vision she saw the impression of another reptilian, sightly smaller and different in appearance to Dragonface, interpenetrating the leader's form. But before she could query Avery about it, the creature moved away from her, seemingly compelled to do so.

'Argh.' It folded forward, hand over its stomach as it looked to He Nuan. 'Get her out,' he ordered, controlling his nausea, as Hudan continued to trail him, delighted. 'Lock her in an antechamber until nightfall.'

'*Although you cannot draw on the cosmic light-force in this place, you emit cosmic light and they cannot abide it,*' the lord explained.

Hudan was surprised to hear this. '*Just as my Shifu claimed.*'

'*Well he — or rather she — would know,*' Avery corrected himself, and his slip of the tongue was interesting, but she did not query it as she was more concerned with the present subject matter. '*They do not even tolerate sunlight very well, as like most carnivores they prefer to sleep off the daylight hours as they find the hunting is better at night. When they have gorged themselves their serotonin levels are high, so anything that further heightens the serotonin in their system, like sunlight, makes them depressed and lethargic ... too much cold has the same effect.*'

'*Serotonin?*' Hudan queried.

'*It's a compound found in the central nervous system that constricts blood vessels and acts as a neurotransmitter. It's found in the gut primarily, and is used to regulate intestinal movements, which dictate our sense of wellbeing and happiness. These creatures do not produce this on their own; they steal it from the pineal gland in the brains of their victims, as this is primarily where it is produced.*'

'*That's what those spiked weapons are for,*' Hudan shuddered.

'*Indeed,*' the lord concurred. '*A lack of serotonin will dull the desire to mate and the desire to take care of offspring. An overdose of serotonin enhances socially dominant behaviour — over the centuries these creatures have experienced both extremes.*'

'*They are far more fragile than I'd imagined,*' Hudan was glad now that she'd done this reconnaissance.

'*But very slippery and very smart,*' Avery said, warning her against becoming overconfident. '*They've not survived this long by accident.*'

'*But they are not infallible.*' Hudan observed them closely to desensitise herself to their nasty appearance.

'*No,*' the lord affirmed, '*and your lady friend is safe enough, for the moment.*' Avery observed Nuan being herded out by a few of her captors, who used staffs to direct her into a passage that led out of the central chamber, as none of the creatures wanted to get too near. '*We should return.*' He held out a hand and Hudan took hold.

In complete silence, they waited for Hudan to return to consciousness. It seemed to last an age; yet barely a quarter of an hour had passed when she began to stir.

Fen was up on his feet and at her bedside in an instant.

'Don't rush her, Fen,' Dan cautioned as he approached.

'I know the procedure,' Fen uttered aside, stopping short of reminding him that he'd been the one who'd instructed Dan in Wu ideology.

When Hudan's eyes flickered open, her attention went straight to Fen. 'She's alive.'

The lad burst into tears of joy. 'Her iron will and love for you is keeping her safe.'

Fen flung himself onto his sibling, and hugged her. 'Thank you, brother, thank you!' Hudan hugged him while the relief sunk in.

'Are you all right?' Dan queried and Hudan opened her mouth to respond.

'She's perfectly refreshed and revitalised as promised.'

Dan frowned when he heard the spectre, whose voice irked him immediately. 'Zhou is greatly indebted to you for that.'

'Then why so gloomy?'

Dan's head spun around as the voice came at him from another direction, and Fen broke away from Hudan, aware that something odd was happening.

'My lord,' Hudan sat up in bed to address his tormentor, as she was not looking directly at Dan. 'Did you see the impression of another reptilian beneath the facade of Dragonface?'

'I did,' the spectre confirmed.

'Why would that be?' she wondered out loud. 'Either they can impersonate each other, which would make it very difficult to know if you'd killed Dragonface. Or, Dragonface is just a persona that the leader of the hive-mind wears?'

'We'll just have to kill every single one of them,' Dan concluded.

Hudan was not so easily reassured. 'If control of the hive-mind just passes to the next strongest in their collective consciousness, even if we kill every one of them here, any hiding further afield will inherit the knowledge and power and come back to haunt us.'

'Then we must hope that is not the case,' Dan said, attempting reassurance.

'Right ...' Hudan's otherworldly friend sounded very determined about something suddenly. *'I'm going to do us all a favour.'*

'What?' Hudan was alarmed as she watched her invisible buddy approach Dan, who took several steps backward when he realised he was the lord's target.

'Come here, this won't hurt a bit.'

'Hudan?' Dan panicked as looked back to her for reassurance.

'Lord, I beg you explain yourself first,' Hudan insisted, rushing to stand between them.

'Is the spook here again?' Fen reckoned, having lost track of the conversation.

'He is the only one on the team that can see spirits shifting about. Don't you think that talent would come in handy about now?'

'To what team do you refer?' Dan exploited the detail to delay the spirit.

'You'll find out, if you manage to live till your dying day.'

The response was rather puzzling. 'Well, of course I shall live until my dying day —'

'Do you want me to unlock your talent or not?' the invisible guest asked impatiently.

'You have tapped into that power before,' Hudan told Dan, recollecting the additional soul-mind he'd spotted within the Great Mother. 'You would have mastered the skill by now had a revolution not hindered your progress.'

'Will it mean I can see your lordly *friend?*' Dan wanted to know.

'*Yes,*' the lord stated in challenge.

Dan moved Hudan aside gently, and stepped into her place. 'Then proceed.'

'What is happening?' Fen observed his lord warily, as Hudan was doing.

Avery pressed his right index finger into Dan's third eye area.

At first Dan felt a tingling against his forehead, and then a pressure, like light-filled water bubbles rushing into his forehead. His eyes were closed and flickered feverishly as energy, distinctly golden in colour, surged into his being via his contact point with the lord. When the experience ended, Dan was immediately destabilised and dropped to the floor.

'You could have warned him.' Hudan came to sit beside Dan to support his quivering form and Fen rushed over to be of aid by placing his calming hands upon his lord.

'Whoa!' Dan released an exhilarated cry; he didn't have any inclination to reproach the lord, as he felt utterly incredible. He squinted at first, blinded — the light volume in the room seemed to have increased tenfold. The first thing he came to focus on was Hudan, and she was glowing all over. 'You look like an undulating rainbow,' he said and smiled, enchanted, and Hudan smiled back equally so. Fen appeared likewise.

'*Look at me.*' The lord cut into the middle of the huddle.

'Argh!' The brightness of Avery's celestial appearance bowled Dan backward and he blocked his eyes.

'*Focus,*' the lord insisted.

Tears of resistance drained from Dan's eyes as he forced his eyes open to view the fair face of a son of the sky.

'*You good?*' the young, scantily clad lad asked.

Dan nodded, and looking at Hudan and Fen, they were almost back to normal.

'*Now we're ready.*' Avery smiled, confidently.

Upon their return to the king's council chamber, they found the Ji brothers awaiting their briefing, along with Jiang Huxin and a handful of Ji Fa's personal guard. 'All things considered I thought it best to keep this matter in the family,' Ji Fa explained. For the truth was, that among their allies, the Ji brothers were the youngest and boldest warriors in the land. 'I will not have my allies perish for a Ji family curse. Zai will remain here in this chamber to safeguard the throne, while we deal with this.'

'You intend to come?' Dan was convinced Fa could not be serious. 'As your chief advisor, I strongly advise against it.'

'This is *my* curse,' Ji Fa replied, not be swayed. '*I* carry the mandate, thus *I* choose who may be of aid to me in this quest, or *not.*'

Hudan placed a hand on Dan's arm to calm him, and moved forward to address the king. 'Brother Fa, Dragonface *wants* you to attend —'

'Then I will not disappoint,' he insisted. 'With all due respect, my brother, what manner of king would subject his loyal warriors to a terror he will not face himself?'

'One who plans to rule longer than a day,' Dan quipped, frustrated.

'I shall guard Ji Fa,' Shi assured Hudan as he stepped forward, and the claim was much to the amusement of his brothers.

'I feel sure our king feels *much* safer now,' jeered Chu, brother number eight and the most warlike of the bunch.

But Hudan knew that Fa could have no greater guardian than Shi, who was obviously prepared to disclose his secret to protect his siblings, even at the risk of their ridicule. 'That would be most pleasing to Tian,' she informed Shi.

'He'll have us tame them and keep them as pets,' Chu warned, to the amusement of all.

'I don't know that it is possible to love our enemy to death!' Zai, the youngest added to the mirth.

'Courage and love are the only two weapons you have against these creatures,' Hudan said, and they hushed. 'Fear them and you will die; hate them and you will die. Should you find yourself in the clutches of the creature, think of what you love most, for love is the one thing that repulses them.'

'My happy place is on the battlefield,' Chu contended, inciting a cheer from most of his brothers.

'Then you ought to fare well,' Hudan granted.

Ji Fa looked pleased that any impediment to his involvement had been set aside, and looked to his chief advisor, who was not quite so content with the decision. 'So, what's the plan?'

The remainder of the king's guard had been posted outside the bolted garden enclosure to keep watch and ensure that nothing came out and no one went in. The huge pen had been found open — Shou had ordered it unbolted before he set himself ablaze, as a present for his enemies. There was perhaps an hour of daylight left and the rain was still falling steadily.

'Keep your eyes peeled for anything shifting about.'

Hudan overheard the Lord Avery advise Dan, who gave a nod as the double-bolt to the enclosure was pulled aside.

Dan sights shifted to Hudan alongside him. 'Be brilliant.'

'Oh, I will be.' She shook the staff in her hand, trying to avoid contemplating any tragedy that the next hour might hold.

Unfortunately, Fen had talked his way onto the battlefield, arguing that his unique talent made him indispensable, even more so than anyone bar his intimate family would realise.

'*Like lambs to the slaughter.*' Daji's prediction was like poison in Hudan's mind, but not even little Fen had the look of a lamb about him this day. Rather, his expression was one of single-mindedness — to get his love back alive.

Of course Daji would think good-hearted men were no match for such evil, because she never understood the power of rightful intention, Hudan mused. *And neither do these creatures.* Her pity for the homeless reptiles welled as they were about to have their delusions of being all-powerful shattered — Hudan truly believed this.

Unlike Zi Shou's guards, who had entered this place in fear, the Ji clan strode inside with a consolidated sense of purpose. But upon viewing inside the pit, even Chu was revolted.

'Bastards,' he uttered as he viewed the mountain of unnamed, unhonoured dead, beautiful women, children and Bi Gan rotting amongst them. 'I'm going to slice you open and leave you staked in the sun for the vultures!' he yelled into the cavernous pit, whereby Du and Zhenduo dragged him away from the hole to calm him down.

'Find a happy place,' Du suggested.

'My sword through a lizard's head!' Chu seethed and then smiled through gritted teeth. 'And I mean that in the most loving and endearing way.'

'There you go,' Zhenduo said and released his little brother.

Du slapped Chu's shoulder to encourage him to keep his spirits light, as they turned back to face the pit, the stench of which was enough to compel anyone to flee the vicinity.

'I had hoped your Wu were deluded, Ji Fa,' Xian admitted, 'but it is obvious we have a fight on our hands this day.' He twirled his sword around a few times to limber up, as he backed up with the rest of his brothers to allow Hudan to draw the creatures out. 'This should be a bit of post-war fun for us, brothers! We haven't had a good family hunt since Shi was born.' His siblings were roused by his fighting mood, and even Shi was amused and feisty.

Dan stopped beside Hudan, and when she looked at him, the expression on his face said everything: primarily, don't die.

'If you're going to kiss her again, Dan, I do wish you'd get on with it!' Wu teased, which embarrassed Dan into a retreat.

Left to their conjuring, Lord Avery asked Hudan, '*Are we ready?*'

With a nod, she turned back to face the pit. Taiji in one hand, the lord's hand in her other, Hudan sang the lowest note of her scale. The base of her staff, she pounded into the ground, whereupon its crystal sphere lit up brilliant red. Higher up the scale she sang through orange and yellow, but with her next note — akin to the heart centre of the body — instead of the stone turning a shade of green, as it normally did, Taiji turned rosy pink. The discrepancy distracted Hudan. '*It's never gone that shade before!*'

'*Not to worry, this energy will come in handy.*' The lord's worried sights edged toward Dan and but resisted going there, needing to stay focused on Hudan. '*Just keep going, stick to the plan.*'

With her next note, the sphere in Taiji turned blue, one of the coolest colours of the spectrum. The pale blue light filled the area, and an icy wind whipped around the enclosure, gathering the falling rain and turning it to snow. The temperature plummeted, but before any of her allies could freeze, she directed the icy wind into the pit, at which point the light in Taiji's sphere fell dormant once more. Hudan closed her eyes to direct the cold front through the tunnel and down into the second pit, which was the dragon's lair.

The snowball of wind and ice hit the chamber at high velocity, extinguishing the firepit and covering everything therein in a blanket of snow.

There was a spine-chilling silence that succeeded the strike as everyone strained to listen for a protest or the approach of the enemy.

Hudan rose into the air to get the best view inside the pit without falling prey to a hidden dragon. '*Do you think we froze them all?*'

The Lord Avery, floating beside her, shook his head. '*They are going to be seriously ticked off though.*' He closed his eyes to perceive their movements. '*Here they come.*'

Hudan saw something travelling through the shadows in the pit beneath and passed on the warning. 'Here they come!' The brothers stood on guard with weapons raised and ready to strike.

The first of the reptilians to rear its ugly head shot a dart in Hudan's direction, which she caught and threw back to him with equal force, but his scaly armour deflected it.

Chu was the first to rush forward to engage the monster in battle, when behind it four more of the creatures crawled out of the pit, then rose onto their hind legs to form a huge wall in front of him. Chu came to a stop and backed up a step, as Du, Xian, Wu and Zhenduo rushed to his aid. 'These things are even uglier than I imagined,' Chu exclaimed, suddenly releasing a war cry; whereupone the brothers rushed at the creatures, who dropped onto all fours, heads lowered.

The reptiles sprang forward and battered their opposition backward. Chu, Du and Wu were sent flying and their opponents scattered, scampering up walls and onto the ceiling grid.

Zhenduo, armed with a long, bladed staff, used his weapon as leverage to side-flip clear of the strike. He spun around to give his opponent a nasty gash on the tail, which bled blue gunk as the creature turned about to retaliate. It gripped hold of Zhenduo around the middle and raised him off the ground to tear him in two, but the warrior thrust the sword at the end of his long staff into the creature's eye, and wailing in pain it released its captive, before falling dead at his feet. Zhenduo was quick to retrieve his weapon.

As Xian ran at his target, he dropped to his knees and slid on the mud under the animal, to thrust his sword into the creature's throat. When he cleared his target he was covered in blue gooey blood, and empty-handed. 'Aw … the stink!' The smell of the creatures was like rotting flesh, and they smelt even worse on the inside. Xian wiped the excess slime away and drew another sword from his back. His victim was still thrashing about trying to pull his sword out of its throat. When it did, it dropped dead on the spot, spurting blue fluid.

Another three reptilians climbed out of the pit to replace them, and one of them had hold of Nuan.

'Nuan!' Fen spotted her and immediately took off in that direction, but Ji Fa grabbed the lad to prevent him rushing in as the reptile holding his love was Dragonface.

'Which one of you is Ji Fa?' the largest lizard asked.

'It talks?' Chu was amazed.

'Sing your heart note, Hudan. Now!' Avery urged.

'I am Ji Fa!' Shi announced in response to the lizard's query.

'No, Shi!' Fa called out.

As Dragonface looked to the king, having found his target, Hudan sang. No moving through the scale this time, her voice attuned itself straight to the heart note and the reptilians cringed, repulsed at the sound of it, while the men were galvanised by its beauty. Hudan flew to the ground and as her staff made contact with the earth, the sphere lit up bright pink. The colour frequency was blinding to everyone for a moment, and it shot a debilitating energy through their enemies, but an empowering, righteous energy through her allies.

'Now!' Ji Fa cried and everyone chose a target.

'Come on!' Dan invited, but for some reason the lizards were avoiding him, so he was forced to chase up an opponent.

Dragonface handed his hostage to the lizard next to him and raced at Ji Fa. In the distraction of the glare of Hudan's heart-light, Shi had stripped naked, and the king was astonished when his younger brother transformed into a tiger and leapt at the creature, bowling it over. Dragonface may have stood taller than the tiger, but the tiger had greater body mass on its side and Shi sounded far more ferocious, with teeth and claws every bit as sharp as his slippery opponent.

The creature was clearly overwhelmed by this development. Noticing their leader in trouble, a couple of his minions ran to his aid, abandoning their battle with Chu and Xian.

'Where did the tiger come from?' Chu asked, and Xian shrugged.

'The enemy of our enemy is our ally.' Xian rushed off to help the animal and Chu, in agreement with Xian's reasoning, followed suit.

Hudan noted another enemy had scampered across the ceiling of the cage. As it dropped toward the king, she blasted the creature with a burst of force from Taiji, so that it slammed into the back wall of the enclosure and fell unconscious. Wu was quick to run it through before it recovered. Hudan then turned her attention to the lizard that held Nuan, but Fen was racing toward the beast at breakneck speed.

'You want something, little girl?' the creature laughed, seeing that his challenger was so young and didn't even wield a weapon. Fen jumped high into the air over the creature's head and, doing a half twist, came to land on the lizard warrior's back. The reptile struggled to swat the lad off with his one free arm, but Fen hugged tight, eyes closed. Hudan realised his tactic as the creature calmed to a passive state.

'You don't want to kill,' Fen told it, and it shook its head to agree. 'Put the lady down.' The creature complied with his wish, and Fen slid from its back to embrace Nuan.

'Fen!' She threw her arms around him.

Hudan turned back to see Dragonface had escaped the tiger by scampering up a wall, and while the tiger aided Xian and Chu to fend off the other two lizards, Dragonface shot a dart from his wristband across the field of battle and Nuan suddenly felt like a dead weight in Fen's arms.

'No!' Hudan and Fen cried out together. Hudan began blasting the creature as it skittered around the enclosure to avoid her strikes. Then she stole a moment to centre herself, and directed her chi to pin Dragonface to the spot. Aiming with her staff, it took all her concentration to keep the struggling animal pinned down, as Ji Fa cried out, 'He's mine!' The king took a running jump and with a swing of his battleaxe, took the creature's head clean off. As the reptilian's head rolled across the ground it changed into another of its ilk.

'Fa! Look out!' Dan cried in warning, as the creature he was battling changed form into Dragonface and left Dan to pursue the king.

Fa turned and was stunned to be confronted by the very dragon he'd just killed, who sank his claws deep into the king's leg. 'A little gift from me to make your remaining time on this earth as miserable as possible.'

The tiger clamped his jaws around the neck of the creature to drag it off the king, and applying more and more pressure, drained the life from his victim, who fell limp in his jaws.

Dan watched the dead animal and his eyes followed an invisible trail of something moving toward the reptilian Chu was fighting. 'There!'

The reptilian before Chu began to transform into Dragonface, but before the shift was completed Chu took advantage and drove his sword through the head of his opponent. 'With love from Zhou, shithead!' He yanked his weapon back out and watched the monster fall.

All the warriors then turned their attention to the one reptilian still active, who assumed the form of Dragonface.

'The curse you have imposed on our land, its rulers and humanity ends today!' Ji Fa told the creature.

'My tribute is not so great, compared with the knowledge I can offer you, Ji Fa,' it said, inviting negotiation. 'I've been alive for hundreds of thousands of years. You cannot begin to imagine what I know.'

'Like a whore you promise delights, but will deliver nothing but disease,' the king replied, making it clear he was not interested in collaboration.

'You are not the only civilisation to exploit on this planet, you realise?' the creature vexed his opponent, the edges of its very large mouth curving to a grin as it pressed a button on its armour and exploded over them.

'Argh!' they all cried in disgust, wiping blue muck and pieces of lizard off themselves. Dan, however, remained focused on the dead creature.

Hudan rushed over. 'Where is he going?' she queried Dan, who shook his head as he looked about them.

'He didn't shift that time. His dark spirit just vanished.'

They both looked at Avery, who nodded. *'Dan's right. He's gone.'*

All eyes turned to the one remaining creature that Fen had taken down with his healing and empathic skills. This creature had not taken on the persona of Dragonface, but was kneeling beside Fen weeping over the dead body of Nuan.

'I'll go check the dragon pit and see if there are any left down there.' The lord vanished from their midst.

'Fen?' Hudan moved to drag her brother away from the creature, but Fen was too overwhelmed by grief.

'The poison worked too fast. She was gone before I knew what had happened!' He collapsed over Nuan's body, weeping.

'So sad,' the lizard sobbed, blue tears of empathy streaming down its snout, one arm around Fen in comfort.

'I'm so sorry, Fen,' Hudan told him, trying to remove the creature's arm from around her brother, but it held tight, shaking its head as it cried harder.

'What on earth?' The king limped over, unable to believe what he was seeing.

Hudan rose and approached Ji Fa to whisper an explanation. 'Fen can pass his emotions on to others. That is he why is such an exceptional healer.'

'Really? Good to know. How long will it last?'

'Difficult to say, really,' Hudan advised.

'We have to kill it,' Dan insisted. 'It could turn into Dragonface at any second. Or this could be a trick.'

'Is anyone going to restrain that tiger?' Chu was wary of it roaming around free. 'And what happened to Shi?' he asked, as he witnessed the tiger transform into the said missing person. '*Oh …*'.

'Bugger me,' uttered Xian. His naked brother rose and giving his stunned brothers a wave, moved to get his clothes and get dressed.

'That explains a lot,' Zhenduo added.

'Shi saved my life twice,' the king spoke up, as his siblings moved in Shi's direction, 'so if I hear one word of ridicule from any of you, or anyone breathes a word about his secret to anyone, I'll have your head for it. Is that clear?'

'Sure thing,' Xian muttered, not really listening, as he pursued his brothers who were keen to speak with their supernatural brother.

'You knew,' Dan accused Hudan. 'He's the father of Huxin's little bundle.'

She raised her eyebrows at his reasoning, and Fa didn't know whether he should be pleased about it or not. 'Well, at least I know what you were being so secretive about.'

'Huxin doesn't know,' Hudan was quick to add, and Fa was even more perplexed, but he had other concerns at present.

'Lock this thing in the strongest cell we have for now,' Fa ordered, indicating the weeping lizard.

'We must kill it!' Dan stressed.

'Yes, we must,' Fa agreed, then posited, 'but we might like to question it first?'

'He might know where Dragonface has gone?' Hudan suggested, as four of the king's guard seized Fen's weeping lizard and easily bound its hands and feet to a pole. 'Their leader certainly didn't seem very concerned about offing himself,' she added, which was making her very uneasy.

'It's probably wondering how we knew about his lair,' Dan proposed. 'An enemy with no fixed address is much harder to root out.'

Fen clearly didn't know how to feel as he watched the pacified creature being bound. 'Something is wrong,' he said, as the lizard was lifted to be carted away. It was writhing in pain and making a straining sound. Before Fen could rise to soothe it, the creature exploded, and the guards dropped their load in disgust.

'There goes that problem.' Fa commented, turning back to his advisors.

'That did not look like a suicide,' Dan observed.

The suggestion sent a chill through Hudan's body as she bowed down to try and pry her shell-shocked brother away from his dead lover. 'Fen, your king has been injured.'

The lad raised his head to view the king, and shifted to kneel before Ji Fa. 'I beg your forgiveness, highness, but I can aid no one like this.' Fen held his hands palm upward his fingers clenched inward like injured claws, and bowing his head in shame, he silently wept anew.

'Perfectly understandable, my brother.' The king leaned on a member of his guard for support. 'Come and see me once you are able.'

The cavern is empty.' Avery startled Dan and Hudan with his sudden reappearance. *'There are no other exits in there.'*

'What's the matter with both of you?' Ji Fa asked, startled by Hudan and Dan as they both flinched at once.

'As we seem to have eliminated Yin's lizard infestation, we should have no problem retrieving the rest of the royal treasury from the dragon's pit,' Hudan advised.

'Tomorrow,' Ji Fa decided. 'I believe we've all had enough adventure for one day.' He wiped more slime from the front of his armour and flicked it aside, revolted.

'I shall have the body of Bi Gan exhumed from the dragon pit immediately and prepared for a decent burial,' Dan granted, knowing this would be his brother's wish.

'At least we can identify him,' the king said, 'unlike all these other poor souls. Once Yin's treasure is retrieved I want this pit filled in and a memorial built here to honour those who suffered under Shou's rule.'

'It will be done.' Dan bowed his head as Fa limped off.

'Good work today!' he called back, as a few of his guard swept the king off his feet to carry him back into the palace proper.

'Come, Fen,' Hudan said gently, encouraging him to his feet, but he pulled away to take He Nuan in hand and carry her from the field.

The remaining Ji brothers fell silent to pay their respects to their fallen ally as Fen passed them by, and then followed him out through the gate.

Left alone amid the slaughter, Hudan turned to her co-conspirator to congratulate him.

'Would you like a hug?' Dan invited, covered in lizard guts and smelling repulsive.

'I think I'll pass,' Hudan decided, having managed to avoid being doused in carnage. 'But congratulations, we made it through the day.'

'Praise Tian,' he returned her smile, clearly grateful for their deliverance.

'*Hey, you two!*' Avery startled them both, and Hudan was a little vexed.

'Are we done here, do you think, my lord?'

'By *all indications, it seems we are,*' he said happily.

'Then on behalf of the people of our land, I thank you,' she said kindly, and he lapped up her attention. 'You are dismissed.'

'*Hey* —' He vanished with a stunned look on his face.

'Thank heaven for small mercies,' Dan grinned, and noting the clean-up crew entering the enclosure, he wiped his hand on a clean part of his trousers and extended it palm up to Hudan.

The gesture made her a little uncomfortable, now that she no longer needed gossip to fuel Daji's anger, but she accepted with a cheeky grin and closing her eyes she envisioned the king's council chamber.

'Hudan?' Dan queried, dismayed and enchanted, as Hudan directed her chi to encompass him and drag him along for the ride. 'I don't *know* …'

'… about this,' he concluded to find he was already elsewhere, grinning deliriously as Hudan released him and he staggered about regaining his equilibrium.

'Dan?' Zai rose from the king's chair, obviously shocked to see his brother appear out of thin air with the Wu, in the middle of the council chamber.

'Is it over?' Huxin came striding toward them to inquire, but stopped in her tracks, repelled by the stench. 'Dear heaven, what happened to you? You smell as horrendous as old Jizi did when he came straight from the dungeon.'

'That, my dear brother, is the sweet smell of victory,' Dan advised.

'The king lives?' Zai queried, sounding more disappointed than concerned.

'You need not fear having kingship thrust upon you, Zai,' Dan said, sarcastically. 'Ji Fa has but a few scratches to show for the battle, thanks to Shi.'

'Shi?' Zai was surprised to hear him singled out for special note.

'Shi saved Ji Fa?' Huxin's ears picked up.

'Twice!' Dan held up to fingers to emphasise.

'I don't believe you.' Zai clearly thought his older brother was playing him for sport.

'I believe a debriefing may be taking place in the imperial bathhouse about now. Which is exactly where I am headed if you want to accompany me?' Dan offered.

'At a distance, perhaps,' Zai replied, motioning for Dan to lead the way.

'Brothers.' Dan bowed out, and left the chamber with Zai trailing behind.

'How I would love to be a fly on that bathhouse wall,' Huxin commented aside to Hudan, once the men where out of sight. But looking at her sister, Huxin found Hudan not so amused.

'Fen saved Nuan from the creatures, only to lose her to a poison dart,' Hudan explained her sadness, and Huxin looked horrified. 'Ji Fa's wound is far greater than just a scratch, and Fen is a mess and incapable of healing him.'

Huxin thought through the problem. 'I should go and see that our king's wound is cleaned properly,' she decided, keen to rush off.

'Huxin!' Hudan was surprised at her. 'Don't you care that our brother is hurting? His lover has been killed!'

'No,' Huxin said quite frankly. 'She was wrong for him, and we never liked her. My duty is to Ji Fa and his welfare.'

Hudan would have called her an animal, but Huxin would take it as a compliment.

'He'll get over it, Hudan,' Huxin advised, not liking the way Hudan was looking at her. 'He *must*. You must make him.'

'Is that how you would feel if it was the father of your pride?' Hudan asked. 'Over him, are you?'

Huxin's expression hardened. 'Fine. I'll go and watch Fen wallow in the loss of that useless whore, whilst our king's wound festers!' she suggested cattishly. 'Unless, of course, you are prepared to brave a room full of naked men to treat him? From what Dan was saying it sounds like they will be in there for awhile, and with an animal wound every second counts? So, be my guest?'

'I should comfort Fen,' Hudan conceded, almost ashamed of her sibling, whose animal instincts ran so contrary to Hudan's own spiritual nature at times that she couldn't help but resent it. Once again, Hudan was left with the responsibility and Huxin did what she liked.

'Off I go to the bathhouse then,' Huxin concluded happily. 'It's a tough job, but someone has to do it. I shall retrieve what I need from Fen's stores.' She waved farewell and was on her merry way.

It was beyond Hudan how Huxin could be so callous. Whether they thought Fen was better off without Nuan was irrelevant; their little brother was heartbroken and rousing him from that melancholy promised to be a more formidable task than the reunification of their land had been.

As anticipated, Fen was inconsolable. To give him sympathy only increased his grieving, and his grief was infectious and then off-putting to Hudan. Tough love seemed the only remedy when Fen expressed a desire to be buried with Nuan.

'Wake up!' Hudan yanked him out of his pitiful state. 'Your king is suffering! He has endless duties to perform in the coming weeks, and only you can spare him from undue pain, so that he might comfort the entire land! Tian chose a life path of service to the Ji clan for you. Nuan was a blessing you picked up along the way, but she was *not* your sacred calling.'

'I can't do it without her,' Fen protested. 'I want to go back to Li Shan with you and Huxin!'

'You know the Great Mother loves you, Fen, but she will not have you back,' Hudan said firmly, regretting having to speak the truth. 'Your place is with Ji Dan now.'

'But I heard the king plans to divide the land into fiefs and assign them to his brothers,' Fen appealed, 'so heaven only knows what corner of the land we shall be sent to?'

Hudan was a little disconcerted to hear this, as she had always imagined Dan and Fen would return to Haojing, where they were a short ride from Li Shan. 'I wouldn't worry too much,' Hudan reassured him and herself. 'I feel sure Ji Fa will want his chief advisor and his Wu healer close at hand.'

As Fen shook his head, it was clear that he had never been so miserable. 'How can I heal? I have no happy place, Hudan, they have been taken from me. Every memory I could use to raise my chi, now only gives me pain for I shall never know such happiness again.'

Hudan took a deep breath … this was really going to hurt. 'Fen,' she held him squarely by the shoulders, 'you claimed to be man enough to take a wife, now be man enough to bury her and complete the task the Great Mother sent you here to do.' She let go of him, to avoid feeling his utter desolation. 'I wish I could let you grieve for years, or end your days with her if you so wish it, but I *cannot*. Your admittance into the Ji family was *not* a free ride, it was a *great* honour, and now it is time for you to prove that the Great Mother was right to let you live.'

Hudan closed her heart to his tears and self-pity to be harsh with him. 'You have until morning to get your wits about you. If you cannot aid our king by then, I shall disown you.' Fen gasped and shook his head, convinced that she couldn't mean it.

'And Huxin *certainly* will,' she emphasised then continued a little more gently. 'Please, Fen, step back from your own tiny world of pain and see the big picture … it has never been more vital that you do so.' With those words, Hudan left him in the mortuary to find her bed for the night. This had been the longest, most trying, but also exhilarating, day of her entire life and she could hardly wait for it to end.

13

ZHOU GONG

The bedchamber of Wu Geng was the most luxurious situation Hudan had ever awoken in. She'd found her way back to this room the previous night, and as it was unoccupied, Hudan had collapsed on the bed.

After yesterday's furore, the room seemed deathly quiet, so Hudan slid out of bed to approach the balcony doors and observe the situation outside. But, upon discovering Ji Dan asleep amid a pile of pillows on the floor at the end of the bed, her heart gave a little jolt in her chest and she froze. *Oh, dear.* She'd never seen Dan sleep, nor appear so peaceful. To honour the rare event, she abandoned her trek to the door, and slid back across the bed to find her shoes.

'Good morning.'

Hudan was startled and twisted about on her haunches to find Dan stretching the kinks from his body. 'I was trying not to wake you.' Hudan sat on her behind to strap on her boots. 'Are beds in such short supply in Yin?' she queried.

'Something like that,' he replied with a smile. 'This was the room I was assigned. But when I entered and found the bed was already occupied, I took the floor.'

The tale made Hudan feel rather guilty, and thankful. 'I robbed you of your bed, I do apologise. You should have woken me —'

'Not at all,' and he waved off the inconvenience. 'It was the most delightful theft I am ever likely to discover.'

Hudan forced a smile, and having no idea how to respond to that remark, she turned her attention back to tying off her boots.

'Your sister caused quite a stir at the bathhouse last night.' Dan rose to kneeling to brush his long hair back from his face.

307

'I'm sure she did.' Hudan wanted to roll her eyes, as she stood up.

'I dare say brother Fa has never been so happy to be infirm,' he added. 'Although Shi seemed a little green.'

'As he would,' she stated deadpan.

'What is to be done about them?' Dan asked, his tone gentle and curious.

'That would be for the Great Mother and Ji Fa to decide, I suppose. But I have far greater concerns this day than my sister's love life. I have to deal with Fen.'

Dan noted it was barely dawn. 'He's probably still with Nuan, poor kid.'

'No doubt.' Hudan turned and headed to the door.

'Brother Hudan,' Dan called to waylay her. 'I know you have a lot on your plate today. If there is anything I can do to help —'

'I'm sure you'll have your hands full also,' Hudan warranted, trying not to take her frustration with her siblings out on Dan. 'Dealing with broken hearts and complicated relationships is really not my forte.'

'Nor mine,' he concurred.

'Especially when there is so much else to be done!'

'Our king is eager to set this city to rights and return to Haojing,' Dan mentioned, in prelude to his next query. 'He said something about needing to perform a rite at Li Shan, when heaven will officially acknowledge his mandate?'

'That is correct.' Hudan confirmed. The rite in question was the last thing she wished to discuss right now, especially with Dan. 'But as we have many ceremonies to organise before then, I really must beg your leave.' She bowed, turned and headed for the door.

'There has been another development that might interest you,' Dan suddenly recalled. 'The prince of Shou, who we thought had been murdered, has been found alive, though barely.'

Hudan turned back, concerned.

'But he has gladly yielded to our king's rule, in exchange for his life and return to his family.'

That was reassuring. 'I guess he'll be wanting his room back,'

Hudan joked, as she retreated, hoping to make it out the door this time.

'Unfortunately for Wu Geng, I outrank him these days.'

Indeed he did. Dan and his brothers would be named princes this day, and by nightfall she suspected that her dear friend would have stepped into the current that would sweep him swiftly toward his huge destiny. The unification of their land was just the beginning for Dan. He had far greater achievements to realise in his future.

Fen was where Hudan had left him, but he'd obviously moved from the mortuary at some stage as he'd gathered mountains of stunted plants, which he was willing into full bloom and weaving over Nuan's bamboo coffin. He'd stopped sobbing, so that was a good sign. 'What do you think?' Fen queried, with a sniffle.

'It's beautiful, Fen. Fit for a princess.'

'My king said he will honour her with cremation in the high ancestral temple here in Yin, this day, when he offers tribute to Tian.'

'That is a high honour indeed,' Hudan agreed, 'but should you not —'

'Fen!' Huxin stormed into the mortuary and was momentarily stunned to see so many flowers — the rain was only just beginning to tinge the wasteland of the East green and to fill the river that flowed through the city. 'You've been collecting flowers while our king lies suffering?'

'It healed me, Huxin,' Fen explained calmly. 'If I had attempted to heal the king yesterday, I fear I would only have made his injury worse. Tian knows I fried a few flowers before I managed to turn my emotions around. But if I can revitalise these plants, I know I can safely heal the king.'

'Well, could you please?' Huxin insisted. 'I cleansed the wounds but they are still threatening to fester and brother Fa is in terrible pain.'

Fen looked to his sister and gave a nod. 'Lead me to him.'

*

In the imperial bedchamber, Ji Fa was in bed, and even stripped naked, he sweated like he was baking in the desert sun. His damaged limb protruded from the covers and liberated from the bandages, it was clear that the five gashes down his left leg were beginning to form pus and weep. Dan was attending the king when they arrived, and had sent all the king's personal servants from the room.

'He has come, my brother,' Dan advised the patient.

'Fen Gong,' the king called out as he raised himself onto his elbows and spied the lad being led into the room by his sisters. 'Praise Tian!'

'My liege.' Fen sped up his pace and came to kneel at the king's bedside. 'I regret that it has taken this long to come to your aid, but my ability to heal is entirely dependent on a perfect state of mental wellbeing —'

'Never mind, Fen.' The king waved off the formality, and motioned him to rise. 'Dan has explained how your unique ability works. I only hope that your talent is as good as his boast.' Ji Fa gritted his teeth to endure the pain.

Dan moved back out of Fen's way as the lad came to stand near the king.

'Be calm, majesty,' Fen requested, and placed a hand on the king's forehead. Fa immediately lay back onto the bed and relaxed.

'That's *amazing.*' The king gave a relieved sigh and it made Fen smile to set him at peace.

'One moment,' Fen requested, withdrawing his touch to place both his hands together and focus himself inward.

Ji Fa's eyes grew wide in wonder as a sphere of white light appeared between the lad's hands. '*Great heaven,*' he uttered, as Fen reached over and deposited the tiny sphere of light into the king's chest and he closed his eyes to absorb the healing force.

Fen then moved his healing touch downward over the king's open wounds, and as his hands passed over the affected areas they closed over and healed up completely.

'It's stopped.' Fa took several deep, thankful breaths. 'Ha hah!' the king cried, overjoyed, and sat up to pat Fen's cheek affectionately. 'What a little miracle you are, my lad. I shall not forget this.' He pulled Fen's head toward him and kissed the top of it, as he would his own son's.

Fen was overwhelmed by the gesture and dropped to his knees at Fa's bedside. 'I only wish I could have acted sooner and prevented my king from a night of torment.'

'I wish I could have saved your betrothed and spared you the same.' Fa gripped him around the back of the neck, and gave him a shake. 'Some circumstances are just beyond our control.'

Fen nodded to accept the king's reasoning.

'Go, ready yourself for the day's events,' Fa said. 'This morning we honour your love as the last to give her life in the war against the Shang, and to pay tribute to heaven for the deliverance of our land from tyranny.' The king looked from Fen to address everyone present. 'This afternoon, we shall set this land to rights in accordance with the tribute I agreed to pay Tian, and set forth the plans the Great Mother and I drafted on Tian's behalf.'

Fen nodded as he rose, drained of emotion in the wake of the healing.

'And I command you all to go eat something before you waste away.' Fa shooed them out, so that he might rise and dress.

'Well done!' Dan took Fen under his arm as they left the chamber. 'For a moment, I thought my brother's was to be the shortest reign in history.'

'It was my honour,' Fen said meekly.

'I cannot eat before performing a sacred rite,' Hudan advised her company. 'What I need is somewhere to bathe and prepare.' She aimed her dilemma in Dan's direction.

'You don't want to use the bathhouse,' he advised, 'I think they shall be cleaning it for days! But there is a small bath in the prince's chamber that you are welcome to use. I shall speak to the interior staff about having it filled for you.'

Hudan felt a little awkward frequenting Dan's chambers, and was about to suggest she find her own room, when a wail of pain was heard from the king's chamber, whereupon they spun around and rushed back to investigate.

Inside they found Fa, half dressed and collapsed on a chair, gripping his wounded leg, his wounds tearing open anew. '*Damn*, it smarts!'

Fen was completely perplexed. 'This has never happened before!' He made for Ji Fa to inspect the wound, which then healed up before Fen got anywhere near the king.

'Oh, thank heavens!' The king felt the relief immediately.

'I don't understand?' Fen dropped to his knees beside his liege, and looked at Hudan for inspiration.

A couple of theories came to mind, the most obvious of which she was loath to test. 'I beg your patience and pardon, my brother,' she said to Fa. 'Fen, will you walk until I call you back, please?'

Fen, understanding her aim, sprang up and walked at a steady pace out of the room and up the hall beyond. When Fen was roughly fifty paces away, the king began to twitch in pain.

'Fen Gong!' Fa called, and as the lad returned the pain eased.

'It would seem that Fen must remain in Fa's vicinity for the healing to hold,' Dan said, comprehending Hudan's actions.

Hudan was not convinced. 'I believe it might be a little more complicated than that, for several reasons, which I shall explain presently. But first, tell me, brother Fa, what were you thinking about when Fen, Dan and I left the room before?'

'Well, I was contemplating the day ahead,' he reflected and then looked to his healer, 'and considering how bitter-sweet the ceremony would be for young Fen.'

'Uh-huh.' Hudan felt she was onto something, but how to prove it. 'This may not be as extreme as expected, but best understood for future reference.'

'Fen, could we try that again, please?'

'Must we?' Ji Fa was beginning to tire of being torn apart.

'Unless you want Fen as a *constant* companion for the rest of your life, I think we must,' she explained, and having it put that way Fa considered he would humour her. 'Only this time I would ask brother Huxin to amuse you while Fen walks away.'

Huxin clapped her hands, delighted by her role in the proceedings. 'May I, majesty?' She motioned to his lap.

'For the sake of clarity,' he concurred, happily, as Huxin

straddled the king's legs to take a seat facing him and plant a passionate kiss upon his lips.

Hudan had been thinking of some light conversation, but Fa was amused so she went with the flow.

'Off you go,' Hudan prompted Fen, who stood gaping at his sister seducing the king. 'Quick as you can this time,' she urged and he ran off.

As Fen disappeared from view, Hudan looked back to note Dan was also gaping at her sister's enthusiasm.

'Ji Fa seems to have no complaint,' Hudan commented.

'None whatsoever,' Dan muttered, and forced a smile. 'So what are you implying? That the state of that wound is dependent on Fa's state of being?'

'Exactly.' Hudan felt Fen must be halfway across the city by now. 'Okay, Huxin, we have proven our point. Huxin!' Hudan called more forcefully, and her sister finally let the king go.

'Feeling better, my liege?' she asked Ji Fa, as she nibbled on his earlobe.

'Infinitely.' He lapped up the last of her affection and stood, setting Huxin on her feet also.

'So, as long as I stay in a positive frame of mind, this wound will not ail me?' he asked.

'You're going to need a lot more concubines,' Huxin joked, and Fa was amused.

'As soon as you get low, you'll need Fen close,' Hudan concurred.

'Well,' Ji Fa concluded, 'all things considered, it could be worse.'

'But why should this be?' Dan asked. 'Fen healed Nuan perfectly well.'

'Either Fen's emotional distress has placed a condition on the healing, or Dragonface infested the wound with his own dark magic. I don't know.'

There was a spark of recognition in Fa's eyes, as he recalled Dragonface's words. 'The creature intended for this wound to ail me to my death,' Ji Fa told them. 'So perhaps this condition is a mix of both your theories?'

Fen, puffing and panting, returned to the king's chamber, pleased to find him well. 'I am much relieved to see you still smiling, majesty.'

Xian, who had come to advise that the people of Yin awaited their king's presence in the temple, was also rather stunned to see his brother's leg healed completely. 'What kind of miracle is this?' He seemed a little wary, and as the next eldest of the Ji clan, was no doubt a little disappointed to see Fa so fighting fit.

Under Shang imperial rule the line of succession had passed from oldest to youngest brother. But under the mandate of heaven, Fa intended to return to the old way of passing kingship onto the oldest son, as only this would establish a clear line of succession.

'We shall discuss this at a later date,' Fa stated, aiming the comment at Hudan. 'Today we reshape the face of our land,' he said with commitment. 'Just as soon as everyone leaves, so that I can get my trousers on,' he added, his bed silk still wrapped around his bottom half.

The sacrificial rite was a solemn affair for Fen, who shed silent tears as he set ablaze the wood beneath Nuan's flowery coffin. As Hudan was leading the ceremonial rite, Huxin was standing by their little brother and being a lot more supportive now that the king was no longer ailing. Despite the lad's distressed state, Ji Fa's healing held firm, and this was a great relief to Dan. Hudan asked him to keep a close eye on their sovereign, as she feared Fen's adverse emotions might affect the ability of the healer's magic to hold, and the funeral prove torturous to their new king. Happily, this was not the case.

As fond as he had been of He Nuan, it was the afternoon's proceedings that proved far more distressing for Dan. In the chamber of government, the king met with the chieftains who had supported his campaign, his officers and his eight brothers. The released former Shang prince, Wu Geng, had been invited, but was still too weak to attend.

The king spoke at some length of how he attached great importance to the people of the land being taught the duties of society. He spoke of measures to ensure a good food supply, the observing of sacred rites and sacrifices and the sanctity of marriage and children under his new regime. For he vowed he would reward virtue and honour merit above all else, even birthright.

The nobles of the land the king arranged in five orders of command, and assigned territories to each according to their contribution to the making of the state of Zhou. One by one the lords of the land came forward to receive their appointments and entitlements from their new sovereign, who gave offices to the worthy, and employment to the able.

In accordance with the magic square of the heavenly field, the king had divided the land into nine provinces, to be ruled by one of his brothers, who would be the overlord or 'Zhuhou' of that state — excluding Ji Zai, who was still too young to rule.

The first of these nine provinces was Zhou, the central ruling state, containing Haojing and Fengjing, where Ji Fa, the Tianzi, would base himself. He conferred the title of 'Yinhou' to the Shang prince, Wu Geng Lufu, who was to remain in the Shang capital to control the subjects of the collapsed Shang Dynasty. The remaining Shang minister, Jizi, would also counsel Yin's new governance, although he had been moved to his estate beyond the palace, and had requested to never set foot in the royal residence again, as the structure held too many horrific memories. As his estate was only a short distance from the palace proper, the old minister's request was granted. Minister Jizi's nephew, Weizi, would not be returning to the East, having chosen to settle his family in Zhou.

Xian, Du and Chu were summoned forth to receive their commissions first. To Xian was given Guan province in the northeast, which included Yin, the Shang capital, which was clearly pleasing to Dan's elder brother. Hence, Xian would now be known as Guan Shu Xian. Du was granted charge of the province of Cai and would be henceforth known as Cai Shu Du. The province of Huo was given to Chu along with the new title Huo Shu Chu. But despite being granted estates and provinces to govern, all three were to remain in Yin until the collapsed Shang state had settled. Their youngest brother, Zai, would remain also, to aid Xian, Du and Chu hold the fiefs nearby to Yin, to help supervise Wu Geng, and to prevent the Shang regrouping to revolt against their new sovereign.

Entrusting these four brothers to rule was a considerable risk in Dan's opinion, but they had proved their worth and loyalty during the recent uprising, and he hoped Fa's leap of faith would finally end the division that had always existed between the brothers, but more so since the death of their father.

The fiefs closest to Zhou, Fa bequeathed to Zhenduo, Wu and Shi. The central eastern state of Cao was awarded to Zhenduo, now Cao Shu Zhenduo. The central southern state of Cheng would be ruled by Wu, now Cheng Shu Wu. To Shi, Fa gave the entire north-east — including the mountain range of Shi's origin — from Jin in the north to Ba in the south. This was tiger country, where the white tiger in particular was revered, and Shi could not have been more honoured. The fief that was the gateway to these regions was called Shao, so Shi would henceforth be known as Shao Gong Shi.

As Dan had aided his brother to draft the appointments and division of land for this meeting, he had not expected to be called forth to receive an appointment, and was rather alarmed when he was summoned before the king.

'To you, my most trusted advisor, I bequeath the patrimonial estate of our ancient forefather, Shaohao, at Qufu,' said Fa with a beaming smile.

The city of Qufu was in the Lu provence on the far east coast of the land and was beautiful country, but it was as far from Haojing as you could get! 'Have I done something to offend your majesty?' Dan felt compelled to ask, and Fa laughed.

'Not at all, my dear brother,' the king assured him. 'The birthplace of the Yellow Emperor is surely paradise for a scholar? Or so I thought?'

As this was the last appointment of the day, and Fa could see he was about to get an argument, he dismissed his council, but remained to hear Dan's grievances.

'Lu is so far from Haojing!' Dan reasoned. 'I can hardly assist you from the other side of the realm! Nor can I study, if my Shifu must be at your side in Zhou!' Dan had another thought, that saddened him. 'Or have you grown weary of my counsel?'

Fa seemed genuinely surprised by the reaction. 'I would much rather have you by me in Haojing, Dan. I was thinking only of your greatest happiness.'

'My greatest happiness lies in serving the realm,' Dan insisted. 'Allow me to send my son, Bo Qin, and his young family to rule in Lu, and permit me to return with you to Haojing.'

Fa shook his head, no doubt thinking him insane to pass over a title, estate and governance of his own province, for an advisory position in Zhou.

'I will never marry again, and I know you want all your Zhuhous setting the right example,' Dan argued further, but now his brother was regarding him with an odd expression.

'I think I see why the Great Mother suggested I grant you Lu to govern,' Fa said, nodding as his thoughts fell into place.

'The Great Mother?' Dan was surprised and then irked to receive this information. It wasn't Fa that wanted him out of the neighborhood, it was Yi Wu.

'Is it Haojing you wish to be near, Dan, or Li Shan?' Fa asked him curiously.

'I need Fen to study, you need me to govern,' Dan replied, avoiding the implication.

'I have Jiang Taigong,' Fa pointed out.

'Our state just doubled in size,' Dan emphasised with amusement. 'Do you wish to kill our prime minister?'

'I also wanted you in Lu to keep an eye on my three other supervisors,' Fa elaborated, giving Dan more of his reasoning.

'My son can be our eyes and ears in the East,' Dan insisted, at his wits' end. 'The only way you are going to prevent me from returning with you to Haojing is if you banish me.'

Fa shook his head, serving Dan a 'you idiot' expression. 'Have it your way, then ... Zhou Gong Dan, it is.'

The pronouncement was a shock. Dan had not realised that he was talking Ji Fa into giving him the destiny that both Hudan and Yi Wu had predicted he'd choose.

'Why?' Dan asked, a smile of confusion on his face.

'Why what?' The king plainly wondered where his brother's mind and attention had leapt to now.

'Yi Wu called me Zhou Gong the first time we met,' Dan explained. 'So why would she then suggest you give me Lu as a province? She already knew that was not my destiny.'

Fa found the events not so baffling. 'Well, destiny is something that you have to choose, Dan,' he said, smiling mischievously.

'You knew I would protest.' Dan grinned broadly and his brother shrugged.

'I hoped,' he granted, a tear in his eye. 'But when I was giving my brothers' provinces, I could hardly expect you to settle for that of chief advisor, Dan … only you would, or could, voluntarily commit such political suicide.' Fa threw his arms wide and embraced him. 'But Tian bless you for it, because heaven knows I have need of you.'

'And my Shifu,' Dan added with amusement, as they parted.

'Especially so now,' Fa rested a hand on his healed upper leg. 'I am very eager to put war behind us, and start building a land that our great forefathers would be proud of.'

'That we will do,' Dan declared, 'I promise you.'

'I have dreamt of it,' Ji Fa disclosed, 'as I have of many things that have come to pass.'

Dan noted Fa gripping the thigh that Dragonface had torn shreds off. 'Does your wound ail you? Should I call for Fen?'

'No,' Fa assured him. 'You've made me a happy man, Dan. I warrant I shall sleep soundly tonight. Now it's time to feast and count our blessings. In a few days, we'll head for home.'

Dan was surprised. 'So soon?'

'I'll leave the weeding and teething problems to our brothers to sort, that's what they are good at,' Fa asserted. 'I have an appointment at Li Shan that is far more pressing.'

'And what does this rite entail?' Dan thought it his responsibility to enquire.

'I have no idea,' Fa said, pleading ignorance. 'All I know is that my mandate relies upon my attendance.'

*

The vast banquet hall at Yin was packed to the rafters and the rice wine, from the emperor's private stores, was flowing freely. The king proceeded to the main table where his brothers and nobles were carousing. Jiang Huxin was waiting to greet him, for she had made it her personal mission to keep Ji Fa in good spirits. Shi watched as the tigress attended on the king and laughed with him, quietly turning green with envy. This had not escaped Fa's notice and he seemed to be doing his utmost to torture Shi for his transgression. Dan, spotting Fen toying with a plate of food, sidetracked to join his ward, who was no doubt feeling as alone as he looked.

'My lord ...' Fen went to stand but Dan placed a hand on his shoulder to keep him in his seat, and sat down alongside him. 'What happened? Where has the king sent us?'

'We are going back to Haojing with him,' Dan reassured the lad, who couldn't believe his ears.

'Permanently?'

Dan nodded in the affirmative as he accepted a plate of food from one of the dining room staff, immediately tucking into the meal as he was absolutely famished. After a few mouthfuls, Dan paused to say: 'Fortunately for us, Fen, you are now indispensable.'

'I think you are the one who is indispensable,' Fen replied, fobbing off the flattery, and went back to playing with his food. 'But that is good news.'

'Our king is eager to get home and attend to the last condition of his mandate,' Dan added, subtly fishing for information, in between putting food into his mouth.

'The goddess rite,' Fen said, nodding in recognition, eyes and mind focused elsewhere.

Dan's eating slowed, as a bad feeling made his gut sink. 'A fertility rite then?'

Fen nodded, still lost in a daze and only half following the conversation. 'A man who cannot please the goddess cannot rule the land.' He looked at Dan and could see he was distressed, and so Fen was too. 'Sorry, I thought —'

'Who will be his goddess?' Dan swallowed hard, unsure he wished to know the answer.

'That will be Tian's decision,' Fen replied.

'The Great Mother.' Dan's jaw clenched and losing his appetite he pushed his plate aside.

'No,' Fen emphasised, seeking to soothe his worry. 'Yi Wu has no say, that much I do know.'

'Then how is it decided ... by the candidate?' Dan looked back to Fa, knowing he would have chosen Jiang Huxin, had she not already lost her maidenhood to their younger brother. *Damn Shi*, he thought, but at the same time he could hardly blame him.

'I don't know,' Fen replied apologetically. 'It has been quite some time since such a rite has taken place on Li Shan ... certainly not within any of our lifetimes.'

Dan nodded, accepting this; he'd learned more than he cared to in any case. The mood to celebrate had fled along with his appetite, and Dan rose to depart and escape the noise. Fen trailed him from the banquet hall.

'I should not have mentioned it?'

'I mentioned it,' Dan reminded his ward as they walked. 'I *had* to know,' he continued, scolding himself for destroying the first peace of mind he'd had in a long time. 'This torture is *endless*.'

'Mine shall be, also.' Fen could completely relate to the prospect of loving a woman he would never marry. 'There is nothing to be done, so why dwell on it? I have no option. I *cannot* mourn her now, for fear of failing our king!'

Dan frowned in empathy and stopped to grip Fen around the back of the neck to lend him strength. 'You are a rock, Fen. Your strength puts me to shame ... for as bad as my plight is, I should still prefer it to yours ...' he conceded, biting his tongue.

'But?' Fen sensed his lord's restraint.

Dan let go of the lad, feeling he had no right to complain. 'I can accept that she will never be mine,' he said quietly to his ward, who was his only true confidant in this affair. 'But the thought that she might be given to my *brother* —' The notion left Dan speechless, and shaking his head.

'I would not lend so much energy to that supposition, if I were you,' Fen warned, 'as, chances are, that will not be the case.'

'Why so? Is Hudan not the most noted and powerful of all the vestals of the House of Yi Wu Li Shan?'

'Yes, but in this instance, I feel Tian will be looking for someone with a temperament more like Huxin,' Fen posed, cocking an eye.

'But Huxin is out of the equation.'

'I said *like* Huxin,' Fen clarified. 'I can assure you that there are plenty of pretty young woman on Li Shan with curious smiles and batting eyelashes who will be more than happy to be goddess to our new king.'

Dan smiled at his ward, thankful for his counsel. 'You are a good man, Fen, to keep on giving, even when Tian has taken so much.'

'Heaven takes when we are on the wrong path, and gives when we are on the right one.' It seemed the lad had conceded that his sisters may have been right about Nuan and himself — they were just not meant to be.

'Then we can only hope we are both on the right track now.' Dan followed Fen's advice and lightened his mood, pushing the distressing notion of the goddess rite to the back of his mind.

At a desk in the outer chamber of Dan's sleeping quarters, Hudan was seated carving characters into bone by candlelight.

She had discovered this afternoon that there was not a spare room to be had within the palace walls at present. With all the rulers of the land in Yin, the accommodation in the palace was beyond capacity. When Ji Fa had learned of the oversight, he'd instructed to have a room cleared for the Wu. But Hudan would not hear of ousting many exhausted warriors from their much needed rest so that she might have privacy. Thus, she had returned to Dan's quarters to find peace and quiet.

She had begun to record the events of the months that had passed since her oracle with Ji Fa, the prophecies of which she'd made account of before setting out on their quest. Now that much of her soothsaying had transpired, events needed to be documented as a testament to that original oracle. Both accounts would be bound and stored together at Li Shan for future reference.

The door opening disturbed her from her work and Hudan looked up to find Dan and her little brother, who immediately backed up.

'I forgot … something.' Fen bowed to Dan and left them.

Hudan frowned at her brother's sudden departure, wondering why he seemed so spooked, but smiled to greet Dan. 'It seems there is not another room within the palace that does not already have several men in it,' she explained why she was still frequenting his quarters. 'Would you mind if I slept in here with Fen?'

'No, you must take the bedroom, I insist,' Dan decreed, but Hudan would not accept.

'I robbed you of a decent night' sleep last night, and I feel Fen will need my company now —'

'You both take it,' Dan stated as he sat down. 'Truly, I won't sleep.'

'Why?' Hudan was alarmed. 'What happened in court today? Did brother Fa give you a province like your brothers?'

Dan nodded to concur. 'Lu.'

The news pained Hudan a lot more than expected. 'But that is farther east? What if brother Fa becomes ill … Fen will be on the other side of country?'

'Fa wants Fen with him at Haojing,' Dan put her mind to rest on that count.

Hudan had hoped it was just the prospect of Fen being so far afield that was upsetting her, but she still felt like her heart was being torn out. 'When do you leave?' she asked, unable to disguise the regret in her voice.

This must have been pleasing to Dan, as he smiled broadly, and Hudan realised he was playing her for sport.

'I knew it!' She wanted to hit him, but instead sent a barrage of pillows hurtling in his direction with a flick of her will.

'All right, I'll confess!' Dan blocked the last of the pillows and then brushed hair from his face to find her listening expectantly. 'I passed the appointment onto my son, so that I may continue to be the king's chief advisor at Haojing.'

Hudan huffed a little breath on the news, and the emotional lump in her throat brought a tear to her eye. 'Why would you do that?' It was unheard of for a man to be offered so much power and just pass it by.

'Everything I desire is in Zhou,' he stated, his eyes intent on her, which made Hudan a little uncomfortable until a realisation made her gasp. 'It is as we foresaw?'

Dan nodded. 'I did not even realise myself until brother Fa pronounced me Zhou Gong Dan.'

Hudan's heart was suddenly brimming with emotion and she was at a loss to prevent tears from streaming down her face.

'Why are you crying?' Dan sat forward in his chair to ask. He knew better than to make a move to comfort her without an invitation.

'I don't know,' Hudan brushed the tears away, 'relief, I guess. It is an odd feeling witnessing a prophecy come to pass. But it is well that you will be by brother Fa, to advise him.' Hudan returned to her work. She hadn't lied, because she *was* relieved, but it was more from knowing that Dan had not made the wrong decision due to his misguided feelings for her.

'And what will you do now?' Dan sat back in his seat.

'I shall return to Li Shan and record all this,' she explained.

'I had hoped to do the same myself,' Dan warranted, and Hudan gave a laugh.

'You shall be too busy making history to log it,' Hudan said, glancing up at him and smiling, 'but I will make account of your great achievements, never fear.'

'I would be flattered to be part of your dossier,' he granted kindly, as Fen finally stuck his head around the door.

'I need somewhere to sleep,' he explained the interruption, looking ready to drop where he stood.

'Take the bedroom,' Dan motioned to the door at the far side of the room.

'No,' Hudan insisted, 'we'll be fine in here.'

Fen meandered in, grabbed one of the pillows laying strewn about the room, and collapsing onto the rug, he curled up and immediately fell asleep.

'That seems to settle that then?' Hudan put down her tools, and Dan got up defeated. 'Sleep well.' She passed him her candle, having no further use for it this night.

Dan smiled, a little deflated as he accepted her offering. It was as if he had more he wished to say, but was unprepared. 'Goodnight.'

Hudan watched him leave, silently thanking Tian for not sending her little brother and her best friend to live in the farthest quarter of the land from Li Shan. Even though she would rarely see either of them, just knowing they were close would be a comfort.

She tossed a pillow down beside her brother, and curled up with her arm around him as she used to do when he was little. Soon they would be leading entirely different lives and this close bond they shared would be gone. 'I love you, Fen … and I am going to miss you more than any soul I have ever lost,' she whispered, knowing Fen was too deep in slumber to be affected by her sorrow. But if Hudan were to be honest with herself, her tears were welling at the thought of bidding farewell to Zhou Gong Dan, whose company and counsel she had come to cherish above all others, including her Shifu.

Recollections of his dreams, of life among the sons of the sky, preoccupied Dan's thoughts and robbed him of sleep — he could not put the otherworldly visions from his mind. The Great Mother knew about these dreams he and Hudan shared, and she knew, as well as he did, that Hudan was Tar-rin — his lover and wife from another life. So what right did the Great Mother have, or even Tian, to keep them apart, or worse, to give her to another in this incarnation?

Also, sleep was made more difficult because Hudan's otherworldly lord had heightened Dan's spirit sight — he could see other spirits akin to the son of the sky attached to the Wu of his acquaintance, and to his brother Shi. Dan recognised these people from the glimpses he'd had of Lu Chen's life — were they all members of the 'team' the otherworldly lord had mentioned?

Worse still were the myriad ghosts he could now see plainly, lurking about the palace — some bitter, some lost, but all human — but no sign of the dark, tormenting spirit that he'd seen pass between the lizard warriors and then vanish.

Even now as he lay there, Dan could see an entity lurking in the shadows in the corner of the room. When the spectre burst into flame, Dan was up on his feet in an effort to discern if the fire was real, or an apparition of the spirit world. As there was no heat emanating from the blaze, Dan figured there was no need to call for aid. The man-sized flame began dancing about the room and laughing, and Dan's body chilled as he recognised the dead emperor's insane mirth.

'Zi Shou,' Dan stated to acknowledge his adversary. 'What do you want?'

'To gloat!' The fire frolicked merrily about him.

'We defeated you,' Dan pointed out, finding the spirit's merriment vexing.

'You think you got me good, don't you, Dan?' Shou's form appeared in the flames and his head flew off to simulate his decapitation. The entity only laughed harder, as the flaming head returned to its undulating form. *'You had NOTHING to do with my defeat. You think I had the courage to kill myself?'* If Shou had still been alive he would have asphyxiated on his own laughter.

'Actually, no, I did not,' Dan said, indignant, endeavouring to remain unaffected by the foreboding feeling building in his gut.

'The curse was loose long before you arrived,' Shou said, his jovial mood turning nasty. *'IT lurks amongst you.'*

'We killed your pet lizards,' Dan reported calmly.

'You haven't destroyed IT, only freed my kindred from IT. And my gift to the Ji family in return is a THOUSAND YEARS of torment.' The flames flared, burnt themselves out and were gone in a fit of laughter.

For the longest while Dan just stood there, at first shocked but hesitant to show it. He didn't want to give the dead emperor anything more to gloat over. He returned to bed and lay there, gradually becoming more frustrated by the ghostly emperor's claims.

When at last daylight began to obscure the night sky, Dan rose and dressed to get an early start — the king would have many matters of state to settle this day, if he intended to leave for Haojing tomorrow, and Dan needed to continue his search for Dragonface. He did have one advantage in that very few knew about his developing second sight, and chances were that his adversary had no idea he could be spotted.

In the outer chamber of his quarters, Dan encountered a beguiling scene that tore at his heartstrings.

On the floor, Hudan was curled on her side sleeping soundly, with Fen folded around her — a situation Dan had only dreamed of being in himself. At some stage during the night Jiang Huxin had crept in, and was circled up behind Fen, hugging both her brothers.

Dan deeply envied the trust and love that existed between this trio, and yearned to share that same kind of closeness with Hudan. There was a bond between himself and his brothers, but genuine affection was not something Dan had experienced, or even welcomed, very often in his life. His wife he'd barely known, and his son had been raised in his wife's household, as Dan had been constantly on the move with his father's armed forces.

A knock on the outer door stirred the sleeping Wu, and the enchantment ended.

Shi entered and, realising he'd woken everyone, then wanted to retreat.

'You have disturbed us all now.' Dan startled his brother further — Shi had obviously not spotted him in the doorway opposite. 'Can I help you with something?'

Shi nodded, and looked to the huddle of Wu on the floor. 'I was hoping to speak with Jiang Hudan.'

Hudan looked surprised as Huxin served her a hate-face.

'It is rather early, Shi.' Dan knew what vexed his brother, as did just about everyone in their close acquaintance, except for Jiang Huxin; the king's threat of death had kept everyone silent on the matter.

'I know today will be busy, so I wanted to —'

Hudan held a hand up to stop Shi's tortured explanation, and stood to straighten herself. 'Brother Dan, might we borrow your room for a moment?'

Dan forced a smile and stepping out of the doorway he motioned them inside.

'I should attend the king,' Huxin decided, turning first to kiss Fen's cheek. 'How are you feeling?' She caressed his face affectionately.

'Better,' he granted, his eyebrows raised in worry as he noted Shi's scowl.

Huxin turned her attention his way and Shi's concern melted into tortured delight once again. 'My lords.' She included Dan in her farewell, and then swaggered purposefully from their midst.

'I am just wanting some advice,' Shi explained meekly to Dan.

'I understand,' Dan conceded, moving past him to address his ward. 'Come, Fen, we have work to do.'

When Fen noted Shi still scowling at him, he approached the tall lord to explain. 'Are you aware that Jiang Huxin and Jiang Hudan are my sisters, as well as my Wu brothers.'

Shi appeared a little confused.

'They are my family,' Fen clarified, whereby the scowl finally left the lord's face.

'No ... I was not aware.' Shi's mood lightened considerably, and nodding in understanding to one another, they happily went their separate ways.

Hudan had a fair idea what this meeting was about, but when Shi closed the door and fell on his knees before her, there was no doubt. 'This is about Huxin.'

'You must help me,' he begged, head bowed, hands clenched together and held high in appeal. 'I can't bear her not seeing me ... her not knowing she carries my pride, not Ji Fa's!'

'Ah,' Hudan groaned, not only fed up with being a relationship counsellor, but also the bearer of interesting news. 'The king is aware of your claim —'

'What!' Shi was on his feet, horrified, for several reasons. 'Yet still he flirts with her?' Clearly, that fact hurt more than his exposure.

'The king is just extracting his own justice from you, Shi, he has no real romantic interest in her. I have it on Huxin's authority that Ji Fa is most unfashionably in love with his wife.'

Shi was stunned to learn this. 'But they are so cold to each other, and have only ever had one child?'

Hudan was aware of this. 'I understand brother Fa's wife has had problems conceiving since Song was born, yet the king has never taken another wife or concubine.'

'I thought that had changed with Jiang Huxin.' Shi expressed his greatest fear. 'She accompanies him *every*where.'

'That was the command of the Great Mother,' Hudan informed, 'but Fa has only ever regarded Huxin as a brother. So if you were worried your claim to her pride was in question, it is not.' Hudan saw much of the tension rush from the lord's body, but his spirit was still repressed.

'You told the king about us?' Shi sounded hurt that she had betrayed his confidence.

Hudan shook her head. 'As soon as you transformed I think Fa knew, but Dan was the first to voice the assumption.'

Shi nodded, accepting that he had instigated his own undoing. 'And soon the Great Mother will know.' He swallowed, obviously fearful of the repercussions. 'What will she do to me?'

'I told you, Huxin had permission, you've done nothing wrong.' Hudan pointed out. 'The question here is whether Huxin is to learn your identity, as her mating was only ever intended to be a hit and run affair … as tigers do.'

'No, tigers have a strong sense of family, it's just that males have a wider territory than their mates, but they do keep in contact always,' Shi informed.

This was news to Hudan and she could hardly argue the fact. 'The king, as the holder of the mandate, is the only one who might plead your cause to the Great Mother, and I warrant it would be to his favour to do so,' she suggested, and Shi was pleasantly stunned. 'The king wants you to marry and you need a very particular kind of mate, so …?' Hudan couldn't believe what was she was saying; did she want to lose both her siblings? The notion saddened her, yet Shi's joy was overwhelming.

'To have my family with me at Shao —' he gasped on the excitement of the notion.

'I did not say the Great Mother would agree,' Hudan hushed him. 'But it will be up to Yi Wu and the mandate to decide if Huxin is told about you, and what should happen beyond that.'

'But just to have that to hope for!' Shi bounded around the place like an excited animal.

'Shi,' Hudan called for his attention and he stilled before she stressed. 'No promises.'

'No,' he confirmed with a slight shake of his head.

'I shall discuss the matter with our king.' Hudan winced and held both hands up to prevent being crushed by one of the lord's huge tiger hugs.

Shi refrained from grabbing hold of her and backed away. 'Sorry, Shanyu, I am just very grateful,' he nodded several times to impress that on her. 'I know you would not wish to part from your twin.'

'Ha!' Hudan's cynical streak came out to obscure her sorrow. 'I have lived with her and I warn you it is *no* picnic.'

'To face the greatest peril every day, would be my pleasure, if it meant I could have her by me,' he replied.

'Be careful what you wish for,' she warned in jest.

'I would make her very happy,' Shi said, quite serious about it.

'My dear brother Shi, from what I hear, you do make my sister *very* happy.' Hudan grinned mischievously, fairly sure that that would be the end of their discussion.

For a second the lord could only grin, no doubt deciding whether he wanted to query that comment or not. 'Well I … I have detained you too long already.' He backed up toward an exit. 'I feel much more at ease, and I thank you … again.'

Hudan nodded, holding her humour until the young lord turned and swiftly fled, then she collapsed into her own devastation; as going home to Li Shan suddenly seemed a lonely prospect.

Your work here is not done. She snapped herself out of her melancholy.

The king planned to leave Yin soon, and they had yet to determine if Dragonface had been destroyed or if the creature had merely shifted elsewhere. The reptilian had shape-shifted his way out of Yi Wu's clutches once before, only to return and curse their rulers once again. The reportedly dead prince of Shang had been found shortly after Dragonface's disappearing act and Hudan needed to make sure that was not just a happy coincidence.

The occupants of the palace at Yin — Shang and Zhou alike — observed Hudan with a kind of wary respect. After ten years subjected to Su Daji, it was going to take a while for the people of the East to realise that the Wu were only ever meant to be benevolent. Yet, it was now a widely known fact that Hudan had ended the drought at Ji Fa's request, hence the veneration she received from the people was most sincere. Much as at Haojing, her mystique gave her run of the palace, as no one dared query her agenda.

As luck would have it, the one-time prince of the Shang finally felt well enough this morning to meet with the Zhou king. Hudan was announced and permitted entry to the council chamber, and there she found the royals and Dan seated in conference. Fen was standing behind the dethroned Shang prince, with his hands upon his shoulders, and Huxin perched on the side of Ji Fa's chair. All the men moved to stand, but Hudan motioned them to refrain. 'Please.'

'The last of my Wu trio,' Fa informed Wu Geng and then motioned to him as he looked back to Hudan. 'Your little brother was just working his magic on Yinhou.'

The new title seemed to pain the prince a little, but some regret was to be expected when you lose a heavenly mandate. 'That is well,' Hudan said, observing the former Shang prince, who seemed gaunt, yet quite vital in Fen's hands.

'Clearly, not all the Wu are of my stepmother's ilk,' he said, and forced a smile to make her acquaintance. 'Our land owes you, and all the Wu of Li Shan, a great debt, Jiang Hudan.'

'I am not entirely convinced that my job here is done,' Hudan told them all, although Dan did not appear surprised. 'Might I borrow Zhou Gong for one moment?' she requested.

'Our talks here are concluded,' Fa granted, 'so you may borrow my advisor for as many moments as you wish.'

Huxin found the king's retort amusing, and added her own. 'We may never see you again, Zhou Gong.'

Hudan served her sister a sweet smile, knowing her spite was just unwarranted bitterness left in the wake of Ji Shi's visit this morning. 'I shall return your advisor presently.'

Dan escorted her from the room and into an antechamber at the far end that was used for just such private conferences.

'Do you see anything unusual around the former prince?' Hudan came straight to the point once she had the newly named duke alone.

'Funny you should ask,' Dan raised both brows, intrigued. 'Since your *friend* turned up my second sight, I've seen beings within the people of my close acquaintance ... you, Fen, Huxin, the Great Mother, even Shi.'

'Shi.' Hudan was really not surprised to hear him named, as he was no stranger to the supernatural. 'Fa too,' she assumed, knowing he was one of the sons of the sky.

'No, not Fa,' Dan said, surprised about this, as was Hudan.

'But Fa is Hreen?' That fact just slipped out and Hudan covered her mouth too late to prevent it.

'The one Tar-rin mentions in our dream?' he posed. 'The time lord?'

Hudan nodded, trying desperately to repress her grin, roused by the thought of that dream. 'He is the only one of us I have ever seen in the Lord ...' *Ang-wei* — the name flashed through her mind but she prevented herself from uttering it '... I mean, the elemental lord's company.' *I must avoid saying Ang-wei's name out loud*, she lectured herself inwardly. For to know an entity's name was to have the power to summon them to you. Fortunately, Dan, knowing very little about the laws of summons, had never asked after it. 'Perhaps that's why the son of the sky's presence is not within Ji Fa?' She shook her head to cast off that curious anomaly and returned to more pressing matters. 'But what do you see in Wu Geng?'

'Not Dragonface, if that is what you were hoping,' Dan replied, sorry to disappoint her. 'I had the same thought, but no such luck.'

'Damn … where is that accursed creature?' Hudan felt in her gut that Dragonface was leading them a merry dance.

'I saw the flaming ghost of Zi Shou last night,' Dan admitted, 'and he claims Dragonface is still here.'

Hudan was most concerned, as Dan hadn't been trained to deal with the supernatural yet, an oversight that needed to be corrected. 'That must have been fairly traumatic. Are you all right?'

Dan was a bit stunned by her concern. 'I … I think so.'

'You must not believe everything you hear from ghosts. Many of them are just thought forms left in the wake of tortured spirits, that have no reasoning capability.'

Dan raised his eyebrows, bemused.

'They are just bundles of bad emotional energy that a soul cannot take with it to the next life, so they must be shed and left behind. Depending on how strong these emotions were in life, will determine how long the thought form will take to dissipate, or how difficult it will be to exorcise.'

'But Zi Shou has yet to be laid to rest,' Dan reasoned, 'and he sounded very pleased to have passed the curse onto the Ji family. I've looked over everyone of consequence these past few days, and I promise you,' Dan eyes widened to accentuate the fact, 'I've seen all manner of spooks hanging around people, and the palace itself, but nothing that looks like Dragonface.'

'And you don't see anything odd about Wu Geng?' Hudan pressed.

'He has a son of the sky within him,' Dan informed her, 'but no one I recognise.'

That seemed to Hudan to beg the question. *I wonder if my Lord Ang-wei would know him?*

'*Know who?*' Avery started them both with his appearance.

'Did you have to summon him?' Dan protested.

'I didn't know I had,' Hudan said defensively. She quietly realised that she had indeed thought the lord's name three times in close succession, which according to the esoteric law of three quests, was enough to summon forth an entity.

'Is that any way to greet a valued ally?'

'You present more like a nemesis,' Dan retorted, and the youthful lord had a chuckle at this.

'Well, since you are here …' Hudan interrupted the banter and asked Avery to go and view the former prince of Shang, to see if he recognised the soul-mind lurking beneath the surface of his being.

With Dan's departure, Wu Geng also requested to take his leave of the king. Wu Geng had no end of praise for Fen in leaving. 'You are a treasure more priceless and mysterious than the Jade Book of Shun; I shall be very sorry to see you leave on the morrow.'

'I should be happy to come attend you again before then.' Fen bowed graciously to accept the praise.

'You would be most welcome,' Wu Geng replied happily. 'Heaven truly smiles on you, my king, to send you such blessed subjects.'

'I am greatly honoured,' Fa concurred.

As Wu Geng's servants entered to carry his chair out, the Shang prince stopped them, and attempted to stand for the first time since he was found in prison — he was very surprised to sustain the stance. 'I thought it would be months, *if ever*, that I felt strong enough to stand again … is there nothing you cannot cure?'

'I have yet to find an ailment I could not remedy, excepting death itself,' Fen replied, and the comment got Ji Fa thinking.

The king watched the Yinhou accompanied from the room and then turned to his tigress. 'Huxin, my darling brother, would you be so kind as to fetch me something to eat. I wish to speak with Fen a moment, man to man.'

Huxin observed her little brother as she departed, obviously still amused to hear him referred to as a man. 'I wonder if Hudan and Dan are ever coming out of there,' she commented as she looked at the closed door at the end of the chamber, and then exited through the guarded door to her right.

'Is that true what you said to Wu Geng just now, about being able to heal anything?' the king queried, and Fen nodded to confirm. 'Then I am wanting to ask a favour, if I may?'

'Something ails my king?' Fen was immediately concerned.

'No, no,' Fa smiled to reassure him, 'at least not when you are near.' Fa continued awkwardly. 'No, I wish to ask on behalf of my wife, Yi Jiang. Since she gave birth to Song, she has been unable to conceive again. Hence I fear my goddess rite shall be a frightful waste of time for those involved, for I want no other concubine.'

'Pardon my asking, majesty,' Fen ventured, 'but do you know what the goddess rite entails?'

Fa corrected his last statement. 'Perhaps I should have said that I want no other *earthly* concubine. During the rite I am required to refrain from impregnating my goddess, so there is no chance of an issue between us that might threaten Song's rule or my queen's standing.'

Fen nodded in understanding. 'But a king is expected to have many heirs, to secure the dynasty. Even if your wife is cured, she does not have so many child-bearing years left.'

'Song will rule after me,' Ji Fa said, sure and proud. 'He probably has a few heirs on the way from the concubines he's taken already! But you know what it is to love one woman above all others,' the king petitioned Fen, whom he knew could sympathise with his view. 'And there is nothing my wife would love more dearly than to bear me another child.' The joy of the notion welled in his heart and brought a lump to his throat, making Fa's voice horse. 'Do you think that could be possible?'

'I believe that is entirely possible, majesty,' Fen allowed in an encouraging fashion. Ji Fa nearly collapsed into tears, and felt urged to hug the lad. 'Thank you, Fen Gong.' He gripped the stunned lad's shoulders to hold him at arm's length. 'I shall make you lord of your own fief one day!'

'I wish only to serve my king, my duke and Zhou.' The lad sounded panicked.

The king play punched Fen's cheek, his fist gently giving Fen's cheek a nudge. 'You have been hanging around my brother too long, you've caught his madness.'

'All I know is how to heal and grow things,' Fen reasoned.

'That sounds like the perfect qualifications to run a province to me,' Ji Fa considered.

'Majesty, please!' Fen fell on his knees to beg, ' Promise me you will never take such action. I wish to stay in the service of Zhou Gong, that is the only thing I shall ever ask in return for my services.'

'Done,' the king granted, shaking his head in wonder. 'You are a strange breed, you Wu, but I praise heaven for you.'

'And we praise heaven for you, majesty.' Fen bowed to the ground in gratitude for their agreement.

The Lord Avery returned from observing Wu Geng in the next room, shaking his head. *'I have no idea who he is.'*

'Pardon?' Hudan felt sure he'd know. 'So he isn't a son of the sky?'

'Well, I thought I was aware of every soul taking part in this time-trekking odyssey …' Avery shrugged. *'Yet I've never seen him before!'*

'Could he be a spy, or working with Dragonface?' A variety of scenarios were darting through Hudan's mind.

'Dragonface doesn't know we are here, so he'd hardly have a spy after us,' the lord informed.

'Might your brother recognise him?' Hudan posed another solution.

'I really don't want to drag him into this,' Avery said, his reluctance showing. *'If he recognises this person, he'll want to get involved and the last time that happened the outcome was … not so good.'*

'The last time this happened?' Dan found this curious. 'Is history repeating?'

'Playing with timelines presents infinite possibilities to alter history much more than you desire, and the more you try to rework one point in time to eradicate unwanted changes, the harder it is to have causality come out in your favour.'

'How many times has this instance been reworked?' Dan wondered and the lord seemed surprised that the duke had understood the principle so quickly.

'Counting the original timeline, this will be the third run-through, but only the second conscious attempt any son of the sky has had at it.'

Both Hudan and Dan were boggling at the information. 'Was Wu Geng dangerous the last time around?' Dan asked.

'*None of us were involved on a super-conscious level last time around,*' Avery advised, '*except my brother, who completely screwed, not only the future of your land, but the future of our entire planet!*'

'He sounds like a handful,' Dan observed.

'*You always thought so,*' the lord grinned. '*I, however, was never meant to be involved in this. This part of history is not really my stomping ground. I'm a bit more of a futuristic kinda guy. You were the ones who chose to come back here and eliminate Shyamal ... sorry, Dragonface.*'

'Is that his real name?' Hudan felt that that knowledge might come in handy one day. A name was even better than an image when it came to enchanting someone.

'*Who knows? The point I'm trying to make is that this is* your *mission, your life ... and, pretty well none of my business.*'

'But the Great Mother said that destroying Dragonface was also your quest,' Hudan appealed.

'*More my brother's really,*' Avery pointed out, '*and we are prepared to wait for history to run its course before we take action ... well, I am prepared. My brother, not so much.*'

'Why can I not see a son of the sky behind Ji Fa, if he is Hreen?' Dan queried, and Avery looked at Hudan and scowled.

'I had to tell him. I couldn't explain it!' Hudan threw her hands up in defence, at which time the ethereal lord obliged them with the reason.

'*Rhun took an alternative route back to the past to the rest of you, because he knew Ji Fa would —*'

'My lord!' Hudan interrupted, preventing Avery from revealing too much.

'That Ji Fa would what?' Dan demanded to know.

'*Be otherwise detained.*' Avery wriggled out of the tricky moment and was now looking eager to leave.

'What is that supposed to mean?' Dan looked from Avery to Hudan. 'If my brother is in some sort of trouble I want to know about it.'

Hudan raised an eyebrow to disagree. 'If you wanted to know brother Fa's future, why did you not keep reading on in the Jade Book?'

The query stumped Dan. 'Should I have?'

'That is, and always was, up to you.' Hudan looked back to the celestial lord. 'Is there nothing more we can do here? Must we wait for Dragonface to rear his ugly head again?'

'The creature won't be hard to find in a peaceful land,' the lord warranted. *'When trouble erupts, Dragonface will be behind it.'*

'And what of Wu Geng?' Dan asked, wanting to know if the former prince was a threat or not. Since Dan and Hudan could not explain their reservations about the son of Zi Shou to the king, or anyone else, their hands were tied.

'We really have no reason to suspect that he is malign at this point. In fact, evidence would suggest quite the opposite is true. All we can we do is keep an eye on him, and as the king is leaving four of your brothers to do just that ...' Hudan shrugged, looking at Avery and Dan..

'We can perform a cleansing rite,' Avery suggested. *'With the aid of my minions, it would be a swift affair.'*

'It would indeed,' Hudan agreed, inspired. 'Such a rite would evict any ghosts or thought forms that might be hanging around the royal palace, including Dragonface and Zi Shou,' Hudan advised Dan. 'It would ensure the creature could not take root here again.'

'At least, not easily,' Avery added. *'Dragonface has built himself a fortress of ill will beneath this palace over the ages. If we disperse it, this place will lose its attraction, and hopefully he'll stay away.'*

'That would be wise then,' Dan agreed.

'It will be a good learning experience for you,' Hudan said, nudging him with her shoulder.

'I should very much like to know how to accomplish such a feat, especially now I have been endowed with spirit sight.' He flashed a perturbed look in Avery's direction.

'Rather go back to blind ignorance then, would you?' he challenged Dan, who stepped back, not inclined towards the suggestion. *'You've got talents you haven't even discovered yet, so you've got plenty to develop in your own sweet time if that is your gripe?'*

'I am grateful to you,' Dan admitted graciously, 'but a little warning about what to expect might have been nice. Will cleansing of the palace be difficult?'

'Not at all. Burn a few bunches of the right herbs, and utter some kind words, and that's about it,' Hudan told him, smiling, but then frowned. 'Although this palace is very large, and we need to cover every single room, the dungeons and the pit included.'

Yesterday, after the ceremony, the Zhou army had began the excavation of the dragon pit and had been hauling treasure out of the hole in the ground ever since. The king felt the job would be too harrowing for any citizen of Shang. The body of Bi Gan had been exhumed, and returned to his brother Jizi for proper burial. The rest of the bones would be buried where they lay as, after a decade of murder, separating and identifying the victims would be virtually impossible.

'Feel free to call on the aid of my minions during your rite and in the future. They shall be at your command henceforth, and thus you should have precious little need to summon me,' he advised Hudan. He looked to Dan and grinned, knowing that that news would make him happy.

'And we were just warming to one another,' Dan said with fake disappointment.

'*Good luck in your quest,*' Avery said to Hudan in parting, and she was sincerely sorry that their association seemed to be coming to an end.

'Is this goodbye, then?' Hudan panicked, knowing the second the lord vanished she'd think of hundred questions she should have asked him.

'I've told you way more than I should have already. Forget the sons of the sky exist, and just live your life, Jiang Hudan,' he advised. She nodded for this had been her Shifu's advice as well.

'I thank you for your aid, and your gift,' she granted. 'You are free to go.'

'I'll see you when your time here is done …' the lord kissed her cheek in parting and grinned as he said '*… mother.*'

Hudan took a sharp breath as he vanished, and looked at Dan, who was equally stunned. 'Did he say, *mother?*' The word was just as foreign to her as the notion itself.

'Does that mean …?' Dan choked on his sentence, and Hudan held a hand up to prevent him saying anything.

'I should inform the king that a cleansing is in order.' She headed for the door, and Dan could only nod, dazed as he was.

Hudan's mind was suddenly reeling with memories of her conversations with the Lord of the Elements and his brother — was Hreen another son of hers? Another deep shock of recognition passed through her.

'*What is your name, lord?*' she recalled asking the Lord of the Elements. His dark-haired brother had shaken his head at her, appearing as bemused as Dan just now.

'*She really doesn't remember anything, does she?*' he'd said. Now Hudan understood his disappointment.

But why tell her to live her life as Jiang Hudan and then drop that past-life revelation on her? Yet that one little word explained so much. And for Dan too most likely — perhaps it was meant to soothe the duke's jealous streak that the Lord of the Elements had played upon so often in the past few days. Whatever the lord's reason for exposing their past association, Hudan decided to follow his original advice and forget the sons of the sky existed.

The king was happy to grant permission for the cleansing rite, and Hudan had Fen round up the herbs they would require for the ceremony. On the king's command Dan had every censer in the palace collected, so they could be filled with the herbs for burning. The interior staff were to carry these vessels through every room in the palace, fanning the perfumed smoke into each nook and cranny, bidding spirits to return to their divine source. Soldiers were instructed to do the same through the dungeons, which had been almost vacated since the Zhou takeover.

Many of the censers were collected in the courtyard at Yin and set alight, and to the wonder of all present Hudan levitated the largest of the smoking vessels and had it proceed slowly to the enclosure containing the pit, just ahead of herself and Ji Dan.

A guard had been posted around the enclosure to prevent anyone viewing the pit of bones, or trying to steal the treasure that was still being hauled up from the depths of the cavern. As night had fallen, there was no work happening, but guards

jumped to unbolt the gate when they saw the floating incense
burner of the Wu approaching.

'As you were, gentlemen,' Dan commented light-heartedly and
nodded to thank the astounded guards, as he followed Jiang
Hudan inside. 'And you might wish to close the gate after us.'

The guards did not hesitate to follow that suggestion.

The bonfire which had incinerated the remains of the alien
warriors was now just a large black mark in the middle of the
enclosure. Hudan brought the censer down to rest at the edge of
the pit.

'We are not going down there?' Dan queried, hopefully.

'Oh, no. Believe me, we don't want to be there while the beast
is being evicted,' she advised and Dan decided to back up and
watch the proceedings at a greater distance.

Hudan turned to face the smouldering censer. After a few
deep, centring breaths, she sang a beautiful, high note, which Dan
recognised from their confrontation with the reptilians. She
thumped the base of her staff on the ground and the sphere in
Taiji lit up rosy pink. Then she said …

'Come wind, come fire, bring heaven unto Earth.'

As Hudan invoked these elements, the smoke exuding from the
censer increased tenfold; the elements were obviously disposed
toward her, just as their lord had promised. She continued her
chant:

'Lift the worthy up to Tian,
to await the next rebirth.'

The rising smoke did not disperse, but formed a roiling mass under
the grate at the top of the enclosure.

'Send light into the darkness,
banish shadow from this place.
Bring peace where there was terror,
evince the glory of heaven's grace.'

Whirling her staff's head, Hudan directed the smoke cloud down into the cavern, while the smoke continued to billow in a steady stream from the censer.

As before, there was a deathly silence in the wake of the psychic attack, but as the ground beneath them began to rumble, Hudan backed away to where Dan was standing and urged him back further still.

A massive force of agitated wind came forth out of the hole, blasting away rocks and dirt from the mouth of the cavern and thrusting the grate off the top of the enclosure. What Dan saw was a seething, dark mass of tortured souls all screaming for release. Dan moved to shield Hudan, having no idea if it could see them or what it might do.

'What —' Hudan queried, as the thought form exploded, knocking them both backward, their hair flying in the wind of its dispersal.

Dan got up quickly for a bright light was emanating from within the pit. '*Whoa.*'

'You see something in the smoke?' Hudan was eyeing the pit curiously.

He nodded, his eyes now glued to the sight of thousands of tiny spheres of light dancing around each other as they ascended toward the sky.

'The souls of the dead,' Hudan supposed, and Dan nodded, moved to tears by the serenity of it.

'They are leaving.' He raised his eyes to the night sky where there was a huge light-filled corridor through the clouds above. 'Great wonders of Tian!' He was so startled he fell back on his behind to land alongside Hudan once again. 'There is a corridor to heaven …' He pointed up and then looked toward the royal residence and centre of government. 'There are souls approaching it from the palace also.'

'I wish I could see it,' she sighed.

When Dan glanced over to find Hudan staring at him intently, he was even more enchanted. He wanted to kiss her, but that was not permitted. Their kiss on the battlefield was to the glory of Tian and thus in compliance with Wu creed, but if he stole a kiss at this moment, Hudan would consider it shameful and an insult to her trust. As bitter as it tasted to refrain from following the impulse — with the king's goddess rite looming — Dan knew an impetuous act could end his friendship with Hudan and the Wu for life.

'Our task is complete,' Hudan said, standing up and snapping out of her fascination. 'We may now return to Zhou, knowing we have done everything that we could do here in Yin.'

Dan looked back to the celestial event in the sky as the last of the soul lights vanished into it and the corridor to heaven was swallowed up by the stormy night sky. 'So it is back to Li Shan for you, to prepare for our candidate's goddess rite,' he said, letting Hudan know that he'd learned more about the ritual in question.

They both stood as Hudan nodded and forced a smile. 'I shall instruct you on the theory and use of your new talent on the return journey, if that pleases you?'

Any reason to keep company with her was pleasing. 'I would be most grateful,' Dan replied, and dropped the topic of the rite.

'An untrained psychic is as dangerous as an untrained warrior,' she stressed jokingly, as he accompanied her from the enclosure. 'You need to be able to defend yourself against supernatural attack.'

When Dan considered the events of the past few days, he was sure that more knowledge would not go astray. 'That is becoming painfully obvious,' he granted, before calling to the guards to request their release.

PART 4

THE SON OF THE SKY

14

THE RITE OF GAO MEI

The journey back to Hoajing was faster on horseback, although the king's party were forced to slow down through every village en route, as the people of the land lined the road to give tribute and praise to their new ruler, who made himself far more accessible to the masses than any of the Shang had ever done.

As the days were spent riding as fast as possible in the saddle or passing slowly through crowds, Dan's otherworldly tuition took place in the evenings — both Hudan and Dan diplomatically avoided raising the topic of the goddess rite for the entire journey home.

Huxin and Hudan bid farewell to the king's party near the Li Shan jetty. Their parting of the ways was not too solemn, as the king and his close acquaintances would soon be visiting Li Shan for the rite of Gao Mei. After the Wu returned their horses to the king's guard and, as this was officially the end of her commission to Ji Fa, Huxin could not resist bestowing a farewell embrace on her charge. The king made a point of keeping his hands off the Wu during the pleasant episode, as Hudan had spoken to Ji Fa of Shi's frustration, and he decided he'd punished his brother enough.

Hudan looked to Shi, who, quietly fuming, released a growl of protest, which distracted Huxin from her amusement.

'What was that?' She looked about warily, perhaps recognising the sound of her lover's snarl.

Hudan had to suppress a laugh as Shi covered his mouth, but Huxin did not notice.

'I'm close to home and surrounded by soldiers. I shall be fine from here.' Fa squeezed Huxin's hand and mounted his horse. 'I shall see you both on the full moon.' The king dug his heels into his steed and guided the animal into the stream of his moving soldiers.

The look on Dan's face was rather cheerless and he remained on his horse, as Shi did, whilst Hudan and Huxin hugged Fen goodbye.

'I wish I were coming with you,' Fen whispered into their huddle.

'The king will surely bring you when he visits,' Hudan said, pulling away. She knew a long drawn-out goodbye would see her in tears.

'Be gorgeous.' Huxin pinched his cheek to tease him, as she might not get the chance again, and served him a wink as he backed up grinning with embarrassment while his sisters blew him kisses.

'I'm going.' Fen turned and ran for his horse.

'Farewell, Zhou Gong Dan.' Hudan approached the duke, as he seemed reluctant to move. Still, he politely dismounted to converse with her. 'It has been an honour to serve Zhou with you.' She bowed to him, and he returned the gesture.

'The pleasure was entirely mine, I assure you,' he replied with some difficulty, and the fact that he was choking on emotion caused a painful lump to form in Hudan's throat also.

Although they would see each other again, the reason for their particular association had now run its course. There was nothing left to say that could be said, nothing more to be done.

'It was a brilliant collaboration while it lasted,' Dan said to relieve the awkward moment. 'It seems a shame it could not have lasted longer.'

'Perhaps the next war?' Hudan grinned.

Dan was amused. 'I'll see what I can arrange.'

Hudan backed up, shaking her head at his wicked retort, but could not wipe the smile from her face as Dan returned to his mount.

As they watched the lords depart and join their moving force, Huxin uttered aside to Hudan, 'I have never seen a man so sick with love.'

'You obviously don't look very closely,' Hudan told her and turned to walk the path toward the Li Shan jetty.

Huxin merely thought Hudan was avoiding the issue and made haste to join her. 'You would have to be blind not to see —'

'Not blind, just *committed*,' Hudan interjected.

'You need to be committed.' Huxin looked back at the departing army as she trailed her sister. 'Zhou Gong Dan is yummy.'

'You are unbelievable!' Hudan finally cracked. 'Why not simply seduce the entire family and be done with it?'

'Don't think that thought didn't cross my mind in the bathhouse at Yin,' Huxin said and grinned broadly. 'Do you want to know who is really well equipped?'

'No!'

'Shi,' Huxin replied just to vex her. 'That young man is going to make some woman very happy.'

Hudan's anger suddenly fled and she started to laugh, hysterically.

'Don't tell me that you have finally found your sense of humour!' Huxin was not going to give her the satisfaction of asking what had tickled her funny bone.

'Oh yes, I found it!' Hudan gasped for breath.

'Do you want the low-down on Dan?' Huxin resumed her teasing.

'If I say no, you will tell me anyway,' Hudan shrugged, tired of playing. She stepped onto the jetty and, with a low note from her throat and a flick of her staff, ignited the torches at the end to summon the ferry home.

'Whoa! When did you learn to do that?' Huxin was impressed.

Hudan raised both brows in unassuming triumph. 'You're not the only one who can be surprising! You were saying, about brother Dan?' she prompted, to Huxin's momentary frustration.

'Wouldn't you like to know?' Huxin changed her tactics, and Hudan was spared a lusty description of every member of the Ji clan.

On returning to Haojing, the king silenced the movements of war and cultivated the arts of peace. He sent his horses south of

Mount Hua and let loose his oxen in the peach orchards of the open country, to show all under heaven that he did not intend to use them again. He sacrificed in the ancestral temple of Zhou and worshipped toward the hills, on one side of the city, and to the rivers, on the other, to solemnly announce the successful completion of the war.

The madness of Zi Shou was at an end.

Shao Gong Shi stayed on at Haojing as the king's guest, as Ji Fa had agreed to allow Shi to accompany him to Li Shan and plead his cause. In the meantime, the king had been relying far more heavily on Shi with regard to governmental affairs, since Zhenduo and Wu had their own provinces to run. This was pleasing to Shi, as it brought him much closer to Fa and Dan. He'd never spent so much time indoors!

The day before the king departed for Li Shan, Fen was summoned to the king's private chambers for his promised consultation with the queen.

He was very nervous, as Fen had never directly spoken with any women who were not Wu and this woman was mother of the nation and the Zhou king's queen.

'Just be yourself, Fen,' advised Dan, who had kindly escorted him to his meeting. 'The queen is bound to like you; all women seem to.' The duke came to a standstill by the door to the royal chambers.

'I have some concerns,' Fen confided in Dan.

'Then voice them openly,' Dan suggested, nodding to the king's master of the interior to have Fen announced.

When Fen entered he was glad to be greeted by Ji Fa, who appeared overjoyed to see him. 'Come in. Oh, forget that!' he said, to stop Fen bowing, and waved him forth.

'I have spoken with my wife. She is most anxious to see you.'

'Majesty, I have some questions I would like to ask before I do this,' Fen ventured to say, and Fa looked at the lad, immediately concerned. 'That is not to say I have any intention of not honouring our arrangement. More that I wish ensure that we enter into this with a clear understanding.'

'What are your concerns?' Fa stopped to query Fen, before entering the next room where his wife awaited them.

'To be clear, majesty, I should discuss this with both you and your queen,' Fen stated, as diplomatic as he could be.

'You wish to ensure I am not pushing her into anything against her will,' Fa said, seeing straight through Fen's carefully chosen words.

'If there are risks, I must know that she is fully aware of them.' Fen was not about to compromise his work ethic, even for the king.

'You are very wise for one so young, Fen Gong, and a little *arrogant*,' Fa warned, causing Fen to bow his head and humble himself. 'But I like that.' The king let him know he was just teasing. 'You are starting to worry me, though.'

'That is not my intent,' Fen stated clearly. 'Forewarned is forearmed, is it not, majesty?'

Fa nodded to accept his reasoning. 'Come then, allow me to introduce you to the little woman,' Fa said, giving Fen a chummy hug around the shoulders.

Fen still felt uncomfortable being hugged by Tian's chosen representative on earth, but then he figured that the king probably felt uncomfortable having to call Fen to heal him every time something upset him. As long as Fen was content, people in general found his presence attractive and were well disposed toward him, and for that Fen felt most grateful and blessed. But it did give him an unfair advantage over virtually anyone, and Yi Jiang was to prove no different — she was utterly delighted by the sight of him.

'I regret we have not been properly introduced before today, Fen Gong. You are as beautiful as your name suggests,' the queen said, flattering him and Fen could feel himself blushing.

Fen had seen the queen on a couple of occasions, and she had always appeared very solemn and hard-looking, but today she appeared vibrant and beautiful. Stripped of make-up and finery, dressed only in a silk robe, she sat comfortably in a cushioned chair, poised as always.

'If it pleases your majesty, I should like to show you how I received this name,' Fen requested.

Yi Jiang looked to her husband, who shrugged, baffled. 'By all means?'

Fen repressed a smile as he rose and collected a long stemmed flower from a floral arrangement, its buds yet to open. Running his hand down the stem, each flower burst into full bloom before the queen's eyes.

'How wonderful!' She was completely enchanted as Fen bowed and offered the flowers to her, and she accepted it like the greatest of treasures.

Fen looked to the king, who rolled his eyes, impressed and grinning.

'I can hardly wait for you to work your magic on me,' the queen ventured, and breathed deep the scent of the flowers in her hand. 'Is it truly possible?'

'Yes, majesty,' Fen replied as he knelt before her once more, 'but there are things we should consider first.'

'My age,' she assumed, a little deflated. 'I am not so old as I might appear, stripped of my regalia.'

'Your majesty is very beautiful,' Fen assured her, 'and your age is not the concern.'

'Oh.' Her mood took an upswing. 'Then please rise and speak plainly.'

Fen stood as requested to consult with the royals. 'There is no doubt in my mind that I can heal our queen.'

Yi Jiang sat very tall, excited.

'The potency of the Gao Mei rite is such that our king, should he execute his part satisfactorily —' the king's mouth dropped open, surprised that Fen had the gall to suggest that he might fail in his duty during the rite '— shall surely beget you with a son.' Yi Jiang clutched Fa's hand, excited.

'But?' Ji Fa knew there was a concern.

'Might I ask …' Fen looked at the queen. 'How difficult was the birth of Ji Song for you?'

The queen opened her mouth to speak, but only a gasp came out at first. 'It nearly killed me,' she admitted, obviously still hurt and bitter about the fact.

'But your majesty did not have a healer such as I to aid your labour,' Fen went on, and raised her spirits yet again. 'But still, there are risks with childbirth that no amount of healing can abate. You are built as you are, and my healing will not change that. If you had a difficult labour the first time around, the chances are number two will be just as difficult. But I will be here for your majesty should you decide to proceed.'

Yi Jiang looked up to the king standing alongside her, and he appeared not so eager now.

'I should leave you to discuss this.' Fen bowed to depart.

'There is nothing to discuss,' the queen decreed.

'Yi?' The king obviously thought they should think twice.

'No, Fa,' she insisted, bravely. 'I will bear the son of the Gao Mei rite, no one else!'

Fen felt there was no arguing with the passion in the woman's voice, and as the king nodded to reassure Yi Jiang of his full support, her mood lightened once again.

'I want you to do whatever must be done. Where do you want to do this?' she asked.

'Lying down would be best,' Fen advised.

'In my bedchamber, then,' she said, standing and directing Fen to the door, but as Fa rose to follow them the queen spoke to him. 'I wish to speak with my healer privately.'

The king frowned, affronted.

'Are you jealous, my love?' She toyed with his mood.

'Yes,' he admitted, with a pout.

'Good ...' She kissed him, and left the king mystified.

'I *trust* Fen, completely,' Fa muttered, striving to assure himself, and made sure his comment was heard by the healer escorting his wife into her chamber. 'Usually, I'd only let a *eunuch* in there —'

That got Fen's attention, and he hastily said, 'I understand completely, majesty.' He bowed and slid the door closed behind them.

Yi Jiang lay on the bed, a little awkward and anxious.

'This will not hurt, majesty,' Fen said, endeavouring to sound professional as he approached the very beautiful woman laid out before him.

'Fen … may I call you Fen …?' she asked politely.

'Your majesty may call me anything she likes,' he joked, amusing her and lightening her mood if only for a moment.

'When you say I shall be healed, just how healed is healed?' Tears began to trickle from her eyes as she opened her robe to reveal a mass of scarring on her lower belly that she would not look at; she would not even look at the reaction on Fen's face. 'They cut Song out of me,' she wept. 'Zhou had to have an heir.'

'It's a miracle you are still alive.' Fen brushed the tears from his cheeks, for he realised this was where the king's deep abiding faithfulness to his queen stemmed from, for his child, his love, had resulted in his lover's mutilation.

'I have never even shown it to my husband. I keep it covered always.'

'Majesty …' Fen called for her attention, and when she looked to him, he held her gaze. 'Once I am done, you shall be as you were before Ji Fa ever touched you.' He grinned and the queen did too.

'As a maid?' she gasped, and pulled her gown around her as she sat up.

Fen nodded, eyebrows raised to emphasis his promise.

'I should give anything for that, Fen Gong, *anything!*'

'Just five minutes of calmly lying down is all I require,' he replied.

The queen burst into a huge smile and lay back upon the bed. When the procedure was done, Fen covered his patient and left her blissfully resting in her bed. The queen must have taken the opportunity to explore the previously scarred area of her body, for as Fen was closing the door to address the waiting king, the queen began to cry out: 'You are a wonder, Fen Gong! That is just amazing!'

Fen quickly closed the door to smother the queen's elation, as Ji Fa was frowning. 'All done, majesty.'

'My queen certainly sounds pleased by your service.'

'Yes, indeed,' Fen said in cocky fashion, 'and I warrant your majesty will be very satisfied with my work also.' He bowed to take his leave, but the king caught his arm.

'Thank you, Fen,' he said most sincerely, 'you can't know what this means.'

'I think I can, majesty,' Fen assured him.

'She showed you? Her scars?'

'What scars, majesty?' Fen said cheerily, at which point the king's smile broadened to bursting and he made for his wife's chambers.

Jovial laughter echoed out of the chamber as Fen departed the royal dwelling, and their happiness gave him a certain lightness in his step. To be so intimate with the royal family was surely the highest honour; Fen just hoped that the new prince's birth would be as blithe an affair as his conception.

The king's party departed for Li Shan early the next morning and to the shock of Dan, Shi, the king's guard and the house staff, Ji Fa kissed his queen farewell at the door of the royal house. 'I shall return,' he said, his forehead resting against hers.

'I shall be waiting,' Yi Jiang smiled, as the king dragged himself away, and she returned inside.

Dan was utterly baffled, having expected the queen to be furious about the day's proceedings. 'How on earth ...?' the duke uttered and glancing at Fen he found him grinning. 'What did you do?'

Fen shrugged, as both Dan and Shi awaited an answer, but he gave them none.

Ji Song was also waiting to see his father off. 'Keep away from my goddess, father!' his son called out.

Fa glanced back with a look of warning on his face, knowing the comment was not for his benefit.

Dan met Song's glare of challenge, his gut churning in agitation — the thought of Hudan being given to Fa was lamentable, the thought of her being given to Song was utterly deplorable. *May Fa rule a long, long time.*

'I love being married!' Fa announced as he joined his brothers and mounted his horse. 'Every man should be so fortunate,' he decreed. Then looking to his brothers, he toned down his enthusiasm. 'I have my work cut out for me. You lot should be taking notes from Fen. I have never seen my queen so easily charmed by anyone.'

'We are pleased to see you in such fine spirits this day,' Fen said, as his brothers seemed to have no comment.

The king grinned at the lad. 'Very pleased by your work, Fen,' the king awarded. 'The queen asks you to name any place in our land and it is yours.'

The lords in their company were astonished, but Fen shook his head to decline. 'We have an agreement, majesty, and that is your only obligation for my services.'

'That is well,' Fa grinned, 'as the queen also stressed that she should never let you leave our vicinity.'

'That suits me well,' and Fen bowed his head in gratitude as the king dug his heels into his horse's side and led the charge out of the courtyard to Li Shan.

A few hours in the saddle saw the pace slow down as they approached the jetty at the base of the mount. The sun was shining and the breeze was warm, yet Shi looked as anxious and melancholy as Dan felt.

'Why did you never tell us about your gift?' Dan queried, snatching his brother from his quiet contemplation.

'Our father told me not to,' Shi explained. 'He was afraid I might be rejected by the family, or hunted for sport.'

'We would never allow that to happen,' Dan insisted, including the king in the equation.

Shi seemed not so certain, and he shrugged. 'The boldness of Jiang Huxin lessened my fears and made my disclosure much easier. It does make me wonder how many more of us are out there, hiding.'

'Not so many as to let this one slip through your fingers?' Dan warranted, and Shi smiled to agree. 'I hope Tian rules in your favour.'

'I wish the same for you also,' Shi replied.

'I have no basis for a ruling,' Dan replied as he forced a smile and slowed his horse to dismount.

'Sorry,' Shi detected the swing in Dan's mood. 'I thought that is why you are here.'

'No,' Dan said, regretful. 'I have an appointment of my own with the Great Mother in regard to my continued instruction with the Wu.'

Their horses were led away by the king's guards who were withdrawing to make camp. Fa was merrily strolling up the jetty path, chatting with Fen, and the lords followed.

'I do not know I if should mention this,' Shi began, slyly, 'but I know that Jiang Hudan feels as you do.'

Dan stopped in his tracks. 'How so?'

'The night you saw us in the garden at Li Shan, Jiang Hudan got upset when I mentioned you —'

'That has been known to happen.' Dan kept walking.

'At first I thought you had hurt her,' Shi continued, whereby Dan served him a scowl, 'but she said that just the opposite was true ... And then confessed that she found you too pleasing for her own peace of mind.'

Dan laughed off the report. 'You are playing with me.'

'I would never wish to hurt you or Jiang Hudan,' Shi explained. 'I just hate to see you so sad.'

'I'm not *sad*,' Dan protested and then calmed. 'I am ... content.'

'Oh,' said Shi, not quite convinced, but he did not push the matter.

'She said that?' Dan finally broke the silence.

'She did.' Shi granted with a smile, as they stepped onto the ferry to join the king and Fen, and there the conversation ended.

Jiang Huxin arrived on the ferry to greet their party, and she made a fuss of the king while ignoring Shi almost entirely, bar a greeting.

'She really knows how to hold a grudge, doesn't she?' Dan uttered in Shi's ear, as they sat on the ferry, watching their hostess chat with her little brother and the king.

'She is jealous,' Shi figured, quietly. 'And so am I, so I guess that is good.'

Dan smiled and nodded at his reasoning. 'If only I should be so lucky.'

From the dock the king and his brothers were led directly to the Great Mother's council chamber for their meeting.

'Fen, you may come with me.' Huxin held a hand out to him, and the lad appeared overjoyed to take it.

'Shall we see Hudan?'

'We shall,' she promised, noting she'd gained Dan's attention. Yet brother Huxin did not tease him as she usually would, but gave him a sympathetic smile.

That was how everyone looked at him now, and the duke had just about had enough of it.

Quietly fuming was probably not the wisest of moods to be entertaining as they were led into the Great Mother's audience chamber, so Dan endeavoured to calm and find his serenity.

The Great Mother was unmasked this day as they knelt before her, Dan to the king's right-hand side, Shi to the left.

'Rise, noble men of Zhou, and allow me to commend you on executing the mandate of heaven in complete accordance with our prophecy. Brother Hudan has delivered a full report,' her eyes shifted to Shi for a moment, 'and I can assure you that Tian is satisfied by your dauntless devotion to heaven's cause.'

'Without the aid of your house, brother Yi, it would not have been possible. Your Wu have played an integral role in our success,' Fa granted.

'You, brother Fa, come before me today as the true Tianzi ... with Tian's grace, you shall leave us with heaven's blessing, having fulfilled our agreement in all regards.'

'I am honoured by heaven's faith in the Ji family,' Fa replied, graciously.

'But it seems I have business with the three of you this visit, and I shall see each of you in turn. Ji Shi, I shall hear you first. Brother Fa should stay and I shall speak with you after Shi, about this evening's proceedings. Brother Dan, if you would kindly take your leave of us, I will speak with you on the morrow.'

The request burst Dan's serene bubble and his resentment oozed forth. 'I respectfully entreat you to speak with me this day.' Dan breathed deeply to contain his panic.

'Today is about our king,' she said. 'There should be no urgency —'

'There is a very great urgency and well you know it,' Dan challenged her, and his king was shocked by the contempt in his tone.

'Dan,' Fa reprimanded him, 'apologise at once!'

Dan gazed at the Great Mother and took a few steps toward her. 'I could speak openly of my concerns,' he proposed, arms held wide in invitation. His brothers knew nothing of the sons of the sky, as far as he knew, and he doubted very much if Yi Wu wanted them enlightened.

'*Dan.*' Fa's tone was most displeased.

Yi Wu's face hardened, and for a moment Dan feared he'd pushed his cause too far. 'Wait outside … I will call for you when I am done with the *more important* matters of the day.'

Dan bowed in appreciation and returned to the outer chamber, with both his brothers frowning at him for upsetting their hostess.

Dan spent the next hour carefully contemplating the forthcoming audience. Shi was the first to emerge from the chamber, and as soon as he exited he breathed a huge sigh of relief. 'She scares me,' he whispered as he approached Dan and took a seat, 'and yet she is very wise and caring also.'

'I am sorry if my outburst made the situation more difficult,' Dan said, sincerely remorseful.

'Not at all. The Great Mother was very kind to me and has given her consent for me to ask Jiang Huxin to be my wife.'

The news tore Dan's heart out. He'd never been so envious, yet he was happy for his brother. 'A pleasing result. Congratulations.'

'But I must wait until after the rite of Gao Mei to approach her, as the Great Mother wants her initiates focussing on their preparation,' Shi added, still not confident enough to be truly excited about the news. 'Now my hope is that she won't reject me.'

Dan had heard Huxin speak of her affection for Shi, and smiled, happy to return his favour of this morning. 'I know the only reason Jiang Huxin did not seduce you months ago was because Fa forbade her, as our king wanted you to find a wife.'

Shi's eyes opened wide in wonderment at the news, and he smiled warmly at his brother. 'Clearly, you and I should speak more often.'

Dan was amused, and his spirits lightened as he nodded to agree.

'Will you stay with me at Li Shan tonight?' Shi asked. 'Our king will want to return to his queen at Haojing immediately following the rite, and will take Fen with him. Should everything not go as I hope, well … it would be good not to have to return to Haojing alone.'

'Of course I will,' Dan said, happy to oblige. 'Provided the Great Mother does not banish me before evening.'

Shi gave a laugh, but frowned in concern as well. 'It might be our king you have to worry about banishing you. He is most displeased.'

'I thank you for the warning.' Dan sat back and took a deep breath to await the reprimand that would come later.

'May I ask why you were so abrupt?'

Dan observed Shi, seeing in him a warrior-like figure of a man, fair-haired like the Lord of the Elements, and not unlike the young male being he had seen within Yi Wu the last time they had spoken. It was the first time Dan had wondered whether Shi knew about the supernatural agenda, and what other secrets he was hiding. 'Do you know anything about the sons of the sky?'

'No.' Shi shook his head and leaned in, eager to hear more. Dan was sorry to disappoint him.

'Then I cannot really explain my reasons for affronting Yi Wu,' Dan said.

'But it has something to do with Jiang Hudan?' Shi asked, and Dan only nodded in response, before returning to his silent contemplation.

A little over an hour later, Fa exited the chamber, by which time Dan had grown very restless, and was up on his feet and ready to enter as the king approached him.

'Speak to the Great Mother like that again and I will have you flogged! Am I making myself understood?'

It was seldom that Dan clashed heads with Fa, and he bowed his head humbly and nodded. 'My deepest apologies, majesty.'

'The Great Mother will see you now.' Fa grabbed his arm as he moved off, and Dan turned back to heed his word. 'She had best give me a glowing report of your encounter, or so help me, I will —'

'— have me flogged, I understand,' Dan stated deadpan, and Fa let him go.

'Come Shi, time to eat.' The king collected their brother and left Dan to his business.

The duke took a moment to truly compose himself before he entered the Great Mother's presence this time. *'Speak always from a place of love,'* Fen had advised in regard to addressing the Great Mother, and Dan endeavoured to abide by that guidance.

When he came before Yi Wu, she did not appear to be in a very loving frame of mind, however. 'I believe we both know why you are so eager to converse this day, so let us speak plainly.'

Dan nodded to indicate that it would be appreciated. 'I —'

'Want Jiang Hudan for your wife,' Yi Wu completed his sentence for him.

'I had not intended to be so bold,' Dan replied, honestly. 'I sought only to have her exempted from the goddess rite this night.'

'On what basis?' Yi Wu sounded appalled. 'This is her life, her calling —'

'On a soul level, we belong to one another,' Dan interrupted, defending his request.

'Not in this life,' she insisted, although she was sounding a little more empathetic now.

The spirit inside Yi Wu suddenly burst through her physical persona and a young lord of the sky stood addressing him in her stead. 'Let me be clear,' this spirit said in a friendly fashion, rising to approach Dan.

The duke backed away warily, for he recognised the fellow from his dreams, and had the peculiar sense that he knew and trusted him, better than he did the Great Mother. This son of the sky was slighter in frame than the one inside Shi, and slighter than the Lord of the Elements. Telmo was build more like a scholar and very pretty for a man — like Fen Gong and the spirit lord who was concealed within the healer.

'You are not another of my sons, are you?' Dan was circumspect.

The fair lord smiled, finding the assumption funny. 'No. You could say I have been something of a mentor to you through the ages, just as Yi Wu is now, and this is why I beg you to listen to what we have to tell you.'

'Which is?' Dan's jaw clenched with a premonition that the news would not be to his liking.

'Shanyu Jiang Hudan and Zhou Gong Dan never fell in love,' he stated clearly. 'They worked together to the benefit of Zhou, but nothing more. This is how this *must* play out if you are both to live until your dying day.'

'What does that mean?' Dan said irritably, as the Lord of the Elements had used the same expression.

'It means … that is how history must unfold to avoid affecting this timeline. You must do what you were destined to do here or the effect on the future will be catastrophic.'

'Why? Why me?' Dan protested.

'Because you are who you are,' the spirit replied, sounded weary of repeating himself. 'And this is not the first, or last, time you will lead a civilisation to greatness. We are aware of the exact time, date and location of your death, and we then plan to recruit you back into our fold. But once you change causality, as Rhun did last time he interfered with your destiny, then all bets are off! We could lose any of you unexpectedly at any time and our higher quest would be thwarted. It is only the dreams from your time with us that have triggered the attraction you have to Hudan now.'

Could it be true? It was a lot to swallow, and Dan was overwhelmed and having trouble processing it all.

'I promised Taren that she would have all the skills required to resume her quest beyond this life. If Hudan marries you, her greatest potential will not be realised, and when the time of her reckoning comes she shall be ill-prepared to deal with it. That is why, even now, without consciously knowing it, she is completely dedicated to the Wu way, which is not just a course of study, but a way of life! Do you really think being a wife would provide her that same satisfaction? It is not that she does not love you, but that she loves her higher purpose more, and so should you.'

'Then just excuse her from the rite,' Dan appealed. 'That is all I ask.'

'I am bound to see history unfold as it should.' The fair lord stated his case again, hoping Dan would finally comprehend it. 'And Jiang Hudan was *not* excused. *Do you see?*'

Dan wanted to scream, wanted to cry, but breathed deeply to contain his frustration.

'If I could offer some advice?'

Dan merely nodded tongue-tied at present.

'You should really have more faith in heaven's sense of fair play.'

'Why?' Dan snapped. 'Was it not heaven that landed me in this torment?'

'By your *own will*,' he replied, and Dan was shocked out of his resentment. 'I should think that feeling as you do about your beloved you must have had a very good reason to voluntarily part from her for this mission.' The lad raised his eyebrows to urge him to consider that premise, before he returned to Yi Wu's chair. 'There is a bigger and far more glorious picture, I assure you. This life you lead now is just a tiny moment in the ocean of Lucian's life. I respectfully suggest that you keep that in mind.'

'Tell me one thing?' Dan appealed, for his own peace of mind. 'Did Zhou Gong Dan ever marry again? Am I expected to spawn more offspring?'

The lord frowned slightly, intrigued, but answered the question. 'Actually, no, he never did.'

In one way that was a huge relief, but in another, rather heartbreaking. 'So, perhaps they were in love, but no one else knew about it?'

'That is very thin ice you are skating upon, Zhou Gong. I'd be very, very careful, if I were you. Unless, of course, you want to have to come back and do this mission again, with the odds stacked even further against us.' Once the lord was seated he withdrew from open view and the feminine persona of Yi Wu returned. Her eyes were closed and when they parted, she regarded Dan fondly. 'Are we done here?'

Dan, still wide-eyed and reeling, nodded his head sombrely. 'It would seem so.'

'So, we leave it entirely up to you whether or not you choose to pursue your affection for Jiang Hudan,' the Great Mother summed up,

Dan clenched his jaw, for in reality it seemed he had no option at all. 'It may have been Fa named in the Jade Book, but I am the one who has been cursed,' he considered, bitterly.

'We, the sons of the sky, are all living under a curse, Zhou Gong.'

'How do you bear it?' he asked in an honest appeal for a cure.

'I channel my frustration into beneficial pursuits, just as you *will* do,' she informed him. 'You know how much there is to be done for our land, yet your mind is distracted from your purpose. The only solution is to let time and distance do this work and cut your ties with Jiang Hudan.'

'All ties?' Dan had hoped they could at least write to one another. 'She wishes to document my work —'

'Which she can follow via a correspondence with her brother, Fen,' Yi Wu insisted. 'If you truly want what is best for the both of you and history at large, you will say your goodbyes this visit and never intentionally seek her for personal gratification again.'

'But if the realm has need of her …?' Dan argued.

'That would be the will of heaven, not yours,' she ruled, and Dan was devastated.

'My heart goes out to you, brother Dan … *it does*,' she asserted, as he glared at her, feeling wounded and unwillingly restrained. 'But you sent me here to guide you, and guide you I must.'

'*I* sent you?' His frown deepened.

The Great Mother nodded. 'You are the captain of this mission. Too much information?' Yi Wu queried, as Dan's jaw dropped and he appeared to be going into shock. 'Perhaps some food and rest might be in order?'

'Yes,' Dan groaned, as his brain felt like it was splitting open in an attempt to fathom the enormity of his destiny, which seemingly appeared to extend far beyond the barriers of this life. The idea was mind-blowing. 'I am immortal?' He staggered and gave a laugh as the room blurred, and his free-wheeling form crashed to the floor in an unconscious heap.

Hudan stood with ten of her Wu brothers in the goddess temple, her face painted, her hair bound up in an ornate head-dress, her body shaved clean of hair and perfumed. Naked beneath her long white veil, she was indistinguishable from every other potential candidate seeking to be chosen to embody the goddess Gao Mei this night for the King of Zhou.

The eleven of them represented the eleven heads of the goddess Gao Mei: the goddess who sees all, and hears all cries from the human world; she who brings children, particularly sons.

One of them would be chosen by the ancient chimera bird, Feng-Huang, which resided atop of the mighty Kunlun mountain range of which Bayan Har Shan formed part. These mountains, which Ji Shi had reportedly sprung from, seemed to be a hotbed of supernatural activity. The legendary bird had a male aspect, Feng, and a female aspect, Huang, and presided over every other bird in the land ... it was known to have the beak of a rooster, the face of a swallow, the forehead of a fowl, the neck of a snake, the breast of a goose, the back of a tortoise, the hindquarters of a stag and the tail of a fish. Feng-Huang would only appear in the most harmonious and joyous of situations. Its coming always heralded the beginning of a new era of imperial rule, and bestowed the perfect balance of yin and yang upon heaven's mandate.

It was exciting to be standing on the threshold of such a rare event. Hudan had been fasting for days and had been given a brew, along with the other candidates, that would suspend inhibitions whilst invoking a calm, euphoric state of being. Even so, Hudan's stomach was in a knot and her head was a mass of conflicting thoughts which fed the whirl of conflicting emotions in her chest, which made her stomach knot tighter. To be honest, she could not decide whether it would be better to be chosen as

Fa's goddess this night or not. If she were to be selected, the event would change Dan's affection for her and he might seek love in more realistic places, perhaps finding happiness as, indeed, he deserved.

What was more worrying was that she stood in the centre of the semicircle that she and her brothers formed around one side of the pool in the temple. Beneath the central circular opening in the roof of the holy space, a stone altar block had been placed; padded and covered in the finest silk, it was for the chosen goddess to lie upon. The one who was chosen by Feng-Huang would prostrate herself on the altar beneath her veil and await the king's pleasure. The other candidates would remain present, their backs turned in silent vigil. The goddess was expected to endure the rite as silently as she found humanly possible: if she vocalised her rapture it was a clear sign of the king's prowess. Ji Fa was expected to abstain from ejaculating during the rite, so that the blessings of Gao Mei were bestowed upon his queen. To seed one of the vestals of Li Shan would be considered a poor show and a bad omen for the Ji family rule.

As Yi Wu entered the temple carrying Taiji, the doors closed and the king remained outside. The candidates raised their voices in song to herald her arrival and to sanctify the holy space. The Great Mother walked across the surface of the pool to stand before the altar facing her initiates, and she sang an oscillating note. The Taiji sphere lit up, and streams of brilliantly coloured light shot out from it, whirling around each other as the rainbow of light rose into the night sky and formed a bright mass.

'Come Feng-Huang,
Of six celestial bodies!
With the face of the sky,
The eyes of the sun,
The moon on your back,
Your wings like the wind,
Your feet of the earth,
And a tail of planets,
Select for our king,

The body of Gao Mei,
Who will channel the next prince
Into the Zhou dynasty!'

Above the temple the mass formed into a huge celestial bird afire with colour as it swooped down into the temple and slowed to hover behind Yi Wu, observing everyone.

Even seen through Hudan's silken veil, the fluidity, brilliance and colour of Feng-Huang's form was mesmerising. Its long tail swirled like seaweed in water and its wings were spread wide and flapped like fine silk in the breeze. But Hudan caught her breath when the undulating apparition made a move, as it was headed straight for her.

When Dan awoke he was briefly disoriented, and then, noting night had fallen, he snapped to attention and came to a sitting position. 'Hudan!'

He realised the rite must have started, and scampered up … he knew not why, as there was nothing he could do to stop it.

'My lord?'

Dan spun around to see Fen. 'What are you doing here? Is it over?'

Fen nodded. 'The king is in the next room awaiting Yi Wu's summons and the goddess's verdict,' Fen grinned. 'But as I could hear her pleasure from outside the temple, I would say the imperial mandate is his.'

Dan grimaced at the news. He knew what Hudan's pleasure sounded like and if he'd been awake he would already know the outcome. The duke charged out of the room and headed next door to see the king.

When announced, the duke entered, holding back his panic. 'Well?'

Fa raised his brow, appearing very ill at ease. '*That* was *really* difficult.'

'But was your goddess … her?' Dan pushed, and Fa frowned.

'I don't think so,' was the best the king could say, as he was too preoccupied with his own frustration at present.

'You don't *think* so?' Dan pushed. How could he have just made love to a woman and not be able to identify her?

'Her face was painted and she was veiled in the moonlight,' Fa said, holding up both hands in apology as Jiang Huxin entered.

'Yi Wu will see you now, brother Fa,' she said, sporting a huge grin.

'Praise Tian for that!' Fa was eager to leave, and moved on immediately.

'Brother Huxin?' Dan caught her arm on the way out, but she was shaking her head before he'd asked the question.

'I wasn't there and I haven't seen her yet,' she said sharply, as she followed the king and Fen to their meeting.

Left alone and agitated, Dan resigned himself to the fact that Hudan was the only one who really knew the truth, and once the house had settled for the night, Dan had a very good idea where he might find her.

Alongside Fen, Huxin was proud to bear witness to Yi Wu's bestowing of Tian's mandate. Yi Wu presented the king with a beautiful ritual set consisting of six jade worshipping items: a bi-disk for the worship of heaven's deities; a cong for earthly spirits; the Guik tablet and the zhang, huang, and tiger plaques were for worshipping the four deities of the four directions.

'Arise Ji Fa, king of our land and holder of Tian's mandate on earth,' Yi Wu said. 'You are free to depart Li Shan, having earned heaven's highest honour for the House of Ji.'

'Praise heaven!' The king rose. 'And praise to you, Yi Wu. My family shall treasure your gift always.'

'I know you are eager to be home,' Yi Wu proffered, grinning at his impatience to leave.

'What are a few hours in a saddle compared to a lifetime of bliss,' the king replied, not about to complain.

'What I meant was,' Yi Wu continued, 'Jiang Huxin has kindly offered to speed you back to your queen via Wu means if that would be pleasing to you?'

The Great Mother's offer made Fa grin with fear and elation. The thought of two hours in the saddle to reach his lover, versus his fear of being whipped through the inner world, was not a real contest. His eagerness to be home won out over his fear of the unknown. 'I would be most obliged for that service.'

'I shall have your trophies returned with your brothers on the morrow,' Yi Wu advised. 'Until next we meet, I wish you every happiness and success, brother Fa.' The Great Mother bowed deeply to him in parting.

'And I you, brother Yi.' The king returned the gesture, and then took hold of Huxin's outstretched hand.

She already held Fen's hand on her other side, knowing the king would not return without him. 'At your leave, majesty,' she allowed, as Fa was looking a little anxious — he appeared more petrified now than he had before battle.

'Fear not, brother Fa,' Yi Wu said kindly. 'for this is not the first time you have travelled thus, nor will it be the last.'

The king forced a smile, a little perplexed by her words, and gave Huxin a nod to get the event over with.

As the light of Huxin's intention began to engulf them, Fa gripped her hand tighter.

'We are here, majesty.' Huxin placed a hand on his shoulder to gently shake him, so that he might realise their passage was over, open his eyes and release her hand.

'What?' He was genuinely surprised to find himself in his private quarters at Haojing, and he gasped with delight when the fact sunk in. 'Jiang Huxin, you are a wonder!' he said, bowing his head to her in gratitude. 'This is truly the end of the road for us,' and he sounded deeply sorry about the fact.

Huxin smiled. 'Go to your queen, majesty,' she urged, feeling tears coming on — she was not usually sentimental. 'I shall treasure our victory always.' She respectfully bowed to him in parting.

Ji Fa, more than a little choked up himself, nodded and managed to say, 'I shall also.' He turned and departed for his queen's bedchamber.

When Huxin turned back to Fen, her tears fell. 'I shall miss him,' she confessed, 'and you.' Huxin flung her arms around Fen and held him tight.

'I expect I shall be seeing more of you than either of us could expect at this moment.'

Fen's claim prompted Huxin to push him to arm's length and hold him there. 'Why?' Her sweetness was gone, and suspicion had taken its place.

'Because that is what I wish for, and I am a very powerful being,' Fen boasted, his grin more confident than it usually was in the wake of such a statement. 'You should really get back to Li Shan and make sure brother Hudan fares well.'

Huxin's eyes narrowed as she was wary and mistrustful that he was not more upset by their parting. 'Have you got another lover you are running off to see?'

'No,' Fen insisted, still grinning. 'Not I.'

Huxin was still looking at him sideways. 'What do you know that I don't?'

'Am I supposed to have an answer for such a question?' Fen raised his eyebrows in his own defence, as Huxin's eyes continued to bore into him.

'All right, I'm going,' Huxin conceded, dissatisfied, but realising that Fen was not going to crack.

'Good,' Fen said. 'Have fun.'

'Why fun?' Huxin asked, delaying.

'Will you just go to Hudan already!' Fen shooed her away, and in a huff Huxin willed herself to her twin.

It was dark, warm and moist where Huxin landed, and it didn't take her long to realise where she was. 'I thought I'd find you here.'

By the light of the moon, Hudan was cleaning make-up from her face in one of the smaller thermal pools around the large pool where the siblings always swam after a big event — it had been their own personal tradition.

'Here I am!' Hudan slurred her words a little.

'So, was it you?' Huxin crept closer, eager to hear the gossip. 'Did you lose your maidenhood to Ji Fa's mighty —'

'Huxin.' Hudan pushed her away. 'A gentle person never tells.'

'What if Zhou Gong asks? And he will,' Huxin warned.

'I am not sure if it would be kinder to tell the truth or not?' Hudan drew a deep uneasy breath and kept rubbing.

'It wasn't you,' Huxin said, ceasing her scrutiny of her sister. 'You are way too tense to have been so liberated this night.'

'You think it would bring me joy to give myself to Ji Fa?' Hudan stood, her voice wavering along with her body.

'I would have thought you would consider it the highest honour,' Huxin stated. For others, this would have been the truth of the matter.

'Honour and joy very rarely coincide.' Hudan staggered toward the larger pool, and Huxin rushed to help steady her on her feet, as her sister was clearly still intoxicated from the rite.

Huxin had only ever seen Hudan like this a few times, and she was usually so much more fun and *honest*. 'Is this you admitting you hold feelings for our brother Dan?' Huxin sidled up close to her sister to ask in a whisper.

Hudan appeared fit to burst, and she growled softly as her defences crumbled. 'I heard their pleasure and all I could think about was *him*.' She clenched her hands frustrated. 'I tried not to, Tian knows I did …'

A giggle of delight escaped Huxin's lips, as she hugged her sister to her. 'There is a human in there, after all.'

Her comment made Hudan laugh, and she mellowed. 'Something the Great Mother told me has changed the way I perceive my relationship to Dan.'

'What did Shifu say?' Huxin was curious, but slapped a hand over her sister's mouth to prevent an answer as a loud roar was heard in the distance, higher up on the mountain. The sound stopped Huxin's heart from beating for a second, and then made it beat double-time.

'That is him!' she breathed, and gripped her sister's arm so tight it made her squeal.

'Ouch!'

'Sorry.' Huxin stroked the injured limb a couple of times to silence Hudan, and then they heard the roar again. 'We'll talk later … I have to go.' Huxin took off so fast she accidentally knocked her sister into the water, robe and all. She waited to see

Hudan surface in a spray of water and silk, coughing and spluttering.

'Are you trying to kill me?' Hudan twisted the heavily ornate headpiece from her tangled mass of hair.

'So sorry,' Huxin giggled, as she stripped the clothes from her body on her way up the path. 'Don't wait up for me.'

Huxin felt a slight twinge of guilt at leaving Hudan alone; her departure would make Fen's absence this night even more obvious to her sister. But her heavenly appointed mate had come to visit her and their half-baked brood, and that opportunity was too rare to miss.

At the top of the path she entered the garden, and was startled to collide with Ji Dan. 'Brother Dan … fancy meeting you here,' she giggled again. The poor duke seemed unsure of what to do with the naked person he found himself holding, and averted his eyes as he set her on her feet and turned away.

'I thought you were … elsewhere?'

'Don't fret, I am leaving and Hudan is *alone*.' She moved away. 'I warn you, she is still quite inebriated, and feeling rather more amorous than usual, so I would tread very carefully if I were you.'

'Did she say —' Dan glanced back to query her, but Huxin had shifted into the tigress.

In animal form her desire turned solely to hunting up her mate and she took off up the mountain in pursuit of him.

Hudan floated on her back on the surface of the pool, her ruined silk robe floating about her like soft seaweed. The night sky was glistening and the moonlight felt intense upon her being. Strangely, she did not feel alone, but rather free to indulge in her own contemplation. If her siblings were here right now they would, most likely, be ducking and teasing her and, upon reflection, this private bliss was far preferable.

'Brother Hudan?'

The sound of Dan's voice shot a wave of fear and excitement through her being, and Hudan drew herself into a tucked position to hear more clearly and locate him.

'May I join you?'

As she spotted the duke at the top of the path, her excitement surged and she gave him a friendly wave. 'Be my guest.' She waved him forth. 'My siblings have abandoned me, although we always swim after sacred rites. It helps us regain our senses.'

'I know,' Dan confessed, as he approached the edge of the pool, and crouched down to speak with her. 'I saw the three of you here on my first night at Li Shan.'

Hudan gasped. 'It was you?' She splashed water in his direction, and he stood and backed away. 'We were talking about you that night —' She remembered, and then grinned mischievously. 'I notice you no longer wear a beard?'

Dan applauded her powers of perception, and she flicked another stream of water in his direction. 'Well, I had to do something to make you see me differently ... as more than another tool you carried around with you. Does it please you?' he asked. Hudan had choked up at his first sentence, but with a deep breath she expelled her regret at treating him so badly in the beginning.

'I think it suits you very well,' she admitted, impishly. 'So, are you going to come in or are you merely spectating?' The invitation came out sounding rather more seductive than intended; it was like her mouth and body had their own agenda and the regular Hudan was not invited.

'Is that permissible?' he queried, removing his boots.

'There is no law in our creed that prevents Wu brothers from bathing together. In fact, we do it all the time,' Hudan was delighted to realise and thinking herself very clever as she intently watched Dan disrobe in the moonlight, captivated by the sight.

Dan did not have the warrior physique that some of his more martial brothers had, but his tall, athletic body was well developed, slender and smooth. Hudan was rather annoyed when he only stripped to his trousers and made a move to approach the pool. 'Are you shy, Brother Dan?'

The duke grinned at her challenge. 'No,' he assured her, 'I merely wished to avoid offence. And you did not bother removing your clothes, I see.'

Hudan immediately stripped the silk from her body, rolled it into a ball and cast it from the pool. 'Do you think you have something down there that I haven't seen before?'

He glanced down at the front of his trousers, and raised both eyebrows to concede, 'Maybe?'

Hudan found his antics amusing and floated her body on the surface of the pool to look to the night sky and let him out of his predicament. When she heard him dive into the water, Hudan tucked back into a wading pose for greater manoeuvrability, and then squealed as she felt him pass underneath her, releasing bubbles as he did so. He surfaced in a spray of water in front of her. 'Brother Dan,' she grinned at his close proximity and took a stroke away from him.

'Brother Hudan ....' he did the same. 'How did the rite go?'

'Well, Fa pleased the goddess very well,' she said, deciding in that second whether or not to tell him the truth. 'Very, very well, from what I *heard*,' she stressed, so that he might realise she was just a bystander to the event. Dan was silent, his face in shadow, so she could not gauge his reaction. 'I believe the other candidates envied the goddess her rapture —'

'And you?' Dan asked, expectantly. Hudan took a stroke toward him, and another to circle around until his face caught the moonlight.

She gave her head a small shake. 'I imagined it was us.'

In one synchronised movement they came together, his kisses warm, tender and moist, their bodies pressed against one another in a sudden frenzy to harness their closeness. The evidence of Dan's passion was pressed hard against Hudan's pelvis and abdomen, and her legs wrapped about him in an effort to maintain the pleasurable pressure of rubbing against him. Dan's hands and arms slid over her body in an attempt to support her in her intent, and it was only as she released a pleasured groan that she realised Dan's lips were moving down her neck.

Then, unexpectedly, Dan let loose a frustrated cry and pushed her away to swim for the edge.

'Dan?' Hudan was left gasping and bewildered.

'You are not yourself tonight,' he conceded, thwarted by his own sense of fair play.

'No, no, no!' Hudan appealed with conviction, desperate to make him understand her seemingly sudden change of heart. 'I think you are wrong. What if tonight I am myself, and it is every other day I wear the mask of someone else?'

The statement turned Dan about, as it struck a chord in him too. 'The Great Mother told you … that we were not meant to fall in love in this life.'

Hudan nodded. 'But the way I see it, you don't have to take my maidenhood and cause some catastrophic event when we spawn a child that was never meant to exist! But, if this is it … if this is all we get in this life, well …' Her voice wavered under the weight of her want. 'Just as we were then, felt wonderful to me, and for the years ahead that we must be apart, I believe Tian owes us this small kindness. I promise you, neither one of us will regret it tomorrow.'

Dan returned to her embrace and their enjoyment with so much enthusiasm that it seemed their momentum had not been disturbed in the slightest. The feeling aroused by their love-play transported Hudan to the place she'd only ever been to in her dreams of Lu Chen. The way he touched her and kissed her — the sounds he made when aroused — it was all so familiar and disarming that she held none of her desire back. And when finally she felt his member — slipping between her legs — ejaculate, his cry of relief triggered her climax, and they collapsed around each other gasping for breath, sighing, and praising the heavens for the release.

'I love you, Zhou Gong Dan,' she whispered into his ear, head resting on his shoulder as he carried her to the side of the pool with the aim of sitting them both down before they drowned.

'I never would have guessed,' he jested with a grin, taking a seat on a rock by the edge, with Hudan still straddling him.

'Share my room tonight,' she said as she snuggled into him. 'Now that I am aware of the purpose behind my cloistered vocation, I am no longer afraid our love will offend Tian. I am only mindful of not defeating our own purpose in the long run.'

'As much as I would love to wake up beside you,' Dan kissed her head, 'I think that might land us both in a lot of hot water.'

Then, considering their current location, they both laughed at the irony.

'I can sneak you in,' Hudan whispered seductively, then nibbled his earlobe, as she'd seen Huxin do to Fa's enjoyment.

'You could do that.' Dan was pleasantly distracted. 'And I certainly could not stop you. But Yi Wu —'

'As long as my maidenhood is still intact,' Hudan silenced him with her fingers, 'he–she should have nothing to complain about.'

Dan grinned, in complete agreement with her reasoning. 'That seems a perfectly fetching compromise to me.'

His tigress was very amorous this evening, rubbing against him, and grooming him affectionately. As she was already with child, Shi was not here to mate with her; he just wanted to be near her and that instinct was entirely human.

On the freshly replenished grass on the mountainside he lay soaking up Huxin's affection and feeling guilty for not having transformed into his human form the second he'd laid eyes on her — he had intended to. But Huxin never gave him this much affection as a man, and he was priming himself for his confession. Dan's insight this afternoon had given Shi some hope of success, and his hesitation was due mainly to fearing that once she knew the truth, this lovely enchantment would end. The lord finally reached a point where he could not bear the suspense any longer and shifted form.

When his tigress found herself licking the face of a man, she sprang away from him and shifted form also. 'Who are you?'

'Jiang Huxin, it is I, Ji Shi.' He moved into the moonlight where she might see him.

'Shi?' Her defensiveness shifted, and she was left awestruck. 'You are a shifter?'

He nodded.

'It was you who saved my sister. It was you who —' She gasped as the realisation hit, and held the little bulge on her naked belly.

'I wanted to tell you, but I had to wait to ask the Great Mother's permission to do so, which I did not receive until today,' he explained, to Huxin's mortification.

'Shifu Yi is aware I betrayed my creed by sleeping with a man?' Huxin wailed, holding her head as if she had a massive headache and was going to be sick. 'I'll be banished for sure.'

Of all the reactions Shi had anticipated, this had not been one of them. 'The Great Mother knows that no one knew my secret, and you are free to stay and live on Li Shan and raise our pride here if you so wish it,' he told her, on the verge of tears, and wary of asking her now what he had intended to.

'Our pride,' Huxin repeated, sounding very upset. 'I hadn't thought to ever see you again.'

'I have thought of nothing else,' said Shi, falling to his knees to appeal for her forgiveness. 'I should have stayed and told you the truth the morning after the yin rite. But when I saw you were human, and a Wu, I fled for fear I had offended heaven. When Jiang Hudan told me you were pregnant —'

'Hudan knew you were the father of my pride all along?' Huxin's frown and anger deepened, and Shi was beginning to realise what Hudan had meant when she'd said that her sister was a handful. '*That* is what has been going on between you two …' Her tone lightened suddenly, and Shi took this to be a good sign.

'Seeing you with Ji Fa, I had to appeal my case to someone,' he explained.

'You were jealous?' Huxin smiled, appeased.

'To the point that I feared for my king's safety,' he confessed.

'So Hudan appealed your case to the king,' she concluded.

'Yes.'

'And the king appealed your case to the Great Mother.'

'Yes,' Shi said more cheerfully, as she seemed to be leading the conversation straight to the crux of the matter.

'And what did my Shifu have to say?'

'Well,' he moved to stand.

'Ah!' Huxin directed him back to his knees. 'I haven't forgiven you yet.'

Shi remained as he was. 'As the West of Zhou is now under my governace, our king wishes me to marry and as you see, my prerequisite for a wife is very particular.'

'So you chose me for lack of options?' Huxin took offence and Shi was on his feet to defend himself.

'I chose you before I even knew who you were. You know I did.'

'Li Shan is my *home*.' Huxin appealed her own cause. 'I am not persecuted here, I am *revered* … and I should never see my sister again if I leave!'

'I know I am asking a lot when you barely know me … as a person,' he allowed. 'But I am not afraid of what I am any more: you made me rejoice in my uniqueness. I believe in the West, where the white tiger is respected above all other creatures, we can build a new home for our pride, and make a haven for others like us.'

'Others?' Huxin had never even considered there were others.

'We came from somewhere, Huxin. I come from the vicinity of the Kunlun Mountains, that I … *we* now rule in their entirety and far, far beyond.'

Huxin choked, overwhelmed, and then collapsed into tears. 'I am not normally this emotional … it's just a lot to take in.' She fanned her face in an attempt to calm down.

'I understand.' He made a move to comfort her, but she held him at bay. Then with a wave of her hand, changed her mind and hugged him tightly.

'I am so sorry,' she cried into his chest.

'What are you sorry for?' Shi asked, a lump forming in his throat as he suspected a rejection was forthcoming.

'This is probably not how you imagined the event of your marriage proposal would be like.'

'I honestly never expected to make a marriage proposal before today.' Shi was deeply immersed in the feeling of her bare form hugged to his — he was attempting to savour the feeling for future reference, when it suddenly went away.

'Did the Great Mother command you to wed me?' Huxin was immediately on guard and regarding him warily.

'No!' Shi whined — why did she have so much trouble believing that he wanted this. 'I fell in love with you the moment I saw you flirting with my tigers in the garden. I am the one who championed this proposal, and by Tian's grace I was granted the opportunity to shoot for the moon.' He dropped on one knee before her to lay it all on the line. 'Jiang Huxin … would you do me the very great honour of becoming my wife?'

Huxin was fidgeting in her stance and tears streamed from her eyes. She was clearly torn, tongue-tied, and feeling under pressure to give him a response.

'Do you not feel as I do?' He rose from his knees to ease the tension.

'I chose you to father my pride … I did not have to go with you that night, but I did so joyfully.'

'But when I am in this form, a man, you do not feel the same way about me?'

'I find you very agreeable, Shi, but as a man … you pose an entirely different level of commitment for me.' Huxin reached out to brush his long hair from his face, and finally smiled again. 'You are not so much why I hesitate … it is me, this place.' She referred to the mount on which they stood. 'And as you say, I do not know you, as a person, very well. If I make a mistake, there is no running home to my family … once I leave I am banished and can never return.'

'I wish to make us a life in Shao that is so fine you will never want to return to Li Shan,' Shi contested, but he also did not want to upset her again. 'If I were permitted to court you for a time, so that you might know me better and have more time to prepare for leaving your home, would that be pleasing?'

When Huxin threw her arms around his neck and squeezed him tight, his heart finally found some peace. 'I should like that very much.'

'Perhaps you can give me an answer once our pride is born,' he suggested, daring to place a hand upon her naked belly.

'I should love to give birth here,' she admitted, her tone lighter now, and devoid of stress, as Shi knelt and placed an ear to her belly.

When Shi felt a movement in her womb and his lover affectionately toying with his hair, he smiled broadly. This was bliss.

Beyond the open window in Jiang Hudan's quarters it was a glorious morning on Li Shan. The sky was brilliant blue and the birds were singing. Dan had been awake since dawn and had not moved from his position curled up behind his lover — the moment was precious, so he wished to stay focused in it and make it linger. He had some concerns about Hudan's reaction when she awoke to discover she'd invited him into her bed, and when she began to stir Dan figured the romance was just about over.

'Hmmm …' To his delight she wriggled in closer to him. 'Good morning, brother Dan.' She glanced back to see him gazing down upon her. 'You haven't been awake all night, have you?'

'I wanted to stay awake,' Dan admitted, kissing her bare shoulder, 'but I couldn't keep my eyes open. I slept like a baby.'

Hudan turned on her back to smile up at him, and brushing his hair back out of the way, drew him into a long kiss.

As the good morning became rather heated Dan thought he should remind Hudan of her commitments. 'Do you not have a class you should be teaching about now?'

'Holiday,' she enlightened him.

A holiday was a rare event on Li Shan and, elated by the news, Dan returned to their fun — disappearing under the sheet, as he kissed down one side of her body.

'What is this?' He flicked the sheet back to admire her bare thigh which had one darker stripe of skin across it. 'That is my birthmark,' she said proudly. 'It's my little bit of tiger.'

'I like!' Dan grinned, as he pulled the sheet completely over them and kissed the mark.

'Hudan,' Huxin said as she slid the door aside and entered, 'do you know where I can find —' She gasped when two people popped out from under the bedcovers. 'Brother Dan! Holy mother!' She ran back and slid the door closed. 'Have you both lost your mind?'

Hudan was a little lost for words, but could not wipe the grin from her face. 'He didn't do anything I couldn't do to myself?' she retorted, recalling Fen's defence and was fit to burst as she shrugged to admit, 'except the tongue thing.' Hudan and Dan were reduced to laughter, and Huxin was having trouble being the responsible one for a change.

'Well … good for you,' she said, adding to their mirth. 'But, the Great Mother is asking to see Zhou Gong.'

'What? Now?' He was naked and dishevelled.

'*No*, when you are finished ravishing my sister,' Huxin stated with a good serve of sarcasm. 'Yes. Now!'

Dan flew into a panic, but Hudan prevented him from going anywhere until he'd kissed her, and when they parted he found himself dressed, groomed and ready to leave. 'You *have* to teach me that —!'

'Just come,' Huxin insisted, with a grumble, 'before we are all in trouble.'

'Thank you.' He kissed Hudan farewell, loath to part from her so quickly, at which point Huxin strode over and, grabbing one of his arms, dragged him away. 'Are you trying to get her banished?'

'Oh, she won't get banished,' Dan replied. 'Jiang Hudan doesn't get banished,' He aimed his cynical quip back at Hudan, who found it amusing. 'Will you come and see me off?'

'Of course I will.' She choked back her emotion and nodded.

'I'll *speak* with *you* later,' Huxin stressed, trying to look displeased, but looking more excited as she shoved Dan out the door.

'Do you manhandle all your guests in such a manner?' Dan asked as she closed the door behind them.

'Only the ones I am personally mad at.' She forced a smile and led off.

'Why are you mad?' Dan was surprised by her reaction when she was normally such a little minx. 'If we did anything wrong, your fingerprints were all over our backs.'

Huxin turned about, her mouth gaping open. 'What do you mean *if*? You took advantage, when I warned you that she was not herself.'

'She is herself now,' Dan said and motioned back to the happy instance he'd been dragged from.

'And tomorrow, when you are gone for good, who will she be then? Not herself, I assure you.' Huxin continued walking, as Dan opened his mouth to respond and pursued her to do so quietly.

'She will feel much as I shall, I expect.'

Huxin rolled her eyes as walked on. 'You will eventually find some other distraction, Hudan will not.'

'No,' he assured her. 'Zhou Gong Dan never marries again.'

Huxin frowned. 'Are you a prophet now?'

'You might say that,' he replied confidently. 'Shall I predict something for you?'

Huxin's eyes narrowed, but she was intrigued by his game as she led him down the stairs. 'Does your prediction have something to do with your brother, Shi?'

'It does,' Dan grinned, and Huxin looked thunderstruck.

'You knew too!'

'When I saw my brother transform into a tiger before my eyes, it was rather hard not to guess,' he confessed, glad to have taken Huxin's attention off his love life. 'Shi loves you very much.'

'He has told you so?' Huxin was immediately pacified when she realised she had a witness to question.

'Many times,' Dan emphasised. 'In fact on one occasion you were there.'

Huxin had a chuckle at the memory. 'You were *so* jealous that day,' she recalled, 'but not any more.'

'No,' he was pleased to admit. 'Nor shall I be in future.'

Huxin, pregnant and extra-emotional, had tears in her eyes. 'I am happy and sad for you both.' She forced a smile, but it was sincere. 'I just hope last night will bring you more cheer than heartache in the future.'

'As long as I know Hudan lives and prospers, I am content.'

'I have a feeling your brother will not be so easily contented.' She led them out of the stairway and across the open courtyard of the cloister toward Yi Wu's chambers.

'And that saddens you?' Dan was surprised.

'Either life I choose, I lose someone dear to me,' she explained. 'How would you feel?'

'No competition. I would stay here with Hudan,' he grinned broadly, to lighten her mood.

'The wisest man in the land and you are no help,' she grumbled in fun. 'I shall miss you, Zhou Gong.'

'For my brother's sake, I hope that it is not for too long,' he replied.

'My wedding would be the perfect excuse to see my sister again?'

'I hadn't considered that,' he replied honestly, his smile as broad as could be. 'But it only serves to make me want to champion Shi's cause all the more.'

Huxin laughed at his resolve. 'So, you think I should stay here with Hudan, and marry your brother. You are as confused as me.'

'Clearly, when it comes to love, there is no reasoning it out, you just have to do as your heart compels you,' he advised, and Huxin took that advice into consideration with a nod and an affectionate gaze as she let his hands go.

'I should announce you.' She entered the Great Mother's chambers, leaving the doors to the outer room open for Dan, as she passed through the doors into the main chamber.

Dan was left alone with Yi Wu as Huxin ushered him in and then left, closing the door behind her. The duke walked forward to address the Great Mother, but only bowed his head in greeting.

'Zhou Gong ...' She remained seated. 'I trust you slept well.'

'Very well,' he replied, raising his eyebrows in emphasis.

'You appear much at ease, my lord,' she observed graciously and not in the slightest bit wary.

'Clarity is a calming force,' he granted. 'I assume this meeting is to discuss my future training.'

The Great Mother nodded to concur. 'You understand, from what we discussed yesterday, that you must be more focused in your efforts to develop your supernatural skills?'

'A captain should be as able as any of his crew,' Dan warranted.

'Precisely.' She stood. 'Fen shall be a good instructor for you, for now. Once you have mastered your own talents, however, you must be taught the art of physical teleportation.'

'Like Hudan.' Dan smiled keen to have her mentorship back.

'Like Huxin.' The tigress was more the mentor Yi Wu had in mind. 'You, Shi and Fen must be competent in this art before your dying day, which, if time holds true, shall not be for some time yet.'

'Why that art in particular?' Dan was curious, and was startled as the young son of the sky manifested his form in Yi Wu's stead.

'Because you require this skill to shift through time, like the rest of us,' Telmo explained. 'If you die without mastering this, you get left behind, and will default back to your old life as Lucian.'

'That does not sound so terrible.'

'Well, that depends ...'

'On what?' Dan was wary of asking, as the young lord had ducked behind his long fair hair, and was peering out from beneath.

'It depends on whether or not any of the rest of our team complete the mission. If just one of us succeeds in killing Dragonface and willingly teleports back to our universe, to the time before we all shifted to this one, then we foil the bad guys in both universes and everyone lives happily ever after.'

'And if none of us completes the mission?'

'Our souls revert to the bodies we left for dead on Kila in the future of this universe,' he replied flatly.

'Left for *dead*,' Dan repeated, not liking the punchline.

'Lost in space, *dead*, yeah! Bad guys win. Game over,' Telmo said. 'You see what I mean now, about this being only a tiny drop in the ocean of what is really unfolding in your soul-life?'

'More and more so,' Dan granted, his consciousness feeling pushed to the limit once again.

'So Fen will continue your training,' the lord summed up, 'but you must not forget the aspirations of the person you are now, in the process. Zhou Gong Dan's life must stay on track.'

'I believe we understand each other,' Dan stated, seriously. 'Hudan and I shall make allowances for the sake of the mission. But ...'

'Ah, here it comes.' The lad waved on the rebuttal.

'I shall be communicating with her,' Dan stated, 'and seeking her company for solace whenever heaven allows me that opportunity. *This* is your captain speaking.'

'Boom, boom!' Telmo was amused. 'Well … I cannot stop you. But I will say this: I am not the judge here, causality is the judge. I would also point out that having unpredestined offspring is not your only concern here … missing an important event because you are seducing your lover could be every bit as damaging.'

Dan had not explored the scenario so far as to consider this.

'Last night, you would only have spent alone in your room. There was very little possibility of any other outcome,' Telmo said, explaining why he'd allowed them to transgress. 'Out there in the real world there are far more possible outcomes, and any one of them could be vital.'

Dan nodded, fully comprehending the spirit's cautionary words. 'Would I be right in saying that this would not be the first time we've cheated history to be together?'

Telmo grinned broadly. 'If you only knew how right you are, you'd be much less of a worry. Am I dismissed, captain?'

Dan felt quite empowered in the wake of this chat, and smiled and nodded. 'I thank you for your guidance.'

'Any time,' Telmo emphasised.

'Until next we meet, I wish you well.'

'Hopefully our next meeting will be as joyous an event as this.' Dan was hoping it would be his brother's wedding.

'I have one pregnant and courting, another having an affair!' Telmo grumbled, as he transformed back into the form of Yi Wu and was seated. 'I'm starting to feel like I'm a matchmaker rather than Shifu.'

'How do you bear the distraction of having so many beautiful women around you?' Dan asked out of curiosity.

'If Hudan was not here, would you be tempted by any of these beauties?' Yi Wu posed.

Dan raised his eyebrows and shook his head, seeing Telmo's point.

'My love awaits me at our final destination, captain. She was not chosen for this mission. And now you know why I am so eager to see our mission executed to perfection, and to make you see that any risk you take, is *everybody's* risk.'

Dan was sobered by that realisation, and nodded as he considered everything he had heard. 'I am grateful for your honesty and your confidence in me to date. I shall do my very best.'

'That is all any of us can do, Zhou Gong,' she said, applauding his resolve. 'You have always, *always*, led us to victory and this life shall prove no different.'

Beyond speech, Dan bowed, exiting through the waiting room and out into the sunshine of the cloister where Huxin, Hudan and Shi were waiting to accompany him to the morning meal.

'What did Shifu say?' Huxin was most eager to know if he'd been found out and scolded.

'The Great Mother said that we make a great team,' and Dan nodded once to confirm he felt the same. 'My Wu training shall continue.'

'Congratulations.' Hudan was relieved and happy for him — and herself, as being Wu meant he would remain unmarried.

'Let's eat.' Dan rubbed his hands together. 'I'm starving!'

'Me too,' Shi agreed, and his stomach gave a loud growl.

'We had best make haste then,' Dan urged them on in jest, 'before he eats somebody.' The notion amused the Wu, and Shi frowned at his brother's quip at his expense.

'I have managed to control myself for the last twenty years,' Shi objected.

'Which is far more than can be said about Dan and his appetites this morning,' Huxin commented, ribbing Dan in Shi's defence, and taking hold of the arm of her intended, she led Shi into the dining hall.

Shi turned back to note Dan was lost for words. 'I have missed something.'

A shy smile passed between his brother and Hudan as the pair entered the dining hall to enjoy one last meal together.

15

THE TWINS AND
SPIRIT TIGER

Over the next month and a half, the heat of summer was replaced by the cooler, drizzly days of autumn, and Shi was a regular visitor to Li Shan. Hudan took advantage of her would-be brother-in-law's weekly visits to send correspondence to Dan and Fen and to keep abreast of events in Haojing.

Zhou Gong Dan had been enthused and absorbed by a commission given to him by the King of Zhou — to design a heavenly city based on the strict cosmological principles of the holy field, otherwise known in mathematics as the magic square. This was to set a design precedent in urban planning that would demonstrate and complement Zhou's new civil laws and structure.

The holy field in its most simplified form was one square divided into nine equal squares and each square was allocated a number between one and nine. The number placement was such that no matter how the numbers were added, across or down or diagonally, they equaled fifteen.

The four squares of even integers at the corners represented yin, and the five axial squares of odd integers represented yang, and so the diagram was thought to demonstrate the perfect balance of yin and yang to achieve a flow of chi. Each segment of the square could then be divided into nine down to infinity.

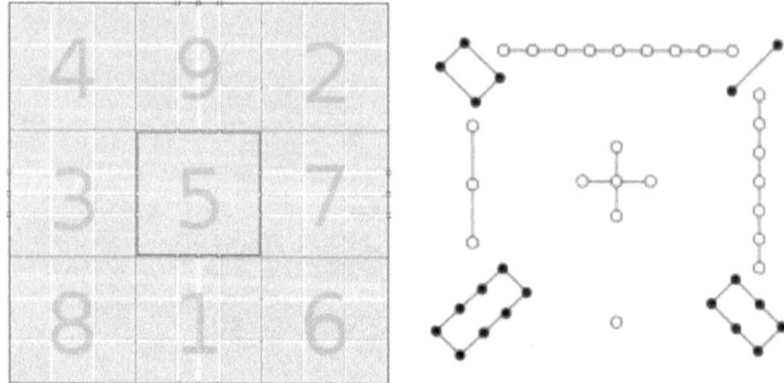

To find a location for the new city was to be Shi's mission, but as the young overlord was otherwise distracted courting a wife, he'd been excused from the responsibility until such time as Dan had drafted his first blueprint.

Fen was also keeping himself busy, training Zhou Gong in Dao Yin and Wu doctrine, researching the ancient art of placement for Dan's urban planning project, and visiting the queen every day to check on her condition. Hudan's brother was pleased to report that the signs that Yi Jiang was with child were very promising: she had yet to bleed, was feeling ill in the mornings and was otherwise eating like a horse, not unlike their own sister, who would have devoured a horse a day if given the opportunity. Due to the queen's morning sickness she was Fen's first priority every morning, and she was always pleased to see him, as was the king. Fen's only frustration was that the queen had found her playful streak and was making it her personal mission to find Fen a love interest. He complained in his letters to Hudan that every day Yi Jiang had a new line-up of lovely handmaidens for him to peruse, no matter how many times he assured the queen that he was quite content with his life at Haojing. 'But it is such a waste of a young, handsome, able and *rich* lord,' the queen would emphasise. Fen was being very well paid for his services and had been awarded land at the base of Li Shan. So whether Fen liked it or not, he was now a Count of Zhou and his name was Zhou Bo Fen Gong.

Since they had first realised their separation was a real possibility, Hudan and Huxin were getting along better than they ever had. And as Huxin's belly swelled, the fact that their days were numbered was more and more apparent — for Shi was winning his battle to gain the tigress' trust and affection.

On this, his last visit before the due date of birth of their pride, Shi brought something he hoped would seal the deal for him.

'What is that?' Hudan queried, seeing the long, thick bamboo container in his hand as she took the smaller bamboo boxes containing her correspondence from him.

'It is a silken blueprint of my estate at Shao,' he whispered. 'I thought Huxin might like to see it and,' he shrugged coyly, 'perhaps make plans for the future? Do you think that would be pleasing to her?'

'I'm sure she shall be delighted,' Hudan replied with a sincere smile of encouragement, her heart sinking at the thought of being the last of her siblings left on Li Shan, and without a courier to and from Haojing. Still, Dan had been joking in his letters about training up some pigeons to replace their tiger express.

'Is she in the garden courtyard?' Shi queried, backing up in that direction, as this was where they usually met, and Hudan nodded. 'Wish me luck.' He did not wait for her retort.

As there was still an hour of good daylight left and it was a pleasant, fine day, Hudan took her mail to the garden to read. This had become her favourite time of the week and she loved being able to sit and read and think of those she cared about — she was going to miss it greatly once Huxin and Shi were gone. She always read Fen's news first, and so slipped the silk from its bamboo coffer and unfurled it to read.

The big news from Haojing was confirmation of the queen's pregnancy, an event which had the Zhou king, and the household at large, overjoyed. Yi Jiang was so thrilled that Fen's prediction had come to pass that she gave him four concubines, but having no idea what to do with them, Fen insisted, upon threat of taking his own life, that she take them back. 'The life of a concubine would be horrid in the service of a man who does not love you,' he had told her majesty.

'But you must pass your healing art on to your offspring,' she had insisted.

'I don't know that it works that way, majesty, having never known my parents,' he had countered. 'I should much prefer a few days off to visit with my sister, Huxin, to ensure it goes well with the birth of her offspring.' The queen had taken back the handmaidens and agreed to allow Fen to visit this coming week. *You must come and fetch me as soon as there is any sign of labour*, he advised Hudan in his letter, and the thought of seeing Dan, even fleetingly, put a large smile on her face.

Dan's missive was all political talk and the intricacies of his current project. Hudan loved how neither Dan nor Fen spoke of their absence, only of the positive progress they were making toward the future. Dan never mentioned their affection, but spoke constantly of how he would take her here and show her this, which was his subtle way of saying that she was always in his thoughts.

'Sister Hudan!' Shi jumped the garden gate to join her. 'I think it's happening!'

'They are early!' Hudan rose to accompany him to consult with her sister, who was seated in heaven's garden — the plans of her new house were laid out before her, as she gripped her belly.

'I think the west wing downstairs for the nursery,' she said as they entered.

'In theory?' Shi queried, repressing his excitement as he approached and sat beside her, wondering if this was the 'yes' he'd been waiting for.

'No,' she shook her head, and smiled at him. 'I am decided … we go, where you go.' She took hold of his face and drew him into a kiss.

Hudan's heart welled at the scene, and her eyes moistened. Once she would have been rolling her eyes and thinking them deluded, but now Hudan knew that love could last beyond death, beyond rebirth, for its source lay in the spirit where it could not be erased or forgotten.

'I could not be happier.' Shi was smiling and crying at once, and Huxin's expression reflected his perfectly.

'Brother Shi said you were in labour?' Hudan queried her sister's calm state.

'The pain has backed off — ah —' Her expression contorted in agony.

'The queen has said I may fetch Fen to your aid,' Hudan told her, as Huxin urged Shi to back off. She was panting heavily.

'Yes, bring Fen, *bring Fen!*' She gritted her teeth to endure the contraction.

'Quickly!' Shi urged her, at a loss to do anything himself.

'I shall inform the Great Mother of my errand,' Hudan advised.

Once she had gained permission, the sun had nearly set. Hudan was hopeful of finding Fen in Dan's company, as they studied together in his Hall of Records in the evenings.

Acting on her intention to join Fen, Hudan arrived to find the men she sought working away quietly in Dan's hall; the duke was drafting plans upon a large framed silk, and Fen was referencing some old bamboo annuals and taking notes.

'Ahem.' Hudan cleared her throat upon arrival, not wishing to startle them.

'Brother Hudan!' they both chanted at once, Dan with a huge smile, Fen with a worried frown.

'Huxin?' Fen concluded, raising himself from his desk.

'Yes,' Hudan confirmed, 'she has gone into labour a week early.'

'I shall advise the queen of my absence.' Fen rushed from the room, but stopped to close the door behind him.

'Brother Dan,' Hudan said, as he approached to greet her.

'This is such a pleasant surprise,' he said, in good spirits. 'You look well.'

'As do you,' she replied, and they both stood politely at a distance observing one another.

'In that other timeline,' Dan posed, taking a step toward her, 'the one we are trying to keep on track, do you think we would be doing anything more than standing here having a polite conversation?' He moved closer to speak more intimately with her.

Hudan considered it an odd question. 'I doubt it. Why do you ask?'

'I would not want to miss anything ...' His lips found hers in a sweet bid for some attention, which he got in a deep, long moment, as Hudan was too relieved to object. 'I long to see you again,' he whispered, afterward.

'The wedding will be at Li Shan and only a small affair. Do you think Shi will nominate you as his witness?' Hudan suggested.

'He owes us a few favours if memory serves.' Dan's lips lingered close to hers.

'Hudan!' Fen's horrified call startled them apart, but what was more alarming was that Ji Song was in his company.

'Highness?' Dan was clearly surprised to see the prince.

'Zhou Gong, you sly old fox,' Song jeered, annoyed. 'You are not trying to have your way with one of the *holy* vestals, are you? That would be a shameful blemish on your otherwise distinguished career.'

'Not at all,' Hudan said in response to Song's accusation. 'I had something in my eye,' she informed the prince, and Dan nodded to corroborate her lie, as she blinked a few times. 'But I believe you got it, thank you, brother Dan.'

'My pleasure,' he said, their secret making them both rather more jovial than warranted.

'Can I help you with something, highness?' Dan queried, and then frowned deeply, as he eyed Song closely, feeling disturbed by something other than Song's mere presence.

'When Fen mentioned Jiang Hudan was here,' Song fixed his sights on Hudan, and his boyish charm came to the fore as he approached her, 'I felt compelled to come and congratulate the legend myself for her amazing conquest of Su Daji. I stand in awe!' He bowed to her, one hand upon his heart, but his intense eye contact did not waver.

'Ultimately, Su Daji took her own life,' Hudan replied, rather more aroused by his gaze then she felt she should have been. 'She was dragged into a role she never wanted, and was happy to die, having tarnished the eternal memory of the man who ruined her life.'

'How sad,' Ji Song said, and his sympathy surprised Hudan; apparently, Song had unexpected depth. 'Still, I should very much like to hear the tale one day.'

'I have made an account of the events of your father's campaign in the East, and I can have a copy made especially for your highness, if that is pleasing?' Hudan proffered.

Although it was clearly less than Ji Song had hoped for, he smiled to accept. 'I greatly look forward to reading your narrative.'

'Your highness must excuse us,' Fen interrupted, as the men vied for Hudan's attention. 'Our sister is in pressing need.'

'I should come with you,' Dan decided, out of the blue, and everyone looked at him wondering about his reason. 'Someone has to keep Shi calm.'

'A good point.' Hudan looked to Fen, who nodded to confirm.

'Please inform the king of my absence,' Dan requested of Song, who seemed a mite baffled as Hudan took Fen's hand in hers and reached out to Dan, who took hold of the other. 'We shall return,' said the duke, with a grin.

'Highness,' Fen bowed, and the three of them vanished from Haojing.

They materialised in the open cloister, and Fen did not have to ask where Huxin was; the lad simply followed the loud wailing that led to their old quarters. Hudan made a move after him, but Dan held her back.

'I need to tell you something.' He swung her around.

'Not now,' she appealed, fretting for her sister. She'd never heard her in so much pain.

'I've seen another son of the sky,' he said, breathing a heavy sigh as he let her go. 'He's in Ji Song.'

'Ji Song?' Hudan hadn't felt any connection to Song before today, but had to admit his gaze had stirred something in her.

'Why him?' Dan was clearly not happy. 'Shi, I can understand. But his highness is completely self-absorbed.'

'Not completely,' Hudan defended the lad. 'He was sympathetic to Su Daji's plight.'

Dan frowned and he rolled his eyes. 'I thought you might have seen through his charming antics, which he pours on for all the ladies, and I mean *all*.'

Now Hudan was frowning. 'Dan, such animosity toward your future king is surely not beneficial.'

The duke hung his head briefly, contrite. 'Still, it is the truth.'

'Perhaps wooing women is his talent.' Hudan shrugged in a non-judgemental fashion. 'Our Shifu claims seduction is a weapon as efficient as any blade.'

Dan seemed slightly offended by her perspective. 'Song is obviously very proficient at his art.'

'You could thank me for lying to his highness just now,' she said, placing her hands on her hips to rebut his jealousy.

'That was kind of you,' he admitted, finding his sense of humour.

'The simple truth of the matter is that, regardless of how you feel about him, Song is clearly one of us,' Hudan stated. 'Do you think the Great Mother is aware of him?'

'That is what I really came here to ask, in fact,' Dan murmured, looking about at the abandoned downstairs area of the cloister.

Most of the residents of Li Shan were in the their beds, though no one could possibly have been sleeping through the ruckus Huxin had been making, which had quietened since Fen's arrival.

'I should go.' Hudan began to walk away and Dan moved with her as far as the landing that led to the hallway to heaven's garden. 'I shall see you after.'

With a nod from Dan, they went their separate ways, Hudan toward her quarters, and the duke into the hallway leading to the garden courtyard beyond, in search of his brother.

The tranquil garden seemed anything but, with Shi pacing about like a caged animal. He was overjoyed when he spotted Dan and near winded him with a hug that was more of a collision of bodies. 'Thank you for coming.'

'My pleasure,' Dan replied after catching his breath. 'How are you faring?' he asked and slapped his brother's back in the hope he would release him.

'I am fine,' Shi insisted, backing off. 'It is Huxin I am worried about! At least the roaring and screaming has stopped now. Huxin keeps transforming; she can't decide what is more comfortable.'

'I see.' Dan didn't envy Fen right now. 'Her brother is with her, so rest assured she is in the best of care.' Dan directed Shi to take a seat.

'No, thanks.' Shi decided he'd rather pace back and forth.

'Has Brother Huxin given you her answer? Am I to be calling her "sister" from now on?'

'Yes,' Shi said and realised he hadn't broken the good news to anyone yet. 'She said, yes!'

'Congratulations!' Dan held his hand hand out to his brother, and they gripped each other around the forearm. 'Jiang Huxin is quite a catch, and our Zhou will be pleased. I wish you every happiness.'

Shi received the good wishes graciously, before his expression soured. 'My only worry is that Huxin's mother died in birthing —'

'She was already wounded and weak.'

Both men were started by the voice of the Great Mother, who was standing at the end of the hallway that led from the courtyard back to the cloister, with two students poised beside her, one carrying a tray of tea and the other a burning lantern.

'Shifu Yi?' Dan uttered, amazed. He'd never seen Yi Wu outside of her chambers or the temple.

'Yes, I do get out and about on occasion, and this event is certainly auspicious.' She motioned her students to place their loads on the table, which they did, and closed the large doors to the hallway as they departed. 'A little something to sooth your nerves, Shi … and it won't hurt us either.' Yi Wu winked at Dan, and motioned them to be seated. This time Shi did not object, for the Great Mother's presence was a pacifying force.

'I thought you might be a little concerned by the sketchy nature of the reports about your mate,' Yi Wu said, as she came to join them and seated herself on the opposite side on the table to them both. 'So, I considered that a first-hand account of how I came by my two most prized students could be in order?'

Dan was sure he looked every bit as eager to hear the yarn as Shi, who nodded in response to the suggestion. 'I would be honoured to know her history.'

'Then I shall tell it.' Yi Wu poured the tea and they each partook of a cup and both men gasped for breath in the wake of the brew.

'Whoa,' Dan emphasised, while his brother thumped the table to endure the passage of the liquid down his throat.

'Ah,' Yi Wu finished her cup, '*special*.'

Shi gave his head a shake — his jaw flapping made a ridiculous sound that amused his company. 'Phew! That was *good*.'

'More?' she invited, whereby Dan covered his cup with his hand.

'I need my wits about me,' he graciously declined.

'I think I shall take my time with this one.' Shi indicated he would like a refill, welcoming the distraction.

'You were saying, Shifu?' Dan had been waiting to hear this tale for a long time, and feared they would be interrupted.

'It was the year of the fire tiger.' She poured tea for Shi and then herself. 'And long before I had the connection to my higher self that I do now, you understand?' She aimed the statement at Dan, who nodded to confirm he followed.

'I don't understand.' Shi was disheartened to be lost already.

'It is not important that you do,' the Great Mother assured him, and Shi was happy again. 'I was trekking deep in the pathless regions of Qiang, toward the source of the three great western rivers.'

'That is where I hail from.'

'I am not surprised,' Yi Wu awarded, 'for it has been one of the stomping grounds of the sons of the sky and their forefathers since prehistoric times.'

Dan was very interested to hear this and immediately aspired to travel there himself, and explore the region.

'It was my aim to find the fabled sea of stars,' Yi Wu continued, 'that is said to lie north of the principal chain of mountains, but I never made it to my destination.' She didn't appear to regret not attaining her goal too much. 'There was a terrible blizzard, and I sought shelter in a cave where I was stunned to encounter a young woman giving birth. She appeared to have been attacked by a wild animal, and as a healer, I was eager to assist her, for the child was crowning and in hurry to be born.'

'Hudan?' Dan guessed, as she had to do everything immediately.

'It was,' she grinned to confirm. 'Yet no sooner had the mother swathed the child to warm it, than she was urging me to take her away and come back later. As I departed to search for alternative shelter, I turned back to note the woman removing her clothes, despite the freezing temperatures. I thought her trying to harm herself and so made a move to caution her … that's when I saw her transform … I turned and ran for my life!'

Shi had a chuckle at her fear. 'It was brave of you to go back,' he awarded.

Yi Wu smiled at his praise. 'I had made a promise,' she concurred, appearing more sombre. 'I regret that I did not get my courage up a little faster. By the time I returned, their mother was dead and the runt of the litter, the only male, had frozen to death on the ice.'

Even Dan winced at the visual image, so Shi was certainly distressed.

'Huxin had pulled herself in between her mother's forearms, off the cold ground and was sucking for her life.'

Shi smiled at the tale of his love's deliverance.

'Taiji was their mother's,' Yi Wu explained, 'and I taught myself how to wield the staff, and then taught Hudan when she was old enough.'

'Hence your quest to find the sea of stars was abandoned?' Dan concluded for his Shifu.

'It was Tian who sent me on that pilgrimage, but I like to think Hudan and Huxin were the true reason I was compelled to take that path. I think if I had known the real reason I was being so compelled, I might not have been so keen. Raising the pair of them, so very different from each other, was challenging to say the very least.'

'So Hudan and Huxin would have had a brother?' Shi mourned for them.

'I have never told them,' Yi Wu confessed. 'But when Fen came along and they became so attached, I felt that soul had come back around to them.'

Dan felt himself getting sentimental, and he sniffled back the emotion. 'I should like to write that tale.'

'I have beaten you to it, but you are welcome to record it for mass consumption if you so desire,' the Great Mother allowed.

'Did their mother say anything about where she was from?' Shi asked, curious.

'We did not exactly speak the same language?' Yi Wu explained, 'although I did ask, and the only reply I got was, Dropa.'

'Dropa? I've never heard of it,' Shi exclaimed, shaking his head, 'but once I am residing in the region and the cubs are older, we shall explore.'

'That sounds a splendid plan,' she conceded, as the doors from the entrance hall were heard to part.

When Shi saw it was Hudan he ran to hear the news.

'It's twins!' she announced.

'Twins!' he conveyed back to the Great Mother and Dan, before turning back to Hudan. 'Of what variety?'

'A boy and girl.'

'One of each!' Shi clapped his hands together. 'But what *variety*?'

'Oh,' Hudan realised his meaning. 'Cubs.'

'Splendid! May I see them?' he requested.

'Of course!' As Hudan moved to lead him, Shi was already whipping his shirt off. 'Shi, this is a cloister of maidens. You might want to wait until you get indoors to transform.'

'Sorry.' He pulled his shirt half on to accompany her. 'I am not really thinking straight.'

In the wake of his brother's excited exit, Dan looked back to his companion. 'Shifu, I need to speak with you about Ji Song.'

'I know your concerns,' she told him, 'but the prince's time among the Wu will come in due course.'

'He *is* one of us then?' Dan was hoping there had been some mistake.

'I'm afraid so,' she said, causing Dan to wonder if his aversion to the prince was far more obvious than he'd imagined.

'Do we have a history, outside of our current circumstances?' Dan queried, suspecting that they did.

'Work on tapping into your Akashic memory, and you shall be able to answer that for yourself.' Yi Wu obviously thought this would motivate him, and she was right — it would.

'Just when I think I have it all figured out, causality kicks me another curve ball,' Dan grumbled.

'Then train harder,' she suggested, 'and you'll be kicking goals in no time.'

Huxin had actually birthed three cubs, but one was clearly smaller than its siblings and was entirely white. Unlike the twins, she was not born squirming, and seemed dead until Fen had taken her in hand. Huxin had given the cub one sniff and then completely ignored it. Once Fen had cleaned the third newborn, he tried to place it back with the others to be fed, but it was quickly barged out of the way by both its siblings and its mother.

Hudan and Shi arrived to find the tigress on the floor feeding the twins, and Fen drip-feeding the runt with his finger from a bowl of goat's milk.

'There are three?' Shi began whipping his clothes off the second he was in the room, eager to join his family, and Hudan turned to face the other way.

'She rejected this one.' Fen was clearly worried for the tiny ball of white fur sucking on his finger, although it made him smile. 'Huxin has not returned to human form to tell us why.'

'I shall find out.' Shi shifted form to join his pride, and walking around behind his tigress, the tiger collapsed onto the floor and began grooming her around the head. Huxin was very receptive and purred loudly.

Hudan sat by Fen on the bed to admire his little bundle.

'I am sorry the prince surprised you at Haojing,' he commented. 'I was not expecting to interrupt anything.'

'You did not,' she insisted. 'I told you, I had something in my eye.'

Fen gave half a laugh and shook his head. 'What happened to "love is the addiction of unfulfilled people"?'

Hudan dropped her innocent front and grinned to admit. 'You were right, and I was … so very wrong.'

Fen, having never won an argument with Hudan before, wanted to grin but was too annoyed. 'You nearly shamed my duke and the House of Li Shan in front of the next Zhou,' he said, his voice low. 'What were you thinking?'

Hudan frowned and pouted, unaccustomed to being in trouble or being lectured by her baby brother. 'You do not have to worry; circumstances dictate that it will not happen again,' she concluded sadly.

One side of Fen's mouth almost formed a sympathetic smile as he looked to their sister and her new family. 'Well, at least love was kind to one of us.'

Hudan bumped heads with her brother, and gave him a hug. He was not really angry with her — she would have felt it in his energy, which was brimming with joy at present. Yet Hudan was angry that her little brother had been forced into a position where he'd been compelled to call her commonsense into question. Even if circumstances did allow such an opportunity again, as it might at the forthcoming wedding, Hudan felt she must not succumb. It had been a mistake to admit her true feelings to Dan and, although the thought pained her like a sucker-punch to the chest, their connection had to be severed.

Once the twins were snoozing in between their father's paws where they had been licked to sleep, Huxin returned to her human form to get herself cleaned up. She was surprisingly unscathed and undaunted by the event; just a little weary and moving slow.

'Can I get you something?' Hudan climbed off the bed to be of assistance, as Huxin pulled on a robe.

'No, I'm good.' She looked at Fen, affectionately. 'Thanks to you, my sweetness.'

'What would you like me to do with this little girl?' Fen referred to the runt sleeping down the front of his shirt.

'She's not a shifter,' Huxin told him. 'There is no human in her, and that makes her a danger to her siblings. Were-tigers and full blood tigers develop at a different rate, so if the twins don't kill her during the feeding process in the first few months, she will outgrow them in a year and ... I can't run the risk.'

'You can't just let her die,' Fen appealed.

'I can and I will,' she told him surely. 'Thank you again for your assistance. I am going to bathe.'

'Huxin?' Fen called her back. 'May I keep her for you, then? Surely, they will be of equal size sooner or later?'

'*Your* choice!' Huxin stressed the point and exited the room quietly.

Fen was left utterly bewildered by her attitude and looked to Shi, who shifted back into human form. Hudan did him the service of returning his clothes to his body, and he was stunned to find himself instantly dressed.

'Many thanks, sister.' He rose with a smile — both the tiny cubs still asleep in his folded arms.

'What say you, Shi?' Fen climbed off the bed to show him his other daughter.

'I do not have a say,' Shi said as he eyed her over and smiled fondly.

'In the tiger world, perhaps,' Fen argued, 'but in the human world you are the head of the household.'

'But the runt is not human,' Shi replied, frowning, and lowered his voice to share his other concern, 'and I should rather have Huxin *in* my household before I attempt to challenge her authority.'

Fen conceded Shi's predicament, to his own frustration. 'Well then, I *shall* take her.' He sounded deeply disappointed that he seemed to care more about the cub than either of her parents did. He dug the slumbering cub out from his shirt to look at her. 'I shall name her Ling Hu.' He rubbed noses with his new charge.

The name meant 'spirit tiger' or 'tiger with inner strength' and it suited her albino colouring well.

'That is a fine name,' Shi agreed. 'I shall inform Huxin of it when she returns.'

This was a subtle hint to Fen that he should take the spurned cub and go, before Huxin came back, and Fen lost a little of his cheer as he returned the cub inside his shirt.

'Come, Fen,' Hudan broke the tense moment, 'I should see you and brother Dan back to court.'

'I shall be sure and tell the king your happy news.' Fen followed Hudan to the door.

'I am indebted to you, brother Fen,' Shi spoke up before the healer departed, 'on *many* levels, and I thank you with all my heart.'

'You just gave me your first-born daughter,' Fen's voice went hoarse with emotion, 'I would say we are even.' He made a hasty retreat ahead of his sister.

'It is for the best,' Shi told Hudan, who nodded to assure him she did not question their judgement.

'Fen Gong was himself abandoned by his parents,' she explained, 'and this event has struck a chord, I would say. But he will come to see that events will unfold in accord with heaven for Ling Hu, just as they did for him.' Hudan followed Fen from the room.

The ominous conversation Hudan knew she must have with Dan before she left his company that evening was looming large in her thoughts as she followed Fen into the courtyard. The notion had dulled the joy around the day's happy occasion, and Hudan just felt cold and numb.

'What are you going to do with a tiger at court?' Dan was saying, as he admired the little cub down the front of his companion's shirt. 'Do you have any idea what she could do to our Hall of Records?'

'Well, I could just move to my property with her,' Fen teased. 'I'm sure the queen would have no problem allowing me to *leave*.'

Dan smiled to concede Fen would get his way. 'You are quite right, every level of diyu would freeze over before Yi Jiang will part with you.' Dan looked to Hudan, and must have noted how forced her smile was. 'Is something the matter?'

'I am just tired,' she advised. 'I should deliver you both back to court, before I do not have the chi to do it.'

Back in Dan's Hall of Records, Hudan bid goodnight to Fen and his little charge, in the hope that he would leave her to speak with

Dan, but her little brother ignored the hint, despite the long awkward silence, and their glares.

'I shall see you in the morning, Fen,' Dan prodded further.

'I would like to see my sister gone before I leave,' Fen hinted right back. 'Just in case she gets anything in her eye.'

'Very well.' Hudan resented being treated like a child. 'Zhou Gong.' She nodded in the duke's direction and vanished.

'Happy?' Dan queried, with more than a little annoyance.

'Nice try, Hudan,' Fen grinned, not looking up from stroking his charge, 'but I know you are still here.'

'Damn you, Fen.' Hudan reappeared beside Dan. 'I can handle this myself.'

'I think handling is your problem,' he backed up a few paces. 'No handling,' he specified.

'Yes, I understand. *Goodnight*,' she stressed, and Fen finally left.

'Am I what you are not handling?' Dan cocked his head, alerted to a change in the emotional weather.

Hudan opened her mouth to answer, but no words were forthcoming, so she merely nodded to confirm.

'Don't,' he appealed, taking a step toward her, and when she took a step away, he was gutted. 'Please —'

'The night of the goddess rite, I made the choice to tell you the truth because I didn't want to hurt you,' Hudan said, 'but it was the wrong choice —'

'No, it wasn't.' He made another attempt to approach, but she maintained the distance. 'You vowed you'd never regret it.'

'I don't regret our bliss, Dan,' Hudan told him, on the verge of tears, 'only that it has to end.'

'Why,' he objected, 'when even the Great Mother has not forbidden it.'

'She cannot take away our free will, only *we* can to do that,' Hudan stated, 'or *I*, if I must do this alone.'

Dan shook his head not wanting to put her in that position, but not wishing to concede the end either. 'I apologise for earlier, but we can work around this.'

'The risk is too great,' she reminded him, desperate to make him see. 'Zhou Gong will be remembered as the father of civilisation, Dan.'

'Yi Wu told you that?' Dan assumed, annoyed by the Great Mother's tactic.

'I will not be the one who shames the brightest star in Tian's sky,' she insisted and ignored his query.

'I don't care about greatness!' Dan finally caught Hudan and wanted to hold her, but she held him at bay.

'That is my entire point.' she reasoned. 'History will care, very much.' She held a hand to his face and regarded him tenderly. 'Farewell, my friend —'

'No,' he implored her not to leave.

'May Tian speed your destiny. I shall await you at the end.' She caught her breath as she broke away from him, and with her inner focus already on Li Shan, she was spirited away.

16

THE BIRTH OF JI YU

If Fen had been attracting a lot of female attention before, now that he had a tiger cub he could not keep the ladies of the queen's court at bay and they would fight over who would mind his charge whilst he tended to the queen.

He was rather grateful for the delightful distraction of Ling Hu in his life. Fen missed his sisters, and Zhou Gong Dan had been a complete misery for weeks!

Even the sight of Fen attempting to teach Ling Hu how to drink milk out of a bowl by himself demonstrating, failed to rouse a smile from the duke.

'No, dopey,' Fen remonstrated, lifting the cub out of the bowl it had walked in. 'We drink it!' He shoved one of Ling Hu's paws to her mouth and she began licking the milk off. 'That's right.' Fen sat the cub down next the bowl, whereupon she stuck her paw back in the bowl and proceeded to lick it off again. 'Well, she's getting it, kind of.' He looked at Dan.

'We have work to do,' he said, looking back to his drafting.

'I'm leaving soon for the wedding,' Fen said, to jolt the lord's memory.

'Ah yes, that is today, isn't it?' Dan remained focused on his work.

'You can still change your mind and come,' Fen stood to appeal. 'Shi very much wants you there.'

'Busy.'

'In that case,' Fen ventured, 'would you mind taking care of Ling Hu for me? I'm afraid Huxin might eat her if I take her to the wedding.'

'Do I look like a wet nurse to you?' Dan looked at Fen to ask, and the lad reached the end of his tether.

'It was not my fault she ended what should never have begun,' Fen decided to get the real issue out in the open.

'Did I say it was?' Dan replied, his mood unchanged.

'Then where did our friendship go?' Fen implored him to answer. 'Why are you treating me like I am the bad guy?'

'Was I?' Dan faked surprise. 'My apologies. We know you have never been led astray.'

'Ah!' Fen saw his beef now. 'I was no one of consequence, nor was my lover. The same could not be said of you and Hudan.'

'Yes, thank you, Fen. That has been made painfully clear to me.' The duke was obviously using a considerable amount of restraint to stay civil. 'I'm sorry if you find my resulting bad mood offensive, but I feel sure it shall improve given time.'

Fen backed down, content they would get past this falling out. 'Please come to Li Shan.'

'Absolutely not.' Dan wasn't budging on that issue. 'But you can leave the cub, I'll take care of her.'

The duke's agreement was pleasing to Fen, and he picked up his charge to hand her over. 'You have to cuddle her to keep her warm.'

'Aw … must I?' Dan grumbled, as Ling Hu was plonked on his lap.

'I shall return this evening.' Fen patted her head, and was off out the door. He paused in the hallway wondering what the duke would do next. Would he, a) put the cub back on the floor, b) cuddle her as instructed, or c) get peed on and become very angry? Fen backed up quietly to see the duke smiling down at the cub as he played with her. It was the happiest he'd seen Dan since the birth, so Fen was content to leave them both.

'Tian, damn it all!' Fen heard Dan holler when he was halfway down the hall, and so he sped up his pace to make good his escape before the duke came after him.

There had never been a wedding on Li Shan, and the cloister was abuzz with excitement. The entire house was decorated with autumn blooms, which proved a much more difficult task without Fen on hand to help.

Ji Fa and Fen Gong were the only outsiders to join the festivities, apart from the groom himself, and as Yi Wu presided over the ceremony in the heaven's garden courtyard, Hudan felt one absence very deeply. It was difficult to know whether to be proud of Dan for not attending, or to feel wounded. Was he feeling the separation like she was, or did he despise her now? It didn't matter, she supposed, as long as history was back on track.

Hudan was getting used to saying goodbye, but she and Huxin had never thought to see this particular day — yet here it was. The king, Shi, Fen and the twins were already on board the ferry.

The cubs were fighting healthy although had yet to do their first shift. The female of the pair had been called Ji Zhen, meaning precious, rare, true and pure. Her twin brother had been named Ji Kao, a name chosen to honour Shi's eldest brother, Bo Yi Kao.

'You take good care of yourself and your new family,' Hudan began, tears welling from the first word.

Huxin forced a smile. 'I wish I could say come and visit us,' she managed to say though choked up. It was rare that Huxin was suffocated by emotion.

'Me too,' Hudan nodded in complete sympathy. 'Have a great life!' She threw her arms around her sister, her smile and tears bursting through, as they hugged tightly.

'I hope you find what you seek on Li Shan,' Huxin replied, 'but if you do not … you know where I am.'

Hudan nodded, too teary to speak as her twin boarded the ferry to join her new husband. Hudan waved them off, smiling on the outside and feeling emptied from within. Once the barge passed out of the cavern, Hudan drew a deep breath to decide if she was going to collapse into tears or maintain a calm state of acceptance.

This was it. The adventure was over and it was back to the rigours of everyday life on Li Shan, but without Fen or Huxin.

When Hudan released her breath without falling apart, she figured that the past six months had drained her dry of every emotion she had. Or was this delayed shock? Whatever the case, she welcomed the small comfort of feeling numb as she turned about and went back to her cloistered life.

During the dry cold days of winter, Dan and Fen made good progress on their urban planning project and on the duke's Wu training — the lord's attitude had picked up after the wedding and he seemed almost back to the man he'd been before Hudan had spurned him.

Ling Hu, now the size of a large dog, had grown strong, and the tigress followed Fen absolutely everywhere. Much to the duke's surprise and relief, she had the same respect for the Hall of Records as her master and only chewed on the pillows and the furnishings in the chamber — she was also very partial to the duke's boots. But her favourite toy was Fen, and through the coldest part of the year that saw Haojing blanketed in snow, the young tigress delighted in using the white camouflage to stalk her master. On a couple of occasions, even Dan fell victim to her stealth. To make the game a little fairer, Fen had taken to dressing in white and covered his dark hair with a white hood. As the winter months at court were a little boring, when the queen's maids caught Fen and Ling Hu at their game, the ladies joined in, and tried to distract the tigress and hide Fen from her. The queen could not have been more delighted and it became a regular event at court until the snow melted into slush, not suitable for ladies to run about on. But they still gathered every afternoon on the balcony to watch Fen toy with the beast ... or vice versa.

A tigress in court was not all fun and games, however, as trying to separate her from her master was impossible. Even in a council meeting with the king, with guards posted at every door, somehow Ling Hu managed to get in without being detected until she nudged up against Fen to announce her arrival.

'How did you get in here? I am so sorry, majesty,' Fen had been forced to apologise, but the king would not hear it. He had been more worried about how the incident reflected on his guards.

By the time the new prince was due to be born, everyone had

given up trying to train Ling Hu to wait for Fen elsewhere. So sweet was the nature of the tigress, that not even the queen was averse to having her present at the morning check-up.

'Good morning, majesties.' Fen entered the royal sitting room where the king and queen were taking breakfast, and Ling Hu was right beside him.

'It is, isn't it?' Fa replied, very chipper.

'Hmmm,' Yi Jiang frowned, rubbing her back. 'It is mornings like these when I have to wonder why I took that beautiful body you gave back to me, and did this to it.' She rubbed her very swollen belly.

'You look radiant,' Fa rebutted her complaint with his normal flair. 'Tell her, Fen.'

'I absolutely agree, majesty,' Fen said with a beaming smile.

'Perhaps once you are done with me, I might agree ...' She smothered a moan as she stood up belly first, and Fa was quick to give her a hand.

'Just a few more weeks and you'll have your body back.' The king kissed her forehead. 'Fen will see to that. And we shall have another son.'

Perhaps the king did not see the fear behind her smile, but Fen saw it, and it made him more determined that, this time around, the queen would endure and emerge from labour in much better shape.

'I praise Tian for you, Fen, every day,' Yi Jiang said once her husband had departed. 'Because of you, I hold no fear for myself or this child.'

'That is well, majesty, for you and your child are my sole purpose for being ... except for Ling Hu here,' he allowed, patting his animal friend on the head.

'Yes,' the queen laughed, 'I do believe Ling Hu is the envy of every lady in my court.'

Fen just grinned, shrugged and went quiet, as he did every time she mentioned ladies in his presence.

'Come, Fen, you must like one of them?' she appealed.

'They are all so lovely, I could not choose,' he joked, diplomatically.

'Then have them all,' she insisted, to Fen's great distress, and the tigress gave a whimper as she picked up on his discomfort. Fen stroked her in reassurance. 'Perhaps not?' the queen said, realising her error. 'Are you sure she is not a shifter like her mother?'

'Quite sure, majesty. I've had word from my sister that Ling Hu's siblings have begun shifting form now, but are only half the size of Ling Hu here.'

'It is rather exotic to have shifters in the family,' the queen said with some delight, as it gave their royal line a superhuman status, 'but visiting the cousins is going to be an adventure.'

'The prince can practise with Ling Hu,' Fen suggested, 'who is also his cousin.'

'Why so she is!' The queen had obviously not considered that, and picked some sweetmeat from the breakfast table to give Ling Hu in return for some tiger affection.

But when the queen moved to rise from cuddling the animal, she gripped her belly. 'Ah!'

'Majesty!' Fen caught her and aided her back to a seat, but even once she was seated, Yi Jiang would not let go of his hand. 'Just breathe,' he advised, allowing her to grip him and absorb his calm.

At last, she gave a deep exhale as the contraction passed. 'I think he is making his move.' The queen turned her sights to Fen, her eyes full of hope and horror.

'Have no fear, majesty,' Fen knelt before the queen, 'by this time tomorrow you shall be a content and happy woman.'

The queen's chamber was prepared and the king notified, and for most of the day Yi Jiang experienced light contractions. It was around dinner time her waters burst and the labour pains became more frequent and long lasting. Fen knew things were about to get intense and, suspecting he may not get another opportunity this side of the birth, he asked to be excused for a moment when the king arrived to check on his wife.

'No, you cannot leave me.' Yi Jiang refused to let him go.

Fen badly needed to relieve himself, and Ling Hu was very restless also.

'I shall just have to suffice for a moment,' the king said, aiding Fen out of Yi Jiang's killer grip, and wrapping it around his own hand. 'I really am quite concerned about this addiction you have to our healer.'

'Just one more day and I shall give him up, but not today!' she wailed in her pain, as Fen and Ling Hu made a hasty exit.

'How goes progress?' Zhou Gong Dan was waiting in the next room, and Fen was surprised to see him.

'I thought you would work through the drama,' Fen said, rapidly heading toward the back doors of the royal chambers.

'Have you seen our king? He is a bundle of nerves!' Dan explained, moving with the young count as far as the door outside. 'So all goes well?' Dan stopped in the double doorway, as Fen and his tigress proceeded across the verandah.

'Of course!' Fen grinned, and gave a wave. 'I shall return presently.' He jogged down the back stairs and ran into the garden after the tigress, who was already waiting at the gate to the outer grounds where he always took her to do her business. Shi had taken his pet tigers to Shao, and so his tigress had the run of the place. When Fen reached her Ling Hu gave a whimper and a growl.

'I am hurrying.' He released the latch, the gate swung open and Ling Hu was off and sprinting across the open grass. Fen followed at a slower pace. There was a lot of cloud cover and the night was black as pitch, so he did not venture far before relieving himself. 'Ah ...' The discharge was a relief and pleasure.

He'd just finished doing up his trousers when he heard Ling Hu whimper and drop. 'Ling Hu!' Fen called softly, as her hearing was excellent. In the silence, he detected a risk to the two beings in his care at present, which set his heart pounding in his throat. His impulse was to run to Ling Hu's aid, but he could not risk being injured himself — the queen took priority.

Fen turned about and ran toward the gate, when the sting of a sharp object lodging itself in his right butt cheek took the leg out from underneath him and he fell to the ground. 'No!' He attempted to yell, but only a small whimper came out. He reached back to pull the offending item out to discover it was a dart, and not an arrow as he'd originally thought. 'I've been drugged ...'

Two dark-clad persons approached and, sitting him up, they drew around his neck a leather band from which hung a dark stone that felt like ice when it made contact with his skin. The charm also felt heavy, and ominous to the point of being nauseating. Or perhaps it was the drugs making him feel woozy? As his hands and feet were bound, Fen blacked out.

The text Dan was reading was highly engrossing and he didn't notice how long Fen had been gone until Ji Fa emerged from the queen's chamber in search of him.

Dan laid aside the bamboo scroll, and looking at the candle alongside him, found it had receded more than expected. 'He hasn't come back in yet?' Ji Fa shook his head.

This was alarming, as it wasn't like Fen to shirk his duties, especially one as important as this. 'I shall grab a lantern and go look for him.'

'I would be grateful,' Fa emphasised, holding his injured leg, which was clearly threatening to flare up.

'Do not become distressed!' the duke ordered his king. 'I shall find him.'

Just as a precaution, and to get the search completed with haste, Dan conscripted a few guards to accompany him into the garden, but it was the duke who noted the drag marks first. 'Please, no,' he uttered, as he followed the marks toward the river.

'Zhou Gong!' one of the guards yelled from the other direction.

'What is it?' Dan called back.

'We found the tigress.'

Dan was afraid to ask. 'Is she alive?'

'She has been drugged, but she is alive.' The response gave Dan hope that Fen was alive also, and he ran, following the tracks which led to the river and vanished as expected.

Dan gripped the hair on his scalp, wanting to rip it out. 'How stupid!' Whoever had hatched this kidnap was brilliant. By stealing Fen, they could take out the queen, the king and the new prince in one foul swoop. Only one being knew about the king's weakness, and Fen's talent — having seen it first-hand. 'Dragonface.'

The duke dropped the lantern and ran back toward the house to inform the king. There was only one person who could find Fen now and that was Jiang Hudan — he needed permission to ride to Li Shan.

Dan was cursing that he had not yet mastered the art of moving via chi. Even riding full speed in the darkness it took an hour to reach the Li Shan jetty, and as he awaited the arrival of the ferry, the torches of summons blazing to either side of him, he prayed to Tian that it was Jiang Hudan the Great Mother sent to investigate.

With all the anxiety of his errand, Dan had not considered how this reunion might play out, or how he felt about seeing Hudan again. *Just keep it professional.*

As the ferry came to dock at the jetty, a white-clad woman disembarked. 'Brother Dan,' came the startled voice, and she slid back her hood to reveal Jiang Hudan.

'Fen has been kidnapped,' the duke said, quickly stating his case for seeking her out. 'The queen is in labour and the king's wound is threatening to recur.'

Hudan's eyes opened wide in horror.

'They've taken Fen via the river and at night,' Dan shrugged. 'By morning it will be too late for the queen and her child, and if they die, you know what that will do to our king. Can you track Fen by psychic means?'

'Yes, of course.' Hudan waved her sisters back to Li Shan. 'Do you wish to come with me?'

'If that is convenient.'

Hudan held out her hands, palm upwards, and Dan took hold.

After some time, when they still stood there, Dan had to comment, 'This is no time for romantic gestures.'

'I am not flirting!' She let go the duke's hands, frustrated. 'I can't find him. I'm being blocked. Which means whoever has my brother has a very good understanding of the dark arts.'

'Well, of course Dragonface is behind this,' Dan warranted. 'Who else?'

'Shh,' Hudan insisted, walking away down the jetty, 'let me think.'

'Perhaps I should just go and leave you to it?' he offered.

'Feel free,' Hudan invited, 'but wherever you are going, I can get you there faster.'

'Where am I going?' Dan was at a loss. 'How on earth am I going to find Fen, if you cannot?'

'Do you have men looking for him already?' Hudan asked.

'Up and down both sides of the river,' Dan confirmed.

'Then let me return us to Hoajing and see if there is anything to report,' Hudan suggested. 'Then we can wing it from there. I might be able to pick up something from the site where Fen was taken. That might help us.'

Dan nodded, as he didn't have a better plan. 'Our dynasty could fall apart in one night.' He took hold of her outstretched hands.

'Not on our watch.' Her smiled was forced but well meaning, and it was the last impression Dan had before light consumed him in a rush, and carried him forth to Haojing.

Led to the spot where Fen had been taken, Hudan focused herself inward to see if any psychic impression of the event had been left behind. She knelt and held her palms close over the earth. 'I'm not picking up anything specific, just a cold, sickly feeling and that could just be my reaction to this event.' She was frustrated. 'But I am not renowned for my clairvoyance.' She suddenly looked to Dan. 'You should try.'

'Me? No,' he declined.

Hudan reached up and, gripping the side of his coat, pulled him down beside her. 'This is no time to be modest.'

'I only see ghosts in the present,' he explained, 'not impressions of the past.'

'Have you tried?' Hudan queried in challenge.

'This is the first opportunity I have had,' he conceded. 'Can you talk me through it?'

'Just still your mind, focus on Fen, and see what impressions you get. You could see an image, pick up on a thought or just have a feeling,' Hudan advised, relieving him of his lantern.

Eyes closed, Dan took several deep breaths, and then held his hands over the piece of earth where they suspected Fen had fallen.

'Ah!' Dan could not suppress the reaction. 'Intense pain,' he pointed to his behind. 'Panic,' he described the feeling. 'They are putting something around my neck —'

'Who are?' Hudan queried.

'I cannot see,' Dan replied, eyes shut tight, 'it's too dark.'

'What is it around your neck?'

'A dark stone,' Dan shivered. 'Ah —' He sounded repulsed. 'It's cold and sickening.' Dan felt very woozy and stood to escape the hold the vision had upon him.

'That is how they are blocking us from finding him,' Hudan concluded and stood also. 'Very well done, brother.'

'I'm sure I shall be thrilled by my development, as soon as I stop feeling ill,' Dan replied, drawing deep breaths to steady his stomach.

'Poor Fen,' Hudan said in sympathy … if this was the reaction Dan had from briefly sensing the dark amulet, what must her little brother be feeling. He had been wearing it for hours!

'Indeed,' Dan was in complete agreement. 'But I don't think any of those impressions are going to help us find him.'

'Oi! Come back here!' a guard was heard to yell from the closed garden gate.

Within moments Ling Hu was trudging all over their crime scene.

'No girl,' Dan complained and then changed his tune. 'Hold on, Ling Hu can find Fen anywhere!'

Hudan felt the tigress's regular method would not help them track Fen in this instance. 'A tiger's sense of smell is not as acute as its other senses …' Then she noted the tigress move further afield, where she started taking deep inhales through her mouth. 'The one scent they can detect efficiently is urine. That's how they track their mates.'

The tigress took off, back past them, toward the river. Dan and Hudan gave chase until the tigress vanished into thin air.

'Whoa?' Dan wondered if he was seeing things, and ran forth to discover that her tracks just ended some distance from the river bank, and they had heard no splash. 'Good heavens!'

'Ling Hu *is* a shifter,' Hudan concluded, amazed. 'Just not the same variety as her kin.'

'She can shift straight from animal to spirit.' Dan followed Hudan's thinking.

'Quickly,' Hudan urged Dan to take her hand, 'let's not lose her. If she finds Fen before we are with her, Ling Hu may be blocked by the dark magic that is hiding him.'

As Dan took her hand, Hudan blew out the flame in the lantern and invoked a desire to find Ling Hu.

Why is it so cold? Fen awoke, trembling. A vast heaviness hung over his being, worse than any morning he'd experienced after a sacred rite. His eyelids felt like they were cemented and, along with the rest of his body, did not want to budge. The cold stone beneath his face compelled Fen to raise himself. His bound hands brought his current plight flooding back and the shock got his eyes open rather efficiently.

He was in the ruins of an old river fort. In front of him, a large portion of a major defensive wall was missing and he could see the river bumping up against it by the light of the waning moon. This dungeon area probably flooded during high tide.

The queen! At that thought, the healer struggled to release himself from his leather bonds.

'The pretty boy is awake,' came the voice of one of his captors, sending a chill down his spine. They were seated right behind him.

Shoved by a foot, Fen was rolled over so he faced them, but unfortunately it was too dark to see them.

'Your king and queen are dying, pretty boy, and you cannot get back there in time to save them.'

'Who are you working for?' Fen asked, trying to contain his angst. If he gave in to fear and the urge to hate these men, then he would lose any chance of swaying them to his cause. He must remain caring and compassionate, and wait for them to get close enough to influence.

'Who could possibly despise your king for deposing the true emperor?' his captor teased, but Fen figured just about anyone still loyal to the Shang was the answer.

'Why would anyone prefer to live under the yoke of tyranny?' Fen said reasonably. 'Ji Fa is a good and fair ruler —'

Three simultaneous lashes across Fen's upper arm turned his appeal into a cry of pain when the triple whip tore through his jacket and the hooked ends stung his skin as they dragged across it.

'Ouch, that has got to hurt,' jeered the kidnapper. 'Do you hate me?'

'We each have our own path to take,' Fen replied, sucking back the pain.

'You got that right, sweet cheeks.' Fen sensed his stalker leering close, and then withdrawing. 'Strip him down, boys!'

'No!' Fen protested as he was grabbed by many hands and knives began to shred the clothes from his body. There was no point in telling himself to remain calm when he wanted to kill every one of them, but his struggles only served to get him cut several times. Finally, Fen was hauled, naked, to his feet and all he could feel was the icy-cold charm against his chest sucking the life right out of him — he had no fight, no influence left in him. His willing himself to be released had no effect on his captors at all. He was at the mercy of heaven now.

'I'm going to make you hate like you have never hated before, boy,' his assailant threatened. 'Up against the wall!'

Fen tried once more to pull free, his heart thumping with fear, as he was turned about and thrown face first against the stone wall. The pain in one side of his head knocked all care from his mind for a moment and he would have dropped like a rock had he not been so firmly supported in his stance.

'The queen's favourite. I can see why!' A hand slapped against his sore butt cheek, and Fen winced … his already grazed face scraping against the sandstone was smarting as much as the penetrating reminder of where the dart had hit his rump. 'What a pretty little arse.'

'You will rot in diyu,' Fen mumbled, furious at the suggestion that there might be rumours circulating about his relationship with the queen.

His tormentor came in close to say, 'I hear her bastard is yours, and now it will kill her.'

'Ah!' As Fen let loose a howl of protest, a commotion erupted behind him and his attackers let him go. Fen lowered himself down the wall, and managed to turn around to see Ling Hu almost sparkling in the moonlight as she mauled his tormentor. Close by, the men who had been holding him, took aim at her with arrows. 'Hide!' Fen yelled. It was the order that usually aroused the fastest response from her, and Fen expected that she would bound away to the closest cover.

As the arrows flew, the tigress vanished, leaving the men visibly shocked.

'That's how she does it.' Fen realised she'd been cheating in their games.

When she reappeared in front of Fen, she scared her attackers into backing further away from him, exactly to where Hudan and Dan silently appeared. The duke drew the sword from the bandit's scabbard before the man even knew someone was behind him, and he turned around in time to lose his head.

Hudan gripped the neck of the last man, who he dropped his weapon. 'Who sent you?'

The man chose to defy her and remain silent. 'Tell me, or the king's guard will torture the truth from you. Your choice.'

He attempted to spit in her face, but the spittle rebounded onto his own, and he recoiled in disgust. As he had lost control of his limbs, he tried to shake it off his face.

'Have it your way. Sit.' She directed him to the ground, where he dropped straight onto his behind.

Next Hudan rushed to Fen, removing her white cloak to place around him. 'Thank Tian you are alive.' She cut his bonds then embraced him. 'Argh!' she cried, repelled and rapidly backing up.

'It's this thing,' Fen explained, removing the amulet.

'It's absolutely repulsive.' Hudan could not bring herself to touch it. 'Are you otherwise unharmed?' She brushed his hair aside to try and view the graze on his face.

'Do not fuss.' Fen was still reeling in his mind from the close call. 'Your timing was impeccable, as always.'

'It was Ling Hu's timing, really,' Hudan said, giving credit to the tigress.

Fen set aside the offensive amulet and left Hudan to go and hug his saviour.

'You should take Fen directly to the king,' Dan suggested. 'I'll keep a watch on our friend here.'

'Stay with Zhou Gong, Ling Hu,' Fen instructed the tigress, as he took hold of his sister's hand. 'Stay.'

Fen vanished with Hudan, and for the first time in her life, Ling Hu complied with Fen's request.

The Wu joined the king in his public council chamber, where he sat on his throne in an almost catatonic state. What was more disheartening was that the king's spirits did not lift upon sighting them; he barely reacted.

'Majesty,' Fen fell to his knees, for clearly they had come too late. 'I have failed you.' His heart welled with sorrow, and tears of remorse tumbled from his eyes.

Fa shook his head. 'You warned us, Fen Gong, but we did not listen.'

'Your son?' Hudan asked, as Fen had his head down and was silently choking on his emotion.

'Ji Yu,' Fa forced a smile, 'he lives and is well. Ah —' The king gripped his wounded thigh.

Upon noting this, Fen suppressed his remorse and crawled toward the king. He thought of his gratitude that Ling Hu had not been harmed by his abductors and focussing on that happiness, Fen reached out and placed a hand on the king's leg.

The tension from the pain left Ji Fa and, given relief, he fell to pieces. 'She was my all, Fen ... and I had to give the nod to butcher her, *again*. But she did not survive this time.' Fa keeled forward, unable to endure his torment. 'I thank you for your service,' he said as he removed the lad's healing hand from his person, 'but I want you to let me die.'

'That would be treason,' Fen appealed. 'I cannot deprive the land of your supreme guidance. Heaven chose you, majesty.'

The king shook his head, not wanting to hear it. 'When Yi passed, I had to hope they would not find you, Fen, because I knew you would keep me living. Yet if you had not spared me at Yin, Yi Jiang would still be alive.'

'Ji Song is too young to rule.' Hudan's voice of reason interrupted the sympathy party. 'Yi Jiang died to secure your dynasty! If you give up now, my brother, you will lose everything we fought for.'

The king raised his eyes to view Hudan, his ire evident. 'Who did this?'

'Someone very patient, clever and skilled in the dark arts,' Hudan replied.

'In other words, that accursed dragon.' Fa stood, angered, but collapsed back on his throne as his leg began to ail once again. 'Damn it all!' He gripped the wounded area.

'Even you, mighty Fa, are having trouble dealing with this curse,' she pointed out. 'Are you really prepared to abandon Ji Song to contend with it?'

'No.' He gritted his teeth and gave Fen the nod to heal him.

'I regret I am now part of your curse, majesty.' Fen reluctantly reached out and placed his hand on the king's leg to force his wound into remission.

'Ahhh ...' Fa relaxed once again, exhausted from the stress. 'Fen.'

'Yes, majesty.'

'Of all my subjects it is you I cherish most. Above Dan, above Jiang Taigong —'

The claim made Fen catch his breath and he shook his head. 'It is only the glamour of my art, majesty. These men are far greater than I could —'

'Despite what has become of our folly,' Fa spoke up over the lad, 'your healing gave me the best year of my life ... and now I face the worst.'

'I shall be here by your side, majesty,' Fen swore.

'I fear you will have little choice in the matter,' because as long as the king maintained his grief his wound would ail him.

'I should return to Zhou Gong who is guarding the captive. We plan to give him to you for questioning,' Hudan informed Fa, and he was pleased by the news.

'I want that creature dead!' The king's resolve hardened, and Hudan nodded in support of his determination and she vanished from their midst. The king turned to Fen. 'I would ask you to prepare my wife's body for burial.'

'You do me incalculable honour, majesty.'

'You did such a beautiful job with He Nuan's casket —' Fa choked and fell silent.

'I shall do my best to do our queen honour, majesty.'

'You might want to heal yourself, first.' The king referred to Fen's arm, which was bleeding long, red stains through the white cloak. 'Forgive me, brother … I have not even asked how you fare?' Ji Fa stood and, raising the lad, he placed him on the throne.

'It is nothing, majesty. I am fine, truly.' Fen quickly stood, uncomfortable with the situation, causing the room to spin and, with a painful crack to the head, Fen passed out cold.

It was darker than before in the ruins. The moon had passed over the site and as the tide was beginning to rise, Hudan found herself ankle deep in water.

'I was hoping you would arrive soon.' Dan tapped her shoulder to let her know where he was. 'I still have the lantern here, if you would be so kind.'

She imaged the lantern burning, and it lit up the cavern as the inner flame roared back into life.

'You do not need the staff any longer?' Dan noted, impressed.

She shook her head, not really in the mood for light banter, and it showed.

'We were too late,' the duke concluded. 'The prince?'

'Lives,' Hudan said, pleased to have some happy news.

'Fa?' he asked more warily.

'Fen is with him.' Hudan gave the best news on that front that she could.

There was a secret she'd been carrying for some time now, which had been preoccupying her mind, and it was begging to be released.

'This is most unfortunate.'

Hudan glanced around to note their prisoner was unconscious, and Ling Hu was missing. 'What happened?'

'Ling Hu and I were just playing a little cat and mouse with him, and he tripped and fell unconscious,' claimed Dan. 'He's still alive.'

'Uh-huh.' Hudan was not sure she believed him, and Dan avoided her questioning gaze as he looked about for Ling Hu. 'She was here just a moment ago.'

'Clearly, we are alone, and that is well,' Hudan piped up, gathering her courage. 'I have something I feel I have to tell you.'

Dan was intrigued and awarded her his full attention. 'What is on your mind, brother Hudan?'

'It's about brother Fa —'

Dan exhaled heavily, clearly finding the subject matter very anticlimactic. 'What about him?'

She didn't know how she could put it delicately, so she just said it. 'He's going to die within the year.'

Dan was mortified. 'You have foreseen it?'

Hudan shook her head slowly, preparing to be yelled at. 'I read it in the Jade Book.'

'You have known since then?' The duke was doubly affronted. 'Why didn't you tell me?'

'What difference would it have made?' Hudan appealed. 'It would have just been another worry to contend with.'

'You managed!' Dan confronted her. 'I am not a child … I am chief advisor to the king! Ji Song will be too young to rule,' Dan gasped, as he realised their biggest problem.

'I know.' Hudan pre-empted his next query. 'Before you ask, I did not read on, and I do not know what happens next.'

'The Great Mother must have known this.' Dan was frustrated. Thinking back over their conversations, he could see now how she'd been priming him for a leadership challenge. 'Sometimes I just want to kill that woman! Man!'

'Dan?' Hudan called for him to calm down when she spotted the discarded amulet her brother had been wearing.

'What!' he roared, annoyed.

'I think we should get away from this thing, before we discuss this any further, as it is bound to make us more unreasonable,' she advised.

'This reaction is not unreasonable, considering what you have just told me,' Dan grumbled, endeavouring to stay civil, but clearly he was struggling.

'Please can we deliver the prisoner to the king,' Hudan suggested, 'and this amulet to the Great Mother for disposal?'

'If you promise not to disappear before we finish our conversation this time,' Dan bartered.

'Done,' Hudan agreed, and was chary of asking another favour. 'Please … could you not mention to the Great Mother that I told you about Ji Fa.'

'It is nothing I could not have found out by myself,' Dan said, making it known he would not be silenced on the matter altogether.

'I would have preferred it were so.'

'It is not like we have not altered history before.' Dan shrugged off the white lie.

But the amulet deadened psychic activity, so Hudan was forced to send it to the Great Mother ahead of them, and after delivering the prisoner to the king, they finally arrived at Li Shan to explain the amulet to Yi Wu.

She had the situation under control. 'I have the stone soaking in salt water, and the morning sunlight will drive out any evil thought form still attached to it,' she advised them. 'Our real concern this night is that Ji Fa will not live out the year.'

Hudan and Dan were shocked to have the Great Mother raise the very subject they were here to discuss.

'It is time for you and Fen to begin Ji Song's Wu training,' she said to Dan. The duke was chagrined as he digested that statement, and nodded to confirm her request. 'Song is not just your next sovereign, but a vital member of your crew, captain.'

'Why?' Dan asked, curious, feeling that his cosmic counterpart did not have the same good judgement of character that he did. 'He is reckless and self-absorbed —'

'He is a risk taker, yes, and he is a thrill seeker also, but doing what we do those traits come in rather handy,' Yi Wu advised. 'He would rather make love than fight,' she admitted, 'but he will fight to the death to protect anything he holds dear.'

'That is what worries me,' Dan muttered to himself.

'He is also an excellent pilot,' she commented.

'A pilot?' Dan queried the term.

'A captain has a ship,' she explained, 'the ship has a driver. He's the driver, the best we have.'

'Right!' Dan had to regretfully concede that Song was vitally important to their mission, in ways he couldn't begin to imagine.

'So you see, you must train him and train him well.'

Dan hung his head submissively, to hide the antagonism he felt. 'Will that be all, Shifu?'

'Hudan may see you back to Haojing now. I am sure you are most anxious to make plans.'

He mustered a nod and took hold of Hudan's outstretched hand, and sensing his need to be absent, she made her farewell brief and returned the duke to his Hall of Records.

The dawn of this horrendous night had finally come. It was silent and still in the huge room, and only a few birds chirping outside disturbed the perfect serenity. When Hudan felt Dan had his sensibilities back, she moved to withdraw.

'Please, linger.' Dan held Hudan's hands just tight enough that she could not easily retreat.

'Our Shifu has ended the discussion for us … there is really nothing more to be said.' Hudan attempted to slip her hands free, but the duke would not let her.

'I miss you,' he began, melting her resistance with his sincerity. 'I miss just being able to sit and speak with you.'

Hudan didn't know what to say. She wanted to tell him she missed him, too, and give him reassurance, but she'd been down that road before and it only made the situation more difficult.

'Ji Song is going to have a goddess rite, I take it?' Dan voiced what was really bothering him.

'Please …' She was tired already and just the mention of the subject drained her. 'With all that is going on in the world, must we go into this now?'

Dan pulled Hudan in close, and her tears welled for the willpower she did not have to resist. 'Do you have any idea how it feels to wonder how many other men in my family will be given their chance with you?'

Hudan's frustration gave her an adrenaline boost and she pushed him away, angry. 'I am tormented too,' she challenged in a harsh whisper, 'but everything I am dictates that I should *not* be. I have a war raging inside of me, every moment of every day. The Wu I was before I met you would never have allowed anyone to compromise her commitment to the creed. Such is the effect you have had on me.' Hudan's fierce streak broke over the welling emotion in her chest and she could not prevent the tears from falling. 'But what do you expect me to do? When I must reason everything from the point of view of the austere initiate I once was. One misguided decision because of my feelings for you and history diverts to some tragic end that all sons of the sky will pay for?'

The fact was a heavy blow to Dan. 'I cannot even fathom the man I was before I met you, let alone reason from his perspective.'

'You must,' Hudan insisted. 'I do not believe this is just some elaborate cosmic test that the Great Mother has thought up for us ...' Dan shook his head, agreeing with her '... therefore the sons of the sky are real, and our situation is every bit as precarious as we have been warned.'

A deep breath didn't seem to ease Dan's frustration at all.

'On the upside,' Hudan added, 'when this mission ends, the constraints that bind us now will be gone.'

'But Song is one of us. He will not be gone.' Dan's grievance had clearly been well thought out.

The door to the hall opened and the master of the interior entered. 'Zhou Gong,' he bowed, 'it is well I find Jiang Hudan in your company for Fen Gong is ailing.'

The news was startling. Hudan had never known Fen to be sick.

'And the king?' Dan queried as they both hurried to assist however they could.

'His majesty is ailing also.' The servant opened the door for them and bowed out of the way to let them pass.

As Fen and the king were in separate rooms, Hudan went to Fen's bedside, and Dan proceeded to the king's chamber.

The duke found Ji Fa in bed, suffering in silence — his cursed leg exposed and bleeding from the newly torn wounds. Upon the announcement of Zhou Gong's arrival, the king sent his servants from the room to converse with his chief advisor in private. 'This is it, Dan. The white guard will be coming for me before long.'

'No, they won't,' Dan said surely.

'You think it will be the black guard?' The king made a jest of his brother's optimism.

'You are not dying, brother,' Dan insisted, as he went down on one knee beside the king's bed, 'now is not your time.'

'We can fight about this, or we can prepare,' Fa reasoned, and Dan went quiet to hear him out. 'I want you to give tribute in the ancestral temple for me, to alert our forefathers to my imminent arrival.'

Dan shook his head. 'I will beseech them for your deliverance, nothing else. Ji Song is too young to rule. He is not ready.'

'You must rule,' Fa told him.

'That is your fever talking,' Dan replied, thinking the king was otherwise joking.

'I have not even broken a sweat yet,' Fa pointed out, 'but it will come, once the infection sets in … which is why I am speaking my mind to you now.'

'Neither by the old law of succession nor the new, am I entitled to rule,' Dan pointed out in a hushed whisper.

'I have not yet disclosed my will on the law of succession,' Fa announced to Dan's utter bewilderment. 'Kill Xian, claim the throne … and your goddess,' Fa added a little incentive.

The duke hated how tempting this idea was. He stood and backed up as if to distance himself from the enticement. 'Why would you even suggest such a thing, when we have six other brothers, half of whom would gladly kill the others for a chance to usurp the throne? Such an indulgence would lead our land into a war that might never end! Only Song can secure a clear line of succession!'

'You said yourself, *Song is not ready*. The chieftains who pay us homage do not yet respect his authority, but they respect *yours*,' Fa insisted. 'It is your words they hear coming out of my mouth every time I speak! *You* are the only one who can preserve the peace ... and no matter how many of our brothers you must kill to do it, you *will* rule when I am gone, and Jiang Taigong is my witness.'

The prime minister emerged from behind a screen on the far side of the king's bed.

'Dear heavens, *no!*' Dan couldn't believe their prime minister would be party to such talk. 'You cannot be serious.'

'Sadly, Zhou Gong, I am quite serious,' the prime minister advised, solemnly. 'Is our new policy not to give the appointment to the most worthy candidate? You are, beyond the shadow of any doubt, the best man for the position. I have the king's will in writing.'

Dan couldn't breathe when Jiang Taigong held up a metal-bound box.

'This is *madness* ... the precedent we would set ...' The suggestion made the duke furious. 'This is not the time to discuss this,' the duke said, backing up toward the door, adamant their ruling would not stand. 'Our king *is not* dying any day soon!'

THE DEATH OF JI FA

The duke immediately set about following the king's order, and took the royal ritual jades gifted to their king by Yi Wu to pay homage in the temple of their ancestors in Haojing. Surely their great forefathers would see the chaos that would ensue if Ji Fa was allowed his way. Dan felt he must enlist the ancients in his quest to keep Fa alive — if only for a year. Even this small reprieve would allow him some time to mould Ji Song into a king who might have a chance of sustaining their dynasty.

You must train him, and train him well. The words of the Great Mother came back to haunt.

I hate that that woman is always one step ahead of me. Dan's jaw clenched in frustration as he crossed the first courtyard of the temple complex at Hoajing.

This complex had been built before the death of their father, who had dared to defy the emperor's order to abandon the worship of their great ancestors. The temple had been reserved as a place to perform marriage, birth and death ceremonies in the past. Only since Ji Fa had come to power had it been used as a regular place of worship and celebration. The complex consisted of two courtyards. The first featured a combat and target area for competition, and a feasting hall with large covered balconies for viewing of tournaments, and beyond the hall lay the second, the musicians' courtyard, the west wall of which was lined with bells and the east wall lined with chime-stones.

At Dan's request, musicians were preparing to play to either side of him, to invoke and entertain the ancient spirits of whom he sought favour and, now given leave, their melodious tones penetrated the sombre morning silence and stirred Dan's emotions afresh.

Although the duke had countless worries this morning, the heavenly bells brought him into the moment and heightened his senses. The fresh air in his lungs and the sunshine on his face suddenly felt like the heavenly gifts they were. He was reminded that he had much to be grateful for: he had his health and his wits, which were what he needed in order to persevere. He knew he would be wise to remember these truths, for collapsing into a state of despair would only allow disease to take root in his physical manifestation. Fen had taught him that and Fen had taught him well. If the duke became ill he'd have a much harder time keeping abreast of the current challenges. Still, if the ancestors would take him in Fa's stead, it would be more beneficial for the land as a whole. He would appeal this case to his forefathers although, having been given an account of future events, Dan held out little hope for winning such an appeal.

The duke approached the stairs of the platform at the far end of the courtyard where the temple of their ancestors stood, with its roof crown and golden-glazed tiles glistening in the sunshine. The pagoda roof had bas relief carvings of tigers looking out from its four outer points. The walls and arches of the temple were red and the tall pillars black, as was attractive to the spirits.

The ceremonial jades had been placed accordingly in the temple — the jade bi-disk and cong on the central altar, and the jades of the four directions at their cardinal points. Dan lit candles and incense before kneeling down before the altar to call upon their great-grandfather, their grandfather and their father.

'Your eldest descendant, Ji Fa, has through his arduous labours been struck by illness. If it be the heavenly charge of you three kings to determine his fate, then take me, Dan, in place of him,' he implored them. 'I am skilful and able, with many talents, many arts. I am well able to serve the spirits. The king is not so talented nor so able. Moreover, he has been mandated to possess the four quarters by the court of the Lord on High. Thus he has the power to settle your descendants upon the lands below, such that none in the four quarters will act without respect, but will all evince awe.

Do not destroy the holder of the mandate that heaven has sent down. You, our former kings, would then have none upon whom to rely for sustenance. I entrust destiny to your guidance and shall divine your answer.'

The duke returned to his Hall of Records, where he consulted the *Yi Jing: the Book of Changes* concerning the response of the three kings by selecting three tubes. Each tube contained one hexagram of the sixty-four hexagrams of the King Wen sequence, and its explanation. These in turn would reveal to Dan the advice of his ancestors in regard to the cause, the action and the outcome of the situation.

In regard to the cause Dan had drawn Hexagram Sixty-three: After Completion.

JI JI
above KAN — THE ABYSMAL, WATER
below LI — THE CLINGING, FIRE

The transition from the old to the new time is already accomplished. In principle, everything stands systematised, and it is only in regard to details that success is still to be achieved. In respect to this, however, we must be careful to maintain the right attitude. Here we have the rule indicating the usual course of history. But this rule is not an inescapable law. He who understands it, is in a position to avoid its effects by dint of unremitting perseverance and caution.

This is a very favourable outlook, yet it gives reason for thought. For it is just when perfect equilibrium has been reached that any movement may cause order to revert to disorder. Hence the hexagram indicates the conditions of a time of climax, which necessitate the utmost caution and the necessity to be on guard against falling into chaos again.

This indicated to Dan that Fa would recover and history would be set to rights, but that the reprieve of a year was short to train the new king — he must be diligent.

In regard to action that should be taken to order to rectify the situation, the duke drew Hexagram Fifty-one: Thunder, the Arousing Shock.

ZHEN
above ZHEN — THE AROUSING, THUNDER
below ZHEN — THE AROUSING, THUNDER

The hexagram Zhen represents the eldest son, who seizes rule with energy and power. A yang line develops below two yin lines and presses upward forcibly. This movement is so violent that it arouses terror. It is symbolised by thunder, which bursts forth from the earth, and by its shock, causes fear and trembling.

There are three kinds of shock — the shock of heaven, which is thunder, the shock of fate, and finally, the shock of the heart. This hexagram refers less to inner shock and more to the shock of fate. In such times of shock, presence of mind is all too easily lost: the individual overlooks all opportunities for action and mutely lets fate take its course. But if he allows the shocks of fate to induce movement within his mind, he will overcome these external blows with little effort.

This told the duke that he had the means within himself to right the current situation, although he did not at this moment understand those means. But whatever the solution was, it would be shocking to him.

The outcome tube contained Hexagram Six — Conflict.

SONG
above QIAN — THE CREATIVE, HEAVEN
below KAN — THE ABYSMAL, WATER

The upper trigram, whose image is heaven, has an upward movement; the lower trigram, water, in accordance with its nature tends downward. Thus the two halves move away from each other, giving rise to the idea of conflict. The attribute of the Creative is strength, that of the Abysmal is danger.

A third indication of conflict, in terms of character, is presented by the combination of deep cunning within and fixed determination outwardly. A person of this character will certainly be quarrelsome.

This is a warning of the danger that goes with an expansive disposition. Only that which has been honestly acquired through merit remains a permanent possession. It can happen that such a possession may be contested, but since it is really one's own, one cannot be robbed of it. Whatever a man possesses through the strength of his own nature cannot be lost. If one enters the service of a superior, one can avoid conflict only by not seeking works for the sake of prestige. It is enough if the work is done: let the honour go to the other.

Dan could hardly believe how accurate this last part of the reading was. It clearly spoke to him of the future conflict in rulership between himself and Ji Song, and what it indicated was that the ancestors agreed with Dan: only Song could establish a clear line of descent, and even if the duke had to perform the young king's duties on the boy's behalf at first, he must do so without seeking any recognition himself. Dan felt the contested possession mentioned in the explanation of the outcome, could just as easily refer to Jiang Hudan, as much as to the throne of Zhou.

Dan was quietly thanking the ancestors for their guidance and reassurance, when his head servant of the interior entered to announce: 'A thousand apologies for interrupting my lord's meditation, but Jiang Hudan is requesting your assistance at her brother's bedside. She insists the matter is of the utmost urgency.'

Dan nodded to acknowledge the request. 'Fen Gong is at the heart of this quandary,' the duke said to himself and so rose to comply, for he had no hope of saving the king without the healer. However, if even Jiang Hudan was concerned for Fen's welfare, how they were going to save him was another matter again.

Fen was still and pale in the bed; his tigress lay down one side of him with her head rested on his chest, and Jiang Hudan brushed tears from her eyes as she stood to greet the duke.

'How is he?' Dan wondered if he'd come around at any time. 'Have you spoken?'

Hudan nodded. 'He feels he failed everyone,' she conveyed, suppressing her distress. 'He claims the king wants him to die and so he shall.'

'Oh no, he shall not.' Dan moved past Hudan to sit by Fen on the bed and stir him. 'Listen to me, Fen ...'

The lad's eyes wavered open and he peered at the duke through thin slits between his eyelids.

'The king does not want you dead, you have misunderstood.' Dan appealed. 'You wanted to die after He Nuan's death, but you got past it, just as Fa will.'

To Dan's frustration, Fen shook his head. 'Never did ...' he mumbled and passed out again.

'Heaven give me patience,' Dan muttered, about to fly into a fit of frustration, when he noticed something different about the young count's appearance. 'Where is his son of the sky?' the duke asked out loud for Hudan's benefit, as the spirit of the said entity was not within Fen as per usual. It could not be Dan's spirit sight failing him, as he could still see Tar-rin inside of Hudan. 'I have never seen one go missing before.'

'*I am here, captain.*' Dan jumped up and swung around so quickly he startled Hudan.

'What is it?' she inquired.

'I just found him,' Dan explained, eyeing over the slightly built, fair lord with large soulful blue eyes, who seemed quite meek and friendly in disposition.

'*Ringbalin Malachi,*' he introduced himself and then explained the situation. '*That dark stone drove me out, and as this incarnation's life is in question, I thought it best to stay evacuated in case I need to make a quick getaway.*'

'Getaway?' the duke queried.

'What is he saying?' Hudan wanted to know, but Dan shushed her, so she folded her arms and sat to await an outcome.

'*If the incarnation dies unexpectedly, before I will myself back to where we came from, I shall die right along with him,*' the lad explained. '*Either way I will be off the mission, and that is not what I desire.*'

'No,' Dan agreed, his mind ticking over. 'Would I be right in assuming you are the healer among us?'

'*Yes, captain,*' he beamed. '*I grow things and heal things, just as Fen Gong does.*'

The duke's smile broadened, and the lord was quick to add: '*But without a body, I cannot employ my craft. Nor can I heal my host body from within against his will.*'

'I have a body,' Dan proffered.

Hudan gasped and stood, having caught the gist of the conversation. 'You have never acted as a channel before,' she warned. 'I have seen women channel, and it will exhaust you.'

'Then you must ensure Fen heals the king once I am done. Will you do that?' Dan asked, pangs of shock reverberating through his person at the notion of letting a completely foreign entity inhabit his form. Still, if that being was akin to Fen, the duke resonated with him as well as anyone and that was a promising sign.

'Of course I will,' Hudan replied, but that was not her worry. 'Can you trust this spirit to leave your form when requested?'

Dan glanced back to the lad and his fair hair drifted over his face as he nodded to convince Dan of his sincerity. *'I owe you both so much … my only desire is to continue to serve your cause and see it through to its completion.'*

'He is Fen,' Dan said to assure Hudan no harm would ensue.

The Wu looked back to her ailing sibling and then nodded to lend her full support.

The duke knelt alongside Fen and looked to the spirit. 'I am at your disposal. Please do what must be done.'

'Well, I have never tried this on anyone else before,' Ringbalin advised, as cautious and wary as Dan himself felt, *'but, here goes.'*

As the spirit moved into alignment with his body, Dan felt his own perception shift out of his form and into an observation position. It was amazing to watch himself summon up a ball of pure chi between his hands and distribute it into his ailing colleague's body, whereupon Fen's injuries healed at once.

When the lad opened his eyes, he did so with a gasp that left a smile on his face. 'The pain is gone.' Fen held his heart rather than his head, and looked at Dan curiously.

'You don't have to grieve for your lover; she awaits in the next life and every life,' the lord told Fen, before withdrawing from Dan's form. As the spirit did so, Dan's consciousness was rushed back into control so quickly he fumbled the transfer and collapsed backward onto the bed.

'My lord!' Fen sat up, concerned.

'He just needs to rest,' Hudan told Fen, leaning over to check Dan's vital signs.

Her touch and the sight of her smiling down at him, took Dan back to their one night of bliss. 'I would give anything to wake up beside you again,' he mumbled, feeling euphoric and in a daze.

'What did he say?' Fen queried, certain he had heard wrong.

'He is delirious,' Dan heard Hudan say, as he struggled to stay conscious and see his plan carried out.

'Dress yourself, quickly, Fen. We must revive the king.'

With Hudan's call to arms, Dan was content to give in to his struggling faculties and sleep.

A pleasant, damp coolness against the skin on his face encouraged Dan to wake, and he was moved to find Jiang Hudan tending him and not one of the servants. She was wringing out the cloth in a large bowl, looking somewhat exhausted and a little dishevelled from the night's events, but content. When she turned back to find the duke awake, she smiled.

'I got my wish,' he noted.

She raised her brow, pleased to oblige and yet annoyed at him. 'Yes, but if you would not voice your secret desires in front of the children, it would be preferable. Fen nearly had a fit.'

'He's not one of ours, too, is he?' Dan was alarmed.

'You are the one who converses with spirits,' she pointed out. 'I was just speaking figuratively.'

'We are alone then, I gather?' Dan hadn't taken his eyes off Hudan to ascertain if anyone else was present, but her openness suggested to him that they were.

'Do not get any ideas, or I shall be forced to knock you out again,' she jested, placing her cloth aside.

'The king —'

'Is recovered and, along with Fen, is visiting the new prince.' Hudan brought the duke up to speed. 'Fen felt the king needed to remember what he had to live for, as brother Fa was none too happy to be dragged back from the brink of death yet again.'

Dan sympathised, but they needed the time with Fa on the throne. 'And now Fa has written his will of succession, naming me as his appointed one.'

'That is insane!' Hudan was horrified.

'If you read on in the Jade Book and know who is to succeed, please tell me, as I do not believe it should be me, despite the good arguments put forward by my king and prime minister in support of their decision.' Dan struggled to raise himself and Hudan gave him a hand, placing pillows behind his back to support him.

'I did not read on, I swear it. And I cannot believe Jiang Taigong is in favour of this,' Hudan said, baffled, as she sat down once more, but beside him on the bed this time and not on her chair.

Dan nodded, solemnly. 'The only up-side I can see is that I would do Ji Song out of his chance with you.'

Hudan was insulted by his reasoning. 'If you dare even take that into consideration, I will personally kill you myself. My virtue is a trivial matter compared to the fate of this dynasty!'

'I have already told you where I stand on the issue of succession,' Dan said, appealing for her to think better of him.

'Your feelings for me must not affect your devotion to your next Zhou. Even if Ji Song has no clue about it, he could not ask for a better Shifu than you. Only you can mould him into a leader greater than Ji Fa … if you set your mind and heart to it.'

'I am sure you are right,' Dan said, forcing a smile, and pinched the skin between his eyes to ease the tension.

Hudan shook her head and continued to give him further encouragement. 'It was truly inspiring to watch you turn today's sad events around. You've obviously been training and studying very hard, and I commend you.'

Dan was shy in accepting praise. 'And yet, I find myself looking forward to the next disaster that will bring us together … however, since I know that it will be Song's goddess rite, I am now dreading our next reunion.'

Hudan frowned in sympathy. 'You must convince Ji Fa to change his will before the year is out.'

'I am painfully aware of that,' Dan assured her, and she allowed him to take hold of her hand. 'We are agreed then, that Song as Ji Fa's successor would be the proper course.'

Hudan nodded. 'I feel sure it is.'

Dan winced, pained that the decision sat so well with his brain, but not with his heart.

'Even if *you* were to have a goddess rite, it would only be a one in eleven chance that I would be chosen for you,' she revealed, and Dan felt slightly mollified to learn this. 'And I would have to send you home to your wife.' Her voice cracked over the notion, and she looked ashamed. 'Honestly … I would rather be given to Ji Song.'

Dan's heart jolted in his chest, as the statement both elated and enraged him at once. 'I will pray every day that that does not come to pass.' He squeezed her hand tighter and Hudan forced a smile.

'Regardless … it is the right path to take,' she confirmed.

So their one chance for the divine to bless their physical union dissolved into the ether, and that smarted on the inside something terrible. But the duke felt he would rather wait until the end of time to be with the woman he loved, than to spend his lifetime with several that he did not — he had been there once before; never again.

It took several weeks for the city to settle down in the wake of the queen's death, and the king's illness fuelled rumours that his rule had been cursed. Then again, the fact that heaven had granted Fa another son ran contrary to that rumour and quashed it. Women often died giving birth, so the queen's death was not seen as a bad omen but rather as an honorable martyrdom for the Zhou kingdom.

Whoever had masterminded the kidnap of Fen Gong had directly contributed to the queen's death, hence Ji Song had taken it upon himself to question the prisoner whom Zhou Gong and Jiang Hudan had captured. Either the prisoner truly didn't know who had paid for his services, or he remained loyal to them to his death. Zhou Gong sent word to his brothers in the East regarding the treachery that had led to the queen's death, and urged them to be diligent in keeping a close eye on Wu Geng and anyone still loyal to the Shang.

Once Haojing was again settled, Dan informed the king of the Great Mother's desire for Ji Song to study Wu doctrine and discipline along with himself and Fen Gong.

'A splendid suggestion,' Ji Fa said, in agreement that such training could only be to Song's benefit.

'If I vow to you to mould the prince into a ruler that all chieftains will respect, will you alter your will of succession?' Dan asked.

'The year Song comes of age, and only if he proves himself worthy, shall I rethink my decision,' the king decreed.

'But majesty —'

'No buts, Dan,' he insisted. 'I have felt at peace since penning that document, and I will not change my mind until fate presents me with a better alternative, and at present there is none.'

'But I —'

'If I nominate Song and die before he comes of age, Xian, as the eldest of my brothers, will expect to be regent. And rather than focussing on maintaining the peace and good relations we have now, Xian will seek war wherever he can find it. No, Dan, I won't have everything we and our forefathers have worked so hard to achieve cast aside in its infancy.'

Dan understood his reasoning completely, but Fa would not live to see Song reach adulthood. 'As you wish.' The duke figured that if Ji Fa could not be talked around by year's end, then he would take him to the family storehouse and they would read together what the Jade Book had to say on the matter.

So it was that Ji Song was excused from his regular classes and training, and was sent by his father to report to Zhou Gong Dan for tuition instead.

The duke's head of the interior announced the prince's arrival, and Song entered the Hall of Records appearing rather put out. 'Why am I here?'

'Good morning, highness,' Fen said chirpily, as Dan was already breathing deeply to endure Song's presence.

'Is it?' the prince queried, as the tigress went bounding up to greet him, and he went down on bended knee, happy to give Ling Hu some affection. 'I am usually in martial training at this time, not in a library.'

'I hear you are already better than most with any weapon,' Dan stated. 'There is no doubting your warrior capabilities. It is your ethics that require some refinement …'

Song was immediately affronted, and stood from patting the tigress.

'… so the Great Mother has requested that we tutor you in the way of the Wu,' Dan concluded, and Song's suddenly cocky smile indicated that he was pleased.

'I thought she might,' the prince said, well chuffed with himself, and Dan just thought it typical behaviour from Song.

'And why is that?' the duke challenged, as he had certainly not seen it coming.

'I told you, Uncle, I have dreams.' Song rubbed his hands together. 'So, where do we start?'

'The first thing you must do is learn the Wu creed,' Fen informed him, which is when Song's tune dramatically altered.

'I am not expected to *live* by that entire creed, surely?' He backed up, warily. 'If I'm expected to be celibate, the deal is off!'

'Do you have *any idea* what ethics are?' Dan was infuriated by his puerile attitude. 'This is not a deal. It is your duty.'

'Oh, no!' Song shook his finger at Dan. 'It is my responsibility to make heirs and lots of them.'

'Once you are king,' Dan corrected. 'The last thing your heirs need is a bunch of older bastard brothers contesting their throne.'

'Well, Uncle, if you were a bit more experienced, you'd know there are ways of avoiding the issue,' Song teased, and was obviously surprised when Dan had trouble suppressing his grin.

'The point is ... and if you behaved ethically, you'd know that —'

'I should not try, if I do not intend to buy,' Song concluded for his uncle, and Dan was again frustrated by the young man's attitude.

'It is about love, not lust!'

'I do not think that is what your father told you when you were forced to marry at my age,' Song posited and Dan could not deny that. 'Besides, there is only one woman for me, and she is not permitted to marry, so ...' He shrugged, and Dan could feel himself frowning at the suggestion.

'A crush is not love,' Dan felt he should point out, 'love is reciprocal.'

'Give me time,' Song challenged. 'If Uncle Shi can manage it, I can.'

Poor Fen jumped into the middle of the debate before it got out of hand. 'Lord Shi's was a special case, for he is a shifter like Jiang Huxin.'

'Well, what if I were to develop the same skills as Jiang Hudan?' Song proposed.

Fen's eyebrows were raised as he stated humbly, 'Pardon my saying so, highness, but that would be highly unlikely.'

'Would it?' Song challenged. 'Watch this.' He walked over to Fen's desk where a pile of bamboo manuals were placed, and holding his hand over them, the scroll on top leapt up into Song's awaiting grasp.

Dan's heart sunk in his chest — he was mortified and somewhat fearful to know such an immature being had so much power at his disposal. 'Where did you learn how to do that?'

'Just happened.' The prince shrugged off the wonder. 'So you see, I am already Wu, and now I know that the Great Mother knows it too.' He was smug as he strolled over and took a seat. 'I haven't had to stick to any creed to get me this far, and I am not about to start.'

'This is most unusual,' Fen said, bemused, and looked to Dan. 'You know what they say about an untrained psychic?'

'What do they say?' Song was curious.

'It is dangerous,' Dan summarised, and Song looked affronted again.

'My lord means to say,' Fen intervened to explain, 'that psychic attack is one thing, but psychic defence is quite another.'

'Well, then, you are compelled to teach me,' Song told Fen, as he was now a mite concerned that he might have a chink in his personal defences. 'I will study hard — that is how I got this far — and I promise I shall do my best to behave ethically, although I'm not too sure how good that is, as I never had to attempt it before.'

Fen seemed happier as he looked at Dan, who was still reeling over why Tian would give the prince more power than he himself had ever dreamt of. Dan nodded and forced a smile. 'That is all anyone can ask, highness. We should get to work.'

'You make it sound like there is some sort of urgency?' Song noted.

'Our king is losing his will to live,' Dan replied; 'there is a very great urgency.'

'But Fen can heal him?'

'Only as long as he wills it,' Fen stipulated.

Song was decidedly more concerned to learn this. 'Then we must find him a new woman —'

Fen was shaking his head. 'It is a fear of being forced to marry again that is driving the king's will to die, along with a deire to join your mother in the afterlife.'

'But surely he realises that I am not old enough to rule?' Song hit upon the very motivation Dan needed to keep the prince focused, and he applauded the prince's powers of perception.

'Thus the urgency,' Dan concluded.

'Have the Wu foreseen something?'

Dan thought hard upon whether to answer and, in the end, merely nodded.

There was a lump in Song's throat that he was finding hard to swallow. 'How long do we have?'

In appreciation of Song's serious reaction Dan decided to do the prince the courtesy of being honest. 'A year.'

Song slapped his palms against his forehead, unable to believe it, and no doubt devastated by the thought of losing his father in close succession to his mother.

Fen was also horrified to hear the news. 'The Great Mother told you this?'

'She did,' Dan said, sorry to admit it.

'People change fate,' Song appealed. 'I have this power, and I shall figure a way to cheat —'

'Fate is not something that is so easily swayed. It has history and causality on its side,' Dan advised, 'and I am speaking from personal experience.'

'We cannot just let him die!' Song was up and in Dan's face, insistent.

'We did not plan to allow Yi Jiang to die either, but it happened! There are forces at play in this land that you cannot yet conceive of,' Dan stressed. 'So, we can quarrel about the inevitable, or we can prepare.'

'Then prepare me,' Song said, accepting the challenge.

Six months back in her cloistered routine and Hudan had almost forgotten the world beyond Li Shan. True, there was little excitement and adventure in her life now, but there wasn't any torment or distraction either. As her chronicling of the reign of Ji Fa to date was completed, Hudan had returned to teaching and honing her craft. She had missed Huxin and Fen terribly at first, but had come to truly cherish her own company and thoughts, and her own quiet time to work on developing the elemental powers that had been bestowed on her. It was Ji Dan whom she entertained in her thoughts most often, but she had disciplined herself to reserve such musing for the night hours which were her own.

On one such evening, when the sun was low in the sky and she could no longer read her text, Hudan stole a moment in the garden to think back on their night together here on Li Shan, which never failed to bring a smile to her face and incite a sigh from her lips.

'Who are you thinking about?'

Hudan gasped upon hearing a male voice and sighting the Prince of Zhou in the garden with her, she sprang to her feet. 'Ji Song! How did you get here?' Hudan felt sure she would have been summoned to go meet any unexpected visitor.

Song grinned. 'How about you answer my question, and then I shall answer yours?'

Hudan rose up and made sure her displeasure was apparent in her stare. 'I do not play games, or make deals. You will answer my question or I shall take you to the Great Mother and she shall have the truth out of you.'

'Never mind then,' he said, waving off the offer. 'I know the answer to my query anyway. I just have to wonder what you see in that old stuffed shirt? I am closer to your age than he is, and we have a lot more in common.'

For a second Hudan was stumped by his brazen disrespect, yet so charming all the while — it was rather unbelievable to witness. 'Are you trying to shame me in some way, brother? For I assure you, that at this point, you have only shamed yourself.'

'I would not wish that, Jiang Hudan,' he said. 'Or should I call you, Tar-rin?'

Hudan couldn't repress a gasp. The claim came out of nowhere, and hit her hard.

'You know that name, right?' he reasoned, venturing closer. 'Does the name Zhe-Fan ring any bells for you?'

'No,' she answered honestly, 'should it?'

'Say it a few times?' Song urged.

'Zhe-Fan, Zhe-Fan, *Zhe* —' Hudan was struck by a memory of a dark-haired young man, not so dissimilar to Song, dressed as a son of the sky, with large wide eyes of pale brown.

'*See you on the other side of the light-field,*' he was saying to her and admiring her fondly. '*You can't miss me. I'm a prince.*'

She then recalled embracing him and telling him that he was always a prince, and that she would miss him.

'*Not if you can't remember me.*'

The memory slipped away, and Hudan returned to the present to find Song holding his arms open. 'How much do you remember?' she asked, fearfully.

'Enough to know we've been close friends before, and are meant to be again.' He moved closer and Hudan backed away, confused by this turn of events.

'How close?' she asked, and held out a hand to keep him at bay.

'Steamy close, actually,' he hinted in a seductive fashion.

Hudan gasped again. A memory of standing in the teeming rain, knee deep in steamy water, in the throes of a passionate embrace with Zhe-Fan, flashed through her mind and blocked all external vision for a moment.

'You remember?' Song suspected she did, but Hudan shook her head.

'You know it is against Wu creed to knowingly lie?' Song toyed and backed off.

'That was another life. I am Wu now,' Hudan insisted. But inwardly the memories of Zhe-Fan had rattled her — had Tar-rin been having an affair? She was appalled to think she could be such a harlot. 'Why did you come here?'

'I hoped you might be able to tell me why I am having these future memories?' Song appealed, his eyes as engaging as in his previous incarnations, and Hudan saw Zhe-Fan in him now. 'I wanted to know if you have them, too? And you obviously do.'

He held his arms wide and then dropped them to his side, a little dissatisfied with the result. 'Do you not suppose that there might be a higher purpose behind it?'

'Zhou Gong is the expert on past-life memory,' Hudan told him and Song was stunned.

'So that was a past life?' Song was bemused.

'More a life, still going on outside of this life,' Hudan said, sharing her limited understanding. 'Zhou Gong's link to the Akashic memory is the talent he has least developed at this stage, but I suspect he still remembers more than I do.'

'Zhou Gong has psychic talent? You have got to be kidding me?' Song was finding the proposition hard to fathom.

'He is Lu-Chen,' Hudan advised, to test just how much Song did remember.

Song was even more rattled to learn this. 'Forget I said anything!' he insisted backing away.

'Wait!' Hudan enforced her will to keep him glued to the spot. 'Tell me what you know of him?'

'Not fair,' the prince said, referring to his feet, but then with a little effort, he stepped out of her hold, and Hudan was gobsmacked. 'It is not that I do not fancy a bit of bondage, you understand, but I would rather be the one in control.'

'Dear heaven,' Hudan mumbled, completely lost for rational thought.

'Admit it, you are impressed,' he goaded, with a charming smile.

All she could do was nod.

'That would make me the first man to ever be beyond your control,' he boasted, and Hudan noted the arrogance that Dan so deplored.

'I would not go that far,' she cautioned. 'I was going easy on you.'

'Is that a fact?' The prince folded his arms to defy her.

'Tell me what you know about Lu-Chen … please,' she thought to add, taking a step closer to him.

'I do not remember him. Just you,' he whispered, taking a step closer.

Hudan slapped her hands together and keeping her fingertips pressed firmly together, she drew her palms apart. Tiny rushes of blue-white lightning passed between her hands, startling Song backward.

'Holy Tian!' Song had obviously seen how bad it was to be struck by lightning.

'I did ask nicely.'

'You would not hurt your next sovereign, surely?' he appealed sweetly with his eyes.

'I am permitted to punish anyone who sets foot on this mountain uninvited,' she stated and took several purposeful steps toward him.

'Best go then.' Song grinned, and vanished, leaving Hudan in a state of utter disbelief for a third time.

'Oh, Tian!' She clapped her hand to her heart in the wake of the visit, shocked and rattled. She had no idea what to make of the visions she'd just had, or how on earth Ji Song had become so powerful, so fast. Was Zhou Gong aware of his student's talent? It was uncertain which of her concerns was fuelling her desire, but Hudan knew she was compelled to seek Dan.

As it was the midnight hour, Hudan was not surprised to be spirited forth to a dark room. It was silent as her eyes adjusted to the moonlit shadows of her new location.

'Am I seeing things?' Dan asked as he sat up in bed, naked to the waist, his long dark hair falling over his shoulders.

'I had to see you,' she said, and the panic in her voice spurred to the duke to her side.

'What has happened?' He gripped her shoulders and pulled her into the moonlight. 'You are crying.'

The anguish of a secret love seemed a trifle compared to the guilt she was feeling, which was even more foreign to her sensibilities and twice as painful. 'Ji Song came to see me —'

'What?' Dan was baffled.

'He just popped in for a visit,' she said laconically, and Dan's jaw dropped.

'Song can teleport!' It took a second to absorb that shock, and then the duke was angry. 'What did he do to upset you like this?'

'No, nothing like that!' Hudan backpedalled a little. 'Song did not do anything apart from be his cocky, arrogant self. His powers rattled me a little, but not as much as the fact that he remembers being a son of the sky.'

'He remembers?'

Hudan nodded. 'The name of his incarnation among them sparked my memories of knowing him ... and I wish it had not.' She slipped free of Dan's gasp, shaking her head in an attempt to overcome her rising dread of coming to the point.

'What did you see?' Dan was alarmed now, and Hudan couldn't stop the tears from flowing.

'I know I was close to him,' she confessed.

'No,' Dan said, not prepared to accept it.

'What if Tar-rin was cheating on Lu-Chen?' Hudan's chest felt like it was about to rip open, and the panic was causing her to hyperventilate. 'Now I question what kind of a life I am going back to among the sons of the sky? I want to remember, but I only see into the future. The past is your domain. But I want you to know that I would not, could not, betray anyone like that. If the woman I was among the sons of the sky could, then ... I do not want to go back to being her.'

'Whoa!' Dan appealed holding both hands up in truce. 'It seems to me that you are not entirely sure what you saw.'

'I saw enough to make me panic. I felt how much it hurt to let him go, before we came here.' She looked at Dan and even in the dim light, she could see him hurting. 'But that makes no sense when I consider how Tar-rin felt when she was with Lu-Chen. I feel that too, very strongly.' She thumped a fist to her chest in frustration. 'You know I do! I am just ... completely baffled.'

'His royal highness is in so much trouble right now,' Dan seethed. 'When the king and the Great Mother learn —'

'No!' Hudan begged the duke not to take that course. 'Song must not know I told you.'

Dan frowned.

'If there was any wrongdoing here, it was mine, or rather Tar-rin's,' she defended. 'I know he was a good friend of hers, so I do not want to betray his trust, or yours. Maybe I have this all wrong?' Hudan was frustrated. 'If I could only remember more.'

'The prince should not have been on Li Shan in the first place.'

'I am aware of that,' she agreed and yet she was wary. 'But he is *powerful*. I have my elemental arts over him, but that is all. I fear he is every bit as masterful as I … in which case it would be most unwise to get him offside.'

'He has you in tears, he broke a holy law and yet you defend him?'

The last thing Hudan wanted was to upset Dan, but he certainly had that tone in his voice.

'I wish now that the Lord of Time had awakened my dormant other, when he had the chance,' she stated, 'so I could know what has gone before. As it is, I can only go with my gut instinct … and that is, that Song is a staunch ally and we should treat him as such.'

It took a moment, but Dan decided to be diplomatic. 'So how do you wish me to proceed?'

'I just thought you should be aware of Song's capabilities, and of his visit …' She bit her lip, contemplating whether to say more. 'And should you remember anything damning about me, in our past life together, I want to assure you that I am not that woman now.'

To Hudan's tremendous relief Dan embraced her, and some of her guilt lifted. 'Clearly … when you are racked with guilt over an affair you *might* have had in a *past* life. In this life, you have done nothing wrong.'

Hudan sniffled, unable to agree as she pulled back from an embrace she should not be having. 'Surely you jest?'

'You're right, you are hopeless,' Dan chuckled, trying reverse psychology and making her smile.

'I will say, when I told Song that you were Lu-Chen, the prince became much more cautious.'

'You told him?' Dan was annoyed to have been exposed.

'Well, Song claimed that he came to me to ask about the future memories he was having,' she justified. 'I told him you were the expert in that department, hoping he might come to you with his queries.'

Dan nodded, finding her reasoning sound.

'He knows something about Lu-Chen, but he refused to discuss it with me,' she said, giving him fair warning.

'I shall keep a close eye on the prince,' Dan advised. 'If he comes to see you again, come straight to me. The chances are he will pursue you, and if I catch him, I can reprimand him accordingly.'

Hudan was glad to have laid the mystery open, and to have a strategy in place to deal with the situation should it arise again. 'Thank you for listening. I feel lightened of a great load.'

'That you should not have been burdened with in the first place, in my view,' Dan replied. 'I suspect Ji Song is making mischief, and if I discover he is playing some kind of game with you, I swear —'

Hudan placed a hand over the duke's mouth. 'Let us hope this is just a terrible misunderstanding.' She began to move her hand, but he kissed her fingers before they departed, and then her palm and wrist.

'I should go.' She was reluctant to pull away, and Dan did not let her go. 'That is not why I came.'

'When I first saw you appear, I thought it was, since it is my birthday,' he explained, both eyes raised in appeal.

'Oh, no, please tell me it isn't!' Hudan felt awful, dumping her woes on him on such an occasion, and not even to be aware of it. 'I am so sorry,' she said, and bowed to him, deeply remorseful.

'No need to apologise, brother,' he assured her, kindly. 'A simple kiss would suffice.'

Under normal circumstances Hudan would have resented being put on the spot, but as it was his birthday, and she felt no harm could come of it, she obliged his request with some fervour. Her penance was disturbingly pleasurable, as he tasted like sweet wine and smelt of sandalwood, but she did not allow it to continue beyond their control.

'Am I forgiven?' she asked, as she slid away.

'You are,' he decided, graciously. 'But ...' His benevolent mood erred on the side of caution. 'Would you be very cross with me to know it is not really my birthday.'

Hudan shoved him backward, annoyed to have been proven so gullible, but not sorry to have had the opportunity to reassure him of how she felt. 'When is your birthday then?' she thought to ask, so as not to be caught out again.

'Tomorrow,' he grinned broadly, and Hudan knew he was just being smart.

'Seriously.' She placed her hands on her hips.

But Dan remained tightlipped. 'I'm not telling you. You'll read up on my astrology and have me worked out by the next time we meet.'

'You flatter yourself,' Hudan scoffed. 'That is not what I intended at all.'

'No?' Dan challenged. 'Then tell me your time and date of birth.'

'Oh, no.' Hudan felt she was wise to his game this time. 'You won't outfox me twice in one evening.'

'I have better things to do, quite frankly,' Dan assured her with a cheeky grin.

Despite his stratagem and coquetry, or perhaps directly due to it, Hudan felt so much more at ease now. 'Onward and upward then.'

'As we were,' he assured, and Hudan breathed easier knowing Song could not spring news of his secret visit with her on his uncle at any point in the future and catch him off-guard.

It was no surprise to note how respectful Song was when he arrived for his lesson the next day, and he seemed relieved to find his tutor in good cheer, and not furious as he had probably anticipated. Dan figured that Song believed Jiang Hudan had kept his secret from his mentor and rival for her affections and was revelling in the fact. Since it had been Dan tasting her affection the day before, he knew her love was securely in his quarter.

The morning session of Dao Yin passed without incident, but during the theory lesson Dan steered the discussion toward the various powers the Wu developed, to see if Song would disclose any of his secrets to them of his own accord.

'So, you have been studying Wu doctrine for some time now, Uncle,' Song commented, looking at Dan curiously. 'Have you developed any psychic skill?'

Cunning, Dan thought, as he gave a nod in confirmation. 'I see spirits.'

'Dead people?' Song queried, sounding spooked.

'Dead, living, abstract,' Dan concurred.

'And that's it?' Song said, sounding unimpressed, but the duke knew he was fishing for something in particular.

'Not at all,' Fen spoke up, proud of his student. 'My lord saw through a wall the other day.'

Song looked back at his uncle, and Dan smiled and nodded. 'Now *that* I envy, Uncle. Such a talent would come in very handy.' The prince grinned mischievously, rubbing his hands together.

'I have also met a son of the sky,' Dan boasted and Song was immediately intrigued. 'It was, in fact, he who heightened my psychic sight.'

'It is true,' Fen assured the prince, 'I was there and so was Jiang Hudan.'

'So you had cosmic help to develop your skills,' Song said in a superior tone. Dan gathered that that was not how Song had developed his talents.

Dan laughed, thinking him clueless. 'I can also see a son of the sky lying dormant inside of you, Song.' Dan shocked the prince with the news. 'And another within Fen Gong,' he added, and Fen was stunned in equal measure.

'You never said so?' Fen was a mite disconcerted by the news.

'It was that entity who aided me to heal you,' Dan said. 'He has your same talent for healing and growing.'

'I wondered how that had come about. I thought I might have healed myself.'

'Well, in a way, you did,' the duke granted.

'That is why I keep dreaming of future worlds?' Song surmised, speaking out loud.

'I'm guessing that the son of the sky within you has the same talents that you are developing,' Dan told him, 'and so you see, you have also had some cosmic help. What do you remember?' the duke asked casually and Song's eyes narrowed in caution.

'I recall arguing with my superior over a woman,' he stated, and Fen was forced to suppress a laugh as the scenario seemed so typical of the prince. But Dan knew Lu-Chen was Song's superior in that other life, so he was not laughing. 'He, my superior,' Song advised, 'doubted this woman's loyalty, but I did not. It was his wife's word he wanted to believe when, in fact, I knew *she* was the traitor.'

Dan was frowning now, having totally lost track of the plot. 'So what happened?'

'I told him to stick his job and went to work for the accused,' Song concluded, punching the air in support of his other incarnation.

'Good for you!' Fen cheered.

'Do you remember any names?' Dan attempted to keep the conversation on track.

'I remember *her* name,' Song teased, a dark expression on his face as he stared his uncle down. 'I remember a *whole lot* about her. Her name was … a bit hard to pronounce actually, but something like, Tar-rin Lin-ox.' Song shrugged as though he was none the wiser, but Dan was reeling.

Did this mean Lu-Chen had not been married to Tar-rin — as the Great Mother had said? Or was Song twisting the truth to his own ends? It was certainly a prime motivation to develop the universal memory Dan had been told he possessed.

'Something on your mind, Uncle?' Song queried. 'You seem distracted.'

'Not at all,' Dan smiled in reassurance. 'I find your recollections most intriguing. How did it all end, I wonder?'

'Maybe it never did end,' Song posed, 'and that is why we are all here?'

'How exciting!' Fen clapped his hands together, inspired by their banter. 'Do you think my sisters are involved?' he asked, and was surprised when both men looked at him, a withering look on their face that he failed to understand. 'It was just a question.'

'No doubt of it,' Dan stated, repressing his urge to ring Fen's neck for opening that barrel of worms right now.

'So you have seen sons of the sky in them?' Fen asked, whereby he and Song looked at him, expectantly — Song overly keen.

Dan nodded to confirm. 'And Shi also.'

Fen was ecstatic!

Song was grinning broadly. 'My father?'

The duke shook his head to the negative. 'His son of the sky is elsewhere at present.'

'What does that mean?' Song demanded to know.

'It is my understanding that we are operating inside of time, whereas the king's other is operating outside of time, along with his brother, the Lord of the Elements.'

Song looked to Fen. 'Do you have any idea what he is talking about?'

Fen shook his head in the negative. 'But I want my sisters back, so I am in,' he grinned broadly.

'Everyone wants your sisters,' Song remarked facetiously. Fen was not amused and neither was Dan.

'Your etiquette and sense of propriety need a *lot* of work, Ji Song.' Fen looked back to the duke. 'So what are we doing here?'

'Just trying to keep history on track at present,' he enlightened them, 'and forget that the sons of the sky exist, until our dying day. At least, that was the Great Mother's advice to me on the matter.'

'The Great Mother is one of them?' Song was always delighted to have another woman involved.

'She knows much about the sons of the sky,' Dan said to skirt around the issue, 'and what is most important in the greater scheme of things, is that you are prepared to ascend to the throne in the near future.'

'Are you saying I have to wait until I die to know what I am really here for?' Song protested.

'Prince Song is here to lead our dynasty and the land to peace and greatness,' Dan said clearly, adamantly.

'But the powers, the dreams —'

'Must be put away, as much as possible, until such time as what you came here to do is done,' Dan lectured, as Song's resistance grew.

'That sucks! It's all right for you, you're old,' Song argued with his uncle. 'But Fen and I are still young! It could be fifty years before we die! And then what? We will be old and decrepit and of no use to anyone!'

'I do not know how it works. I am only passing on what I was told,' Dan stressed.

'By the Great Mother?'

The query sounded like a threat, and Dan suspected the prince was about to do something very rash. Before he could warn him not to take such action, the prince vanished. 'Oh dear,' said Dan.

'His highness is out of control!' Fen was panicking. 'I hope for his sake he was not going where I think he went.'

Dan cocked an eye, feeling Song would find the Great Mother less accommodating and harder to defy than he expected.

Still. Quiet. Get your bearings. Song had trained himself to recite this instruction upon materialising anywhere. Through trial and error, he had learned that he could not teleport himself anywhere, or to anyone, that he did not have a clear visual image of — so the closest he could get himself to the Great Mother was the central cloister at the House of Yi Wu Li Shan. A quick scan of the area confirmed that no one had seen him arrive, and he made his way swiftly to the Great Mother's chambers.

As he reached the doors to the outer chamber, they unexpectedly parted before him, and finding the room beyond empty, the prince entered cautiously. When the doors on the far side of the chamber opened in invitation, the prince proceeded, feeling welcome; when the doors behind him slammed closed, making him jump, Song relinquished any hope of a warm welcome.

Song had never had a private audience with the Great Mother before, and so had never seen inside her council chamber, which he entered reverently and quietly.

On this rainy afternoon the Great Mother was seated at a desk, applying ink to bamboo. Her face was veiled; only her eyes were exposed. As she was so completely focused on her task, Song cleared his throat to let her know he was present.

'I am very aware you are here.' She did not disturb herself, but finished what she was writing.

'Do you not wonder how I got here?' the prince queried.

'I know how you got here,' she replied. 'Why do you think I am veiled?'

'Are you not impressed?' Song tried the tactic that had worked on Hudan.

'Not in the least.'

'But I am Wu —'

The Great Mother put down her pen and stood. 'You are a disrespectful upstart, show-off and womaniser, and you always were!'

Song pulled his head in. 'I resent … some of that.'

'Tough!' she said, as if he were no one of consequence. 'And I shall tell you something else for nothing. These traits have seen you pulled from our missions before, so I would be very wary, dutiful, gracious and attentive to your lessons, young prince, or you shall find yourself off the team once again.'

'There must be some mistake.'

'I do not make mistakes,' she replied 'but you *surely* do. If you ever set foot on this mount again, uninvited, I shall withdraw our holy mandate from your dynasty and leave you to it.'

'But Great Mother, I have these dreams —'

'Forget them. Accomplish all that Ji Song must,' she proffered, 'and you can create a peace that will extend far beyond your lifetime. Only then will the sons of the sky come for you.'

'Then tell me mine is a short reign,' Song pleaded.

'I should hope not. You have yet to even wed or bear an heir … legitimately,' she added, and Song was frustrated. 'And before you even ask, the answer is no.'

'What was the question?' Song queried.

'No, you cannot wed Jiang Hudan. No, you are not meant to be with her, nor was she ever yours.' The Great Mother crushed him with the information. 'You have a strong bond with her, but she is not the love of your life, Song. That mystery still lays ahead of you in this life, and so your future in Zhou is not so grim and meaningless as you think. Indeed, for most of your life, the sons of the sky will not be given a second thought. You will be too busy.'

Song felt the wind had rushed from his sails; he felt depleted and Yi Wu seemed raring to go. 'I have a list of works for you to begin work on, that your father has given his prior blessing to,' she advised. 'Let us have tea and discuss it.'

Song nodded to be polite, sincerely wishing he'd never come.

When the prince returned to Haojing, he was dazed, despondent and not very talkative. He had a bamboo scroll in his possession that he handed to Dan.

'What is this?' The duke unfurled the document to read.

'We have a lot of work to do,' was all Song said, ahead of excusing himself for the rest of the day. 'I need to … process.'

'That is exactly how I feel every time I speak with Yi Wu,' Dan sympathised, still reading, as Song turned and headed for the door. 'I note that finding a wife for you is high on the list of priorities,' the duke said, eager to see Song thus distracted.

The prince halted and looked back at the duke — the chore of fielding candidates would have fallen to the queen, and the king was certainly in no fit state. 'You pick one that makes political sense, Zhou Gong. I could not care less who she is.'

'That is not how our new system of marriage is supposed to work,' Dan pointed out. 'That is hardly going to serve to make for a happy family life, highness.'

'If that is the aim, my baby brother will be next king on the throne,' Song insisted and his frustration fuelled his departure.

Fen exhaled heavily, discouraged. 'You have your work cut out for you, my duke.'

'A bit of divine guidance would not go astray,' Dan considered.

'*Yi Jing: the Book of Changes?*' Fen suggested, ready to fetch the scrolls.

'No. I have something else in mind, an experiment.' Dan was quietly mulling over something Hudan had said the night before.

'*I wish now that the Lord of Time had awakened my dormant other, when he had the chance, so I could know what has gone before.*'

Fen had been teaching Dan the Wu laws regarding summoning entities, and one of these — the law of three requests — stated that to summon any entity, you must know their name and recite it three times. He may not have known the name of the Lord of the Elements — Hudan had gone to great lengths to keep that secret — but Dan did know the name of the Lord of Time, and if he could awaken Dan's sleeper within so that he could fathom the past, surely the path forward would also be clarified.

Once the house had settled for the night and there was no danger of being disturbed, Dan steadied his nerve. The Lord of the Elements had not wanted his brother involved in the worldly affairs of this time, but as the elemental lord had not offered up his name for counsel if required, the duke felt compelled to proceed with what he had.

He requested the counsel of the Lord of Time and summoned him: 'Hreen, Hreen, Hreen.'

The duke caught his breath as a young son of the sky manifested before him, pale of face, with large round eyes as dark as Dan's own. His hair was dark and straight, and fell long around his face and shoulders as Fen's did. He was attired entirely in black and the clothing covered him like a skin: his boots covered his shins to just below the knee and had fasteners up the side. These were made of what appeared to be metal, but the strange back material must have been extremely lightweight, as the lord's movement did not appeared hindered in the least. The belt around his waist had wonders hanging from it, the purposes of which Dan could not imagine — weapons, or tools, perhaps?

'Hello, father,' the lord said, grinning broadly. 'You *never* call.'

'That actually worked.' The duke was amazed.

'Technically, no, as I am not a creature of the otherworld like my brother,' and the lord held an arm out for the duke to feel. 'I am as living as you are.'

When the duke felt the strange skin covering the lord's arm he was astounded. 'That is why your spirit is not in Ji Fa.'

The lord winked at him, just as Fa used to when they were siblings with no titles or responsibilities. 'I just happened to be around, checking up on the team, as I do from time to time. I sure as hell have nothing better to do at present. Still, if my brother finds out we've spoken, he's not going to be happy.' Rhun looked about the room, warily, and with a wave of his hand put out the flame in the lantern. 'No plants,' he noted, 'no airflow.' The shutters on the windows were closed. 'You don't have any water in here, do you?'

'No,' replied Dan curiously.

'No precious stones or crystals?'

'Nothing like that. Why?'

'If there are no living elements present, there are no elementals to report back to his lordship,' Rhun explained.

'It's a good thing I did not summon you out of doors!' Dan exclaimed.

'A very good thing,' the lord concurred, taking a seat opposite the duke. 'So what is on your mind?'

'I want you to return my cosmic memory.'

Rhun forced a laugh and shook his head. 'If I was permitted, do you not think I would have already? Besides, that task you, in particular, can accomplish on your own.'

Dan was discouraged by the response.

'Why do you feel you need it all at once?' the lord asked. 'I am sure this has something to do with mother.'

'That's right!' Dan's eyes lit up. 'If we are your parents, then Lu-Chen cannot have been married to someone else.'

'Hah! If that is your worry, then have none!' The lord cut through the air with his hand in emphasis. 'I have known you both through many, many lifetimes, and you have never chosen anyone but her, unless you were forced, deceived, or enchanted.'

Dan was baffled and frustrated! 'Then where does her close connection with Song come from?'

'Ah ... now I see,' Rhun nodded surely. 'You've had this problem before.'

'Why am I not surprised?' Dan was not sure if he should be hopeful or alarmed.

'The soul in question is fiercely protective of mother as they are very much alike; like twins or twin-souls say, and have often incarnated as siblings ... whereas you are more a soul mate. Do you see? Even when they are not related they still feel that strong bond.'

Dan nodded. What the lord was saying made perfect sense. 'So, what did I do about it in the past?'

'You aided him to find his own soul mate,' Rhun said, stating the obvious.

'She is a son of the sky also?' the duke asked, wondering if there were others he hadn't found yet.

'She is, but she was not chosen for this mission,' Rhun was sorry to say.

'Then she shall not be so easy for me to spot. *If* she is even incarnate in this time.' Dan had the feeling he would be looking for a needle in a haystack.

'Oh, she is bound to be,' Rhun encouraged, 'and will surely cross paths with your prince eventually.'

'But I have to find him a wife now!' the duke said in desperation. 'Can you give me some inkling of her character at least?'

'Well, I never actually met his better half, but I had known a few past incarnations of her and …' His brow furrowed as he brought her to mind. 'She is tenacious, and will probably seem completely indifferent to your prince's charms … but the more immune she appears, the more interested she is. Oh, and she is very likely more martial than he is — he tends to find assertive women attractive.'

'Which is why he finds Hudan so alluring,' Dan mused, understanding. 'But the only women like Hudan are Wu, who do not marry.'

'Do not be so sure, or you'll just make the task much more difficult.' He grinned broadly in support. 'Anything else?'

The lord had done Dan an admirable service, and although Dan did not want to be seen to play favourites, he liked Rhun more than his tricky brother and, wished to return the kindness. 'Were you there at Yin when we attempted to take down Dragonface?'

'*No.*' The time lord was obviously annoyed. 'My brother trapped me in an obelisk whilst that was going down, and now we've lost that son of a bitch again! What of it?'

'I saw a son of the sky in Wu Geng, the last Prince of the Shang, that I did not recognise and your brother didn't either,' Dan disclosed. 'Hudan asked him if you should be consulted, but he —'

'Doesn't want me involved, I know,' Rhun concluded, frowning and obviously finding the news interesting.

'What did you do last time around that made things go so horribly wrong?' Dan had wondered this ever since the lord's brother had first mentioned it.

'The creature you call Dragonface stole my time-hopping transport and destroyed my planet in my absence. Meantime, I made you and Hudan aware of one another, romantically speaking, and you ran off together, resulting in decades of war when it should have been peaceful, and then Dragonface returned and took full advantage of the chaos. It was then that my brother aided me to steal my transport back and I returned home to discover that I had been the one to cause the very disaster that I had fled into time to escape!'

Dan's jaw was dropping open. 'So how did we get involved.'

'Fortunately for me, I had already recruited your beloved to quantum jump across from your parallel universe and warn me of the threat to my people. You and all the other dormant souls you see in those around you, came with her, and volunteered to help me right this mess.'

'There is more than one universe?' Dan had not considered this, let alone that you could jump between them! 'Hudan did all this?'

'Oh yes,' Rhun said proudly, 'she is quite the strategist where reworking time is concerned. You don't call her Time —' The lord bit his tongue. 'Nearly did it.'

'What?' Dan was dying to know.

One of the window shutters rattled as the wind rapped against it, and Rhun stood, looking nervous. 'Nothing.' The lord closed the subject. 'I shall investigate that other matter.'

'Must you go?' The duke could have spoken with him all night.

'I'll be around,' Rhun assured him. 'Good luck with your lady hunt.'

Moments after the lord vanished, the shutters on the window burst open and the duke's eyes widened in wonder as he saw faint impressions of beautiful women in the wind that whipped around the room. The spectres wound about each other as they searched the interior, completely ignoring Dan. When they found nothing of interest, the ghostly ladies fled back out the window and the wind died out.

The duke slapped his hands to his face, mind-blown by the events of the evening. With every contact he had with the sons of the sky, his own expansive nature and purpose became clearer and more real to him. How could he not be awed and inspired by what the distant future held in store? He'd been told several times now that he could recapture his ancient memory and he now aspired to pursue that goal with far greater vigour.

Over the next several months the prince continued to train and study diligently, and the screening process for his queen began in earnest. Across the kingdom nobles were invited to send forth their daughters for the prince's consideration. The candidates were physically screened by the queen's sister, and if they were found to be exceedingly beautiful, and maidens still, they were referred to Zhou Gong and Zhou Bo Fen Gong for an interview. If the candidate was found to be of pleasing character and intelligent, they were granted a private audience with Ji Song. Neither Zhou Gong nor the king would allow the prince to forego the responsibility of choosing his own life partner and possible future Queen of Zhou.

Each evening after dinner, Ji Song interviewed potential spouses, which he found a little tedious, for the girls were so nervous and stuffy by the time they got to meet him, that they just bored him to tears.

This particular evening had been more of the same until the last woman on his list, Yin Hui Ru — granddaughter of the esteemed Shang minister Jizi, just outside of Yin proper — entered their audience, completely cloaked in black.

'Is this a joke?' Ji Song stopped slouching in his throne and sat up as she came to kneel before him. 'How am I to know if I find you pleasing, if I cannot see you?'

'Please forgive my deception, highness. I am not here to seek the position of your queen, but to warn you of an impending threat,' she informed him.

Her voice was pleasing enough and Song was curious. 'If you wish to converse with me, then remove your hood at least.'

'Are you not listening —'

'*No*. I am not listening to anyone who will not look me in the eye,' he said, insistently.

'Highness.' Hui Ru flung her hood back to reveal a head shaved clean like a monk. 'It is most —'

'What on earth?' He wondered what she was thinking, doing this to herself, for her face was very beautiful. 'Am I supposed to find this attractive?'

'No, highness,' she stated, 'that is the point. I have no desire to be your queen, only to warn you that I suspect there is a threat to the peace that your father has so recently established in our land. This marriage nonsense was my only means to get to Zhou.'

Song laughed at her charade. 'I cannot imagine how you got through the screening process.'

Hui Ru rolled her eyes, impatient with the distraction, but humoured him. 'I had my maid stand in for me at those interviews, hence the cape.'

'I see,' he chuckled, delighted, as he descended the stairs to observe her more closely. 'You have gone to an awful lot of trouble to get here,' he warranted.

'Yes, I *have*,' she emphasised, 'because some kind of creature has possessed my grandfather and I believe that, through him, it is influencing events in the Yin court.'

When Song heard her story he laughed out loud. 'If your aim was to be memorable, you are surely that!'

'Highness, I know it sounds fantastic, but in the East we have heard that such creatures frequent the Yin court —' Hui Ru gave up trying to explain herself, as the prince was laughing too hard to hear her.

'I can see why you sent your maid to the interviews in your stead.' Song curbed his mirth, circling her, wondering what kind of a figure was under the robe. 'You never would have got past Zhou Gong with that story!'

'Oh!' she exclaimed, furious. 'What would you know? You are just a boy! Clearly, I need to see the king.' She stood and turned to leave.

'Just a boy, am I?' Song was tired of hearing that. 'You won't think so on our wedding night.'

'What?' She swung back around, horrified.

'You are definitely the most interesting and enterprising female I've seen,' he announced, happily.

'No,' she said.

'And the best news is that I don't have to do any more of these damn interviews,' Song muttered to himself. By the time he looked back to her, she had a blade to his throat.

'Marry me, and I shall kill you!' she threatened, and was confused when Song grabbed her backside, one cheek in each hand.

'Now that's my idea of foreplay,' he grinned, but looking down and noting the attire beneath her robe, he frowned. 'The dressing like a boy thing is a little kinky for my —'

'I am not your property.' She forcefully shoved him backward, and Song played along, as he quite enjoyed being dominated for a change. Hui Ru backed him up to his throne, which she shoved him onto and then aimed her blade toward his groin area. 'And I will never consent!'

'Steady on,' Song protested, not too worried. 'Think of the children,' he entreated, with a charming smile.

'My house is under *threat*. Do you not understand?' she asked, slowly and plainly.

'Well, if you marry me, it will be under threat no longer,' the prince replied, loving her dramatics.

Hui Ru was shaking her head at him, as if he should be taking her seriously and he was. This was, by far, the most amused he'd been in ages.

'Guards!' he called to have her escorted to back to her quarters.

'No wait!' she begged him. 'You are making a terrible mistake.'

Song shrugged. 'I'll live with it.'

'Idiot!' she yelled as she was hauled away kicking and resisting. 'I demand to see the king!'

'You shall see him at our wedding, sweetness.' Song blew her a kiss, and looked to the master of the interior who had entered with the guards. 'Find her a dress, so I can see what kind of form she has. And no more haircuts.'

'Give me a sword, and I shall show you my form!' Hui Ru threatened.

'I cannot give you my sword until our wedding night, my love, but it is good to know you are so keen,' he teased her. She was in a silent fury as the master of the interior closed the door on the departing scuffle, and Song collapsed into his chair, content with his choice.

She was not Jiang Hudan, but would be a feisty challenge to follow his goddess rite.

News that Ji Song had finally chosen a bride gave Dan the best night's sleep he'd had in ages, but the awakening proved not so blissful.

'My lord? *Brother*, please awake!' Fen was stressing about something …

'What did she ruin this time?' Dan figured Fen's tigress must have knocked over the ink again, or chewed up his new boots.

'The king is ailing.' The serious tone of the lad's voice got Dan's attention. 'And he has ordered his guard to keep me out.' The young count swallowed his pain. 'He is asking for you.'

Dan did not bother to tidy himself, but made for the king's chamber with Fen hot on his heels.

The healer was halted at the door and the duke entered alone, to find Jiang Taigong and Ji Song already with him, along with several of the king's house staff in various states of dishevelment.

'What are you doing?' Dan went down on bended knee beside the king. 'Let Fen in here to heal you.'

'I cannot do it any more, Dan,' Fa said, appealing for his indulgence, and gripping Dan's hand in his. 'This wound tears open a least once a day, and I cannot put her from my mind … you understand?'

The duke comprehended the plea, knowing if he had to go a day without thinking of Hudan, he would have died long ago. He nodded to show his understanding. 'But I must speak with you alone,' the duke said. He had to get Fa to rewrite his will before he became too incoherent to do it.

'No, stay!' the king ordered those who had moved to leave upon hearing the duke's request. 'Dan knows my wishes and there will be no discussion. Our prime minister has my will in writing. Promise me, Dan, *promise* that you will see it done.'

Fa was sweating fiercely, as the wound had been left to fester, no doubt at the king's own order, and it smelt as bad as the creature who had given it to him. Dan had to wonder if his brother was already beyond reasoning with. Put on the spot, the duke nodded to console his brother, then stood and backed away. 'I shall return presently.'

As Dan left the room the prime minister pursued him.

'What do you intend to do?' Jiang Taigong asked, knowing the duke would not act against his own good judgement without protest.

'Just the man I need,' Dan said, inviting the prime minister to follow him.

'Where are we going?' Jiang Taigong was uncomfortable to be running around in his bed attire. 'Should we not at least dress ourselves properly?'

'There is no time for propriety,' the duke insisted. 'Come, Fen, I could use a second witness.'

'Witness?' Fen was concerned.

'Walk now, query later,' the duke urged, not prepared to speak further until they were away from prying ears.

'If the king intends to die, let me give him the elixir of waking sleep to ease his passage from this world?' Fen implored the duke as he kept pace with him.

'Not to sound cruel, Fen, but I need the king to have his wits about him just a little bit longer.'

When Dan led them to the family storehouse complex, Jiang Taigong had a fair idea what he was up to, and as they waited for Heng, the storehouse guard, to unbolt the door the prime minister was feeling most unnerved.

'It is the only way to be sure,' the duke said in justification, as the door to the storehouse opened and he was handed a lantern to guide the three of them down to the lower level.

'What can I get for you this evening, my lord?' Heng asked.

'I need the Jade Book, and the metal-bound coffer containing the king's last will and testament.'

Heng was cautious, as the two items named were currently the most prized in his care. 'And the prime minister agrees?'

Jiang Taigong was uneasy, but trusted Dan's judgement. 'I do.'

'I shall return,' Heng disappeared up the dark stairs.

'What exactly are we doing?' Fen was concerned about what the said items amounted to when put together.

'We are deciding the course of history,' the duke stated plainly.

'Or rather,' Jiang Taigong added, 'allowing an ancient book to do that for us.' The prime minister made his disapproval plain.

'It has been right up until now,' Dan challenged.

'Perhaps because of people like us?' The wise old man raised his eyebrows in question, and although Dan saw his point he could not agree.

'I know the author of this book made an accurate account of how history originally was, and this is how it must be again.' Dan was determined, and as soon as the treasure was unbolted before him, he found his place and read: *Ji Fa of Zhou will unite and rule over all the land* — He turned the tablet over, as Hudan had, to read what had shocked her into abandoning her research. — *but will die two years thereafter. King Cheng, son of Fa, will succeed under the regency of his uncle, Zhou Gong. They suppress an eastern rebellion to secure a peace that survives them both.*

'It is as I thought, and not as the king has willed it,' Zhou Gong informed his company, and moved aside to allow the prime minister to read for himself.

'King Cheng?' the prime minister queried.

Clearly, Cheng was a posthumous name, as it was a tradition to pay tribute to their kings and founding fathers in this manner. Even Dan's father, Ji Chang, who had never officially become king, had been given the posthumous title of King Wen, as he'd been considered to be knowledgeable, benevolent and kind.

Cheng meant 'to succeed, to be accomplished and sincere', which hardly seemed a fitting description of Ji Song at present, Dan had to admit. 'It does state, the son of Fa,' the duke pointed out, 'which is clearly not I.'

'But the king has two sons now,' Jiang Taigong pointed out.

Dan did not even want to consider trying to hold the regency until the younger prince grew to manhood. 'Let us just assume for the moment that the text refers to Song.'

'So what do you suggest we do. Forge the king's will?' Jiang Taigong jested, but lost his cheer when the duke nodded.

'You penned the first will for the king's signature, did you not?' the duke said, implying how easily this task could be carried out.

'I do not think I should be here,' Fen said, horrified by their talk.

'Fen Gong, do you not agree that Ji Song should rule?'

Fen was stunned by the query. 'Yes, of course. That is the only way to define a clear line of succession … and the Great Mother has foreseen it.'

'I have consulted the ancestors on this issue and they say the same.' Dan made sure Jiang Taigong noted the lad's view. 'But our problem is that my brother has willed me the throne.'

Fen gasped in panic. 'That would certainly bring war; we must change the king's mind.'

'I have appealed his decision, all year,' Dan replied, and Fen ran out of protest and fell silent. 'No, gentlemen, I am sorry to say this weighty decision has fallen squarely in our quarter. The future of the Zhou dynasty must be rewritten by us here and now, and placed in an identical coffer to that of the king's, which will be hidden away by Heng to bear future witness to what we have done here this morning. May future generations judge us as having chosen wisely for the greater benefit of our land.'

'There will still be a rebellion, Zhou Gong: the text states as much. Xian will demand the regency.'

'But if we take this suggested path it promises we shall overcome,' Dan pointed out. 'If the king gets his way, we may not fare so well, with every brother I have and Song against us. As much as I hate to admit it, Song is our best way forward.'

When Jiang Taigong finally nodded, that was the duke's biggest obstacle gone, and it was a huge relief to him. For Dan knew that on a higher level of awareness he was achieving an even more important directive — history would stay its course.

'Now, may I have permission to offer the king some pain relief?' Fen begged. 'For he is obviously to have no further say in worldly affairs.'

Dan nodded to confirm the request. 'I shall join you at his bedside as soon as we are done here.'

Fen nodded.

'Not a word to anyone, Fen Gong, not so long as I live,' Dan asserted. 'Swear it to me.'

'I believe in you, my lord,' he replied, sounding shaken. 'If this is what you say must be done, then there is nothing to discuss, now or ever.' He bowed out of the proceedings and scampered up the stairs.

Jiang Taigong appeared to have a bitter-sweet taste on his tongue as he watched Fen depart. 'If only men had the same kind of faith in our young prince, our worries would be fewer.'

'Before I hand over the regency, Song shall be respected by his elders.' Dan was not hearing any more reasons for a change of heart now. 'I promise you.'

The prime minister did not appear so certain. 'Then, let us do what we must and be content with it.'

As the death of the king would cast the land into a state of chaos that would only be stabilised upon the crowning of the next king, Fa waived pain relief in order to maintain his sensibilities and spent his final hours advising his son and nobles.

There was no time to prepare a huge funeral or to undergo a three-year mourning period, as they had been at liberty to do with their great father, Ji Chang. Ji Fa had not ruled long enough, nor did their young dynasty have the time or resources to waste on such veneration. If they were required to quash a rebellion in the wake of his death, the king commanded that they do so without hesitation.

It was also the king's wish that Song take good care of his baby brother, which the prince claimed went without saying, for he had already formed a close attachment to his only sibling. It was not often Ji Song showed vulnerability, but in the face of losing his father, he could not prevent the tears from silently streaming down his face. The idea of ascending to the throne at such a young age was far more daunting to him then he would ever admit openly.

Fa's final request was to be buried on Li Shan behind the temple of Heaven, next to his queen, where they might listen to the sweet music of the Wu for so long as their spirits dwelt on earth.

Dan was gutted as he watched his older brother breathe his last. There was no long-standing friend he trusted or loved better than Fa, and he wept bitterly upon his passing, along with everyone else who had known him for the unassuming and honourable man that he was. The duke feared that the potential for a truly great and wise ruler died along with Ji Fa.

In the wake of his death, the king's spirit stayed in the room and, as the duke was the only one who perceived this, he had the room cleared before attempting to communicate.

'*I know what you have done, Dan,*' said the spectre, and Dan bowed down upon hearing his brother's voice.

'Forgive me, brother, but the Jade Book —'

'*I am aware of why you have defied me,*' he granted, '*and I understand that you could not confide in me without disclosing my own passing. Song is not yet the best man for the position, but I trust you will make it so. I support your decision, and trust you to see our great forefathers' aspirations brought to full realisation.*'

Dan rose, astounded to be vindicated. 'I shall not fail you in this.'

'*Be at peace, brother.*' Fa bowed to Dan, and the duke returned the sentiment. By the time he rose again, the spectre of his brother had vanished and the duke drew a deep breath for strength. His diplomatic skills were about to be tested to their limit, and Dan inwardly braced himself to face the consequences of his decision to refuse the throne.

18

THE REGENT OF JI SONG

Naturally Song suspected nothing of the micro-conspiracy that had swept through the court just prior to his father's death, as he had always fully expected to be king. But when he learned Dan was to be regent until he came of age, Song was none too happy. 'Why not Xian? He is the eldest of my uncles?'

'Your father left Xian as far east as possible for a reason,' Jiang Taigong pointed out. 'He is prone to war and thus not always of sound judgement.'

'This will not affect your marriage plans, or your goddess rite,' Dan added to reassure him. 'Only to speed them up, as we need your rule established quickly. In order to rule, you need to be granted the Great Mother's blessing on your reign via the goddess rite. And so that the Gao Mei rite is not wasted, you must be married, so as to pass her blessing on to your queen.'

'What do you mean "so that the Gao Mei rite is not wasted"?' Song queried, finding the phrasing curious.

'You will be briefed by the Great Mother before the rite takes place,' Dan advised, carefully avoiding that explosive subject for the moment. 'I suggest that after the funeral we accompany the king's body for burial on Li Shan, and stay for the rite of Gao Mei. Upon your return to Haojing you can immediately marry and —'

'— make little princes, I get the picture And what do we do when Uncle Xian takes offence to your regency? Are you prepared to kill your own brothers?'

'I promised your father I would kill every single one if that proved necessary to keep the peace.' Dan repeated his vow for Song's benefit.

'But I know you, Uncle, you do not give up power easily.' Song warily waved a finger at Dan. 'You gave up an entire province to maintain your influence over my father, and therefore the entire land —'

Dan was insulted by the prince's summation of his actions.

'How do I know you will hand over rule at the due time, and not use your considerable influence with the chieftains to usurp me?'

Jiang Taigong felt compelled to interject. 'I assure your majesty, Zhou Gong Dan is not such a man, but Guan Shu Xian definitely is.'

The duke held up a hand, thankful for the prime minister's support, but he was eager to settle this score himself. 'If I could retire to a large library in the middle of nowhere, I would be perfectly content for the rest of my days. I have no desire to rule, or even be at court, but until you come of age, I shall remain to advise you at Haojing as per your father's will.'

'And what of my will?' Song was obviously wondering how much free rein he would be allowed to have.

'You are the king. I serve you, majesty, and my resources are at your disposal.' Dan bowed his head to Song, although as a Wu he was his equal and not bound to do so.

'Until we have a conflict of interest,' Song figured.

'I feel very sure it will never come to that,' the duke replied confidently.

'I feel very sure it will,' Song replied, managing to get the duke's hackles up with the certainty of his statement. 'But we shall see. In the first place, I shall not be taking you with me to Li Shan. I will be taking Fen Gong.'

Dan was angered and entirely speechless for a moment. He had hoped to see Jiang Hudan and tell her what he had learned from Hreen, but apparently the prince intended to make it much more difficult for him to see her. So he sucked up his disappointment and managed an indifferent tone. 'Of course, majesty. There are many preparations I must to attend to.'

'Impressive,' Song assessed his uncle's demeanour and was satisfied for the moment. 'I shall not detain you.'

The duke gladly seized the opportunity to make a shrewd withdrawal.

The morning of Ji Fa's funeral, Ji Song personally went to check whether his bride-to-be was in any fit state to attend the service with him.

It had been reported to the prince that Yin Hui Ru had caused such a commotion with her unladylike behaviour and delusional rants, that she'd been moved out of the women's quarters and into a locked chamber in the palace that was usually reserved for important political prisoners. The house physicians were questioning if she was even mentally fit to be Queen of Zhou. Given these alarming reports Song felt that he should take a second look at his choice and see if she still tickled his fancy.

When the door was unbolted, Song entered to find Hui Ru hanging upside down from a rafter in her sleepwear, doing stomach crunches. 'Why are you not dressed?'

'Give me my clothes back and I will happily oblige.' She backflipped down to confront her visitor; her clothes were half hanging off her petite, fit form, and she wasn't at all worried that he was copping an eyeful of her bountiful cleavage.

'You cannot go to the king's funeral dressed like a poacher, or like this,' and he indicated her present clothing.

'The king is dead?' she said, clearly devastated.

'Some days now,' he replied.

'This is terrible news!' She backed up and took a seat on the bed, on top of the clothes that had been laid out for her to wear. 'Praise Shangdi for Zhou Gong.'

'Zhou Gong!' Song was sick to death of hearing how admired his uncle was. 'I am king! I am the Tianzi and thus the highest authority in the land.'

'But Zhou Gong is the wisest man alive, everyone knows that!' she told him and had no qualms in saying so. 'If I were the late king I would have named Zhou Gong my successor, in alignment with the new Zhou policy of awarding the office to the man most able. I feel sure Zhou Gong would take my troubles seriously.'

'Zhou Gong knows, just as I do, that there is no such thing as monsters or demons,' Ji Song reasoned.

'Oh!' Hui Ru gave a cry of frustration. 'Is there no one in the four quarters who will believe me?'

'You can stop the act,' Song appealed. 'You have my attention!'

'It is *not* an act!' She appeared at her wit's end, and Song was certainly nearing his.

'Then we will find a cure for this madness of yours —'

'The *cure* is for you to ride east with me, and kill the *thing* that is posing as my grandfather!' she challenged, and Song threw his hands up in complete bewilderment. 'What is necessary for you to take me seriously?' Hui Ru stood and took slow purposeful steps toward him. 'You want my body? Take it! I don't care! I shall sleep with every man in Haojing if it means I get my revenge.' She came to a stop before him.

I can see now why my advisors are so concerned, Song frowned, not knowing what to make of her. 'What kind of a lady would say such a thing?'

Hui Ru appeared tempted to be offended, but decided better of it. 'You are right, majesty, I am not the manner of woman who would do the Zhou honour as queen.' She knelt before him. 'Please, let me go and choose another more worthy. And allow me to pursue my quest to seek aid for my house, I beg you.' She bowed all the way down to the ground.

'I see your game now,' Song acknowledged and backed up few paces, offended. 'I am not eager to wed either, but I have no choice!'

'No, majesty, you misunderstand —'

'I could have you quartered for offending your king thus,' he shouted. 'You speak of defending your family from a beast! That beast is *you*, for you have *no* honour.'

Her hardline attitude changed as her mind ticked over, and she realised the volatile position she had placed herself in. 'I will dress for the funeral, if you still wish it,' She bowed to the ground again.

'So you can slip away at the first opportunity?' Song was not stupid. 'Or shame yourself beyond redemption before we wed? I think not.'

She raised her head to look at him, her large dark eyes afire with the conflict raging in her mind.

'The next time you need bother dressing is for our *wedding*,' he advised her sternly. 'And you had best be ready, willing and perfectly able, or I will have your house *burned to the ground*, along with everyone in it! Better that, than have you shame the house of the great Minister Jizi with your cowardly nonsense! Do you understand?'

She was openly weeping now, which only added to Song's disgust — he'd never purposely made a woman weep before. But as she was sobbing for shame, he was not moved by her performance. 'I understand, majesty. You are most gracious,' she said through gritted teeth.

The king was too irate to speak, but merely breathed heavily to maintain his composure as he exited the room and slammed the door in his wake.

'Bastard!' she yelled, and every muscle in Song's body tensed to prevent him from going back in there.

'Your majesty.' The head of the interior was waiting to hear what was to be done about the girl.

'I uphold my choice,' Song replied, jaw clenched in determination. 'I shall wed Yin Hui Ru tomorrow evening, when I return from Li Shan. *Do not* let her out of that room before then.'

The master of the interior was naturally completely mortified to hear this. 'If your majesty is certain.'

'Never more so.' Song was no scholar, and he was certainly no monk, but there was one rule his father had taught him to live by and that was to always leave a woman better than he found her. Whatever was truly behind Hui Ru's troubling behaviour he would expose it eventually, and hopefully he would do it with somewhat more patience than he had just displayed. It did not feel good to have reproached the woman he intended to marry, but Hui Ru obviously needed to grow up and do her great family honour, just as he must.

After his quarrel with Hui Ru, the funeral of Ji Fa was even more of an emotional drain for Song. The day was one of the longest of his young life, and the fact that he was suddenly expected to lead such a ceremony made it all the more harrowing.

The guarded procession out of town took an age, as people came from far and wide to farewell their late king, who had returned prosperity, stability and peace to their everyday lives. They also came to hail their new sovereign and it felt decidedly surreal to have the fate of the entire land resting in his hands.

It was like a beautiful, peaceful dream to finally be standing on the Li Shan jetty, with Fen Gong, his tigress and a handful of guards, to transport the large, ornately carved coffin containing the king's body. It was a few hours to sunset and yet an ample waxing moon rose over the steamy waters of the lake. Even the guards were quiet to show their respect for the occasion and the serenity of the place, as the torches of summons were set ablaze.

Song breathed deep of the warm moisture from the thermal waters and felt instantly revived, then turned to note Fen's hand on his shoulder. 'Thank you, my friend,' said Song, realising that he had the healer to thank for the sudden lift in his spirits.

'Thank you, majesty, for bringing me to visit my home,' Fen said, looking about proudly. The land abutting the jetty had been awarded to him by the late queen. 'I miss my sisters.'

Song grinned but made no derogatory comment.

'Very good, majesty,' Fen awarded, noting his restraint.

The king nodded. 'Not really. If I meet a Wu who reads thoughts, I am done for.'

Fen grinned. 'Honesty is also an admirable quality.'

'What I should I have said,' Song considered, 'is that … now that you are no longer required to be at the king's bedside every day, you shall be more at liberty to visit at least one of them.'

The young count was excited. 'I should love to take Ling Hu to visit her siblings.'

'You may do so immediately upon our return to Haojing,' Song granted.

'But your wedding, majesty?' Fen pointed out.

'Will be a very small, speedy affair, I should imagine,' Song advised, 'and your presence is not required. It is far more important that you are here with me on Li Shan, as Zhou Gong is such a boring travelling companion.'

'I have never found him so,' Fen said in defence of his lord.

Again Song grinned, but chose not to comment, as he turned his sights to the approaching ferry.

They need not have bothered with the soldiers, as the black clothed Wu who guarded the ferry had no problem raising and drawing Ji Fa's coffin on board their craft. Much to the king's and Fen's disappointment, it was not Hudan who was sent to greet them, but another of her ilk, and upon their arrival at Li Shan, Ji Song was led straight into a meeting with the Great Mother.

Yi Wu was not veiled today, and Song was rather smitten by her as she was far more attractive than expected. He wondered if this woman could possibly be the Great Mother, but when she spoke, he recognised her voice well enough. As he could find anyone by thinking about them, Yi Wu's decision to expose her face to him was flattering and a vote of confidence that he would gain her blessing on his reign.

The Great Mother expressed her deep condolences for the loss of her dear friend, Ji Fa, and advised that he would be laid to rest at dawn behind the temple of Heaven alongside Yi Jiang. 'You have some mighty boots to fill,' she emphasised, and then smiled in reassurance. 'But you will do your forefathers proud, brother Song. I have foreseen it.'

It was refreshing to have someone show some faith in him. 'I trust in your word, Great Mother, although many will not.'

'You may be a young man, Song, but you are an old soul. You must allow others time to see your potential, for you have yet to fully realise it yourself,' she counselled. 'Your first step along that path to greatness you will take tomorrow; so let us discuss that, shall we?'

Song's goddess rite would take place in the afternoon, so that he might return to Haojing by nightfall to be wed; there was no formal crowning — once the king died, his successor was sovereign. The Great Mother then discussed the purpose and particulars of the rite of Gao Mei, and Song got a rude shock when he discovered his goddess was to be chosen for him by Feng-Huang. The fact that he must abstain from ejaculation throughout the entire rite so that he might seed his queen was more than a little alarming, so he was not looking forward to the ride back to Haojing. Unless, of course, he used Wu means to get back there. He understood now, what Dan had meant when he'd suggested that the rite would be wasted without a wife! The expression on his face must have said it all.

'What did you expect, my young friend? No rite of passage is easy,' Yi Wu contended. 'This is a holy order, not a brothel.'

'I understand, Great Mother.' Inside, Song was raging to think that his uncle obviously knew the conditions of this rite and had never thought to set him straight on the matter. The prince considered Dan was probably feeling smug and superior right now, knowing what a slim chance it was that Song's aspiration to have Hudan as his goddess would be realised. But still, a chance was more than the duke had, and Song praised Tian for that. 'Is that all, Great Mother?'

'There is one more thing I need to make very clear to you.' Yi Wu leaned forward in her chair. 'The Wu in you must remain hidden from everyone who is not already aware. You must not use your power in front of anyone you do not intend to kill.'

'I had not planned to,' the king replied. 'My people will certainly not respect me if they believe I acquired my throne via supernatural means.'

Yi Wu smiled, satisfied. 'Wisely spoken. The powers must be developed and kept in reserve for another time.'

The assertion was interesting and Song wished to know more about that other time, but as he opened his mouth the Great Mother shook her head.

'On your deathbed, it shall be made clear,' she advised.

'But what use shall I be as an old man?' he appealed.

'I am older than you can imagine, and my soul-mind is older still. Do you think I have reached the end of my usefulness?'

'No, Great Mother,' Song said, humbly. 'I meant no offence, I am just curious about the many mysteries of this order that I do not understand.'

'Heed your mentor, Ji Song, and before long —' The Great Mother broke off her sentence as the young king appeared so aggravated by the advice. 'The lessons you find so tedious are more important than you think, for everything on earth is connected and has meaning. If you do not listen to the counsel of others, you may spend twice the amount of time, and endure far harder lessons, in gathering the knowledge and experience you need in order to understand the bigger picture by yourself. For we are all one.'

When Ji Song exited into the cloister, he was reeling from information overload, emotional exhaustion and stress. There was a novice of the house waiting to show him to his quarters, but as there was still an hour or so of daylight left he requested instead to take a turn in the garden. The young king was led to the gate in the heaven's garden courtyard, which he'd never even noticed before, and there he excused his guide.

Song had been made aware that Hudan often spent time in the garden at this time of day, and at the fork in the path he heard laugher and followed it down the low road toward the thermal pool.

To the king's utter delight, Fen was in the water, and Hudan was just climbing out of the heated pool, her fully naked form steaming and glistening in the last of the sunlight. On her left thigh Song noted the dark stripe of a birthmark, and grinned. Such a mark made her easily differentiated from other women, and he wondered if Zhou Gong had ever seen it. *Probably not.* He considered his uncle too refined to seduce his way underneath the skirts of such a woman. 'Brothers!' he called loudly to announce himself and Hudan wound her drying cloth around her as Fen waved the king forth.

'Come in, majesty, this is just what you need.' Fen swam about, appearing completely revitalised.

'I feel you are right about that,' he awarded, looking at Hudan. 'If that will cause no offence?'

'Not at all, I was just leaving.' Hudan walked past him toward the exit pathway, as Song began to strip. 'I have made up your old bed,' Hudan advised Fen, 'if you'd like to sleep in our room?'

'I would like that, very much,' he said, grinning broadly.

'Why do you always get to have a slumber party with the girls?' Song jested, and then looked to Hudan. 'Afraid I might pop in for a visit?' He stripped his shirt away to show off his perfectly crafted body.

'Not at all … I know your majesty is far smarter than that.' Although her retort amused him, her smile faded. 'I was very sad to learn of the death of your father. I am so sorry for your loss.' Hudan bowed her head to quell her grief. 'Brother Fa was a dear and treasured friend, and a compassionate and wise leader of men.'

'I hope that some day you will consider me in the same terms,' Song said, accepting her condolences with a gentle smile.

Hudan nodded once, her smile genuine this time. 'I must also congratulate you on your engagement. I wish you every happiness.'

'I thank you,' he accepted, not keen to dwell on the subject. 'But nothing would make me happier than to see you tomorrow.'

The look of challenge on Hudan's face told him he did not need to elaborate on that comment, but he felt he would anyway.

'Would you not be honoured to be my goddess?' the young king asked. He wondered how well she could mask the feelings for his uncle that she was not permitted to have.

'Majesty?' Fen cautioned. 'My brother is not your subject, do not presume to treat her as such.'

'Fen,' Hudan held up a hand to silence him. 'His majesty is just teasing,' she said coolly. 'He has not yet learned to respect and treasure his allies. At present he takes everyone for granted, as we were so loyal to his father. But beware, brother, lest you find yourself without anyone to watch your back.'

'I am sorry,' the king pleaded, 'but I fail to see what I have said to cause offence?' The Wu knew he was toying with her, but she was the one in the wrong not he. 'Is it wrong of me to aspire to live my dreams?'

She appeared to be pained by his words. 'Only if they serve the greater good of *all*.'

Song put on a baffled expression to pose: 'And who would not be served in this instance?'

Hudan met his questioning gaze and stared back at him defiantly. Yes, he knew her secret, but in this instance the duke should not be a factor. 'Fen?' The king looked to the count, who turned his rueful sights away and would not answer.

'You want to play with me?' Hudan drew his attention back to her, and she had a dare in her eye. 'Game on.' She grabbed her clothes and departed up the path.

'I thought your diplomatic skills were improving,' Fen commented, 'but obviously I was mistaken.'

'Just tell me the cause of my offence?' the king requested of Fen, but the young count grew tried of the game and ducked under the water.

It was not until the morning of the royal wedding that the master of the interior came to inform Dan that no one dared enter the locked chamber of the king's betrothed.

The duke was alarmed at this, but curious to be brought up to speed on the king's chosen bride.

'My humble observation is that the king's queen-to-be is delusional and violent.'

'She is martial, you say?' Dan was intrigued by this point. Could Song have randomly chosen his perfect match? 'I don't recall interviewing any candidates who fitted that description?'

'That is why I felt my duke must be informed. Apparently, Yin Hui Ru deceived this house by sending her maid in her stead to the interviews, hence I fear she may not even be a maiden! And she will let no one near her to confirm the fact.' The master panicked. 'Her uncouth behaviour only serves to vindicate my fears ... she openly called his majesty *a bastard*,' he whispered, his expression filled with horror.

But the tale brought a smile to Dan's face. 'I like her already.' He thought it best to meet with the girl at once, and accompanied the master of the interior to her chamber.

As the door beneath her opened, Hui Ru teetered on top of the door trim, bracing herself against the ceiling corner. The guard moved to accompany the visitor into her room, but they paused in the open doorway and Hui Ru took this to be her cue to swing down and take them both out.

'I shall be fine —' The lord was saying when her foot connected with his jaw and he was sent reeling backward, along with the guard beside him. Their heads collided with the floor and both were knocked unconscious.

Hui Ru came to land outside her prison door as the head of the interior rushed to the lord's side.

'Zhou Gong!' The servant shook Dan in an attempt to revive him and her heart stopped beating.

'That is Zhou Gong?' she gasped, immediately regretting that she'd picked this moment to make her escape. He had come to speak with her! It was alarming to discover she had just kicked her best hope of support in face.

'You will burn for this!' the house servant threatened, waving an accusing finger at her. A sweeping kick to his jaw silenced him.

Hui Ru quickly dragged the three men into her prison cell, and stripped the guard of his amour to disguise herself.

Unable to revive Zhou Gong, Hui Ru stood and bowed to him. 'A thousand apologies, Zhou Gong. I pray I have caused you no severe injury.'

On the way out, Hui Ru locked the door behind her and slipped through Haojing's guard posts unchallenged.

The duke was shaken awake, and was instantly aware of a blistering headache as he sat up. 'Fetch Fen Gong!' he commanded.

'He did not return from Li Shan with the prince,' the head of the interior explained, 'but was granted leave to visit his sister at Shao.'

The duke collapsed back onto the bed at that news. 'Then let me rest.'

'Wake up, Zhou Gong, we need to talk!' Ji Song's voice boomed, and he sounded quite irate. 'Leave us!' he said to all others present.

Through bleary eyes, Dan perceived the young king pacing as his house staff and physicians fled the room.

'Did my betrothed do this to you in order to escape our vows?' the king demanded, as Dan struggled to sit upright. 'Because if she did, I will have the house of Minister Jizi burned to the ground, exactly as I promised her I would.'

'What?' Dan staggered to his feet upon learning of Song's intentions. He attempted to cover for the girl. 'I let her go, as she would not consent to the marriage.'

Song cocked an eye, challenging his uncle's statement. 'In that case, I shall have our head of the interior and her guard executed for lying, as they said Yin Hui Ru attacked you. From the look of you, I would say they are telling the truth, but I will heed the words of my regent, of course.'

Dan's head was throbbing and he knew he wasn't reasoning straight. 'They are telling the truth,' Dan admitted. 'But to burn the house of a respected man of Shang is hardly going to promote —'

'Hui Ru knew the repercussions when she did this to you ... to me!' Song seethed. 'I have gone to *considerable* pains to secure the Great Mother's blessing on my reign. I have the erection from hell, and no goddamn queen!'

Dan found it difficult not to be amused by the young king's grievances and it showed.

'Funny, is it?' Song said, smugly. 'It was the apple of your eye who gave me this encumbrance. I can still feel her pleasure coursing all over it.'

The notion got Dan's adrenalin pumping, although he had expected such a claim from Song. Whether it was the truth was quite another matter. 'How could you possibly tell, when your goddess was veiled and masked?'

Song's smile broadened. 'Jiang Hudan has a tiger stripe across her left hip.'

The truth of his words plunged an emotional dagger deep into Dan's heart, and his chest caved in as painful shock waves reverberated through his being.

'So you *have* seen it ... you old deviant.' Song sounded impressed, but he continued taunting his uncle. 'Still, she was a maid when I took her, so I guess she never really let you in.'

Dan flew at Song, who vanished and reappeared behind him. 'I told you there would be a conflict of interest. And as it seems you have blatantly lied to me on several counts already, I really cannot see that this partnership is going to work out.'

'You want my resignation?' Dan was fuming. Not the will of heaven, nor history, nor his dead brother would enable him to overcome the loathing he felt in this moment. Never had he wanted to kill a man so much, not even Zi Shou.

Song grinned. 'I shall tell everyone you did the right thing and abdicated the regency in favour of Uncle Xian.'

This had been Ji Fa's worst nightmare, and what he had attempted to avoid with his original will. But now Dan wanted to terminate the alliance as much as Song did. The duke had strived to form a bond with the king, but he would not be the object of his emotional abuse and ridicule any longer. He could not guide and support someone he could not abide to be near.

'Whatever pleases your majesty,' Dan granted.

'Will you leave court?' Song inquired.

'I expect so.'

'And where will you go? To your son's province in the East?' Song emphasised the fact that Dan had done himself out of a province and his political career. 'Or will you run to the Great Mother at Li Shan?'

'Does your majesty think you will have need to call on me in the future?' Dan queried him back.

'I very much doubt it.'

'Then it should hardly make any difference where I go,' Dan retorted.

'Stir up trouble for me and I shall hunt you down, Uncle,' Song warned.

'I swear to you, majesty, you shall never hear from me again.' The duke bowed to see him on his way.

'I shall have your horse saddled and brought around to the courtyard,' the king said, and departed, happy with the outcome.

The thought of Song pleasuring Hudan fuelled Dan's desire to get out of the palace, and he quickly collected the few belongings he could not leave behind, such as the qin Ji Fa had had fashioned for him.

'Zhou Gong!' Jiang Taigong entered ahead of being announced as he was in too much of a panic to endure formality. 'Tell me it is *not true* ... surely you would not resign the appointment our late king awarded you! Whatever our Zhou has done to offend you, or you him, you must overcome for the greater good.'

'The king is a youth and as yet has no understanding,' Dan snarled, continuing to pack his things into saddlebags. He had no desire to debate the matter further. 'The one who has offended the spirits is I, Dan.'

'No!' The prime minister would not believe it. 'I know you, Zhou Gong. You are covering for him.'

'You have it backward. And I am just Ji Dan now, my friend,' he pointed out, as he hooked his bags over his shoulder and picked up his qin case before bowing to Jiang Taigong, the longest serving advisor of the court. 'Farewell, Jiang Taigong. It has been an honour to serve Zhou with you.'

The prime minister watched with sadness as his longtime ally and co-conspirator departed. 'Heaven help us if the Jade Book was right,' Jiang Taigong commented after him.

No longer was Dan going to take the responsibility for history running its proper course. Tian had dealt him a cruel blow this day, and if the prophecy of their victory never came to pass, then let it be on heaven's conscience. Dan was fleeing this new regime before Song decided he'd much prefer to see his uncle locked in a cell.

PART 5

THE DROPA

19

SANCTUARY AT SHAO

The frosty dawn found Ji Dan approaching the Li Shan jetty, numb from cold and thought. He'd been in two minds about coming here, which is why the journey had taken all night. The notion of seeing Hudan in the wake of being bended to the will of his nephew was harrowing. He didn't want to see the regret in her eyes, or worse, that she had none! But he felt the Great Mother had to be told what her new candidate was planning; perhaps she could advise on what Dan's next move should be.

Dan left his horse to graze and began walking the tree-lined track toward the jetty. About when he was noting that the wafting warm wind that blew across the thermal lake was not so prominent this morning, he spied a strange anomaly up ahead and ran to investigate.

The Li Shan jetty was gone! The lake had been reduced and was now a few large pools scattered around the rocky base of the mountain. The rocks were not wet or mossy and, as Dan ran in the direction that the ferry usually took, it seemed more like the lake had never existed rather than that it had disappeared overnight!

The cavern that marked the entrance to the Wu fortress was nothing but a large hollow, with a gaping hole through to the surface above, where the staircase to the cloister had once been.

There is no temple. Dan suddenly recalled Huxin's words on his first morning on Li Shan. *What if I told you none of this is really here? We are not really here … Time, space, reality,* individuality, *are an illusion created by heaven to understand earth.*

'You can't do this!' Dan collapsed to his knees under the weight of the implications and was distraught beyond reason that it could have vanished. He may have always been a loner, but he had never been without support before — without a home, or purpose! In the absence of the Great Mother's vindication and Hudan's love, he had nothing!

Did Song lie about obtaining the Great Mother's sanction on his rule? Had the new king offended the great House of Yi Wu Li Shan, or was it Dan's own forbidden love that had done it?

'If I have offended heaven, then tell me what I must do to make amends!' His voice echoed loudly round the cavern, but was not answered. 'You have no right to take her from me! Or to give her to another!' he yelled out, his frustration boiling over, but he was immediately repentant and bowed down to allow his tears to flow. 'Please don't take her away ...'

Exhausted, wounded and utterly baffled, Dan fell on his side and rolled over to stare at the ceiling of the cavern.

Perhaps I am still unconscious and this is a dream? The pain felt real, but as his eyelids wavered and then closed and his conscious thoughts dulled, his torment was slowly diluted into the dream state of a fitful sleep.

Today we shall reach Shao. Fen took comfort in the thought as he awoke curled up against his warm tigress. He had no desire to rise and face the winter morning chill, but a strong urge to stretch the kinks from his body after lying under a tree all night compelled him to move.

Ling Hu took the opportunity do the same, then suddenly rolled over and sat up to give a bemused whine.

'What is —'

A hand slapped over Fen's mouth and he was startled out of his wits. 'Boo!'

When Fen heard Hudan's laugh, he was relieved to turn about and behold his sister. 'Brother Hudan!' He embraced her tightly. 'I am overjoyed to see you!' He held her at arm's length to look at her. 'How it is you are here, on the road to Shao?'

'Do you remember that quest the Great Mother kept saying I'd embark on one day?' Hudan posed with a large smile, and Fen nodded. 'That day finally came. And, as I was headed this way in any case, I wanted to take the opportunity to see my sister first.'

'I am taking Ling Hu to visit her siblings also,' Fen said, overjoyed to have another travelling companion for the remainder of the journey. 'The three of us together again … I could not ask Tian for a better gift!'

Hudan moved to greet and pat the tigress. 'It is indeed a happy coincidence.' She pulled her cloak tighter round her, as the wind chill and sky were threatening snow, and then looked to the road, eager to get moving.

Fen's stomach rumbled loudly, and Ling Hu whimpered, concerned for him. 'I hope it isn't much further.'

'Well, I'm not supposed to do this …' Hudan manifested a ripe juicy pear in her hand, which in the middle of winter was an amazing treat, and tossed it to her little brother.

'Thank you!' He rose to stand with Hudan, and Ling Hu whimpered to plead the case of her stomach. Hudan directed Ling Hu to the road, where a small boar suddenly appeared, and the tigress took off after it.

'Why did you not take lodging in a village? Surely you could sneak Ling Hu in, given her little talent?' Hudan queried, retrieving her staff from the ground and trailing the lioness to the road at a much slower pace.

'Old habits die hard,' Fen explained, untying his horse's reins from a tree branch to lead her back to the road. 'And if Ling Hu gets bored while I am sleeping?' He shook his head to indicate the outcome was not good. 'If we sleep out here, she knows I'll freeze to death if she leaves me, so it's safer all round.'

Hudan smiled. 'I'm impressed by the lengths you will go to to make the relationship work.'

'Well, she's my responsibility,' Fen said, as he caught up to Hudan. 'You wouldn't lead your child anywhere you knew they might get into trouble, right?'

'Quite right,' Hudan agreed. 'You are an excellent parent. But then, I always thought you would be.' She ruffled his hair affectionately and Fen edged away from the attention, even though he secretly missed being teased by his sisters.

'So tell me of your quest,' Fen said, liking the idea of walking for a bit as it was warming his frozen limbs.

'I am taking Taiji home,' Hudan replied, admiring the staff in her hand.

'You are going in search of the Star Sea?' His heart began beating fast in panic as she nodded enthusiastically. 'Over the mountains, in the middle of winter?' He raised his eyebrows in disbelief.

'Better when the snow is hard than when it is melting,' Hudan advised. 'Besides, I have my talent to extract myself from any bad scrapes, and elementals to keep me warm if need be.'

'Really!' Fen was freezing. 'Would you mind sharing some of those?'

At that moment the sun penetrated the heavy morning mist, which began to break up in the warmth. Fen looked at his sister sideways, and Hudan laughed and shook her head to indicate it was purely a happy coincidence.

'Eat your pear,' she encouraged, pulling a carrot from thin air to feed to his horse. 'If we ride, we should make our destination by lunch.'

As Ling Hu had only just killed her breakfast, they continued to stroll as Fen ate. 'But why are you returning the staff? How do you know if there is anyone to return the staff to?'

'Our mother came from somewhere … brother Shi came from somewhere, and even your origins are in question?' Hudan said. 'I want to know where home is, who my people are, really.'

'But Li Shan is your home?' Fen didn't understand her sudden need to trek off into the wilderness.

Hudan forced a smile, and Fen wasn't sure what it meant. Did Li Shan not feel like home to her now that he and Huxin had left? 'Is there something you are not telling me?'

'Probably.' She inhaled deeply, as if it was her first breath of fresh air in an age.

'Hudan …' Fen took hold of her arm to bring her to a halt. 'If you have trouble —'

'No trouble,' she assured. 'There is nothing wrong with wanting to find one's clan.'

'But what if you do find them ... will you stay?' Fen was starting to fret that he'd never see her again.

'Fen, I can find you with a thought,' she reminded him, 'so I shall never be far afield.'

That was comforting. 'I wish I could do the same. The Great Mother said I must learn the art of thought motion.'

Hudan placed an arm around him and squeezed. 'Then perhaps it is time Huxin and I taught you.'

'So you intend to stay at Shao a little while.'

Hudan gave a noncommittal nod. 'We shall keep an eye on the weather and see how it goes.'

Shao was located in a valley that opened to the east and was surrounded by hills on the other three sides. The location was strategic to control the pass through the Qin Ling mountains of Qiang and the upper Jia-ling River.

The fields of the outlying farms were dormant at this time of year, but the village outside the stronghold was busy at the midday hour of this brisk sunny day.

'To think our sister is the first lady over everyone and that *this* is only the gateway to all Shi's provinces,' Fen said, and gave an impressed whistle.

When considered that way, the fact was rather surreal, and Hudan wondered how Huxin was coping with her life as a ruler, wife and mother? She was suddenly very excited at the prospect of seeing her sister again and learning of all that had transpired during the last year or so.

At the end of the thoroughfare through town, they came to the stronghold's estate. Fen announced himself as Zhou Bo Fen Gong, and Shanyu Jiang Hudan's name was well known in these parts, so the huge gates of the fortress were opened to permit them entry.

Inside the gates, they both dismounted and were led by a guard across the courtyard to the stairs of the main house, at the top of which Huxin and Shi stood, appearing very official. Huxin descended the stairs to greet them formally. 'Welcome to Shao,' she said as she came to stand before them, her expression serious.

'My brothers,' she broke into a smile and flung her arms open wide to hug them both. 'I cannot believe you are both here!'

'I feared you might have become reserved and ladylike,' Fen grinned, mocking Huxin's boisterous welcome.

'We do not stand on formality here,' Shi assured from the top of the stairway, and Hudan broke away from her sister to scale the stairs and hug Shi. 'You both appear to be thriving.'

'We love it here!' Huxin told her, grabbing Fen's hand to drag him up the stairs with her. 'I cannot wait for you to see the twins!'

'But where is Ling Hu?' Shi queried, looking about for the albino tigress.

Huxin came to a stop, also interested in the answer. 'Did you not bring her?'

Fen frowned and grinned at once, as he eyed the area. 'Ling Hu, there is no need to be nervous,' he called. 'You can come out.'

'Come out?' Huxin queried with a frown, as there was nowhere to hide in the immediate vicinity.

Fen let go of Huxin's hand and walked away from everyone. 'Here, girl,' he called quietly. When the tigress still did not appear, Fen gave a quiet whimper, at which time Ling Hu manifested alongside to lick his face.

Huxin and Shi were both completely floored by this occurrence, and Huxin lowered her hand from where it had momentarily hidden her shocked expression. 'She is like you!' Huxin exclaimed in wonder, looking at Hudan who was grinning broadly.

As Huxin moved to be introduced to her extraordinary offspring, Hudan noted Shi's amusement. 'This is going to add a whole new dimension to hide and seek,' he told her, chuckling.

The twins, Zhen and Kao, spent much of their day romping around the huge courtyard enclosure that was an extension of their large nursery. They still had the appearance of cute and fuzzy cubs, no bigger than a small dog or a human toddler, which is exactly what they were. Huxin had been teaching them the game she had been taught by Wu Yi as a child, where she would call out 'skin', or 'fur', at any given time, and they had begun to compete to see who reacted and transformed the fastest. This was important training, for they needed to be able to maintain one form or the other according to their will, and not just shift randomly, as they did more often than not at present.

Their party watched the cubs in the courtyard, rumbling with each other, from inside the nursery. The cubs were blissfully ignorant of the fact that they had an audience.

'Shall we go meet your siblings?' Fen asked his tigress, who raised her eyebrows, worried, whimpered and vanished again.

'Scaredy cat,' Fen teased, 'they're not going to bite —' He observed Kao clamp his jaws around his sister's head. 'Well, maybe they will? But you are bigger than they are.'

'And I was worried she would be too aggressive with her smaller siblings,' Huxin said, boggling at the timidity of her spirit daughter.

'Just don't threaten Fen,' Hudan warned, letting them know the tigress had a dangerous streak. 'She seems to read situations according to his feelings.'

'Are you scared of your niece and nephew?' Huxin asked Fen, playfully poking him.

'Of course not.' He considered his feelings. 'Perhaps it is more that I am anxious for this reunion to go well.'

'Then let us proceed.' She smiled nervously, and then looked back to the courtyard. 'Zhen! Kao!' Huxin called, and the twins broke off their combat to come bolting toward her.

'Skins!' she cued. Both cubs skidded to a halt to focus on their transformation. Once complete, and finding themselves on all fours, the twins propped themselves onto their unsteady feet and tottered over to their parents. Kao reached his mother just ahead of Zhen, who cast herself into her father's awaiting snuggle.

The scene was heartwarming as it was rare to see a noble family so close and attentive to one another. Huxin, who had a good serve of yang in her, and Shi, who was very yin in nature, were a perfect balance and obviously very much in love with each other and their children. Hudan, who did not have a maternal bone in her body, still felt her niece and nephew were the cutest, happiest babes she had ever laid eyes on.

'You need some clothes,' Shi told Zhen.

'No!' She shook her head.

'No?' Shi made a 'brrrr' sound, wrapping his fur-lined vest about her. 'I think you'll get cold.'

But Zhen's attention had been diverted to the other side of the room and her eyes lit up as she pointed and said, 'Tiger!'

Kao turned about in Huxin's arms and squealed with delight upon seeing the pure white tiger vanish.

The toddlers gasped and wriggled their feet to get down on the ground, and Huxin looked to Fen as she let them go.

'It will be all right,' he assured her. 'Ling Hu's had plenty of practice with the prince.'

Zhen and Kao were searching the nursery cautiously and when Ling Hu suddenly appeared again, they both released an ear-piercing squeal of shock and ran laughing back to their parents waiting arms.

Ling Hu ran to Fen, who gave her plenty of praise and reassurance.

Utterly delighted by it all, Hudan couldn't wipe the smile off her face, as it had been some time since she'd felt so grateful just to be alive and in the moment. Life was simple here in Shao — the last outpost before the wilds of the mountains to the east, south and north. Strangely, it already felt more like home than Li Shan ever had, and something told Hudan that she would be in no hurry to leave.

I believe I made the right decision, she told herself. Hudan may have missed this happy occasion if she had chosen differently. Such good fortune was surely a sign from Tian that she was on the right path.

In her heart she felt at peace with what she'd done.

To Hudan's delight, Huxin and Shi practised Dao Yin in the morning, and Fen joined them to make it a real family affair. They then ate together and Fen joined Shi in the afternoon to attend to state matters, affording Hudan and Huxin time to catch up on the events of the past year.

They spoke of the loss of Ji Fa as they strolled through the winter garden, and reminisced about their adventures with him. Hudan conveyed the story of Fen's kidnapping and of how Ling Hu's gift had been exposed during that dramatic rescue.

'I must say I am surprised to see you and Fen here and no Zhou Gong.' Huxin held both hands, palm up, in wonder. 'You haven't said a word about Ji Dan all afternoon.'

Hudan was disturbed by the topic. 'What do you want to know?'

'Is he still your guilty pleasure?' she asked openly, as there were no servants within earshot in the garden and a good steady breeze to drown their conversation.

Hudan shook her head. 'We were nearly caught by Ji Song, the night the twins were born.' She knew Huxin would find the information juicy.

Huxin gasped, unsure of whether to frown or smile. 'Not dull!' She was happy for Hudan, and Hudan served her a look that implied she thought her quite demented. 'So where is he?'

'Back at Haojing, serving the royal adolescent, I imagine.' The comment caused Huxin to grip Hudan's arm with both hands as she nearly collapsed laughing.

'I thank heaven Ji Song has yet to summon Shi to the capital,' Huxin said, but toned down her mirth as she spied the head of the exterior rushing double-time up the path behind them.

'My lady. The master told me to let you to know we have another guest …' He appeared very excited. 'Zhou Gong is here!'

Hudan's heart leapt into her throat at the announcement.

Huxin raised her eyebrows, utterly delighted. 'Not at Haojing, after all.'

'The relevant question being why not,' Hudan mused, folding her arms in bafflement. She drew a deep breath for courage.

'Let us go find out … shall we?' Huxin pulled her sister back toward the house.

Once Shi had sent a servant to inform his wife that they had another surprise guest, he looked back at Dan, who'd collapsed into a chair in the council chamber. He'd never seen his older brother appear so dishevelled. 'What has happened?'

'I quit the regency,' he informed them bluntly, through barely parted eyelids.

'No, you cannot have!' Fen exclaimed. 'What of our late brother's wishes?'

Dan held his head, which clearly ailed him. 'It is better this way,' he replied, eyes lowered to the floor, despondent. 'There will be no revolt.'

'Have you been drinking?' Shi noted Dan's words were a little slurred.

'The House of Yi Wu Li Shan has vanished from the face of the earth!' Dan blurted out.

'You *have* been drinking,' Shi deduced.

'Hudan is gone!' he mumbled, tears of distress rimming his eyes.

'No, Hudan is here,' Shi was happy to inform him, although deeply concerned for his brother's mental health.

When Dan looked at Fen and he nodded to confirm Shi's statement, he was overjoyed. But his happiness quickly deteriorated into horror as he found his sobriety. Reaching up, Dan grabbed hold of Shi by the shirt to appeal. 'Please ... I cannot face her like this!'

After a close whiff of him, Shi had to agree. 'Right you are,' Shi said as he released himself from Dan's grasp and asked his master of the interior to have a bath prepared.

'Why did you quit?' Fen moved in close to get Dan to focus. 'And what do you mean, Li Shan has disappeared?'

'House, lake, jetty, ferry, gone! Poof!' Dan twirled his hands once to mark his words. 'I was starting to wonder if any of you were really here.' He gave Fen a couple of friendly slaps on the cheek, happy to see him in the flesh, then had a more serious concern. 'Did Song receive the Great Mother's mandate?'

'Yes,' Fen nodded, 'I was there when he did, and she predicted that one day he would be remembered as Zhou Cheng.'

'Yi Wu said that?' Dan was clearly baffled to hear this. 'What *was* she thinking?' He forced a laugh. 'Song is not accomplished and is anything *but* sincere. The Jade Book prophecy unfolds,' he said mysteriously. 'But then the Great Mother was the author, so

494

her actions are not *so* remarkable. Still, at present I have more faith in the babe *Yu* living up to the name *Cheng*.'

Both Fen and Shi stood with jaws flapping in the breeze in the wake of Ji Dan's rant, which was bordering on treasonous and was arrogantly disrespectful to the Great Mother.

'You are not yourself, brother,' Fen croaked, finding his voice.

'We should get you to a bath and rested before you see *anyone*,' Shi suggested, giving Fen a hand to get Dan to his feet. Only once he'd recovered from whatever trauma he'd been through would they be able get any sense out of him.

'Come, I shall heal your head,' Fen said, noting his lord was bloodied both on his forehead and the back of his skull.

'I have dreamt of little else all week.' Dan was grateful as he staggered to standing. He leant heavily on Fen to make good his timely retreat to the guest chambers.

When Hudan and Huxin arrived to greet Zhou Gong, Shi apologised for dragging them inside so quickly, as Dan was weary from his journey and needed to rest.

'But why is he at Shao,' Hudan asked, 'when he should be at Haojing advising the new king?' The pained look on Shi's face told Hudan something wasn't right.

'My brother has had a bump on the head, and until Fen is done with him and he has had time to rest, I shall not be able to tell you.'

'He is hurt?' Hudan was alarmed.

'Not beyond Fen's healing,' Shi pointed out, 'but Dan has been through something traumatic —'

Hudan was already heading for the guest quarters. 'I should see him.'

'He does not wish to see you until he has recovered.' Shi's statement stopped her in her tracks.

'He knows I am here?' Hudan swung back around to rejoin the conversation.

'He does,' Shi confirmed.

'And he does not wish to see me?' The hurt she felt caused her voice to crack, and she cleared her throat, as a painful emotional lump had formed in it.

'Not until he has had a chance to recover,' Shi repeated, and Hudan found that very curious.

'Since when has he needed his strength to face me?' If he was ailing Dan usually wanted her near ... there was something seriously wrong.

'Please do not worry,' Shi said hastily, hating that he'd upset her. 'He is very eager to see you, and was overjoyed to learn you are here.'

She forced a smile, so that her brother-in-law would not feel bad. 'Please let me know as soon as he is prepared to grant me an audience,' she said graciously, and backed up a few paces to turn and make for the door.

'Hudan —' Huxin moved to go after her, but her sister held up a hand to bid her stay.

Quickly departing the halls of governance, Hudan took another turn into the garden, where she hoped to work off her discontent.

Some time in nature practising her craft had lessened Hudan's tension, and despite Ji Dan's all too obvious absence at the dinner table, she suppressed her intuitive concerns and made the most of the happy occasion. Fen joined them late, to report that the patient was resting peacefully and should be as right as rain by tomorrow.

I can be patient, had been Hudan's mantra for the evening.

Dinner was a lovely drawn-out affair, and she enjoyed playing hide and seek with the family before the twins' bedtime. The adult banter around the fireplace afterward continued well on into the wee hours of the morning over too much warmed wine. Only at festival time did they ever have nights like this together, and all four of them might have fallen asleep in front of the fire, had the head of the interior at Shao not humbly suggested they call it a night.

Hudan had actually fallen asleep on Fen, but once roused and sent off to her room and having changed and settled into bed, she was wide awake again. Her inebriated thoughts turned to Dan, in the room down the hall. She was starting to really worry about him, as he never rested this much. *I should check in on him,* she thought, and clambered out of bed, then stood up and swayed about a little. 'I am good,' she decided as she found her balance.

She managed to walk a straight, quiet, line down the hallway and, looking back to ensure no one had been alerted, she collided into someone and made a muffled sound as a hand was slapped over her mouth.

'Hudan?' She was swung around to view her assailant.

'Aaan!' Hudan hummed, as the lord dragged her back into his room, where a lantern was still burning.

'I was coming to see you —' they both said at once, as Dan let her go to close the door. Hudan suppressed a laugh and tottered about in the wake of being released, as it felt like the room was swaying.

'Are you … drunk?' Dan queried her unusually good cheer, and Hudan pinched her index finger near her thumb to imply 'a little'. 'And I was concerned about you seeing me thus!' He gave a laugh, amused to see her so uninhibited.

'You were drunk …' Hudan raised her eyebrows, intrigued, as she found her centre and stilled. 'That's why you didn't want to see me?'

'That, and …' He hesitated to spoil her good mood. 'After what happened at the Gao Mei rite, I wasn't sure you would want to see me.'

'Why? What happened?' Hudan queried, and Dan was curious about her response.

'His majesty told me that you were chosen as his goddess,' Dan informed her, and her eyes grew wide in comprehension. 'He identified you by your birthmark.'

Hudan was so angry she couldn't speak for a second. 'His boast to you is impossible as I left Li Shan immediately after Ji Fa's burial, before the goddess rite even began.'

Dan breathed a huge sigh of relief. 'The Great Mother allowed you to forgo the rite?'

Hudan shook her head. 'I chose banishment.'

Dan caught his breath.

'However sordid our love life might have been in another life, I am not about to repeat those shortcomings in this one.' Hudan became teary; the wine was making her over-emotional.

'No ...' Dan took hold of her hands. 'Hreen said that you had always had a connection with the son of the sky within Song, but that you had never been his.'

'I'd like to connect with him right now!' Hudan threatened under her breath. Then as the full wording of his statement fully sank in, she did a double take. 'When did you speak with the Lord of Time?'

'More important is that I did, and he assured me you have never willingly betrayed me, nor I you.'

The moment they both realised all was well between them, their lips met and their bodies entwined. Hudan had not expected to be awarded the opportunity to see Dan before departing on her quest, so this was another happy blessing from Tian. But in the midst of their mutual emotional delirium, Hudan realised there were still questions to be answered, and she pulled away, compelled to question him. 'Why are you here at Shao?'

Breathing heavily in the wake of their affectionate outpouring, Dan appeared pained by the question. 'I too chose banishment,' he confessed.

'You quit the regency, when brother Fa wanted you to be king,' Hudan was horrified. 'Why?'

'The Jade Book said Cheng, son of Wu would rule,' Dan said, defending his actions.

'And?' Hudan knew there must have been more as Song was too young to rule alone.

'I am not playing this game any more! I shall not be responsible for keeping history on track according to Yi Wu's will, when even she has abandoned our cause!' Dan seated himself, as the romantic mood took a dive.

'What are you talking about?' Hudan was confused and hoped it wasn't the wine making her vague.

'Li Shan is *gone*, without a trace that it ever existed!' Dan spelt it out for her. The devastation and shock she felt upon learning this must have been written on her face, as he added more gently: 'I thought you had gone, too.'

The sorrowful look on his face melted her heart, and Hudan came to kneel before him, feeling a little overwhelmed herself. 'I had expected that once my quest was done, the Great Mother might take me back, but clearly that will be not be the case.'

'Your quest?' Dan sat forward in his seat.

'I am to return Taiji to Bayan Har Shan,' she advised, and Dan's interest was piqued by the notion.

'I have had a mind to go there myself,' he said. Hudan forced a smile, thinking it a delightful dream that had no basis in reality.

'Who did the Jade Book name as regent?' Hudan reverted to her previous query, and Dan slumped back in the chair, bored by the topic.

'Zhou Gong,' he admitted. 'Apparently, we are to put down a rebellion in the East together,' he stated with a good serve of irony, 'which our new Zhou is about to spark by setting fire to the House of Jizi!'

Hudan was perplexed and slapped her hands down hard on Dan's knees. 'Why are you still here!'

'Song will not listen to me as Fa did.' He stood to distance himself from any further attacks. 'He wanted me gone, so I left before he could gang up with Xian against me and *I* ended up rotting in prison! Now that the Great Mother has up and fled, I have no hope of bringing our young upstart into line.' Dan threw his hands up in despair.

Hudan breathed deep to reflect on the circumstances, and raised herself upright in the chair. 'If the House of Li Shan has departed, it is because, in heaven's eyes, the crisis has passed … perhaps it is not as grave as you think?'

'Song meant to crush me when he lied about you …' Dan suddenly twigged, and was floored in retrospect. 'I knew I was not his favourite person in the world, but I had no idea his malice was so deep-seated. The slanderous claims he made about you are unforgivable.'

'Song is a boy, a child!' Hudan emphasised. 'He *envies* you, and hates that you are so well respected. He covets what you have because he feels he has something to prove *to you*. Not because he despises you, but because he secretly idolises you.'

'He has a strange way of showing it.' Dan was not convinced.

'You must go back,' Hudan informed him timidly. 'As it is, Zhou Gong Dan has not reached his potential and never shall, if he no longer exists.'

'Not if Song bowed down to the ground and *begged* me,' Dan insisted. 'I am coming with you.'

Hudan tactfully decided to avoid that and redirected the conversation. 'Why does Song intend to burn the House of Jizi?'

'Because he picked the granddaughter of Minister Jizi to marry, and she overpowered me so she could flee before Song returned from his goddess rite,' Dan advised.

'You lost his bride on their wedding day and Song is still carrying the goddess' blessing?' Hudan queried, thinking this would be particularly frustrating for Ji Song.

'He has probably frittered the blessing away on half the young females in Haojing by now,' Dan imagined. 'There will be little princes springing up in the capital like daisies next fall!'

Hudan had to chuckle, although it was no laughing matter. 'Still, our king must have been very vexed when you spoke.'

'He wasn't the only one. His bride had just knocked me unconscious and then I awoke to an interrogation!' Dan was angry just thinking about it. 'I had been warned she was martial, but I had no idea she was going to swing down out of the rafters and ambush me!'

'Wow!' Hudan was impressed. 'Not your average lady of the aristocracy, then?'

'The pity of it is that, according to Hreen's description of Song's perfect match, she fits the bill.'

'You learned the law of summons,' Hudan said, figuring out how Dan had contacted the Lord of Time.

'Yes, but apparently that law does not apply to Hreen, for he is of the physical realm.' Dan was delighted to teach Hudan something she didn't know. 'He claimed he pops in and checks on the team from time to time, so our meeting was just a timely coincidence.'

'Really.' Hudan was impressed by his tale, but eyed the room warily. 'That is a little off-putting.'

'Forget I mentioned it,' Dan grinned, and Hudan returned the sentiment.

'So ...' Hudan summed up. 'You are telling me that you know the young King of Zhou is about to make a grave error in judgement, and you are choosing to step aside and do nothing?'

Dan shook his head, obviously not liking her summation. 'I have waited an age to be alone with you. Could we not revel in the joy of being banished, just for a few days?'

'Our child king has been left unsupervised for a week already,' Hudan commented drily.

'I just want to be with you,' Dan said, articulating his heartfelt feelings on the matter. 'You left Li Shan on the same day, for the same reason. If that is not fate, then what is?'

That was a very good point, Hudan conceded, biting her lip as she considered the coincidence.

'You have no home any more,' Dan stated as he neared to speak with her more intimately. 'Return to Haojing with me, as my wife, and I will go.'

'Zhou Gong Dan never marries again.' She repeated what the Great Mother had foretold.

'No one need know,' Dan encouraged. 'Unless our king is of the mind to covet you, in which case we shall speak up. We can ask our siblings here to bear witness.'

Hudan had not even considered that now she was not Wu, the king could marry her on a whim, and keep her locked away for life — unless she was married to someone else. Were they changing history, or just uncovering what had never been recorded and lost over time? 'I will marry you tomorrow evening.'

Dan's joyful gasp was premature, she felt, and she covered his mouth with her fingers.

'But,' she added earnestly, 'only if you will then allow me to complete my quest, whilst you return to Haojing to aid the king.'

'Allow me to accompany —'

'No.' Hudan made it clear she was not open to a compromise. 'I promise I shall complete my task as swiftly as possible and return to you, but every day you remain with me is a day closer the king's soldiers will be to the House of Jizi.'

'I cannot stop that now. I am not as accomplished at thought movement as you are,' he appealed.

'Huxin is,' Hudan said, tearing down his excuse. 'We have four days at best. If we marry tomorrow, then day after we must take action to stay abreast of the situation.'

'All right,' Dan grumbled, deciding he could live with that. 'I accept.'

'Then consider it an engagement,' Hudan grinned and sealed their deal with a kiss. The outcome was mutually beneficial, and she never had to worry about being given to any other man beside the one she truly loved.

Ji Dan requested a family meeting in Shi's council chamber late the next afternoon, and you could have knocked Huxin, Fen and Shi over with a feather when Dan announced that Hudan and he intended to marry that day.

'What?' Shi retorted, as they looked at him expectantly.

'This is stunning news,' Huxin said, not knowing whether to jump for joy, or voice a caution.

'But what of your vows?' Fen asked.

'I have left Li Shan for good,' Hudan advised, looking at Dan with a smile. 'The Great Mother said that my heart clearly lay elsewhere and that I should follow where it led.'

Huxin was excited and rushed to congratulate them both. 'Then this is surely a most auspicious occasion! You must give me time to plan such an event.'

'It must be today,' Dan replied, sorry to dash her plan of a big celebration. 'Tomorrow we go our separate ways.'

'What?' Huxin was dumbfounded by this turn of events.

'And as our time together is to be so short,' Dan looked back to Shi, 'we would rather appreciate it if you would be witness to us doing the honours now.'

'You two could not be accused of being sentimental!' Huxin stewed in her disappointment only briefly.

'We would also greatly appreciate it if we could keep this event just between those of us here in this room,' Hudan added.

'Who else needs to know anyway?' Fen said immediately, smiling in approval.

'Well, the king should be informed,' Shi pointed out.

'I shall inform the king,' Dan proffered, 'when the time is right.'

'So, you have not quit the regency,' Shi assumed.

'That remains to be seen. I will return to Haojing, and I hope to persuade you all to aid in getting me reinstated.'

All three were eager to be of service in any way they could, and both Dan and Hudan were very grateful for the support.

'Let us start by seeing you married,' Shi suggested.

Their host led the couple to a small altar within the house, and Dan and Hudan knelt before it. They were instructed to firstly bow down to heaven and earth, secondly, to bow to the ancestors, and thirdly, to one another. Once pronounced man and wife, Shi asked them both to rise, and after a brief round of congratulations, the happy couple swiftly made themselves absent for the remainder of the day.

In the interests of making the most of every minute of their wedding day, Dan had not closed his eyes to rest until dawn the following day and then slept until after noon.

On waking, Dan thought himself the luckiest man alive, until he realised he was cuddling a pillow and that his wife had fled, leaving a silken note on her pillow where her head should have been.

'Argh,' he groaned, feeling he should have known better then to think Hudan would delay her quest any longer than their negotiation stipulated. 'Would a goodbye have been too much to ask?' He took hold of the silk and smiled as he pressed it to his face, for it smelt like Hudan — not just the perfume of it, but the smell of ink always reminded him of her.

My darling husband, I believe I have thought of a way to complete my quest swiftly — I look forward to joining you in the next few days at Haojing.

Dan kissed the silk, thankful for the good news. 'If the quest is to be so swift, I could have gone,' he muttered to himself.

That thought spurred him from his marital bed and he made haste to dress and find his sister-in-law.

'Could you possibly talk me through the process of instant physical relocation?' he requested, when he found Huxin in the dining room supervising the twin's mealtime.

'Would you not like to eat first?' Huxin queried. 'I thought you two were never coming out of there.'

'No, thank you.' Dan had never been so eager to try his hand at the skill, and he felt that his desire, coupled with the amount of chi that was surging through his being this morning, might give him the edge he needed to step up to the challenge. 'Just the tutorial would be excellent.'

'Have you lost your wife already?' Huxin figured out the reason for his request fairly quickly. 'I think you really must be instructed, or you shall never keep up with her. Follow me.'

She left the servants to finish off her motherly duties and led him to a quiet place in the garden. 'Firstly ...' she said, noting how Dan was shivering already; in the next instant, Dan felt himself rugged up in a fur-lined coat and boots. 'Learn to dress for where you are headed.'

'Noted.' Dan smiled, thankful for her foresight. 'What next?'

'Three things prevent teleportation,' she began. 'One — a lack of chi, and you have an abundance of that this morning, I feel.' She grinned, and he grinned to confirm her intuition. 'The second obstacle is a belief that the task is not possible, but as you have experienced the phenomena first-hand, your mind already accepts it as possible.'

'What is the third obstacle?' Dan asked, keen to move on.

'Fear of success,' Huxin concluded. 'But since it is clear that you want this, you may well make a go of it. However ... weren't we supposed to be heading back to Haojing today?'

'Today or tomorrow,' Dan said, insisting they had a little time up their sleeve. 'The Great Mother said it was important that we learn this art, and I believe my best chance of succeeding is today.'

'Fair enough,' Huxin granted, 'but if you are not back here by this time tomorrow, I'm coming after you.'

'Understood,' Dan conceded. 'I thank you in advance for your assistance.' He bowed, greatly indebted.

'Don't be silly, we are family!' Huxin pulled him upright. 'Now, as you have experienced physical teleportation before with Hudan, you are familiar with the sensation. So, all you need do is invoke that same light-filled feeling, whilst focussing on your destination, or in this case, your subject.'

'That is all?' It sounded too easy and Dan wished he'd asked for instruction before now.

'That is all,' Huxin confirmed. 'You either have it, or you don't.'

'Well, time to find out.' Dan took a few deep breaths in preparation and then closed his eyes to tap into those other occasions when Hudan had reduced his being to pure chi energy and spirited him elsewhere.

The light filled his being with a tingling sensation even more intense than a post-sexual euphoria and he lost his stomach to a sensation of it being swallowed by his heart centre, as he focused his will on locating Hudan. In a rush of motion, like being caught in a river surge, he was cast forth into the mountain ranges of Qiang.

Dan stood in disbelief when he found himself on a frozen mountainside with nothing but other snow-capped mountain peaks around him. 'Where on earth?' he uttered, having never seen this place before.

Hudan was nowhere to be seen, but before him lay footprints in the snow, which he assumed must be hers. Curiously, there were no tracks behind him, they just started here and headed into the thin forest ahead. *Hudan must be willing herself from one peak, within her sight, to the next.* If that were case then she had to be close by, and so he rushed to catch her up.

When he cleared the trees on the other side of the forest there was a large open expanse of snow that Hudan was halfway across. 'Hudan!' he called, and ran toward her.

Heart beating ten to the dozen, Hudan realised she had made a fatal mistake attempting to cross the snow-covered slope on foot, for she could hear subtle cracking in the ice beneath her with every step she took.

She had been willing herself from one mountain peak to the next, but once she had reached this one, Hudan's will to be teleported forth had had no effect. Hudan thought it might be due to the wind whipping up the snow here and making visibility bad, so she had ventured forth onto the snow-covered mountainside to get a better look at the peak she wished to reach. Then she heard the sound of cracking ice beneath her, which seemed to indicate that she was not walking across solid ground. She'd come to a standstill to decide whether she should keep moving forward or attempt to retrace her steps.

'Hudan!'

The sound of her husband's voice struck the fear of heaven into her for the second time in as many minutes, and as she turned she felt the ground crack beneath her. 'Dan, go back!' she yelled, horrified to see him running toward her.

'No, I'm coming with you!' He did not slow down.

'*Stop!*' she screamed to make him listen, tears streaming down her face. 'The ice —'

A crack as loud as thunder stopped Dan in his tracks. Further down the slope from where Hudan stood, the snow began to disappear into a sinkhole — the entire ice sheet was about to collapse. 'Transport yourself out of there!' he yelled in desperation.

'I tried already,' she yelled back, and began to run toward him, 'Go!' she urged him.

But Dan refused, watching the ice face crumble away from the slope and fall into an oblivion that was threatening to engulf them both. 'Run faster!' Dan spotted a rock peeking out from the snow to his right and dived onto it. He braced himself on top of it and held out a hand toward her.

The shifting ground beneath her made her lose her footing, but by using her staff for leverage she stayed upright and, reaching out with a her free hand, she gripped hold of Dan's. The ice sheet cracked at the base of the rock suddenly and Hudan slid off her feet as the chunk of ice she was on tilted, but did not fall.

'Ah!' she gasped as she could not get a foothold, and bits of ice slid around her to plummet into the deep abyss below.

'Hudan, drop the staff!' Dan said, straining to hold her. 'I need your other hand to pull you up.'

'No!' She took a deep breath and cast it over the top of Dan to safety, but her exertions put an extra strain on his grip. Both their hands were sweating and slippery and Dan was being pulled over with her. 'You must return it, when you have finished with Song,' she told him, tears streaming down her face as she felt the chunk of ice beneath her slipping. 'Let me go —'

'No!' he insisted, dangerously close to losing his grip and balance. 'Give me your other hand.'

'Zhou Gong must not die today!' She tried to pry his hand away from hers. 'You must live!'

'No, goddamn it!' He allowed himself to slip down onto the ice sheet with her and pulling her close to him, they both plummeted into the abyss. 'Hreen!' he yelled until the velocity of their dive forced him to silence, and they hugged close as they spun out of control.

The frantic dropping spinning motion receded, and Hudan became aware that there was ground beneath her feet. She was still clinging to Dan and all that could be heard was the sound of the wind whipping around them.

'Are we dead?' Hudan opened her eyes, and Dan ventured to do the same.

'You are dead.' Their attention was drawn to Rhun, who was standing on the snow-covered mountainside nearby them, and he was pointing at Hudan.

'You,' the time lord pointed to Dan, 'are not supposed to be here, and must go back.'

'You heard my call?' Dan was astonished.

'No, I was here to pick up Hudan,' the lord explained. 'This is her dying day.'

'I am dead?' she whimpered, and feeling herself all over, she felt as alive as she ever was.

'As far as history is concerned, yes.'

'No,' Dan protested, 'this cannot be how it ends.' He gripped Hudan's hand tighter. 'I marry her one day … and the next she *dies?*'

'Well, that's history for you.' The time lord threw his hands up to imply it was beyond his control. 'And that's why there is no record of the marriage,' Rhun informed him, 'as you will have any record destroyed upon your return.'

'You know about our marriage?' Dan wasn't really surprised.

'Nothing gets by us,' Rhun assured him, 'but it is not why Hudan is being taken out of the equation. It just happens to be her time.'

'Where are you taking me?' Hudan queried the lord. 'And why did my chi fail me just now?'

'Because this entire area is shielded by an invisible force field that prevents anyone using supernatural powers here … unless, of course you are wearing one of these.' He flashed the metallic bracelet on his wrist. 'A Dropa security measure.'

'Dropa?' Both Dan and Hudan were curious about the word. 'What does that mean?' Hudan ventured to inquire.

'He is not permitted to know, and you will find out soon enough,' Rhun told them.

'My staff?' Hudan wondered where it was, and Rhun conjured it forth and saw it back into her possession. 'I believe this has something to do with Dropa as that was the only word my mother uttered just before she died.'

'A fair assumption,' Rhun granted, 'but I am not saying anything until after you say farewell to father.' When Hudan caught her breath, overwhelmed by the suggestion, the Lord of Time rolled his eyes and added, 'Which is never a snappy affair.' He clicked his fingers and looked at Dan. 'Ah … I investigated that issue you asked about.'

'Yes?' Dan confirmed, and Hudan wondered why they were being so secretive.

'I do know him. He was something of a nemesis to you in the past.'

'Who are you talking about?' Hudan jumped in, curious.

'The concerns of this time are no longer your affair,' Rhun told her plainly, 'so please mind your own business, or I shall be forced to make you absent.'

'You should not speak to your mother like that.'

'I could just leave you to it?' he proposed, backing away with his hand raised in indifference, and Dan relented.

'Please … continue.'

'Thank you,' Rhun said, sauntering back toward Dan. 'However, the soul in question was seeking to reform his behaviour when he tricked his way onto this mission.'

'Tricked?' Dan queried the point, and the lord nodded.

'So whether Khalid is friend or foe now, I really cannot say.' Rhun shook his head and added, 'So be very careful with him. He was once as powerful as Hudan … well, almost.'

Dan was worried, but nodded to confirm he'd bear that in mind. 'Have you any idea where Dragonface is hiding?'

'Until I have my team back, his royal etheric-ness will not allow me investigate.' Rhun looked at Hudan and smiled. 'We'll see if he can maintain his stance, once I have mother on my side.'

'Who said I will take your side?' Hudan objected and Rhun grinned. 'Oh, believe me, once you are brought up to speed, you'll take my side, because somewhere in your super-conscious you have way more information about this mission than either Avery or I do.' Hudan's mind boggled at his claim and she just stared at him. 'So would you please say your goodbyes, and we can get on?' Rhun suggested.

'But I never got to say goodbye to my family?' She now greatly regretted sneaking off before anyone had awoken.

'Not to worry, you'll get to say hello to them again upon their death,' Rhun proposed by way of compensation, and he moved away to give them some space.

The notion was surreal and not of much comfort to Hudan. Then her attention returned to her husband of one day. 'You would have died with me.' The fact brought tears to her eyes as he hugged her to him.

'I wish I had,' he said, sincerely.

Hudan allowed the fear and sorrow to wash over her and found a spark of inspiration beneath. 'You do not have time to die.' She roused a smile as she pulled back to look at him, yet Dan could not return the sentiment. 'But when you do complete your destiny … I shall be there to bring you home.'

'Wherever that is?' His brow furrowed as he found his sense of humour.

'I shall investigate,' she vowed, 'and bring you up to speed when next we speak.'

'If I do not find my Akashic memory first, that is. Your absence will surely provide impetus for me to tap into that.' He breathed back his emotion and Hudan was doing the same.

'I want to go back to yesterday,' she told him, desperately trying to contain her regret. 'I am so sorry I was so insistent on getting my task completed.'

'It seems you cannot fight fate,' Dan said. 'You were not to know Yi Wu was sending you to your death.'

As they prolonged their goodbye kiss, Hudan could feel the time lord's impatience, and through no fault of her own she was torn from Dan's being and drawn into the light-field toward an unknown destination.

20

THE RISE OF
ZHOU CHENG WANG

When Shi, Fen Gong and Ji Dan arrived in Haojing unexpectedly, the young king was curious to learn the reason for their visit so they were granted an immediate audience.

As Dan could now teleport himself about, Huxin had reluctantly remained at Shao — for the sake of the children, Shi did not want her embroiled in a civil war. But, just as the Great Mother had always cautioned, Huxin also warned Dan not to use his abilities in front of the uninitiated, and he agreed he would be cautious. He had, however, used his new ability to speed his small party to Haojing. Ling Hu had followed under her own steam.

'You promised I would never see you again,' Song complained from his throne, the second he caught sight of his uncle. 'Yet here you are. Come to beg for your old position back?'

'Not at all, majesty,' Dan said, bowing deeply, as did his companions, and then stood straight to state what was on his mind. 'I have come at Jiang Hudan's request to prevent you from making a grave error in judgement.'

The mention of the Wu's name pacified his majesty a little. 'Why does my goddess not appear to me herself to voice her caution?'

As Hudan had come to him as a maid on their wedding night, Song's lie no longer got a rise out of Dan, and he let the comment slide. 'That would be because Jiang Hudan is dead.' Dan's voiced wavered under the strain of delivering the news.

'I do not believe you!' Song stood, enraged, and then gave a laugh, feeling he was wise to what was going on. 'This is part of brother Hudan's game with me —'

'No, majesty,' Fen interrupted, stepping forward, his solemn expression conveying that this was no laughing matter. 'Game over. Ji Dan speaks the truth.'

'Li Shan has vanished back into legend with her, leaving the fate of the land in our hands,' Dan advised, and Song seemed a little daunted by that proposition. 'So, for the sake of clarity, would you please tell me again why you had to threaten to burn down the house of your betrothed?'

'I would think that it is obvious!' Song was agitated. 'She fled!'

'Pardon my asking, majesty —'

'I did not do anything!' the king objected, preempting Dan's query. 'She was the one who tried to deceive me. Yin Hui Ru has no honour.'

'But *how* did she deceive you?' Dan strived for understanding.

'She created a *fantastic* story, about her grandfather being possessed by a creature, and claimed the only reason she had come to Haojing was to seek my aid to be rid of it,' Song spat out, disgusted by her wanting to weasel out of her duty.

'A creature, you say?' Dan's mind was suddenly going ten to the dozen.

'Why?' Song was clearly ill-at-ease with his uncle's reaction.

But Dan's mind was back in Yin as the pieces of the puzzle fell together. *'You smell as horrendous as old Jizi did straight from the dungeon,'* he recalled Huxin saying. She had been commenting on the stench of the lizards on him, following their battle with the creatures. 'Minister Jizi wasn't in Yin when we performed the clearing rite on the palace,' Dan said, with all the force of his revelation.

'Dragonface is hiding in Minister Jizi!' Shi concluded on Dan's behalf and they looked at each other in shock.

'Ji Fa left Minister Jizi to advise your brothers,' Fen seconded their panic. 'He could well have been behind my abduction and the death of the queen. Dragonface saw my talent at work the night we drove him out.'

'It saw you pacify someone, not heal them,' Dan pointed out, 'but the ousted Shang prince, Wu Geng, knows how Fen's healing talent works.' Rhun had warned that the soul-mind hiding within Wu Geng might be powerful, and could even be antagonistic. 'Perhaps they are working together to overthrow us?'

'Who or what is Dragonface?' Song demanded.

'A shape-shifting creature that we ousted from its lair beneath Yin,' Dan replied.

'That wasn't in Hudan's chronicle!' Song complained.

'Your father did not want the event made common knowledge,' Dan explained, as Song's expression became increasingly mournful.

'You mean Hui Ru was *not* lying to me?' the young king squeaked. 'She really does need my help?'

All three of the lords nodded in harmony.

'But … I have sent an order to Xian to burn the minister's house down. It should be arriving as we speak!' The king was flustered. 'I cannot make her entire family suffer more, if there is already such a curse within their house!'

'That is, if Dragonface doesn't kill the force our brothers send to carry out his majesty's order,' Shi added.

'We have to do something,' Song said, spurred on by his own guilt.

'We?' Dan asked. 'I have no power to do anything.'

Song met his uncle's glare of challenge. 'I order you, Zhou Gong, to resume your regency and fix my bloody mess.'

Dan grinned to accept his reappointment, and Song grinned also.

'Which, I might add, is not entirely *my* fault, as I was not fully briefed on the situation in Yin,' he said, with a frown of disapproval.

'My fault entirely.' Dan accepted that blame gladly.

'Still, I guess I should also mention that I have already advised Xian of your resignation, so he may not be overjoyed by your reappointment.'

'I never expected him to accept your father's will, in any case,' Dan advised.

'I want my queen back,' Song advised them. 'And I don't want her to hate me, so … how are we going to impress her?' He looked at Dan, who was considering their next move.

'I believe we should pay your betrothed a surprise visit.'

'No one seems to know where she is,' Song advised them.

'But you know what she looks like,' Dan said, suggesting they use his new skills. 'My guess is that the future queen headed toward home, and is probably in hiding, which should serve our purpose well.'

The four men and the spirit tiger joined the runaway bride in a clearing in the woods, where Hui Ru was beating up Ji Song's messenger. She ripped the small container with the king's message from the staggering soldier and with one final punch to the jaw, she knocked him to the ground unconscious. 'Thank you very much,' she said triumphantly, 'but I think an entirely different set of orders is in order.'

'Such as?' Song queried from behind her, and glancing back to see her company, she sprinted for the messenger's horse.

'Ling Hu, bring her back,' Song requested and with a nod from Fen, Ling Hu vanished and reappeared between Hui Ru and her means of escape. She was startled into backing up and collided with the king, who grabbed her from behind.

Hui Ru threw her head backward to headbutt Song, who released her, and staggered back to be caught by his subjects.

'I am here to help you,' the king protested, holding his throbbing head. 'Is that not what you wanted?'

'Like I would believe you,' she said, skittish and searching for an escape route.

'Well … I believe you,' Song said sincerely, now standing on his own two feet. 'We are here to help with your monster problem.'

Hui Ru ceased looking for an exit and grew angry. '*Now* you believe me!' She threw her hands up in disgust! 'After I had to *fight* my way out of the palace, and negotiate my way home, across country, *alone … now*, you decide to believe me!'

'His majesty was not made aware of the curse at Yin until

recently,' Dan said in defence of Song's previous restraint, 'which is entirely my fault.' He bowed to her in apology.

'You are Zhou Gong?' She recognised him as one of the men she had knocked out at Hoajing.

'I am,' he confirmed. 'Might I ask how you came to realise the creature had converted your grandfather's body?'

'My grandfather was never fond of drink,' she explained, 'and it likes to drink, a lot! When it drinks it cannot maintain its disguise properly and I see the dragon beneath.'

'That is very interesting to know, and it's entirely plausible,' he advised the king, who nodded to accept his word for it.

'I told you Zhou Gong would believe me,' Hui Ru impressed on his majesty, and then looked back to the Duke of Zhou. 'I apologise for any injury I caused your esteemed person, but I had to escape and deal with my grandfather, *and* his majesty's threat to my family!' She waved the message in her hand, and Song gritted his teeth and remained quiet.

'It is greatly fortunate for us that you did.' Dan held out his hand and invited her to give the missive back.

'What do you intend to do with it?' Hui Ru hesitated.

'I intend to burn it,' Dan advised. 'Then, as per his majesty's request, we shall go to Yin, recruit my brothers and destroy the creature living within your grandfather.' At least that was their intention and he hoped they could carry it out.

'And find my grandfather,' she added, but was alerted by the sorrowful look on Dan's face.

'I am sorry to tell you,' he said gently, 'but the creature can only assume the form of someone it has killed.'

'No …' Hui Ru's fighting spirit crumpled before their eyes, and she fell to the ground and collapsed into tears.

Dan looked at Song to comfort his bride, but the king held up his hands and shook his head, knowing she would protest. Dan went down on one knee before her. 'If it is any consolation, Shanyu Jiang Hudan performed a cleansing rite at Yin and released the imprisoned souls from the bondage of the beast.'

She raised her tear-stained face, enchanted by his words.

'So the two great men Jizi and Bi Gan now rest in peace.'

Hui Ru nodded, and thankful for the reassurance, she handed Dan back the metal container. 'I trust your word, my lord.' Hui Ru served Song a look that implied his word was still in question.

In Dan's books, this was a good sign, as Rhun had claimed that the more aloof Hui Ru was with the king, the more interested she was. 'Then let us proceed to Yin and discover what kind of a reception awaits us there.'

The capital seemed devoid of people and subdued, even for the cold season.

'Where are all the guards?' Shi uttered aside to Dan, as they trailed the king, Hui Ru and Fen across the courtyard toward the council chambers.

They had expected to be met by all four of their brothers, but when led into the council chamber, Wu Geng was again seated on the throne at Yin.

'I believe that is my seat,' Song challenged, as he entered and the former Shang prince did not rise.

'That seems to be a matter of some debate at this time.' Wu Geng lifted his frail form from the throne, aided by his servants, and it was painful to watch.

'Never mind,' Song insisted the Shang prince sit back down. It was going to be agony trying to watch the man try to stand and speak. 'Where are my uncles?'

'They have returned to their estates for the winter, along with their troops … that's what they told me to say, should anyone inquire.'

'But the truth is?' Dan prompted, moving close to view the being within Wu Geng.

'They are amassing a force to claim the regency for Guan Shu Xian.' He raised his eyebrows at their frowning faces. 'Are you really surprised?'

'Only by the speed of his revolt,' Dan allowed.

'Your brothers are spreading rumours among the central and eastern tribes, that Zhou Gong plans to usurp our new majesty, and that is why Zhou Gong has assumed the role that was rightly Guan Shu Xian's.'

'Zhou Gong is regent, because that was my father's wish!' The king approached Wu Geng to question him further. 'Why was I not informed about this sedition sooner?'

'Is my missive not the reason you are here?' Wu Geng was looking more concerned now. 'I grant that you got here rather swiftly.'

Dan noted Wu Geng appeared outwardly puzzled, but the son of the sky within him was grinning. 'We do have Wu in our service, who alerted us to trouble at Yin before your missive reached us.'

'Ah, yes, your Wu.' Wu Geng's eyes drifted to Fen. 'Your lovely sisters appear to be absent?'

'One of my sisters, Jiang Hudan, has died.'

'Really?' The former Shang prince didn't seem to believe Fen. 'That is surprising news, to be sure.'

The tigress gave a growl, as Fen was irritated by Wu Geng's reaction.

'I think he is working with Dragonface,' Fen said, stating his feelings outright, and Wu Geng was impressed by his bold statement.

'The creature did not see me jailed because we were close,' Wu Geng told them. 'I never did like the reptile much.'

'Is that Wu Geng speaking, or Ca-Lid?' Dan asked, and Song nearly had a fit.

'I know that name!' His expression turned stormier than the sky outside, which rumbled loudly to echo Song's ire.

'You do?' Dan was surprised to hear this, and became concerned when the young king unsheathed his sword. 'What do you remember?'

Song swung his sword at Wu Geng, stopping a hair's breadth short of slitting his throat. 'That I am supposed to kill him.'

'Majesty!' Shang Hui Ru yelled, and fell to her knees. 'Please, do not kill my cousin. Please.'

'Really, cousin,' Wu Geng raised an eyebrow and hadn't flinched at all. 'This body is a frightful bore. His majesty would be doing me a great service. I know where we are ultimately going, and if you send me off ahead of you, well … all the better. You are not the only ones who can play time games.'

Song was so stunned he dropped his sword and backed up.

'I am lost!' Shi looked at Fen, who shook his head, also baffled.

'How much do you remember?' Dan queried — even he was shocked out of his wits.

'How much do *you* remember, *captain?*' Wu Geng grinned and when Dan was not prepared to answer, Wu Geng continued. 'If you want my help, I am happy to give it, but if you are not prepared to give me the benefit of the doubt, *this once*, then just kill me now and send me home.'

'Where is home?' Dan queried.

'Sermetica, next universe on the right,' he replied smartly, and the duke thought he joked as Dan had no memory of such a place.

'That is absolutely correct,' the king said, looking at Dan, confounding him again.

'Or if you are talking about our last stopover in this universal scheme,' Wu Geng went on, 'that was the planet Kila, other side of the galaxy, about three thousand years from now.'

It felt like someone had sucked the air out of the room; Dan was having trouble breathing as he fathomed that statement.

'I can confirm,' Song swallowed hard, 'some of that.'

'Have you all been drinking?' Hui Ru appealed. 'Never mind about your little fantasies, we have to do something about that monster in my house!'

'I believe you will find Minister Jizi has fled,' Wu Geng announced casually, as everyone queried his claim. 'When Guan Shu Xian announced his intention to contest the regency, our dear old minister up and left. He claimed he was going north, which seems to rule out that direction: what lizard would head for the snow? No, south would be my guess.'

'My family?' Hui Ru wondered what had become of them.

'I insisted the minister leave them all in my safekeeping here at Yin.'

Hui Ru burst into tears of joy and bowed down before Wu Geng, 'I thank you, cousin. I am eternally in your debt.'

Wu Geng looked at his majesty, to see if he was still inclined to kill him, and it seemed he was conflicted on the issue. 'My dear cousin,' his sights turned back to Hui Ru. 'There is nothing amiss here and nothing more to impede your union with his majesty, which our family feels will unite and bring peace to the land.'

The king clearly hated the thought that he now owed Wu Geng a favour; he didn't trust him, just as the Lord of Time had not.

Hui Ru raised her eyes to her relative, not entirely ill-disposed toward the notion. 'Only if his majesty will gift me with your life.'

Wu Geng grinned to refer the petition back to his majesty. 'Call it a wedding gift,' he suggested.

Song inhaled deeply to suffer the idea, and looked to Dan for his opinion.

In all honesty, Dan did not want to kill him, as Wu Geng obviously remembered much of the team's history. 'The question is, do you want Hui Ru as your queen, or not?' Dan referred the decision back to the king.

Song looked back to Hui Ru, and she was observing him expectantly. 'I do.'

'So Wu Geng lives?' She rose to confront Song, and he smiled.

'I might be persuaded,' he grinned and Hui Ru's face filled with anger, but to the relief of all, she smiled at him instead.

'Excellent!' Wu Geng sprang from his chair — clearly he was not as weak an invalid as he had been making out. 'But here is the problem … today is my dying day,' he announced, happily. Everyone stared at him in amazement.

'Pardon?' Dan queried.

'You kill Wu Geng for conspiracy, and he is history.' He looked at Dan. 'So I guess we need to arrange some kind of inter-dimensional relocation program for me.'

'A what?' The king was annoyed not to comprehend his raving. 'Did you lose your mind in prison?'

'Come on,' Wu Geng appealed, feeling he was being toyed with. 'I know you must have one …' He turned to Dan. 'For I know there is no way Jiang Hudan is dead. The time lord will never let her perish.'

The king looked at Dan, as he'd gone very quiet. 'Do you know what he is talking about?'

'Perhaps.' It was unwise to commit.

'So, Hudan is not dead?' the king asked. Fen was most interested in the answer too.

'It is my guess,' Wu Geng ventured, to save Zhou Gong a painful explanation, 'that Jiang Hudan is dead to this world, but still very much alive. She has merely slipped through the veil between inner time and outer time, which is exactly what I need to do.' His head swivelled in the Duke of Zhou's direction, eyebrows raised.

'But I do not have the authority to organise such a thing!' Dan objected. 'The sons of the sky have their own agenda.'

'The sons of the sky?' Hui Ru was immediately fascinated by the phrase, which made the young king grin.

'You're the captain of this mission, right?' Wu Geng challenged Zhou Gong. 'So you tell Rhun to get his butt down here and pick me up.'

'I don't take kindly to orders.' The statement echoed around the room ahead of the time lord's appearance in their midst.

Shi moved to draw his weapon on sighting the oddly clad stranger, but Dan discouraged him. 'He is an ally,' he said to convince Shi.

'I know him.' Song frowned at the stranger, who nodded to him in recognition, and as Zhou Gong appeared more relieved than worried, the king held his tongue.

'He is Wu? He looks *different*,' Hui Ru queried Song quietly, and he shook his head.

'I believe he is a son of the sky,' he mumbled, not entirely sure, but keen to hear what the stranger had to say.

'You told me you intended to reform,' Rhun accused Wu Geng, or rather the soul inside of him. 'Then you tricked your way onto this mission. You are not supposed to be here.'

'How am I to change my fate, without this chance to prove myself?' he entreated, and fell to his knees before Rhun to implore his mercy. 'If you kill me, my soul-mind will be absorbed back into the light-field and I will be reborn Khalid of Sermetica, and this whole damn mess will begin again! Is that what you want? Because it is not what I want.'

Rhun eyed the man at his feet cautiously. 'You are as slippery as a snake, Khalid, and just as deadly. Don't think I am not aware of it.'

'I can use those skills for your ends,' he proposed. 'I have!' He motioned to the king, who now held the favour of his bride.

'You allowed Dragonface to slip through our fingers again,' the lord noted. Wu Geng was not ashamed.

'I do not have a team to back me up,' he stated. 'You took him on alone and failed. I was not about to make the same mistake.'

Rhun was frustrated that the statement irked him, but also made good sense.

'I have suffered my entire life in that creature's company, so I could be of greater service to you,' Wu Geng said, throwing out one last appeal. 'I possess knowledge that can help you. Just give me this chance.'

'Please, lord ...' Hui Ru didn't know who the fantastic stranger was, but was moved to implore him. 'Wu Geng has suffered long in this house and has always done his best to defend our family from the evil within Yin. I truly believe he is a good man, and to be trusted.'

Rhun looked at Dan, who wished he was more informed. He could only go with his gut feeling in the moment. 'I believe any repentant man deserves the right to make good his name.'

'Thank you, captain,' Wu Geng said in appreciation of the vote of confidence.

The time lord then looked to the young king. 'And what say you, majesty ... as you are the one with the vendetta against him?'

Hui Ru caught her breath and looked back to Song with pleading eyes.

'Not in this life,' he replied diplomatically, and Hui Ru smiled with relief.

'And you two?' Rhun turned to Fen and Shi, who both backed up a step as the time lord's attention shifted their way.

'I have no idea what is going on,' Shi told him, and held up both hands to pass on making any comment.

Fen was not so fast to absolve the man in question. 'Did you tell Dragonface about my talent?'

The former Shang prince shook his head. 'Guan Shu Xian figured it out when Ji Fa was miraculously healed of his wounds, and his queen of her inability to give birth. Yi Jiang's adoration of you was well known, and you were the only Wu still housed at Haojing,' Wu Geng concluded. 'It is my belief that Guan Shu Xian plotted, under Jizi's guidance, to bring down the last king, and he now plans to do the same to you, Ji Song.'

Fen looked to his tigress. 'Is he telling the truth?'

Wu Geng shrank back warily as the animal approached him.

'If you are not lying you have nothing to fear,' Fen vowed, so the former Shang prince closed his eyes and calmed, while Ling Hu stalked around him without incident. 'That is good enough for me.' Fen said.

'How long ago did my uncle's war party leave here?' the king asked before the witness vanished for life.

'Four days ago,' Wu Geng advised. 'It will take time to rally the clans in winter, and Zhou Gong is respected and liked so not all shall heed Guan Shu Xian's right to be regent. You have perhaps two weeks before he brings rebellion to your doorstep.'

'Then there is no time to waste!' Hui Ru was rather more eager to defend the throne of Zhou than anyone had expected. 'I shall rally my kinsmen, and we can quash his treason from the East and the West.' The princess strode from the chamber, but turned back to her stunned male company to add. 'I shall see you all around Mengjin.'

'That's her!' Rhun looked at Dan. 'Well spotted.'

'Hey, I found her,' Song said, seeking credit where credit was due. 'Who is she?'

The time lord found this funny. 'Why is it you can remember Khalid, you can remember Taren, but you cannot remember your soul mate?'

'My what?' The king protested. 'Do not answer that, I do not want to know —'

'That your womanising days are over,' Rhun teased him. 'I am afraid so.' He shared a laugh with Dan, as he lifted Wu Geng from the floor. 'I shall get this one out of your hair, as it seems you have a war to be getting on with. Good luck with that … see you all around dead-time.'

The time lord vanished, along with Wu Geng, and the four men left behind were stupefied.

'No more secrets!' The king was the first to speak. 'Clearly, we each have knowledge we are not sharing with the group, so let us make a pact here and now to trust each other.'

'Honesty is a righteous thing,' Dan allowed, his eyes boring into the king's, and he felt sure Song knew why.

'I think you already know that Hudan was not my goddess,' Song conceded, humbling himself. 'It was a cruel blow I dealt you, Uncle … I spoke in rage, without thought of the consequences. I deeply regret that Jiang Hudan has left this world thinking that I meant her harm and disrespect.' The king bowed his head to indicate his remorse. 'Please forgive my insult to you, and to the legend of Shanyu Jiang Hudan.' He bowed to the duke to beg forgiveness.

'It is forgotten,' Dan granted.

The king gave a nod in gratitude and looking aside to Fen he found the healer scowling. 'I know, my ethics need a lot of work.'

'To Hoajing then,' Shi said, wanting to motivate them into action. 'We have to raise an army.'

'Here's hoping that respect for Zhou Gong is as widespread as reported,' the king said, looking at his uncle.

For once Dan was confident and he braced Ji Song's forearm, and Song returned the gesture of solidarity. 'We shall quash this rebellion and establish a peace that will survive us.'

The king nodded in agreement. 'Are we really going to leave my bride to rally the East? She may be of the mind to kill *me*?'

Dan was not so worried. 'I believe she will surprise everyone.'

Upon their return to the capital, a war council was called and a major announcement was composed by Zhou Gong for the king. Copies of the call to arms were produced by every scribe available, and signed by both the king and Zhou Gong, then witnessed by Shao Gong Shi. Each summons was placed in a small coffer and sent via messenger on horseback to every ally Zhou Gong trusted this side of the great Huang He.

Lords of my friendly states, directors of my departments, my officers, and the managers of my affairs, I make a great announcement to you. I, Song, who am but a little child, must diffuse the elegant institutions of my predecessor and display the appointment, which he received from Heaven. Ever mindful of his great work, I dare not restrain the majesty of Heaven in sending down its inflictions on criminals. The enlightening of the country was wise — the ten men who obeyed knew the charge of God and the real assistance given them by Heaven. At that time none presumed to change the rules prescribed by the Tranquillising king. And now, when Heaven is sending down calamity on the country of Zhou, the authors of these great distresses make it appear, on a grand scale, as if the inmates of our house mutually attack one another, and you are perplexed as the decree of Heaven is not to be changed! Heaven, in destroying Yin, was doing husbandman's work. Heaven will thereby show its favour to my predecessor, the Tranquilliser, who I am following, and whose purpose embraced all within the limits of the land! I must proceed, when the divinations are all favourable! It is on these accounts that I make this expedition in force to the East. I will go forward with you from all the states, and punish those vagabond and transported ministers of Yin. There is no mistake about the decree of Heaven!

Within days, chieftains, nobility and the men under their charge, began amassing at Haojing and many of these had yet to hear the announcement, but they had heard the news of Guan Shu Xian's call to arms and were compelled to defend the will of the late King Fa. The late king was now revered as Zhou Wu Wang — the martial king.

As they marched east toward Mengjin, their ranks swelled, and they were joined by the forces of King Wu Wang's brothers, Cheng Shu Wu and Cao Shu Zhenduo. By the time they reached the crossing point at the Huang He, the king received word that the rebel force was amassing just south of them at Luoyi. The more alarming news was that the Princess Hui Ru had joined forces with Guan Shu Xian to avenge the overthrow of the Shang dynasty, for Xian had promised to give back the Shang capital, Yin, to her.

'Well, I for one am surprised,' Dan commented as they observed Hui Ru from horseback. Across the battlefield, she had positioned her horse right alongside their rebel brothers, blowing Song kisses and waving.

'I am surprised,' Shi granted.

'I'm not.' Song was disappointed and then very angry, as he glared at her. 'I should have known better than to trust a woman. I want her alive.'

Song's allies who had Wu ability had agreed not to use any supernatural force to win his battle. With this in mind, Ji Song had left Fen Gong at Haojing — if anyone died of their injuries this day then it was the will of heaven.

'Xian is mine,' Dan advised his companions.

'I do not think so,' Song said, begging to differ. 'Who is king again?'

'You are,' Dan granted, 'but it is me he is rebelling against.' The duke felt he had the right of way in this instance.

'He orchestrated the death of both my parents,' Ji Song stated, ending the debate, and Dan bowed to his will. The king was young and impetuous, but he was a finer swordsman than Dan, most certainly.

'I think your queen has other plans.' Shi sensed the truth when Hui Ru unexpectedly released a war cry, and swung her sword to the right, taking off the head of Huo Shu Chu, whose body fell from the horse alongside her. Xian's army erupted into chaos and began fighting each other.

'Holy shit!' The young king was pleasantly surprised as he dug his heels in and led the charge forth. His uncle Xian was firmly in his sights.

With the influx of the opposing forces into the chaos and commotion, the recruited clans abandoned the field, and the three remaining ringleaders were surrounded. 'This is our fight!' Song jumped from his horse to challenge Guan Shu Xian, whereby Cai Shu Du and Ji Zai dropped their weapons and backed away.

'My beef is with Dan, majesty, not you!' Xian kept his weapon poised, inviting Dan to take Song's place with intermittent glares of challenge.

'Zhou Gong is my father's appointed regent. He and I are one!' Song circled Xian, just an underdeveloped child next to the hardened warrior figure of his uncle.

'That is not what I heard?' Xian challenged, limbering up the wrist of his sword arm.

'Everything you hear is a fabrication of your own sordid mind, Uncle,' Song stated. 'That's what happens when you consult with demons!'

Xian was taken off-guard by the comment and by the king's fierce attack. Dan felt Song must be employing more power than was humanly possible, for his fury was unrelenting.

'Would you deny that you were behind the kidnapping of Fen Gong?' the king ceased his attack long enough to ask, which was enough time for Xian to recover and start fighting back.

'More likely that you or Zhou Gong staged that one,' Xian countered. 'After all, you profited most.' The tip of Xian's sword scratched the king's cheek as he bent backward to avoid a strike and Dan was forced to jump from his horse to prevent Hui Ru rushing in.

'Finish that arsehole!' she encouraged the king. She was disinclined to break free of Zhou Gong in case she injured him.

'Your queen has a mouth like a jun-ji,' Xian said, insulting the king's choice of bride.

Song grinned, proud. 'Aw, you're just upset that your rebellion was quashed by my incredible woman!' Song taunted, and the forces gave a cheer as Hui Ru took a bow.

'I shall be sure to pay her due attention when you are gone!' Xian vowed and Song's mood darkened as they lashed out at one another with their swords. The king was now utterly oblivious to anything beyond killing his uncle, who was armoured and powerful, but Song was swift, agile and audacious.

As much as the duke wished to put himself in Song's place, he observed the chieftains and nobles cheering their new king on and realised, as did young Song, that if he won this battle he would also win the respect of his peers and his rule would be consolidated.

With youth on his side, the king ran his older uncle in circles until he began to tire. Song then resumed his attack with gusto, managing to scar Xian's cheek in return. 'Give it up, Uncle, even if you win, you lose! Your armies have fled; your allies have surrendered and will be treated leniently. I offer you one last chance to confess your treason and live beyond this day.'

'Give me the regency that is rightfully mine,' Xian said as he lashed out with his sword. Song ducked and swung around behind his uncle, and as Xian spun about, the king took his head clean off.

A cheer of support sounded from the captivated audience, but as Song held his sword high in victory, the field hushed. '*Tian has spoken* ... and is in agreement with the Tranquillising king! Zhou Gong is regent and let no man question his right henceforth.'

'Long live the king!' Shi yelled, and the chant was echoed by all who remained on the field.

Yin Hu Rui approached and knelt before the king. 'The Shang are beholden to you, my king, for quashing the unrest in the East, and hope that our majesty sees our valour this day on the battlefield as proof of our devotion.'

'Arise,' he invited and she stood before him. 'Does this mean you accept my proposal of marriage? And I must say, I love what you can do with an army.'

'I love that you entrusted the duty to me without question,' Hui Ru replied.

'Then I shall make you a general, as well as queen, if you so wish it,' Ji Song told her.

'He knows the way to that girl's heart,' Shi whispered to Dan, who was amused.

'Then my answer must be yes,' Hui Ru replied, smiling broadly, as was the king.

Taking hold of her hand, he held it high. 'East and West unite!'

As there was not a man on the field who did not reside in one direction or the other, the roar of approval was unanimous.

Shao Gong Shi disappeared during the ensuing revelry for some time and returned by dusk to make an announcement to the king. 'This is it! I have spent the afternoon surveying the area and I believe this is the perfect location to build Zhou Wu Wang's heavenly city.' A lot had happened since Shi had been given the assignment, but he had not forgotten his brother's wish, and also felt that strategically their new capital should be between the East and the West.

Dan was impressed by Shi's notion, and Ji Song agreed. 'Let construction on Zhou Wu Wang's vision begin, so that we all might marvel at the glory of heaven here on earth.'

In the wake of the battle there was much rearranging to be done. Ji Song banished the last of his troublesome uncles, Cai Shu Du, but Ji Zai, due to his young age, was pardoned for the crimes committed through his alliance to his brothers and granted a small province to govern until he proved his worth. The other provinces were split and incorporated into the provinces of his remaining uncles, and he endowed the former Shang Prince Weizi, who had fled to Zhou some time before, with a patrimonial estate in Song, in order that the Shang sacrifices should be continued.

Once the new capital was erected, there would be only two overlords in the land, however. Ji Song intended to rule the East from the new city, and Shao Gong Shi would govern the West from Haojing under the title of Grand Protector. As regent, Zhou Gong would accept no entitlements but intended to dedicate himself to the council of Ji Song and the building of Zhou Wu Wang's holy city.

The king, his queen and general Hui Ru, the Lord Regent and the Grand Protector pacified the lands of the tribes in the valley of the Huai River, and within two years the lands of the East were settled. At this time, the patrimonial lords all came to the Zhou ancestral capital, Haojing, to offer their submission.

21

BAYAN HAR SHAN

'So you see, us dumb boys did fine, even without your assistance,' Rhun said, relating the outcome of the revolution against Zhou Gong's regency. He was hoping this would end Hudan's objections to having been pulled away from her life at such a crucial point in history.

'Well, at least Song and Dan found their solidarity,' she commented, pleased about that.

'Not really,' Rhun enlightened her. 'They'll spend the next ten years clashing heads over whether the word of the Zhou represents the word of heaven, or whether the Zhou should rule according to the divinations of heaven.'

Hudan rolled her eyes, thinking that it would be just typical of both of them.

'But they did manage to stay allies, thanks to the negotiating prowess of Shao Gong Shi, Feng Gong and Xi Wangmu.'

Hudan gasped. 'The Great Mother returned?'

Rhun shook his head. 'In the wake of Yi Wu's absence, your sister was vested with the title.'

'Just as I predicted,' Hudan grinned, delighted.

She had been brought to the crystal cavern where she had first met with the Lord of the Elements and been introduced to Rhun, but the time lord's otherworldly brother was not here at present. It was clearly a place of the physical realm, although the light emanating from the crystal clusters all through the cavern gave it an otherworldly appearance. The glow was not as intense as it had appeared in her dream state, yet there was still more than enough light to see by.

'But what became of Fen?' Hudan wanted to know, wondering how the crystalline minerals therein managed to glow of their own accord in complete darkness.

'He stayed with Zhou Gong, of course, and never married,' he informed her. 'Together they brought to fruition the holy city of Chengzhou, which set the standard for urban planning for thousands of years to come.'

Hudan was impressed by their achievement. 'That certainly is a mighty destiny.'

'And that is not to mention the numerous laws and important documents Zhou Gong wrote before his death, detailing the offices of the Zhou government and the guidelines for establishing proper governance of the people.'

'So was there any more civil unrest?' Hudan was curious to know how long the peace had lasted.

'Not in Song's lifetime, nor that of his son,' Rhun was happy to report. 'The Grand Protector, as tutor to Song's heir, Ji Zhao, saw to that.'

Hudan's eyes opened wide. 'Shi lives a *long* time then,' she reasoned.

'As does his spouse.' Rhun clasped his hands together, hoping they could now get on with more important matters. 'So, Jiang Hudan … are you ready to have your cosmic memory reinstated?'

She was a little alarmed by the proposition. 'Then what?' She hoped that the answer was not to wait around for however long it took for the rest of their team to die of natural causes.

'Well … my brother will be assisting us to do a little time-hopping and collect the rest of the team.' Rhun was clearly ecstatic to be moving forward with his own mission, finally. 'Once we have everyone together, and your memories are restored, I shall take you to the Dropa.'

'You mean, I don't have to wait decades to see any of our team again?' Hudan was delighted and much more eager to move on now. 'But what of finding Dragonface?'

'Well, in order to get Avery to cooperate with my little time-hopping exercise, he made me agree to wait until the entire team was together and brought up to speed before deciding on our next course of action.'

'That reasoning seems sound to me.'

'I am sick of arguing the matter, so whatever gets us there fastest.' Rhun gestured with his palms out, appealing to her to answer his original query. 'So? Are you ready to get your Taren back?'

With a deep breath, Hudan had second thoughts. 'I am not going to lose Jiang Hudan, am I?'

'No,' he assured her, 'you'll just have many more memories.'

Hudan found a smooth rock to sit upon and gave him the nod to go ahead. '*Timekeeper* awaken,' Rhun said.

The influx of memory was not a violent experience, as Hudan had imagined, but like the gentle rise in consciousness when one awakes from a long sleep.

'Taren …' Rhun queried her stillness and silence. 'Are you in there?'

Her eyes slowly parted wide with awareness. 'Oh, my stars, I made it through ancient Zhou!' She looked at Rhun. 'Well done, governor.' Hudan remembered now that Rhun was the ruler of the planet they were trying to save.

'Welcome back,' he said, and grinned broadly.

Hudan cocked her head to one side. 'You know, technically I am not your mother,' she told him, amused by his deception when she was in Zhou.

'Well you were, in yet another earth life,' Rhun granted, 'so I know she's in there somewhere.'

Hudan nodded, for indeed she remembered portions of that life too, thanks to the thought recordings made by the incarnation in question, and left as reference material in the Institute of Immortal History on Kila — although none of their team, bar Rhun, was immortal any more. Back in the universe she'd come from, it was not unusual to live a thousand years, for the aging process was much slower. The earthly body she was wearing at present was not gifted with such DNA, so Hudan was as vulnerable to death and aging now as she had been before Rhun had fetched her. The only advantage she now had was her memory of their quest.

'And besides,' the time lord added, 'we couldn't have Dan thinking we were trying to make off with his girl … never a wise move around any man.'

'Dear, sweet, Dan,' she smiled fondly. 'I can hardly wait to bring him back on board.'

'Then let's get to it,' Rhun suggested, ahead of summoning his brother to join them.

When the elemental lord appeared, he smiled broadly. 'Hello, mother.'

'My lord Avery,' she replied, bowing to him. 'Please, call me Hudan, or Taren. As neither of those incarnations have ever given birth, mother is just a little strange.'

'As you wish,' the fair lord granted, holding out a hand to her. 'You need to come with me, Hudan.'

'Where are we going?' she queried, as she took hold of his hand.

'Outside of time,' he replied. 'Rhun will take the time chariot forward in time, and summon us forth once he is there, so that, in effect, we can quantum jump.'

'Sounds feasible.' Hudan granted, now reasoning with Taren's scientific knowledge — for Dr Taren Lennox had degrees in genetics, quantum theory and astrophysics. 'Who is first on the pick-up list?'

Avery went to answer, but Rhun jumped in first. 'Let's … just keep it as a surprise, shall we? Meet you back here in, well … no time.' The lord walked over to what appeared to be a crystal cluster, but whipping an invisible cover away, it was obvious that the reflective cloth created this illusion, for the time-hopping chariot of the ancients was underneath.

As Rhun climbed on board the futuristic-looking transport — which had actually been constructed on Atlantis some twelve thousand years before the time they now inhabited — a sweet-smelling mist, filled with tiny lights, arose within the cavern and veiled everything else from view. The atmosphere felt electric and Hudan's entire being buzzed with the kind of euphoria that was associated with a rapid influx of chi, or cosmic light — rather like the sensation of thought projection, but far more intense!

When the glistening haze cleared, Rhun was gone and the light emitting from the crystals in the cavern was far more brilliant — as they had appeared when she'd seen this place in her dream state. Hudan could no longer feel the lord's hand in hers as he'd shifted into his spirit form for their short otherworldly sabbatical.

'*So how does it feel to be back?*' Avery asked, making conversation while they awaited Rhun's cue to return to the physical realm.

Hudan was overwhelmed by the peace and tranquillity of the heavenly waking dream state she was in. '*It feels like home,*' she was happy to admit.

'*Imagine how it will feel once the entire team has been assembled,*' Avery commented. '*Speaking of which, I hear Rhun now.*'

'*I cannot wait to see who is with him!*' Hudan grinned broadly, feeling she had never been so excited in all her earthly life, but the otherworldly atmosphere no doubt had something to do with that. Every molecule of her being was over-excited and had to be in order to resonate at the same frequency as the otherworldly realm she was inhabiting.

'*Going down,*' Avery warned, as the light-filled mist arose again.

The decrease in her vibratory rate brought Hudan crashing back to the heavy feeling of being physically present on earth and confined by the relentless grip of time.

What was worse was that when the mist cleared, Rhun's first recruit turned out to be Wu Geng, the ex-prince of Shang.

'What is going on?' Hudan had never seen the soul-mind inside this character, and she still could not. 'Is he the one you warned Dan about before you brought me here?'

'One and the same,' Rhun granted, but Hudan had already figured out who it had to be, and her sights narrowed in suspicion.

'Khalid,' she deduced, immediately irked by his presence.

'Doctor,' he replied and bowed to her, knowing she was really the one in charge of this time-hopping escapade.

For Taren was the original timekeeper who had recruited the other members of the team. The captain may have called the shots on-board their vessel, but off-board Taren was in charge.

'How on earth did you get to ancient Zhou?' She placed her hands on her hips, completely baffled.

'The same way you did. I found an ancient incarnation and jumped right in,' he answered happily, taking a moment to admire their location.

'You should not have brought him here,' Taren said, still perturbed. Now Khalid could find this place with a thought, wherever this place was, and she'd still not been brought up to speed on that, either.

'The captain approved it,' Rhun defended.

'But he remembers nothing!' Hudan countered.

'His majesty also approved, and Song remembers enough to know he'd vowed to kill Khalid.'

Hudan inhaled a deep breath and looked to Wu Geng. 'Why did you come?'

'I need to get along.' Rhun headed for the chariot to make his next jump forward. 'Take your time with the witness. It makes no difference to me.'

'No, wait,' Hudan urged him. 'When you go to get Zhou Gong, I want to be there.'

'Bugger!' Rhun slumped in his seat to wait for her. 'Then make it snappy.'

Hudan wanted to kill Rhun for having the chariot and their arch-enemy in the same room. But then, neither Avery nor Rhun really knew much about Khalid. He was from her universe of origin and he and Taren had quite a long and unpleasant history. Her sights returned to Wu Geng. 'Well?'

'I taped the past-life regression session you each did to find these incarnations. When I discovered that I had indeed been alive in the target location, and time, in question, and that my incarnation had spent most of his life being oppressed by your target enemy, I saw it as an opportunity to be of benefit to the righteous for a change.'

'You saw it as an opportunity to keep pace with us through time, you mean. So that when we return to stop you causing an inter-universal disaster, you will land with your memory intact and be ready for us.' Her eyebrows rose questioningly.

'There is that,' he granted. 'But, what if I were to *land* ...' he used her terminology, 'and I was on your side? Then what? A double victory all round.'

'When you return, you will be subject to the sway of your father's demonic creation,' Hudan pointed out.

'Whoa, this is interesting,' Avery muttered and took a seat to listen.

'I can sever that influence,' Wu Geng assured her.

'By destroying the Soul Keep that your father used to create the anomaly. I know,' Hudan said. She knew that was how to destroy the curse that had driven Khalid's mindset back then and given him additional power ... the trouble was she had never seen the Soul Keep, nor did she know where Khalid had hidden it. Since Khalid had accidentally hitched a ride with them into this universe, he'd been cut off from his evil influences and had been behaving himself, but his dark black eyes, unchanged in the incarnation he was filling, were so very hard to trust or read. 'Do you really expect me to take you at your word on that?'

'No,' said Khalid, frankly. 'However, if I prove myself during this mission against the creature, then maybe you will?'

'Good argument,' Avery conceded, and Wu Geng bowed his head in gracious thanks. 'Shall we get on?' the lord suggested. 'I can take him with me, or leave him here to rot. Your call?' Avery put it to Hudan.

'You defended my right to live back on Kila,' Wu Geng said to her. 'I hope you will do the same now.' He bowed deeply to her, and stayed bowed as he awaited her answer.

But Hudan was still torn. 'Why did Song forego Zeven's vendetta?' she mused. As she asked this she noted how well she could suddenly wrap her mouth around the names she'd found so difficult, or recalled incorrectly, during life.

Wu Geng rose to reply. 'Because I saved his bride's family from Dragonface and put him back in her favour.'

'Of course,' Hudan huffed with emphasis, 'it had to have something to do with a woman.'

Lord Avery and Rhun chuckled at her observation, as the soul-mind in question had been their uncle once upon another time.

'I do not know the soul in question very well,' Wu Geng told them, 'but even I know that women are the centre of his universe. If I might add, Fen Gong's albino tigress sniffed me and gave me the all-clear also.'

Uncertain, Hudan looked to Avery for his opinion. 'I told you, it is your call. I am already more involved in this affair than I should be, but you cannot pick your soul group, can you?' He threw Rhun an exasperated look, and Rhun grinned a little too sweetly.

'I do not believe I have a soul,' Wu Geng said.

'Of course you do,' Avery shot back, 'it's just not one of ours.'

'You must have a soul to be still surviving beyond the reach of your father's demons,' Hudan agreed, and if he had an independent soul, then it could be developed and turned into an ally. 'Very well, you are on the team,' she decreed, to Wu Geng's great relief. 'Zeven will be with us presently, and I will make it his responsibility to keep an eye on you.'

'Oh, goody,' Khalid replied drolly, 'more violence.'

'I shall ensure he is fair with you,' Hudan vowed, as she moved to take a seat behind Rhun in the chariot, taking her staff along with her.

The transport was controlled by a telepathic control plate on the centre of its dashboard, which Rhun placed his hand upon; with his desired destination in mind, Rhun set a course for ten years hence and, submitting his intention, activated the ignition and they were swept forth into the future.

The exhilaration of their time-shift was intense, then the thrill of the propulsive sensation stopped abruptly. It was apparent to Hudan that moving forward in time via artificial means was far more radical than moving backward through time via natural channels. Hudan was surprised to discover that they were in the same crystal cavern — it appeared that they had not moved anywhere.

'That was awesome!' Hudan lifted her arms into the air, exhilarated. 'I've never moved forward in time before, only backward.'

'In Taren's lifetime, you mean. My mother, Tory, zipped forward and backward all through history,' Rhun said as he got out. 'The chariot is safe here ... best to use regular teleportation from this point.'

'Good show.' Hudan climbed out also and then looked at Rhun expectantly; the latter looked back with the same regard.

'Well, go get him,' Rhun prompted her. 'You know what he looks like, you don't need me.'

Hudan smiled broadly. 'This is it! Thank you,' she thought to add.

'Thank you, actually.' Rhun was quick to respond. 'You are the one doing me the favour.'

In the long run, that was true. 'I shall return.' With the thought of Dan, her world lit up and she was sped forth to his vicinity.

It was night. Early autumn, if the swell of the river before her and the cool, drizzly rain were anything to go by. There was no moon, but on the far side of the river, men with lanterns and drawn weapons were scouring the shoreline. *What is going on? Where is Dan?*

In the light that was reflecting on the river from the lanterns Hudan spied someone break the surface of the water near the bank closest to her and then drag themself out of the flow and onto the rocks. Was it Dan? Why would the Duke of Zhou have an armed force in pursuit of him?

'Dan?' she stopped short of her target to query.

'Hudan?' He looked about to find her rushing toward him. 'Please tell me, that you have come ... to take me away ... from all this,' he spluttered.

'Yes,' she assured, 'it is time for the timekeeper to awaken.'

'I managed to awaken the timekeeper in me years ago,' he didn't mind boasting as she put her staff down to help him out of the water. 'I told you your absence would make me work harder and it did.' Dan collapsed on the bank puffing and coughing water. 'I feel so *old*,' he complained, arching his head backward to take in more air.

'Well, you made it across a rushing river, so you are still doing pretty well,' she observed, crouching down to speak with him. 'But why are you swimming a river in the middle of the night? Who do the soldiers belong to?'

'The king,' he replied. 'I handed over full rulership to him three years ago, and since then he has been trying to persuade me to resign as his chief advisor and govern a province. We have had a difference of opinion over whether the Zhou's word, without any divination, is the word of heaven? Which it cannot possibly be, as what man can be completely unbiased and fair without divine counsel? The holder of the mandate must still be answerable to, and judged by, heaven.'

'Never mind about the particulars of your falling out,' Hudan said, urging him to the point. 'Surely such a detail did not cause all this?'

'I refused to be removed from central governance and so I resigned.' Dan cut the tale short. 'The king refused my resignation and threatened to have me hunted down as a criminal if I left.' Dan motioned to the force across the river. 'This is the king making good on his threat.'

'That rotten little ingrate!' Hudan stood and took up her staff, enraged.

'Now that you are here for me,' Dan interjected, 'I really could not give a damn how I am remembered.'

'That is not how history would have it.' Hudan took a few steps backward and the sphere in the staff lit up deep red. 'Let us see how the little king copes with heaven's wrath, now that you are no longer around to advise him.'

'What are you going to do?' Dan asked as he found his feet and stood. Hudan hummed a beautiful note that turned the light in Taiji a soft pink as she rose into the air and out of his reach.

In her mind's eye, Hudan willed her chi to the surface of her body and she began to glow. Her rain-soaked form dried, as an invisible elemental cocoon directed the storm to pass around her.

Dan was besotted by this vision of her. 'You are just as you appeared my first night on Li Shan ... which seems a hundred years ago now.'

Hudan smiled at his sweet sentiment, but turned her sights to the force on the opposite bank.

When she was spotted floating over the water's surface, the men gasped in awe and alerted one another to the phenomenon — none dared to attack for fear of tasting the wrath of the staff in her hand.

'Taiji!' One of the soldiers pointed to the staff to alert his company. 'The weapon of the Wu, Jiang Hudan!'

'But she is dead!' cried another, who had dropped down to kneel by the man beside him, who hissed, 'That is the point!'

Mesmerised by the heart-light of Taiji, and Hudan's celestial appearance, the men fell on bended knee to listen to her speak.

'Good men of Zhou …' She amplified her voice, but kept her tone gentle. 'You may cease your search for Zhou Gong. I, Shanyu Jiang Hudan, have been sent by heaven to deliver him to the mount of immortals, where he shall reside with his great brother Zhou Wu Wang, and others of their chosen ilk, forevermore. I ask that you deliver this message to the king from me …' The light in the staff turned deep grey as a whirling storm appeared to erupt from within the sphere. Hudan withdrew her chi, her form ceased to glow, and the mood became more foreboding. 'Tell the king that heaven is appalled by his treatment of our beloved son, Zhou Gong. Our fury will rain down upon him until the disrespect and injustice that drove the brightest star in Tian's sky to his death has been righted.'

'Huh?' The soldiers were disturbed — they'd obviously been expecting good news.

'The sons of the sky have been dreaming of Zhou Gong, and your Zhou will now dream of him too! Every night he shall know the bitter remorse of having forsaken the counsel of his most divinely knowledgeable ally. And if the one chosen to carry heaven's mandate still stubbornly refuses to repent his disservice, and not show due honour to his most beloved advisor, I have to wonder this … on his dying day, will the sons of the sky send for Zhou Cheng, as they have for Zhou Gong? The king's resolve in this matter will decide.'

Hudan willed herself back to Dan's side and vanished from the sight of the mystified search party.

When Hudan reappeared beside him, Dan was alarmed to view the stormy whirlpool churning about inside the Taiji sphere. 'With all due respect, I do not believe you have the right to judge Zhou Cheng on heaven's behalf.'

'But Taiji does,' Hudan retorted. 'Being a polarising force, it judges without bias.' She backed away from him.

Dan's second sight picked up on the many spectres of nature that were rushing toward Taiji from every direction; they were akin to the spirit-like beauties which had burst into his quarters one night in search of Rhun. As they wove around the head of the staff in empathy with the motion of the whirlwind within, the wind force around Hudan built in momentum and Dan was forced to back away.

With a cry, Hudan directed the enchantment skyward toward the East with the head of her staff — whatever curse befell Ji Song, it would not affect the provinces of Shao Gong Shi. As the elemental force sped forth and penetrated the cloud, a mighty clap of thunder boomed and the sky lit up with electrical activity. The wind increased without warning and was so intense, the rain fell at a steep angle toward the East.

'No, Hudan, you will destroy the autumn harvest,' Dan appealed for the sake of the people, as he was battered by the storm being sent to avenge him.

'All Ji Song has to do is be truly repentant in his heart, and any damage will be undone,' she replied.

'I have no wish for the people of Zhou to suffer for the sake of my veneration.'

'If your life's work is not properly venerated then many, many more people will suffer in the future. Besides, the events of this time are no longer your concern. So, stop protesting and give me your hand.' Hudan extended her hand toward him.

Dan observed the huge force of nature now bearing down on eastern Zhou, and found it difficult to relinquish his worldly concerns. 'But what if Song fails to wake up to himself?'

'I had to leave before the eastern revolution!' Hudan emphasised how hard that had been. 'But as Rhun went to great pains to point out, you managed without any help from me. Let it go, Dan … it's time to step back into the larger scheme of things.' Hudan held out her hand again.

'As much as I have looked forward to this day, I shall miss this place and time.'

'I expected that might be the case when you up and left for ancient China ahead of us all!' Hudan ribbed, as Taren had been waiting a lifetime to scold Lucian about that. 'I thought you'd died during our recon exercise!'

As Dan took hold of her hand, her cocoon of calm encapsulated him and the drenching rain and ripping wind ceased battering him. 'It's nice in here,' Dan remarked, able to observe the stormy night from a place of shelter, and enjoy the pleasing feeling of being dry and warm. 'I'm sorry if I made you worry,' Dan turned his dark eyes her way to appeal on Lucian's behalf, 'but I'd had so much difficulty teleporting that when my soul made contact with his incarnation, I did not want to leave for fear I would not achieve the feat again.'

'I forgive you.' Hudan was pleased to have distracted him from his earthly concerns, and wrapping both hands around the back of his neck, she kissed him all the way back to their contact point.

'No wonder it has taken so long!' Rhun was slouching in the time chariot and looking extremely put out. 'We are on real time here, you realise.'

'Apologies, I was detained cursing Ji Song,' Hudan informed him.

'Oh, yes,' Rhun noted, 'I remember that little storm.'

'How did the young king fare?' Dan wanted to know if the people had suffered for long.

'I guess we shall find out when we collect Song,' Rhun said. 'But I shouldn't worry too much. There was one man upset by your death whom the king did trust and respect beyond all others.'

'Fen Gong.' The thought of his dear friend made Dan smile, and he was more hopeful that things had turned out well.

Hudan eyed the cavern, pleased to note it was just the three of them. 'Excellent. Your brother is not here yet.'

'I have not summoned him yet,' said Rhun, wondering what was on her mind.

'You haven't aged a day,' Dan mumbled, having caught his first good glimpse of Hudan in natural light.

'That's because I have barely been parted from you a day,' she explained, with a grin. 'We've been doing some time-hopping.'

Dan was disgruntled to learn this. 'But I have had to live ten years without you!' That hardly seemed fair. 'And I am now twenty years your senior, instead of ten!'

'Hey, be thankful,' Rhun interjected, 'your brother Shi lives until he's sixty-three!'

The comment left Dan flummoxed, and he was suddenly most thankful to have died when he did.

'But you are still *gorgeous*.' Hudan admired him — not a grey hair in his head at forty-five — and she was compelled to kiss him, as she had never been so free to do so.

'Oh, for heaven's sake!' Rhun appealed. 'When this chore is done I shall find you a room, I promise. But for the moment, can we *please* focus!'

Both Dan and Hudan turned their undismayed gazes his way.

'Why do you *not* want me to summon the boy wonder?' Rhun was obviously intrigued by this.

'No sinister reason,' Hudan assured him. 'I just do not think it wise to have Khalid and the chariot in the same place. It is regrettable that he has seen it at all, as he used to be able to thought-project himself about as we do, and probably still can. Now he can find the chariot with a thought! I don't trust him, and the chariot was how Dragonface got the jump on you last time around.'

'Hmmm … my fault then.' Rhun realised that in his rush to get the task done he'd been careless. 'It is probably about time the chariot had a revamp,' he considered, looking it over. 'If it does not appear as it did when Khalid saw it, then he cannot find it again. But I might wait for Zeven to weigh in on the design aesthetic. In the meantime, while we gather the rest of the team,

I'll get Avery to drop Khalid at our final destination ahead of us. We have people there who can watch him.'

'We do?' Hudan was curious, and then smiled as she figured it out. 'Yi Wu.'

'Telmo,' Dan corrected.

'I knew him as Taliesin,' Rhun shrugged, 'but yeah, whatever! Give me a moment and I shall arrange it.' The time lord went quiet to introvert his attention, and then a short while later emerged to announce, 'All sorted.'

'You can telepathically connect with your brother?' None of Taren's crew had been able to employ telepathy over a vast distance, but way back, a few timelines ago, Taren had witnessed Rhun use this talent to save Avery's life.

'On the whole, annoying,' he admitted, 'but handy at times like these. Avery will be here presently.'

'So we have a moment's grace, then,' Dan established, as he grabbed Hudan and pulled her close as he'd rarely dared to in life.

'Lucian is definitely back,' she noted with glee.

'Which makes me your husband twice over.'

'Don't mind me ...' Rhun grumbled, envious of their outpouring of emotion.

'Aw ...' Avery commented airily, as he arrived to witness their heated kiss. 'More little brothers and sisters on the way, hmm?'

Hudan's enthusiasm waned and Dan turned to study the lord Avery. 'That's right, I remember now. You are the baby of the family.'

'My twin sister is, actually,' Avery smiled, sweetly.

'No, Dan's right,' Rhun awarded, 'as Thea does not exist at this point in time.'

'Gosh,' commented Hudan, sensing the friction in the air, 'it is so lovely to have you together again in the one room. I'm not too sure about bringing anyone else to this reunion.'

'Huxin is next,' Rhun posed.

Hudan's grin broadened, and she clapped her hands together. 'Let's go!'

Given leave to continue, Rhun disappeared into the future on the chariot, and Hudan and Dan vanished into the otherworld with Lord Avery.

Nothing could have prepared Hudan for the sight of her twin sister as an old woman of sixty-seven years — her honey waves of hair had turned white and thin, her body was hunched and her skin sagged on her bones.

Huxin wept as she stroked Hudan's smooth young face. 'Time has not touched you. I cannot see what use I can be to the sons of the sky as I am,' and she held out her bony wrinkled hands to show Hudan how they'd aged. 'My tiger form is not much better, I'm afraid.'

'I feel sure there is a method to Rhun's madness.' Hudan looked at him, and he nodded to reassure her it was so. 'One marvel at a time.'

Repeating the process once again, it was Shi's turn to shock, as Dan now appeared twenty years younger than his favourite baby brother. Shi was delighted to see them again, but none more so than his wife, Huxin, whom he embraced. 'I did not last a year without you, my love,' he confessed, as they rocked back and forth in their hug.

'How are Zhen and Kao?' Huxin pulled away to ask.

'The children are fine, the grandchildren are fine, and so are the great-grandchildren,' he declared.

'Holy smoke, Shi,' Dan exclaimed, 'where on earth did you find mates for them all?'

'There are many more were-tigers like us in the western mountains,' he said happily. 'Once word of our legend spread, numerous others sought sanctuary at Shao.'

'I'll always remember Shao with great fondness myself.' Hudan grinned up at Dan, and he responded likewise.

'*Do not* start kissing again,' Rhun objected. 'We are on a roll, let's keep the momentum going.'

Ji Song was brought forth as a nuggety old man of fifty-three, still dressed in battle armour that was splattered in blood.

'I thought there was no more unrest in Zhou?' Hudan queried Rhun as he released Song from his influence.

The king looked down at his attire, realising there was a misunderstanding. 'I nearly had a nasty hunting accident … this blood belongs to dinner,' he explained humbly, as he was finally forced to confront Hudan and Dan. 'I owe you both an apology —'

'You'll have to save it.' Rhun slapped Song on the back and, waving his hand repeatedly, urged Avery to be gone with the lot of them.

On their final return to the crystal cave, Fen Gong, aged sixty-one years of age, and Ling Hu — the albino spirit tiger — were waiting. The tigress had managed to defy her tiger lifespan, which should have ended half her lifetime ago, and she was still not on her last legs, though she moved at a slower pace these days, in tune with her keeper.

'It seems the mission now has a pet,' Rhun commented, and the tigress growled to object to his inference.

'That is my daughter you are talking about!' Shi warned the time lord, and even aged, Shi was a bigger man than Rhun.

'Sorry, I meant to say, a new team member,' the time lord awarded kindly. 'She just sort of … followed us.' He held up both hands to imply there was not much to be done about it.

'Oh goodness,' Fen cried with glee to see everyone, and Hudan especially. 'Our big brother looks like a baby, Huxin!'

'And you are an old man.' Hudan was shocked to see their visibly time-worn forms; the years with her siblings that she had missed were painfully apparent.

'He's still cute though.' Huxin pinched his cheek, proud of him. 'And he had women chasing his marriage suit right to the end.'

Fen shook his head to deny it was even worth mentioning. 'I have my life companion.' He motioned back to Ling Hu.

'I am worried about you, Fen,' Song commented.

'If I recall correctly, Zeven, you are the worry,' Fen grinned. 'And always were.'

Rhun let loose a loud whistle to draw everyone's attention, and they fell quiet. 'Finally … a moment's bloody silence! Listen up —'

'What the hell do you plan to do with a bunch of geriatrics like us?' Song was baffled and impatient. 'You should have killed me twenty years ago!'

'Have you taught him nothing?' Rhun referred the query to the captain.

'I went through it with him many times,' Dan sighed.

'I know about changing causality, blah, blah, blah … I am just saying that most of us are a little past our prime.' Song held up both palms in wonder.

'I know you have questions,' Rhun allowed, covering up the chariot with its reflective cloak. 'And if you would be so kind as to all join hands, I'll take you to the answers.'

'Hey, that is cool!' Song split from the huddle to check out the camouflage cover, and when Fen followed, Rhun threw his hands up in frustration.

'Okay, you've got your team,' Avery said to his brother in leaving, 'but I want to be consulted before any of you set foot in any period of earth history again. Are we clear?'

'Clear as vodka, bro!' Rhun replied drily.

'I want my wife back!' Avery hissed, a little disturbed by his brother's attitude.

'I will stop Shyamal, and we *will* return to Kila, just as it was before this lot ever landed there,' Rhun vowed to Avery in all seriousness.

'Is there a plan?' Song wondered. 'A plan would be good about now.'

'I actually thought the plan was to kill the reptilian during our lifetime here,' Huxin said, wondering why they were not more concerned, as Rhun had restored her timekeeper memory when he'd picked her up.

'When I returned here on the chariot for the second time,' Rhun began, 'I realised —'

'*I* realised,' Avery corrected his brother.

'*We* realised,' Rhun granted, 'that we could not take out Dragonface without radically changing history. I had no idea he'd been so involved in events here on earth. And as bad as those events are, change them, and everything changes. We've learned a lot about our enemy through your interactions with the reptilian, and we've gained a far better understanding of what it is going to take to destroy our target without screwing up earth history or Kila's future. You all have bodies functioning on this planet —'

'Yeah, barely,' Zeven complained.

'And you are all free of your historical responsibilities,' Rhun concluded. 'So, now we can focus on our purpose.'

'I repeat, is there a plan?' Song wasn't feeling any more informed.

The time lord returned his brother's wave goodbye and the lord Avery left them to it. 'Telmo is waiting to answer all your questions,' Rhun said impatiently. 'If you would just humour me a moment and hold hands!' he prompted.

Everyone joined the circle, and once they were holding each other's hands, the time lord saw his team to their final destination at Bayan Har Shan. Ling Hu followed.

As they emerged from the light-field, Hudan and her companions were blinded by the glare of the midday sun hitting the snow around them — the sky above was azure for as far as the eye could see. The high plateau fronted up to a mountain bluff that had several cave openings up its face and one at the bottom. In the mouth of the lowest of these stood Yi Wu and a tiny little woman, only half her size, who Hudan recognised from her appearances during holy rites held on Li Shan.

'Shifu Yi!' Hudan made haste to address the pair ... she was the only one young and energetic enough to run. She stopped before the women, looking at the one more unfamiliar as she knelt to address her. Her large indigo eyes were almost too piercing to look at. 'Are you Dropa?'

'That is the name of my clan,' the woman granted kindly.

'Then I believe this belongs to you?' Hudan held out the Taiji staff with both her hands to complete her quest. 'Taiji has served Zhou well.'

'You have been a worthy guardian, Jiang Hudan, just as Telmo insisted you would be,' the tiny woman said as she reclaimed her property, regarding the tool fondly.

'Telmo?' Song queried the announcement, whereupon Yi Wu shifted form into her younger male inner persona.

The king was repulsed. 'Posing as a chick is really low! To think I actually found you attractive!' Song shuddered at the thought now.

Fen, Shi and Huxin were also surprised to note his deception, and then doubly shocked to see Wu Geng surface from the cave beyond. The ex-prince of Shang was absolutely beaming with health and appeared more youthful and vibrant than he ever had in life. 'You all finally made it!' he exclaimed, pleased to see them. 'Thirty years is quite a bit of waiting around, but I've learned a lot.'

'Thirty years?' Hudan looked him up and down. 'But you look younger than when I last saw you.'

He grinned broadly, displaying a perfect set of white teeth. 'The Dropa have a really wonderful genetic restoration program here. I highly recommend it.'

'Absolutely, yes!' Huxin exclaimed, ready to head inside the cave. 'I shall have whatever you had.'

Shi and Fen were also pleasantly curious about Wu Geng's boast. 'No wonder Yi Wu never aged a day,' Fen muttered to his brother-in-law as they trailed after Huxin, who was being aided inside by Wu Geng.

'But who are the Dropa?' Hudan asked the tiny woman, as she stood to follow the others.

'My people crashed here about twenty thousand years ago,' she began, and continued telling her story as she turned and walked alongside Hudan. 'And the DNA of my people runs through you all, and through many others in the surrounding regions ...'

When Dan moved to follow their party, he was annoyed to have Song delay him. 'I really want to hear that account,' he complained, but his resistance lessened when he saw how grim Song appeared.

'Please,' Song implored him, 'I cannot carry this guilt any more. Please hear my apology, or I am going to *burst* or go mad!'

'Song, I forgive your trespasses against me, truly.' Dan lightly punched his shoulder, and smiled to reassure him. Yet the absolution only served to make Song appear more upset. 'Does this have anything to do with Hudan's cursed storm?'

'Only in so far as the disaster served as a trigger for my epiphany,' Song said, and looked Dan in the eyes. 'And now that I have my timekeeper memory back in its entirety, more than ever I need to clear the way between us, captain.' He swallowed hard on his regret.

'To a large extent we've all been operating in the dark,' Dan warranted, 'but if it makes you feel better, go ahead and purge; I won't stop you.' He found a rock to lean against and got comfortable as he prepared himself to hear his pilot out.

EPILOGUE

THE METAL-BANDED COFFER

The year of the Duke of Zhou's death, before the autumn harvest, a fierce wind blew, battling with thunder. The grain was bent low, and even great trees were uprooted. The eastern state of Zhou was in terror.

When Ji Song was told that the misfortune was a curse sent from heaven to repay his ill-respect of Zhou Gong, his animosity toward his deceased uncle only increased. Fen Gong, who had fled to Haojing in the wake of Song's decree to hunt Zhou Gong to his death, had been dragged back to Chengzhou by the king to assist with the calamity now afflicting the East.

When Fen Gong was brought before the king and his queen, the Grand Protector, Shao Gong Shi, accompanied him. In the twelve years that Song had known Fen Gong, he'd never seen him appear so fiercely hostile. Ji Song's most trusted advisors knelt before him, but clearly it brought them no joy to do so.

'My uncle has conspired with the spirit of your sister, Jiang Hudan, to bring this curse down upon Zhou,' the king stated.

'If that is what our majesty truly believes in his heart is the truth,' Fen replied, 'then I predict the curse of heaven will last long.'

'What are you implying?' Hui Ru asked, taking offence at his tone.

'I am implying ...' Fen raised his baleful sights to view the young royals, 'that you are both deluded!'

'Fen?' Shi cautioned from beside him, and Hui Ru stood, insulted.

'I will have your head for —'

'Then take it,' Fen Gong said, defiantly, 'but I will have my say first! How can you, in good conscience, sit upon the throne in this heavenly city, having destroyed the selfless visionary who put you both where you are?'

'I did not bring you here to be lectured, Fen Gong,' the king warned, then descended the stairs to confront him. 'I want to know what must be done to counter this hex. Are you going to tell me, or shall I have the wife of the protector dragged before me for questioning?'

Shi stood rigidly, provoked by the threat, but Fen placed a pacifying hand on Shi's shoulder and then turned to the king. 'I know exactly what must be done, majesty,' he said.

'I knew I could rely on you, Fen Gong.' The king retreated to a less threatening distance.

'We shall find the solution at Haojing,' Fen concluded.

'At Haojing!' Both the king and Shi were alarmed at the news. The king disliked this as the ancestral capital was a week's journey away, and Shi's concern was that Haojing was where his family presently resided and he didn't want them embroiled in the family feud.

Ji Song's eyes narrowed. 'You had best not be toying with me, Fen Gong.'

'When your majesty has shown no mercy to a man of such greatness as Zhou Gong, I realise that I am of far less worth.'

The reply got both the king and queen fuming. 'Do you wish to keep your tongue?' Hu Rui seethed.

'At least until you cease to need my advice,' Fen replied tartly.

'Show the respect due to your king, or I promise to sever some body part and you won't be needing it any more.' She glared down at him, and Fen held his tongue, though his look of disdain did not alter.

The king's friendship with Fen Gong was the one casualty from his battle with Zhou Gong that he truly regretted. It hurt him personally that Fen Gong was more loyal to his controlling uncle than he was to himself, but he hoped their friendship would recover given time.

*

Before they set off on the final leg of the journey to Haojing, Ji Song made it clear to Fen that he wished to waste no time in addressing the curse as soon as they reached their destination. Fen Gong confidently assured Song that there would be no need for delay.

Once inside the courtyard at Haojing, Fen dismounted and did not even greet Huxin before heading toward the Ji family storehouse. Zhou Cheng followed him, and Shi cast a cautioning look in his wife's direction as he kept pace with his companions.

'Why are we here?' The king was feeling uneasy. He'd never ventured into the family storehouse, as he had no interest in old texts or relics that were not war- or weapons-related.

'All will be clear soon enough.' Fen knocked, and when the hatch opened, Fen rattled off the list of names that was Dan's entry code.

'My lord!' Heng exclaimed. 'I feared I would be forgotten now the great Zhou Gong has departed this earth.'

Hearing his uncle referred to in this way yet again was starting to vex Ji Song, to the amusement of Fen Gong.

'I have our majesty in my company,' he informed the custodian, 'and the Grand Protector also has business to attend here this night.'

'Majesty! And my lord!' Heng unbolted the door immediately.

Fen bade Shi escort the king downstairs, whilst he ascended with Heng to the upper storage room to advise of their requirements.

When the count returned with two coffers, the king was sorely deflated. 'How is reading going stop the storm in the East?'

Fen held out to the king the more ornate of the two coffers. 'Trust me.'

'I recognise this —' The king frowned as he accepted the container from his advisor.

'It is your father's last will and testament,' Fen told him, 'but it is most unlike the altered article that you know, which at Zhou Gong's request was penned by Jiang Taigong the night your father died. This document is Zhou Wu Wang's true will, penned by Jiang Taigong at your father's request, over a year before his death.'

'Zhou Gong changed my father's will!' Ji Song was furious and Shi was shocked out of his wits.

'How do you know this?' Ji Song demanded, as he opened the coffer.

'I bore witness to the event,' he admitted proudly, although the king's rage intensified.

'I knew it. Xian was meant to be regent all along!' The king laid out the document to read in the lamplight, but as he did, his rage gradually turned to bemusement. 'This cannot be ...' The king looked up from his reading, disillusioned.

'What is it?' Shi ventured to ask.

The answer was painful to articulate. 'My father wanted Dan to be king.' Song was distressed as he thought back over the events that had transpired in the wake of Zhou Wu Wang's death. 'Zhou Gong could have had the crown; he could have had his chance with the goddess,' he realised, looking at Fen in bewilderment. 'Why?' Tears rimmed the young king's eyes, as he felt the bitter sting of regret.

'Because it was the will of heaven,' Fen Gong advised. 'I can show you Zhou Gong's divinations on the matter.'

'Heng!' The king called for the storeman.

'Yes, majesty.' He came forward from the shadows and bowed.

'Do you confirm Fen Gong's account of events?'

'Yes,' Heng said with certainty, 'this truly happened. But the Duke of Zhou ordered us not to speak of it while he was still living.'

The king held the text and wept. 'There is no further need for divination,' he said. 'The Duke of Zhou served the royal house with assiduous effort, but I, young and foolish, understood *nothing*. It is now that heaven has moved in its awesomeness to bring the virtue of the Duke of Zhou to light.'

'Zhou Gong once told me that he wished to be laid to rest in Chengzhou,' Fen enlightened the king. 'This was to make it clear that he would never depart from you, majesty.'

The revelation further fuelled the king's grieving. 'I had not planned to pay homage to Zhou Gong Dan anywhere, but to let his memory slip from history as though he'd never existed.' Song clenched his jaw, determined. 'But I shall build a memorial for the duke alongside the tomb of King Wen. This will demonstrate that I never presumed to treat the Duke of Zhou as a subject.'

Both his advisors were smiling at him now, and nodding their heads to second his decision. 'That shall be pleasing to heaven,' Fen warranted.

'What is in there?' After receiving such a shock from the first coffer, Ji Song was hesitant to ask after the second one that Fen was holding.

'This is a parting gift from Zhou Gong to you, majesty.' Fen passed the item to Song, who was too shattered to bring himself to read the missive at present.

'I shall cherish this,' the king assured Fen, although he could barely speak, he was so choked with emotion. 'Thank you for having the courage to set me straight. You have been a true friend to Zhou Gong, to Zhou, and to your king this day. It is clear to me now why heaven has seen fit to punish me, and the path to redemption is now obvious.'

With the king's change of heart, a reverse wind blew across eastern Zhou, the grain was blown upright again and the people of the state replanted the trees that had been toppled. In the end, there was a bountiful harvest that year.

A memorial to Zhou Gong was erected beside that of the king's late father, hailing him as Yuán Shèng — 'The First Sage'. All the duke's proposals on governance passed into law, and Ji Song finally conceded that the holder of the mandate ruled via the divinations of heaven, as Zhou Gong had always contended, feeling the Duke of Zhou's point had been vindicated during the final clash. Had Song only taken a moment to consult the Book of Changes before banishing his uncle, Zhou might never have been cursed, and he might still have kept his most loyal advisor.

Only once the king had made this peace with his uncle's great memory did he finally open the inheritance left to him by the Duke of Zhou.

The gift took the form of a cautionary text entitled, 'You Many Gentlemen, Be Never Slack.' It read:

In the past, the Shang king Zhongzong solemnly attended to heaven's mandate with the utmost care, fashioning ordinances to rule the people, always fearfully alert lest he should dare to become self-indulgent. For this reason, Zhongzong enjoyed his throne for seventy-five years. When the throne passed to Gaozong ...

GLOSSARY

Bi-disk — a flat jade disc with a hole in the centre, with ornate surface carving. Used in Zhou for the worship of heavenly deities.

Bo — title, equal to a Count; can also mean 'the eldest child'.

Censer — vessel for the burning of incense; these can vary greatly in size and material of construction.

Chi #1 — (also Qi or Ki) life energy, life force, energy flow. Literal translation is: 'breath, air, gas'.

Chi #2 — traditional Chinese unit of length equal to one foot.

Cun — traditional Chinese unit of measure equal to an inch.

Cong — a tube-shaped implement with a circular inner section and a squarish outer section, i.e. a hollow cylinder embedded in a partial rectangular block. Used for the worship of earthly spirits.

Dao Yin — a series of breathing exercises to cultivate chi; the precursor of Qigong and Tai Chi.

Diyu — 'earth prison', hell, the eighteen levels of the Chinese underworld.

Dizi — a Chinese transverse flute; most commonly made of bamboo but can also be wood, stone or jade.

Gong — title, equal to a Duke, when used preceding a person's first name.

Jinzita — 'gold word tower' — Chinese flat-topped pyramid, sometimes stepped.

Huang He — the Yellow River.

Qin — (or Guqin) an ancient Chinese string instrument of the zither family; favoured by scholars and the literati. Legend has it that during the life of Zhou Gong the qin developed from a five-stringed instrument to a seven-stringed instrument.

Shan — Chinese word for 'mountain'.

Shangdi — the Shang name of the ruler of heaven.

Shu — term with which Zhou kings address feudal lords; also means 'uncle'.

The Wu — female shamans of ancient China who ruled over the affairs of heaven. They were not answerable to any man, not even the emperor.

Tian — heaven/sky.

Xibo — Leader of the West Lands.

Yi Jing — the 'I Ching', also known as 'the Book of Changes'.

Yinhou — title meaning 'lord of Yin'.

Zhou — the name of the state ruled by the Ji family; this name came to encompass most of China; it was also the central province of the nine provinces of Zhou.

Zhuhou — title meaning 'Overlord'.

BIBLIOGRAPHY

558

Books

Hausdorf, Hartwig, *The Chinese Roswell: UFO Encounters in the Far East from Ancient Time to the Present*, New Paradigm Books, Florida, USA, 1998.

Horne, Charles F., *Sacred Books and Early Literature of the East: Ancient China*, Kessinger Publishing Co., Montana, USA. 1997.

Shaughnessy, Edward L., *Before Confucius: Studies in the Creation of the Chinese Classics*, State University of New York Press, Albany, USA. 1997.

Web references

Chinese clock http://theabysmal.wordpress.com

Dashu, Max, 'Wu: Female shamans in Ancient China' (article), www.suppressedhistories.net

www.ingramcontent.com/pod-product-compliance
Lightning Source LLC
Chambersburg PA
CBHW050608110726
47899CB00001B/20